27

WILLIAM DIEHL

27

HEINEMANN : LONDON

William Heinemann Ltd
Michelin House, 81 Fulham Road, London SW3 6RB
LONDON   MELBOURNE   AUCKLAND

First published in Great Britain by William Heinemann 1990
Copyright © 1990 by William Diehl

Grateful acknowledgment is made to the following for permission
to reprint previously published material:

CPP/Belwin, Inc., and International Music Publications: An excerpt from
the lyrics to "Don't Sit Under the Apple Tree" by Charles Tobias, Lew
Brown, and Sam H. Stept. Copyright 1942, 1954 Robbins Music
Corporation. Copyright renewed 1970, 1982 Robbins Music Corporation.
All rights of Robbins Music Corp. assigned to EMI Catalogue Partnership.
All rights controlled and administered by EMI Robbins Catalog, Inc.
International copyright secured. Made in USA. All rights reserved. Used by
permission.

Freddy Bienstock Enterprises: An excerpt from the lyrics to "Strange Fruit"
by Lewis Allen. Copyright 1939 Edward B. Marks Music Company.
Copyright renewed. Used by permission. All rights reserved.

MCA Music Publishing: An excerpt from lyrics to "Lover Man (Oh Where
Can You Be)," words and music by Jimmy Davis, Roger "Ram" Ramirez,
and Jimmy Sherman. Copyright 1941, 1942 by MCA Music Publishing, a
division of MCA, Inc., New York, NY 10019. Copyright renewed. Used by
permission. All rights reserved.

Warner/Chappell Music, Inc., and Songwriter's Guild of America as agent
for Jay Gorney Music and Glocca Morra Music: An excerpt from the lyrics
to "Brother Can You Spare a Dime" by J. Gorney and E. Y. Harburg.
Copyright 1932 by Warner Bros. Inc. Copyright renewed. All rights
reserved. Used by permission.

Warner/Chappell Music, Inc.: An excerpt from the lyrics to "Love for Sale"
by Cole Porter. Copyright © 1957 Warner Bros. Inc. (renewed). An excerpt
from the lyrics to "She's Funny That Way" by Billie Holiday. Copyright
1928 Chappell & Co. An excerpt from the lyrics to "I've Got a Crush on
You" by George Gershwin–Ira Gershwin. Copyright 1930 Warner Bros.
Music (renewed) New World Music Corp. All rights reserved. Used by
permission.

A CIP catalogue record for this book
is available from the British Library
ISBN 0 434 19248 1

Printed in England by Clays Ltd, St Ives plc

*To the four people who love this island
as much as I do:*

*The late, great Bobby Byrd,
my daughter, Temple,
Mark Vaughn,
and always, for Virginia*

"What is past is prologue."

William Shakespeare
The Tempest

BOOK ONE

"What other dungeon is so dark
as one's own heart!
What jailer so inexorable
as one's self."

Nathaniel Hawthorne, 1851

The creature was a terrifying specter. A bizarre distortion, part human, part animal, this scarred, panting, wild-eyed obscenity seemed proof that all things in nature are not perfect and that even God in his infinite wisdom is sometimes capable of a monstrous blunder.

The face was a network of red, ridged scars, one of which stitched his left eye shut. The nose was a crushed lump, its nostrils flattened against a pale, cadaverous face like the snout of a pig. Thick lips revealed tortured, broken teeth which overlapped as if, in a divine afterthought, had been jammed haphazardly into the gums. His hair was a thick, blond, twisted mane that tumbled down both sides of his face, framing and accentuating its abnormalities.

His body had not escaped the ravages of natural disorder. He was short, barely five feet tall, bent over by a bowed spine, his shoulders jammed against his neck in a perpetual shrug, one foot turned inward and slanted so he walked on its side in a curious limp that lacked rhythm and cadence.

Misery permeated every pore and sinew of this tortured being.

His onc good eye hinted at the angry soul encased in this crippled cage of skin and bone; a fearful gray, glittering orb, unable to conceal his unbridled hatred for the normal humans who, on those rare times when he had been seen, were so revolted by his hideous deformities that they turned their own eyes away from him in horror.

Only his arms and hands seemed to have escaped the uncontrolled genes which had molded him into a human disaster. His arms were powerful and muscular, his hands long, expressive, even delicate. And yet, as if their beauty reminded him of what might have been, he kept them tucked away under his armpits, making his peculiar gait even more ominous.

A night predator, he emerged only after dark to forage for food, to steal what little money he required.

And to kill.

Shrouded by a long, dark green loden coat, its hood concealing his face, he stalked the shadows, dodging the police and the brownshirts, looking for victims. His rage was such that he hunted only the most beautiful and innocent-looking women, and when he found them he killed them, disfiguring their bodies with a ragged butcher knife as if he were getting even with the fates for what they had done to him.

In this, the spring of 1932, he had butchered no less than two dozen women over a period of three years.

The Berlin police were confounded by this monster serial killer who seemed to vanish in the city's shadows. Clues were nonexistent. There was no pattern to his crimes other than the victims' youth and beauty.

To everyone who read the newspapers or listened to the radio, he was now known as *Der Nacht Hund,* the Night Dog.

In deep shadows, *Der Nacht Hund* lurked ten feet above the grim, dimly lit alley that wound between the Berlin city hospital and the morgue and ended a block away at the Gelderstrasse bus stop. He had pulled himself, hand-over-hand, up into the shadows by the pipes that ribbed the alley wall. There he waited and watched as the night shift ended and the doctors, interns and nurses drifted out, jabbering as they walked to cars or down the alley below to the bus.

Fifteen minutes passed. He had been watching the alley for several nights, perched in its shadows, checking the nurses, seeking out that perfect beauty and waiting for the moment when she might drop her guard and walk down the alleyway alone.

Der Nacht Hund was infinitely patient.

Two nurses came out of the staff door of the hospital and waited under the bright lights of the emergency entrance for several minutes. One was short and stout, the other, taller and slender with long equine features.

The tall one moved out of the light and lit a cigarette which she shared with the other one. They giggled mischievously, passing the cigarette back and forth, watching lest a doctor or senior nurse catch them. Women were forbidden from smoking on the hospital grounds; if caught, the two would be sternly chastised. In fact, the night supervisor frowned on women smoking at all, considering it a common and filthy habit suitable only for men.

They finished the cigarette, looked back at the exit, then the shorter one shrugged. They proceeded down the alley toward the bus stop.

The third woman was young, barely in her twenties, with an angelic face that exuded innocence and wonder, a delicate beauty who had been in nurse's training for only a few weeks. As she exited the hospital, she looked around and called out, "Anna? Sophie?"

No answer.

She approached the mouth of the alley cautiously, and leaning forward peered into its gloomy depths. Fifty yards away the alley curved. She could see the long shadows of her two friends cast against the brick wall by the street lamps at the bus stop, could hear faint laughter.

She huddled into her coat and walked rapidly after them.

The loden coat made a slight flapping sound as he dropped toward his prey and she turned a moment before he landed behind her.

She caught a brief glimpse of his warped features but before she could scream he lashed out with one hand, slamming it over her mouth and shoving her against the alley wall. Her eyes bulged in terror; he immediately struck her in the temple with his other fist, a sharp, hard punch that knocked her unconscious. She made a slight whimpering sound, her knees buckled and as she dropped straight down he gathered her up in his arms and whisked her into a doorway.

There was not a sound. The alley was suddenly empty.

"Cut!"

Fifty feet away, the director rose from his canvas chair and applauded.

"Wunderbar, wunderbar!" he said in a thick German accent

as he walked across the eerie Gothic movie set toward his stars. "That should whiten their knuckles."

The girl walked out into the set with a sigh.

"Wonderful, my darling," the director cooed, and brushed her cheek with his lips. He was a slight, esthetic man, ramrod straight with the manners of a duke.

"Thank you, Fritz," she said, genuinely pleased by the compliment. This was only her third film, the first in a costarring part. She was still awed by her luck at playing opposite Johann Ingersoll, Germany's most popular actor, and being directed by Fritz Jergens, one of Germany's best-known directors.

The creature emerged behind her.

"Excellent, Johann. Magnificent as always." Jergens shook the monster's hand. "You can go to lunch. Freda, we will do your close-ups before we break."

Ingersoll merely nodded. Remaining in character, he crossed the set in his strange crablike gait and entered a dressing room in the corner of the sound stage.

His valet, Otto Heinz, was waiting as usual. As the actor pulled the door closed, the small, gray-haired man poured Ingersoll a small snifter of brandy. Ingersoll suddenly seemed to grow a foot taller, straightening his shoulders, standing up to his full height. He shook his shoulders out, took out the grotesque plate that covered his real teeth and placed it in a glass cup which Heinz held open for him. He carefully removed the shaggy wig and, as Heinz placed it on a head mold on the corner of the makeup table, the actor dropped wearily on a chaise lounge in the corner of the room.

"It will soon be over," Heinz said, standing behind him. Short and in his late fifties, Heinz still had the body and arms of a weightlifter. He kneaded his muscular hands into Ingersoll's shoulders.

"Ten more days," Ingersoll sighed in a voice that was refined with only a trace of an accent. "This has been the most difficult one so far. Those stunts in that grotesque posture . . . and the makeup! My God, I will think twice before I ever go *this* far again."

Heinz laughed softly. He knew the agony of enduring seven, sometimes eight hours a day in the heavy disguise. It was unbearably hot under the layers of latex and cosmetics, uncomfortable to the point of pain. But he also understood Ingersoll's drive to make each character more startling, more frightening and original than the previous one. Ingersoll created his own makeup, arising several hours before he was due on the set, applying it himself, assisted only by Heinz, who was also his valet, cook and chauffeur.

"You say that on every show," Heinz said.

"This time I mean it. I will swear it in my own blood."

"Of course."

Heinz had given up his own respectable career as a top makeup man to become Ingersoll's servant and confidant. He was a key figure in one of Germany's most popular mysteries— *who was the real Johann Ingersoll?*

The star had made seven enormously popular horror films, five of them talking pictures, and was being compared to the great American actor Lon Chaney. Yet nobody knew *anything* about Johann Ingersoll. There were no photographs of him except in the grotesque makeup he invented for each picture. His biography listed only his films. He never granted interviews and went to unusual lengths to protect his real identity. Adding further to the mystique was Ingersoll's eccentric habit of arriving on the set each day in makeup and leaving the same way, sneaking through the underground tunnels that led to the furnace rooms and the adjoining sound stages, scurrying to some predetermined spot where Heinz was waiting with the limousine. For four years he had eluded both the news reporters and the fans who tried to peer behind the masks, to unveil the real Johann Ingersoll.

The ploy was a publicist's dream and had enhanced the celebrity and stardom of the actor. His stature was now equal to that of Conrad Veidt, Emil Jannings and Peter Lorre. Together they were the four most popular actors to emerge from Germany's young film industry.

There was a soft tapping at the door. Ingersoll groaned.

"Now what?"

"*Ja?*" Heinz said.

"It is Friedrich. Sorry to intrude but it is important."

"Come, come," Ingersoll said impatiently.

Friedrich Kreisler was a tall, intense man in his mid-thirties, a bon vivant who dressed in the latest fashion, wore his fedora jauntily cocked over one eye and affected a monocle and cane. He was Ingersoll's attorney, agent and manager, and Ingersoll had made him a rich man in a bankrupt Germany where such a feat was virtually impossible. Only one person other than Heinz knew the truth about Ingersoll and that person was Kreisler. It was Kreisler who had created the idea of the movie star nobody knew, who had accompanied him on his first screen test when Ingersoll had stunned the studio by arriving already made up as a character of his own diabolical imagination. It was Kreisler who negotiated all the contracts and who handled all of Ingersoll's business affairs.

To everyone else, his friends and neighbors, Ingersoll was Hans Wolfe, a reclusive Berlin businessman who frequently spent weeks at a time abroad.

"So, how does it go?" Kreisler asked.

Heinz rolled his eyes as if to say "don't ask."

"I need rest," Ingersoll said.

"Three months when you finish. We don't start *Das Mitternächtige Tier* until spring."

"It will take me that long to create the character. I have already done a werewolf once; this one must be different."

"Ah, you go skiing in Austria for a month, think about it around the fire at night."

"I suppose."

"I . . . uh . . . you have a visitor," Kreisler said tentatively.

Ingersoll looked up sharply.

"I do not take visitors on the set. You know that," he snapped.

"I think perhaps you will make an exception this time."

"No exceptions!"

Kreisler took a letter from his pocket and handed it to Ingersoll.

"He's outside," the agent said.

Ingersoll turned the letter over. There was an official wax seal on the back. His intolerance with the intrusion was obvious as he ripped open the envelope and unfolded the note. It read:

Herr Ingersoll,

     This will introduce Dr. Wilhelm Vierhaus, a member
of my personal staff. I will be in your debt if you will give
him a few moments of your time on a matter of the utmost
importance to us both.

     It was signed "A. Hitler."

Ingersoll was shocked when Vierhaus entered the dressing room—the visitor's body might have been a creation of his own. Vierhaus had a hunchback, a small distortion on his left shoulder which he partially concealed with a cloak. He held his head true instead of cocked to the side and stood as straight as his physical deformity would permit in an attempt to minimize it. Thick glasses magnified keen, scrutinizing blue eyes. His hair was neatly trimmed and short but not in the crew cut one might expect of someone in the Nazi hierarchy. Were it not for the crippling defect and the thick glasses, Vierhaus would have been handsome for his features were cleanly chiseled and perfect, his jaw was firm and hard. Everything about Vierhaus exuded strength except the physical trick birth had played on him, a black joke which he managed to minimize with a sense of confidence and self-assurance. His handshake was firm and deliberate, his smile warm and genuine.

"Please forgive this intrusion," he apologized. "But I was advised that you are a hard man to approach at the end of the day. Herr Kreisler suggested this might be the best time to talk."

"Of course, of course," Ingersoll answered. Heinz placed a small salad and a cup of tea on a tray in Ingersoll's lap.

"Will you join me in some lunch?"

"*Nein, nein,*" Vierhaus said waving his hand. "*Danke.* I had a late breakfast. But please, go ahead, I know your time is limited."

Ingersoll nodded, toying with his salad as he studied Vierhaus through his gray eye.

"So, *Herr Doktor,* why should I suddenly be so important to you and the Führer?"

"It is quite simple," Vierhaus said. "Our Führer is a great fan of yours, *Herr Schauspieler.* He has seen all your films, some of them several times. He is having friends to his retreat at the Berghof a few weeks from now, a weekend of conversation and perhaps skiing if the early snow is good. He would be pleased to have you join him."

Ingersoll was surprised—no, *elated*—by the invitation. Although he tried his best to remain calm, his heart pounded with excitement. He had just been invited to the leader's most private retreat, the house known as the Eagle's Nest high in the Bavarian Alps above Berchtesgaden.

Hitler wanted to meet *him*!

"I understand you will finish *Der Nacht Hund* in ten days," Vierhaus hurried on. "So it should be perfect for you. The party is not until the first week in February. The Führer's private plane will take you from Berlin to Munich and his car will carry you on from there. I assure you, it will be a most exciting weekend."

"I'm sure of that," Ingersoll replied. The hideous makeup helped him to conceal his excitement. Even for the Führer, Ingersoll did not want to appear overly enthusiastic. "And of course I am flattered by the invitation. Heinz, do you have our schedule handy?"

"I'll get it, sir."

"If there's a conflict . . ." Vierhaus said.

"*Nein,* nothing that can't be switched around," Ingersoll answered quickly.

"Excellent. He can count on you then?"

He was unable to conceal his delight any longer at the thought of meeting Germany's new leader, for he was an ardent supporter of the Nazi party and an unabashed admirer of Hitler. Ingersoll, like many Germans, saw, in this brash, magnetic leader, the answer to the country's problems. Hitler preached a different kind of patriotism from the Kaiser and his predecessors. There was fire in every word, energy crackled around him like lightning. For the first time since the war, *someone* was restoring pride to the people, giving them hope, promising revenge for the terrible injustice the Allies had wrought at Versailles. The thought charged his memory and sent it tumbling back in time.

When Ingersoll joined the German Army in 1916, everyone assumed the war was almost won. And things continued to go well. Europe was one big trench from the English Channel to the Black Sea and the news from home was always encouraging. The Turks had killed 6,000 British soldiers at Gaza in Palestine. In the snow and rain at Caporetto, Italy, 400,000 men had deserted after 10,000 of their comrades were killed in two days and another 40,000 wounded. And in a single day at the Somme, over 19,000 British soldiers had died. Russia was torn by revolution, fighting the Germans on its borders and its own people in the streets of Petrograd and Moscow. There were rumors of mutiny all along the front where it was said that the British and French alike were dropping their guns and running. Encouraging news indeed!

But on his first furlough in 1917, he realized that rumors of victory were lies. In Berlin, the cost of the bloody three-year war had turned the city into a civilian battleground. There wasn't enough food and the country was going bankrupt. On his first day home, he had been caught up in a street riot, watching in disbelief as German troops fought strikers in the streets. Huddled in a doorway, he was numbed with horror.

"Go back to work or be shot," an army captain demanded. "Kaiser's orders!"

When the strikers refused, he ordered his men to fire into the knot of civilians. There was chaos as the soldiers, on horseback, charged the group, trampling men and women under hoof, slashing them with sabers, gunning them down.

That night in a restaurant, Ingersoll was served horse meat. When he complained, the waiter, who was missing a leg and wore an Iron Cross on his jacket, snapped, "They're eating horse meat in Paris, too! When you get to the front you will realize there are no farms left, only mud and wire."

"I've been to the front!" Ingersoll snapped back.

It was the first time it occurred to Ingersoll that Germany might lose the war. Returning to the horror of battle, Ingersoll was shocked to see German troops dropping their weapons and fleeing in disorder before the American Marines who had now entered the battle.

The American Marines, nicknamed the Devil Hounds, charged maniacally, screaming as they came. As they screamed, the Germans ran, tumbling over each other, wallowing through the mud, screaming in pain and terror as their ranks broke in disarray. In final desperation, the Germans launched deadly poison gas bombs. But, in a final twist of fate, the wind changed and the deadly clouds drifted back into the German ranks. Gasping for breath, they clawed feverishly for their gas masks. Many had thrown the cumbersome masks away and now they attacked their own comrades, desperately ripping away at the lifesaving devices they had carelessly discarded.

Ingersoll cowered in a shell hole, his ruined mask filled with muddy water, until finally he pulled a mask off a dead Englishman and got it over his face. The gas stung his hands and neck. Then he looked up and saw the American Marine standing over him, his rifle pointed at him, the point of his bayonet at Ingersoll's throat. The young German dropped his gun and slowly raised his hands in the ultimate gesture of surrender.

Returning to a devastated homeland, Ingersoll, like thousands of other soldiers, found himself scorned by civilians and betrayed by the Kaiser and his politicians. He became one of millions of impoverished Germans, begging for food, wandering from town to town looking for work, rootless and alone and damning to hell the British, French and Americans for humbling the motherland and driving her to her knees. The living nightmare of returning in disgrace to a devastated and bankrupt homeland, to breadlines and street brawls and political chaos, still haunted him. Sometimes he awoke at night soaked in sweat. The vivid memory of being cold and hungry, of sleeping in an alley covered with a sheet of tar paper, was as real as if it were happening at that very moment.

He had joined the National Socialist party in 1928, a few months before the chance meeting with Freddie Kreisler that had changed his life forever. Although he had never been active in the Nazi party, it had introduced him to **Mein Kampf** *and the genius of Adolf Hitler. He read and reread* **Mein Kampf,** *even underlining certain passages and memorizing them.*

While on holiday near Braunschweig he had journeyed to the town out of curiosity to witness a Nazi rally. He watched in awe as hundreds of Hitler's brownshirts goose-stepped up the cobblestone streets.

"Heil Hitler! Heil Hitler!" *echoed through the ancient town.*

Women held up their children to see the savior and threw flowers before his car, their eyes glassy with adoration. The men threw their arms out in the Nazi salute and continued the chorus.

"Sieg heil! Sieg heil! Sieg heil!"

But it was that night, when Hitler made his speech, that Ingersoll recognized the true power of the man. Thousands crowded into the town square, their faces transfixed in the flickering light of torches, hypnotized by the sound of his voice and by the stern discipline of his stare. It was a Gothic opera, a blend of choreography, chorus and aria that both chilled and excited the actor.

What had been called the Führer's Fingerspitzengefühl, *his "fingertip touch," was immediately obvious to Ingersoll. The man had a talent for moving rich and poor alike with an intoxicating brew of political strategy, superpatriotism, and rousing oratory. Angrily, he publicly damned the Allies, refuted the Treaty of Versailles and encouraged Germany to refuse to pay its devastating reparations. He was preaching a new and inspiring kind of national patriotism, discarding the yoke of defeat with his fervor and passion.*

Ingersoll also admired the actor in Hitler, for the Führer savored his performance with an uncanny sense of timing, knowing just when to pause, to wait for the crowd to answer his oratory.

"Heil Hitler!"

"Sieg heil!"

"Sieg heil!"

And there were two other things. First, his attack on the Versailles treaty. Ingersoll had never been political. He had gone to war because it was the patriotic thing to do, to fight for family and for Germany. But at Versailles, the Allies had overlooked that, had forgotten the millions of men who had returned broken in mind, body and spirit. After all, one man's hero is always another man's enemy. And so they had unleashed their victor's venom on all of Germany instead of the politicians who had led them into war, had stripped Germany of honor and resources and left a country dispirited, bankrupt and divided by chaos, a nightmare place stripped of hope. The heart of the country and its people had been pierced by the sword of the avengers and, in the wake of war, anger and hate fired the need for retribution, for another match somewhere in time. The ink was not yet dry on the peace contract and already, from beer halls to breakfast nooks, there was talk of getting even. And no voice had been louder than Ingersoll's.

And there was this other thing, this thing with the Jews. As a child, Ingersoll has listened to his father, an alcoholic failure, revile the Jews, blaming them for all his family's misfortune. Ingersoll had accepted the stereotypical harangues as truth. The old man's fury infected the son until Ingersoll harbored an almost psychotic contempt for Jews. Ultimately, bigotry rather than courage became Ingersoll's sticking post and subconsciously he turned his obsessive passion inward, harnessing it and forging it into the frightening, antisocial monsters he invented for the screen.

So Hitler's inspired intuitionism enhanced the Führer's allure, firing

Ingersoll's creative sensitivity into an inferno of hatred and anger. Hitler's racial attacks were like a tonic to Ingersoll and he found himself believing in the Führer with an intellectual ardor fueled by passionate racism. Proselytized by the power, baptized by the drama, Ingersoll soon became part of the throng, lashing out with his arm and joining the chorus.

"Heil Hitler!"

"Heil Hitler!"

"Heil Hitler!"

So this personal invitation was euphoric indeed, an unexpected bonus from a career that already had carried Ingersoll far beyond his wildest dreams.

"Absolutely," he said, barely able to conceal his enthusiasm.

"Excellent! Our Leader will be delighted, as am I. I also am a fan. I think you are a genius, Herr Ingersoll, and I have heard the Führer refer to you as a national treasure."

"Really! Well . . ." Ingersoll was almost stammering. "What can I say."

"You have already said it," Vierhaus said with a smile. "The Führer's chauffeur will pick you up Friday morning, February 4th, at six A.M. for the flight to Munich."

"I know the area. I've skied there."

"*Gut.* Are you a meat eater?"

"*Ja.*"

"Herr Hitler is a vegetarian. He calls people who prefer meat 'corpse eaters.'"

"That's a bit severe."

"The Führer tends toward the extreme in his opinions, as you probably know."

"I eat everything but fish. Anything that breathes through a hole in the side of its neck makes me nervous."

Vierhaus chuckled.

"You must tell him that. He has a keen sense of humor. Well, if there is a change, I will be in touch with Herr Kreisler. Otherwise we'll see you on the fourth. Good luck with your film."

They shook hands again and Vierhaus was gone as quickly as he had come. Ingersoll sat back with his mouth open.

"Hitler wants to meet *me*!" he breathed.

"And why not, my friend," Otto said, laughing with joy. "As Hitler himself says, you are a national treasure. Enjoy the moment, it is just the beginning."

Outside the studio, Vierhaus settled back in his Mercedes and smiled. The man was bedazzled, he thought to himself. Everything we have learned about him is true. He is the perfect choice.

Done!

And now *Der Führer* would complete the transformation.

The first step in the fiendishly conceived plot Vierhaus simply called *Siebenundzwanzig*—27—was complete.

Ingersoll sprawled on the chaise lounge in the living room of his town house, freshly bathed, swathed in his silk robe, sipping champagne and staring out at the Helgestrasse. The events of the day raced through his mind. He had awakened that morning feeling unusually stressed and tired. There were a lot of reasons. The picture was three days over schedule and there was another week to go. It had been a difficult shoot from the start. That new girl, whatever her name was, had been tense and insecure since the first day, requiring take after take. His makeup was more difficult than usual to put on and became painful after only two or three hours. Every muscle in his face ached after nine hours encased in the twisted mask of rubber and aluminum.

But the visit from Hitler's envoy had made up for all that. Only two years before, Ingersoll had been one of the millions of dispirited, homeless Germans scrambling for a living. Now here he was, rich and famous, and Germany's new savior wanted to meet him, indeed had invited him to the Eagle's Nest!

Mixed blessings.

He felt both exhausted and elated. And restless. And the more champagne he drank, the more restless he became, the stronger the familiar stirring became. He knew the symptoms, just as he knew that before the night was over he would know both ecstasy and humiliation.

As always, he tried to fight off the compulsion. He thought of taking a sleeping pill—except the nightmares that accompanied his strange obsession were sometimes worse than the reality.

He held up the champagne glass and stared at it. His hand was shaking, an almost imperceptible tremor. He put the glass down and squeezed his hands together. The compulsion became stronger. The stirring began. Finally he buzzed for Heinz.

"I've changed my mind about dinner," he said. "Will that be a problem for you, Heinz?"

"Of course not. I've just started cooking."

"Good. Call the Ritz and get me a suite on the second floor, will you? Tell them I'll be ordering dinner for two."

"Right away. Will it be Mr. Sanders tonight?"

"Yes. And lay out my tuxedo, please. I feel a bit elegant tonight, Heinz. I feel like celebrating."

"As well you should, Hans."

"Yes. It has been a significant day, hasn't it?"

"I'll get things ready."

After Heinz left the room, Ingersoll downed the rest of the champagne and went to a corner of the room. He slid back a tall bookcase and opened the safe behind it. Inside were thick envelopes of cash: American dollars, British pounds, French francs. Everything but German marks. With inflation as high as it was it would take a safe full of marks to buy a bowl of soup. He opened one of the envelopes, counted out five hundred British pounds and stuffed them in a pocket of his robe.

Two hours later, Ingersoll checked into the hotel where he was known as Harry Sanders, a fiftyish English art dealer with thick white hair and an elegantly trimmed beard. Sanders was a welcome guest. He usually arrived with only a small, black suitcase, ran up impressive bills, stayed only one night and always paid in British pounds. He went up to the suite, checked it out, then left the hotel immediately to begin cruising the Helgestrasse in his Mercedes.

Driving through the dark streets, he was light-headed with anticipation. Less than two blocks from the hotel he passed four brownshirts standing in front of a jewelry store. One held an old Jewish man by the collar while two others stood with their faces inches from his, berating the old man, who was wearing a yarmulke. The fourth uniformed storm trooper was painting a six-pointed star on the wall beside the display window. Ingersoll stopped his car, turned off the lights and watched as the SA troopers began pushing the old man from one to the other, in a circle, spinning him around as they did. They pulled the skullcap off and threw it in the gutter. Then they began punching the crying old man, spinning him and punching him until he fell to his knees. The biggest of the storm troopers stepped back and kicked the man in the chest. He fell to the ground, drawing up into a fetal knot with his hands over his head. The storm troopers were laughing as they circled their cowering victim, taunting him, kicking him, screaming insults at him. Then the big one picked up a garbage can and shattered the display window with it. The glass showered down in a rain of gleaming daggers and splashed across the sidewalk. The SA stood back and appraised their destruction. Satisfied, they went off down the street laughing and singing.

The old man did not move. He lay curled on the sidewalk, shaking. Ingersoll sat for a few minutes watching him. Finally there was a stirring in the shadows; two men scurried out and helped him up.

Well, the actor thought bitterly, that old Jew learned his lesson.

For a moment, Ingersoll wondered about his dispassionate response, for he felt no pity for the helpless old man. Certainly he despised the drunken, brawling brownshirt louts. They were animallike in their stupidity. But these were extreme times and extreme measures were necessary. Sooner or later the Marxist Jews would get the message. While the rest of the Germans wallowed in debt, the Jews grew richer, hoarding their money, controlling the banks, supporting the Communists who *wanted* to destroy the economy.

Sooner or later they'll figure it out, Ingersoll thought as he drove on. Sooner or later they would all close up shop and get the hell out of Germany. And the sooner the better.

She had long, dark hair which was tied with a bow in the back but her skin was fair, almost pale, and she had exquisite deep brown eyes. She could be Italian, he thought, or Spanish. She definitely was not German. She wore very little cheek rouge and a modest amount of lipstick, not the heavy theatrical makeup the German whores troweled on. Greek maybe. He had been driving around appraising the whores on the street for almost an hour and he was getting impatient. He stopped the car and studied her as she eyed the men entering and leaving a bar called The Happy Club.

Twenty-three or four at best. Nice legs and a trim little ass. His groin tightened. He drove up beside her and stopped the car. She leaned over and looked in the window.

"Well, now ain't you the fancy one," she said. The accent was cockney. He was surprised but it was definitely cockney. Ingersoll was an expert on dialects and accents.

"And aren't you the English one. London I'd guess."

"Well ain't you the smart one, too, ducks. East End, actually."

"What are you doing in Berlin?"

"Now what does it look like I'm doin', dearie?"

"I mean, why here," he said caustically. He could not deal with street whores pleasantly, as hard as he tried.

"Say, you're an English toff, too, ain't you?"

He ignored the question.

"What *are* you doing over here?" he repeated.

"Not that it's any of your business, but I'm on holiday and I've run a bit short. And let me give you a hint, sweetie, I can show you a few tricks these German ladies ain't never heard of. Why, I doubt they could *imagine* the kind o' time I can show you."

"And what is this extraordinary performance going to cost me . . . ducks," he said with a sneer.

"Y'know, that's a problem with me. I still haven't worked out this business about marks . . ."

"Tell me in pounds, I'll work out the equation."

"Gaw, you do have a way of talkin', don't you, luv?"

"The *price*," he said coldly.

"Tell you what, we'll start off with a massage. That'll take yer edge off. Then you can really enjoy the rest of the show."

He felt degraded and unclean but he was growing hard thinking about what would follow. This would be enjoyable, he thought.

"*How much?*" he demanded again.

"Ten pounds and the massage is free."

He threw back his head and laughed. "Don't be ridiculous."

"Now look 'ere . . ."

"You never got more than a fiver in your life, *dearie*. I'll pay you seven-fifty for the night."

Negotiating was part of it, part of the compulsion.

"Aw, now, I gets twenty fer the night, you know that's fair. Seven-fifty for one trip."

"Ten for the night."

" 'Ere now," she whined, "give a girl a break, whyn't ya? Don't have to be such a tough one. Make it fifteen and throw in a smile."

"Twelve-fifty. You can forgo the massage and I'll forgo the smile."

"You'll be sorry about the massage."

"Get in the car."

He was a weird one, she thought. Usually her parties wanted to get right to it. This one had called up a fine dinner, then ordered her to take a bath, had given her fresh clothes and even a bottle of perfume. He wasn't in any rush. So here she was in a suite in the fanciest hotel in town, staring at herself in the full-length mirror. The dress was Victorian, draped to the floor. The black corset underneath squeezed and shoved her breasts until they bulged over the top of the dress. A garter belt supported the black hose he had given her.

I look like I just came from the theater, she thought to herself as she dabbed the perfume behind her ears and knees and in the crook of her elbow.

She walked back into the bedroom and stopped in surprise. The older gentleman was gone. In his place a younger man sat on the sofa in the opposite corner of the room. He had short blond hair, was clean shaven and was wearing a black mask that covered the upper part of his face down to his lower lip.

"Where's the other gentleman?" She demanded.

"I *am* the other gentleman," he said.

"What's this all about?"

"Harmless games. Do you object to a little playacting?"

"Gaw, you are a strange one, all right."

"Come over here."

She crossed the room and stood in front of him with her hands on her hips.

"Now reach up under the dress and masturbate," he said softly, almost a whisper. "But don't let me see you. Keep the dress down over your hand."

"*Wha—?*"

"Do it."

She slid both hands up her thighs until he could see the edge of the corset. She shook her hands and the dress flopped over them.

"There is no hurry," he whispered. "Enjoy yourself."

He began to sweat. His heartbeat increased. He could feel his pulse pounding in his temple.

"No hurry," he repeated.

"C'mon, guv, you reach a certain point, you can't slow down, y'know."

"What do you like best about it?"

"Why, comin', o' course. Don't we all? Ain't that the best part for you, luv?"

His blue eyes glittered behind the mask. He licked his lips.

"The best part is after."

"After?"

He was breathing heavier and was almost out of breath.

"Reach out with one hand and take off my tie."

When she did he could smell the musky odor of her sex on her fingers. She slowly drew one end of the tie until it fell loose. The hand under her dress was moving faster and her legs were beginning to quiver. She closed her eyes, lowered her chin to her breasts and licked the top of them as she stroked herself faster.

"Yeah, guv, oh yeah," she groaned.

"Stop," he ordered.

"What?"

"Stop. Unbutton my shirt."

"C'mon now . . ."

"*Do it.*"

She was out of breath and her face was flushed but she did what he asked. Her hands shook as she undid the buttons. When she was finished he took the shirt off. He sat on the sofa and leaned back on his elbows.

"Undo my pants . . . now reach in and stroke me for awhile . . . now you can do yourself again . . . stop! No, not me, you . . . take off the dress . . . yes, now the corset . . . slowly, no hurry . . ."

He saw her full breasts burst free of the tight corset,

watched her as she slid the corset down, stared at the black triangle of hair that glistened a few inches from his face. Her hands stroked him to life. He lay back.

"Now you again . . . yes, like that . . . not so fast, build up to it again . . ."

She couldn't control it.

"Can't wait, luv." She closed her eyes. Her arm was moving spasmodically.

He watched her hand moving faster and faster, watched her stroke him with the same cadence. She begin to tremble, to stiffen and he felt himself about to explode.

"Stop!" he cried out. But she paid no attention.

"*Stop it!*" Her gripped the hand that was stroking him around the wrist. His grip was so tight it hurt her but she still didn't stop. Instead she stroked herself faster and began to moan.

Ingersoll rolled slightly to one side and lashed out with a vicious right cross, punching her in the mouth as hard as he could. Her head snapped back, her body sagged; she fell sideways to the floor and lay there unconscious.

He sat up on the sofa and took a deep breath, composing himself. His chest heaved, twice, three times, then he was calm. He stared down at her, watching the bruise on her jaw turn black, and he began to chuckle.

She came around slowly and just as slowly became aware that her hands and legs were tied to the four corners of the bed. He was inside her, thrusting like an animal. Her mouth was gagged with a cotton cloth. She looked up, terrified. He was leaning over her, his mouth half open, sweat pouring from his chin and when he saw her look up he straightened up and hit her again, not as hard this time but enough to split her lip. She could feel the lip going numb, the salty flow of blood in her throat. She tried to scream. He hit her again and now he began to pant as he hit her, punching her in the chest and ribs and face, although the blows became less and less brutal as he built to a climax with each punch. She was almost unconscious again when she heard him cry out and felt him fall forward on top of her. His head fell beside hers. His heart was pounding against her bruised ribs. She could feel him begin to soften inside her.

She began to moan in pain. If he heard her he paid no attention.

He left her tied and bleeding while he went into the bathroom to shower. When he came back the white wig and beard were restored. He untied her but left the gag in place; her shattered lips were swollen around it. He helped her get dressed, threw the bloody dress and corset and the black mask in the suitcase.

"We're going to leave by the back stairs, the way we came in," he whispered in her ear. "I want you to keep your head down, understand me? Understand?"

She nodded.

"You act drunk. If we pass anybody, don't look up. You make one sound and I will break your neck like a dead twig."

He held her up with one arm and carried his bag in the other. She kept her head down as he had ordered but no one saw them. He shoved her roughly into the front seat of the car and slammed the door, then drove back toward the Helgestrasse in silence. She stared at the floorboard, pressing a towel to her shattered lips.

Two years, chasing rides on freight trains, sleeping under railroad bridges and in the corners of dark tunnels, stealing to eat. Sometimes there had been laboring jobs, brutal work moving railroad tracks or clearing brush for a handful of marks that would barely buy a good meal. And sometimes there had been enough left over to pay one of the whores that lived near the rail yards—old whores, too sick or burned out to appeal to anyone else, smothering his rage in momentary passion while the humiliation burned his soul like a branding iron. A good-looking man like himself, a handsome man, a war hero for God's sake! Reduced to haggling over pennies with filthy, smelly human relics no self-respecting man would endure, screwing in tattered tents or on the ground when the weather was warm enough. But since no respectable woman would have anything to do with the wanderers, it was a momentary relief from the agony of poverty.

He could no longer remember exactly where he was that night. Brandenburg, perhaps, or Münster. Days and places had become a jumbled nightmare in which every place looked the same. Littered rail yards with feeble campfires to keep warm. Hands scabbed and blistered and encrusted with dirt. The endless sound of coughing. A warm summer night. Soft grass underneath them. And he looked up and saw the faces, lined up and peering over the edge of the ravine. Grinning, tooth-rotten mouths and hollow eyes, lined up and peering from the darkness. His rage had been tumultuous. He had thrown pieces of coal at them, grabbed one by the hair and flogged him with a stick.

"We paid her to watch," the feeble voice pleaded.

And turning back he saw her lying there, her dress around her waist, laughing at him.

"You want a show, I'll give you a show," he bellowed. He had mounted her as a bull mounts a cow, roaring with anger, striking her with his fist as he thrust himself into her until he was spent and collapsed on top of her and only then did he realize she was dead.

His first instinct was to run. But the old men had seen him. So he dragged and carried her to a nearby overpass and waited until a train came, hoisting her limp body over the railing, dangling her at arm's length until the train was almost on him, then dropping her in its path.

By morning he had hopped another freight and was miles away and the dead whore was an ugly dream. But it was a dream that would not die and so when he was obsessed, when the compulsion would not go away, he relived the nightmare. And when it was over there was no remorse, no guilt, no anger left in him. Only blessed relief and dreamless sleep.

He returned her to within a block of where he had picked her up, pulled up to the curb and turned off the car lights.

"Look at me," he said softly.

She stared at the floor of the car for several seconds but the softness of his voice made her finally look up at him. One side of her face was black and blue. Her eye was almost swollen shut. Her lips bulged.

He held up a sheaf of pound notes and wiggled them in front of her good eye.

"Two hundred pounds, luv. Now which do you want? Do you want this two hundred quid or do you want me to drive to the police station so you can turn me in for whacking you about? Two hundred, luv, think about it. Couldn't make that in a fortnight, could you?"

She looked at him for a long time before she slowly reached out and took the money.

"Get out," he ordered.

The girl moved painfully out onto the sidewalk. Ingersoll pulled the door shut behind her and the tires squealed as he raced off into the darkness.

Ingersoll awoke at four A.M.. The two months since the strange professor had visited him on the set had flown by. They had worked feverishly editing the picture and he had seen the rough edit of *Der Nacht Hund* the night before. Everyone agreed that it was his best film to date. They had added simple titles so he could carry it with him to Berchtesgaden for a private showing to the Führer. It would be the first public showing. The premiere was set for late February at the Kroll Opera House and would be a gala event.

For two hours, he and Heinz worked on his makeup. He had decided to go as a middle-aged businessman with latex masking that moved his hairline back, giving him a partially bald look. Heinz built up the bridge of his nose to give it a hard, almost hooked appearance; rubber fleshed out his cheeks and jowled his jaw line. Gray streaks in his thinned hair, a gray mustache and goatee and wire-rimmed glasses with clear lenses finished the process. He put on a tweed double-breasted suit and wore his fur-lined black trench coat.

He smiled in the mirror at the older man who looked back: a forty-five-year-old, respectably affluent, slightly paunchy businessman.

At precisely six A.M., a uniformed sergeant arrived at the door and whisked him in one of Hitler's private cars to the airport for the two-hour flight to Munich. He was treated like royalty. By 8:30 he was having coffee and pastries at the old Barlow Palace facing Munich's Königsplatz, waiting to be picked up by Hitler's personal chauffeur.

In the lobby, Ingersoll sensed Hitler's presence everywhere. In January, the old palace had been opened as the headquarters for the Nazi party after months of renovations. It was now called the Brown House and had been redesigned by Hitler's personal architect, Albert Speer. The cost had been staggering although nobody knew what the changes had actually cost. "Blood flags" from the Beer Hall Putsch and other early Nazi street battles snapped in the wind over the entrance and the place seemed to be a hive of activity. Dispatch riders wheeled up on motorcycles. Officers marched briskly in and out of the building, their riding boots clacking on marble floors. There was a constant ringing of telephones. The place was antiseptically clean, smelling of cold steel, leather, and boot polish.

Hitler's dynamic charisma dominated the place even though Ingersoll knew he was in Berchtesgaden, one hundred miles away. This was the heart of the Nazi party, the nerve center of the New Germany. One could almost hear the Führer's voice as he dictated Germany's future from behind the walls of his vast first-floor suite of offices.

He had only to wait a few minutes before the chauffeur arrived in Hitler's open Mercedes.

"Shall I put up the top?" the chauffeur asked. "It's quite cold."

Ingersoll shook his head. He knew the drive south to the Bavarian border in the Alpine foothills was one of the most beautiful in all Germany and he wanted to enjoy the scenery. A blanket and his heavy coat would suffice. The chauffeur gave him a hat with ear flaps and then raced off down the main highway toward the Führer's hideaway.

Hitler, usually a late sleeper, had awakened as first light cast long red shadows into the bedroom. He lay wide awake, staring at the ceiling for several minutes before he slipped out of the bed he shared with Eva Braun and walked through the bathroom into his sitting room.

Four days earlier, Hindenburg had named him chancellor of the German Republic.

Chancellor!

He was Chancellor of Germany.

He held out a hand and stared at it. As the new president of the Reichstag, the nation's parliament, Hitler had the laws of Germany in the palm of that hand.

Chancellor Hitler.

He had strutted around the room in his bathrobe laughing aloud and repeating the two words over and over again before ordering up coffee and sweet rolls and drawing his bath.

Now Hitler stood at the window of his sitting room, as he often did, gazing north toward Braunau am Inn, his birthplace, and then east toward Vienna, remembering with rage the words which had once torn at his heart.

Nicht zur Prüfung zugelassen.

He tapped a forefinger on his cheek and chuckled with self-satisfaction. Ingersoll! One of the world's most famous actors at his command, on his way to the Berghof, he thought. Now it was he who humiliated those miserable middle-class fools in the Waldviertel who had laughed at him when he was young, called him the "cemetery fool" because he sometimes sat all night on the wall surrounding the medieval graveyard staring at the stars and dreaming. They had ridiculed his dreams of becoming another Rembrandt as had the stupid masters at the Vienna Academy whose words, even after twelve years, still stung.

Nicht zur Prüfung zugelassen.

"Not admitted to the examination."

Twice the Academy in Vienna had rejected him, twice they had humiliated him. The bastards had refused to even let him take the examination for admittance to art school! He gazed across the foothills and forest toward the place he still hated. Waldviertel, "the wooded quarter," that borderland of brutal soil, medieval architecture and narrow minds where he was born, that dreary and depressing corner of Austria which had rejected and humiliated him.

He had only bad memories of that hard land and its people who had once thought of him only as an argumentative, willful, arrogant and bad-tempered young man, so disliked that they ridiculed him behind his back. Even his one friend, August Kubizek—old Gustl—thought he was a bit strange.

None of them understood. Then.

But they did now.

He laughed aloud, pounding a fist into the palm of his other hand.

None of them knew his torments as a child. None of them understood his dreams.

"Imbeciles!" he said aloud as he paced the room. He frequently talked to himself in the privacy of his office.

In the dark corners of his mind, Hitler sometimes planned the most vicious kind of retaliation for the officials at the Vienna Academy who had smashed his early dreams, forcing him to sell his hand-painted postcards on the streets to earn enough to eat and pay the two kronen it cost to spend the week in the cold, filthy men's home along the Danube. They had sentenced him to three years in the gutter, a derelict wandering Vienna in a mindless trance, cold and hungry. He still feared and hated the winter. And he hated the Jews who bought his postcards. He hated them because they had pitied him. Pity was a word that turned to ashes in his mouth.

Well, nobody, *nobody* laughed at him anymore. Five nights before he had stood in the window of the Chancellery for four hours while thousands marched by under torchlight, screaming his name and singing the "Horst Wessel" song, the Nazi anthem. The excitement of that night still clung to him. Now they threw flowers at his feet, exhibited his early architectural paintings in a special section of the Vienna museum, raised their arms in stiff salute and howled *Heil Hitler* when he drove through the city. And in the Waldviertel they pointed to the place where he was born, now a cheap, pink-plastered inn, and bragged that the life of the new savior of Germany had begun in that very house. Perhaps that was retribution enough.

He stood at the window, smiling, his groin throbbing with excitement, and incanted softly to himself:

"*Heil Hitler, Heil Hitler, Heil Hitler.*" And giggled.

The 150-kilometer drive to Berchtesgaden had taken two hours and by midmorning they were on the way up the dirt road toward the mountain stronghold. As they drove through the eight-foot wire fence with its top strands of electrified wire, past the guard dogs and the sentries, and up the dirt road that led to Hitler's retreat, Ingersoll could see the Berghof, Hitler's mountainside chalet, etched against a thick forest of pine trees. The house itself was smaller and simpler than he expected, but the setting, perched as it was 3,300 feet above the village in the Bavarian Alps, was stunning.

Staring at the chalet, Ingersoll recalled a recurring theme from Hitler's speeches:

"Absolute authority comes from God, absolute obedience comes from the Devil."

It was one of Hitler's favorite aphorisms for it justified what he called *Machtergreifung,* his seizure of power in Germany.

Was this the hideaway of God or the Devil, Ingersoll wondered? Was Hitler's vision for Germany ordained or Mephistophelian?

Not that it made any difference. For Germany now had a leader who scoffed at the Allies and trampled the miserable Versailles treaty underfoot. His was a divine vision, regardless of its roots.

Ingersoll was an avid student of neo-German history, knew that much was based on lies or, rather, "propaganda." He knew that the "Horst Wessel" song was named after a miserable pimp who had been elevated to martyrdom by Nazi lies, that even the *Machtergreifung* was a lie. Hitler had not seized power, he had bought and bartered it. But Ingersoll accepted Hitler's manipulations as the actions of a political genius who had to resort to sordid intrigues to win; to sellouts in smoke-filled rooms, to millions of marks in graft from the Ruhr's wealthy industrialists like Krupp and bankers like von Schroeder, to his use of the brownshirt storm troopers who terrorized the population, to lies about the power the Jews never had. Hitler wove fantasies around them, blamed them for the rise of Marxism and Communism in Germany and for the desperate depression that by now had twenty million Germans unemployed and near starvation.

Ingersoll accepted that, too, since his hatred of Jews was as virulent as was Hitler's, just as he recognized that misery and destitution had become Hitler's strongest allies. The more helplessly the Germans were mired in poverty, the more they turned to this strange political agitator who sometimes made five or six speeches in a single day, orchestrated by goose-stepping storm troopers waving swastikas, and who proclaimed that he would single-handedly rid Germany of her debts and her enemies, grant land to farmers, socialism to workers and anticommunism to the wealthy, although he never explained how he planned to accomplish any of this. And while he had never actually won an election, he had won enough votes to manipulate the aging and senile Hindenburg into naming him chancellor of Germany, the new head of the Reichstag.

Hitler was a mere step away from becoming dictator.

Ingersoll accepted that inevitability as a small price to pay. If chicanery and lies were the road to success, Ingersoll earnestly believed that in Hitler Germany had found the perfect leader to exploit them. And he felt a kindred link to him since Ingersoll's own good fortune had paralleled Hitler's.

Now he was to be the personal guest of Germany's new chancellor. His nerves hummed with the electricity of expectation as they approached the chalet.

Professor Vierhaus knocked softly on the door to the sitting room, usually a forbidden place to everyone but Eva Braun. But on this morning he had been invited to have coffee with the Führer and talk about *der Schauspieler*—the Actor—which is how Hitler referred to Ingersoll. Vierhaus was flattered. Hitler, a late sleeper, usually arose around eleven A.M. looked over the morning reports, and didn't appear until noon.

"Come, come," was the impatient response.

He had only been in Hitler's private sitting room once before. Entering it now, he remembered how surprised he had been the first time he had seen it. The sitting room was small and rather bleak with high ceilings, a simple chandelier and thick double doors. Two French windows overlooked the valley, their heavy drapes and cotton curtains pulled back. His desk was angled in one corner near the windows. There was an easy chair, a bookcase and a sofa with three hand-sewn throw pillows. That was it. Two expensive but worn Oriental rugs partially covered the brilliantly waxed dark oak floors. There was a rather dreary landscape over the sofa. A wolf painting near the desk. A photograph of Hitler addressing a meeting somewhere hung on the wall beside the desk. A coffee service was set on the corner of the desk. Nothing more.

Hitler was seated at his desk writing.

"I'm working on my acceptance speech," Hitler said without looking up. "Give me just a moment, I don't want to lose the thought."

"Shall I leave and come back later?"

"No. Just a moment."

Vierhaus stood as straight as possible, lifting one shoulder to balance the hump on the other side of his back, trying to minimize the grotesque posture caused by his deformity. Hitler looked over at him.

"Sit, sit, Willie."

"Yes sir."

Vierhaus sat down. Hitler continued writing, his scratching pen the only sound in the room except for the wind which moaned through the eaves outside. He stopped, the pen poised at his lips, then scribbled out another sentence.

"This will be the most important speech of my life," he said, staring at the paper. "I must challenge them as never before."

"Yes, *mein Führer.*"

The little man finally put his pen down and leaned back in his chair, reading what he had written.

"Listen to this, Professor. 'We must raise the German people by their own labor, their own industry, their own determination and daring, their own perseverance, so they will perceive Germany, not as a gift, but a nation created by themselves.' What do you think?"

Vierhaus thought for several moments before answering.

"Excellent, Führer, excellent. Powerful. I would consider only one small suggestion."

Hitler glowered but said nothing.

"Where you say 'they will perceive Germany,' perhaps 'perceive' is a bit too intellectual. Accept might be more understandable to the public."

"Humph," Hitler snorted. "Seems a bit weak, that word accept." He did not take criticism well but even as he disagreed he drew a line through the word "perceive" and wrote "accept" over it.

As a clinical psychologist, Vierhaus knew and understood Hitler's contradictions far better than did most of his henchmen. He encouraged them and used them to fuel Hitler's most outrageous schemes, many of which he himself had subtly planted in the Führer's mind. Here was a man whose personal sanctuary was modest at best but who had spent millions on the renovation of Brown House. A man who decried the use of alcohol yet drank beer, champagne and wine; who loved sausage but decried eating meat; who hated hunting but eagerly encouraged the murder of his political enemies and Jews; who could coo like a dove one moment and go into fits of rage an instant later, driven out of control by rampant paranoia; who ate meagerly in public but whose cook, a grossly fat man named Willy Kannenberg, produced exquisite seven- and eight-course meals for him; who demanded radical self-discipline yet indulged himself in sweets, fruit and cream cakes and literally drowned his tea and coffee in sugar and cream; who publicly encouraged and rewarded the marriage of purer Aryans yet kept a mistress.

"It is wiser to have a mistress than to be married," Hitler had told Vierhaus once, then added with a wink, "Of course, this only holds true of an exceptional man."

Psychotic behavior patterns all, yet Vierhaus accepted them, even encouraged them, for he also saw the other Hitler. Pale, slight, his thin brown hair draped over one eye, here was a man so common he should have been easy to ignore but who was, instead, a man who could not be overlooked in *any* company. Self-assured, confident, dignified, his flashing, cold-steel eyes signaled the fanatic within and the cutting-edge mind that lurked behind the spurious smile. People were awed in his presence without knowing why.

Vierhaus understood it all. Unlike Goebbels, Göring, Himmler and the rest of the sycophants who agreed blindly with everything Hitler said, Vierhaus recognized both the genius and the madness of the man. He had recognized it nine years before when he had first seen Hitler at Landsberg prison. Here was a political prisoner who was living in relative splendor, his cell decorated with flowers and pictures, a special cot in the corner, his meals specially prepared for him, writing a book which outlined his plan to overthrow the government. Amazing, Vierhaus had thought, this little man with incredible self-assurance around whom power seemed to energize. If they did not put him in a madhouse or assassinate him, he could become a very dangerous man.

Now he marveled at the understatement. What was it Nietzsche had said? *All greatness is tinged with madness.* How accurate.

Hitler was standing with his back to the door, staring out the window.

"My father never understood the world," Hitler said without turning around. "He accepted everything that was handed to him." He turned and glared at Vierhaus. "That is what has been wrong with Germany. They have accepted what was handed to them. But they are learning. Yes, Willie?"

"Yes, *mein Führer,* they *are* learning."

Hitler smiled and stamped his foot on the floor.

"Chancellor, Willie. I am *Chancellor* of Germany."

Vierhaus bowed slightly. "And I salute you, Chancellor Hitler."

"Chancellor Hitler," Hitler echoed.

He poured himself a cup of coffee, doused it with cream and sugar and gestured to Vierhaus to join him.

"I have a thought to share with you," Vierhaus said very softly as he fixed his coffee.

"Not this morning," Hitler said quickly. "You know the rule, Willie, no business at the Berghof. It can wait until we are back in Munich on Monday."

"Of course, of course," the mind doctor answered quickly. "I just thought it would be something for you to mull over. I admit it is a rather daring plan but . . ." and then he sank the hook for he knew just how to lure the little man into his net, "it could resolve the Communist problem."

Hitler sat down at his desk and stared at Vierhaus.

"By God, you are a devious one, Willie," he said. "Perhaps that is why we get along so well."

"*Danke, mein Führer,*" Vierhaus said with a grin.

"And what do you suggest, *Herr Doktor,* that we kill all the seventy-seven communists in Parliament? Hmm?" He chuckled and sipped his coffee.

"Yes," Vierhaus said, leaning forward and speaking almost in a whisper. "But first we must have a reason to get rid of them."

Hitler stopped smiling. His jaw tightened and his eyes turned snakelike.

"And what would that reason be?"

Vierhaus stared straight into his eyes.

"Burn the Reichstag," he said.

Hitler looked perplexed for several moments, then his lips curved into a smile.

"You are a mad one, Willie," he said.

"I am deadly serious."

"Burn the *Reichstag!*"

"Think about it, *mein Führer,*" Vierhaus continued, his voice still almost a whisper. "It is *to all Germans* the most sacred building in Germany. Right now, the Communists are the strongest party in the country. If the Reichstag were put to the torch and the Communists were blamed for it, the people would be outraged. Excuse enough to bring the party down once and for all. Then focus attention on the Brown House as the new seat of government. You rid yourself of the Reds, throw the parliament into chaos . . ."

"And use parliamentary decree to take over once and for all," Hitler interceded.

"You are a step ahead of me."

"A dangerous move, my friend," Hitler said, his eyes narrowing.

"I have heard Hermann talk about a secret passageway from the residence to the Reichstag. Easy enough to arrange the fire. Then all you need is a scapegoat. I am sure Himmler or Göring can arrange that."

At first Hitler was astounded but as he listened, the plot began to take shape in his own mind. Daring? Yes. Audacious? Yes. Possible? He tapped his cheek nervously with a finger.

"Just a thought, Herr Chancellor. Something to mull over. But if it is to be done, it must done quickly."

The plot turned Hitler's mood. He had been jocular, now he became dark and brooding. Vierhaus realized he had to change the mood back.

"It's a dismal old building anyway," he said lightly, pouring himself another coffee. He looked at the Führer and smiled.

Hitler stared back for a moment more, then his face softened and he leaned back and laughed.

"So, Willie, you have stirred the pot again. Does that mind of yours ever rest?"

"Occasionally."

"When you are asleep, eh?"

"No. Sometimes my best ideas come in dreams."

It was a clever response for it appealed to Hitler's fascination with dreams, psychism and astrology, and Vierhaus knew it.

"Well, I will consider your Reichstag idea, Willie. Perhaps

it is not as crazy as it sounded," Hitler said. "Now let's talk about the Twenty-seven project. Talk to me about *der Schauspieler.*"

Vierhaus leaned back in his chair and stared at the ceiling for a moment. Then he began to recite the information.

"A devout party member and an ardent supporter of the Führer. A war hero like yourself. He was still in his teens when he won the Iron Cross at Belleau Wood . . ."

"For what?"

Hitler interrupted whenever the mood served him; Vierhaus was accustomed to that. He also sensed a tinge of jealousy in the question. Hitler had also won two Iron Crosses, a rare achievement for an enlisted man. It surprised him that the actor had also earned such a distinction.

"He destroyed a tank and two squads of American Marines before he was himself wounded. He returned to the front and was captured near the end of the war at Cambrai, the day the wind shifted."

"I hate to think about that day. A tragedy for us. Was he gassed then?"

"No, he managed to kill an Englishman and take his mask."

"Resourceful, *ja*?"

"Very," Vierhaus nodded. "He was born near Linz . . ."

"Ah, an Austrian."

"Yes. And quite proud of it. His born name is Hans Wolfe . . ."

"Wolfe, eh. A good name. A significant name."

"Yes, *mein Führer.* His father was a storekeeper. He died early on, when the boy was ten. The mother taught school. She died while he was in the army. He studied engineering at Berlin University but quit in the early twenties. He became one of the wanderers, a lost soul for almost two years. . . ."

"Was he in the SA?"

Vierhaus shook his head.

"No. He joined the party in Nuremberg in 1927. A year later he auditioned for a small part in a film and ended up getting the leading part. That's when this charade of his began. He lives in Berlin as Johann Ingersoll and has a summer place outside of Munich where he uses his real name. And . . . he contributes heavily to the party."

"Excellent. Personality?"

"Arrogant, demanding, self-centered, explosive. Also extremely intelligent and well read. He can actually quote long passages from *Mein Kampf*."

"Really!" Hitler said, obviously pleased.

"Yes. He can also be quite outspoken, even insulting at times, and I hear he has quite a cynical sense of humor. On the other hand, those who know him as Hans Wolfe in Munich think he is a businessman. To them, he is charming and generous. A totally different personality when he is away from the studios."

"So, he is two different people then?"

Vierhaus nodded. "And apparently he has no problem switching back and forth."

"A *real* actor."

"Yes, Führer. And quite an athlete, too. Expert skier and swimmer, did some boxing in the army. An avid mountain climber and hunter."

"Women?"

"A bachelor, but he has frequent affairs."

"Not homosexual?"

"*Nein, nein,*" Vierhaus said hurriedly.

"And he knows *Mein Kampf,* eh?"

"An obsession with him."

"I hope he is not uncomfortable, being the odd card here this weekend. Everybody else knows each other."

"I think that will appeal to him."

"Oh?"

"It sets him apart from the rest of us. Reminds everyone he is the star."

Hitler glanced at Vierhaus. "Not in *this* house," he said.

Vierhaus laughed. "He is egocentric, Führer, not crazy."

Hitler laughed and slapped his knee. "So, now the question is, will he do it?"

"I think, *mein Führer,* that will be largely up to you."

Hitler nodded, then strolled back to the window. Far below he saw the Mercedes whisking up the narrow road, dust fluting out behind it.

"Ah," he said, rubbing his hands together. His tone did not conceal his excitement. "The actor has arrived."

"Excellent!" Vierhaus said. "The play begins."

"Herr Ingersoll," Vierhaus greeted the actor at the front door, "Welcome to the Eagle's Nest."

The hunchbacked professor stared intently at Ingersoll, who was surprisingly nonchalant. A cool fellow, all right. He led the actor into the large foyer.

"And is this the real Ingersoll we're meeting or another character you've created?" he asked with a smile.

Ingersoll shrugged off the question with a cryptic answer.

"Perhaps there *is* no real Ingersoll," he replied, following Vierhaus into the main hallway of the chalet. Behind him, two servants followed with his luggage and five heavy reels of film.

"Ah, you brought the film!" Vierhaus cried. "Excellent. The Führer will be delighted. He has assigned you to the room opposite his, on the northwest corner. I think you will find the view breathtaking."

"Thank you, Doctor."

"You may thank him personally. He's looking forward to meeting you."

"And when will that be?"

"Not too long now. The Führer likes to keep business to a minimum when he's here. He sleeps late and reviews the morning reports. He usually comes down about lunchtime."

"Herr Professor, shall I take the film to the projection room?" one of the servants asked.

"Excuse me for a moment while I make sure everything is done properly," Vierhaus said to Ingersoll and went off with the servants. Ingersoll was left alone in the hallway.

The actor was impressed by the cleanliness of the chalet. The wood floors were polished to a sheen and he saw not a speck of dust anywhere. Somewhere in the back of the house, a canary started warbling, then another joined in from somewhere else, then a cockatoo answered shrilly and another. There seemed to be birds everywhere, the house echoed with their chirping. Ingersoll strolled to the edge of the library and looked in. The books were all bound in leather. In the dining room, the table had been set for the evening meal. Ingersoll casually picked up a cup and looked at the bottom. The entire service was the finest Meissen china; each plate, saucer and cup were engraved with Hitler's initials and a swastika. The goblets and tea service were gold.

Nothing pedestrian about the Führer's taste.

There were several valuable paintings hanging in the downstairs rooms but one instantly galvanized Ingersoll's stare. It was almost life size and framed in gold leaf. A shielded lamp ran the length of the top of the frame, casting a soft light down on the painting. The subject was dressed in a peasant blouse and a pink skirt, the colors bright and cheerful but not garish. A striking woman, young and exquisitely beautiful, he thought. There was a disarming sense of innocence in her pale blue eyes, yet a boldness in the arrogant tilt of her chin. Ingersoll felt himself aroused by her impish innocence, a spectacularly sensuous combination.

Who was this woman whose picture dominated the hallway?

As he stared up at it he suddenly felt as if he were being watched. He looked around but the hall was empty. He stared up the stairway and for an instant thought he saw someone moving in the shadows at the top of the stairs. Then he turned his gaze back to the portrait.

At the top of the staircase, Hitler stood in the deep shadows staring down at Ingersoll, watching the actor's almost hypnotic attraction to the painting.

Look at the way he stares at her. There is hunger in that look.

There *was* sexual ardor in his stare and Ingersoll made no attempt to hide it. Hitler was seized by a momentary rush of jealousy. He turned abruptly and went back down the hall to his sitting room. Once inside he sat on the edge of the chair as though perched there, his fist pressed against his lips, fighting back an overwhelming sense of longing, anger and remorse.

Watching Ingersoll stare at the portrait he understood the

actor's sexual attraction to the subject. He too had stared at that picture with the same longing, the same desire. The same perverted fantasy.

He began to shake uncontrollably. First his knee began to bob, then his hands quivered. He beat on his legs with his fists and muffled the cry of anguish that hurt his throat. He fought back the tears of rage that burned the corners of his eyes. Time had eradicated the need. Only resentment remained.

How dare she! How dare she defy and humiliate me. How dare she rob me in such a way.

It was a question he had asked himself many times in the eighteen months since Geli Raubal had killed herself. His maid, Annie Winter, had found Geli with Hitler's Walther 6.35 wrapped in a towel, its muzzle still pressed against her chest.

I can't live with your rage and your anger, sometimes I think it would be better to be dead.

She had said the same thing many times and in a variety of ways but he always scoffed at her, derided her, *dared* her.

And then that awful night she had taken the dare and it had fallen to Rudolf Hess and Gregor Strasser to hush up the potential scandal, just as they had handled the blackmailers who had managed to acquire the obscene nude paintings he had done of Geli.

Just as they had subdued him and watched over him for days because he, too, was raving on the edge of self-destruction.

September 18, 1931, a date that was scorched into his memory, like the date of the Putsch and the date Hindenburg had named him chancellor. Except that this date was a nightmare from which he could not escape.

Ingersoll was still staring at the painting when Vierhaus returned, walking with that curious kind of swagger he had affected to minimize the hump on his back.

"She's exquisite," Ingersoll said, still staring up at the face in the portrait. "Who is she?"

"Geli Raubal, the Führer's niece. His favorite sister's daughter. He adored her. She was killed a year and a half ago. A tragic accident. He still hasn't fully recovered from the shock."

"I can understand why," Ingersoll said.

"Well, let me show you to your rooms," Vierhaus said,

leading Ingersoll up the stairs. "You can freshen up. The Führer should be down shortly. He usually takes lunch at the tea house down by the mountain overlook. By the way, there are a few rules you should be aware of. The Führer does not permit smoking in the house, he detests the odor. But he has no objection if you smoke outside. He also does not permit the keeping of diaries or writing letters from here, either. And he can't stand whistling."

"Whistling?"

"Yes. Drives him crazy. Are you a whistler, Herr Ingersoll?"

"Sometimes. I find it a comforting diversion."

"Not here. The Führer is a vegetarian although there may be meat dishes for the guests. Also he is a teetotaler, but, again, there will be wine and champagne for his visitors."

"He sounds quite tolerant of others," Ingersoll said.

"Oh yes, the Führer is a most tolerant gentleman. . . ."

He came downstairs precisely at noon. Ingersoll was surprised at how small Hitler was in person. And he wasn't sure what to expect. Would this be the serious, stormy Hitler he had seen so many times, speaking in Berlin, Nuremberg and Munich, the forceful leader, demanding and getting the adoration of thousands, berating the British and French, damning the Jews and Communists? Or would it be the more affable Hitler he had seen in crowds, often speaking in low caressing tones, bowing low from the waist and kissing the hands of the young *Fräuleins*, kissing the foreheads of the children, making jokes with them.

He was dressed in a gray wool double-breasted suit with the Wehrmacht insignia over the breast pocket, a smiling man, pleasant and friendly. The affable Hitler.

"So," said Hitler, "we finally meet. I am an ardent fan of yours, Herr Ingersoll. I've seen all your films, some more than once. You have brought great credit to Germany. Thank you for accepting my invitation."

"I am flattered that you asked, *mein Führer.*"

"I trust your room is satisfactory."

"Lovely."

"Good. Good! I usually take a noon stroll down to the tea

house for lunch with my guests but since you and Willie are the first to arrive and he has a few things to do, perhaps just the two of us can go down together."

This man in an ordinary lounging suit, projecting a patriarchal image of kindness and affability, is this the man who will change the world?

Servants helped Hitler and Ingersoll on with their wraps. Hitler wore a heavy greatcoat. The chancellor wrapped a thick muffler around his neck and, flexing his shoulders, smiled at Ingersoll.

"Sure you're up to a walk in this weather?" Hitler asked.

"Looking forward to it."

The wind sliced up the mountainside with an edge as sharp as a knife. Hitler was hunched down in the thick greatcoat, its tall collar wrapped around his ears. His gloved hands were tucked under his armpits. Two armed guards followed twenty or so feet behind them, just out of earshot. As they approached the overlook, the entire valley spread below them. Snow glistened in the noonday sun.

Ingersoll stopped at the overlook halfway to the tea house and pointed out over the mountains. "That's where you were born, isn't it? Over the mountains there in the Waldviertel?"

"Yes. Braunau. A terrible place. Not as bad as Vienna but a terrible place."

"What's so terrible about it?"

"It's known as the wooded place. Very harsh," Hitler said, not hiding the bitterness in his voice. "Harsh land, harsh people, dreary, medieval. For centuries it was prey to every marauding army that invaded southern Germany. Sacked by the Huns, by the Bohemian Ottakar II. By the Swedes during the Thirty Years' War. Even Napoleon marched through it in 1805 on the way to Vienna. The fools in the Waldviertel have a legacy of defeat. Defeatists all."

Hitler's voice began to rise as anger took the place of bitterness.

"We have too many people in Germany today who feel the same way," he went on, slashing his fists against his thighs. "That's why I must throw that damnable Versailles treaty back in the Allies' faces. Pride, *pride,* Herr Ingersoll, that's what I will give back to all my people. I must make defeat an alien word to all Germans."

"You have already started, sir," Ingersoll said.

"*Danke,* Herr Ingersoll," Hitler said with genuine pleasure. He stamped his feet against the cold.

Cajole and flatter.

"What do they call you? Johann? John?"

"Hans, actually," Ingersoll said.

"Ah, your proper name." And Hitler smiled.

So, they want something, Ingersoll thought. *They've gone to a lot of trouble to check me out. Do they know everything? Do they know all the secrets of Johann Ingersoll? Was this to be some kind of blackmail?*

He dispelled the notion as paranoia.

"Don't be alarmed," Hitler said. "It's Himmler and his SS. They're overly cautious. Security, you know."

"Ah yes, security."

Hitler's breath swirled from the folds of the collar.

"I don't like the winter, Hans," he said. "When I first went to Vienna to study it was an endlessly bitter time . . . for two years my only mistress was sorrow and my only companion was hunger. But the thing I remember most was how cold it was."

He stopped and shivered, huddling deeper into his great coat before going on.

"In the winter I was never warm. It is beautiful here, looking out at the snow on the mountains, listening to it crunch underfoot, but the cold cuts me like a saber."

"Should we go back to the chalet?"

"*Nein!* It is a fear I must deal with. Someday I will overcome it. Perhaps I will get badly sunburned, eh, and then I will fear the warm more than the cold. Ha! Besides, I am sure you know what it is like to sleep on cold pavement."

"Not as bad as in the trenches when it rained," Ingersoll said. "My greatest fear was drowning in mud. When the rains came I was terrified the trench would slide in on me. After dark I would crawl out and sleep with the dead ones. And then in the morning I'd crawl back in the ditch. To prefer sleeping with the dead, now that's fear."

"You were a good soldier," Hitler said.

"So were you."

"We still are, Hans. The war is just beginning."

"The sooner the better."

"Spoken like a true Nazi."

"I have read *Mein Kampf* a dozen times, memorized passages, spoken them aloud just to hear their power," Ingersoll said enthusiastically. "I've read all your works, *mein Führer.*" And he recited:

"*Ohne Juda, ohne Rom,*
Wird gebaut Germaniens Dom!
Heil!"

"My God," Hitler said, surprised, "I wrote that, let's see, that was in . . ."

"Nineteen-twelve."

"*Ja,* 1912," he said with surprise and repeated it:

"*Without Jews, without Rome,*
We shall build Germany's cathedral!
Hail!"

"I was twenty-four years old at the time. People laughed at me, you know," Hitler said.

"A prophet must always endure scorn."

"You are a student of Nietzsche, too?"

"I am familiar with his works."

"You are quite the scholar, Hans Wolfe," Hitler said, impressed. "Do you like music? Wagner?"

"Very much."

They continued down the path toward the tea house.

"Do you know when I was a boy in the Waldviertel my friend Gustl and I wrote an opera. An outrageous thing, filled with madness, violence, murder, miracles, mythology, magic, suicide. Oh, it was quite Wagnerian."

Suddenly Hitler's mood swung again, this time from nostalgia to petulance. His voice grew slightly louder, its pitch a shade higher.

"That is another thing about the fools down there," he went on. "They do not even under*stand* Wagner. Only *I* understood the magnitude of Wagner's vision, Hans. *Only I understand that the creation was an act of violence, and so all creation must continue on a path of violence.*"

Just as suddenly his voice lowered, became almost a whisper. He leaned closer to Ingersoll.

"This is the beginning. Last Monday when that doddering, senile old fool made me chancellor, that was the start of it. First there was the Holy Roman Empire, then the Prussian Hohenzollerns and now the glorious Third Reich. We are going to change the world. We are going to obliterate Versailles. Obliterate the Jews and the Gypsies and the Communists. We are going to create a population of pure Aryans, smarter, stronger, better-looking than any other race in history. We are *going* to do all this." He stopped for a moment, his eyes blazing, his breath coming in short, wispy breaths. "Do you believe that, Hans? Do you believe that the Third Reich now exists?"

"Yes, *mein Führer,*" said Ingersoll. He was staring transfixed by the simple power of Hitler's voice. He had heard or read all the words before, in various speeches and in books. But he had never heard them performed with such mastery. And he did believe it. There was no question in his mind.

"The Third Reich is you, *mein Führer,*" he blurted passionately. And impulsively he stepped back and threw out his arm in the Nazi salute. "*Heil Hitler,*" he said. "Hail the Chancellor."

A faint smile played on Hitler's lips. He lifted his hand in response. They walked on down the footpath.

The tea house looked like a large, enclosed gazebo on the edge of a cliff at the foot of the overlook walk. As they neared it Hitler picked up the pace, anxious to get out of the cold. They rushed inside and slammed the door against the freezing draft. A white-uniformed servant snapped to attention and saluted.

"You may go to the kitchen, Fritz, we can serve ourselves."

"Yes, *mein Führer,*" the soldier said and vanished.

Outside, the wind whirled the snow into twisting devils that danced past the frosted windows. Inside, a giant fire snapped and sent glittering sparks twirling up the chimney.

"Ah," Hitler said, closing his eyes. He opened the coat and held it like a shield in front of the fire, gathering in its warmth. "Fire is a great cleanser," he said. Staring at the blazing logs, he saw instead that towering Reichstag ablaze. His mind conjured twinkling sparks floating over the city.

A table had been set in front of the fireplace. There were plates of homemade breads, pastries, cheeses, and thick sausages cooked until their skin had burst. A large china teapot squatted in the center of the table, the tea steeping in its own steam. Two bottles of wine had also been opened and were sitting on the table.

"The walk here is good discipline. Are you a disciplined man, Hans?"

"When it's necessary."

"Good point. One of the reasons I come to this place is to relax." He placed a finger on one of the wine bottles.

"Red or white?"

"I think I prefer the red."

Hitler poured them both a glass of the red, then took a knife and sliced off a bit of sausage and put it in his mouth. He closed his eyes for a moment, savoring the spicy bit of meat before washing it down with a sip of wine.

"Forget the discipline for a day or two, yes?"

"An absolute necessity, *mein Führer.*"

"Exactly, exactly. Help yourself, Hans."

Hitler fixed himself a plate of bread, cheese and sausage, poured more wine in the glass. Warmed by the fire, he took off his coat and threw it over a chair, pulled another one close to the hearth and sat with his legs outstretched, crossed at the ankles. He sighed with contentment. Ingersoll drew up a chair and sat beside him. They both stared, almost transfixed, at the fire as they spoke.

"I never discuss politics here at the Eagle's Nest," Hitler said. "We come here to relax and forget the problems, hmm? However, Herr Ingersoll, I think it would be profitable for us to understand each other, eh?"

"If you wish, *mein Führer.*"

"I am curious about something," Hitler said. "I know you had bad times for a year or two before you became an actor. Why didn't you join the *Sturmabteilung*? A good Nazi like you, belonging to the brownshirts would have given you prestige."

"I couldn't do that," Ingersoll answered.

"Why not?"

"It's a personal matter," he said with some hesitation.

"One you cannot share with your Führer?"

Ingersoll thought for a moment before answering.

"I didn't come here to make enemies."

"It will not go beyond this room, Hans."

Ingersoll thought about that for a few moments. On the one hand he feared his own prejudice would infuriate Hitler, and yet his instincts told him that Hitler would respond favorably to honesty.

Besides, why was he really here, he wondered? Were these political questions merely curiosity? Or was there some darker motive behind the discussion? Ingersoll flipped the two options over and over in his mind, like spinning a coin. Finally he opted for candor. After all, he was a national idol. His popularity transcended politics or ideology.

"I am afraid my opinions are somewhat . . . snobbish," he said finally.

"Snobbish?"

"The brownshirts are not my kind of people. I understand their function is necessary but . . . they are loudmouth bullies, boisterous and . . ."

"Yes? And?" Hitler's eyes bored into his but Ingersoll did not look away.

"And then there's Ernst Röhm. He is . . . there is something about him . . . Röhm is a lover of little boys," Ingersoll said rather harshly. "A sadist. A drunkard . . ."

"You know Röhm?"

"I met him once. Back in '25, '26, in Berlin. He was making a speech. Cold sober he was incoherent."

"He was not picked for his oratorical skills—or his good manners, for that matter."

"Yes, *mein Führer,* but . . ."

"Your instincts about Ernst are correct," Hitler said. "He has failed to give the SA a soul of its own." Hitler stood up with his back to the fire and shrugged his shoulders. "It has no pride or direction." He thought for a moment more, then added enigmatically, "These things eventually outlive their purpose."

He paused again.

"Besides, Röhm has pig eyes," Hitler said, changing the mood again and chuckling at his own insult.

"I wouldn't want to spend the evening with Attila the Hun either, but he was very effective."

"Precisely. I see you understand that even rats can serve a useful purpose. He serves a purpose, a very necessary purpose. But I assure you, he will have no voice in the future of Germany. He is uncouth," Hitler said abruptly.

"Exactly!"

Ingersoll was obviously a student of politics, his observations were accurate. *Die Sturmabteilung,* the SA, were Hitler's personal storm troopers. Ruffians and thugs, most of the brownshirts had originally been recruited from prisons or from beer halls where they were bouncers. They had become an undisciplined paramilitary force. Marching through the streets, smashing windows, beating up Jews, guarding political meetings and privately engaging in blackmail and extortion, the SA had become dangerously out of control and so Hitler had brought Ernst Röhm, a compatriot from the old Putsch days, back from a diplomatic post in Bolivia to head it. Hitler still needed this private police force of his, but he had his own plan for dealing with them. He had created the SS, the *Schutzstaffel,* putting one of his closest friends, Heinrich Himmler, in charge. It also had a satellite, the SD, a security service engaged in counterintelligence in Germany and abroad. It was the SD in which Wilhelm Vierhaus played a vague but obviously important role. Hitler's plan was to build the SS into the most fearful organization in the Nazi party, shifting its power until it was stronger than the SA and then . . .

But each thing in its time.

"I realize I probably seem like an elitist . . ." Ingersoll started to say.

"You *are* an elitist," Hitler said matter-of-factly. "There is nothing wrong with that. It's one reason you are here."

"I have little in common with Röhm and his brownshirts other than politics. I prefer to support the National Socialist movement in other ways."

Hitler's eyes narrowed and he leaned forward slightly.

"Such as?" he asked.

"Financial contributions. Encourage my associates to join the party. Defend your ideas to those who, uh . . . don't fully understand them."

"So, you are a good Nazi then?" Hitler asked.

Ingersoll thought for a moment before he answered.

"Perhaps I am a good Hitlerite, *mein Führer*. That might be a more accurate way of putting it."

"What do you mean?"

"I see the party as a means to the end. To me, it's a necessary glory show. There are too many buffoons and hooligans."

"Buffoons and hooligans?" Hitler echoed with surprise. Vierhaus was right, Ingersoll was certainly outspoken. Ingersoll could sense Hitler's growing irritation.

"I would follow you into fire, *mein Führer*," he quickly added, "But there are some I'd prefer to shove into the flames."

Cajole and flatter. Hear him out.

"As I told you, I've read *Mein Kampf* cover to cover many times. It is always on my nightstand. It is a great book, greater than the Bible. I agree with everything you say, particularly regarding the Jewish problem."

"*Herr Schauspieler,* tell me the truth. How do you really feel about the Jews?"

"I hate them," Ingersoll said, his voice taut and low. "I hate their Marxist tricks. Their whining . . ."

"*Ja. Ja! Very* good. They *are* whiners. And you're right, they are the backbone of the Marxist movement. They've had fourteen years, *fourteen years* to show us what they can do and all they have produced is rubble. Look around you. *Rubble!* The secret to our success, Hans, is that we are honest. We deal honestly. We seek only what is fair, what is proper. What is right for Germany."

He smiled, an understated smile, a momentary manipulation of the corners of his mouth that was almost a smirk. He sat down again, perched on the edge of his chair and leaned toward Ingersoll with fists clenched.

"We *must* take the Jews out of the marketplace, out of the banks, out of our industries. Perhaps even . . . rid Germany totally of this *Jude* scourge. Would you agree?"

Ingersoll smiled in return and nodded. "Yes, but how? And how will you justify what we do to the rest of the world?"

Hitler's mood changed radically. His face turned red. His voice rose fervently and rage simmered deep inside him. He glared out the window.

"Justify? We justify *nothing*! The rest of the world? Who in the rest of the world? The French?" He snorted indignantly. "How can you have an understanding with a man who is choking you as you speak? The Americans with their Monroe Doctrine? My God! The ultimate hypocrisy. They exclude would-be immigrants if they are *undesirable*. Regulate their numbers. Demand certain physical standards, insist they bring in a certain amount of money, interrogate them about their political beliefs. Listen, my friend, one learns from one's enemies. Anyway, there is a way we can deal with the Americans. The Communists say that power comes from the barrel of a gun. Well, I'll show them power, all right. I'll show them the barrel of our gun." He smashed his fist into his open palm and stamped his foot on the floor. "How can they blame us for doing the same things, eh? I don't give a damn about the Jews in other countries. But here, this is *Germany's* business. This is *our* business."

For a moment it seemed to Ingersoll as if Hitler had forgotten he was in the room. He seemed to be speaking to all the unseen hordes of disenfranchised Germans out there somewhere. And his fervor was hypnotic. Ingersoll's heart began to race. Then just as quickly the voice became quiet again. He turned back to Ingersoll, his eyes still burning with the fever of power.

"As for the British? Compromisers, that's their style. The Britishers are tough and proud. And they are exploiters. England is a psychological force embracing the entire world. They are protected by a great navy and a very courageous air service. But these things will be dealt with in their time.

"I say the hell with the rest of the world," he whispered, leaning over Ingersoll. "Another year and ours will be the most powerful political party in history and all Europe will be on its knees before us. Tomorrow we will *be* the world, my young friend."

So, Hitler's mind was already preparing *for war,* thought Ingersoll. *To him it is an inevitability.*

Hitler paused, saw the unconcealed excitement in Ingersoll's face.

"You believe that, don't you, Ingersoll?"

Entranced, Ingersoll nodded.

He is hooked, Hitler said to himself. *Der Schauspieler is ours.*

"And you want to be an important player in this crusade, don't you?"

"Yes!"

"More than just making contributions to the party, yes?"

"Yes, *mein Führer*!"

"And so you shall, Herr Ingersoll," Hitler said, patting Ingersoll's knee, "so you shall."

Looking over Hitler's shoulder through the frosty window, Ingersoll saw Willie Vierhaus scurrying awkwardly down the icy footpath toward the tea house.

As cold as Vierhaus obviously was, he stood outside the tea house and knocked. Hitler waved him in.

"My God it's cold out there," he complained as he burst through the door. "That trooper out there says it's ten below freezing!"

He scrambled to the fire and immediately stood with his back to it, hiding the mound on his shoulder. He closed his eyes and shivered as the crackling flames warmed him.

"We'll have to start a war in Africa, Willie, just so you can be comfortable," Hitler said.

"Worse, much worse," Vierhaus answered. "Dust. I think dust is worse than the cold."

"Everybody to their own discomfort," Hitler said. "Hans hates mud worse than cold. You hate dust worse than cold."

"And you, *mein Führer,* what do you hate worse than cold?"

"Failure," Hitler said.

"Sometimes they go together," Vierhaus said. "Napoleon met both in Russia."

"The trouble with the French is they always put more on their plate than they can eat," Ingersoll said, fixing a sandwich.

"The trouble with the French is that they have no stomach for fighting," Hitler added. "They'd rather make love than win a battle."

"At the Somme I saw a whole battalion of infantry turn their backs on us and run," Ingersoll said, nibbling on the sandwich and washing it down with a swallow of wine. "As far as the eye could see, nothing but French behinds."

"A lovely sight, I'll bet," Vierhaus said and laughed.

"Absolutely beautiful," Ingersoll answered.

"Probably running back to Paris to find a bottle of wine and a *Fräulein* for the night," Hitler said, chuckling. "Can you believe they actually think their Maginot line will stop us. Ha! A concrete cow fence is going to stop the *Wehrmacht*? I can hardly wait for that day."

He snipped off another piece of sausage and chewed it passionately, rolling the meat around on his tongue, sucking every gram of juice from it before swallowing.

"It's beginning to snow, Führer," Vierhaus said. "The plane from Berlin may have a problem landing in Linz."

"I'm sure Hermann will not let his pilot turn back. The head of the *Luftwaffe* will not denied by a little snow."

"Well, there is good news. Albert's plane has landed. He is on his way up from the village at this very moment."

"Splendid!"

"I left a message for him to come on down when he arrives. I trust that's all right?" Vierhaus said.

"Yes, yes," Hitler quickly agreed. "I am anxious for Speer and Hans here to get together. Two creative geniuses matching wits, that should be stimulating."

He stood up and joined Vierhaus in front of the fireplace, his back to the flames, his hands clasped behind his back.

"I had hoped Leni Riefenstahl could be here but she is finishing a film. When Leni is finishing a film she is as if . . . in a trance."

"Fritz Lang thinks she's one of the greatest cinematographers alive today," Ingersoll said.

"*One* of?" said Hitler. "She is *the* greatest cinematographer alive today. That is why she is the official cameraman of the Third Reich. Take Speer, for instance. Speer has majestic vision. It is impossible for him to think small. If I asked for a pebble he would deliver me a mountain."

"I saw the Brown House this morning," Ingersoll said. "It's magnificent."

"Tell him," Hitler said. "He loves to be flattered, although he tries not to show it."

"I hope he brings the Nuremberg model," Vierhaus said.

"Everything Albert does soars," Hitler said. "He is my architect because he lifts Germany's spirits. But the stadium at Nuremberg, it will be a symbol. I will promise you this, when we hold the rally to celebrate its completion, every German will know that the Third Reich is their destiny."

He stood in front of Ingersoll and clenched his fists tightly against his chest.

"You see, what I am talking about is pride, *Schauspieler.* Hitler is pride. Speer is pride. Wagner is pride." He paused for effect, leaned an inch closer to Ingersoll. "Johann *Ingersoll* is pride."

Now for the *pièce de résistance.*

He leaned closer to Ingersoll, glancing for a moment at Vierhaus, then settling his hard, almost fevered stare on Johann Ingersoll.

"I am sure you are familiar with the *Schutzstaffel,* the SS, my personal elite corps. More powerful than the army, the SA, and the police all put together. Himmler is in charge. You have seen the uniform?"

"The black is very impressive," Ingersoll said.

"You have brought great credit to the Fatherland," Hitler went on. "It would be to my advantage, and I think to yours, if you would accept a commission in the *Schutzstaffel.* "

Ingersoll was stunned. "A commission? For doing what?"

"You will be my personal representative in the world of the arts. Wearing the uniform at official events will give the SS added prestige and respect. I was thinking perhaps . . . *Colonel* Hans Wolfe."

A colonel! Ingersoll said to himself. *My God, a colonel in Hitler's own elite corps.*

"I am flattered, *mein Führer.* "

"You will accept then?"

"With honor, sir!"

"Excellent! Willie, get me the Bible from that table over there. I will administer the oath personally."

"Yes, *mein Führer.* "

Vierhaus got the Bible and handed it to Ingersoll.

"Raise your right hand and repeat after me," said Hitler.

Ingersoll held the Bible in his left hand and raised his right. Hitler repeated the oath of the SS:

"I swear to thee Adolf Hitler,
As Führer and Chancellor of the German Reich,

Loyalty and bravery.
I vow to thee and to the superiors
Whom thou shalt appoint
Obedience unto death,
So help me God."

Ingersoll repeated the entire oath verbatim.

Hitler smiled and held out his hand.

"Congratulations, Colonel. I will put you in touch with my personal tailor in Berlin. Your uniform will be my gift. Along with this."

Hitler held his hand out. Vierhaus took a package from his coat pocket and gave it to him. It was wrapped as a present, a long slender box, about a foot long, four or five inches wide. Hitler offered it to Ingersoll.

"Congratulations," he said with a smile. Yet, as Ingersoll met his gaze, he saw more than a smile. He saw pride. And he saw anticipation.

The actor slowly took the package in both hands and stared at it a moment. Subconsciously he hefted it once or twice, a throwback to his childhood when the heaviest gifts were always the best. It was heavy enough.

"Open it, open it," Hitler said impatiently.

Ingersoll put it on the edge of the table and took off the wrapping paper. It was a mahogany box. Inside was a dagger, the official SS long knife, ebony handled with a gleaming double-edged blade almost a foot long scabbarded in black leather. On the hilt was the official SS insignia, two jagged lightning streaks in gold. He turned it over and on the opposite side of the handle was a golden eagle perched on a wreath which encircled a diamond-studded swastika. He drew the dagger from its scabbard. Just below the hilt, pressed into the steel, were the initials "A.H."

Ingersoll was struck dumb. In a matter of moments he had been commissioned a colonel in the SS and presented with a personal gift signed by the Führer.

He looked at Hitler with adoration.

"I can tell you this now," he stammered. "Although we have been keeping it a very guarded secret. I've made five horror films in less than two years and frankly, I want to get away from these thrillers, play a dramatic part. Stretch my talent. We plan to have the world premiere of *Der Nacht Hund* on February twenty-seventh in the Kroll. On that night I plan to appear as myself and end this publicity charade. It's become a terrible burden. Now I can go as *Colonel* Hans Wolfe. The publicity impact will be even greater!"

Hitler looked at Vierhaus for a moment and pursed his lips.

Now is the time, Hitler thought. *He is ready.*

Hitler began to stride the room, hands behind his back, slapping a fist into the palm of his other hand. He stared at the ceiling of the room as he spoke.

"You have a unique combination of talents, my friend. You are a superb actor. You speak four languages fluently, you are a master of dialects and accents. You are a master of disguise, a soldier and a survivalist, an acrobat. You believe in the Third Reich. And . . . you are a killer. Two squads of American Marines in one encounter, correct?"

He stopped and looked down at Ingersoll.

"Yes, Führer, that is correct."

"Was it difficult? The killing, I mean?"

Ingersoll stared at him for a few seconds and smiled. "On the contrary, Führer, it was very satisfying," he said.

"There, you see," Hitler said, spreading his arms to his sides. "Unique talents. One of a kind. Did I tell you, Willie?"

"Yes, *mein Führer,* you told me," Vierhaus agreed, accepting the fact that the plot had suddenly become Hitler's.

"Is the Third Reich your dream, Hans?"

"Yes."

"The most important thing in the world?"

"Yes."

"More important than your career, even life itself?"

"Yes!"

Hitler poured himself another glass of wine. His gaze was riveted to Ingersoll's. He sipped the wine and leaned forward again and nodded.

"I believe you. And I believe that if I told you I had an impossible mission to be performed, a mission requiring great personal sacrifice, one which would require giving up your name, your career, your fortune—*everything*—I do believe that if I asked you to take on such a mission, you would say yes."

Ingersoll said nothing. Hitler's words had put him in a near trance of ecstasy.

"Even if this mission meant living in a country you detest for years, six, seven, perhaps?"

Now Hitler leaned closer, his voice a whisper.

"Even if I tell you this mission is so secret that I cannot tell—even *you*—what it will be. Only the professor and I will know, until it is time for you to act. Even then I believe you would accept such an assignment."

"It would be an honor even to be considered for such a task," Ingersoll whispered back.

"Well, Hans Wolfe, so you are. You are the man I want to carry out that mission."

Stunned, Ingersoll looked back and forth between the two men.

Is he serious, he wondered. *Is this some kind of a test of my loyalty, my trust in him?*

"There is within the SS a highly guarded unit called *Die Sechs Füchse,* the Six Foxes. It is headed by Professor Vierhaus. There are only five members, including himself. Each of the other four is a unique individual, like yourself. Each has been given a specific mission to perform. Each is known by a code name known only to Willie and myself. Even Himmler does not know their identities or their individual objectives. There are no written reports and no records kept by the Six Foxes. The reason is that these missions are so sensitive, so secret, that we cannot afford even the slightest breach of security. The individuals themselves do not know the nature of the assignments. Obviously if they were caught and gave up the secret, that mission would have to be abandoned. And each of these missions is *vital* to the future of *Deutschland.*"

"I understand," Ingersoll said.

"The agents of *Die Sechs Füchse* report only to Vierhaus and he reports only to me. The particular assignment we have in mind for you would, in the event war is imminent with the United States, paralyze their war effort and neutralize them. It would, we are certain, keep the United States out of the war. In other words, Hans, this mission could directly affect the outcome of our struggle. So, if you choose to accept and are successful, you will be the single most important war hero in the history of the Third Reich."

Ingersoll's excitement flooded over. He began to speak but Hitler held up a finger.

"Before you say anything, Hans Wolfe, you must understand if you accept this job, both Hans Wolfe and Johann Ingersoll must die. You would become a man without an identity. A number."

"A number?"

"Willie . . ." Hitler said.

"You would be known only as *Siebenundzwanzig.*"

"Twenty-seven? Why twenty-seven?"

"You will understand in time," Vierhaus said. "Between the three of us, we will shorten it to Swan. I would suggest that we move your personal fortune to Swiss banks, although you would have to promise never to draw money from these accounts until the mission is complete. Upon your death, your property would be sold and those funds, too, would be deposited in Switzerland. We cannot afford to establish the remotest kind of paper trail. Does that make sense?"

Almost in a state of shock, Ingersoll merely nodded.

"You will be trained in every facet of espionage, sabotage and survival," Vierhaus continued. "When you are ready you will be the most competent agent in the German intelligence system. And then you would go underground until the time is right. And that, dear sir, could be," and he paused before completing the sentence, "five to eight years from now."

"What would I do for eight years?"

"Wait," said Hitler. And then he smiled. A genuine, uncomplicated smile. "Become an American. A plain, insignificant American."

Ingersoll could not speak. The awesome scope of Hitler's proposal had short-circuited his thinking powers. Too much had happened in the last few minutes for him to rationally sort it all out. Only one thought was beginning to come through: *to become another person, in another country. What an acting job. The world's greatest acting job. . . .*

"Wealth, recognition, fame . . . all these things are yours," Hitler continued. "To give all that up for *any* reason is almost unthinkable." Hitler stared into the fire. The flames crackled in the now total silence. "There have been many sacrifices made for the glory of *Deutschland* and there will be many, many more. But none will be greater than what I have proposed to you . . . Colonel Wolfe."

Ingersoll barely heard the words. *The glory of* Deutschland *. . . none will be greater . . . almost unthinkable . . . Colonel Wolfe . . . The world's greatest acting job. . . .*

Ingersoll entered his room and quickly shed his suit jacket, replacing it with a black turtleneck. He and Heinz had devised a simple mask that on superficial inspection looked like the *Nacht Hund* makeup. He unpacked the black cloak and shook it out.

Dinner had been electrifying. The air in the dining room seemed to crackle from the combined power of the people around the table, though there had been only subtle references to politics and the problems of state. Ingersoll wondered what, if any, significance there was to the seating arrangement. Hitler, Herman Göring, Heinrich Himmler, Joseph Goebbels, Eva Braun at the foot of the table, Ingersoll seated between Eva and Albert Speer, then Walter Funk, Vierhaus and Rudolf Hess seated at the Führer's right. It seemed obvious that Hess and Göring, who were sitting on either side of Hitler, were the two most important men in the hierarchy.

They all had listened enrapt as Speer described his plans for the stadium and several other state buildings. Speer was different from the rest of them, more concerned with architecture than its political ramifications. When he talked about buildings it was with such passion one could actually envision the towering structures.

Himmler, on the other hand, seemed bored and uncomfortable with the conversation that rambled from architecture to the depravity of the Communist artist Picasso, whose first art exhibit was the talk of Paris, to motion pictures, to Hess's theories on the occult and numerology, to Wagner's *Rienzi*.

Hitler was fascinated by the story of Cola da Rienzi, who freed the fourteenth-century Romans from the oppression of the noblemen only to be stoned to death because he gave the people freedom they didn't want. A lugubrious tale at best.

"I was twelve or thirteen when I first heard *Rienzi,*" Hitler said. "I sat up all night thinking about it. About the lessons to be learned from it. Heinrich, what did you learn from *Rienzi?*"

"That he was a fool," Himmler said in a humorless monotone.

"How so?"

"He should have known there is no such thing as a benevolent leader. The tool of power is terror. Physical . . . and mental. And the only way to assure victory is through the total annihilation of all enemies within the state. Scare them to death. Or kill them."

"You mean the Jews?" Hitler said.

"Jews. Dissidents," Himmler said with a shrug.

"You're talking about millions of people, Heinrich," Hess said. "What are you going to do, poison all the matzoh balls in Germany? A difficult thing to do."

There was a ripple of laughter.

"Oh I don't know," Himmler answered. "The Turks disposed of eight hundred thousand Armenians between 1915 and 1917. *Eight hundred thousand,* using only the crudest methods. I should think with proper ingenuity and planning, sophisticated techniques . . ." He shrugged again, letting their imaginations complete the sentence.

"Rather a dark interpretation of *Rienzi,*" Vierhaus offered.

"Wagner is dark," Himmler said flatly.

Was he talking about *all* the Jews in Germany, Ingersoll had wondered. Impossible.

"And what lesson did you learn, Führer?" Goebbels asked, shifting the conversation back to Hitler.

"Never give anything to the people until you have convinced them they want it," Hitler answered and laughed. "Nobody should know that better than you, eh, Joseph? It's your job to convince them."

They had all laughed and moved on to a lighter subject.

"I understand they are using hypnotism now as a means of interrogation, is that true, Willie?" Göring asked.

"It's not really that new," Vierhaus answered. "Psychiatrists have been using hypnotism for years to get inside the mind."

"I was hypnotized once," Ingersoll said.

"Really?" Hitler said. "Why?"

"We had a hypnotist in a film I was working on. I was curious, I did it out of curiosity."

"What happened?" Vierhaus asked.

"I hate oysters. So I asked him to hypnotize me and make me like oysters. He did it! I sat there and ate an entire plate of raw oysters. And relished them. I asked him to do it again, before I started *Der Nacht Hund.* I told him to make me feel the pain of being crippled. And then let me recall those feelings at will while I was making the movie."

"And . . . ?" Vierhaus leaned forward slightly.

"I could actually invoke pain when I was in costume."

"Amazing," Vierhaus said.

"So it might be possible under hypnosis to ask questions which the subject might normally be reluctant to answer?" Himmler asked.

"I should think so," said Ingersoll. "Of course there is a danger."

"And that is?" Hitler asked.

"Well, supposing I was hypnotized and told I was a pig and then the hypnotist suddenly dropped dead of a heart attack. Would I think I was a pig forever?"

There was a moment of silence. Then Eva began to laugh.

"That's a very funny notion," she giggled. Everyone else began to laugh, too, except for Himmler. He smiled, but only for the briefest moment. Ingersoll watched his eyes and knew that, from the way they darted, Himmler was thinking, *Would it work?*

For the most part, Ingersoll sat through the meal entranced. These were the elite of Hitler's elite. Men who had simply been names and faces before tonight now were his peers, handpicked by Hitler to mold his ideas into the new German order.

Each of them was different, each had a specific objective. Himmler, head of the SS, a little no-nonsense man with no sense of humor and a mind as cold as a crypt, seemed incapable of frivolous conversation. The perfect man to lead the SS.

Göring, bulky head of the *Luftwaffe,* the state police, and Reich Master of the Hunt, the World War ace who had shot down twenty-two British and American flyers. He had been Hitler's closest friend and confidant since they had marched side-by-side at the Bürgerbräukeller Beer Hall Putsch of '23 and Göring had taken two bullets in the thigh. Göring was the court jester, constantly making jokes, many times on himself.

Goebbels. The midget with a club foot. Cadaverous, pushy and cynical, with a nervous laugh, he had written, after first hearing Hitler speak at the Zirkus Krone in Munich in 1926, "I am reborn." As the master propagandist he seemed the perfect man to spread the Gospel of the Third Reich.

Walther Funk, the mousy little man with dodgy eyes and very little to say. The party's money genius. It didn't seem possible that this quiet, involuted, self-deprecating man had whipped Thyssen, the steel magnate, Schnitzler, leader of the chemical cartel, and von Schroeder, head of the banking trust, into line and kept them and the other industrialists there. His promise that Hitler would get rid of both the Communists and the labor unions had lured the industrial power of Germany into the Nazi party. A schemer, Ingersoll decided, probably best at executing the ideas of others.

Speer the architect, young, handsome, with the bright-eyed look of the idealist, the youthful genius seemed a bit awed at being in such powerful company. Speer, who had little to say except when he was talking about buildings, was the dreamer who would create a phoenix from the ashes of Germany's defeat.

Eva Braun, the vivacious little girl from the village who appeared to be Hitler's current girlfriend. Frivolous, pretty in a common way, but empty-headed, she was apparently an innocuous diversion for the leader.

Vierhaus. Deformed, persuasive, an enigma who apparently had no title but held an autonomous position within the Gestapo and reported to no one but the Führer. Could he be the Iago to Hitler's Othello?

And Hess. Dark, handsome, quick-witted and sarcastic, Hess was the mystery man. He had transcribed much of *Mein Kampf* from the Führer's notes while Hitler was still in prison and was probably closer to Hitler than anyone except Hermann Göring. His role in the hierarchy was vague to Ingersoll, although as Deputy Führer he was next in line of succession, the crown prince of the Nazi party.

Was he, like Vierhaus, a back-room planner, an unheralded advisor working in the shadows? Or was he simply a confidant whose opinion Hitler respected and whom Hitler trusted to carry on the dream if something happened to him?

Hess had another bond with the Führer, an uncommon interest in witchcraft and the occult. After dinner, assisted by Hess, Hitler told the future using an old-fashioned divining process. In the eerie light of candles, Hitler held a spoon of lead over one candle, dripping the molten lead into a bowl of cold water, then Hess read the misshapen blobs, predicting an amazing and successful year for the Führer, much to the Führer's delight.

Ingersoll reluctantly had excused himself on the pretense of making sure the film was properly prepared for the screening. But he had other things to do. He had conceived a crazy stunt, daring and dangerous, but one his showman instincts could not resist.

Dressed all in black, he slipped a pair of ice spikes over his shoes, put on a pair of thick work gloves and took a long length of coiled rope from the case. Wrapping his black cloak around his shoulders, he stepped out on the icy balcony.

He had studied the front wall of the chalet earlier in the day. The screening room was on the same level as his room but two balconies away. Normally it would have been a simple stunt to climb up to the roof and down to the screening room but the building was encrusted with ice. Even though the wind had died away, snow flurries drifted down, making it difficult to see up to the roof and making the stunt doubly dangerous. And then, of course, there were the guards constantly patrolling the grounds. But Ingersoll was determined to go through with it.

He swung the loop of coiled rope around, letting it out as he did in a widening circle, and tried to hook it over the cornice on the roof. It missed and fell over the side of the balcony, sending a cascade of broken ice to the ground. Ingersoll flattened himself against the wall as one of the guards peered up. But the guard could see nothing, his vision impaired by hundreds of twinkling snowflakes, and he walked around the corner. On the third try, the rope slipped over the cornice and caught.

Pulling it taut, Ingersoll worked his way up the face of the chalet, his spikes biting into the patches of ice imbedded in the wall. Once he was on the steeply eaved rooftop, he loosened the rope. Balanced on the edge of the roof with no safety line, he could feel the ice shifting underfoot. Snow sprinkled into his eyes and mouth.

He bent his knees slightly for added balance and swung the rope around again, this time attempting to hook the cornice over the screening room balcony. It was difficult to judge in the dark and the falling snow. Each time the rope missed, shards of ice clattered down fifty feet to the garden beneath him.

His heart was throbbing with excitement as he continued to try to loop his line over the cornice. Finally it caught. He started to pull it taut but as he did, the icy patch underfoot crumbled and he felt himself slipping over the edge. He reached out with one hand, grabbed the roof, felt his hand slide off and pitched over the side into the darkness.

He plunged downward, grasping the lifeline, wondering for an instant whether it would catch and break his fall. Then he felt the snap of the rope, the shock through his wrists and elbows and felt himself arcing through the air. He smacked against the side of the chalet and his gloved hands began slipping down the length of rope. He let go with one hand, grabbed the rope a foot lower and frantically twisted it around his wrist. It stopped his slide. He was dangling six feet above the balcony.

"Where is *der Schauspieler*?" he heard Göring ask from inside the room. "He is late for his own show."

"You know these artists," he heard the woman answer.

He slid down the rest of the rope to the screening room balcony and sighed with relief, a specter in black hunched against the wall.

Inside the dimly lit screening room, Hitler had settled in his usual chair with Göring on one side and Eva on the other. The rest of the guests found seats around him. Vierhaus was worried. Hitler had no patience when it came to tardiness. Where was Ingersoll?

Suddenly the French doors leading to the balcony burst open and a hideous specter in black whirled dramatically through the doors.

Everyone in the room gasped.

Eva screamed.

Himmler reached for his Luger.

Hitler bolted back against his seat, his eyes as wide as a full moon.

"Mein Führer, Damen, gentlemen," Ingersoll said, "may I present *Der Nacht Hund."*

He swept the mask off his head and leaned over in a deep bow.

Ingersoll sat on the bed in his room.

What a day this had been, a personal victory for him. The screening had been a triumph. And his little stunt had, once the outrage disappeared, thrilled the Führer with its daring.

The actor stepped out on the balcony and lit a cigarette. He was exhausted and needed time to think, to plan his future.

One floor below the masters of the Reich were talking business, something both Hitler and Vierhaus had said was usually forbidden.

Somebody opened the doors to the terrace below and he could hear the voices, pick up an occasional word or phrase, although he was not trying to eavesdrop. He was intoxicated by the thought that twenty feet below him, the destiny of Germany was being planned.

"I say do it," he heard Göring's boisterous voice say. "And quickly."

". . . very risky," somebody said, perhaps Funk.

"Of course it's risky," Himmler said. "So what . . ."

The voice faded away. There was more muffled conversation and he picked up occasional snatches of sentences.

Goebbels: ". . . must convince everyone it was a Communist plot."

Hitler: "That is your problem, Joseph."

"Göring: ". . . worry, I know the perfect scapegoat . . . a half-wit who lives . . ."

Himmler: ". . . five days and I will convince him he is the head of the Communist party for the entire continent," followed by a chorus of laughter.

More muffled talk and then he heard Göring finish a sentence: ". . . to arrange the fire."

The *fire?*

There was more muffled talk. He stepped closer to the edge of the balcony to hear better and heard a snatch of something Göring was saying: ". . . a tunnel from . . ." and he faded out again. Moments later . . .

Himmler: "A rat bomb perhaps . . ."

A rat bomb? Ingersoll wondered. So did Hitler.

"A rat bomb?"

"Simply starve a rat for a day or two. Prepare the fire in the heating ducts in the basement, set a trap so it will ignite the fire when the trap is sprung. Then we let the rat loose in the duct. A hungry rat can smell food for miles. When he takes his meal, poof. The building is old, it will go up like a dry Christmas tree."

What building, Ingersoll wondered. *And why?*

Someone walked out on the terrace below. Ingersoll snuffed out the cigarette in a drift of snow beside the door and stepped back inside.

Why? he thought. And what was it Goebbels had said, *blame it on the Communists?*

He sat at the writing desk in the corner of the room trying to put his mind back on the film. There were several minor things he wanted to change. But he could not shake the events of the day and Hitler's outrageous proposal to him.

His decision was sudden and irrevocable.

He got up suddenly and cracked the door to his room a couple of inches. He heard the sitting room doors on the first floor open, the muffled voices of men saying their good nights, a ripple of laughter. He left the door ajar and went back to the table.

At the foot of the stairs, Hitler turned to Vierhaus and whispered, "Well, what do you think, Willie? Will our *Schauspieler* accept the challenge?"

"I think there is no question," Vierhaus answered confidently.

"Well, after tonight, I don't think his courage could ever be faulted."

"In fact," Vierhaus answered, "after his stunt tonight I would say he is a man who *enjoys* taking risks. Perhaps without thought of the consequences."

"How do you come to that conclusion?"

"He risked his life scaling your icy wall and he was not at all concerned with what your reaction might be. He simply didn't care."

"Hmm. Are you implying there may be some hidden surprises with this fellow?" Hitler pressed on. "That he may have, what do you call them, fatal flaws?"

"Not at all. I think he's the perfect man for the job."

Vierhaus was shading the truth a bit. He knew all human beings harbor hidden surprises. Vierhaus was a trained psychologist, a conditioned skeptic who impulsively looked beyond the surface. He knew that within that cold cell of the mind there were obsessions, compulsions, dark impulses, secrets, even imaginary companions, and the line between the neurotic and the psychotic was thin indeed. The neurotic submitted to those passions. The psychotic was a victim of them.

Thus far he had only intelligence reports on Ingersoll on which to base his judgment. Simple facts—Himmler's people were not interested in interpretation, they were collectors of data—and the data had not permitted a reliable analysis of the man. Now, after a day and night in which to observe Ingersoll, some questions had crept into his mind.

Sitting in the darkened theater, Vierhaus had focused on the actor. His entrance through the French doors had been a startling piece of showmanship—but did it indicate something else?

Was Ingersoll an eccentric artist? Or was there some dark secret lurking inside his head that could at some crucial moment explode like a volcano and endanger the entire mission?

In short, was this man eccentric, neurotic or psychotic?

Or was he all three?

Vierhaus simply did not know but he had his own megalomania and was confident that if the actor accepted Hitler's proposal, he could control and master the man. It was a risky assumption but one he had to take. He had convinced the Führer that Ingersoll was perfect for the job, it was too late to back away now.

Five minutes passed before Ingersoll heard the footsteps mounting the stairs and coming down the hallway. He leaned over his notes. He heard the footsteps stop and a moment later a tap on the door. He turned, acting startled. Hitler was peering in the doorway.

"Excuse me, Colonel Wolfe, your door was open."

Ingersoll scrambled to get to his feet but Hitler waved him back down.

"Stay down, please. I didn't mean to intrude."

"Please come in," Ingersoll said. "I was just jotting down some notes on the film. Little things, you know. A snip here, a snip there."

Hitler pushed the door open but did not enter the room. He stood framed in the entrance with his hands behind his back.

"Always the perfectionist, eh?"

"I suppose I am. It drives the technicians crazy."

"Then you should get better technicians."

"I keep hoping we have the best."

"Well, I did not mean to disturb you. Thank you again for the film. As you can tell, everyone was thrilled by it. I will watch it many times more, I am sure. And thank you for coming to my home."

"It is the highlight of my life, *mein Führer*. It is I who thank you." He paused for a moment and then said, "I would like to repay the kindness . . . in a small way of course, I'm afraid I can't match the significance of the dagger."

"Usually a German shepherd puppy goes with the commission. To be a companion during the training period. But in your case, it seemed inappropriate."

"One of my vices is fine wines," Ingersoll said. "I have about two hundred bottles of vintage French reds and whites at my country house. I would like you to have them, Führer."

Hitler was genuinely surprised at the offer. Then the significance of the gift slowly sank in. His expression turned quizzical, then curious, then his eyes widened and he smiled broadly.

"That is a very generous gift, Colonel."

He paused, his eyebrows rounded into question marks.

"When Hans Wolfe dies," said Ingersoll, "the wine will be delivered to you."

Hitler clenched his fists to his chest. His expression was one of pure joy.

"So you agree then?"

"Yes," Ingersoll said, rising to his feet, "I would be honored to become *Siebenundzwanzig.*"

"I am sure that was a difficult decision for you."

"Yes. And there is something else that is difficult."

"What might that be?" Hitler asked.

"There are two problems we must deal with," Ingersoll said and calmly explained what they were.

Hitler did not flinch. His expression did not change.

"You shall learn," he said to the actor, "those are the kinds of problems we deal with extremely well."

Their eyes met and slowly, very slowly, Johann Ingersoll raised his hand in the Nazi salute.

Adolf Hitler saluted back and smiled.

The five-day-old newspaper lay on top of a scattered pile of current papers on an oak table in the living room. The inside pages had been pulled out so the carryover lay beside the front page opener.

FILM IDOL INGERSOLL
DEAD IN CAR CRASH
Valet Also Dies in
3,000-foot Alpine Plunge

By
Bert Rudman
Herald Tribune Correspondent

BADEN-BADEN, Germany. March 7. Johann Ingersoll, Germany's newest movie star, vacationing after the triumphant world premiere of his new film, "Der Nacht Hund," was killed instantly today when his touring car skidded off a mountain highway near here and plunged 3,000 feet to the ravine below.

Otto Heinz, onetime makeup artist who quit films to become Ingersoll's personal attendant, was also killed in the crash.

The two victims were identified by Friedrich Kreisler, Ingersoll's attorney and agent.

"It was difficult for him," said Burgermeister Louis Brunch, of nearby Baden-Baden, where the bodies were taken after their recovery by alpine teams. "Both bodies were horribly mangled in the fall."

Ingersoll was a bachelor and had no heirs, according to Kreisler, who was obviously stricken by the death of his friend and client.

Ingersoll was a colonel in the SS and a personal favorite of Adolf Hitler. He shocked some of the guests at the premiere by appearing in full SS uniform for the first time.

"Germany has lost a national treasure," Chancellor Hitler told the press. "He was on the verge of becoming one of the world's great film stars and as such would have brought new glory to the Fatherland."

Ironically, the film's world premiere, a gala affair held at the Kroll Opera House, was overshadowed by the burning of the Reichstag which was discovered during the party that followed the screening. Guests crowded the balconies of the theater to watch the blaze a few blocks away or rushed to the scene from the party.

Ingersoll's last film, "Der Nacht Hund" was praised by critics as his most difficult and terrifying role. His work was compared favorably to that of American film star Lon Chaney.

Fritz Jergens, who directed Ingersoll's final picture, praised him as an "astounding performer who seemed to actually get inside the grotesque characters he played. He had great potential as a dramatic actor."

Ingersoll was known as an obsessively reclusive star who was never seen without makeup. He went to extraordinary lengths to conceal his true identity from press and public alike. In his two-year rise to international stardom, no pictures were ever released or taken of Ingersoll. Biographical data was sketchy at best. The only known photos of the actor are stills from his films. Publicity stories included only the names and background details of his films.

Ingersoll leaned over the table, chortling with glee, rereading the story and sipping a glass of wine. He was dressed in his black SS uniform, the dagger hanging ominously from his hip in its ebony scabbard. The uniform fit him perfectly. Hitler's tailor had done a magnificent job.

Imagine, he thought, *being upstaged by the Reichstag*. He strutted around the room, stopping for a moment in front of the hall mirror to admire himself. The uniform was a marvel of stark elegance. Coal black, its stiff puttees arcing from hip to knee, ending at the top of dazzling black riding boots. The death's head on the field cap, the sterling silver belt buckle, emblazoned with the words "Loyalty Is My Honor," the silver SS runes on one collar like double bolts of lightning, all stark against the black wool uniform. He straightened his shoulders and pulled in his chin.

"*Achtung,*" he snapped at the reflection.

Ingersoll strolled back to the table, rustled through the newspapers and reread part of one of the stories on the fire.

> Marinus van der Lubbe, a Dutch Communist, was arrested while the building was still ablaze and charged with setting the fire.
>
> Marshal Hermann Göring, head of the State Police, said van der Lubbe was found hiding in Bismarck Hall, behind the Reichstag. According to Göring, van der Lubbe readily admitted setting the blaze "for the glory of the Communist Party."
>
> Göring also said Communist pamphlets and other paraphernalia were found in van der Lubbe's apartment.
>
> "It was clearly a Communist-inspired tragedy," Göring said. "It is a miracle nobody was hurt."

What a brilliant political move! Even the revelation that van der Lubbe was nearly blind and mad as a hatter had been largely ignored by the German people. They didn't care. A frenzy of reaction had started almost immediately. In the five days since the fire, thousands of Communists had been arrested. The political power of the party had been broken. On the pretense of protecting the state against violence from the Communists, Hitler had announced a decree "for the Protection of the People and the State" and in a single stroke he had revoked all the freedoms guaranteed by the Constitution.

Five days since the fire and the man was now ruling Germany by decree.

Ingersoll went to the kitchen to refill his glass. *Hitler is now the Emperor of Germany,* he thought. *He is the* ruler *of Germany.* Laughing aloud, he raised his glass in a silent toast to the Führer.

Then he heard a key click in the front door lock, heard the tumblers clink.

My God! he thought. *It's Friedrich. He's the only one who has a key. What the hell was he doing here?*

He heard the door open, the floors creak, the door close. He moved to the edge of the kitchen door and sneaked a look. Kreisler was taking off his coat. He looked at the table, walked over to it and began leafing through the papers. He looked around the room.

"Hello," he called out, confused. "Is someone here?"

Well, Ingersoll thought. *What the hell.*

He stepped into the living room.

"Hello, Freddie," he said casually.

Kreisler was stunned, shocked to speechlessness. He stared at the ghost standing before him.

"My God," he said and his voice was barely audible. "My God, it's you, Johnny!"

"In the flesh, pardon the pun."

"I don't understand . . . what in God's name . . ."

"It's a long, rather involved story, Freddie. Relax. I'll get you a glass of wine. Châteauneuf-du-Pape, twenty-nine. Incredible year."

"What in hell is going on?" Kreisler demanded, finding his voice. "My God, what kind of publicity stunt have you dreamed up now? Where's Heinz? How did you get him in on this?"

"Heinz is dead. For real."

"Then who was that other poor devil I identified? He was wearing your clothes. He was . . ."

"I have no idea who he was, Freddie. I never saw the man. I don't know anything about him and I don't want to."

"What happened? Did Heinz pick somebody up on the road? How did he get into your clothes?"

The lie came as easily as whistling a tune.

"He was Heinz's lover," Ingersoll said. "I assume they

were going down to the village from the ski camp. The road was icy . . ."

"But why did you . . . ?"

Kreisler stopped and looked Ingersoll up and down, realizing suddenly that he was wearing his SS uniform.

"And what are you doing in that uniform? What's come over you, Johann? What is going *on*?"

There was no way to lie to Kreisler. No way to explain. Freddie had made an error by coming to the house. A fatal error.

"What are you doing here, by the way?" Ingersoll asked.

"I wanted to check the place over, figure out what to do with all these antiques, the paintings. The wine. You've got a fortune in wine downstairs, Johnny."

"It's all taken care of. The house will be closed up as is. Caretakers will keep it up. The apartment in Berlin will be sold."

"What are you doing in that uniform?"

Ingersoll stared across the room at his friend. His face turned cold.

"It may be the last time I'll get to wear it for a long time," he said.

"You shouldn't be wearing it at all."

"Why not," Ingersoll said proudly. "My appointment was made directly by the Führer."

"Christ, Johnny, do you know what that madman's up to? He's abolished the Constitution, taken away all our rights. He *decreed* it, for God's sake. He decreed away all our rights. Freedom of speech, freedom of the press, freedom to think, to make a phone call, to send a damn *letter* without having it intercepted. The SA is tearing up Berlin. Hitler's become a damn *dictator* in just a few weeks."

"Days, actually," Ingersoll said smugly. "Oh, the process of getting elected chancellor, building up the party, all that took years. But actually he's completely taken over a failed, corrupt, rotten government, and done it in only *five days*."

He laughed and held up five fingers.

"How can you support this, Johnny? You're a creative artist . . ."

Ingersoll cut him off.

"I'm an actor in scary movies, Freddie, that's all. Until now.

Now I've been invited to play an important role in the greatest revolution in history."

"This isn't a revolution, it's banditry. Common theft. He's stolen the rights from the people. He's . . ."

Ingersoll waved him quiet.

"The Third Reich will change history, Freddie. You don't have the imagination to see that. You have *no* imagination, Freddie, that's why you're the agent and I'm the actor. I want to be a part of all this. I'm tired of sneaking around in fake whiskers and wigs. Tired of torturing my body in those ridiculous getups. I've got more money than I'll ever spend." He picked up the paper and held it toward Kreisler. "Great notices on the picture. And a wonderful obituary. Time for Johann Ingersoll to die."

"And become a Nazi blackshirt?"

"Become a Nazi *patriot,*" Ingersoll snapped back. "I'm giving up everything, *everything,* for my country."

"No, you're giving it up for that little man with the Chaplin mustache."

"You're truly straining my patience, Freddie."

"Oh, come on, we've been friends too long for this kind of . . . of . . . for God's sake, Johann, I'm your friend. I'm concerned about you."

"And your ten percent?"

Kreisler's shoulders sagged.

"I was a successful lawyer when I met you and I am still a successful lawyer," Kreisler said. His voice trembled from the strain of the confrontation. "I can certainly live without the frills your ten percent allows me. I didn't know you felt that way, Johann. I didn't know you felt I was cheating you."

Ingersoll's mind was racing. He had an image of the night of the premiere, just after the fire in the Reichstag was discovered.

At the first news of the fire, everyone at the party had rushed to the windows and balconies. A few blocks away, flames scorched the night sky and glowing embers swirled up through the twisting smoke.

Ingersoll had laughed at the irony. The fire had ended his gala celebration. And now he understood the conversation he had overheard at Berchtesgaden. He had led Vierhaus away from the crowd and back down the mezzanine to a quiet corner.

"Do you think the Communists are behind this fire?" Ingersoll asked casually.

"No doubt about it. I predict a quick arrest and the downfall of the Communist party for committing this atrocity."

Ingersoll raised his champagne glass to Vierhaus.

"Another victory for the Führer."

"You are a nervy one, *Schauspieler,* I'll say that for you," Vierhaus said. "Showing up in that uniform and that severe disguise has raised a lot of eyebrows."

Ingersoll had covered his crown with skinlike rubber latex and deepened the shadows in his cheeks. Bald, almost skull-like, wearing the stark SS uniform, he had startled the sellout crowd, many of whom were foreigners.

"And perhaps softened some attitudes?" Ingersoll had suggested.

"I think the Führer might take issue with your choice of words. He will not put up with softened attitudes. Blind obedience, that's what he—we all—require. Did the Führer ever mention the German shepherd puppies to you?"

"Yes." He was apologetic. "He said SS trainees are usually given a puppy when they begin their training. But in my case . . ."

"Do you know the significance?"

Ingersoll hesitated, shrugged. "They are excellent watchdogs, great pets."

"And an important part of the ritual of acceptance," said Vierhaus. "Normally, any officer in the SS must undergo vigorous training. At the beginning he is given a shepherd puppy as a companion through the course. Dog and man come to rely on each other. And on the day they finish their training and take the oath of allegiance to the Führer, they are ordered to slit the dog's throat."

"What?" Ingersoll had answered with some skepticism and not a little shock.

"What better way to show that we are loyal to only one master. That we have only one friend, Adolf Hitler, and that we will follow his orders with blind obedience."

Ingersoll said nothing. His eyes narrowed and he peered at Vierhaus with a strange new respect.

"The German people must also learn blind obedience," Vierhaus continued. "If you are not *of* the party, you are *against* it. A good rule of thumb. It simplifies things."

Ingersoll nodded agreement. "And now the Reichstag burns," he said. "A fortunate misfortune."

Vierhaus laughed at the contradiction. "Exactly, my friend. A decrepit symbol dies, new ones will take its place. The Third Reich is just that, a new order of things for *Deutschland*."

"A new order of things." Ingersoll echoed the words. Staring deeply into the eyes of the professor, he had said very matter-of-factly, "I think it's time to die, Professor."

"I'm sorry, old friend," Ingersoll said, putting his arm around Kreisler's shoulder and leading him toward the table covered with newspapers. "Forgive me, all right? I lost my temper. You know how that can be. Can't let politics stand in the way of a good friendship, can we?"

He pointed to the papers on the table.

"Think about it. A chance to read my own obituary. Don't you see, I couldn't resist the temptation. You know me. Could I really pass it up?"

"That's why you did this? To read your own obituary. Is that why you accepted a commission in the SS?"

"I am a Nazi, Freddie. You have known that for years. I never concealed that from you."

"But to present yourself in public in that uniform. Do you realize what this has done to your standing in foreign countries? The United States will not book your pictures anymore. Neither will England or France."

"The hell with all three of them. One of these days we will have a Johann Ingersoll retrospective in Paris, London, New York."

"I don't understand. What are you going to do?"

"Not me. Us, Freddie. What we're going to do."

"What the hell *are* we going to do?"

"We're going to die, Freddie," Ingersoll said. His hand swept up from Kreisler's shoulder, grabbed the back of his hair and snapped his head back. The other hand drew the long knife from its scabbard and swiftly drew the gleaming blade from just below Kreisler's left ear straight across to his right.

Kreisler did not feel the cut at first, the SS knife was that sharp. Then he felt a burning sensation under his Adam's apple. He looked down and saw geysers of his own blood gushing from the gaping slice in his throat.

He tried to scream but managed only a wracking gurgle. He couldn't breathe. He grabbed for Ingersoll but the actor stepped back and plunged the knife upward, under his ribs and into his heart.

Kreisler's eyes rolled back and he fell like a rag doll in a heap on the floor, landing in a kneeling position, his forehead on the rug and his arms stretched back toward his feet.

Blood flooded the rug.

Ingersoll leaned over and wiped the blade clean on Kreisler's suit jacket and put it back in its sheath. He rolled Kreisler over on his back and stuffed several newspapers in the wound to stem the bleeding. Kreisler stared up at him with vacant eyes. Ingersoll closed them with one hand. Then he rolled Kreisler up in the rug. He felt a rush of adrenaline. He started to get hard and he was almost out of breath. He leaned his head back, breathing heavily through his mouth. The rush of excitement continued for a full minute or two, swelling his groin, pumping blood into his temples. Then he slumped down on the edge of the table with a gasp of air.

In a few moments, he was able to walk across the room to the telephone and put in a long-distance call to Vierhaus in Berlin.

"Professor Vierhaus here," came the oily answer.

"This is Swan."

"Swan?"

"Yes, Swan. You understand?"

"Of course."

"I had to take care of part of it myself."

"I *don't* understand."

"I just killed Freddie Kreisler. He's rolled up in a rug in my living room at the Bergen House. I had no choice."

Vierhaus paused for only a moment. Ingersoll could almost hear the gears clicking in the professor's head.

"Have you finished your business there?"

"Yes. All the papers are in a strong box in the wine cellar. I trust you will handle all those affairs for me."

"Of course."

"You know about the wine, yes?"

"Yes. I am sure the Führer will enjoy every bottle. Now listen carefully. I want you to leave there as quickly as you can. Leave in Kreisler's car. Wear his coat and hat. Drive to the train station in Bergen. Leave the car keys under the seat. Someone will be there to meet you."

"How will I know him?"

"He'll be watching for Kreisler's car. You'll know him, he'll address you as Herr Swan. We'll take care of the body."

"Thank you."

"It's not all that much trouble," Vierhaus said. "I'm . . . sorry you had to do it. We had more elaborate plans."

"Unavoidable. By the way, remember what you told me about the dogs?"

"The dogs?"

"The German shepherds."

"Oh, yes, of course."

When Ingersoll spoke next, he spoke with just a touch of pride.

"I don't think I'll be needing a dog when I begin training," he said.

Felix Reinhardt dashed through the summer shower from the streetcar stop to the two-story building on the edge of the last art colony in Berlin—if it could be called that—most of the artists and writers having left the city in the wake of the Nazi putsch. He huddled in the vestibule of the gaily painted building, a short, serious man, on the stout side, his black hair and mustache shaggy and uncut, his deep-set eyes peering out from behind thick glasses, his suit rumpled. The rainstorm had come up suddenly, catching him without an umbrella, so now he shook the rain off his jacket.

Reinhardt climbed the stairs to the second-floor studio. A bell over the door tinkled gently as he entered the bright, cheerful loft. Partially complete sculpture littered the big room which was lit from above by two enormous skylights. He closed the door and began whistling the chorus of the "Blue Danube Waltz."

In a small compartment off to one side of the studio, Oscar Probst peered through a small hole in the wall. He wore an apron over his gray pants. He pulled off the apron, using it to wipe ink off his hands before draping it over one of the two tables that contained the fonts for his ancient, foot-powered Angerstadt printing press.

In the studio, Reinhardt heard the ceiling-high bookcase in one corner groan as Probst slid one side of it away from the wall and stepped into the studio. The bookcase hid the entrance to the tiny printing shop.

"Felix, you are early," Probst said with a smile. He was a cheerful man, younger than Reinhardt, handsome and clean shaven with short-trimmed blond hair and an air of optimistic naïveté that was a sharp contrast to Reinhardt's persistently dark and gloomy countenance.

"I have some changes in the lead story," Reinhardt said, taking a folded sheet of paper from his inside pocket. "Not much, just a few things."

"It is no problem," the younger man answered. "The foot pedal broke on me again. I'm afraid the old press is about to give up for good. Anyway I'm behind about half an hour."

Every two weeks Probst printed a four-sheet underground newspaper called *The Berlin Conscience.* It was one of the last free voices left in the city. Its editor was Felix Reinhardt. Probst also manufactured passports for political dissidents escaping from Germany. In fact, Probst was probably the best passport counterfeiter in the country.

Both the *Conscience* and his passport service were extremely dangerous enterprises. In public, Probst professed to be an ardent Nazi, a sham that had enabled him to escape detection by the Gestapo. Reinhardt was internationally famous. His articles appeared in newspapers in London, Paris, and New York, occasionally in *The New Republic.* He had escaped the wrath of the Gestapo only because he was so well known internationally but his situation grew more precarious by the day. His telephone was tapped and he was often followed. The Gestapo was looking for any reasonable excuse to silence Reinhardt forever.

Both men knew they were marking time with disaster. *The Berlin Conscience* was high on the Gestapo's hit list and both men knew they would be killed if they were caught.

"One more issue," Probst would say every other Thursday. "We have to stop, Felix, they're getting too close."

Reinhardt knew Probst was right. Every issue drew them closer to disaster. Yet every fortnight brought new revelations, new atrocities and decrees that both men felt compelled to reveal to the people, so they continued their dangerous enterprise. Sometimes Reinhardt would awaken sweating in the middle of the night, his discomfort caused by the hot breath of the Gestapo, whether real or imagined.

"So, the pedal is fixed," Probst said. "Give me the corrections and I'll make them. Go have a beer. Come back in thirty minutes."

"Can I bring you something?"

"No, thank you. Go out the back way to the *Hofbräu* across the street. You won't get too wet."

"*Danke,*" Reinhardt said.

Felix Reinhardt could not have known when he left that his best friend had less than a minute to live. In fact, if Probst's printing press had not broken down, Reinhardt would have died with him.

As they spoke, a gray command car pulled up in front of the building and four *Sturmabteilung* jumped out. The brownshirts were led by a stout, granite-faced sergeant, his nose streaked with the broken blood vessels that are the sign of a heavy drinker. They moved quickly, entering the stairway to the second floor and taking the steps two at a time.

Reinhardt was on his way down the back stairs when the SA crashed into Probst's studio.

"Oscar Probst?" he heard a gruff voice demand.

"What do you want?" Probst answered.

Reinhardt sneaked back up the stairs when he heard the commotion. He peered through the half-open door just as one of the brownshirts grabbed the tall oak bookcase at the rear of the artist's studio and sent it crashing down. He kicked open the hidden door behind it and stalked into the small printing shop, looked around, picked up several sheets of copy from a table and quickly read them.

With a roar of anger, he tossed the papers in the air and putting a shoulder under the edge of one of the two tables where type fonts were stored, hefted it over. It smashed to the floor and hundreds of lead letters cascaded out.

"No, no!" Probst said and rushed toward the big man in the brown uniform. The brownshirt grabbed Probst by the shirt front.

"Traitor," he snarled and shoved him back across the room. Then he turned over the second table.

"You swine!" Probst screamed.

They were his last words. The SA sergeant entered the studio and marched to the door of the printing room. As Probst charged forward again, the sergeant drew his Luger and shot him. The bullet tore into Probst's chest and knocked the artist backward. His knees buckled but he didn't fall. He looked at the SA sergeant with a mixture of surprise and horror.

The sergeant's attack on Probst spurred on the other three brownshirts. They all pulled their pistols and the room exploded with gunfire. Several more shots tore into Probst's body, knocking him against his desk. He fell backward across it, arms outstretched, his legs dangling to the floor. Half a dozen bullet holes had chewed up his sweater. Blood began to ooze out.

Reinhardt held his hand over his mouth to trap his own scream of horror. He could do nothing for Probst, so he bolted down the stairs, his eyes darting back toward the rear door of the studio as he rushed down the steps sideways, expecting to see the *Sturmabteilung* assassins come after him. Instead he heard them smashing things in the print shop and in Probst's studio. Then there was a dull thud and someone yelled, "Fire!"

My God, Reinhardt realized, *they're setting the whole building on fire.*

He slipped out the back entrance into the rainy afternoon crowd that scurried along the street and walked away as quickly as he could.

Ahead of him a woman on the street pointed behind him toward the building.

"Look," she cried out, "that building is burning."

Reinhardt didn't stop or turn around. He tried not to run, not to be too obvious but he was overwhelmed with fear, fear that they were right behind him, fear that they would shoot him in the back. He half-ran, half-walked to the corner a block away, then he stopped to look back for the first time. Flames broiled out of the second-story windows of the freestanding building. Reinhardt's heart was racing and his mouth was dry. He leaned against the building to get out of the rain and watched.

A few moments passed. Two brownshirts emerged from the back door, looked up and down the street. A Nazi command car, its red and black swastika flags flapping from the fenders, wheeled around the corner and stopped beside them. The ugly sergeant who had fired the first shot at Probst stood up in the open car and pointed up and down the rain-soaked street. His orders were interrupted by the arrival of a fire truck.

Reinhardt squeezed tighter against the wall. Standing in the shadows, he watched as the firefighters dawdled setting up their hoses. Several SA stood around, encouraging them to take their time.

"Too late anyway," one of them said. "The building is gone. Why waste water, eh? Let the rain put it out."

They all began to laugh.

The roof of the building was now ablaze, the flames snapping up at the sheets of rain.

The brownshirts fanned out from the building, looking through the gathering crowd. Several of them had photographs which they showed to the people staring at the fire.

"Listen to me," one of the SA yelled to the crowd while he held up a photograph. "You see this man, Felix Reinhardt? I know you recognize his picture. He is very famous. We have orders to arrest him for crimes against the Führer and the Fatherland. Anyone who hides him or fails to turn him over to us will be shot. Has anyone seen him? Speak up!"

Reinhardt hurried away from the scene. The nearest tram stop was two blocks away. A crowd was already gathered there, huddled under umbrellas. He headed straight for it, holding his head down against the driving summer rain. He could not return to his house, they would be watching it. Nor could he risk a taxicab. He needed the security of a crowd. A few more people gathered at the streetcar stop and he crowded in with them, holding a newspaper in front of his face, pretending to read as he peered over the top. He tried to slow his breathing but he had never been this afraid in his life.

Two blocks away the streetcar rounded the corner and crept toward them. It was still a block away when two brownshirts started down the street in his direction. The rain began to slacken. They stopped and looked up and down the street, started to cross toward him, stopping occasionally to show the photograph to wet and annoyed pedestrians.

Sweat mingled with the rain dribbling down the side of Reinhardt's face. He could feel its dampness under his arms, spreading down under his jacket.

The streetcar pulled up and he clambered aboard. It pulled away with a groan as the two brownshirts reached his side of the street. One of them walked briskly alongside the streetcar as it pulled away, peering intently in the windows. Reinhardt turned his back to the brownshirt, watching the SA's reflection in the window as the stormtrooper walked the length of the car checking the pedestrians from outside. He could feel his own heart beating in his temples. He closed his eyes and took several deep breaths, exhaling slowly to calm down.

Thank God, he missed me.

He rode the bus for seven or eight blocks until the passengers began to thin out, then got off and flagged down a taxicab.

"Take me to the American embassy," he told the driver. "It's on the Munich highway."

"Yes, I know it," the driver said. He looked in his rearview mirror. "Are you an American?" he asked.

"No, no," Reinhardt answered quickly. "I . . . I'm a carpenter. They want me to do some work for them."

"Make them pay good, eh?" the driver said with a smile.

"Oh yes, they will pay dearly," Reinhardt answered, trying to look relaxed.

When they were two blocks from the embassy he saw the two touring cars parked across the street from its arched gate. Two men in black raincoats, their black felt hats pulled down over their eyes, were talking to the Marine guard at the gate. Four others sat in the cars across the street with the doors standing open.

The Gestapo.

"Stop here at the tobacco shop," Reinhardt said suddenly. "I need to get some cigarettes."

"Right. You want me to wait?"

"Not necessary. It's only two blocks more. The walk will do me good."

He paid the driver, entered the store and bought a package of cigarettes, then left, walked away from the embassy and turned a corner. He hurried to a phone booth halfway down the block and stood with his back to the street as he gave the operator the American attaché's private number. He was sweating again, his breath labored. He could taste fear in his mouth. It seemed forever before the secretary answered.

"Colonel Meredith's office."

"The colonel, please," Reinhardt said as he checked both ends of the street.

"Who may I say is calling?"

Were the phones tapped? he wondered. *Could he take a chance?*

"Please, it is a matter of life and death. May I speak to the colonel."

"Can't you give me your name?" she asked.

He hesitated a moment then said, "No. Just give me the colonel, for God's sake! *Please.*"

There was a pause. For a terrible moment he thought he'd been disconnected. Then he heard a click and a blessed human voice.

"This is Colonel Meredith. Who is this, please?"

"This is an old friend, Colonel. You told me if I ever needed help I could call you . . ."

"I recognize your voice, don't say any more," the colonel interrupted. "Are you close by?"

"Yes."

There was a pause.

"Two blocks, three blocks?"

"Two blocks east. Side street phone booth."

"Do you remember the place we went for frankfurters?"

Reinhardt looked over his shoulder. An American food store known as The Brooklyn Delicatessen was directly across the street.

"Yes," he said, and wondered why he was whispering.

"Go there now. Immediately. I'll have somebody there in two minutes."

"*Danke.* Please hurry."

Reinhardt walked briskly across the street and entered the store. As he walked in the proprietor was answering the phone. He listened for a moment, looked at Reinhardt, said something, hung up and jerked his head toward the rear of the store.

Reinhardt went straight down the aisle and through a set of curtains into a tiny, cramped office with a rear door, an old rolltop desk stacked high with correspondence, and shelves of canned goods lining one wall. He waited, peering cautiously through the curtains. He could see the phone booth across the street. Moments crawled by.

A Mercedes pulled up at the booth and four SA troopers jumped out. One checked the booth, the other three looked up and down the street. Then one of them pointed at the store.

Panic seized the tousled little man. He turned and rushed out the back door.

Two men stood just outside the door, huddled in raincoats, hands stuffed in pockets, rain trickling off the brims of their hats. One held open the rear door of a sedan. A third man sat behind the steering wheel. Steam curled from the exhaust of the car.

"Herr Reinhardt?" one of them said.

Reinhardt's terrified eyes jerked in their sockets.

"It's all right, sir," said the taller of the two, grabbing him by the arm. "I'm Major Trace, U.S. embassy. Get in the car, quickly."

"They're right behind me. The SA are right behind me!" he cried as he jumped in the backseat. The two Americans followed, one in the front, Trace in the back with Reinhardt. The car roared away before they got the doors fully closed.

"On the floor, please," Trace said firmly. Reinhardt dropped on his knees on the floor and the major threw a blanket over him.

"No matter what happens, don't move," Trace said.

Huddled under the blanket, Reinhardt almost vomited with fear. He felt the car skid around a corner, heard its horn blaring. The next few seconds seemed like hours. He felt the car slow down for an instant, then stop. He could hear muffled voices outside the car.

My God, I am caught, Reinhardt thought. *I am dead.*

Then the car started up again. A few seconds later, Trace said, "Okay, sir, you can breathe easy, you're on U.S. soil."

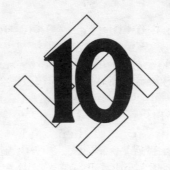

Keegan stood in the entrance to the main embassy salon, appraising the guests and listening to the band in the ballroom attempting to play jazz in a tempo that was more Victor Herbert than Chick Webb.

Keegan could not remember exactly what the occasion for the party was, there was *always* an occasion, but Wallingford had drawn a good crowd. There were the obligatory hangers-on, a few dull foreign diplomats, and, as usual, several officers of the German SS in their snappy black uniforms. There were also some new and interesting faces. The diminutive German actor with the pop eyes and the voice like an angry bee, Peter something, who had become an overnight sensation playing a child molester, was standing alone in a corner while in the opposite side of the room the English playwright, George Bernard Shaw, was holding forth to a large, mesmerized group, while the German actress Elizabeth Bergner, star of Shaw's play, *Saint Joan,* stared up at him adoringly.

There were several other new faces. A half dozen beautiful women. Wallingford did have a good eye for pretty ladies.

One of them was a new international film star. She stood on the far side of the room, and was immediately attracted to the tall man in the tuxedo who seemed to command the doorway as if he owned it. She was also aware that everyone else had seen him too. A murmur of whispers swept the room.

"Who is he?" she asked her escort, an American military attaché named Charles Gault.

Whispers always started the moment Keegan entered a room. He attracted rumors the way J. P. Morgan attracted money. Men usually glared at him with disdain, women stared

at him with hunger. Royalty doted on him and the café society
of England, France, Germany and Italy pandered him. Keegan
materialized wherever the action was, slightly aloof, with an
acerbic wit that intimidated men and an arrogant half-smile that
dazzled the ladies. There was also a hard edge to his charm, a
toughness that enhanced the rumors and added a hint of danger
to his allure.

"That's Francis Scott Keegan," Gault answered.

"So that's Keegan?" she said in a soft, husky voice, without
taking her eyes off him.

"His notoriety always seems to precede him," Gault answered.

It had. She had heard about this brash American playboy
who was supposedly richer than Midas. Had heard that he had
sired two or three illegitimate offspring among the rich and
titled. That he was an American war hero. That he was a gangster with a price on his head. That he was an active member of
Sinn Fein, the Irish rebel army. That he once cleaned out a
Greek shipping magnate in a poker game and then gave it all
back—with a shrug. They always added that. *With a shrug.*

"I've even heard he's a Russian nobleman, got out just
ahead of the revolution," Gault whispered.

"He's no Russian nobleman," her dusty voice answered.
Keegan entered the room now, stopping to speak to Jock Devane, the American ambassador, and his wife Cissy.

"You will be at the lawn party Sunday, won't you, Francis?"
she asked.

"Wouldn't miss it for the world," he said, kissing her hand.

"I've already picked you for my badminton partner."

"Good," he said and, leaning over, he confided, "I'll work
on my backhand for the rest of the week. We'll cream 'em."

He moved on, shook hands with a Nazi SS officer, exchanged pleasantries with the wife of an American industrialist
and rarely took his eyes off the actress.

"Interesting," she said.

"Want to meet him?" asked Gault.

"Oh, he'll be over," she said with assurance.

As Keegan made his way casually through the room, stopping here and there to exchange greetings or kiss a perfumed

hand, he was aware that one guest, a small man with a hump on his back, seemed intently interested in him. Keegan ignored him but was constantly aware of his presence.

His course through the room eventually steered him straight to the actress.

"Hello, Gault, how're things with the army?"

"Dull as usual. Francis, have you met Marlene Dietrich?"

"No," he said, kissing her hand then looking directly into her eyes, "but I saw you in *Morocco* and I've been weak-kneed ever since."

She laughed. "Should I be complimented?"

"Absolutely," he said.

"And what do you do, Mr. Keegan?"

"Francis."

"Francis."

"Not much of anything," he answered. "I suppose you could say I'm on an extended holiday. A little business now and then."

"How nice," she said. "And when you're not on holiday?"

Absolutely stunning, Keegan thought. Killer eyes and a taunting voice that was both promising and forbidding at the same time. She took out a cigarette and he lit it for her.

"I don't remember," he said with a crooked, almost arrogant smile, and changed the subject. "Are you doing a movie now?"

"I am going back to Hollywood next week," she said. "I'll be starting a new picture next year."

"What's it called?"

"The Devil Is a Woman."

He grinned impishly and said, "How appropriate."

"There's a touch of the devil in *you*, Mr. Keegan," she said, leaning closer to him, staring him straight in the eyes.

"Have you heard the latest?" Gault said, realizing the conversation was about to get away from him. "This morning Goebbels ordered all the American telephone exchanges to fire their Jewish employees. They can only hire members of the Nazi party in the future. And the embassy can no longer make contracts with Jews. Can you imagine, the Germans telling us who to hire and who to do business with."

"It's their country," Keegan said casually.

"No, it's Hitler's country," Miss Dietrich said. "The irony is that he has never been elected to anything. He lost the election to Hindenburg and Hindenburg appointed him chancellor."

"How do you feel about him?" Keegan asked the actress.

She hesitated for a few moments, looking around the room before answering. "I think he is an enemy of anyone who is creative or intellectual."

"I'll never understand why the Germans didn't resist him," Gault said.

"It takes courage to resist him, Charlie," Keegan said. "We kicked hell out of Germany. The Versailles treaty bankrupted them. They haven't got anything left to resist with."

"Whose side are you on, anyway?" Gault said, obviously annoyed by Keegan's defense of the German people.

"It's not a question of sides. Those are facts."

"They started the war and we finished it. What would you have done, slapped their wrist?" Gault snapped back.

"Americans never have understood European politics," Keegan said. "You know what they say, when Roosevelt was elected he forgave all his enemies; when Hitler was elected he arrested all his friends. A difference in point of view."

"Point of view?" Gault answered. "The *Sturmabteilung* are his personal police. They beat up people in the streets every day."

"C'mon, Charlie, things aren't that much different back in the states. The SA beats up Commies over here, we call the veterans Commies and beat them up in Washington. The Gestapo confiscates the Jews' property, our banks confiscate people's homes. The SA beats up Jews, the Ku Klux Klan lynches Negroes. We have the same soup kitchens, the same hobo camps, the same unemployment. Hell, we just got lucky. We got Roosevelt, they got Hitler. And believe me, there are people back home who think FDR's just as dangerous as Adolf."

"Not so loud," Gault hissed, looking around as though he expected someone from the State Department to jump out from behind the potted plants.

"You don't see Hitler as a threat to America, then?" Miss Dietrich asked.

"Hitlers come and go," Keegan said. "The Germans want him, they've got him. It's none of our business."

"Not *all* Germans want him," she said.

Keegan's look got hard for a moment.

"But you all have him," he said. Then the grin returned. "Hell, I like the German people. I get along with them."

"I hear they almost got you at Belleau Wood," Gault said.

"Yeah, well, we made a deal, the Germans and me. I forgave them for the war, they forgave me for the peace."

"Isn't that convenient," Gault said sarcastically.

"Look, Gault, I've made a lot of good friends over here. I'm sure some of them are in the Nazi party, hell it only costs six marks a month to belong. I don't ask them, it's none of my concern. If Hitler's their cup of tea, then I say they're welcome to him. It's none of our damn business what the Germans do."

"Please," Miss Dietrich pleaded, "can we change the subject? I am so tired of it, everyone you meet these days talks politics, politics, politics."

"It's the national sport," said Keegan. "We've got baseball, you've got the storm troopers."

She scowled painfully at the analogy.

"What brought you here?" Keegan asked her, attempting to remove the scowl.

"Haven't you heard? The American embassy is *the* social center of Berlin this season." Her lip curled into a faint and delicious smile.

"I hope that doesn't get back to Wally Wallingford," Keegan said. "His head's already ten sizes too big for his hat."

"Speaking of the devil." She nodded over Keegan's shoulder.

Wallace Wallingford was the protocol chief of the embassy and its social director. He was a slight man in his early thirties, tense and formal, with blond hair that was already beginning to thin out and anxious, watery eyes. Like many career diplomats, Wallingford affected an air of superiority, an attitude which intimidated some. But on this night he seemed nervous and distracted. Tiny beads of sweat twinkled on his forehead.

"Marlene, darling," he said, kissing her hand, "how generous of you to come."

"You're delightful, Wally," she said, "but you do have a tendency toward overstatement."

"And how are you, Francis?" Wallingford said.

"Just fine, Wally. Generous of you to ask."

Wallingford glared at him for a moment, then took his elbow.

"Marlene, may I borrow him for a moment or two?"

"Of course."

"I'll be back in a minute," Keegan said as Wallingford led him away.

"You've got to do something about that band, Wally," Keegan said.

"Like what?"

"I suggest deporting them. The sooner, the better."

"Just keep smiling and listen," Wallingford said softly. "You know where my office is on the second floor?"

"Of course I know where your office is. And stop talking without moving your lips, you look like Edgar Bergen."

Wallingford affected a frozen smile and said casually, "Wait about five minutes. Then go out on the terrace and come back in the side door. I'll meet you up there."

"Damn it, Wally, I was talking to the most beautiful, the most sensual, the most . . ."

"Don't be difficult, this is very serious," Wallingford said, still with that frozen grin. "Five minutes." And he moved back into the crowd.

Keegan looked back toward Marlene but Gault had already swept her onto the dance floor. The little hunchback was nowhere to be seen. Keegan went to the terrace and lit a cigarette.

From an alcove in the ballroom, Vierhaus continued to watch Keegan as he casually puffed on his cigarette, picked a carnation from the flowers at the edge of the garden, and fitting it into the slit in his lapel, strolled into the garden, vanishing into the damp, moonless night.

Keegan walked around the corner of the building, went back in through a side door and went up the stairs two at a time. Wallingford was waiting for him in the upper hallway.

"All right, Wally, what the hell is this all about?"

"You know who Felix Reinhardt is?" Wallingford asked nervously.

"The writer? Sure. He's the one who called Hitler the greatest actor in the world and said they should have given him a stage instead of the whole country."

"The whole *world's* the son of a bitch's stage," Wallingford said. "Reinhardt's here in my office."

"Why doesn't he come downstairs and join the rest of us peons?"

"Because he can't," Wallingford said, lowering his voice in exasperation.

Keegan laughed. "What's the matter, is he on the lam?"

"Exactly."

They entered Wallingford's office, a large, book-lined room that smelled of leather and pipe tobacco. There were two men in the room. Keegan knew one of them casually. His name was Herman Fuegel, a tall, gangly, awkward-looking American immigration officer who worked in the embassy. Fuegel was an American but his parents had migrated from Germany and he was fluent in the language.

The other person was Felix Reinhardt. He was sitting on a sofa in the corner of the room, a heavy-set man in his early forties with thick, black hair that tumbled almost to his shoulders and deep-set, dark-circled eyes. His tie was pulled down and he was disheveled and nervous. A partially eaten plate of fruit and vegetables sat on the coffee table in front of him.

"Mr. Reinhardt, this is Francis Keegan, an American. We can trust him. Francis, this is Felix Reinhardt."

"My pleasure," Keegan said. Reinhardt merely nodded. It was obvious he was deeply disturbed.

"They killed Probst," he blurted suddenly. "You wouldn't believe it. They just walked in his office, four of them, and emptied their guns into him." He made a gun from his forefinger and fist and said very slowly, "Bang . . . bang . . . bang . . . like that, over and over until their guns were clicking empty. Bang . . . bang . . . then they burned the building with him inside. It was . . . worse than awful. Worse than . . ."

"Easy," Wallingford said, handing him a brandy. The writer sipped it and seemed to calm down.

"Who's Probst?" Keegan asked, bewildered by the entire scene.

"A young German artist," Reinhardt said. "We put out *The Berlin Conscience* together. He also counterfeited passports for us."

"Us?" Keegan said. "Who's us?"

Reinhardt stared at him for a moment. "Enemies of the state. Communists, Jews, anyone who disagrees with our great Führer," he said bitterly.

"They killed him for making phony passports?" Keegan said with disbelief. "Who? Who did it?"

"The *Sturmabteilung*," Reinhardt said.

"Am I missing something here?" Keegan asked. "Here we are, standing in front of an immigration man, and we're talking about phony passports."

"Christ, Keegan, you are thick," Wallingford said.

"As long as he has papers nobody will question him," Fuegel explained. "But if he comes in without papers, we have no choice but to deport him."

"Even if you know his papers are phony?" Keegan said.

"As long as he has a passport and a hundred dollars in his pocket, there'll be no questions asked. But he must have papers."

"Christ, what a silly game."

"Not silly, Keegan, necessary," Wallingford said. "If we permit German refugees to enter the country without passports, there will be hell to pay with the German government. We've got to maintain some semblance of diplomatic relations with Germany. We have to know what the hell's going on here and we can't do it if they shut the embassy down."

"So you're on the run?" Keegan said to Reinhardt.

"*Ja.*"

"Running for his life," said Fuegel.

"What did you do?" Keegan asked quietly.

Reinhardt looked up slowly and said, "I disagreed with Hitler. Unfortunately I am also a Jew. That's what I did, sir. I have a big mouth and a Jewish mother."

"You've read his articles," Wallingford said. "He's an enemy of the state."

"What the hell's he doing here? Half the SS is down in the living room," Keegan said.

"There was no place else for him to go," Wallingford said. "No place safe."

"What am *I* doing here, Wally?"

"We have to get him out of Germany tonight."

"*Tonight!*"

"There's a warrant for his arrest. Specifically he's been charged with sedition for publishing *The Berlin Conscience.* If they catch him, he's finished."

"What do you mean, finished?"

"For Christ sake, Francis, you heard what he said. The brownshirts broke into his partner's place this afternoon, shot him in cold blood, then burned the building. You know what's going on here!"

Keegan thought about the storm troopers on their nightly forays, torch flames whirling in the wind as they drove through the streets in their open trucks, chanting their persistent dirge, "Down with Jews, Death to Jews," as they sought their prey. It was a common sight and like most people in Berlin, Keegan had become immune to its dreadful portent. Like most foreigners, he was reviled by the brownshirts but felt powerless to do or say anything against these drunken bullies with their insatiable appetite for violence. They had more power than the local police and they traveled in packs like hungry predators. Besides, it was a temporary thing, he thought. It would pass. And if the German people did not feel compelled to speak out against them what could *he* do? After all, it was their country. Germany was going through the trauma of revolution—death and fear were the companions of revolt. So he had learned to shut out the sounds of shattering glass and the cries of the victims, to turn his eyes away from the *Sturmabteilung* as they looted Jewish stores, beat up the owners, and painted crude, six-sided stars on the doors.

Keegan shook his head and his eyes opened fully. "I'm sorry," he said. "I don't get involved in local politics." He leaned over to Wallingford, and added, "This isn't your problem either, Wally."

Wallingford turned to Reinhardt. "Will you excuse us a minute," he said, and led Keegan into the adjoining office.

"We can't just ignore him," he said flatly.

"I admire him for going to bat for his country, but it's *his* country. We have to *live* with these people. It's none of our damn business."

"Listen, Reinhardt is one of the few outspoken German

writers left," Wallingford said, his voice brittle with tension. "His articles and editorials have a strong impact on Germans. Hell, he could be nominated for a Nobel Prize this year—if he lives that long." He paused for a moment, then leaned over and said softly, "President Roosevelt wants him out."

"Ah," Keegan dragged the word out, "we get to the pay-off."

"Call it anything you want, we need to move quickly, Francis."

"What do you mean *we*?"

"This is *every*body's business. This man is a symbol. We need to get him out of Germany."

"*You* need to get him out of Germany. You blow this and you'll end up third assistant attaché in some banana republic with tarantulas for a staff. Hell, you got the whole damn diplomatic corps, spies crawling out your kazoo and you want *me* to find *you* a forger. What am I supposed to do, go over to the Kit Kat Club and ask around? Why don't you just grant him political asylum?"

"It's too late for that," Wallingford said, lighting a cigarette. "This man is a very hot potato, he's been accused of treason. Asylum would not go down well at all, not well at all. My instructions are to get him out of Germany tonight and keep the government out of it. You've got a plane. Let us use it to get him to Paris. It's two hours away. I'll take care of the rest of it."

"So that's what this is all about. You want my plane."

"Just to fly him to Paris. Two hours, for God's sake."

"First of all it isn't just my plane," Keegan said brusquely. "It belongs to four of us, a Frenchman and two Brits are in on it with me. We share it and we schedule a month ahead so we can all make our plans. I'd have to check with all three of them and I don't even know where they are right now. It could take hours. And if the Nazis find out, and they will find out, they'll probably confiscate it. I can just see myself explaining that to my Parisian partner. *You're going to have to eat a hundred and fifty thousand bucks, Louie, Hitler decided to use our plane for weekend picnics.*"

"Listen to me," Wallingford said desperately. "If they catch this man they're going to execute him."

"Then don't let them catch him. Just leave me out of it. This isn't my fight."

"It's everybody's fight. You'll learn that soon enough."

"Stop preaching. Call in your intelligence chief and lay it off on him."

"*I can't involve them, damn it!*"

"You're a real case, you are. You can't get involved because you're a diplomat. Fuegel can't get involved because he's in the immigration service. Reinhardt can't get involved because he's on the dodge. But *I* can get involved because I'm just plain good old Frankie Keegan, rich American sucker, that it?"

"No one would suspect you," Wallingford said. "We get him out in your car, take him to the airport and he'll be in Paris before morning. All he needs is a passport."

"For the last time, I'm not going to get involved in local politics. What's the matter, don't you know anybody else with an airplane?"

"Nobody that's here now, no."

"That's flattering."

"Look, we're not talking about politics here, we're talking about a man's life," Wallingford implored. "You heard what the SA did to his best friend. You know what they'll do with Reinhardt? They'll take him over to the basement of Landsberg prison and behead him. *Behead* him!"

"I don't believe that."

"That's the way they do it these days. I can show you intelligence reports. Last month they beheaded three university students simply for *distributing The Berlin Conscience.* This guy *writes* the fucking paper. You wonder why he's panicked?"

Keegan shook his head.

"*Damn it,* Keegan!" Wallingford sat down heavily on the secretary's chair and shook his head. "There isn't any politics here anymore," he said wearily. "It's a one-party situation. There won't be another election in Germany until Hitler is dead."

"Well, there's your answer," Keegan said. "Knock off Hitler."

"You've got a lousy sense of humor." Wallingford's shoulders sagged. "I gave you credit for more guts than this."

"Look," Keegan answered angrily. "Once and for all, I

don't play politics, particularly German politics! The Germans adore Hitler. He drives down the street and everybody's out *heil*ing away, throwing flowers in front of his car. Germany's in love with him. And Reinhardt's a traitor to Germany!"

"He's *not* a traitor, he's a writer who is speaking out against things he feels are wrong."

"One man's traitor is another man's patriot." Keegan tapped Wallingford in the middle of his chest. "Know what I think? You got caught with your pants down on this. You knew this guy was in hot water but you didn't have a plan. Now FDR wants him smuggled out of the country and you're up against the wall."

"I'll admit I wasn't prepared for the President's reaction. Besides, it happened too quickly. Some miserable little *Juden-jäger* probably turned Reinhardt and Probst up."

"*Judenjäger?*"

"Jewhunters. It's what they do for a living. Trace family trees, look for a Jewish connection, report rumors to the Gestapo. Sometimes they are Jews themselves trying to stay out of trouble."

"Stool pigeons."

"Right. Stool pigeons."

"Call in your people," Keegan said, patting Wallingford on the shoulder. "Tell them what the President wants and cut them loose. You don't have any choice. Hell, I think the plane's in Paris anyway and even if it wasn't we couldn't find a pilot this late at night." He turned to leave.

"I thought I could count on you," Wallingford said.

"That's what you get for thinking, Wally," Keegan said without turning around. He went back to the other room.

"Good luck, Herr Reinhardt, I'm sorry I can't help you," Keegan said to the terrified little man. "I can do this for you. If you get out, there'll be ten thousand dollars on deposit in your name at Chase Manhattan Bank in New York to help you get started in America."

"That's most kind of you, sir. Thank you." Reinhardt turned to Wallingford. "Perhaps the Black Lily?" he asked.

"What's the Black Lily?" Keegan asked.

"You don't want to be involved," Wallingford said, "so stay out of it completely."

"Fair enough," Keegan nodded, and left the room.

When he got back downstairs, the actress was gone. The little man with the hump on his back was still there, though, and he watched Keegan's every step as Keegan left the embassy.

In Der Schwarze Stier Verein, Berlin's most notorious nightclub, nobody paid any attention to Francis Keegan. The downstairs room was nothing more than an elaborate beer hall, a mob
scene, crowded, smoky and boisterous, the heat oppressive.
Keegan decided he would stay long enough to have a nightcap
and hear the singer.

As he weaved through the crowd toward the bar, the manager, Herman Braff, pushed his way through the dancers toward
him.

"What an honor, what an honor," the chubby little sycophant babbled. "I am always flattered when you come, Herr
Keegan." Herman's tuxedo was a disaster of wrinkles and sweat
stains and his shirt was soaked down the front. Rivulets of perspiration dribbled down his face which he dabbed constantly
with a handkerchief.

"Looks like a great night for you, Herman," Keegan said.

"Lots of beautiful ladies." Braff winked. "Just your type."

"How about the new singer?"

"*Nein, nein, nein.*" Herman shook his head vigorously, waving off the idea with his hand. "Not your type at all."

"I came to hear her sing, Herman, not to propose."

The German laughed. "Not to propose, that's a good one,"
he said. "Your type is . . ."

He put his two hands out in front of his chest as though he
were carrying a large bundle, then rolling one hand across his
buttocks in an imaginary parabola.

"Wonderful, Herman, you should be up there on the stage
doing impressions."

Keegan shook his head sadly at the grinning manager and
looked around the packed club. Smoke clouded the ceiling, the

odor of stale beer was overpowering and the band was loud, dominated by the tuba and drums. There were young couples at most of the tables, some dressed in brown uniforms with swastikas on the arm, most of them thick-necked, blond and garrulous. Stag men stood two and three deep at the bar. The chorus line was dancing furiously on stage, as though trying to finish their number as quickly as possible. On the packed dance floor, couples undulated, mauled each other and ignored the stage show.

"How about those two in the corner booth?" Herman pressed on, nudging Keegan's arms with his elbow. It was important to Herman to impress Keegan for Keegan was a trend-setter. If he liked a place, he would draw others to it, expatriates who spent their American dollars and English pounds freely. "They are Americans. And they're with two boys. College students I would guess. They look bored."

"I came to Europe to escape Americans," Keegan said, squinting his eyes and peering through the swirling haze toward the corner, studying the two women as best he could. Both were brunettes, stunning, perfectly coiffed and dressed to the teeth. One, in a shiny, glittering short formal, her black hair cut in a pageboy, looked absolutely defiant, as if challenging every man in the room to try and pick her up. There was something about her, something familiar. Perhaps he had seen her photograph in the rotos. Perhaps she was an actress. The lack of visibility in the room prevented any real scrutiny.

Vanessa Bromley and Deenie Brookstone were ready to ditch the two American boys who had brought them to the club. Vanessa had tired quickly of their stupid college talk and under-graduate mentality. After all, she had come to Berlin not as a sightseer, but, as she put it, "to raise almighty hell," which definitely did not include being squired by two Dartmouth boys who knew her parents.

"I didn't come over here to end up with the same ninnies we left behind," she said.

Now the boys had sealed their fate by refusing to take them upstairs, to the private club called Das Goldene Tor where the nightclub act was supposedly more shocking than the one at the Crazy Horse in Paris.

"They're naked all over," Deenie had whispered earlier in the seclusion of their suite. "Men *and* women."

"Why are you whispering?" Vanessa asked.

"I don't know," Deenie answered, still whispering. "It's just so . . . *scandalous.*"

"Only if we're seen. I'm sure nobody from Boston would be caught dead there."

"I'm real nervous."

"Will you stop *whispering.*"

"I can't help it."

Now the two absolute juveniles were preventing them from learning firsthand just how depraved the show really was.

"They're both virgins," Vanessa said with disgust, watching them thread through the crowd toward the men's room. "You can just tell."

"So am I," Deenie said weakly.

"Don't be silly!"

"I am."

"Deenie, you're nineteen years old. How come we've never talked about this before?"

"I don't know. It just never came up. How long . . . when did you . . ."

"Christmas holiday last year."

"Who . . . ?"

"Donny Ebersole."

"Donny Ebersole!"

"What's the matter with Donny Ebersole?"

"Donny Ebersole. He's . . . so . . . *little.* He's not as tall as you are."

"Size has nothing to do with it," Vanessa snapped back.

"Was it . . . fun?"

"Not the first time."

"You did it more than *once?*"

"Well, once you start what's the difference? I mean, we just did it all the way through the holiday, Deenie. And yes, it was a lot of fun."

"I just always figured I'd wait until I got married."

"Oh, for God's sake, Deenie, grow up! This is 1933." She thought for a moment, then added, "Maybe we ought to leave. Take a cab around town for a while, then come back."

"Will they let us in upstairs without escorts?"

"Oh, who knows?" Vanessa said, obviously getting annoyed by Deenie's constant blathering.

They were both aware that most of the men at the bar were staring at them, and why not? They were both gorgeous women and Vanessa was wearing what she called her "shimmy" dress, a white, form-fitting number, covered with rhinestones, that ended above the knee. She glittered like a handful of polished diamonds and when she walked the shimmering garment turned every step into an invitation. A rhinestone tiara topped off the package. Vanessa suddenly felt oppressed by the crowded room.

"I am not going to waste this evening on these two jerks," she said. "Come on, let's leave and come back a little later. Maybe they'll get the idea and leave."

"What if they don't?"

"We'll snub them when we come back."

"Vanessa!"

"Deenie, will you kindly please just *grow up*."

"At least we should wait until they come back. That's the right thing to do."

"Deenie, if you keep doing the right thing all your life, you're going to be a virgin when you're fifty."

At the bar, Keegan waited impatiently for the chorus to finish its work. A voice behind him said, "Francis?" He turned to find Bert Rudman, a reporter for the *Herald Tribune,* standing behind him. Rudman was one of their better-known correspondents, a good writer relegated at first to personality pieces, lately spending more time on European politics. They had known each other briefly in France during the war and had renewed their friendship during the year Keegan had been in Europe, bumping into each other all over the continent. A pretty boy who looked ten years younger than the thirty-five he claimed to be, Rudman was wearing a leather trenchcoat with the collar turned up and a brown fedora.

"I thought that was you," Rudman said. "Haven't seen you since that terrible bash in Rome."

"The Italians throw the worst parties in Europe."

"No, the Russians throw the worst parties in Europe."

"The Russians don't throw parties at all, Bert. It's against the law to enjoy yourself in Russia."

"Speaking of parties, are you going down to Bavaria for the Runstedts' boar hunt this weekend?"

"My horse is running at Longchamp. I'll be in Paris."

"He's been doing well," Rudman said. "I've been following him."

"I've made a little money on him this season. If he shows anything in Paris, I might try him out in the States."

"You mean you'd actually go home?" Rudman was surprised. He had heard all the rumors about Keegan. Some, like the bootlegger story, he believed simply because he had met Keegan in an army hospital on the Western Front when the kid was barely eighteen and stone broke. Now he was a millionaire. It had to come from someplace. The fact that he thought his friend was an ex-gangster only made Keegan's friendship more alluring. But Rudman feared if he pried too deeply into Keegan's personal life it would damage their friendship. Keegan was aware of Rudman's caution and while he would never have held it against the newspaperman if he did pry a little, he let Rudman think it would.

"Just long enough to run him at Belmont and Saratoga," said Keegan. "See how he shows up. I've got a little filly coming along who'll wear him out in another two years. What brings you to Berlin, anyway?"

"Three guesses," the reporter answered, looking around the room at the swastikas. He leaned forward and spoke directly into Keegan's ear. "My editor in Paris thinks World War Two is going to start here sometime in the next five minutes."

"Here in this saloon?"

"In Berlin, schmuck."

"Incidentally, you ought to get rid of that coat, everybody'll think you're with the *Schutzstaffel*."

"That's very funny, Francis. This coat cost me a month's salary."

"You wuz robbed."

Rudman looked hurt. "It's the latest fashion," he said.

"Yeah, if you're in the SS."

"You can be a real bastard when you want to be."

"Ah, don't be so thin-skinned." Keegan laughed. "You look beautiful. Did you take the train in?"

"No, I drove from Paris. I thought about you, kiddo. Went right through the park at Belleau Wood. That hospital where we met is a big cow barn now."

After fourteen years, Keegan remembered that day very well. The war was over for Keegan but it was the first time he had understood what was going on. It was Bert Rudman who had finally put it all in perspective for him.

By the spring of 1917, a whipped Woodrow Wilson, reelected as a liberal idealist with a clear vision for the future of the country, had watched his own rigid policies lead the country into archconservatism. He was finally forced to admit the inevitable: They were on the verge of war. After a passionate speech in which he urged the Congress to declare war on Germany, Austria-Hungary and the Turks of the Ottoman Empire to save the world "for Democracy," he returned to his office in the White House with the cheers of the senators and representatives still clamoring in his ears.

His secretary was shocked by his appearance. He looked worn out, defeated, old and sick.

"Are you all right?" she asked with alarm.

He shook his head sadly and dropped heavily into his chair.

"My message today was a message of death for our young men," he said. "How strange it seems to applaud that." Then lowering his head to his desk, he wept.

His message started a wave of patriotism in the country. Hamburgers became Salisbury steaks; sauerkraut was "liberty cabbage." Germans quietly slipped to the courthouse and changed their names. Conscientious objectors were beaten up and thrown in jail. Either you were for the war or you were a traitor, and thousands of young Americans were inspired to take up the fight. Keegan was one of them. Only eighteen, he joined the Marines and six months later he was in the first Marine battalion to land in France.

Jocko Nayles, a tough street fighter from Brooklyn, only three years Keegan's senior, took Keegan in tow on the boat ride to France.

"How old're ye?" he asked.

"Eighteen," Keegan answered, trying to sound tough.

"Eighteen, then! Jesus, Mary and Joseph. Well, ye just stick with me, kid, I'll get you through this."

Together they had marched down muddy French roads toward the Marne River where they were baptized in fire, where Keegan had seen his first German and killed his first man. The meaning of these skirmishes was lost in the terror of hand-to-hand combat, of sky bombs showering shards of metal down on him from overhead, of the flashes of shells that temporarily blinded him, and of the mines underfoot. In horror, he saw his buddies struck down in rows like grass before a scythe and finally felt the burning punch in his shoulder, felt his knees give out, and he fell, not knowing how badly he was hit or whether he would live or die.

To Keegan, the war was five hundred yards long and a hundred yards wide and scattered with helmets and weapons and body parts. He could not relate to anything beyond his field of vision. Whether they were winning or losing, why they were there, were questions that did not even occur to him.

When the battle was over, Jocko had come back and found him huddled in a shell hole, a dirty handkerchief stuffed in the bullet hole in his shoulder, had picked him up and carried him back to the field hospital, had nursed over him for days until his fever broke and infection passed.

A month later he was back with his unit, wallowing through the mire on the outskirts of a French town called Château-Thierry, headed for the Marne River only seventy miles from Paris.

To Keegan, the length of the French and German border was one great muddy battlefield, its trees reduced to stumps, its fields coursed with twisted barbed wire and miles of trenches, its villages reduced to rubble. For mile after mile, the disgusting perfume of death hung in the air like a fog. Mud-caked and broken, soldiers, driven to the edge of insanity, hunched in their trenches, cursed the rain and the shells which intermittently poured down on them, dreamt of home, faced chattering machine guns, aerial bombs, mines and an equally insane army of Germans in a crazy leapfrog of battles in which thousands sometimes died in a single day. All to gain a few miles of decimated earth.

"This is where we stop 'em, lads," a youthful lieutenant told them as they trudged toward the enemy. "Else they'll be in Paris before Christmas."

From Château-Thierry they headed north toward a game preserve called Belleau Wood, singing songs as they marched. One platoon singing one song, the second answering with another.

K-K-K-Katie, K-K-K-Katie,
You're the only g-g-g-girl that I adore,
When the m-m-m-moon shines, over the c-c-c-cowshed,
I'll be w-w-w-waiting at the k-k-k-kitchen door.

Answered by:

You may forget the gas and shells, parley-voo,
You may forget the gas and shells, parley-voo,
You may forget the gas and shells,
But you'll never forget the mademoiselles,
Hinky-dinky parley-voo.

They were singing as they approached the park. The Germans fired the first shot.

This time, Keegan went down with a shell fragment in the leg. He dragged himself to a battered wall where he found three Marines clustered around a machinegun, dead long enough that bugs had begun to feast on them. Then there was a lull in the battle and he leaned his cheek against the wall, biting his lip to keep back the pain. An uneasy silence fell on the glen where he lay.

He was surprised by the first of the Germans. They were on horseback, like a ghost posse, suddenly materializing in the swirling smoke of battle. The hooves of their horses were wrapped in gunny cloth and their halters and cinches were greased to cut down the noise. They moved slowly and silently over the battered ground, their guns at the ready. Keegan started firing and he kept firing, his teeth rattling as the heavy machinegun kicked and thundered under hand, firing until the barrel of the gun was glowing red, warped from the heat, and the ammo belts were scattered empty around him.

When he stopped, the world stopped. There was not a sound. Not a bird singing, nor the wind sighing, nor even the cries of the wounded. There was silence. Before him was a grotesque frieze, as though the horses with their legs stretched up in the air and the men sprawled like sacks around them were posing for a photograph. Only then did the ghastly pain from the hole in his leg fire his brain and he screamed and passed out.

In the hospital he found Jocko Nayles, his face half covered in a bloody bandage, his bloody eye socket swollen with pus, lying in his mud-caked uniform raving with fever. This time it was Keegan who urged his friend away from death.

The French gave him the Croix de Guerre and the Americans a Silver Star and his second Purple Heart. He had been in Europe only four months.

It was at the coffee bar in the hospital that Keegan first met Bert Rudman, a cocky young man starched and clean in a field coat and campaign hat, scratching out a story with a stub of pencil on a grungy sheaf of folded paper.

"Hi," Rudman had greeted him holding out his hand, "I'm Bert Rudman, Herald Tribune *out of Paris."*

"Keegan," was all the youngster had mumbled back.

"Were you at Belleau Wood?"

"I think so."

"How bad is it?" Rudman asked, nodding toward his leg.

"Bad enough to get me home." He paused for a moment and then, "Did we win?"

Rudman had stared at him for a moment, the significance of his question slowly sinking in. Then he smiled. "You sure did, kiddo. Kicked the Kaiser's ass right back where it came from and then some."

"That's good," Keegan said.

"Hell yes, it's good. Know what they're callin' you Marines? Devil Hounds. Is that a Croix de Guerre on your shirt?"

"Yeah. Some frog general gave it to me."

"What'd you do?"

"Damned if I know."

"Well, you must've done something, trooper, that's hot stuff in the French Army. Say, could I impose on you? I'm writing this piece on the battle, you know, kind of the big picture of what happened. Can I read it to you, you bein' there and all?"

Keegan nodded. "Sure."

Rudman had sat there, reading from his tattered papers, stopping occasionally to scratch out a correction or take a sip of coffee as Keegan listened in awe, not because the words were that stunning, although it was clear that Rudman knew how to write, but because for the first time he understood the panorama of the battle he had been part of: the decisions made by the officers, the attacks and counterattacks, the strategy and terrible price that had been paid to drive the Germans back across the Marne and break their march toward Paris.

He was struck by the realization that what had been a traumatic and monumental moment in his life had been an infinitesimal part of the battle, by the insignificance of his part in the brutal encounter. And as Rudman

*read on, the story gathered a kind of chilling energy unto itself and Keegan
began to feel its power.*

*"Belleau Wood is silent now," Rudman said, wrapping up the
lengthy tome. "What was once a beautiful picnic spot has been reduced to
tree stubs, great gaping holes in the ground, and mud. It is as if the earth
itself at Château-Thierry has been mortally wounded and lies bleeding at
the feet of the victors.*

*"Perhaps this is the beginning of the end for the Germans who sought
this war and have paid so dearly for it. For while our victories are clear,
the cause of this war is still clouded and obscure. Perhaps we will learn
that from the peace, for until we understand why this war happened, we
can never be sure it will not happen again."*

He looked over at Keegan, who sat speechless.

"Well, what you think?"

*"Why, it's great. Just great," Keegan said softly and took a deep,
slow breath. "They really call us Devil Hounds?"*

*"You bet. You boys fought like hell out there. And you really think
it's good, the story I mean?"*

Keegan nodded emphatically.

"Okay. O-kay! Say, what'd you say your name was again?"

"Francis Keegan."

*Rudman scribbled a phone number and tore it off the bottom of one
of the sheets of paper.*

*"Look here, Francis, here's my number. You get back to Paris, call
me. We'll have dinner together, on the* Trib.*"*

"Can I bring my buddy? He lost an eye in the fight."

*"An eye! Goddamn those Krauts! Why, sure enough, bring him
along, we'll make a night of it. And say, thanks for listening, okay?"*

"Sure. Thanks for letting me hear it."

"No kidding," Keegan finally said. "A cow barn, eh. No plaque
or anything to commemorate the occasion?"

"Nothing but a salt lick."

"I'm insulted," Keegan said. "Are *you* insulted?"

"Cut to the quick."

"So they've got you covering politics now, huh?"

Rudman nodded, "Hear about Hitler's speech in Munich?"

"He makes a speech every time his auto stalls."

"Not like this one. Talk about choreography? They were

climbing the walls before he was through. You could hear the mob *heil*ing Hitler in Brooklyn. It was scary. I still get goose pimples thinking about it. He's got something, this guy. He's dangerous, Francis. Did you read my piece on Munich?"

"I read it," Keegan said.

"And . . . ?"

"A little hysterical."

"Hysterical! Have you seen him? Heard him speak?"

"Sure. That line about Hitler being a demonic vision of God was lovely. Keep writing stuff like that you'll lose your visa—or end up with a bullet in the back."

"Now who's being hysterical? They're not going to fool around with the *Herald Trib.*"

"Look around you. You think these crazies give two hoots in hell about your credentials? Poor old Sid Lewis got his brains beat out down in Rome for using the wrong adjectives about Mussolini."

"That's not what happened at all," Rudman said. "Sid was queer. He got in a lover's quarrel with some fascist he picked up in a bar and got his head bashed in."

"Count on you to know all the dirt. You ought to start your own little monthly newsletter. All the news that's unfit to print."

"That's very funny, Keegan. And what have you been up to?"

"I'm the embassy badminton champion. Me and Cissy Devane."

"My God, that's really impressive," Rudman said sarcastically.

Keegan waved his arm toward the crowded club.

"Take my word for it, pal, they're the ones you have to worry about. Hitler's all talk."

"You sound like the isolationists back home. You should read *Mein Kampf,* it's all laid out there."

"I've read *Mein Kampf.*"

Rudman looked surprised and said, "Well, I give him two years, three tops. He'll have the Saar back, Austria, Poland, probably Czechoslovakia. He's already using the Versailles treaty for toilet paper."

"Rudman, I came here to be entertained, not to listen to lectures on the rise and fall of the German Empire."

"Okay," said Rudman, and abruptly changed the subject. "Okay. What's this Gold Gate I've been hearing about?"

"Sex show upstairs."

"Any good?"

"If you like naked men and women covered with oil rolling around under bad lights."

"I do," Rudman said with a leering grin. "Shall we?"

Keegan shook his head. "I came for the singer."

"Does she sing covered with oil?"

Keegan rolled his eyes. "She's coming on next. As soon as they round up that herd and get them off the stage." He nodded toward the chorus line, all of whom were at least ten pounds overweight. As he spoke they lumbered into the wings.

"I'll be where the action is," Rudman said and headed upstairs. "Dinner tomorrow night?"

Keegan nodded and waved him away because now the stage lights were lowering. They went out. Keegan could barely discern the tiny woman who came out on the darkened stage carrying her own stool. She put it down in front of the microphone on the corner of the stage and sat down. The piano man started playing trills, warming up. Then the baby spot faded in on her.

He was immediately taken by her appearance. She was barely five feet tall, thin, rather frail. Her face was narrow to the point of being gaunt and her sharply honed cheekbones seemed etched into her face. The result was an almost haunted look, an impression strengthened by large, saucerlike eyes that gleamed in the tiny light and seemed almost tear-struck. A simple, long black dress accented the aura of vulnerability that surrounded her. He had to strain to hear her name when the emcee introduced her. Jenny Gould.

She stood without speaking for a few moments, just long enough for Keegan to worry that perhaps something was wrong, that she wasn't going to perform. Then she began to sing.

The voice startled him at first. It was low, throaty, a torch-song voice that tortured every word of the Cole Porter song she chose to interpret, not as a cynical dirge, but as a metaphor about love gone sour.

Love for sale,
Appetizing young love for sale,

If you want to try my wares,
Take a chance and climb the stairs,
Love for sale.

The crowd was ill mannered and inattentive. Chattering, laughing, clinking glasses, creating a constant babel that underscored every word she sang, and Keegan finally moved down the bar closer to the stage to hear better. He was mesmerized by her. When the song was over there was a smattering of applause, except from Keegan who wore out his hands clapping.

He thought she glanced over at him as he applauded, but couldn't be sure, felt foolish in fact at how pleased he was that she might have noticed him. Then she began her second song and he was, once again, caught in the magical, sensual spell she was weaving.

In the darkened room, Vanessa suddenly decided it was time to make a break for it. The boys were trapped on the other side of the room. The singer was into her second song and Vanessa snatched up her purse and stood to leave. From the bar there was a smattering of wolf whistles mostly lost in the clamor. She stalked across the room, her dress swaying in sparkling waves as she walked. Deenie struggled to her feet, trotting after the haughty beauty. Then Vanessa stopped so suddenly that Deenie bumped into her.

"Oh my God," Vanessa said half-aloud.

"What is it?" Deenie asked.

"Somebody I know," Vanessa said, her mouth curling into a sly smile.

"From Boston?" Deenie asked wide-eyed.

"Oh yes, he's from Boston all right."

"Oh *no!*" Deenie cried out and turned her back to the bar.

"Don't be silly. If there's one person in Boston I'd prefer to be seen by, it's him. C'mon."

She grabbed Deenie's hand and dragged her through the crowd, ignoring the looks and the comments. She stood ten feet behind Keegan, waiting for the song to end.

"Which one is he?" Deenie whispered.

"Shhh."

*   *   *

The second song was a German tune Keegan was not familiar with. Then she sang "Someone to Watch Over Me" and every syllable was plaintive, every word a plea to be loved, every note a heartbreaker.

There was a smattering of applause, again except for Keegan. He looked around the room, wondering if all these people were crazy. Didn't they know what was happening up on stage?

The set was over. He had barely been aware that she'd sung several more songs. Her voice had mesmerized him, hypnotized him. He couldn't remember the last time he'd been so thrilled.

She left the stage rather meekly and, to Keegan, the rest of the room came back into focus. He caught Herman's eye and urgently waved him over.

"She's wonderful!" he told the damp little manager. He realized he sounded too excited but he didn't care. "She's absolutely—"

Herman rolled his eyes. "Unfortunately you are the only one who seems to think so." Then, looking over Keegan's shoulder, he saw the two American girls coming toward them.

As they walked down the length of the bar, Vanessa was aware that the little sweaty man in the soggy tuxedo was talking about them, his eyes darting toward them, then away. And she was also aware that the tall man with his back to them was staring at her in the deco mirror behind the bar. She led Deenie right up to him, standing behind him, less than a foot away, staring up at the back of his neck. He finally turned around and looked down at her.

Deenie caught her breath. Her impression was immediate: he's rich. That was always number one on Deenie's checklist. The man was rich, fashionable, handsome and self-confident. With his shock of black hair and gray eyes and persistent, arrogant smile, he epitomized what, in her mind, was the classic continental playboy. Definitely dangerous, she thought.

"Something?" He asked it pleasantly, but he was annoyed. He wanted to rush backstage, to meet the singer.

"You don't remember me, do you?"

All he could remember was that voice, the sunken eyes. *Love for sale* . . .

The girl reached up and pulled lightly on his lapel, interrupting his reverie, and when he leaned toward her, she whispered a name in his ear. His reaction was immediate and startled, although he quickly recovered his composure. He stared back at her, his gray eyes intent and inquiring.

It had been three years since anyone had called him that and this woman was perhaps nineteen, twenty at best. He made a quick study. She was tallish, maybe five-seven, slender and busty with turquoise eyes and jet black hair. Her face was angular, her features perfect. Her full mouth curved down at the corners except when she smiled and she wore very little makeup. The diamond choker around her long, slender neck was the real thing. A well-groomed, self-confident snob with money, he decided, and her long *a*'s pegged her from Boston. Who the hell was she? And how did she know that name?

And then she repeated it aloud.

"Frankie Kee."

"My God," he said finally, "you're not Vannie Bromley!"

"Vanessa Bromley," she corrected. "Nobody's called me Vannie since my sixteenth birthday."

"That makes us even. Nobody's called me Frankie for a couple of years, either. Where did you hear that name, anyway?"

"Daddy," she said. "I was eavesdropping after a party once and he was telling mother all about you. I gathered it was kind of his personal secret. He swore her to silence."

"And you?"

"Never told a soul. Too good to share."

"How are old David and Linda?"

"The same. Stuffy but nice."

"What *are* you two talking about?" Deenie finally interrupted.

"Oh, I'm sorry. This is Deenie Brookstone. Remember her?"

"Your father's Earl, right? Merrill, Lynch?"

"That's right," she said brightly. "Should I remember you?"

"Probably not," he said and let the subject die. "What are you two doing in this place?"

"We came to see the show. The one upstairs. Our dates are absolute dinosaurs. Personally I think they're afraid to go up."

"Hardly the place for proper Bostonians," Keegan said.

"Who said anything about being proper?" Vanessa's green eyes worked over every line in his face. There was no doubting her intentions.

Jesus, Keegan thought, *here I am in the worst den of iniquity in Europe and the daughter of the president of the Bank of Massachusetts is sending out very definite signals.* She had turned into a real dish. Big trouble, but a real dish. His dilemma ended abruptly with the arrival of their dates.

"What's going on?" one of them demanded in a voice that sounded like it was pitched an octave lower than normal. Vanessa turned to him, linked her arm in Keegan's and said, "We've just run into an old friend."

"Oh?"

"Francis, this is Donald, this is Gerald. Donald has blond hair, Gerald has brown hair. That's how you tell them apart."

"Take it easy," Keegan growled under his breath. He held out his hand.

"I'm Frank Keegan," he said, "friend of the family."

Donald, the blond, shook hands, then stuffed his in his pockets and shifted uneasily from one foot to the other. Gerald, who was built like a football player, was more aggressive.

"We've decided to go to the *Speisewagen* for breakfast," he said, ignoring Keegan's hand. "A lot of the gang will be there."

"I'm sick of the gang," Vanessa answered. "We're going upstairs."

"C'mon," Donald whined. "Your old man'll nail us to the wall if he finds out we took you up there."

Vanessa looked at Keegan for support. "Is it *that* bad?"

"Pretty risqué," he said.

"*How* risqué?"

"About as risqué as it gets."

"See?" Donald said.

"Well, we just won't tell him."

"No!" Donald said firmly. "They'll find out. Parents always find out those things."

"Donald," Vanessa said firmly, "get lost." And she turned her back on him.

As Donald started toward her, three burly Nazi youths in brown shirts walked by. One of them slammed into Gerald's back. He turned angrily toward them.

"Watch it, buddy," the football-type snarled. The brownshirt bristled. He turned to his two friends, scowling, and said, "*Buddy . . . buddy . . . Was ist los, buddy, eh?*" He turned back to Gerald and leaning against him forced him back against the bar.

"*Schweinehund,*" he said viciously.

Gerald shoved back.

"What's that supposed to mean?" he said to nobody in particular.

"I think he called you a pig," Deenie said without thinking.

"Just a minute . . ." Keegan started, but Gerald was already bristling from the insult.

"Well, tell him he's a goddamn clown in that Boy Scout uniform," he said. "I can take all three of these assholes with one hand behind my back. We'll just step outside and . . ."

Vanessa covered her eyes with her hand. "Oh my God," she moaned, "he thinks he's back on fraternity row."

Keegan waved Herman over to the bar and whispered quickly, "Get these brownshirts away from here or you're going to have a riot on your hands. Give 'em a free pitcher of beer, anything."

Herman flashed his most sincere smile and herded the three Germans back into the club, jabbering in German as he did.

"Let me tell you something, boys," Keegan said coldly. "These guys have all the nickels on their side of the table. Do you understand the situation here?"

"We're Americans," Donald said with bravura, "we don't have to take this stuff."

Keegan kept talking.

"These people have the heart of a weasel, the soul of a rutabaga and pure muscle between the ears. They work in packs. You start something, there'll be a dozen of them all over you. Just ease on out the door and go on over to the *Speisewagen.* Forget it. No face lost, okay, it's a no-win thing."

"You're a real hero type," Gerald said.

"Listen, kid," Keegan said, and his voice became harsh and brittle, "I don't like the odds. I don't want to spend the rest of the night sitting beside you in the hospital or calling your folks to tell them you've just become part of the cobblestone walk out front. This isn't football weekend at Harvard, these people are dangerous."

Deenie's tiny voice piped up. "Please," she implored. "I'm frightened."

"Ahh . . ." Gerald said in disgust.

"We're going to the American diner," Donald said as assertively as he could. "Are you two coming or not?"

"No," Vanessa said.

"Then good night."

"Vanessa . . ." Deenie began.

"What, Deenie?"

"I think we better go."

"Don't be silly!"

"I want to go with them."

"Then go. The key is at the desk. Enjoy your breakfast."

"You really should come along, you know," she said, her voice barely audible in the din.

"Good night, Deenie."

Deenie and the two boys left the club. Vanessa turned to Keegan.

"Guess what," she said. "You're stuck with me."

"You have a real stubborn streak, lady," Keegan said.

"No," she answered firmly, "I just know what I want . . . and I usually get it. Are you going to take me to Das Goldene Tor?"

He thought for a moment and shrugged. "Why not," he said. "But I have something to do first."

When he got backstage, Jenny Gould was about to leave the club, having finished her last set for the night. She stood near the door, wrapped in a raincoat, waiting for a sudden downpour to clear.

"Miss Gould?" Keegan said.

She turned abruptly, startled to hear her name. She stared at him with her big eyes.

"Yes?"

"I'm Francis Keegan," he said. "I wanted to tell you how much I enjoyed your singing."

"*Danke,*" she murmured, looking away.

"I was wondering . . . if we . . . might have lunch tomorrow," he said.

She seemed frightened by the suggestion, her eyes darting toward the door as if hoping the rain would suddenly stop.

"I don't think so," she said, managing a weak smile. "If you'll excuse me, I must go."

"It's raining so hard," Keegan said with a smile. "At least let my car take you home."

She looked at him again, then shook her head.

"That's very kind of you," she said softly. "But I must refuse."

And just like that she was gone, huddled against the rain as she scampered out the stage door and down the alley toward the street.

When he got back to the bar, Vanessa studied the look in his face. "It looks like my last obstacle has been removed," she said. "Shall we go upstairs?"

They entered a room that smelled of perfumed body oil and candle wax. At its center was a carpeted circle perhaps twelve feet across and on it were two large mats covered with yellow satin sheets. Around its perimeter were a dozen head-high candlesticks, which provided the only light in the room. Behind them, three tiers deep, were the loges, each with a full-length, thick-piled couch big enough to seat four. Eight to each tier.

The price for the one-hour show was a hundred dollars a person, payable in either American dollars or British pounds, enough money to feed a German family for a month.

A tall, lean hawk of a man in tails strolled among the boxes, greeting the patrons, his long, aesthetic fingers caressing the hands of the women as he brushed his lips across them. Conrad Weil was the owner of the club and had spawned the show that was to follow, a manifestation of his own corrupt fantasies. The Gold Gate was a private club, by invitation only, and the man who extended the invitation was Weil. He also could waive the rules at the door if you looked prosperous or important—or if he did not have a full house, since there was only one performance a night.

Drinks were provided by three men and three women, their bodies oiled and glistening in the gloomy light of a half dozen blue spotlights. The women, although heavier than Americans preferred, were young, voluptuous and handsome. The men were built like Charles Atlas and looked like they had a combined IQ of twelve. All were blond and wore loincloths. The women were bare-breasted.

They took orders and delivered drinks without expression, their robotic attitude ingeniously designed to separate them from the audience, to assure their inaccessibility and heighten the erotic expectation of the show that was to follow.

Vanessa immediately responded. Her cheeks flushed. Her breath came a little faster. Mesmerized by the promise of the evening, she was the perfect spectator, an affirmation of Weil's perverse creation. And she did not escape his eye. The moment they entered the arena, Weil saw them, watched her as she walked to the couch and sat down, her dress twinkling, reflecting the blue lights like stars on a clear night. She sat with her chin up, accentuating the long, regal sweep of her neck. She was keenly aware of her allure, flaunted it in fact, and Weil was hooked and reeled to her like a trout on a line.

"Francis, an honor to see you again," he gushed, without taking his eyes off Vanessa. And to her, "I am Conrad, your host," as he kissed her hand.

"Conrad, this is Vanessa, a friend of mine from the States."

"Ah, *Fräulein* Vanessa, what a marvelous distraction," he said. "You will make life difficult for our performers. No one can take their eyes off you."

She was properly dazzled by his schmaltz.

And Bert Rudman was dazzled by *her*. He sat across the room next to a heavy-set, Teutonic man with a thick mustache who slumped on the couch with his chin on his chest, nodding as if by rote as Rudman jabbered in his ear. Then Rudman saw Keegan. He looked at him with exaggerated surprise. And then he saw Vanessa and his mouth gaped.

Keegan smiled, first across the room at Rudman, then at Vanessa. When their eyes met, he realized the room and the anticipation of the show were having an effect on him, too. He wondered if the sudden hunger showed on his face.

The music began softly, built slowly. It was Oriental, an eerie melody dominated by bells and drums. Its tempo, slow and sensuous, segued into a soft, steady beat and two blue spotlights faded on, each focused on one of the pallets. Three women and three men wearing yellow silk robes seemed to materialize from the shadows, emerging into the spotlight, standing back to back. They were all dark-haired, not an Aryan in the bunch. The women, more sensuous than beautiful, looked French. The men were more Mediterranean-looking, possibly Greek or Italian.

Weil had selected the cast of his erotic show personally. During a search that had lasted several months, he had assembled six women and six men for his show, rotating the members of the cast each night since only three couples were required for each performance. Weil himself had choreographed the exhibition, sitting in different places in the auditorium and giving directions as the sex-actors performed for him.

At first their moves were subtle. They began to sway slightly with the music. As the tempo picked up, their movements became more pronounced, more provocative. They brushed briefly against each other at first, barely touching, then moving away. In the soft light of the masked spots, they looked at first like a moving sculpture.

Vanessa stared at them transfixed.

They moved out slowly, widening the circle of the spotlight, and broke into groups rather than pairing up. Two women and one man, two men and one woman. The two men began stroking and petting the most petite of the three women, moving their hands lightly over the silken robe, touching every part of her body. She swayed with them and began to hum very slowly as they kissed her neck and shoulders, slipped their hands under the robe, burnishing her body with oil. Finally, they removed her robe. One of her partners stood behind her, glossing her stomach and breasts with oil. Her breasts swelled, the nipples hardening. The other partner used the oil to glaze the insides of her thighs, moving up slowly, slowly, higher, until . . .

A tiny cry slipped from her throat. She fell back against the other man while the one continued to knead oil into her with the flat of one hand, his fingers tantalizing her. Her knees buckled and they lowered her to the mat, never losing a stroke, always massaging her breasts and mound. The tempo of the music increased.

The other two women concentrated on their subject, who stared unblinking as their fingertips flitted across the silk.

One of the women opened her robe and moved against him, swaying to the music. The other girl dropped her robe off her shoulders and stood naked, caressing both their backs, also swaying in cadence with them. The first woman shrugged her shoulders and dropped her hands straight to her sides. Her robe slid down her back and fell away.

They removed the man's robe slowly until it too fell away. It was obvious he was aroused. One of the women leaned down and took a bottle of oil from under the corner of the mat. Both girls oiled their hands, then began to spread the oil over his body, starting just under his chin and moving down to his fingertips, across the flat of his stomach and down to his groin. He closed his eyes and his head fell back and they lowered him to the silk sheet. Hands and lips seemed to devour him, stroking, kneading, urging him toward a climax.

"Seen enough?" Keegan whispered in Vanessa's ear.

She opened her mouth but nothing came out, so she just shook her head, never blinking or taking her eyes off the sexual gladiators. The music grew faster and with the increase in the beat, the activity in the center of the arena became more frenzied. Vanessa's fingers dug into Keegan's thigh and she sank deeper into the down cushions of the sofa.

The two *ménages à trois* became totally impassioned, oblivious to the room full of voyeurs. The two women urged their male performer erect with lips and hands while he felt for each of them, touching them, arousing them until they stretched out beside him, one stroking, the other kissing him.

On the other silk pallet, the woman began to moan, rocking her hips slowly back and forth while the men kissed and petted and stroked her entire body. She arched her back, her breathing erratic and labored. Finally one of her partners lay on his side, lifted her leg over his hip and entered her. Her cry—half anguish, half joy—shocked the spectators. But only for a moment. She moved with him, head back, eyes closed, mouth slightly open, her lips trembling as the other partner kissed her body, first her breasts, then her stomach, moving down until all three were moving in concert.

"Oh my God," Vanessa muttered under her breath. She moved tighter against Keegan, began to stroke his thigh with her fingertips. Keegan put his arm around her shoulder. She snuggled under it, her breasts crushing against his side. She was breathing heavily as they watched the performers reach their climax.

And it was over. Somehow, the performers were gone and the lights were up. The audience began murmuring.

"Now you know the secret of the Gold Gate," Keegan whispered, but she was too entranced to answer.

They drove back to the hotel along deserted streets, the SA predators having finished their foraging for the night. She clung to him and he took her mouth between a thumb and forefinger, puckering it up and softly kissing the swollen lips. She responded with a moan, her tongue searching for his, her arms wrapped around his waist, pulling him to her.

"I want to see your room," she whispered.

"It's just like yours."

"No it isn't. Deenie isn't in it."

"You know, the Our Gang kids were right. Your father would drop dead on the spot if he saw us now."

"Who's going to tell?"

"How about Deenie?"

"No way."

"Why not?"

"I'd rip her little heart out and she knows it."

A bottle of Taittinger champagne wallowed on its side in half-melted ice in a silver bucket. A towel was thrown casually over it. She poured a glass but there was not a bubble in it.

"Flat," she moaned.

Keegan got a lemon from a plate in the kitchenette, pared six or seven inches of peeling from it, and dropped the yellow curl into the champagne glass. It began fizzing crazily the moment the peel hit the wine.

"How clever," she said.

"I used to be in the business," he smiled.

"I keep forgetting."

"No you don't. Not for a minute."

She snuggled against him, put her hands in the small of his back and leaned into him, staring up, her mouth slightly ajar. She unbuttoned his shirt and ran her tongue across his chest and around his nipples. "They get hard, just like mine," she said with surprise. She dropped the slender straps of her dress over her shoulders and wiggled out of it. It fell around her ankles. She was naked underneath, her body youthfully trim, her breasts full, and she stood on her toes and rubbed her hard nipples against his.

She reached up and put her hand gently behind his head, drew it down and kissed him, her lips soft and full. He wrapped his arms around her, lifted her slightly and, slipping his leg between hers, lowered her on his thigh.

She whimpered and looked at him through smoky eyes. "Oh yes. Oh yessiree, Francis."

She moved his hands with hers, cried with joy every time they found the perfect spot, her response reckless and candid and open. She moved with her feelings, unhampered and uninhibited, embracing and coddling her own passion without a trace of modesty or conscience. She asked him what to do, followed his whispered instructions and then experimented on her own. And she transferred her joy to him. Stroking, kissing, touching, she finally rolled over on top of him, squirming to his touch until suddenly almost by accident he was inside her.

She was stretched out on her stomach beside him, propped up on her elbows.

"Frankie," she said earnestly, "that was even better than I imagined it would be all these years."

"You mean you coveted me as a child?" he said, feigning shock.

"I was thirteen. That's not such a child."

"I'm glad I didn't know," he said. "I probably would have had a terrible guilt complex."

"Why should you have had a guilty conscience over the way I felt?"

He stared up at the ceiling for a moment and said, "That's a good point. Something subconscious, maybe. I don't think I care to pursue it."

She laughed and ran her fingernail very lightly across his bottom lip and he almost jumped out of bed.

"Tickle?" she asked.

"My nerve endings are still twitching."

"I know, isn't it terrific! Want to do it again?" She suggested eagerly.

"Give me a little while to recuperate."

"Humph," she said, pretending to pout. She leaned closer to him and put her chin on his chest.

She lay across him, her legs straddling his, her warm body pressed against him, smelling of expensive perfume. He stroked the small of her back, caressed the perfect swell of her buttocks.

"No one's ever made love to me like that before," she murmured, suddenly.

"Made love to a lot of men, have you?"

"Two," she confessed. "Little boys, always in such a hurry. I didn't know you could make it last that long, or that it would get better and better . . . 'n better . . ."

She closed her eyes, squirming a bit to get comfortable. In a few moments her breathing was deep and constant and he felt her body soften in sleep.

He slid out from under her and walked to the window. The sun was ablaze at the edge of rooftops, throwing slender crimson shadows down the wet streets. The city seemed clean and innocent and silent, its solace disturbed for a minute or two by an ice truck that rattled up the street and vanished around a corner. Then all was quiet again.

He drew the drapes and took off his robe and slid back in bed beside Vanessa. She groaned in her sleep, slid one leg across his hip and cuddled up close to him. In minutes, he too was asleep. It was eight-thirty when the phone rang for the first time. It rang every thirty minutes after that but Keegan didn't hear it. He was dead to the world.

A loud banging on the door finally awakened Keegan. He put on a robe and went into the living room of his suite, closing the bedroom door behind him. When he answered the door, Bert Rudman rushed past him without waiting for an invitation.

"Where the hell have you been?" he demanded. "I've been calling you all morning!"

"I was tied up," Keegan groaned.

"It's almost noon."

"It was dawn before I got to bed."

"Look, old buddy, I need your help. Did . . ."

Rudman stopped abruptly and stared open-mouthed over Keegan's shoulder. Keegan turned to find Vanessa standing in the bedroom doorway wrapped in the bedsheet.

"Oh . . . I . . . uh . . . I . . ."

"Vanessa," Keegan said. "Vanessa Bromley. This eloquent person is Bert Rudman."

"How do you do?" she said and pulled the sheet up a little higher.

"Now what the hell's so important?"

"I'm onto a hot story but I can't pin anything down. I know Wally Wallingford's a friend of yours and I thought . . ."

"Not anymore," Keegan interrupted. "Want some coffee?"

"Great."

"I'll call down and order it," Vanessa said.

"What does Wally have to do with this scoop of yours?"

"You know who Felix Reinhardt is?"

Keegan hesitated. "Yes," he said. "I know who he is."

"Apparently he was arrested sometime during the night, although I can't confirm it. The way I get it, he was with an American officer attached to the embassy when he was nabbed and there's a big diplomatic stink brewing. But nobody'll talk to me."

"What was he arrested for?"

"From what I can put together, he was editing *The Berlin Conscience* and a man named Probst was printing it. Yesterday afternoon the SA raided Probst's print shop. A big gunfight broke out, then a fire. Probst was shot and his place burned to the ground. They had the whole damn *Sturmabteilung* after Reinhardt and caught up with him about two o'clock this morning."

"Where did you hear that?"

"The Nazis had a press conference and announced the details on the Probst part of it. I pieced the rest of it together, y'know, a little bit here, a little bit there, but I can't confirm anything. The Nazis are staying mum on Reinhardt."

"It didn't happen that way."

"What?"

"The Probst part of it. It didn't happen the way you said. He wasn't even armed. The SA kicked in his door, shot him in cold blood, then set his place afire."

"How do you know?"

"I pieced it together."

"C'mon, don't be a schmuck. Where did you hear that?"

"From an eyewitness. That's all I can tell you. Just don't print that official Nazi bullshit."

"When'd you find out about this?"

"I don't know, Bert, sometime during the night."

"And you didn't tip me off?"

Keegan didn't say anything. Rudman had never seen this expression in his friend's eyes.

"You consider this eyewitness reliable?"

"As reliable as you can get."

Rudman's eyes narrowed.

"It was Reinhardt, wasn't it? You talked to Reinhardt."

"I've told you all I can. Don't push me." He looked down at Vanessa. "Why don't you go put something on," he suggested.

"All I've got's my dress from last night."

"There are half a dozen bathrobes in there. Take one."

She walked out of the room, the sheet dragging along behind her.

"Phew," Rudman sighed appreciatively.

"Don't get any ideas," Keegan said.

"I've already got so many ideas I couldn't . . . ah, forget that." He stopped and waved his hand. "At least talk to Wallingford, okay? See what you can find out for me."

"Wally isn't speaking to me right now."

"What the hell did you do to him? Wally speaks to *every* body."

"I didn't RSVP one of his parties."

"Ah c'mon. Take him out for a drink or something, Francis, I'm hurting for a lead right now."

"Believe me, Bert, the guy will not give me the time."

"Try."

There was a long silence. Then Keegan quietly said, "All right, I'll try."

"Thanks, buddy. I'll be at the *Trib* office and then the Imperial Bar."

"I didn't know the Imperial had a pressroom," Keegan said sarcastically.

"The Imperial Bar *is* a pressroom," Rudman said. "Everybody in the press corps hangs out there. Goebbels even drops by in the afternoon with his latest proclamation."

"Well, that's a break, you don't even have to go over to the propaganda ministry to pick up his latest lies."

"It's a starting place," Rudman said. "He gives us his lies and we boil out the truth."

Rudman started for the door, stopped short. "You know," he said, "this is the first time I've ever known you to change your mind about something."

"Maybe it's because I want to know the truth myself."

"Well, that's another first," Rudman said, and left.

George Gaines was standing inside the door of the embassy when Keegan entered. He looked up sharply, his face drawn up with anger.

"What the hell are you doing here?" the attaché asked harshly.

"I came to see Wally," Keegan said quietly. "What's your problem?"

"*You* are," the major answered. "You're *every*body here's problem."

"What the hell's that supposed to mean?"

"You know damn well what I mean. Trace spent the night in Landsberg prison. God knows what happened to Reinhardt. And poor old Wally's been recalled."

"Recalled!"

Gaines started up the stairs to the offices and Keegan fell in beside him. When one of the Marine guards stepped in front of Keegan, Gaines waved him aside. "It's okay," he said.

"That Nazi bastard lifted his passport," Gaines said as they went to the second floor. "With a little help from you . . ."

Keegan cut him off. "Look, I don't get paid to stick my neck in a noose because Roosevelt snaps his fingers," he growled angrily. "So Trace spent the night in jail. Big deal. He's okay, isn't he?"

"He's okay," Gaines begrudgingly admitted.

"If I'd been with Reinhardt *I'd* be dead now, I wouldn't just have to worry about my damn passport. I don't have diplomatic immunity, George."

"Tell Wally about it. He's the one whose career just got flushed." Gaines nodded toward an open door. "There's his office. Although I don't think he's too anxious to talk to you."

As Keegan started to enter the office a Marine came by carrying a large cardboard box. Keegan stepped around him. Wallingford's inner door was open and Keegan could see him in the office, taking pictures off the wall.

"It's all right, Belinda," Wallingford said. He walked back to his desk, his arms stacked with framed photographs as Keegan entered his room. Wallingford carefully placed the pictures in an open box on his desk. The rest of the room was almost cleared out.

"I heard they gave you the boot," Keegan said.

"Come by to gloat?"

"Come on, Wally, I didn't stick Reinhardt in that car with Trace. Hell, I'm going to miss you. You throw the best parties in Europe."

"That's all it means to you, isn't it?"

"No, I'm worried about you. What're you going to do?"

"Go back to Washington for reassignment. It's the end of my career."

"What the hell happened?"

"I screwed up, that's what happened. Almost got Trace arrested for espionage. We tried to sneak Reinhardt out of the country in an official vehicle but the Gestapo stopped them. Roosevelt apologized to that little freak in the Reichstag and I got recalled. I'm going to have to quit. It's like getting courtmartialed in the army. Win or lose, you're finished."

"Didn't the intelligence people help you?"

Wallingford stared at him for a moment, then sat down on the corner of his desk.

"Listen, Keegan. We don't *have* an intelligence system. Every other country in the world is up to their ears in spies but we don't have a spy among us. And you know why? Because my boss, the mighty Cordell Hull, says it's ungentlemanly to pry in other countrys' affairs. *Ungentlemanly!* So, we play by the Marquis of Queensberry rules and they play with a billy club. That's what happens when the secretary of state is a gentleman."

"I'm sorry, pal . . ."

"Hey, it's your country, too. And I'm not your goddamn pal."

"C'mon, Wally, we've had some pretty good times together. How about those weekends in Paris. That trip down to Monte Carlo last spring . . ."

"Christ, is that what life is to you, just one long goddamn party?! Reinhardt is dead! According to our best sources, they tortured him for hours and when he bit off his own tongue to keep from talking, they forced him to drink battery acid. Of course, we can't confirm it but it sounds right. Felix is dead and my career's in the toilet and what the hell difference does it make to you? You'll find another party to go to."

"I'm sorry about Reinhardt. And I do care what happens to you. My friendship for you doesn't have anything to do with him."

"I asked you to help me and all you did was worry about your goddamn plane. We could've gotten him out."

"Maybe."

"What's it going to take to wake you up and see what's going on here?"

"I see what's going on . . ."

"No, no. You don't see what's going on. You drive past the bloody storm troopers beating up some pawnbroker or doctor, but you don't really *see* it. At least it doesn't register. You think this can't happen back home? Let me tell you something, *pal,* Hitler was absolute dictator of Germany less than a month after Hindenburg appointed him president and the Nazi party had less than forty percent of the vote in the last election. Hitler didn't have a majority of anything, he was never elected to anything. He just took over. He threw out the Constitution and took over. Every time the arrogant little bastard opens his mouth he insults Americans. And he's making racism accept-able. Hell, *fashion* able. Not only here—everywhere, *every* where! The other day I heard a couple of our secretaries giggling over the latest Jewish joke."

"That's human nature."

"You call it what you want, I call it prejudice. Hitler wakes up that sleeping giant in everyone, he makes it desirable to flaunt hate. He has the key, Keegan. Pride. He appeals to their pride." He paused for a moment, then asked, "What do you want, Francis? What are you after?"

"I don't know, Wally."

"Well, I *do* know. See, I'm just an everyday jerk from Phila-delphia. I planned my whole life out. The diplomatic corps, that was it for me. That's what I wanted, worked my ass off to get it. And you know where I wanted to be?" He jabbed a forefinger toward the floor. "Right here. Berlin. From the moment I en-tered the diplomatic service, this is where I wanted to be. Know why? Because I knew it was going to be *the* hot spot in the world. I *knew* it. I knew I could make a name for myself here if I played it just right. And I was doing great until last night."

He turned back to the shelves and stacked the last of his possessions in the box on the desk. He kept out one book and opened it to a random page.

"Collected speeches of Woodrow Wilson," he said. "My hero, Mr. Wilson. Great vision. Sold out by his own country. You know, the day Woodrow Wilson asked Congress to declare war on Germany he also warned them not to be too hard on the losers when we won the war or they'd rise up and strike back. Had a lot of vision, Mr. Wilson. You paint a mouse into a corner and a tiger comes out. Nobody paid any attention to him. We left Germany with nothing and now the tiger is loose and America sleeps on, as fucking usual."

"You're an angry man, Wally."

"I'm a scared man. People like you scare me. You're sophisticated enough to understand what's happening."

"You don't belong in the State Department. Go back home and run for the Senate or something."

"I couldn't get elected meter reader," Wallingford said with disgust. "Nobody wants to hear what I've got to say. By the time they wake up it'll be too late."

"People are sick of gloom and doom," said Keegan. "They've had their fill of war. Now they're trying to get over the Depression. They're looking for good times, not threats."

"Typical attitude."

"I'm calling it the way I see it."

"I'll admit you have a certain roughneck charm, Keegan, but as far as I'm concerned it's all veneer," said Wallingford wearily. "I've heard about your mother being a countess and all that romantic crap and that's all it is to me, crap. Underneath it all, you're nothing. Just another crook who got rich."

Keegan nodded ruefully and turned to leave the office.

"I've got this theory, Keegan," Wallingford went on. "If you're not against something, you're for it. When you turned your back on Reinhardt, you kissed Hitler's ass."

"Take it easy . . ."

"No, I won't take it easy. And you're right, this doesn't have anything to do with Reinhardt or my job. I asked a friend for a favor and he turned me down, that's what it's about."

"One hell of a favor."

"You would have been doing yourself a favor, too. You and a lot of other Americans think Hitler's a flash in the pan, but he's going to start gobbling up Europe and the only way we're going to stop him is to go to war again. Now if you'll excuse me, I've got to be out of the country by six P.M. Deported, isn't that ironic? Thousands of people desperate to leave Germany and I'm being thrown out on my ass."

Wallingford walked past Keegan to the doorway and summoned the Marine sergeant.

"That's the last box, Jerry," he said.

"Yes sir," the Marine answered, and carried it out. Wallingford looked around the office once more. It was stripped clean of everything personal. He started to leave and then turned back to Keegan.

"You know, I hope I never see you again, Francis," Wallingford said, and there was a tone of sadness in his remark. "It will just remind me what a poor judge of character I am."

He left Keegan standing alone in the empty office.

The Imperial was the most elegant bar and restaurant in Berlin. Its domed ceiling towered two stories over the deco and bronze interior. Tall French doors separated the garden restaurant from the bar, where fresh flowers brightened every table and the waiters in their white, gold-trimmed uniforms hustled stoically about the room. The place was buzzing with activity when Keegan arrived, the crowd a strange mix of reporters in their blue suits and flowered ties, tourists in white, SS officers in black uniforms, and the usual smattering of Gestapo agents, easily identifiable in their drab gray suits, their impersonal eyes suspicious of everything and everybody.

Rudman was sitting at a corner table, scratching out notes on the usual sheaf of curled and wrinkled note paper.

"Why don't you get yourself a real notebook?" Keegan asked, joining him. "Looks like you retrieved that pile of scrap from a garbage pail."

"Force of habit," Rudman answered. "Besides, notebooks are too organized. How's your girlfriend?" Keegan just nodded, "I did a little checking. Nice family background—if you like money."

"That's enough," Keegan said.

"Did you see Wally?"

"Long enough to get insulted and say goodbye."

"Goodbye?"

"He's been recalled."

"What?"

"Forget where you heard what I'm going to tell you."

"Naturally."

"Wallingford set up Reinhardt's escape. A military attaché named Trace was driving him across the border and they got nailed by the Gestapo. The damn fool was in an embassy car. To avoid an international stink, Roosevelt has officially apologized to Hitler and Wally and Trace have been deported."

A waiter appeared and Keegan ordered a double martini.

"Jesus! How about Reinhardt?" Rudman pressed on eagerly.

"The way I get it, the Gestapo tortured him for several hours, then forced battery acid down his throat. He's dead. It will probably be written off as a suicide."

"Can I use this?"

"You can do whatever you want with it, just don't mention my name. I don't want to join Wally and Trace on the boat home. Anyway, I'm sure Herr Goebbels will be over here gloating about it by the cocktail hour."

"Poor old Wally. Everybody writes him off as an alarmist."

"He *is* an alarmist."

"He's a visionary, Francis. He sees it the way it's going to be."

For the first time, Keegan didn't argue. He didn't feel he had the right to argue just then, not with Felix Reinhardt on his conscience.

"Here comes the Bank of Massachusetts," Rudman said.

Keegan turned to see Vanessa enter the Imperial. She spoke to the maître d', who led her toward their table.

"She's leaving for Hamburg tomorrow," Keegan said. "Going back on the *Bremen.*"

"What a shame."

"Let's not talk politics in front of her, okay?"

"I've got to file this piece," Rudman said. "And I need to get more background on this Trace fellow. You know anything about him?"

"He's a major."

"Everybody in the military over here seems to be a major."

"It has a nice ring to it."

"Good afternoon," Rudman said cheerily as Vanessa approached the table.

She nodded at him politely, then smiled sweetly at Keegan.

"How did it go at the embassy?" she asked.

"Diplomacy is rampant over there," Keegan chuckled.

"I hear you're leaving us," said Rudman to Vanessa.

"Yes. My daddy has taken a cottage at Saratoga every year

since I was born. He still thinks I'm ten years old and *dying* to go to the afternoon tea dances."

"It'll be a nice place to dry out," Keegan said with a snicker.

"I never liked the afternoon tea dances, even when I was ten. And I don't *want* to dry out."

"Well, Berlin won't be the same without you," Rudman offered with a sincere smile.

"What a sweet thing to say. Did you hear that, Frankie?"

"I've been listening to his malarkey for years."

"How can you stand him?" Rudman said, fishing for his wallet. "He's such a cynic."

"It's all bluff," she said.

"Put your wallet away," said Keegan. "I'll spring for your beer."

"Bloody generous of you. I'm sure I'll be bumping into you in the next day or two. If not, maybe I'll swing over to Paris for the races, if you think that nag of yours really has a chance."

"She'll run their legs off."

"You have a racehorse?" Vanessa asked. "I didn't know that."

"He's got half a dozen racehorses," Rudman said. "And I bet there's a lot you don't know about Mr. Keegan." He smiled, stood up, kissed her hand and left the table with a wave.

"Have you two been friends long?" she asked.

"Since the war," Keegan said. "He's a good guy, but he's going to get in a lot of trouble."

"Why?"

"He's obsessed with the whole Nazi thing. If he's not careful he'll end up like Reinhardt."

"Oh no, the little man you were talking about this morning? What happened to him?"

"He's dead," Keegan said, taking out his wallet and studying the check.

"Did they . . . did they kill him?"

Keegan looked around the crowded bar without answering her. "Let's get out of here. I don't like the company."

"All right," she said. But she didn't move, she leaned back in her chair and studied his face. His expression scared her a little bit. And not much scared Vanessa Bromley. She took a long-stemmed rose from the tube vase in the middle of the table and stroked it slowly and gently down Keegan's cheek. "I have a wonderful idea."

He looked up at her questioningly.

"Dinner in the room. I'll charge it to the bank. I really don't feel like getting dressed again tonight. Besides, most of my things are packed."

"I suppose you'll be wanting to borrow another bathrobe," he said softly.

"The train doesn't leave until one tomorrow," she said.

"I just happen to be free until one tomorrow," He took her hand. "Let's vamoose."

He paid the check and they headed for the door. As they approached the revolving door leading to the street, a short, ferret-faced man in an SS uniform limped into the bar, accompanied by several officers. He stared at Vanessa for a moment, then nodded with a smile as they passed him.

"That little man has a club foot," she whispered when they were outside.

"That little man is Paul Joseph Goebbels," Keegan said. "Master liar of the master race."

She shivered. "Are they all so . . ."

"Ugly?" Keegan offered.

"Yes, ugly."

"Heart and soul," Keegan answered, hailing a cab.

She cuddled against him and stroked his cheek with her fingertips. He could feel her relaxing as she had the night before. And just before she went to sleep, she murmured, half under her breath, "I hope I haven't fallen in love with you, Frankie Kee."

A moment later she was asleep.

He lay there for several minutes, regaining his breath. He rolled her gently on her side and looked over at her, admiring her naked body. What a revelation she had turned out to be. Who would have expected such passionate abandon simmered inside that once-mischievous teenager? She was a remarkable sex partner. Totally inexperienced, she was unhampered by modesty and accepted each sexual discovery with a rare mixture of wonderment and joy. So why did he still feel a tinge of conscience? Was it because he had known Vanessa as child? Or because her father was a friend of his? Was it because he still thought of her as thirteen (an embarrassing and uncomfortably erotic consideration)? Or was it just an unfortunate Catholic response—a sense of guilt because it felt so good.

Or perhaps she had opened a window he thought had been shut forever.

There would always be the rumors, of course. One could expect that. But rumors could be ignored, even turned to one's advantage. The most romantic story about Keegan, the one most often repeated, had him the only son of an Irish countess and a New York bartender who had parlayed his inheritance into a fortune on the stock market, had sold short and got out clean before the crash.

It was a story Keegan liked. It had drama, it had romance, it had a touch of tragedy and a touch of mystery. There was also a semblance of truth to it, so he never disputed it. He never repeated the story as fact, either. Keegan never talked about himself at all, he let others do the talking.

Then there was the other part of the story. That Keegan had made his fortune as a bootlegger while attending Boston College, dealing only with the families of rich college friends.

Another rumor, also not without some merit.

"But what does he *do*?" the proper Bostonians would be asked, and the answer was usually the same. "He's . . . rich."

A perfectly respectable response. . . .

Actually Rose Clarke was a countess and Clancy Keegan was a bartender. When they married, she bought the bar for him and when she died during the influenza epidemic of 1903, Keegan followed close behind, the victim of a broken heart, its shards awash in a sea of Irish whiskey.

Francis, only five at the time, was reared by his trustee, his father's brother Ned, a sly entrepreneur who took his stewardship seriously and managed the bar into a classic East Side watering hole. Ned Keegan reasoned that a bar need only to attract hearty drinkers to be a success and so he concentrated on the heaviest drinkers he knew, reporters and politicians. He pandered to them, providing extra phones for the reporters and a couple of nicely appointed rooms on the second floor for those times when they either couldn't make it home—or simply required a little privacy for a couple of hours. There was an unwritten rule that the second floor was a kind of neutral ground for both the politicians and the reporters, as if a papal decree had proclaimed it off limits to inquiring minds.

Many a devious political plot was hatched in the scarred oaken booths of the Killarney Rose—to be unhatched just as quickly by eavesdropping journalists, yet the two sects kept coming back. Gossip and news was a commodity of the place, to be bartered, sold and traded between drinks, and so The Rose, as it was known to regulars, prospered. And while Ned Keegan tried to keep his young charge out of the place and under the watchful eye of the Sisters of the Immaculate Conception, his efforts failed. By the time he was fifteen, Francis was bussing tables. At sixteen he had graduated to tending bar.

Like all good bartenders, Francis mastered the art of carrying on one conversation and listening to another at the same time. He never wrote anything down—but he had a long memory. It was at The Rose that he learned his most valuable lessons: never repeat anything he saw or heard; the quickest way to a politician's heart was through his wallet; bribery was only illegal if one got caught; all sin was relative. It quickly became patently clear to young Francis Keegan that one man's meat was indeed another man's poison.

By the time he was twenty, Francis had fought as a doughboy in the trenches in Europe. When he returned in 1918, a hero from the war, Ned offered to buy The Rose from him.

Half a million dollars.

Not bad for a kid with only a couple of Purple Hearts, a Silver Star, and two years of bartending to show for his twenty years.

"Now what're ye gonna do?" Ned asked.

"I'm going to get rich, but first I'm going to college," Keegan answered. "Up in Boston. There's a lot of class in Boston and there's no such thing as a rich bum."

He had been there less than a year when he called Jocko Nayles and invited him to lunch at The Rose. It had been two years since he had seen his wartime buddy. Nayles's clothes were neat but showing wear and he wore the mottled tan of a man who spends long, hard hours working in the sun.

"What've you been up to?" Keegan asked him.

"Y'know, kid, I'm on the docks."

"You like it?"

"Nobody likes it, it's a living."

"I've got a better idea, Jocko. I've got an idea where we can make a couple of million dollars a year."

"Yeah, sure. What're we gonna do, rent out the White House?"

"Jocko, I got half a million dollars. We buy a couple of fast boats.

We make a trip to Scotland. We set up a deal, a thousand cases of scotch a month . . .''

"That's bootlegging!"

"Of course it's bootlegging."

"You wanna go to jail?"

"Listen to me. Everybody drinks. I've got friends who buy booze by the case. Rich guys. Connected people. We keep our clientele very select. We make a run a month. I'll set up the sales, you handle distribution. The cut's fifty-fifty."

Nayles looked at him for a very long time before he decided the kid was serious.

"Make it sixty you, forty me," he said finally. "You're footin' the bills."

Keegan smiled. "Quit your job," he said, "we just went into business."

In the next few years, Francis Scott Keegan, the proper Bostonian college student, split his studies between business and the arts. He read voraciously and listened to music constantly. During the same time, he also was known variously as Frank the K, Scotch Frank, and Frankie Kee, a nickname whose subtle patriotic reference was lost to most of Keegan's business competitors. Keegan had studied how territories were divided among the more noted gangland mobs of the day: Alfonse in Chicago, Louis the Lep in Brooklyn, Dutch Shultz and Frankie C in Manhattan, Willie Knucks in Philly, Legs in upstate New York, Nukey Johnson in Jersey and of course Luciano, Charley Lucky, who called all the shots. Boston was wide open, nothing but nickel rollers there. Nobody in the mobs paid much attention to him. Unlike his competitors, who bought scotch from offshore freighters for four dollars a bottle, cut it three or four times and sold it for eighteen dollars a fifth, Keegan paid three-fifty a quart and sold it to his customers uncut for fifteen dollars a bottle.

The fact is, Keegan liked to think of himself as a connoisseur of good liquor, a booze steward to the very rich. He never thought of himself as a bootlegger. Hell, everybody he knew drank. Keegan just didn't like the sound of the word. Besides, he really wasn't in the shabby end of the business. No bathtub gin, no homemade poison. His specialty was Scotch whisky imported straight from Edinburgh, perfectly aged and light as mist.

His circle of friends at Boston College were all rich or near rich, a snobbish set which suited Keegan just fine. They were all potential customers—and they all had friends who were potential customers.

"I know this wonderful bootlegger but he's shy," Keegan would tell them. *"I'll put the order in for you."* And the goods were delivered like milk to the back door. His was definitely a select clientele: two governors, half a dozen senators, one of Broadway's brightest comedy stars, half a dozen Catholic bishops spread from Jersey to Connecticut to New York to Massachusetts, and one future president of the United States. He performed a service, got rich and everybody was happy. Well, almost everybody.

When the word got around, Arthur Flegenheimer, who had adopted the name Dutch Shultz so it would fit into newspaper headlines, blew up and went to the big man himself.

"Lookit here, Lucky," Schultz told Luciano, *"we got this Irish asshole, this Frankie Kee, he's sellin' uncut scotch less'n we're gettin'.* Uncut. *The word gets around, it ain't good for business. It's unfair competition, I say, and I say we burn the little shit and be done with it. An object lesson."*

"So do it," Luciano answered around a mouthful of pasta. *"Why the hell you askin' me for? It ain't like you're gonna bump off Calvin Coolidge."*

Keegan fit comfortably into the schizophrenic life-style he had adopted. He read six newspapers a day, everything from The New York Times to the Boston Globe to the New York News and Mirror to the Racing Form. He studied everything from the stock market to the morning lineup at Hialeah. And he had a way with language. He could turn his Irish brogue on and off at will, and had a keen perception of the differences in cadence and vernacular between the two worlds he had chosen, the social world of Boston and the underworld of the East Coast. He was as comfortable being Francis Keegan, discussing a fluctuation in the stock market with a Boston banker, as he was being Frankie Kee, discussing the pros and cons of a gangland rub-out with a Sicilian mobster. It was one of many lessons he had learned tending bar in the Killarney Rose saloon. When in Rome, talk like the Romans, when in Boston, speak as a proper Bostonian.

The Boston Ambush, as he would refer to it later in life, was a particularly cowardly act, the first perpetrated by Shultz. Keegan had been to the theater. As he got out of his car, a black Ford squealed around the corner and he heard someone yelling, *"Shoot, shoot."* He dove behind the car as a half dozen shots rang out. He felt the ping in his side, then the burning, deep in his back, and he knew he had been shot. The shooter, a Philadelphia gunsel named Harvey Fusco, never made it back to Philadelphia to spend the ten thousand he was paid to do the job. When the Manhattan Limited pulled into Broad Street station, Fusco was found sitting in his compartment, the New York Daily Mirror in his lap, his eyes crossed and staring up at the bridge of his nose at the single .45-caliber bullet hole there.

Frankie Kee was never a suspect. He was in Boston General in intensive care when it happened. Since the authorities didn't know Fusco's bullet had put him there no connection was ever made. For the record, Francis Scott Keegan's attack went down as an attempted stickup. As for Keegan, he was never sure who had disposed of Fusco. It was one of those unclaimed favors one simply takes for granted, savors and forgets.

So Shultz tried unsuccessfully to give Frankie Kee the big gift—the concrete overcoat and the deep swim. But Keegan, touched with the luck of the Irish, always proved equal to the challenge. Each time the Dutchman failed, his assassins felt the sting of his Irish vengeance in strange, sometimes almost supernatural ways. One of his attempted assassins was kicked to death by a racehorse in a stable at Belmont Park. Another choked to death on a chicken bone during a birthday celebration in Reuben's Restaurant in Manhattan.

"Listen, pal, I never lifted a finger against anybody," Keegan once told Albert A at a meeting in Providence, Rhode Island, where Anastasia had been sent to put Frankie Kee in a box and Dutch Shultz out of his misery. "It's just that bad things seem to befall people I particularly don't like. And Albert, I particularly don't like you as much as anybody I know."

Anastasia, probably the New York mob's top killer and a man unaccustomed to insults, was so astounded he didn't say anything in response. At first he didn't even tell anybody that this smartass mackerel snapper from Boston had insulted him. Then his anger got the best of him. When he decided to start his own Boston Tea Party, Arnold Rothstein stepped in.

A few days after the Anastasia meeting, Keegan was in The Rose for dinner, his Uncle Ned serving the best Kansas City sirloin east of the town itself. Ned slid into the booth opposite him.

"I heard this rumor that you put the double hex on Albert A," he whispered in his Irish lilt. "Tell me it's a lie. Tell me yer not mixin' it up with them Guineas. Jesus, Francis, they'll cut off yer jewels n' have 'em fer breakfast."

"Now why would I do a silly thing like that, Unc?"

"But you talked to him, didn't ye. Ye had a conversation with Albert A."

"He wanted to buy my Rolls."

"So what'd you tell 'im?"

"I told him him no dice. Told him it wouldn't fit him."

"You told Albert A that*? That it wouldn't* fit *'im?"*

"Yeah. I told him he was too small for it. He shrank another two inches when it sank in."

"Why ye do things like that, Frankie? Ye better watch yer step, son, them dagos have a short fuse."

"Been tried, Unc." He wiped his mouth with his napkin. "I've got a meeting to go to."

"What're ye gonna do, sell a bottle a scotch to the mayor?" Ned said with a snicker.

"I'm going uptown to Central Park."

"Central Park is it?"

"A meeting with A.R."

"Rothstein himself! Are ye crazy, then?" Ned shook his head. "I'll tell ye this, boy, when I die they's gonna be hell t'pay. When I get to heaven yer old man's gonna kick my ass to Baltimore and back fer lettin' you go astray."

"And well he should," Keegan answered with his cockeyed smile.

Arnold Rothstein, who had been known as A.R. since his teens, was a democrat in the true sense of the word. Every day he held court on the same bench in the southwest corner of Central Park just off 59th Street, listening to deals, requests for loans, entertaining favors. Want to shack up with a chorus girl? Ask A.R. Want to buy a load of whiskey and willing to pay the interest? Ask A.R.. Want to fix a cop, bribe a judge, dispose of a witness, fix the 1919 World Series? Ask A.R. Want to lose a bundle in a poker game? Sit across the table from A.R.

Keegan had leaned on the stone wall on Central Park South watching him for about ten minutes. Not as trim as his pictures showed him to be, Keegan thought. Getting bald. But you could sense the power in the man, sitting with his back ramrod straight in his gray pinstripe and polka dot bow tie. All brains, thought Keegan. There sits the most powerful gangster in the world. More powerful than Capone, Luciano, Costello, any of them. Just sitting there in the sun feeding the pigeons. It's a crazy world.

Finally he strolled down the path and stood in front of the big man. Rothstein looked up at him for a moment through narrowed eyes, then held out his hand.

"*You must be Frankie Kee,*" *he said.*

A little cross-eyed, Keegan thought. He took the hand.

"*Francis Keegan, Mr. Rothstein,*" *he answered.*

"*Call me A.R. Everybody calls me A.R. Take a load off.*" *He patted the bench. Keegan sat down.*

"*Where's Jimmy Noland?*" *Keegan asked, using Legs Diamond's real name.*

"*Know Legs, do you?*"

"*Never met the man. I've always heard you want to meet Legs Diamond, find Arnold Rothstein.*"

Rothstein laughed. "*That's a kick in the ass,*" *he said.* "*The way I heard it, you wanna meet A.R., find Legs Diamond. He's over at the Plaza having a coffee. I told you this was just you and me. I'm not a welcher.*"

"*I've heard that too.*"

"*Good. We'll get along.*"

"*What's to get along about, Mis . . . A.R.?*"

"*It comes to me you had this thing with Albert A, up in the country.*"

"*It was in Providence.*"

"*Anything past 125th Street is country to me, son. So anyway, it comes to me you insulted him. Something about a car.*"

"*What it was, Anastasia proposed a merger. I'm supposed to give up my little specialty business and pitch in with Charley Lucky, Costello, Capone, that whole Sicilian bunch, right? And they send Albert A to talk the deal. That's what it was. Anyway, he got a look at my car and got all hot and bothered to have it.*"

"*And you told him it was too* big *for him.*"

"*Something like that.*"

"*That's rich, that is. I admire your moxie, pal. The little bastard really blew his cork, y'know. You're lucky he didn't start World War Two right there on the spot. I'm sure you know Albert's specialty is the big knockover.*"

"*The conditions weren't right.*"

Rothstein laughed again. "*Knowing Albert, I gotta agree with you,*" *he said.* "*He's not one to go face-to-face with anybody.*"

"*Well, he was a very pushy guy, you see, and I figure he came to me wanting something, so pushy was not the right attitude.*"

"*You're large on attitude, are you?*"

"*No, I'm large on if you want something you say 'please' and 'how about it,' not 'gimme.'*"

"I'd say that's reasonable. Unfortunately, Albert A is not a reasonable fellow. He is definitely a 'gimme' guy."

"He's a back-shooting son of a bitch. He kills for wages. He smells like death. And he has hyena breath."

"Hyena breath." Rothstein laughed. *"That's great. You're full of 'em."*

"Anyway, he is definitely not the kind of a man you send to talk business. Not if you're serious anyway. You send a negotiator, somebody who talks give and take. Somebody with a greased tongue and the long schmooze. So what we did, we moved him around some before we sat down to talk. Spooked his tails. Anastasia's a planner. He couldn't take me on because he was out of his element, he didn't have a plan. And his back-shooters were lost."

"Very clever. So you think he came to kill you?"

Keegan looked at Rothstein and raised an eyebrow.

"No, I think he came to borrow a smoke."

"I must admit, sending him to negotiate anything was poor judgment. Not mine, incidentally. I'm simply here to mediate some differences."

"That's why I don't believe it, A.R. That's why I think it was not a proposal made in good faith. It was a setup that went sour. They thought they were dealing with one of the Katzenjammer Kids."

"What exactly do you want, Francis?"

"What do I want? Nothing. Not a single, solitary thing. Zip. Just leave me alone. I've got a little specialty business. Hell, it's a nothing to you guys. Somebody got a wire up his ass on this thing. I do a thousand cases a month, your people do twenty thou. If they wanted to do twenty-one thou, no big thing. See what I mean, what's the dif? A couple of times they tried to knock me over and for what? A thousand cases a month?"

"Three times they almost pulled it off," Rothstein said with a note of fatherly caution in his tone.

"But they didn't," Keegan answered. *"So why are we here, Mr. Rothstein? Have you got a beef with me?"*

"You wanna know the truth?"

"That would be nice."

"I wanted to meet the man told Albert Anastasia he was too small a guy to fit in a goddamn Rolls-Royce."

"That's the whole of it?"

"Look, Francis . . . that's what you prefer, isn't it?"

"That's my name. I never have gone in big for monikers."

"Or publicity."

"Or publicity. I'd rather have my face on the post office wall than the front page of the Daily News.*"*

"That's very smart. Anyway, the whole of it is this. You are doing business with some very important people. People I would like to get next to. Like the governor, for instance. So I thought maybe we could work a little something out. You wash my hand, I wash yours. You know how that works. I'll put Albert back in his box, tell the Sicilians to lay off. You got no more troubles. Shit, son, let's see, a thousand cases a month at your price, that would be about, uh, two and a half mil a year, correct me if I'm wrong. We got another two, three years before they repeal the stupid law. We're talking a lot of gelt *here, seven, eight million bucks and nobody hassles you anymore."*

"And for this?"

"For this maybe you could put me in touch with some of your people."

"I never met the governor."

"You have access."

"I'm afraid I couldn't do that, A.R."

"Oh?"

"Look, let's get to the bone, okay? I know these people socially. As far as they know, I've got a damn good bootlegger. They give me the order, I take care of things for them. I never see a dime at that end. So, you see, if I even suggested such a thing, that somebody should parlay with you, that would come down badly on me and *you. You've got Tammany in your pocket, but it doesn't work that way up in Albany. It would not just blow a good thing for me, it would have the state boys up your ass with a searchlight. So what I'm saying to you, I'm giving you some advice. It's a bad call, A.R. You don't want to do that. It'll give you a headache aspirin won't cure."*

Rothstein looked at Keegan with his mouth open just a hair. He was impressed. The kid made sense to him. Keegan knew the lay of the land upstate. He'd been operating free as a sparrow for three, four years now. On the other hand, Rothstein's corruption did not spread that far. He did not own any state cops or any upstate people that amounted to anything.

"That's sound thinking, Francis. You're fast on your feet."

"I'm just calling it the way I see it. Why bite a tiger in the ass?"

"I must say, I could use a man with a head like yours. Most of my people think with their guns and their balls. You give 'em two and two, they gotta take to the weekend to come up with four. Muscle they know

about Brains? Shit, they think you go twenty miles south of Yonkers, you fall off the planet. I don't suppose you'd be interested in a little change in professional direction at this time?"

"That's a flattering offer but I like things as they are."

"Tell you what I'm gonna do, Francis. I'm gonna go back and I'm gonna tell Frank and Lucky to leave you alone. That I owe you one. I appreciate good advice. I give it out a lot but I don't get much back. I can understand why you backed Albert A down. He didn't know what to make of you. How many guns you have on him after you cut him out from his pack?"

Keegan's smile broadened. "You'll never know," he said.

"I guess I won't." Rothstein smiled back. "Pleasure meetin' ya, Francis Keegan. Good health."

"You too. Mind if I ask you one question?"

"Shoot."

"How much did you make on the Series fix?"

Rothstein laughed. "You'll never know," he answered.

Less than two weeks later, Arnold Rothstein, the great fixer, the man who devised the criminal blueprint for the Mafia, a blueprint they followed almost to the letter, was in a card game with "Titanic" Thompson and "Nigger Nate" Raymond, two West Coast gamblers. Rothstein dropped $320,000 and walked out without paying, claiming the game was rigged. An hour later he was dead with four bullet holes in his back. Nobody was ever booked for his murder. But Rothstein was good to his word, even in the grave. Nobody in the mob ever bothered Keegan again.

Francis Scott Keegan, Bootlegger to the Kings. He laughed thinking about it.

What the hell, he thought, why close the window. In retrospect he liked the view. How many people did he know who had snookered Albert Anastasia, the most dangerous man in America, and Arnold Rothstein, its greatest fixer, both in the same week, who had defied the mob and lived to tell about it and who had sold short in the market in September, two months before the bottom dropped out, and made a killing?

And anyway, this had all started because Vanessa had called him Frankie Kee. So if his conscience was having a problem dealing with her, forget it. *Little girls grow up.* And grow up she had. Hell, it was too late to worry about it and besides, his head was throbbing from lack of sleep and too much champagne and he was in no shape to deal with his conscience or his memories and here it was, dawn again, and every muscle in his body ached.

He scribbled a note to her and put it on the pillow beside her, then he covered her up and headed for the steam baths in the basement.

He had heard her whisper to him when she thought he was asleep. He, too, hoped she wasn't falling in love with him.

She was a nice kid, Vanessa. Beautiful, charming. But in the two days he'd been with her, something strange had happened to him. He hadn't been able to stop thinking about the singer, about Jenny Gould. Her voice haunted him, her eyes pierced him still.

He hoped *he* hadn't fallen in love—with a German torch singer he didn't really really.

A burly blond sat behind the desk, dozing.

"Is Werner at work yet?" Keegan asked in German.

"*Nein,*" the young man, said shaking his head, and told him in German that the masseur was not due in for another hour. Keegan went back to the locker room, stripped, wrapped a towel around his waist and entered the empty steam room. He poured a bucket of water over the hot, glowing coals in the corner of the small room and sat with his elbows propped on his knees, letting the hissing steam urge the poisons out of his body.

He was dozing when he heard the door open and close.

Through the swirling steam he saw the little man from the embassy party, swathed in towels to cover the unfortunate hump on his back, smiling across the room at him.

"Good morning," the little man said in almost perfect English.

"I suppose," Keegan answered.

Was he a guest in the hotel? Keegan wondered. What was he doing here at seven in the morning? Was he following Keegan? Or was Keegan's hangover making him a little paranoid?

Keegan couldn't have cared less at that moment. The hangover was now a thunderstorm in his head and he was trying to avoid any kind of movement or thought.

"Have you been in Berlin long?" the humpback asked finally.

"I move around a bit, but I spend about half my time here."

"You like Berlin then?"

"I like the chaos. Reminds me of home."

"Chaos?"

Keegan looked over at him. "You haven't noticed?"

"The chaos is over," the professor said. "The Führer has the country under control."

"Ah, that's reassuring."

"Are you one of those Americans who thinks Hitler is some kind of human devil?"

"I don't think about it at all. Believe me, not at all."

"You know what I mean."

The little bird's trying to get a handle on my political views, Keegan thought. *What the hell's his game?*

"Chancellor Hitler's a bit radical for a lot of Americans, how's that?"

The professor laughed and nodded vigorously.

"A bit radical, *ja,* I like that. That's quite funny."

Keegan leaned forward and stared over at the humpback. He wiped the flat of his hand across his flat belly, sweeping away the puddles of sweat that were collecting around the towel at his waist. He smiled faintly and the smile stayed on his lips.

"And how about you, do *you* think he's a bit radical?" the little man asked.

He's fishing for something, Keegan thought. *Well, whatever he wants he'll have to work for it.* So Keegan did not take the bait.

"I told you, I don't think about it. I'm your typical tourist. I spend money and give the economy a little boost, that's all."

"Your name is Keegan, is that correct? I saw it when you signed in at the desk."

"Keegan. That's correct. You are?"

"Vierhaus. Professor Wilhelm Vierhaus."

"Pleased to meet you."

"Keegan, Keegan. You are Ire?"

"Also correct. Irish-American. My parents both came from Ireland."

"Ah, what part?"

So that's it. He figures I'm an Irish patriot, an English-hater. This guy wants something. Maybe I should play his game, lunch with the little guy. Pick his brains, subtly, of course, and pass the info on to Wally in the states, just to show him I do have feelings about what's going on.

"Belfast," Keegan said. "They weren't interested in politics either."

"Ah. And were you in the war?"

"You ask a lot of questions."

"Please forgive me. Just curious. I don't often have an opportunity to talk with Americans."

"Yes, I was in the war. The other side."

The professor laughed again. Keegan's smile remained the same, a little arrogant, a little mysterious. He poured another bucket on the coal pile. Steam hissed and swirled into the room. Keegan leaned back, closed his eyes.

"I don't suppose you have a cigarette tucked away in that pile of towels you're wearing?" he asked the professor.

"Sorry. I left them outside."

"Excuse me a minute."

Keegan got up and stepped outside the steam room. He opened his locker and took out his pack of Camels and lit one. There were two men in hats standing in the hallway outside the club room, trying hard to ignore him.

He went back inside and sat down.

"Hope the smoke doesn't bother you."

"Not a bit, not a bit."

"I've got a hangover, Professor. It may be terminal."

"I'm sorry to hear that."

"That's okay. I don't want you to think I'm unfriendly."

"Not at all."

They sat in silence for a minute or two, Keegan leaning back against the wooden slats with his eyes closed, smoking, the professor sitting uncomfortably, staring at the floor.

Now what's he going to do? Make his play or call the game? Keegan didn't have to wait long to find out.

"I am in charge of a small bureau. It comes under the Ministry of Information, although I pretty much am left alone. To my own devices, so to speak."

"Uh huh."

"Mainly I keep the Führer up to date on what's happening in the world. Social notes, political notes, that sort of thing. Attitudes, he's very interested in attitudes. But . . . he is so busy . . . he doesn't have time to keep up with everything. You understand?"

"Kind of like . . . social intelligence."

"*Ja,* that's very good. Very good. For instance, we don't think the American people understand how devastating the peace treaty was to the Germans. Do you think the peace at Versailles was fair? An honorable peace?"

What the hell does he want? Keegan was tired of playing games. He leaned forward again, staring through the steam, still smiling. *An honorable peace?* he thought.

They came home on a French liner, all smelling of linoleum and brass polish, with an arrogant staff and food that was too rich and sometimes spoiled. It took too long and many of the men were sick along the way, lining up along the rail, puking away from the wind in solitary agony. Along with this sweeping sense of malaise and mal de mer *was a sense of apprehension, the hangover of battle. As much as they despised the war, there was that side of it that relieved them of responsibility, that directed life for them; when they got up, what they ate, what they did, where they went, all laid out by the omnipotent "they" that ruled their being from taps to reveille. "They" are sending us to the front today; "they" are ordering us to charge; "they" are the dictators of our daily lives.*

Nobody really knew who "they" were, it was a collective noun that encompassed the nameless, faceless, voiceless architects of their victory. Soldiers had only to respond. To march, fight, die, lie wounded in hospitals or, if lucky, to emerge unscathed except for the scars that all war leaves on the mind and soul and which, for now at least, they could ignore because these were the wounds that did not bleed, did not blind or cripple or sterilize their victims. That pain would come later, in nightmares and memories.

And so they were flush with victory and apprehensive of peace. Now they would once again assume responsibility for their own lives, to feed and clothe themselves, to find jobs, mend relationships, to look for love to replace the hate which is the driving force of all men at arms.

In his secret heart, Keegan felt he had been seduced by the victory marches and the speeches and the posters of an angry godlike Uncle Sam pointing his finger at him and demanding, "I want you." Keegan had surrendered his youth to the Marines and though he never doubted the urgency of the war or the need for victory, he harbored a resentment that somehow he had been betrayed, not by the politics that had drawn him to Château-Thierry and Belleau Wood as much as by the lie that all war is glory and all victory is sweet. When the horns stopped blaring, the wind swept the confetti into the sewers and the music died away, he ultimately perceived victory as a fat prize shared only by politicians and profiteers who quickly shunned those whose blood served up that gluttoned calf.

So on a cold December morning, he and Jocko Nayles huddled against

*the railing of the ship, each searching for that symbol which most repre-
sented home, a skyline, a statue in the harbor, a bridge spire reaching into
the fog.*

"Whatcha gonna do?" Nayles asked Keegan.

"I don't know, I've got a piece of this bar," Keegan answered.

"Got it made, huh?"

*He was nineteen and did not know whether he had it made or not.
He knew only that tending bar and listening to the ward heelers and
muckrakers sniping at each other and listening to his uncle reading the
morning headlines and waking to the smell of stale beer and rancid cigar
smoke was not what he wanted to do for the rest of his life.*

"I guess," he answered. "How about you?"

"Worked on the docks. Guess m'job'll still be there."

"Does it . . . seem kind of scary to you? Going home, I mean?"

"Yeah. You too, huh?"

"Yeah."

*"Well, it'll all come out in the wash. We oughta keep in touch
. . . y'know, after all this."*

"Sure."

*But after that morning and the parade down Fifth Avenue in their
pegged breeches, puttees and campaign hats and carrying empty guns
through the ribbons of paper and confetti and the ardent joy of the crowd,
they had been separated in the crowd and Keegan would not see Jocko
Nayles again for two years.*

"There's nothing honorable about war *or* peace," Keegan told
the professor bluntly.

"Rather cynical, isn't it?" Vierhaus answered.

"Oh I don't think cynical nearly covers it. They haven't
invented a word that describes my feelings on the subject."

Keegan poured another bucket of water over the rocks and
another cloud of steam hissed into the room.

"Butchery and boundaries, that's what war's about," he said
quietly, without passion, anger or malice, still smiling. "There's
nothing good or decent or honorable about it. Nothing to be
proud of. Nothing heroic or proper. War is the religion of rich
men and politicians. It's their church. What it is, Professor, is a
disgusting enterprise dedicated to the destruction of the young
by a bunch of vindictive, impotent, scabby old men who envy
youth."

He stopped for a moment to take a drag on his cigarette. Then still smiling, he went on:

"When a war ends, what we ought to do, we ought to turn the bastards on both sides over to all the blind, legless, armless, insane leftovers they created. They ought to be flayed, skinned alive and burned on the steps of the banks where their profits are stored."

He stopped, took another drag and carefully ground the cigarette out on the hot coals.

"Then we should bury them together in common lye pits, strike their names from all human records and monuments and obliterate the sons of bitches from history. And that's better than they deserve."

Vierhaus was somewhat stunned by Keegan's response, not so much by the severity of his opinion as his nonchalance.

"Well," the professor stammered, "you certainly seem to have given it some thought. That's an impassioned viewpoint."

"Nothing passionate about it, *Herr Professor*, they don't make soap strong enough to wash away the stink of death or whiskey strong enough to wash out the bitter taste it leaves in your mouth. It's a foul, stinking, disgusting business. Now if you'll excuse me, this hangover's so bad I may be hospitalized before the day is out."

"My sympathies."

"*Danke.*"

"And my sincerest apologies."

"No apologies necessary. Anyway, it's all politics."

"I see. Am I to assume you have the same dire attitude about politics as you do about warfare, then?"

"I have no attitude at all about it."

"But the Jew, Roosenfeldt, seems to be doing a respectable job on your home front."

Keegan laughed, although even a chuckle was painful to his throbbing head. "It's Roosevelt. And he isn't Jewish."

"Really? I had heard otherwise."

"Well, either you heard wrong or somebody's pulling your leg."

"Pulling my leg?"

"An American expression. It means they are making a joke at your expense. Personally I don't give a damn what anybody says about him, but I hate to hear a silly lie like that perpetuated by an intelligent person like yourself."

"*Danke.* I guess I should take that as a compliment."

"It was meant as one."

"I'm sorry you are indisposed. I love to discuss issues with Americans. Perhaps when you are feeling better we could have lunch."

"I'd love to have lunch with you someday but you've probably heard the extent of my opinion about everything," Keegan answered.

"Oh, I doubt it, a man with your education and experience."

"What do you know about my education and experience, Professor? We just met five minutes ago."

"Uh, yes, that's true. Uh, may I be . . . honest with you, Herr Keegan?"

"That would be refreshing."

"I know about you. Your war record, your success in business. I did seek you out. Nothing mysterious about it, really. I thought perhaps we might talk about something which could be mutually beneficial."

"That's what I like, Professor. In my country we have a saying, One hand washes the other.'"

"That's very good. That says it precisely. I will be out of the city for a few days. Perhaps when I come back I can, how do you Americans say it? Give you a ring?"

Keegan stared at the professor for a moment, a hard stare, then he nodded slowly. "Why don't you do that. When you get back, give me a ring."

Vanessa almost missed her train.

"One more time," she suggested when he returned from the steam room. "It may be years before we see each other again."

They had lost track of the time.

She pulled down the window of her compartment and kissed him.

"You may be the Bootlegger to the Kings to them," she said with a laugh, "but you're my white knight."

As the train started to roll out she reached up suddenly, whipped off her hat and threw it to him.

"My favor," she said brightly. "Wear it proudly in battle."

He watched as the big steam engine lumbered out of the great domed train station, then he walked the several blocks back to the hotel. He was surprised to realize he was going to miss her. Not exactly for her company, more for her potential. It was a waste, he thought. Vanessa would go home, finish college, get married by arrangement, have two-and-two-thirds children and be dead of boredom by the time she was fifty.

When he got back to the hotel he suddenly changed his mind and took a cab to *Der Schwarze Stier Verein.*

The club was virtually empty except for the cleanup people. It smelled of stale beer and cigarette smoke. He went to the back and took the stairs to the second floor. Conrad Weil lived in an apartment that occupied the front side of the building, adjacent to the windowless Gold Gate club. His knock on the door was answered by Weil's valet, an elderly man who regarded everyone and everything with dour suspicion.

"I'll see if Herr Weil is in," he consented grudgingly.

The apartment was a model of art deco, done in shades of blue and green. There was not a sharp corner on a table or chair in the living room. Fluted lamps cast spots of light on the ceiling, bathing the entire room in indirect light; the bar in one corner was smoked glass and lit from below. A large picture window overlooked downtown Berlin.

In a few moments Weil entered the room dressed in dark pants and a red silk smoking jacket. Weil would be elegant in the shower, thought Keegan.

"Well, well, so you finally came by for a visit," Weil said with a smile.

"Sorry I didn't call first," Keegan said. "It was a spur-of-the-moment thing."

"Whatever reason, I'm delighted. How about a brandy? It's Napoleon, the dust is still on the bottle."

"Why not?"

"So, is this a social call or business?" Weil asked as he poured them each a generous snifter. His hawklike features seemed ominous in the reflection of the lights from the bar.

"I need the address of the singer, Jenny Gould."

"What for?"

"What do you think for? I'm going to sue her for not taking requests."

Weil clicked his tongue. "I never get used to your American sarcasm," he said. "Are you smitten with her, Francis?"

"I don't know, Conrad, that's what I expect to find out. I thought maybe she'd be here rehearsing."

"She does not work here anymore."

"What!"

"My customers were complaining."

"About what?"

"They did not like her singing. Or more precisely, they did not like the songs she was singing."

"You mean the brownshirt assholes with the crooked crosses on their sleeves?"

"Unfortunately, the SA thugs are my customers. We had a scene here last night. She was singing a song, an American Depression song, 'Brother Can You Spare a Dime,' I believe it is called. There was a lot of restlessness in the crowd, then they started yelling at her to sing a German song. She kept going. Then from the crowd someone yelled, *Jude!* And somebody else joined in. Then one of the brownshirts stood up and screamed *Heil Hitler* and another joined and another until the whole room was on its feet. I dimmed the lights and got her offstage. Then the mob began singing 'Horst Wessel' and suddenly my beer hall became a Nazi rally. The point is, my friend, Jenny Gould is not even Jewish."

"And you fired her anyway, as good as she is?"

"Good has nothing to do with it. You think that bunch knows what good is?"

"Why the hell did you hire her in the first place?"

"An error in judgment. I thought she might give the place some class. But if she had continued here I would have had a riot on my hands every night. All someone in the crowd has to do is yell '*Jude*' to create a riot."

"Whether it's true or not?"

"Truth is immaterial, dear Francis. In Germany, it has become the ultimate insult. And before you get too hot under the collar, *Ire,* I found her another job making the same money."

"Where?"

"A few blocks away, at the Kit Kat Club. It is more suited to her singing anyway. A very sophisticated audience goes there to hear American jazz. There are a lot of American tourists. At the Kit Kat there will be no trouble. Brownshirts do not frequent it."

"It's a dive!" Keegan said sourly.

"*Ja,* but a very nice dive. You think the *Stier* is a symphony hall?"

"All this because they accuse her of being Jewish," Keegan said, shaking his head.

"Come, come, Francis, you know it is a sin to be a Jew in Germany nowadays. Or a Communist, a Social Democrat, a Gypsy or an artist. Any minority, anyone who disagrees. There is no such thing as dissent. I could be arrested for even talking about this. How have you managed to ignore it?"

"I didn't ignore it, it wasn't any of my business before."

"Ah, and now suddenly you make it your business, *ja?*"

"I'm only interested in the girl."

Conrad shook his head. He sat beside Keegan on the sofa, legs crossed and his snifter poised on one knee. He leaned close to Keegan, speaking almost in a whisper.

"You are a charming rascal, Francis. Here suddenly you are having an attack of conscience over this young woman. Suddenly you are outraged, *ja?*

"That's right, suddenly I'm outraged."

"Don't you understand, my friend, their outrage is far greater than yours. Theirs is inspired hate. Acceptable hate. Racism is the accepted order of things here. In Germany it is unpopular not to hate. Not to hate is nonconformity. We are a closed society and conformity is required. Our leaders repeat the same lies over and over and over until they become a kind of national truth."

Conrad stood up, wandering around the room as he spoke.

"You know what I did before I became a . . ." he waved his hand around the room, "saloon keeper? Hmm? I was a schoolteacher. *Ja,* a teacher of history at the University in Heidelberg. I quit because a teacher by nature is a nonconformist, a rebellious creature, likely to disagree simply to stimulate an argument. The war made that impossible."

"What did the war have to do with it?"

" 'I fear the real danger in war is that conformity becomes the only virtue and those who refuse to conform will pay the penalty.' Do you know who said that?"

"Nope."

"Your own Woodrow Wilson, on the same day he urged your Reichstag to declare war on Germany. He understood that conformity is essential during a war because patriotism demands conformity and since conservatives are usually conformists, it follows that you must be conservative to be patriotic. Say it enough, it becomes the truth."

"I can't believe the whole country buys that. Hitler won't last."

"You are wrong, Francis, Hitler will last because he is at war already." Conrad tapped his head as he said it. "He burns books if the ideas do not conform to his, closes newspapers down if they disagree with him, attacks artists because they are unreliable, because they think. And the irony is that it is all done in the name of freedom and patriotism. Understand this, to be a German today, you must be a fascist, otherwise you are a traitor. To be a fascist you must hate Jews. What do you do when you hate something? Eh? You get rid of it."

"And you support this?" Keegan said.

"Come, come, my friend, why so surprised?" Weil held his hands out at his sides. "Have I ever in the year or so we have been friends, have I ever shown you any pretenses? I am not a hero or a revolutionary. I am a devout coward. I run the most degenerate saloon in Europe. I have become rich pandering to the basest of human frailties. Do I think it is right, what Hitler is doing? *Nein.* Do I oppose it? *Nein.* Do I support this Nazi party?" He shrugged. "I am like a blade of grass, I sway with the winds of the times. For that reason, I say save yourself a lot of grief, forget this girl. Sooner or later she will have trouble again. It is the way of things."

"I don't think I want to do that."

"You have heard her sing once, met her for thirty seconds, you do not even know where she lives. And already you cannot tear yourself away from her."

"Very funny."

"But true."

"I don't want anybody telling me what I can and can't do."

Conrad shrugged. "Very altruistic. Unfortunately, not very practical in Germany these days."

"What's her address, Conrad?"

Weil heaved a sigh. "She lives at 236 Albertstrasse and she starts tonight at the Kit Kat. Two shows, nine and eleven."

"Thanks," Keegan said and, polishing off the brandy in the snifter, stood up.

"You are a man who has always avoided trouble, Francis. At least since I have known you. Why start now?"

"Maybe you just haven't known me long enough, my friend."

When he got back to the hotel, Keegan went to the flower shop and sent Jenny Gould two dozen roses. No card.

Willie Vierhaus hurried up the steps of the Brown House and down the long marble hallway to the Führer's office. Every Tuesday morning at precisely 11:45 A.M., Vierhaus reported to Hitler to provide him with party gossip and other news of interest. The meeting always lasted twelve to fifteen minutes, until Hitler went to lunch.

When he entered the anteroom, Hitler's secretary held her finger to her lips, her brow furrowed and troubled. Hitler's voice, high-pitched and furious, echoed through the paneled doors.

"I don't want to hear that, you understand? Not one more word. That's hogwash, hogwash! You are a stupid man, Plausen. I thought you were a smart man but you are stupid. Stupid, stupid, stupid! Get out. You are relieved of your duties. Pack up your things and get out."

"Yes, *mein Führer. Heil Hitler.*"

"Out!"

The door flew open and Plausen, a tiny mouse of a man who worked in the procurement office, rushed past, his face as white as chalk. From inside his office, Hitler saw Vierhaus waiting and waved him in.

Vierhaus entered and raised his arm in a salute. *"Heil Hitler."* Hitler waved a half-hearted salute in return but his mood changed immediately. Hitler's mood always improved when Vierhaus arrived. He adored intrigue and gossip and Willie Vierhaus provided him with both.

"So, Willie, what is the news? Brighten my day. So far it has been dismal. A morning dealing with idiots like . . ." He waved vaguely toward the door.

"I am sorry, *mein Führer.*"

"Tell me some juicy news, eh." He smiled fleetingly in expectation.

"Well, sir, you know General Romsdorf?"

"Third Division. Of course, of course."

"His wife Fredie is having an affair with a dancer in the Berlin Ballet Company."

"A ballet dancer!" Hitler cried out, clasping his hands together and pressing them to his lips.

"*Ja.* Not even a featured dancer. He is on the chorus."

Hitler stifled a giggle. Then his face grew serious.

"That could present a problem. Romsdorf has a very important post."

"Yes, *mein Führer.*"

"Not to mention that Romsdorf is extremely proud of his . . . manliness." Hitler stifled another giggle.

"Yes, *mein Führer.*"

"In fact," and he giggled out loud, "he fancies himself somewhat of a ladies' man."

Vierhaus felt comfortable enough to laugh along with Hitler.

"Poor old Romsdorf," said Hitler. "I pity the poor dancer. When our general finds out, the young man will be off to Dachau. Any other news?"

"A rather dull week, I'm afraid. There are the usual rumors about Röhm. He is becoming more of an embarrassment. Outrageous stories about his preference for young boys. He seems to be more brazen about it than ever. And I hear he is drinking more heavily than usual."

"He has always been a drunk and a queer," snapped Hitler.

Ernst Röhm was more than an embarrassment, he represented a deep, personal hurt to Hitler. He had brought his friend from the Beer Hall Putsch days back from South America and made him head of the brownshirts, one of the most powerful posts in Germany, giving him carte blanche to deal with the Reds and the Jews. But Röhm wanted more. Now he was actually challenging Hitler's authority and talking about running for president of Germany, a traitorous affront to his mentor.

"The problem is . . ." Vierhaus began.

"The problem is, the SA has six hundred thousand members!" Hitler roared, his voice rising to a near scream. He snapped his head angrily, took a deep breath, and began pacing. When he spoke again his voice was almost a whisper.

"The only way I can deal with this problem is with my own personal guards, Willie, but it will be another year before the *Schutzstaffel* has the proper strength for that." He waved his hand again. "I know, I know. Another year and he grows that much stronger." He stopped pacing and leaned toward Vierhaus, his eyes narrowing. "We cannot destroy the SA until my SS is stronger than they are. And that is the only way to deal with Röhm and his bullies. Destroy them."

"Yes, *mein Führer.*"

"But thank you for telling me. I must keep up with his . . . his perversions." His expression changed radically again, becoming more relaxed. He had said what he had to say about the SA.

"So," he said pleasantly. "I understand it was your man in the American Embassy who turned in Reinhardt."

"Yes, *mein Führer.* A porter. A *Judenhascher,* actually, but very reliable."

"Heinrich is a little put out," Hitler said, strolling around his desk, his hands clasped behind his back. "He would like to take credit for the whole affair. It annoys him that you have these *Judenhaschers* and special agents working for you."

"Did he complain, *mein Führer*?"

"No, no, no, no, of course not," Hitler answered, waving off the suggestion. "Heinrich is no fool. He knows it was my idea to set up your little unit."

Actually Vierhaus had come to Hitler with the idea for an elite unit within the SS but all of Hitler's close associates were accustomed to having the Führer take credit for good ideas. Hitler had treated the suggestion as a joke at first but finally he had given Vierhaus a small budget and permission to train five men. Vierhaus had managed, by conscripting stool pigeons and menial workers, to expand his unit to twenty-five or thirty.

He had begun the practice of using Germans of mixed blood, usually an eighth or sixteenth Jewish, as agents, promising them freedom from persecution as long as they were effective. Known as *Judenhascher,* Jewhunters, they were frequently used to gather information on other Jews, often spending weeks poring over family records, looking for a great-grandmother or second cousin who might have a trace of Jewish blood. Vierhaus turned the reports over to Himmler's SS and the files of information grew thicker every day, waiting for Himmler to put them to whatever dark use his mind might contrive.

Hitler laughed and slapped his hand on the table.

"You know what I like about you, Willie? You are a practical man. So, tell me more. Were you there when they interrogated Reinhardt?"

Vierhaus nodded.

"What did he tell us? What about the Black Lily?"

"He claimed he never heard of it."

The phone rang and Hitler whirled and snatched it off the hook. "No, no, no!" he yelled and slammed it back down. He spun back toward Vierhaus.

"He's a liar!" Hitler bellowed, his face turning red. His fist slammed down on the table. "Of course he knows about it! He helped start it!" He composed himself, taking a deep breath, then he began tapping his cheek with his forefinger. "It is important to crush these organizations quickly, Willie. These fanatics. Fanaticism is contagious. I want that to be your first priority. Break them. Break the Black Lily."

"Isn't that the job of the Gestapo, *mein Führer*?"

Hitler waved his hand frenetically in front of his face, shaking his head as he spoke. "Göring has other things to worry about. Do not concern yourself with politics."

"Yes, *mein Führer*. Reinhardt also told me something else interesting. The American I told you about, Keegan?"

"The *Ire*?"

"Irish-American. Apparently the deputy ambassador, Wallingford, tried to borrow Keegan's plane for Reinhardt's escape and Keegan refused."

"Ah, perhaps your instincts about him are correct."

"I made it my business to have a talk with Keegan early this morning. He is quite the cynic and I get the definite feeling that he is unhappy with things in America. He particularly distrusts bankers and businessmen, says they were the only winners in the war."

"True, quite true," Hitler said, his head bobbing in agreement. "What did you have in mind for Keegan?"

"I am not sure. He is very rich and quite independent.

Knows everybody—in the embassies, the military, government people, most of the royal families here and in England. A man like that, if he is sympathetic with your vision, *mein Führer,* could have many uses. He knows court secrets—who might be vulnerable to blackmail: homosexuals, bankrupts, influential people whose taste exceeds their bank account."

"I agree. Just be careful dealing with him," said Hitler. "Never trust Americans. Too idealistic."

"Yes, *mein Führer.*"

"What of *Siebenundzwanzig?*"

"His training goes very well. Ludwig reports that he is an excellent student. He learns quickly. Incidentally, I am trying something—it is a bit devious."

"Of course," Hitler leered. "What else would I expect from you?"

"I have introduced another student in the training course with Swan. Swan is not aware of this, of course, but the man will be his replacement if there should be an accident or if he gets caught. Swan thinks the new man is training for a totally different assignment. It is a good opportunity to compare them."

"I needn't tell you to be cautious in dealing with Twenty-seven," Hitler said, his face hardening into stern lines again. "He is a great catch but we could lose him if he becomes disillusioned—or if he thinks we do not have complete faith in him."

"I will keep that in mind, *mein Führer.* I am going down to visit the camp in person."

"Very good. I will be anxious to hear your report. Have you worked out the details of the operation?"

"I'll be ready when he is."

"Excellent. I'm proud of you, Willie."

"Thank you, *mein Führer.*"

"And, Willie, don't forget," He held up a single finger. "The Black Lily."

"Yes, *mein Führer. Heil Hitler.*"

"*Heil Hitler.*"

Swan plunged down the steep side of the mountain, the wind thundering in his ears. He was in total control of his downward pitch, his course so steep it was almost like leaping off a cliff. He ignored the danger of the drop run just as he ignored the beauty of the Alps surrounding him and the pain of the effort in calf, thigh and shoulder. He was totally concentrated, his eyes focused one hundred feet in front of him, scanning back and forth to check for boulders, small trees or other obstructions hidden by the deep snow. If he perceived any threat he altered his course as little as necessary to avoid it, never sacrificing speed as his skis skimmed the snow beneath him. He was racing against the stopwatch in his mind.

A mile away, near the base of the mountain, a tall, muscular man in white snow camouflage stood shin-deep in the snow, sweeping the side of Hummel Peak with his binoculars. He was nearly six-five and in excellent physical shape, deeply tanned from hours on the slopes. He was bald as a mountaintop with a long, triangular face and pale, analytical eyes. His only insignia was the silver SS eagle on his cap. Suddenly he stopped and backtracked an inch or two. The skier was a mere speck streaking down the side of the mountain.

"There he is," he said. "About halfway down. Good God, he must be doing seventy miles an hour."

Vierhaus watched the speck as it plunged down the steep, clean side of the tall Dolomite peak, then raised his binoculars. Through the glasses, he watched the black-clad sportsman as he sped down the slope without veering, snow showering in his wake.

"I hope he does not injure himself," Vierhaus said.

"That will not happen," the tall SS officer said. "Swan will never injure himself. Swan will never have an accident. He would not permit it."

"You don't like him, do you, Ludwig?" Vierhaus said.

"There is not much to like or dislike, actually," Ludwig answered. "He is very much a loner, never joins us for a beer at night. He's civil to his teachers and the other students but that is as far as he goes. He is totally dedicated to perfection."

Ludwig lowered his glasses for a moment.

"On the other hand, he is quite the actor. He actually outwitted the entire staff three or four times by disguising himself."

"Is that so?" Vierhaus said.

Ludwig raised the glasses again.

"He can even be quite charming when he is not himself," Ludwig added.

Confident, unswerving, the skier reached the bottom of the steep slope and disappeared into the trees at the base.

"I must say, you have picked the perfect spot for this training facility. Why did you pick the Dolomites?"

"Mostly for the snow. The mountains are capped year-round. And it is isolated. Nobody blunders onto this camp. The people in Millstadt think we are a border station. Italy is only twenty or thirty kilometers from here."

"It seems a pleasant village."

"Very friendly and totally isolated."

"Tell me more about Swan," Vierhaus said.

"Best student I ever had," the tall SS trainer said. "A very smart man. You tell him a thing once and he has learned it. He has already mastered everything my five instructors and I have taught him."

"You think he is ready to leave?"

Ludwig pondered the question for a moment. Vierhaus had recruited the colonel from the SD, the intelligence department of the SS, where he was considered too tall to be an effective field agent. It was an unfortunate loss to the SD for Ludwig was one of the shrewdest men Vierhaus had ever met. He was an honor graduate from the university in Berlin and an excellent judge of character. Vierhaus had put him in charge of training—or eliminating—the agents Vierhaus recruited and Ludwig had devised a program which was both physically and mentally exhausting, designed to break the toughest of men.

"Perhaps," Ludwig said finally. "Perhaps a little longer. Just to make sure he's perfect. After all, we originally planned the course for one year. It has only been seven months."

"There is no rush," Vierhaus said. "Any task, understand Ludwig, *any* task! He must be at ease in any task. How about attitude?"

"Cold as an iceberg. Nothing bothers him. He survived three weeks alone in the mountains and we set him loose with nothing but his weapons. I honestly believe he *gained* weight out there."

"Weapons?"

"A remarkable marksman and he wields a knife like a circus performer. The Okinawan, Ashita, says Swan is the best jujitsu student he has ever had. The man has hands of iron."

"Will he kill if the time comes?"

"In the blink of an eye. He would kill his own mother if it were expedient."

"Interesting. And you think he will follow orders, this loner?"

"He will do whatever is necessary to complete his mission. Quite simply, he has turned himself into a machine."

"And those things you cannot teach a man?"

"He is sly, wily, quick, dangerous. An adroit liar. And like I said, quite an actor. He is just paranoid enough to be properly cautious. And as you can see, not only an expert skier, but absolutely fearless. Quite a find, *Herr Professor*."

"And the other one? Kraft?"

"He has his specialties. A quiet killer that one, but not as versatile as Swan. He is almost as good in some areas."

"How canny is he, Ludwig?"

"Canny? Not in a class with Swan. Let me give you an example. We had an exercise—to blow up a warehouse which was very heavily guarded. Three of the men were caught trying to invade the building but as far as we could tell, Swan never went near the place. Then he came to me and told me to get the guards out of the place, it was going to blow up. Two hours later, boom! It was gone. Pulverized!"

"How did he do it?"

"A rat bomb."

"Really?" Vierhaus said with surprise.

"You are familiar with the rat bomb?"

"I have heard of it," Vierhaus said after a moment.

"He crawled up the sewer line under the place and set the trap. He used Limburger cheese to make sure the rat would smell it. It worked like a charm."

"Do any of the other trainees show Swan's promise?"

Swan shot out of the thicket of pines at the foot of the mountain, leaning forward on bent knees to keep up his speed, moving soundlessly toward them.

"*Nein.* They are good, but not like this one coming here. I tell you, Professor, he is frighteningly efficient."

"Does he scare you, Ludwig?" Vierhaus asked casually.

Colonel Ludwig smiled and shook his head. "Nobody scares me, Professor, I am beyond that. No, I marvel at him. He was only here a week and I realized he could bypass desensitization training. My God, he could teach it! He is the perfect SD officer. What the Führer *dreams* of, this man *is.*"

"Would you like to go up against him?"

Ludwig stared quizzically at Vierhaus for a moment or two before he nodded slowly. "*Ja.* An interesting challenge. He has an uncanny ability to focus on a single objective, to make instant decisions based on knowledge, instinct *and* logic, and react immediately. Most men I know in this business operate on gut instinct. Logic rarely enters into it."

"Does he learn from his mistakes?"

"Swan does not make mistakes."

"What are his weaknesses, Ludwig?"

"His only weakness that I can determine is impatience. When he learns something he means to test himself immediately."

"Hmm. That could be a serious problem. This man may be undercover for years before he is activated."

"Then you will have to find other ways to keep him occupied. He has a taste for danger."

Vierhaus began to chuckle.

"Is something funny?" Ludwig asked.

"I was just thinking, wouldn't it be ironic if we have *over* trained him."

"It isn't possible to be overtrained, *Herr Professor,*" Ludwig said. "Kraft and the other three in training are excellent prospects but it would take two, three years for them to be in Swan's class and by that time God knows how good he would be."

"I congratulate you, Colonel," Vierhaus said, shaking the tall man's hand. "You are doing remarkable work here. So what is next?"

"A competition."

"A competition?"

"Yes. I am going to pit Swan against Kraft on a very difficult climb and race."

"Why?"

Ludwig shrugged. "Just to see who comes in first. To see how they react in a challenge situation, under actual stress. There are some things even training can't imitate. It should be quite revealing."

"But dangerous, Colonel, if your training is as good as I suspect, they could be *too* keen on winning. They might take unnecessary chances."

"I agree," Ludwig said with a smile. "But that is part of it, Professor, to test their judgment. It is not just winning, it is a test of their skill and their judgment. It will certainly be interesting, don't you think?"

"A bit diabolical."

"Oh yes."

"Do they know about this contest yet?"

"They never know anything in advance, Professor. Surprise is part of the training."

"I wonder if Swan suspects that Kraft is being trained as his backup."

"God knows what he suspects—or thinks."

Swan swept across the remaining half mile and cut sharply to a stop a foot in front of Vierhaus and Ludwig. His breath was even and unlabored as it curled from his lips. Ice caked the rims of his goggles and the collar of his jacket. He shoved the goggles up on his forehead and nodded. Vierhaus realized that he was seeing Swan, undisguised, for the first time. His straw-colored hair was long and uncut and he wore a full beard. His eyes were turquoise blue and as intense as a hawk's. He wore no hat. Small knots of melting ice glistened from his long locks and his facial hair.

Quite a handsome devil, Vierhaus thought to himself.

"*Herr Professor,* good to see you again. It has been a while."

"And you, Colonel Swan," Vierhaus answered, shaking his hand. "That was quite an impressive display."

"*Ja.* About a second and a half under my last speed, I should say."

Ludwig looked at his stopwatch. "Actually 1.2 seconds," he said and laughed. "If you go any faster, Swan, we'll have to supply you with wings."

"I thought perhaps we might have dinner tonight at my hotel, just the two of us," Vierhaus suggested.

"I really must decline, Willie," Swan replied. "The next day or two could be difficult ones and I must be in top form."

"Oh? Why so?" Ludwig asked innocently.

"Time for the match between Kraft and me, isn't it?" Swan answered. "I cannot afford distractions." And laughing, he headed for the base cabin.

"How did he know that?" Vierhaus asked. "I thought it was to be a surprise."

"*Ja,*" Ludwig answered with obvious annoyance. "So did I."

The cabin at the base of the mountain was small, with two bedrooms, a kitchen and the large living room which was the planning and lecture center. One entire wall was covered with a six-foot-square detailed map of the local area.

Kraft was smaller than Swan but huskier, with a bull neck and bulging arms that swelled his cotton sweatshirt. He was clean shaven and his dark hair was trimmed close to the scalp. He sat at rigid attention, in sharp contrast to Swan who was slouched back in his chair. Kraft had given up a promising career as an Olympic skiier to join the Six Foxes. He was a former honor student, fluent in English, French and Italian.

Swan ignored his adversary. Instead he stared with narrowed eyes at Ludwig, listening to every word his tutor said.

"This is the exercise," Ludwig was saying. "You will climb the side of the Hummel, here." He used a pointer to show where the exercise was to begin and its eventual course. "You will go up the west face, which is about thirty-five hundred feet, then cross here to the back side and ski down the reverse face. The objective is to retrieve this flag before your opponent."

He held up a small red Nazi banner with a black swastika in its center.

"Will we be scored on anything other than speed?" Kraft asked.

"The object is to retrieve the flag," Ludwig repeated. "You will have fifteen minutes to study the chart. That's all. *Heil Hitler.*"

"*Heil Hitler,*" the two men said in unison, raising their arms in the Nazi salute. Ludwig and Vierhaus left the cabin. Swan and Kraft studied the chart in silence, Kraft scribbling notes to himself while Swan stood close to the map and stared at it without expression. *This exercise is a chess game*, he said to himself. *A very dangerous chess game.* The back slope was a glacier formed by melting snow in the warm August afternoons and then refrozen at night.

There were two courses down the slope. The one on the west side of the glacier was faster but far more dangerous with a deadfall of at least a thousand feet along half its length. The eastern trail had sporadic deadfalls and a natural shelf halfway down to break the run. The two trails merged halfway down the slope. After that it was a drop run all the way down—a piece of cake. The crucial decision would be whether to risk the run down the western wall or cross to the east side.

Ludwig's instructions were simple—retrieve the flag. That was the operation, so the test was one of skill, intelligence and speed, not heroics.

He concentrated on the map. Since they were climbing up the west face, he would have to cross over the glacier to get to the east run, a dangerous task in itself. One slip and he would plunge 1,500 feet down the glacier to certain death.

Ludwig had devised a devilish contest.

"Well, Swan, good luck. May the best man win," Kraft said, offering his hand.

"The best man is going to win," Swan said without looking at him. Ignoring Kraft's outstretched hand, he turned abruptly and left the cabin.

*   *   *

By noon Swan had reached the crest on the back side of the Hummel. By his calculations, he was two or three minutes ahead of Kraft. He wasted thirty seconds, staring out across the valley, focusing his mind on the map. The peak of the Hummel broke away to the east while the west run, the more dangerous of the two, started only fifty or so yards away around the ledge of the mountain. Skiing across the glacier on the back side was more than risky, it was foolish. And there was another factor, the wind. It howled madly around him, twisting the snow into whirlwinds. But by skiing around the front of the crest he could cross to the other side on good powder. Two hundred yards across, he figured, and Kraft was closing on him.

Retrieve the flag. Ludwig's only instructions.

He jumped off and skied around the front side of the peak, headed across to the other side, leaning forward on his skis with his back to the harsh wind, letting it carry him across. He would force Kraft to take the dangerous west run. He sped across the crest, cut sharply as he reached the east side and whipped around the peak to the back side, stopping a few feet from a precipitous deadfall.

He was standing on a small ledge just above the trail down the side of the glacier. He studied the trail for a moment, watching the wind sweep the snow out across the frozen river. *Good powder*, he thought. Below him the glacier spread almost the entire width of the mountain's face: gleaming, melting ice sliced with narrow, deep fissures formed by rivers of melting ice and snow.

Swan looked up toward the peak of the Hummel, thirty yards or so above him. A wide and dangerous overhang of snow clustered near the crest of the mountain. Rivers of melting snow poured from its jagged rim to form the deep cuts in the glacial face of the mountain. Here and there deep cracks appeared in the broad snow overhang.

An avalanche waiting to happen, thought Swan.

He looked to the west. The natural path coursed down through the trees, a steep run, almost vertical in places. Directly below Swan, his trail was hampered by boulders and stunted trees. It was a slower run but safer. From the rim of his eye he saw Kraft emerge on the far side of the glacier. Kraft had achieved the peak, too, and only seconds behind him. But now

Kraft had an open avenue to the faster, more dangerous run. Would he take it? Or lose valuable time chasing Swan to the easier side of the slope?

He will operate on pure instinct, thought Swan. Kraft had made his decision before reaching the crest, basing it on the maps. Now he was cornered. He could not afford to cross the melting river of ice that separated them. He has to make the western run. And as he watched, Kraft hopped in the air, swung his skis around and started down the western face. A fatal decision.

Swan jumped into the air, shoved himself over the ledge with his poles and started straight down the east run. Below him was a straight course halfway down the steep slope, then a ridge of boulders formed a natural shelf that spread east to west halfway across the mountain's face. He plunged toward the shelf, keenly aware that Kraft was already seconds ahead of him on the opposite side of the glacier. To his right, steep cliffs raced past. He watched for patches of ice that might throw him over as he vaulted down the narrow trail. Far to his left he could see Kraft, seconds ahead of him, fighting the wind as he raced along the dangerous west trail. Swan reached the shelf and leveled off, twisting to a stop.

Kraft was still vaulting ahead but he was coming to a flat spot in the run. He would have to cross a hundred feet or so of glacier at the end of the run to get to the final slope. He watched Kraft slow his downward run as he approached the dangerous path across the ice river. *He'll have to stop for a moment and study the roll of the ice*, Swan thought. *He's not stupid enough to run it blind*.

Swan reached into his jacket and took out a Luger. He aimed it back up the mountain toward the snow that clung to the peak of the mountain and fired a shot, then a second, then a third.

Below him, Kraft twisted sideways, leaning into the mountain, felt his skis slapping the rough snow at the edge of the glacier. He stopped a few feet from the edge of the deadfall. The valley sprawled a thousand feet below him. He was out of breath and his goggles were cloudy. He dropped them around his neck and studied the roll of the glacier.

Then he heard a shot. And another. And a third. He looked up the mountain. What the hell was Swan doing?

The huge drift on the peak of the Hummel groaned in the wind, shuddered as the sound waves of the shots swept up to it. The cracks widened and popped like skyrockets. Weakened, the great drift of snow suddenly broke loose. A wave of snow, ten feet deep and fifty yards wide, suddenly fell away and thundered down the mountain.

Swan shoved himself off the shelf with his poles and dropped down on the broad slope. Leaning as far forward as he could, knees bent, he pitched down the slope, ahead of the wall of the snow, veering away from the glacier and hugging the very edge of the eastern deadfall.

Kraft looked up at the thundering wave of snow that rumbled down toward him. Trapped, he made his move, his skis rattling over the crusted glacier bed as he skied downward and sideways, ever closer to the dropoff. He was almost across when the skis whipped out from under him. He fell, grasping desperately for a ridge, a fissure, anything to stop his slide toward the edge of the cliff. His fingers dug into the ice. The sharp edges peeled away his gloves and sliced into his fingers before they dug into a crack in the ice and stopped his slide.

He looked up in terror as the freight train of snow above descended on him with fury, swept into him, filled his mouth and blinded him a moment before it swept him over the side. Lost in the great fountain of snow, he plunged a thousand feet to the floor of the valley.

Swan never looked back. He could hear the terrifying roar of the avalanche behind him but he kept skiing faster and faster, eyes ever alert for obstacles as he swept out onto the last slope, rocketing toward the base of the mountain. He was dangerously close to losing control as he sped down faster and faster, using every muscle to keep from falling. He didn't think about the avalanche behind him. He just kept going. . . .

Swan pulled his goggles down around his neck and shook the snow from his blond mane. Squinting in the bright sunlight, his eyes afire with excitement, he said, "By God, did you see that? I was only a few feet in front of that snow slide." He looked back up the mountainside. "Where's Kraft?" he asked.

"He didn't make it," Ludwig said without emotion. "The avalanche caught him. He went over the west face."

"Bloody shame," Swan said. "Good man, Kraft. But he should never have tried the west run."

"Why do you say that?" Vierhaus asked.

"Much too unpredictable," Swan answered. "In this hot sun that summer snow is unstable. A strong wind could have kicked it off. And the run itself was too risky. A serious error in judgment. Your instructions were to retrieve the flag, not get killed."

"Is that why you chose the east face?" Ludwig asked.

"Yes. It was dangerous enough, but not suicidal. The mission was to get to the top and then come down as quickly as possible, to beat Kraft but not kill myself doing it. Martyrs don't win wars, gentlemen, they are merely pretty faces in history books. Kraft made a fatal error in judgment. My job was to capitalize on his mistakes, not worry about him."

"I thought I heard pistol shots just before the slide started," Ludwig said.

"Really?" said Swan. "Probably the drift cracking up. It sounded like an explosion."

He unbuttoned his jacket. "My mission was to take the flag at the finish line, Colonel," he said, taking the standard from under his jacket and folding it neatly. He handed it to Ludwig.

"My compliments, sir."

"Any further questions about Swan's qualifications?" Ludwig asked.

"No," Vierhaus said. "No questions. But I want you to give him this." He handed Ludwig a slender, solid gold Dunhill cigarette lighter about three inches long. It had smooth sides and a small, hand-carved wolf's head, the mascot of the SS, on top.

Ludwig rubbed his thumb up the side of the lighter. It was almost sensual to the touch.

"It is a graduation present," Vierhaus said. "Tell him to keep it always. As a reminder of who he is."

"So. You think he is ready now?"

"*Oh yes,*" Vierhaus said with a smile. "I think he is ready."

BOOK TWO

"The fates lead the willing.
and drag the unwilling."

Seneca

She sat on a tall stool on the corner of the tiny stage with only a pastel spot on her, a piano, tenor sax and bass providing subtle background for a voice that hardly needed it. She had no arrangements, every song was improvised. The lights darkened in the small club, the announcer introduced her, there was a piano trill and the soft light faded in as she started singing.

> *"I'm not much to look at,*
>   *Nothin' to see,*
>   *Just glad I'm living,*
>   *And happy to be,*
>   *I got a man*
>   *Crazy for me*
>   *He's funny that way."*

She sang in English and her accent added to the allure. Within a few notes she owned the room.

Keegan sat at the same table for hours every night. He sent two dozen roses every day, no card, assuming that sooner or later she would connect the flowers with the crazy American who came every night and sat through every performance—but she ignored him. Finally he attempted to arrange a meeting only to be told by the manager that she did not like Americans. Keegan had never before been spurned by a woman so resolutely, and he was so totally discouraged by her lack of response that he stopped going to the club.

The approaching winter became the winter of his discontent. It was a mild winter and Keegan spent most of it in the south of France in a small town called Grenois. He had decided to winter one of his racehorses there, to get her ready for the summer season at Longchamp. The mare had shown promise on the American tracks as a two-year-old, now Keegan wanted to see what she would do on the European circuit. Keegan's trainer was Alouise Jacquette, Al Jack for short, from Larose in the Delta country of Louisiana. The Delta was known for quarterhorse racing, so named because the horses are flagged off and run wide-open down a quarter-mile straight track. After ten years, Al Jack graduated to thoroughbred racing where he became known as a keen judge of championship horses and a superb trainer. He was six feet two inches tall and had the posture of a West Point cadet. He dressed in a suit, vest, tie and Panama hat at all times, even when he was in the training ring with the horses. Al Jack was a man who believed that racing was a gentleman's game and he dressed accordingly.

"When they speak of mixed blood," he would tell you proudly, "they speak of Al Jack. I am one-quarter Cherokee Indian, two-quarters Cajun and one-quarter Negro, and the only one who knows more about horses than Al Jack is God himself."

When he was working, Al Jack had little to say. He would express approval or disapproval by the tone of his chuckles. Al Jack was a man who chuckled all the time. If he told you the world was about to end he would chuckle while he gave you the bad news. After a while Keegan learned to tell which were good news chuckles and which were bad news chuckles. There was also a disaster chuckle but Keegan had only heard it once, when Al Jack discovered they did not have crawfish in France. Luckily, he soon discovered that snails were a reasonable substitute and became addicted to escargots. So they were up at dawn every day, working out the horses until late afternoon when they would walk to the village and stuff themselves on escargots, washing it down with Châteauneuf-du-Pape.

"Got us a winner, *mon ami*," Al Jack would say in his Cajun patois. "This lady goin' take the purse every time she go outa that gate."

"If she doesn't, it's off to the glue factory with her," Keegan would answer and they would laugh and order more snails.

"You know my dream, Kee? My dream is that I save up enough money to buy her first foal when she retires."

"You got it, Al. Call it a bonus. When she starts losing her speed, we'll breed her."

"That's a damn generous thing t'do, Kee, but I do believe I'd feel better paying for the pony."

"We'll talk about it later."

It was a pleasant enough time, the days filled with hard work, horse talk and good food, but he could not get the singer out of his mind. He never talked about her but she had his heart in her hand and was never far from his thoughts. He and Bert spent the Christmas holiday in Spain trout fishing, then Rudman was off to Ethiopia for a month to report on the country many believed would be Mussolini's first conquest, his dispatches appearing almost daily on the front page of the *Trib*. From there it was on to Spain for two months to report on the civil war everyone felt was imminent. Rudman's style continued to become more formal, more subjective, tougher. With each dispatch he seemed to be more masterful at interpreting the volatile politics of Europe for his readers. His fixation on Hitler, the Nazi movement and the advent of fascism in Germany, Italy and Spain earned him a growing reputation as one of Europe's most respected correspondents. Keegan spent a month skiing in the Swiss Alps after Rudman left, spent a few weeks in Berlin, avoiding the Kit Kat and doing the usual party rounds, frequently bumping into the little hunchback, Vierhaus, Hitler's personal gossip, who was always pleasant to the point of obsequiousness. Then Keegan returned to France.

In early March, Keegan and Al Jack moved to Deauville, where they drove the few miles to the beach every morning to let the filly run in the surf, strengthening her legs and building her endurance for the longer European tracks. Keegan followed his friend's career avidly and was delighted when Rudman finally returned to Paris and came to visit them.

"She learnin' to run backwards," Al Jack said proudly, since most of the European races were run from right to left, the opposite direction from the way Al Jack had trained her in the states.

"So, tell me about it," Keegan asked Rudman as they sat in the dunes watching Al Jack put the mare through her paces. "What's Ethiopia like?"

"Hot, dismal, dirty, dry, sand everywhere—in your hair, your eyes, your coffee."

"Is there going to be a war?"

Rudman nodded emphatically. "Within a year the Lion of Judah will be in an Italian cage."

"That's depressing. How about Spain? How are the ladies?"

"You know the type. They don't get insulted when you invite them home and they don't get mad when you don't invite them to stay for breakfast. Spain's very depressing. Civil war's just around the corner. It's going to be brutal."

"That's the way war is, Bert."

"I don't mean that way. Listen Kee, I saw an airfield outside of Madrid with a couple of dozen Heinkel bombers parked in hangars. The Loyalists are all using German weapons. Wait and see, Spain's going to turn into Hitler's personal testing ground."

"You're getting to be quite the political oracle, aren't you, pal?"

"Trying."

"We got some fine horse there, boss," Al Jack said, climbing up the dune and standing ramrod straight in his Sunday finest, his cap pulled down to his eyebrows, as Keegan and Rudman watched Rave On romp in the surf, her breath steaming from flared nostrils as she bucked and jumped in the chilly water.

In mid-April they were ready to move on to Paris where she was stabled at Longchamp, perhaps the most elegant racetrack in the world. Most of the tracks—Chantilly, St. Cloud de Maisons, Évry and Longchamp—were within forty miles of Paris. The plan was to run her in *La Coupe de Maisons,* then on to Chantilly for the French Derby and after that to Longchamp for the opening of the season in May, building up to the prestigious *Grand Prix de Paris* in June and the big one, *L'Arc de Triomphe,* in September.

Once they had Rave On settled at the stables in Paris, Keegan joined Rudman in Berlin.

"You're not going to believe it," Rudman said when they met for dinner. He was brimming with excitement. "I was just offered chief of *The New York Times* bureau here."

"You're kidding! Will you take it?"

"Take it! Hell, it's the plum job in Europe. Goebbels has been threatening to lift my visa, now I'll be too important for the Nazis to throw out."

"Be careful, buddy," Keegan said, and he was obviously concerned. "These bastards'll kill you."

"They wouldn't dare," Rudman said with a grin.

He went off to the States for a month of indoctrination and returned looking fit with the latest news and gossip from home. He was full of enthusiasm for Roosevelt and the future of America and had glowing reports on the Broadway season, babbling on about the new dancer, Fred Astaire, the star of Cole Porter's new show; about James Hilton's novel *Lost Horizons,* which he had read on the boat over; and André Malraux's *Man's Fate,* which he read on the way back; about a movie called *King Kong,* about an ape that attacks the Empire State Building; and an animated cartoon based on the "Three Little Pigs." He had also fallen madly in love with Greta Garbo after seeing her in two movies. For the first time since leaving, Keegan felt a tinge of homesickness. But the excitement of the coming racing season at Longchamp and Rudman's return soon dispelled that. His horse, Rave On, was looking good and timing well. Rudman would not start the new job until midsummer, so they would have two months to pal around.

"Ever feel like going home for good?" Keegan asked.

"I can't, my future's here," Rudman said. "You know what my editor at the *Times* said? He said I have a keener perception of the political dynamics of Europe than any other reporter alive."

"Good. Can we have that for dinner?"

"You son of a bitch."

"Well, hell, you ought to. You have politics for breakfast, lunch and dinner. You've let your social life go to hell."

"I see things keep getting worse here. Now they're boycotting Jewish stores," said Rudman. "Did you know Jews have been banned from business? Even from schools."

"It's no secret, they brag about what they're doing every day in that Nazi rag, *The People's Observer.*"

"Know what I heard today that they're *not* bragging about?"

"Hitler's a transvestite," Keegan said.

"Probably, but that's not it. I hear they built a prison camp outside Munich for political prisoners and they're building twenty more—*twenty*—just for Jews. I got a source who says they've arrested more than a hundred thousand people and shipped them to these camps without a trial or anything. They're starving prisoners, beating them."

"You better make sure about that," Keegan advised. "Seeing's believing."

"They don't conduct tours for the press."

"I'm just saying you've got great credibility. Don't give Goebbels a chance to shoot you down."

"What's to doubt anyway? We're talking about a whole country that doesn't have a moral bone in its collective body. It isn't politics, anymore. It's gone beyond that. I'm sure you're sick of all this anyway, you've been living with it every day. What's been happening with you? Still mooning over that singer?"

"Who says I'm mooning over anybody?" Keegan demanded.

"C'mon, Kee, you've been dragging your tail for a year over that girl. Hell, she's probably got a beau, maybe she's even married by now."

"She's not married and she doesn't have a *beau*," he said, mocking Rudman's use of the antiquated term.

"So—you *have* been keeping track of her?"

"I heard it somewhere."

"Uh huh."

"Get off the singer, okay?"

"Sure. I just never saw you knuckle under like this before."

"Knuckle under?"

"You send her flowers for a week, she brushes you off, you give up."

"I didn't give up."

"What would you call it?"

"I lost interest."

"Francis, this is your old pal, remember? You act like a lovesick drugstore cowboy."

"Damn it!"

"Okay, okay. But if it were me and I was swooning over this dame . . ."

"She's not a dame—and drop it!"

"Hey, it's dropped." They sat in silence for a moment, then Bert said, "But, you know, if she started getting the flowers again and she realized how serious you are and tenacious . . ."

"Rudman!"

"I know, drop it."

Silence fell over the table for a couple of minutes.

"I would like to hear her sing," Rudman said.

Keegan glared at him.

"Hey, she's an entertainer," Rudman said, his hands held out at his sides. "So let's go be entertained."

The minute she started singing, Keegan was sunk.

"Some day he'll come along,
 The man I love . . ."

Rudman watched Keegan as he sat totally enthralled.

The next day Rudman sent her an enormous spring bouquet and charged it to Keegan. No card. They returned to the club that night, and the next, and the next. And each day Rudman sent more flowers. At the end of the week he told Keegan what he had done.

"She sings like a bird and if you're not going to pursue her, I am," he threatened.

And so it started over again, only this time Jenny Gould sensed his persistence. Out of curiosity she asked around and found out who he was. Every day for a week she received two dozen roses and every night the American and his friend reserved the same table at the edge of the stage at the Kit Kat, although he made no attempt to contact her or speak to her. He just sat and stared and applauded. Then one afternoon he showed up at her door.

"It's lunchtime." He was as awkward as a schoolboy. "You have to eat. I mean, you'll get weak and faint in the middle of a song if you don't eat. And I just happened to be driving by and . . ." And she looked out at the car and back at him and finally sighed and took his arm and he led her out into the lovely late spring day.

He had arranged a picnic in a small park near the Opera House with a vase of flowers, champagne and sandwiches of *Kasseler Rippchen,* the little smoked and pickled pork loin she discovered he loved, frankfurter sausages, boiled eggs and sauerkraut, and for dessert there were several kinds of pastries. He had a windup Victrola and several radio transcriptions a friend

had sent him and they sat on the blanket and listened to Billie
Holiday sing "My Man" and "Stormy Monday Blues." He was
gracious and interested in her and funny and delightful and
caring, things she least expected of this man everyone described
as a rich, reckless American playboy. After that day they were
together constantly. She moved into a small flat on the outskirts
of Berlin soon after they met. They spent the days together and
at night he sat faithfully at his customary table and listened to
her sing. When he finally left to return to Paris for the opening
of the racing season she lasted only three days without him.
There had been three and four phone calls a day and finally she
called him late one night.

"I have never been this sad in my life," she told him.

"Come to Paris, Jenny," he said. "Let's give it a real
chance."

"But my job . . ."

"With a voice like yours, you'll never have to worry about
a job."

The next day he sent the plane for her.

The tan filly snorting like an engine thundered by them, her
long legs snapping out, the jockey perched way forward, almost
on her neck, going light on the whip. Keegan popped the button
on his stopwatch as she streaked by. His face brightened.

Jenny's eyes gleamed with excitement. "What do you
think?" she asked.

Keegan studied his stopwatch. "Not bad, not bad at all. If
it doesn't rain she just might take the roses." He looked up at
the bright, cloudless sky. "But she's not a mudder so pray that
the skies stay clear."

"A really gorgeous filly," Rudman said. "Where did you get
her?"

"Picked her up at a claiming race at Aqueduct."

"Maybe you've got another Cavalcade on your hands."

"She's good," said Keegan, "but I don't think she's got the
stuff to be a Triple Crown winner."

"She looks so beautiful, stretching out those long legs of
hers," Jenny said. "Why did you give her such a ridiculous
name?"

"What would you call her?" Keegan laughed. "Honey Bunch?"

"Something other than Rave On."

"Rave On's a great name," Keegan said.

"It does not make a bit of sense to me."

"It's an American expression," said Rudman. "And you're right, it doesn't make any sense."

"It's not supposed to," Keegan said. "I once knew a race-horse named John J. Four Eyes. Now *that* doesn't make sense."

Jenny looked hopelessly at Rudman who waved off the re-mark with a grin. "I can't begin to explain that one," he said as they walked across the infield of Longchamp racetrack toward the gate. The jockey, a Parisian whose name was Jaimie Foulard, slid out of the saddle and landed in front of Keegan.

"C'est magnifique, c'est wonderful!" He said enthusiastically.

"She can win, can't she?" Keegan asked with some confidence.

"Qué será," he said with a shrug, then winked.

They walked back to the stables and watched Al Jack, who was wearing a white linen suit, wash the filly down and brush her out. He did so without getting a spot on the suit.

"You luck out on this l'il ma'mselle," Al Jack chuckled. "Yes suh, you reached in the jar an' you come up with a gold marble."

"You reached in the jar, Al Jack," said Keegan. "We'll know how golden the l'il old marble is after the third race."

Al Jack looked up and smiled.

"Ma'mselle will give it all, Kee, you can deposit that in the bank. If she don't win, it just isn't in the cards. This lady puts her heart in the pot when she enters the gate."

Jenny softly stroked the filly's long nose. "Like velvet," she said with a look of wonderment.

"Tell you what, Al Jack. If she wins today, she's yours," Keegan said.

"What you say, Mistah Kee!"

"She's yours. I never saw anybody love a horse as much as you love that one."

"No, no way, suh," Al Jack, shaking his head. He wasn't chuckling. "Why, hell, *ami,* I couldn't pay her feed bill."

"I'll cover you for the season, you pay me back with your

purses. You can winter her on the farm in Kentucky and I'll take her first foal when she retires."

Al Jack broke down, laughing, tears bursting out of his eyes. "Why, I don't rightly know what to say."

Keegan smiled at him. "You've already said it, friend," he said, patting the trainer on the shoulder. Al Jack turned to the horse.

"*Hear* that, ma'mselle? You must win today. If you never won a race before or since, you got to go straight today. You hear what I say, lady?"

"That was one helluva thing to do, Kee," Rudman said as they headed back toward the parking area.

"Yes," Jenny said. "It was beautiful."

"I wouldn't own the horse if it wasn't for him," Keegan said, waving off their praise and opening the morning paper. "He picked her. He made her a winner. You got to be involved if you're in the racing game and Al Jack lives for it. It's just a hobby with me. Anyway, I wanted to share my luck."

"What luck?" Jenny asked.

"Being here with you," Keegan said with a broad grin, then he saw Rudman's photograph in the paper. "Hey, you made page two with a photo," Keegan said, showing them the story announcing Rudman's appointment as Berlin bureau chief.

It was a perfectly adequate sketch, recounting the usual biographical data, most of which Keegan already knew. Rudman was from Middleton, Ohio. His father owned a clothing store and had for thirty years, his mother was a housewife. No brothers or sisters. He had a journalism degree from Columbia University and was in Europe on a graduation trip when America entered the war. Keegan learned two new things about Rudman from the article; he had written his first dispatch for the *Herald Tribune* on speculation, having hitched a ride into combat with the Rainbow Division of the U.S. Army and covering their first encounter with the Germans during the Aisne-Marne drive, coverage that was good enough to earn him a correspondent's job at the age of twenty-three. He had also done some wrestling in college.

Keegan looked Rudman up and down. "You don't look like a wrestler to me," he said.

"Oh? And just what's a wrestler supposed to look like?"

"You know, thick neck, a chest like Mae West, shoulders like an elephant, that kind of thing."

Rudman nodded slowly. "Uh huh. With a dumb look on his face? You left that out."

"Yeah, that too. I mean, you're no skin and bones but you don't look like any wrestler."

"That's a very prejudiced attitude," Rudman said rather loftily."

"What do you mean, prejudiced?"

"To you all wrestlers are the same. They all have thick necks, their chests are popping through their shirts and they have a collective IQ of four. That's a prejudice. Not an important one but a prejudice just the same."

"You're a real trick," said Keegan. "I don't know anybody else who could turn a discussion of wrestling into a lecture on bigotry."

"Also they left out that I play a mean ukulele."

"Thanks for warning us."

"Well, anyway, it's great, Bert," Keegan said. "Think about it, here we are at the big social event of the Paris season. It's almost mandatory to show up if you have any social standing at all and here we are with a famous person."

"Right," Rudman said, half embarrassed. He tapped Jenny's arm. "Now that gent over there in the double-breasted tweed suit and the thick mustache studying the form? He's famous. That's H. G. Wells, a very important writer."

"I know who H. G. Wells is, silly. We do read in Germany, you know. Look at those two SS in their uniforms. That makes me sick."

Two German SS officers in their formal black uniforms were stalking the crowd, dope sheets in hand. They stopped to talk to a well-dressed couple.

"That tall one?" Rudman said bitterly. "That's Reinhard von Meister. Believe it or not, he's a bloody Rhodes scholar."

He nodded toward the taller of the two, a captain, who was lean to the point of being emaciated, with intimidating, vulture-like features and blue eyes so pale they were almost cobalt, all of which seemed appropriate with the uniform.

"He's the military attaché to the German ambassador here. Actually he's nothing but a damn *Spion* and everybody knows it."

"Who's the old fud with the young wife talking to him?" Keegan asked, nodding toward a couple on the far side of the paddock.

"She's not his wife, she's his daughter. That's Colin Willoughby, *Sir* Colin Willoughby, used to write a society gossip column for the *Manchester Guardian* called 'Will o' the Wisp.' "

Sir Colin Willoughby was a somewhat stuffy Britisher, trim, handsome in a dull sort of way, his mustache trimmed and waxed, his fingers manicured. He held himself painfully erect, his posture military, his attitude full of arched-eyebrow superiority. He was elegantly dressed in the blue double-breasted suit and red tie that seemed to be the uniform of proper Englishmen that spring and his silver hair was trimmed perfectly.

His daughter, Lady Penelope Traynor the widow, was equally as stunning. Her posture painfully correct, her features classic from the perfect, straight nose and pale-blue eyes to petulant mouth, she was almost a gendered reflection of her father. Like him, she had a cool, tailored, untouchable air that detracted from her natural beauty. Only her red hair, which was longer than the fashion and tied in the back with a bright, red bow, was a concession to femininity.

"So that's old 'Will o' the Wisp,' " Keegan said. "I've been reading his trash for years."

"He's given up trash. He's become a political soothsayer. 'Will o' the Wisp' is now 'The Willow Report.' Old Willoughby's been through it. His wife died two years ago and the daughter's husband was killed last year."

"I remember that," said Keegan. "He got killed at the Cleveland air races."

"Right. Tony Traynor, he was an ace in the war, knocked down twelve or thirteen kites. She's Willoughby's assistant now, goes everywhere with him."

"And he's covering politics at Longchamp race track?"

Rudman shrugged. "Maybe they're on holiday like me."

"Maybe she's your type," Keegan said. "Why don't you give her a fling."

"Not that one. She's all iceberg," said Bert.

"Well, you know what they say, only the tip shows," Keegan said with a wink. "Eighty percent is under the surface."

"Believe me, this one is ice to the core," Rudman said.

"The ultimate English snob. Come on, I'll introduce you. Let's see if he acknowledges my appointment."

Rudman led Keegan through the crowd toward them.

"*Bonjour,* Sir Colin, good to see you again," he said.

"Well, Rudman, good to see you. Been a while," Willoughby said with a condescending smile.

"These are my friends, Jennifer Gould and Francis Keegan," Rudman said. "Sir Colin Willoughby and his daughter, Lady Penelope Traynor."

"A pleasure," Keegan said, shaking Willoughby's hand. Lady Traynor regarded Keegan with aloof contempt, as she might regard a train porter or restaurant waitress. At another time, Keegan might have been attracted by her aura of inaccessibility but now it annoyed him, as did Sir Colin. As in Bert Rudman's case, events had altered Willoughby's career, elevating him from a kind of society gossip to a political observer. But whereas Rudman dealt with the reality of Hitler, Willoughby pontificated, his rampant editorializing devoid of even a semblance of objectivity.

"I see you've been to Africa and Spain," Willoughby said, "Very enterprising. Is it true you're to take over the *Times* bureau in Berlin?"

"Yes."

"Hitler is simply full of himself right now," Willoughby said dourly. "He's full of his success. In a few months he will realize he must conform to a more moral world viewpoint. I think the man thirsts for recognition and acceptance. I've met him, y'know. Did one of the first English interviews with him."

"And we expect to interview Mister Roosevelt this fall when we're in the States," Lady Penelope said.

"Well, you know what they say," Willoughby remarked. "In America, you elect someone to office and then sit back and wait for him to fulfill all the lies he told to get elected. In Europe, we elect a man and sit back and wait for him to make mistakes."

"I'm really sick of politics, it's all anyone talks about," said Jenny. "This is Paris, not Berlin. Why don't we change the subject. Francis has a big race coming up today."

"Right," Keegan agreed. "Anyone care to discuss horses?"

Lady Penelope glared at him with a look of pure contempt.

"I've heard your interests run to the mundane," she said.

Jenny bristled. "That is ill-mannered and untrue," she said suddenly. "And I should think someone with your privileges would know better than to speak that way."

The British woman recoiled in surprise. Jenny had surprised even herself with the outburst and her cheeks flushed.

"There's nothing mundane about a good thoroughbred," Keegan said with a crooked grin, trying to overlook the exchange. "Isn't that why we're all here?" He turned to Lady Penelope. "What do they call you, Penny?"

"You may call me Lady Penelope," she snapped back and, wheeling around, she walked away.

Willoughby shrugged. "You'll have to forgive my daughter," he said apologetically. "Her sense of humor hasn't been just right since her husband's death."

"Perhaps I was being a bit too familiar," Keegan answered. "Extend my apologies."

"Of course. By the by, Keegan, should I bet on your horse?"

"I'm going to," Keegan said as the stuffy Britisher left.

"That's telling the spoiled brat," Rudman chuckled.

"I am sorry," Jenny said. "It just burst out."

"You sure let the wind out of her sails," Keegan said and laughed. "She looked like she'd been whacked with a paddle."

"I say we have brunch at Maxim's on me and get back for post time," Rudman said.

"We have to pass," Keegan said, wrapping his arm around Jenny's waist. "We have previous plans."

"Oh?" Jenny said. "And can't Bert join us?"

"Nope," Keegan said, leading her toward the Packard. "We'll see you in two hours at the post party."

Rudman watched them walk across the parking area and get in the back of his car. He had never seen Keegan so excited and happy. It was the opening of the Longchamp racing season, a major social event in Paris, and they had been generous, sharing their days with him so he felt no slight when they decided to slip away for a couple of hours before the races started.

Rudman was so absorbed in his good feelings for Keegan and Jenny, he didn't see von Meister cross the parking lot toward him.

"Herr Rudman," the Nazi said. "It is nice to see you."

Rudman glared at him. "That uniform seems out of place here," he said brusquely.

"You will get used to it."

Rudman started to walk around the tall Nazi but von Meister stood in his path.

"By the way," he said. "You have an employee in your office, a photographer named Marvin Klein."

"That's right."

"Perhaps *The New York Times* did not receive Reichminister Goebbels's order. You cannot hire Jews to work in Germany anymore."

"We didn't hire him in Germany. He's an American."

"Well . . ." The German smiled. "Don't concern yourself."

As Rudman started to walk away, von Meister said, "Your friend, the one who owns the racehorse, what is his name?"

"Keegan."

"Ah yes, Keegan. I believe his girlfriend—or is it his wife?—no girlfriend, I imagine . . . I believe she is German."

"So?"

"Just curious. I am always interested in German girls." The German chuckled. "So . . . tell him I hope his horse wins. I bet on him."

"Poor old Bert," Jenny said as they got in the car. "We must find him a woman so he can share our happiness."

"Old Bert'll do all right. His mistress is his job. If he gets too lonely, he'll go get his trenchcoat and he'll have to beat them off with a bat."

"Stop that. You give him such trouble."

"I'm showing my affection. It's the only way men can show affection for each other without getting arrested."

She tossed back her head and laughed. "Sometimes you make me laugh and I am not even sure why." She snuggled against him. "I am so happy, Kee." For a month now they had been living in a dream world. The subject of Hitler and politics was rarely mentioned.

"Someday we'll look back on these days and realize how special they are," Keegan said tenderly.

"Promise?"

"Absolutely. Falling in love is a magic time."

"Are we falling in love, Francis?"

"A *fait accompli* for me, my love," Keegan said softly. "I fell in love with you that night at Conrad's, the first time I laid eyes on you."

"What a lovely thought."

"You *are* a lovely thought," he said.

"Oh Francis, it has been so wonderful it makes me nervous. I am so happy."

He laughed. "That may be the nicest thing you've ever said to me."

"Nicer than 'I love you'?" she said, taking his arm in hers and squeezing against him.

He looked down at her with surprise. "You've never said 'I love you,' " he said. "Not to me."

"I just did."

"Very obliquely."

"Then I will say it directly," she said looking up at him with tears in her eyes. "I love you. *Je t'aime. Ich liebe dich.*" She reached up and barely touched his lips with her fingertips. "I do love you so, Francis. When we are together, my chest hurts but it is a good hurt. When we are apart, it is painful."

She cupped his face between her hands and barely touched his lips with hers. They brushed their lips together, their tongues flirting with each other, as the chauffeur drove them away to a park he had selected near the Seine on the edge of the Bois de Boulogne, where the track was located.

They spread a blanket and he wound up the Victrola and put on "Any Old Time" by Lady Day and she leaned back and sang along softly.

"I learned that song listening to Billie Holiday on the radio," she said. "Have you ever seen her?"

"Once. A friend of mine, John Hammond, insisted I go up to Monroe's, that's a Harlem nightclub, to hear this new singer who turned out to be Lady Day. She was—I don't know how to describe her—heartbreaking and heavenly at the same time. I remember we stayed there until dawn. She could smile and tear your heart out. You've got the same quality, Jen."

He sat up suddenly. "Jesus, what's the matter with me!" he said. "John Hammond is a good friend of mine."

"Who is John Hammond?"

"He's a top producer for Columbia Records, one of the biggest. He's put some of the jazz greats on the map. Listen, I'm sure he would flip out if he heard you sing. We'll call him from the hotel tonight. You can audition for him over the phone."

"You are crazy . . ."

"Crazy serious. I promise you, one song and he'll offer you a contract."

"No, no. I couldn't . . . not over the phone. Long-distance like that."

"Jenny, stranger things have happened. America's a funny place."

"Do you miss it?" she asked.

"I don't know, I guess I do," he said. "I think maybe I'll have to go home for a while. I've been gone a very long time." Then a moment later: "You'll love New York."

She sat up suddenly. "What?"

"I said you'll love New York. We'll go there on our honeymoon."

"Honeymoon?"

"Marry me, Jen. I adore you. I will devote my life to making you safe and happy."

She seemed troubled and did not respond immediately. "I want to marry you, Kee. And I thank you for asking me. I don't know . . ."

"Jenny, in one night you'll hear every great jazz artist alive. We'll do the Apollo and the Harlem Opera House, the Savoy, Cotton Club . . ."

"I don't think I'm ready to give up on Germany."

Keegan barely missed a beat. "Okay, we'll stay over here. You'll be my wife, that makes you an American citizen. They can't touch you."

"Oh Kee, for such a worldly man you are so naïve. Don't you see, they can and will do anything they want to. Would you give up your citizenship and become a German? Stay here not knowing whether you can ever go home? Would you do that, Francis?"

He didn't answer.

"The difference between us is that you know you can go home anytime you want to. If I went to America I could never come back. Kee, my father fought for this country just as you fought for yours. He died in 1916 fighting for the Kaiser. I cannot walk away from Germany thinking I did nothing to try to make it better. Did you give up on America because things went badly? Did you do that? Is that why you live in Germany now?"

"No," Keegan answered. "That's not why I left."

"Tell me, I want to know all about you," she said softly. "Maybe it will help me."

For all his adult life, Keegan had prided himself on never looking back. The past was the past, too late to change, so forget it. But in the last few months he had been forced into introspection, by Vanessa, by Vierhaus and now by Jenny. It all seemed far too complex to explain and even Keegan did not fully understand why he had left America to become a nomad in Europe. He had never discussed his past with anyone before, not even Bert. He didn't answer her immediately and when he finally started talking it came out like a flood as he tried to put it all in context. His mind drifted back to the terrible summer of 1932, to Washington, and a night that had changed his life forever.

"I was in Washington," he began. "I don't even remember why. A hot summer night. I ran into an acquaintance of mine named Brattle from Boston and he invited me to dinner on his yacht. It was moored in the Potomac River, at the edge of the city."

The night began with shock, shock at the sight of Bonus City, which they passed on the way to the dock. For three months, army veterans and their families, calling themselves the Bonus Army, had been camped in Washington, demanding a five-hundred-dollar bonus that had been voted them in 1924. Although it wasn't due until 1945, they desperately needed it now.

Keegan was unprepared for the awesome spectacle of twenty thousand ex-soldiers and their families living in squalor around the Capitol and White House. For while this was the year of the Washington Bonus March, it was also the year the twenty-month-old son of America's greatest living hero, Charles Lindbergh, had been kidnapped and murdered. A shy and reclusive man, the "Lone Eagle," as he was known by everyone in America, had conquered the Atlantic Ocean alone in his single-engine plane. Lindbergh, his wife Anne and their new baby were as close to royalty as one could get in America and so the tragedy dominated the news from the night the child was stolen from his New Jersey home until his body was discovered seventy-two days later and then onward as the murder investigation intensified and became a national obsession.

Other news had also overshadowed the march. In France, President Charles Doumer was assassinated in a Paris bookstore. The relatively unknown governor of New York, Franklin D. Roosevelt, was challenging Herbert Hoover for the presidency. Olympic swimming champion Johnny Weismuller had become an instant movie star grunting "Me Tarzan, you Jane" and five other lines of dialogue in *Tarzan the Ape Man.* A machinist named George Blaisdell invented a cigarette lighter which he called a Zippo.

Author Erskine Caldwell had shocked the country with *Tobacco Road,* his novel about life among sharecroppers in the Deep South and there had been threats of book banning in Boston and in the South. Aldous Huxley's *Brave New World* stunned everyone with its dismal science fiction view of life in the future while, on the radio, *Buck Rogers* was introduced, presenting a completely different vision of the future.

In Oklahoma, where years of poor farming practice had depleted the land a devastating drought finished the process, adding hundreds of thousands of farmers to the country's 13 million unemployed. There were two thousand hunger marchers in London; New York's Mayor Jimmy Walker resigned from office in the midst of a juicy scandal; young John Wayne was fighting for his life every Saturday afternoon in a matinee serial called *The Hurricane Express;* Herbert Hoover announced Prohibition a failure and encouraged state liquor laws; and Flo Ziegfeld, who had redefined the meaning of the term showgirl when he created "The Ziegfeld Girl," died in Hollywood with his wife Billie Burke at his side. Walter Winchell, radio's dark prince of gossip, commented in the Stork Club one night, "This is one helluva year," and there was no arguing the point.

Little wonder these stories and others had crowded the veterans' march off the front page and finally out of the newspapers and off the radio altogether. Washington had become an enormous "Hooverville," a name synonymous with the temporary, ragtag villages all over the country that housed the millions of nomadic, dispossessed, jobless people wandering the land in search of lost dreams. As the weeks dragged into months, the plight of the veterans became just another footnote in this, the worst year of the Depression so far.

The Bonus Camps were a ragtag collection of lean-tos, tents, cardboard shacks and crates, sweltering in one of the hottest summers in Washington history. Here and there, makeshift gardens struggled in the heat to produce stunted tomatoes and hard-eared corn. Women bathed their children in tubs with water from the Potomac and Anacostia rivers. The crowd was neither unruly nor threatening.

As they drove past the miserable campsites, Keegan realized how easily he might have been one of them. Jocko Nayles, who had driven him down to Washington in the Pierce Arrow, had commented, "Jesus, Frankie, these are our guys. We fought with them. Things bad as they are, why don't they pay 'em?"

"Haven't you heard?" Keegan had replied. "Hoover says the Depression's over. He wants them to go home and starve to death so he doesn't have to look at them."

The trouble was, most of them had no homes or jobs to go to. In this, the most dreadful summer in the nation's history, there were thirteen million people unemployed. The suicide rate was three times normal. And the President of the United States, Herbert Hoover, continued to preach what was by then a warped and illogical litany, that the economic recovery of America was in full swing, that the greatest danger was from "Prohibition gangsters who've turned our streets into battle-grounds" and that the family would be the resurrection of America. Hoover, of course, wasn't talking about the families who had lost their jobs, their homes, and their dignity in a desperate and failed economy wrought by arrogant millionaires. He was talking about the "decent families" who still had jobs, who earned a living wage, sat by their Atwater Kent radios at night listening to *Jack Armstrong the All-American Boy* and *Li'l Orphan Annie,* and who drove to church each Sunday in their Fords and Chevrolets.

Decency in the minds of Hoover and his ilk was directly related to those who worked, paid their taxes and made monthly mortgage payments, it did not relate to those forgotten men who had lost everything because of an orgy of indulgence promoted by the nation's captains of industry and championed by Hoover's predecessor, Calvin Coolidge, who had preached that "prosperity is permanent." It was a lie, of course, and Coolidge, foreseeing the coming calamity, had chosen not to seek a second term in 1928, leaving Hoover to become the fall guy for the worst depression in written history. Eight months after Coolidge left office, the house of cards had collapsed.

"The country's in a helluva mess, Jocko," Keegan had said. "Count your blessings."

Keegan had squirmed through dinner, listening to Brattle rave about the "Commies camped on the White House lawn" and spouting phrases like, "Why don't they get jobs like decent people," although he had inherited his money and had never worked more than half a day in his entire life. He had blathered on about conditions in the country in an arrogant sermon typical of the attitude of those who had actually benefited from the Depression.

"And these goddamn Bonus Marchers, they ought to get the hell out of here," Brattle said, "go home and get a damn job. Contribute something."

"Come on, Charlie," Keegan said, "These aren't malingerers. They can't *find* jobs, for Christ sake. You've got to have a college degree to get a job as an elevator man in Macy's. Since the first of the year, a quarter of a million people have lost their homes."

"And five thousand banks have gone into the hole because of it," Brattle snapped back. "People don't meet their responsibilities. Jesus, there's eleven million farmers out there holding off the banks and insurance companies with goddamn shotguns, refusing to pay their mortgages."

"Yeah, and they're burning corn because it's cheaper than coal and killing their livestock because they can't afford to feed them," Keegan said. "You can't relate to any of this, you've never been broke. It'll hit you one of these mornings when you wake up and wonder why you don't have steak with your eggs."

"Whose side are you on, anyway?" Brattle asked edgily.

"I didn't know there *were* sides."

"Hoover's got it under control," said one of the guests, a youngish man wearing a striped jacket and a straw boater. "Did you see the *Tribune* this morning? Gross National Product's up, economy's looking brighter . . ."

"That's bullshit and you know it."

Brattle's wife gasped.

"Sorry," Keegan said, "I forgot where I was for a minute."

"Well, I should hope so," Brattle growled.

Keegan leaned back in his chair and picked up a copy of the afternoon *Star* from a chair. He held it up for everyone at the table to see.

"Here's our great president in his celluloid collar and button-up shoes telling a troop of Girl Scouts how great things are. 'Nobody has ever died of starvation in this country,' he says. Then we turn to this little three-paragraph yarn on page twenty-six." Keegan read it slowly: " 'The New York City Welfare Department said today twenty-nine people died of starvation in June in the city and 194 others, mostly children, died of malnutrition.' " He paused for a moment. "Which page of the paper do you read?"

There was a momentary pall over the conversation, then Evelyn Brattle said cryptically, "Well, that's New York City for you."

A young woman shook her shoulders. "It's the stock market," she peeped. "Too many people were playing the stock market who didn't know what they were doing."

"That's right, darlin'," Brattle said smugly. "Listen, investors lost seventy-four billion dollars in the stock market, Francis, that's three times what the war cost, and most of them were upper middle-class jerks who shouldn't have been in it in the first place."

"But they pumped it up for people like us, right, Charlie?"

"You're beginning to sound like a goddamn Bolshevist."

Keegan had laughed. "Same old story," he countered, "if you don't think like I do, you're a Red."

"Well, hell, it's a natural process," Brattle said, brushing off the comment. "The world goes through this kind of thing every thirty, forty, fifty years. Leans out the population. Gets rid of the runts."

Never mind that many of those destroyed were bankers, brokers, their own peers, a fact that was obvious from the number of homburgs and chesterfield coats in the soup kitchen line-ups. Brattle's attitude was typical; the rich "leaning out" the runts of the litter. So Keegan suppressed his disdain. There was no discussing it further with the people at Brattle's table. Theirs was the hardened attitude of the fats against the leans.

About nine o'clock, Keegan heard the unmistakable sound of gunfire. A few minutes later the sweet, stinging odor of tear gas drifted out across the river.

Then came the other sounds: the faraway screams, the neighing of horses and the bizarre creaking of tank treads on cobblestones. And suddenly the night seemed lit by dozens of fires.

"By God, it's started!" Brattle cried out. "Hoover's finally moving on the bastards."

The dinner party pressed against the railing of the yacht, searching the night for a view of the battle. Then another yacht cruised past and someone yelled, "Hey Charlie, they're crossing the Eleventh Street Bridge!"

Brattle had immediately ordered his captain to move the yacht out into the river and down to the bridge, there to join other yachts and pleasure boats crowded near the shore to watch the tawdry spectacle. They moved in closer for a better look, lying close to the bridge, where a major named Eisenhower had set up machine guns to prevent the ex-soldiers from moving back into the city. They watched as a chunky major on horseback, wearing pearl-handled revolvers, ordered his men to douse the ragged main village on the edge of the Anacostia River with gasoline and burn it. The scene became nightmarish. Flames broiled into the black sky and horses and men with brandished sabers galloped to and fro in front of the crackling inferno. Tear gas bombs were lobbed through the night and burst on the sidewalks as women and children ran screaming before the onslaught.

Keegan suddenly felt a desperate need to know what was happening. He stood on the deck of the yacht horrified by what the army was doing to its own ex-comrades in arms, recalling a time fourteen years before when he had been a small part of the catastrophe that had started all this.

At that moment, standing on the deck of Brattle's yacht, Keegan felt a desperate need for a Bert Rudman to describe the full sweep of what was happening around him. Could this incredible attack on the veterans be happening all over the city, or was this an isolated incident of violence? He had to know.

"By God, they're cleaning that bunch of Commies out," Brattle proudly proclaimed, slapping his leg.

"They're not Commies, for God's sake, they're army veterans," Keegan cried out angrily, and whirling on his heels, ordered the yacht's long boat to take him back to the pier.

On the way to the hotel, Jocko had skirted what had been the major thrust of the army's attack on the Bonus villages, the streets littered with used tear gas canisters and remnants of canvas and cardboard houses. As they passed an abandoned park, Keegan told Jocko to stop.

Keegan got out of the car, threw off his jacket and tie and

walked down a knoll, out into the remains of one of the tent
villages, now a scene of devastation. Nothing was left standing.

A man in a tattered shirt, its right sleeve folded up over the
stub of his missing arm and pinned at the shoulder, wandered
numbly toward him, stumbling through the remnants of the
camp, silhouetted by the fires of the main camp several blocks
away. He stopped for a moment and stared at a ragged sign,
"God bless our home," fluttering feebly from a shattered tent
pole.

Tear gas tears had made scant streaks in the dirt on the
man's cheeks. On his shirt were pinned a Purple Heart and a
Silver Star. He moved on, stumbling in shock through the
wreckage of the Bonus village, staring bleakly at the ruined
tents, the burned lean-tos, the shattered remains of chicken
coop houses and cardboard shacks, and the trampled gardens
and broken suitcases and ragged remains of clothing. He looked
under pieces of cardboard and canvas.

"Tommy!" he yelled. "Tommy-boy, it's yer dad."

He almost bumped into Keegan, so intent was he on examining the wreckage scattered around him. He looked Keegan up
and down, studying his freshly laundered shirt and Palm Beach
pants.

"What the hell're you doin here?" he demanded with hatred in every syllable.

"Looks like the Argonne the day after," Keegan said softly.

"You was there, at the Argonne?"

Keegan nodded.

"No worse than this," the man croaked bitterly.

He started to babble, his sentences running together almost
incoherently. "We fit with honor there, this is our shame, they's
dishonored the flag and the army, that fat pig in the White
House and his pimp, MacArthur. It's a parade! m'boy Tommy
says this afternoon and we all goes up there to Pennsylvania
Avenue and we're standin' there watchin' the army paradin'
down the street, some of us even cheerin them . . . then . . . then
they come down on us, they come down on us, cavalry, a whole
battalion of machine gunners. I seen the standard of the 34th
Infantry, too, my very outfit and them with their bayonets
pulled, oh goddamn, can you believe it, we all thought it was
some kind of parade, the army was comin out to support us,

some of us cheerin' like that. Jesus, man, we don't have guns, we don't have bayonets er horses, for God's sake they had tanks. *Tanks* come at us! Suddenly that bastard suddenly up and orders a charge. Oh, that miserable polo-playin' sonofabitch dandy, Patton, with his fancy goddamn ivory-handled goddamn guns ordering those soldiers, *soldiers*! Our own goddamn comrades, cutting us down with their sabers like we was wheat in a field at harvest, runnin' us down like we was pigs in a sty, oh, I seen 'em spear two young lads no older than my Tommy and they trampled half a dozen women under their horses, women and children has died here today . . . a baby lies back there dead in his maw's arms of tear gas, goddamn, of god, god, *damn*! Got to find m'wife and boy, he's only seven, got away from me when they come down on us with them fuckin' horses. Chasin' after his dog and my Emma went after him and I lost 'em both in the smoke and the dark and the gas. Oh goddamn, *goddamn* those miserable bastards. They's dishonored the flag, every man who ever raised a gun to defend it, every man who ever fit for his country and wore his uniform proudly. Well, I spit on the flag and never again will I be able to salute it without my heart tearing apart inside me. The shame, the shame. . . ."

He wandered off through the haze, still babbling, breaking the monotone of his outraged dialogue occasionally to call after his wife and child.

The blue haze of tear gas now stung Keegan's eyes and the skin on his arms. Framed against the sky's orange glow, he saw Patton, a block away, astride his white horse, leading it through the destruction, stopping occasionally to praise his marauders with a "Well done" or "Good show." Keegan stumbled back through the battlefield to the car where Jocko Nayles was leaning against the front fender, tears gushing from his good eye.

"I don't believe this," he said. "We fought side by side with some of these boys, Frank."

"I know, I know," Keegan had answered, trying to regain some semblance of composure. "Let's get out of here, Jocko."

They had gone back to the hotel, slept fitfully and left before dawn for the two-day drive back to Boston. By the first light of dawn, the main highway leading from Washington had looked like the aftermath of Gettysburg or Atlanta. Women, children, tattered men, confused and lost, straggling like robots along the two-lane blacktop highway, a vagabond population with no place to live, nothing to eat and no hope in their tortured eyes on an aimless pilgrimage to nowhere, for they had no homes to return to. Under every bridge and beside every railroad crossing were ragged Hoovervilles, tent cities filled with decent men who rode the rails from one desperate camp to the next in search of hope; men who had lost faith in their institutions, the banks, the manufacturers, the insurance companies, their leaders.

They stopped for gas and Keegan had bought a morning paper, hoping to get the same sense of the tragic sweep of the night's events that once he had gotten from Bert Rudman's story of Belleau Wood, yearning to know what misguided insanity had sent an army against these men who had once faced death for their flag. But the stories were fragmented, inconclusive, inaccurate. On the front page, Hoover praised MacArthur for "delivering us from the siege of Washington" and later in the story: "Beware the crowd—it destroys, it consumes, it hates—but it never builds."

Keegan crushed the paper and threw it on the floor.

"When we got to New York we drove up to Roosevelt's campaign headquarters and I wrote him a check for two hundred and fifty thousand dollars. It wasn't just that, it was a lot of things, that just brought it all to a head. Anyway, a week later I left and I've been here ever since." He stopped for a moment, watching a group of swans paddling down the estuary toward them.

"And now you miss it and you want to go home," she said. "You have not given up on America. Some of us have not given up on Germany either."

He nodded slowly. "You made your point," he said. "But Jen, you have to go on living. People still fall in love and get married, have kids. Hitler can't stop that. Politics and love don't have anything to do with each other. That's oil and water. Sure, things are bad, that's even more reason to get out. Marry me, darling. Come to America. Give it a chance. When things settle down here, we'll come back."

"I love you desperately," she stammered, "but I . . . I . . ." She stopped, trying to sort out all the threads of the dilemma, and sensing her dismay he reached up and laid his hand on her cheek.

"Hey," he said tenderly, "forget it for now. Look at the swans."

The swans moved slowly past, drifting aimlessly with the current.

"Did you know the only time swans utter a sound is when they're making love and when they die?"

"Oh, you made that up," she said.

"Absolutely true," he said, placing his hand over his heart. "That's why they call a dying man's last words his swan song."

She laid her hand on his chest and fear flickered momentarily across her face. He leaned over and kissed her. Her lips, soft and full, parted slowly and her tongue caressed his lower lip.

"Never fear," he whispered. "There'll be no swan songs for us."

Spring came early that year, bringing with it relief from the winter snows, much-needed rain and honey-sweet prairie winds which urged the first sprouts of corn and wheat above the ground and promised that 1934, like the five years before it, would be a fertile and prosperous year. Once the land of the Delaware and Potawatomi Indians, the central plains of Indiana were extremely fertile, abounding in lush produce and hogs the size of ponies, of which the Hoosiers were justifiably proud. This was the sweet land of Booth Tarkington and James Whitcomb Riley, a land settled by Scottish, Irish and German descendants who only begrudgingly acknowledged that Cole Porter, writer of "dirty" songs for blue Broadway shows, was also from the Hoosier State.

There was a small billboard on Route 36 that read: "Drew City, Indiana. Founded 1846. Home of 2,162 happy people," under which someone had painted "and one old grouch." A signpost a hundred feet past it had arrows pointing northwest toward Chicago, one hundred and forty miles away, to South Bend, eighty-one miles north, and Indianapolis, seventy-two miles to the south.

Drew City was a typical mid-American town, located on the southeast bank of the Wabash River, along the route of the Illinois Central Railroad, and proud of its heritage—the Battle of Tippecanoe having been fought near Lafayette, twenty or so miles away. The town was surrounded by miles of fertile, sweeping fields of yellow wheat, head-high stalks of juicy corn and the sweetest tomatoes in the country, if you listened to the farmers talk on Saturdays in front of Jason's hardware store or in the park across the street from the courthouse where they congregated to trade lies and gossip once a week. There were four churches in town, which was about a third Catholic, the rest being Lutheran, Episcopal and Presbyterian. There were two Jewish families, no colored people and a small community of Mennonites a few miles east of town.

The main drag, called Broadway although it was barely two lanes wide, was actually Highway 36. The streets were paved for three blocks on either side of the main street, and there was a small park at the edge of town on the bank of the river with a baseball diamond maintained by the Masons, half a dozen cooking fireplaces, and several wooden tables. The Illinois Central was located on the far side of the river, crossing a bridge to the outskirts west of town. Neither isolated nor along the main traffic routes, it was a prosperous town for the times, for while it had felt the sting of the Depression, there had been five or six years of good harvest and the town's two industries, a machine mill and switching station for the Illinois Central, and a shoe factory, had both survived the ravages of the Depression relatively intact.

There was nothing quaint or unique about Drew City. It was a plain American small town, a town of stucco, brick and wood, of galvanized iron rooftops, cornices and Victorian parapets, squatting in the flatlands of northern Indiana, distinguished only by its citizens who had the same ailments, problems and minor victories as folks in any other town of its size. The business section was actually only two blocks long. There were stores on the first floors of the two-story brick buildings and above them, professional offices. Dr. Kimberly, the family doctor, was over the Dairy Foods and Dr. Hancrafter, the dentist, was across the street over Brophy's Dry Goods Shoppe. The town lawyer, William Horton, who drank a lot, was over Aaron Moore's Drug Emporium, his sign reading "W. B. Horton, Atty at Law," and on the line under it "Wills—Divorces—Complaints." Horton's office was perfectly placed since he started each day in Aaron's drugstore, hunched over one of the tiny round tables in the front of the store by the soda fountain, nursing his hangover with a B-C fizz chased with black coffee.

The town had its share of ne'er-do-wells, alcoholics and eccentrics but it had escaped the collapse in morals and the increase in alcoholics and gambling brought on by the Roaring

Twenties and the Depression. When the *Literary Digest* reported that seven out of every ten people, evenly divided as to sex, had relations prior to marriage, it was a shock to the nervous system of the town and a subject to be discussed in whispers in Mildred Constantine's beauty salon and over weekly bridge games where backseat petting was still regarded by some as a sin and an overture to unmarried pregnancy and even worse, abortion, a word never spoken above a whisper in public.

True, teachers and the police were paid in scrip, slips of paper which were like promissory notes from civic employers, a promise to pay when things got better, but scrip was honored almost every place in town. The bank had survived the crash and the town had only one suicide, an accountant for the railroad who had been playing fast and loose with company funds until the crash cleaned him out. He had gone down to the picnic grounds by the river, finished off a pint of bathtub gin he got from Miss Belinda Allerdy's and done himself in with a shotgun.

"Nobody jumped outa any windas here," Ben Scoby, president of the bank, once bragged.

"That's because the tallest building in town's only two stories high," his daughter Louise pointed out.

"Well, now, we got the water tower," Ben countered. "If you were real determined you could go up there and take a leap."

Hoboes still came to back doors looking for odd jobs to earn a sandwich or a piece of pie. But, as in most small towns in America, they were treated decently, and occasionally they even found work in the fields or at the railroad yards on the outskirts of town. The chief of police drew the line at Hoovervilles, however, and when makeshift camps began to develop he was quick to urge the peripatetic unfortunates to move on. Violence was virtually unheard of here, except for an occasional fistfight over some buxom cheerleader at a ball game, and the chief of police, Tyler Oglesby, who was also mayor, often lay in bed at night, listening to the mournful sigh of the ten o'clock freight rattling through on its way to Lafayette, secretly thanking his lucky stars that in twelve years he had never drawn his gun from its holster except to clean it.

All that was soon to change.

* * *

When Fred Dempsey moved to town from the bank in Chicago, Louise Scoby was a tall, slender, raw-boned woman, her straw-colored hair usually tied in two pigtails that framed stern, heavy features. Her splendid figure had been disguised under loose-fitting cotton frocks since she was a teenager and she wore little makeup to soften her windblown, sun-ridged features. She had the look of early pioneer stock, a hardy woman, stern-faced and formal, whose attitude some folks considered haughty.

Then Fred had come to the bank and soon afterward there had begun a subtle change in Louise. Little things through the months. She began to wear lip gloss. Then a slight dusting of face powder. She began plucking her eyebrows. She had her hair cut shorter, then shorter still, and then curled under. On occasions, such as the Saturday night dance at the YMCA, she appeared in silk dresses and sweaters that implied there was more to Louise Scoby than had once met the eye. But the biggest change had little to do with lip gloss and silk and hairstyling. Her features seemed softer and she smiled a lot. Fred Dempsey had kindled a glow in Louise Scoby and it became obvious to the folks of Drew City that she had finally found a man who measured up to her haughty standards.

Dempsey was a tall, muscular, quiet man, his balding black hair graying at the sides and widow-peaked over steel-gray eyes encircled by thin, wire-framed glasses. His thick black mustache also showed the gray of his years and while he never discussed his age, it was known around town that he was forty, almost the perfect age for Weezie Scoby, who would soon turn twenty-five. Dempsey was a pleasant man, well educated and well informed. He had moved up rapidly at the bank, from assistant teller to teller to loan manager. He made it his business to know the people of Drew City and to be a friendly banker, not the intimidating ogre that most people conjured in their minds when they had to make a loan to buy a new plow or get one of the new plug-in refrigerators or buy an automobile. Dempsey was sympathetic. When he did turn someone down, he did so with compassion and a suggestion that they should try again in a few months.

He also spent a lot of time with little Roger Scoby and even that boy had emerged from his shell. He was no longer the sensitive, sequestered little kid who barely mumbled "hello" and looked at his feet when he spoke. Roger had turned into a typical seven-year-old and at least part of the credit had to go to Dempsey, for while Ben Scoby was a pleasant man, honest as a ten-cent piece, the kind of man for whom the description "salt of the earth" was invented, he had never spent proper time with his son. He adored both his children and although it had taken him almost a year to recover from his wife's death, recover he had, only to settle into a dull, complacent routine at the bank. He was secretly pleased when Louise and Fred started dating. Ben Scoby knew in his heart that it had been unfair to burden his teenage daughter with the responsibilities normally reserved for motherhood. She had grown older than her time under that yoke, and Fred Dempsey seemed to have rekindled her youthful spirit. And so it seemed to Ben Scoby and to the wash-line gossips of Drew City that this was truly a match made in heaven.

Louise reserved Saturdays for Roger, for shopping, getting her hair done. And for Fred Dempsey.

Although the Scobys lived less than a mile from town, Roger was permitted to go into the village only on Saturdays and on special occasions, his father reasoning that once a week was enough temptation for a seven-year-old. So it was always a special experience for him. There was a sense of security for the small boy, knowing week by week that everything was still there, still in the same place and unchanged. Well, almost. Occasionally a new store would open or change hands, like the new Woolworth's Five and Ten. The manager, whose name was Jerry, had come from back East in the fall to get the store started and had once given Roger a kite that came all the way from Japan and then flirted with Louise. Roger was old enough to tell *that.* She was polite but she let it be known that Fred Dempsey was her man. Roger kept the kite anyway and once at the park Jerry had helped him get it aloft. He liked the young manager, but not the way he liked Fred. Next to Paul Silverblatt and Tommy Newton, Fred was his best friend. Besides, Fred and Louise were going steady and he worked in the bank for Roger's dad so it was all perfect. Roger had his loyalties in order, kite or no kite.

Every Saturday, Louise and Roger would walk into town together. He would tuck his hand in hers and he always managed to get on the right side of the street and steer Louise past the filling station and garage, its floor slick with oil and grease. The station scared him, though he wasn't exactly sure why. It wasn't the stacks of tires or the rows of motor oil on sagging shelves, or the pungent odor of gasoline heavy in the air. It was the oil pit. To Roger, there was something dangerous and foreboding and mysterious about the gravelike hole in the floor. And he secretly admired Frankie Bulfer, whose father owned the station, because he was only seventeen and he went down in the dread hole with his little light and worked on automobiles. Roger would stand at the garage door and watch, his eyes saucerlike, and listen to the clicking of ratchet wrenches and the hissing of the air hose as Frankie performed his operations on the bowels of the boxy automobiles that straddled the pit over his head.

There followed the Dairy Foods, which was fairly new and was the high school hangout and the only place in town where you could get Coca-Cola at the fountain. Then came Otis Carnaby's grocery store, Mr. Hobart's meat market, the Christian Science reading room, which Fred had explained was kind of like a small library. Then there was Barney Moran's Lunchroom with its oilcloth counters and cracked linoleum seats and the welcome odor of strong coffee and pancakes and burned toast and the sounds of bacon and sausage sizzling on its blackened grill. And finally his father's bank, the Drew City Farmer's Trust and Guarantee Bank, which was on the corner.

Across the street in the middle of the block was Roger's favorite place of all, the Tivoli Movie Palace, framed on one side by The Book Shoppe, run by the spinster lady, Miss Amy Winthrop, and on the other by Lucas Bailey's General Store, a place of velveteens and sateens and buttons on little cards and galoshes and dress patterns and bib overalls and cellophane shirt collars. There was a smattering of toys—red wagons, jigsaw puzzles, stamps for collectors, wooden whistles—in the store but its real allure to Roger was the glass case near the cash register filled with penny candy. Roger usually spent a nickel, half of his weekly allowance, at Mr. Bailey's, poring over the trays of jujubes, caramel swirls, jawbreakers, all-day suckers, twists of red and black licorice, chocolate kisses and Necco wafers, painfully making his choices. He saved the other nickel for the matinee at the Tivoli.

The most taboo alcove on the main street was Joshua Halem's poolroom, adjacent to the general store. It was forbidden to boys until they were fourteen for it was here the men gathered to tell the latest bawdy stories and occasionally resort to less than studious language. Roger and other young boys would gather around the front window thick with years of grease and dust, peering past the NRA and WPA signs with the Blue Eagle and the slogan, "We do our part," at the forbidden green felt tables lit by Tiffany-shaded lamps. Old Halem, who had lost a leg in the war and had a genuine, honest-to-God pegleg, was always perched high on his long-legged stool near the front, his wooden spike sticking straight out, overseeing every table, and when he frowned at the youngsters scanning the pool parlor and gave them his evil eye, they would scatter.

Then came Isaac Cohen's furniture store, a dark and cramped place with rows of chairs, beds, mattresses, rockers, cribs and sofas, all jammed together, and beside it, Nick Constantine's barber shop smelling of talcum powder and shoe polish where Roger had received his first haircut and where he went once a month to keep it trim. Above it on the second floor was the town's beauty parlor run by Mildred, Nick's wife, and on the corner across the street from the bank, The Zachariah House, a rundown hotel where traveling men and drummers could spend the night on sagging springs for two dollars. The only legitimate bar in town was in the rear of the lobby, a place forbidden to children *and* women.

One of Roger's favorite places was Jesse Hobart's butcher shop, for it was there he had seen his first real-life "miracle." Mr. Hobart had brought the chicken from the back where the pullets were in cages and held it up, all flapping wings and clucking, for Louise to inspect. "Nice fat one," Hobart had told Louise. "Should dress out at about five pounds."

"That'll be perfect," she had answered and turned her head as he whirled the chicken around at arm's length until it was totally dizzy, then laid it on the wooden block and *whap!* chopped off its head with his big, shiny cleaver. Usually, the dark deed done, Hobart would stick the chicken, neck down, in a bucket until it stopped twitching, but on this day it had jumped —*jumped!*— out of his hand. The headless pullet had run frantically around the store, blood spurting from its neck, bouncing off the counters and slipping in the sawdust until it fell, twitching, on the floor and Hobart had retrieved it. Louise had become faint and stepped outside, later confessing she had a difficult time cooking it. Roger had been five at the time. It was one of his most amazing memories.

Roger had described the headless chicken incident in detail many times to Poppy Scoby and later to Fred. Bending his head down to his chest and folding his arms up under his armpits, he ran around the kitchen bumping into things as the chicken had done. He flailed his arms over his head and made disgusting squishing sounds as he described the blood spurting from the running chicken's neck, and then he collapsed on the kitchen floor and imitated the pullet's last violent twitching moments as he concluded his description of the bizarre incident. Poppy had explained that it was a reflex action and that the chicken was really dead all the time, which only made the phenomenon more intriguing to Roger.

On this particular Saturday when they got to the market, and after two years of thinking about it, Roger mustered the courage to request a repeat performance. He cried out, "Put him on the floor and let him run around," as Hobart began whirling the chicken around. Louise turned immediately to him, shocked.

"Rogie, how dare you even *suggest* such a thing! Don't you dare, Mr. Hobart. Roger, go outside and wait."

"Aw, Weezie . . ."

"Out, young man."

Fred was sitting on the bench in front of the hardware store, as he always was on Saturday morning, chatting with Mayor Oglesby. Roger ran down the wavy, heat-buckled length of sidewalk to him.

"Weezie wouldn't let Mr. Hobart do the dead chicken trick," he complained as Louise brought up the rear.

"Aw," Fred sympathized, "what a spoilsport."

"Don't you start," she scolded.

"Tell you what, I suggest we go to the Dairy Foods and have a soda while Weezie's getting her hair done. Then when she's done we'll go to Barney's and have a hot dog and drop you by for the matinee at the Tivoli."

"Yeah!" Roger yelled, jumping up and down even though

they had roughly followed the same schedule every Saturday for the past six months. He looked up the street at the marquee of the Tivoli. Johnny Weismuller in *Tarzan the Ape Man* and Chapter four of *Hurricane Express,* plus "selected short subjects"—which meant a cartoon, too.

"Oh boy," he whispered, "*Tarzan!*"

Louise rolled her eyes.

"It's a jungle story," Fred said reassuringly. "A lot of wild animals."

"I *know* the movie, Fred," Louise said with mock anger. "All right. I'll finish the shopping and pick up the chicken after the show."

"Hooray," Roger said, then reaching up, he whispered to Fred, "Can we go by Mr. Bailey's, too?" And Fred winked and nodded.

Saturday afternoons were special times for Fred and Louise. They deposited Roger at the matinee, finding out exactly when he would be out, then walked to her house, got her Buick and drove the three blocks to the small frame house he had rented. The house was one of the few that had a garage. It was attached to the house, enabling them to enter and leave without being seen by the neighbors. Since Fred frequently borrowed Louise's Buick and washed it in his driveway, nobody paid much attention to him when he drove home in it. Louise sat on the floor in the front seat, often getting the giggles because of the charade they played to outwit the local gossips.

The Saturday "parties" had been his idea. Roger usually met Paul and Tommy at the theater so he was happy, and that gave them two hours together. When they got to the house, their lovemaking was frenetic and hungry. This Saturday was no different. As she crouched on the floor of the car she reached up, sliding her hand under his thigh and stroking the inside of it.

"What happened to that shy young lady I met nine months ago?" he wanted to know.

"She discovered what the word love really means," she said, rubbing her head against his leg.

"And what's that?"

"It means having fun. It means feeling *sooo* good."

Dempsey had avoided the relationship with Louise Scoby

for several months but eventually he was drawn into it. Roger had adopted him quickly as a father figure and as their friendship grew, so did Dempsey's relationship with his sister. There was a danger that, in this small town, marriage would be inevitable, but Dempsey finally dismissed that notion. The idea of marriage did not appeal to him but he would worry about that when he had to. In the meantime, she had proven to be a furious and passionate lover.

Once inside the house, a demon seemed to be released in her. She had suppressed her desires for years, acting as mother and sister to Roger and daughter and mistress of the house to her father. None of the men in the town appealed to her, she had known most of them since childhood. Then Fred Dempsey had sneaked into her life. It was natural for Ben to invite his new employee home to dinner. Roger wasn't the only one who had taken to him immediately. She had secretly been attracted to him the first time he came over. But he was shy, a very private man who took the bus to Chicago to visit his ailing mother once a month and rarely talked about himself. Even his opinions seemed guarded and noncommittal. But when he talked about art and books or the theater or music, she was drawn immediately to him, sensing the same repressed passion within him that she had endured since puberty.

The first time they had made love was in the backseat of the Buick out beyond the railroad switching station. They had avoided it for weeks, their petting getting more impassioned every time they were alone together as they explored and touched and were lost in the ecstasy of discovery. Finally she had suggested they get in the back. The moment he closed the door she had unbuttoned her blouse, baring her ample bosom to his hungry kisses. Then he had touched her and he had taken off her panties and guided her hand to him. It had all been done in such a rush that she still only remembered parts of her first seduction. She remembered only that he was considerate and gentle, that she had enjoyed every moment of it and had almost fainted when she had her first orgasm.

The moment they entered the house she threw off her blouse.

"Let's take a shower together, I've been thinking about it all week," she said, taking his hand and leading him up the stairs to the bathroom. But when they got there and he started to undress her, stroking her flat stomach and teasing her breasts, she frantically took down his pants and once having freed him, pulled her to him.

"Do it now, right here," she breathed and he lifted her and sat her on the edge of the sink and stroked her until she began to moan and stiffen and when she cried out, he entered her.

Dempsey lay on his back with his eyes closed, relaxing. They were both naked. Louise sat cross-legged on the bed at Dempsey's feet, rolling a cigarette. Dempsey liked to roll his own, preferring the sweet taste of Prince Albert tobacco to harsh cigarette tobaccos, and Louise had become a superb cigarette maker. She held two of them up, one in each hand.

"Beautiful," he said. "You're becoming an expert in all my vices."

She lit them, keeping one and putting the other between his lips. He took a deep drag and let the smoke ease out slowly toward the ceiling.

Not a bad way to spend Saturday afternoon, he thought.

"How much time do we have?" he asked.

She looked past him to the Westclox alarm clock on the night table.

"Forty minutes," she said.

"Time for another quickie."

She straddled his legs and leaned over him, brushing her nipples lightly against his.

"I don't like quickies," she whispered, "they always leave me wanting more. Why don't we go to the dance at the Y after dinner tonight—and leave early. You can think about it while we're eating."

"I spent fifteen minutes longer at the hairdresser than usual this morning because everyone wants to hear about *Anthony Adverse,*" Louise said as they finished dinner. She had been first on the list when the best-seller arrived at the public library. "And all they want to hear about are the . . ." She looked over at Roger. ". . . bawdy parts."

"What's bawdy parts?" Roger asked.

"The love parts," she answered quickly. He made a face and lost interest. The boy fingered the two-inch-thick stack of Cops 'N' Robbers bubble gum cards carefully wrapped with a worn and dirty rubber band that lay beside his dinner plate.

"Tommy's got two John Dillingers. *Two! And* a Melvin Purvis," Roger complained. "And he wants five of my cards for one of his John Dillingers. Don't seem fair."

"Doesn't seem fair," Louise corrected.

"It's business, son," Ben Scoby said. "Called the law of supply and demand. He's got the supply, you've got the demand."

"But he's my friend!"

"Don't count in business matters," Scoby said.

"Doesn't," Louise corrected.

"Doesn't," Scoby said with a frown.

"You and Fred do business at the bank with your friends," said Roger.

"Different," Scoby said, and started explaining collateral and interest and payments to the seven-year-old, who quickly tuned him out and concentrated on how he was going to get the Dillinger card away from Tommy Newton without severely depleting his own collection.

"Which card is worth the most?" Fred asked.

"Oh, John Dillinger by far," Roger said. " 'Pretty Boy' Floyd is second, but he's nowhere near John Dillinger."

Scoby sighed. "Here I am in the banking business and my son's primary interest in life is to acquire a gum card with the face of the worst bank robber in history." He shook his head. "What's the world comin' to?"

"It's supply and demand," Roger answered, and they all laughed.

Dinner at the Scobys' was routine. The conversation centered around Roosevelt and how he was handling the economy, and the baseball season, and the county fair coming up in two weeks, and what the Dillinger gang was up to now, and whether Jack Sharkey had the stuff to whip the German, Max Schmeling, for the heavyweight championship of the world. That was about as close as they ever got to German affairs. After all, Europe was half the world away from Drew City.

"Tell you what, Rog," Dempsey said. "I've got to go up to Chicago this weekend and see my mother. Maybe I can find you a John Dillinger up there."

"Really!"

"Maybe. Can't promise but I'll check around."

"Why don't you take the Buick," Louise offered. "I won't be using it and you can get back a lot earlier on Sunday."

Dempsey reached in his pocket and took out the makings of a cigarette. Roger watched with rapt attention as he pulled a sheet of the thin paper from the packet and curled it with his forefinger into a little trough, then shook tobacco out of the package along the length of the curve of paper, rolled it into a tight cigarette and licked the paper and sealed it.

When Dempsey took out his lighter, Louise held out her hand. He put it in her palm. She loved the sensual feel of its smooth, gold sides, rubbing her thumb up and down its length and across the unique wolf's head on the top, before she snapped it open and lit his cigarette.

Dempsey finally shook his head. "I'll take the Greyhound like I always do," he said.

He walked home in the cool spring rain and when he got to Third Street he stopped across the street from the old Victorian house that sat by itself in the middle of the block. Shoulders hunched against the rain, his hands stuffed in his pockets, he stared at Miss Beverly Allerdy's parlor, where the shades were always drawn and you could hear the loud, Negro blues music playing inside the jaded walls and men sneaked in the back door and there was a lot of laughter. Women's laughter. He wondered how far the ladies would go in this small town. He could not risk visiting the house. As he stood there he felt the familiar urge again, felt the familiar tightening in his crotch and the anger building up.

Dempsey had invented the story of an ailing mother in Chicago when the familiar urge had first come over him. Since then he had taken the four o'clock bus to Chicago every six or seven weeks, checked into the Edgewater Beach Hotel and employed one of the most expensive party girl services in the Midwest, girls who were willing to endure his sadistic games for the right price. He had been thinking about taking the trip for several days. The need was building in him.

He decided he would bring up the trip to Chicago again and accept Louise's offer of the car for the weekend—after a reasonable protest, of course. It might be interesting for a change, cruising the streets of Chicago, looking for something different.

As he walked home in the rain, Dempsey thought about what he had learned about Americans in the nine months since he had come to Drew City. They were generous. Too trusting. Good friends when they got to know you. They were crazy for fads. They loved sports and entertainment and elevated ballplayers and movie actors, even the very rich, to a kind of royalty status. They were radically independent. Their slang expressions changed from one place to the next, impossible to keep up with. Everyone went to church on Sunday. They all seemed to have an unusual fascination with the weather. And the entire nation seemed to gather around their radios every night.

But most encouraging of all, thought 27 with satisfaction, they were complacent.

Indiana Highway 29, a long, slender finger of concrete, stretched south from Logansport to Indianapolis under a bleak and threatening sky. A black Packard hummed toward the town of Delphi, its five passengers dressed in suits and dark felt hats except for the man sitting in the front next to the driver. John Dillinger wore a straw boater, which had become somewhat of a trademark for him.

"Car's hummin' like a bee, Russ," Dillinger said to the driver.

"Put in new plugs and points, new air filter . . ."

"Can the crap, okay?" Lester Gillis, who called himself Big George but was known to the world as Baby Face Nelson, growled from the backseat. "I wouldn't know a spark plug from the queen of hearts and I don't wanna."

"Everybody straight on the plan?" Dillinger said, leaning sideways in the seat and facing the three in the back. They all nodded confidently. "We need to go over it again?"

"Nah, we got it, fer Chrissakes," Nelson said.

"You can be a real pain in the ass, y'know that, Lester," said Dillinger.

"Don't call me that. I told you, I like to be called George."

"That makes a lot of sense," the driver chuckled. "I suppose if your name was George you'd want us to call you Percy."

"Watch your mouth."

"Awright, awright," Dillinger said. "No need to get hot. We got work to do."

Nelson settled back and shook his shoulders. His short temper overrode a lifelong inferiority complex—he was only five-four, and he resented the fact that Dillinger was *the* most wanted man in America when Nelson felt he rightfully should have been

Public Enemy Number One. But his own gang had been shot out from under him and he couldn't operate alone. He calmed down.

"How come you do all this planning?" he asked Dillinger.

"Learned it from the expert."

"Who's that?"

"Herman K. Lamm."

"Who?" Homer Van Meter asked, speaking for the first time since breakfast.

"Herman Lamm. You ought to know that name, he's the father of modern bank robbery. When you say you're takin' it on the lam? That expression is named for Herman Lamm. Robbed banks for thirteen years before they grabbed him."

"C'mon," Van Meter said skeptically.

"Where'd you meet him?" Nelson asked.

"Didn't. You remember Walter Dietrich?"

"Yeah, retired, didn't he?"

"Laying low," Dillinger said. "I knew Wally when I did my first stretch at Michigan City. He ran with Herman Lamm for thirteen years. *Thirteen* years without gettin' caught. Lamm's secret was planning, execution and speed. He cased everything, drew plans just like mine, never stayed on the spot more'n four minutes. And he always knew how to get out."

Dillinger was a man of average height with thinning dishwater-blond hair, dyed black, and a high forehead. His intense blue eyes were disguised by gold-rimmed glasses with clear lenses. And although Dillinger had spent painful hours having his fingerprints altered with acid and his face lifted, vanity prevailed. Dillinger was a ladies' man and he continued to sport the thin mustache ladies loved and which, with the pie-shaped straw hat, was his trademark.

The other men in the car were Harry Pierpont, a dapper, gaunt man who liked to be called "Happy"; Homer Van Meter, who said very little and had been with Dillinger the longest; and Russell Clark, a lean, hard-looking man who some people thought resembled Charles Lindbergh. Clark was an ex-mechanic and a fine driver.

Van Meter, Clark and Dillinger were old pals. Nelson was a latecomer to the gang and Dillinger was having serious second thoughts about him. Nelson liked to kill and had done so many times, a violation of one of John Dillinger's unwritten laws—no killing. Thus far Nelson had violated the rule only once—he had killed a cop while trying to rescue Dillinger from the police. Dillinger could hardly complain.

"What's the name of this town again?" Russell Clark asked.

"Delphi," Dillinger answered, his voice Indiana-flat, crisp and authoritative.

Russell laughed. "Well, if it ain't on the map now, it will be after today."

"Delphi," Pierpont said. "What kinda name's that?"

"It's Greek," Dillinger answered.

"How come they named a town after a Greek?"

"Beats the shit outa me," Dillinger answered with a shrug.

"What the hell's that?" Van Meter said suddenly.

Half a mile ahead of them, a state trooper was stopping traffic. Cars were backed up ten deep.

"What the hell . . ." Clark said.

Dillinger looked to their right and left. Ahead of them, past a cornfield, was a dirt road.

"There," he said, "grab a right there, Russ."

Russell didn't even slow down.

"Grab a right here. *Here!* Damn it, Russell."

Clark braked the Ford down and screeched rubber as he skidded into the dirt road.

"What the hell's going on? They having a cop convention er sompin?" said Homer.

"Goddamn it, Homer, shut the hell up. Just keep drivin', Russ. Just drive on here like we're regular people."

"Jeez, lookit the smoke," Van Meter said.

To their left a pall of black smoke broiled up from the town.

"Christ, the whole town must be burnin' up."

"Well that's just fuckin' great," said Homer.

Dillinger clawed a road map from the tray under the dash and opened it.

"Where the hell are we?" he said to himself, tracing a finger across the center of the map.

"We're gonna run outa road."

"Here we are," Dillinger said. "Hey, we're okay. Grab a left at the next road. We'll come back out on the highway just south of town. Hell, it's perfect."

"It's an omen," Pierpont said. "We probably woulda screwed up anyways. And it's beginning to rain."

"We're not through for the day," said Dillinger. "Not by a long shot. And rain's good, keeps people inside."

"Where we goin' now? A picnic," Nelson sneered.

"Yeah, a picnic about twenty miles down the road. They're serving tea and crumpets at the other bank."

"What other bank?"

"Homer and I cased three banks, yesterday," said Dillinger. "We'll take the number two bank. Probably be just as fat. And they stay open on Fridays until three o'clock. We hit 'em at quarter to three—it'll be dark three hours later."

"I don't like it," Homer Van Meter said. "I told you, these one-horse towns with one way in and one way out make me nervous."

In the front seat, John Dillinger shook a Picayune from his pack and lit it.

"Trouble with you, Homer, you're a crepe hanger."

"I try to figure it all out ahead of time, like you do, Johnny."

"You wanna hit a big town again?"

"I didn't say that."

"We tried that in East Chi, look how that went. Charlie gets killed. A bank guard gets knocked off and I end up in the cooler. Now everybody thinks I'm a killer. I'm always the one gets the heat."

"That's cause you're famous, Johnny," Nelson snickered jealously.

"I don't like bein' blamed for somethin' I didn't do," he snapped.

"What do you want me to do, write a letter to the *News* and confess?" Nelson said, and he laughed.

"Hell, Johnny writes letters to the papers all the time," said Pierpont. "Even sent a book to old . . . whatsisname?"

"Matt Leach," said Dillinger proudly, "*Captain* Leach, head of the Indiana State Patrol. Sent him a copy of *How to Be a Good Detective.*"

"Damn fool stunt, you ask me. No use makin' them any madder than they are already," Van Meter replied.

"C'mon, Homer," Dillinger replied, "they can't get any

madder than they are and they can't come after us any harder."

"Still makes me nervous," Van Meter said. "Gonna be a lot of people in the street, Friday afternoon. Payday, all that."

"Nobody's gonna get hurt," Dillinger said flatly. "They'll lay down like a buncha tank fighters. Four minutes, we're on our way to Indy. Time they get themselves together and call the G-men we'll be halfway there. It'll take the feds three, four hours to drive down there from Chicago."

"How about the state cops?" Pierpont asked.

"They can't find their nose with their hanky," Dillinger answered.

"Damn one-horse town," Van Meter mumbled.

"With the fattest bank in Indiana and three cops in the whole town counting the sheriff."

"I'm for that," said Clark. "Look what happened to Charlie Mackle, messing with the G-boys."

"Charlie was a damn fool," Dillinger said with a touch of irritation. "Walks right into Melvin Purvis who's sittin' with a tommygun in his lap. Listen here, this Purvis ain't just an ordinary G-man, he's nuts. Hoover gave him a clean hand to get rid of us all. I don't care to mess with those people, do you?"

Nobody answered.

"So we keep to the small towns with the fat banks."

"Maybe we oughta retire," Pierpont said.

"We got two hundred bucks, if we're lucky that is, between the five of us and you want to retire," Van Meter said and laughed. "You going to Rio on fifty bucks, Harry?"

"I mean hit a string of 'em. Maybe run down the line, catch four, five banks in one day and call it quits."

"Won't work," Dillinger said, shaking his head. "Gives Purvis and his boys time to get a line on us. Hit and run, hit and run, that's the way. Keep 'em off balance."

"I say we go in blasting, kill anybody that twitches and shoot our way out. Scare the shit outa everybody," said Nelson.

"You keep that chatterbox of yours down, hear me, Lester?" Dillinger said in his hardest voice. "This town's just barely breathin'. They ain't gonna give us any trouble."

"Know what I heard?" Pierpont said. "I heard Purvis always lights a cigar before he goes after somebody. Calls it a birthday candle. He's supposed to have a list of twenty-two guys. Says when he's got twenty-two candles on his cake, he's gonna throw a party."

"Twenty-two," Dillinger said. "Wouldn't you know it would be twenty-two."

"Got himself a machine gun squad, now," Nelson said. "His motto's 'show 'em no mercy.' "

"College kids," Dillinger said. "Jump a foot when their shoes squeak. The whole thing with Purvis is, Floyd and his bunch killed a federal man when they hit Jelly Nash in Kansas City. The guy was a personal friend of Purvis."

"What d'ya mean, hit Jelly? They was trying to spring him," Pierpont said.

"No way. Conco told me himself. They wanted to get rid of Nash, he had the talkies. The cops got trigger-happy and they ended up knocking over Nash *and* four cops, including the G-man."

"And that kicked Purvis off his rocker?"

"I guess so. He's got a very short fuse."

"So let's not light it when he's in the room," Pierpont said.

Dillinger laughed. "That's good, Harry."

"What's the name of this bank again?"

"The Drew City Farmer's Trust and Mortgage Bank."

"How big's the town?"

"Three thousand or so, most of 'em farmers out in the field. The town's two blocks long, bank's in the middle of town. I doubt there's two hundred autos in the whole county."

"What're they gonna chase us with, horses and buggies?" Clark snickered.

"Yeah. Like Jesse James," Nelson answered.

"Shut up and listen. This is the setup," Dillinger said. He took out a sheet of typing paper with a sketch of the bank and held it up for all to see. "The bank's on the corner, door faces the intersection, kind of catty-corner. The cages are on the left when you go in. Big shots are in an open area on the right. The teller windows are three feet high, so we use a pyramid. I'll take the door and the stopwatch. Go for twenties and under, you know how tough it is to pass a C-note these days. Homer and Lester work the vault, Harry and Russell clean out the tellers' windows. We'll drive through town once, check it out, then drop off Lester and Harry, then Homer and me. Russ parks the car in front of the bank. Remember, once we're in, we got four minutes."

"How about guards?" Pierpont asked.

"One old-timer in the bank."

"He's about seventy," said Van Meter. "Probably can't see past his nose."

Dillinger went on. "The cop station's two blocks away. There's a phone box here, just inside the bank door, I'll take care of that. We'll call in a fake accident from up the highway here, that'll get the sheriff outa town. So we got two cops and grandpa in the bank." He chuckled. "Hell, boys, we got 'em outnumbered."

The young policeman ducked into the bank and shook the rain off his raincoat. He walked across the floor with his weekly scrip check in hand and presented it to Dempsey for his initials. Luther Conklin was a local boy who had played football in high school, then spent two years at the state college. He was Tyler Oglesby's deputy. He had been on the force for eight months and everyone in town was proud of him.

"How are you today, Luther?" Dempsey asked, scribbling his initials on the green slip of paper.

"Just fine, sir. Hear about the fire up in Delphi?"

"No. When was this, last night?"

"Goin' on right now," Luther said earnestly. "They called down for help. Sheriff Billings's on his way up there to check things out. That new Five and Ten they got is burnin' up."

"Well, I hope nobody gets hurt," Dempsey said.

The bank teller honored Conklin's script and counted out his twenty-five dollars. He walked out of the bank counting it. Dempsey looked at the clock over the door. Ten more minutes and he'd be through for the weekend and on his way to Chicago. His mouth started to get dry thinking about the trip.

Clark guided the Packard slowly down Broadway, turned right, went down a block and turned back the way they had come. They drove past the police station as a young cop entered the front door. The police car was parked in the driveway.

"Well, guess we know where the laws are," Dillinger chuckled. "Swing back around up at the corner, Russ. We'll let Homer and Lester out."

The two men got out of the car and walked casually toward the bank as Russell drove through the intersection one more time. He went down half a block and let Harry Pierpont and Dillinger out. They walked back past the harness shop toward the bank, their guns muzzle-down under their raincoats. When they got to the bank, Van Meter and Nelson were crossing the street toward them.

"Okay, let's do it," Dillinger said and they entered the bank. A moment later, their partners came in behind them.

Dempsey, as he always did, looked up as the men entered the bank. Strangers, he thought. Then he took a second look. The one in glasses looked vaguely familiar . . .

Dillinger swung his shotgun out from under his coat. The man behind him twisted the "Open" sign in the doorway over to "Closed" and pulled the shade on the front door.

"All right, everybody." The man with the shotgun yelled a loud, harsh, no-nonsense command. "Shut up and listen to me. I'm John Dillinger and we're here to rob this bank. Don't you scream, lady, just swallow it, I know a screamer when I see one. All of you just shut up and sit down on the floor. Make yourselves comfortable and don't ring no alarms or yell or make a sound, otherwise some folks could get hurt. That there's Baby Face Nelson and he has a very itchy trigger finger. *Four minutes, Homer!* Now we don't mean to hurt nobody, you understand. We're just here to make a withdrawal."

He laughed as he peered through the window, pointing the shotgun at the ceiling. There were six employees and four customers in the bank. Van Meter, Clark and Pierpont all dropped to their knees and Nelson ran up their backs and sprang over the teller's window. He shoved one of the two women back and opened the door. As Dillinger stared at his stopwatch, the other three got up and went into the business compartment. The vault was open.

Dillinger stared through the window and saw a police officer walk down the opposite side of Broadway.

"Christ," he said under his breath, "a copper."

Tyler Oglesby had left Luther Conklin to handle the phone

while he did his three o'clock rounds. He had planned to go to the bank but the shades were drawn and the closed sign was out. He checked his watch. Either he was slow or Ben Scoby was fast. He went into the barber shop.

"Hey, what's this we hear about a fire over in Delphi?" Nick Constantine said as he entered.

"Yeah," Tyler answered. "Big fire. Still out of control. Lester went on up to help. . . ."

Probably gone to get a haircut, Dillinger thought as Oglesby entered the barber shop. He turned back to his hostages, strolling past them, his shotgun butt resting on his hip. He took out a cigarette and put it in his mouth, lit a wooden match with his thumb.

"One thing I want to make clear," Dillinger said as he lit the cigarette. "I ain't no gangster, I am a bank robber. Gangsters are scum, they work for the likes of Capone and that bunch and they get paid for bumping people off. You know what they say about John Dillinger, he's got the fastest brains and the slowest guns in the country. I ain't no killer, regardless of what you might've read in the papers. *Three minutes, Homer!* We rob banks because the banks rob you! Take your homes, charge you to use your own money, act like they's holier than God. They don't deserve no better than what we give 'em."

Back in the vault, Baby Face Nelson was throwing money in a bag held open by Homer Van Meter.

"Why the hell does he have to walk around jawin' like that," Nelson snarled, stuffing packets of twenties in the bag. "Makin' a damn fool of all of us."

"Keeps their minds off things, Lester," Van Meter answered. "Just do your job there and let Johnny do things his way. This's gonna be one hell of a haul." He grinned broadly as he shook the bag and let the loot settle in the bottom.

"Lookin' good, Johnny," Van Meter yelled.

Dillinger checked the front door again. No sign of the copper. He reached in his coat pocket, took out a pistol and waved it toward the ten people sitting on the floor.

"See this? This is my good luck charm. This is a wooden gun. That's right, *wood*! Carved it out of the top off a washboard and colored it with bootblack. Walked out of the Crown City jail with it, right past the National Guard and everybody else and drove off in the sheriff's car. Ain't a jail made can hold John Herbert Dillinger, folks."

Dempsey sat on the floor, holding his knees, and he thought about the situation and could not help smiling. Dillinger saw the smile. He walked across the bank floor and leaned over Dempsey.

"You think this is funny, pal?"

"No, Mr. Dillinger," Dempsey answered.

"Well, I like a man with a sense of humor, friend. Here, have a cigar."

He slid a cigar in Dempsey's inside jacket pocket. "If you don't smoke, you can frame it."

He looked at the stopwatch. *"Two minutes, Homer."* He strolled back to the front door as he spoke, never excited or hurried. He opened the blind an inch and peered out. No sign of the cop. He turned back to the group on the floor.

"Hell, times bein' what they are, a man can't get a decent job if he wants to. Listen, I was born in Mooresville, right down the road. Did my first time in the State Reformatory. I'm just a hometown boy when you get right down to it. My pap runs a grocery down in Mooresville just like that one across the street. I'm wanted in seven states, hell I'm wanted in states I ain't even *been* to yet! Not that we ain't taken our share of banks, mind you. Hell, we took down over a dozen banks. Harry Pierpont, the dandy there, he's been in on fifteen, sixteen. And Homer Van Meter must've robbed, what, twenty banks, Homer?"

"Twenty-two," Van Meter called back from the vault.

"Twenty-two. You know, there's a number that just seems to dog me. I was born on the twenty-second of the month, stole my first car on the twenty-second, was paroled on the twenty-second. I took my first bank on the twenty-second and escaped the G-men up in Wisconsin just a month ago on the twenty-second. Now here it is the twenty-second of May. *One minute, Homer.* Well, you gents and ladies will remember this day for the rest of your lives, May 22nd, 1934, and you will tell your grandchildren that you was in the Drew City bank the day it was held up by the John Dillinger gang. Sure is more excitin' than sitting around with a fly swatter, whackin' flies, now ain't that a fact, everybody? People'll come from far and wide just to visit here and you will talk about this day for years to come and when you do, you will tell everybody that Johnny Dillinger wasn't a bad sort, he was mannerly and pleasant and didn't hurt a soul and took no money except what was the bank's. *Ten seconds, boys, wrap it up.*"

"Lot more here," Nelson yelled from the vault.

"I said *wrap it up.*"

"Johnny," Harry Pierpont said, looking out the window. "Across the street, that copper's comin' out of the barber's."

"Damn!" Dillinger thought for a moment. "Okay, Russ, go out and get in the car and crank'er up just like normal. Don't show your weapon. If he comes on toward the bank, put the drop on him and tell him to stand fast and no harm'll come to him. Tell him who we are. Soon's you got the car hot, we'll pile in. Go on now."

"Right," Clark said.

Across the street, Tyler Oglesby stared at the bank. His watch still said five minutes to three. He decided to go over anyway, he was sure Ben would let him deposit his scrip.

As he started across the street a man exited the bank and got in a black Packard parked on the corner. Oglesby smiled at him as he approached the car and then the man swung his hand up and pointed a .38 at him.

"Stand fast there, copper. This is the Dillinger gang. You make a move and a lot of people could get hurt."

Oglesby stopped short. His mouth fell open. And then the door to the bank burst open and four men came rushing out carrying bank bags. Without thinking, Oglesby grabbed for his pistol, clawing it out of the holster and backing up at the same time.

Russell Clark fired. Oglesby felt the bullet hit his chest. It felt like somebody had punched him very hard and he fell over on his back. He heard people screaming and the screeching of tires but they seemed very far away. He felt numb all over and then the world seemed to spin away from him as he felt like he was falling into a deep, dark well.

The people of Drew City seemed frozen in time, staring with disbelief at Tyler Oglesby who lay spread-eagled in the middle of Broadway, staring up at the rain. Dempsey was the first to get to him. He ran from inside the bank and dropped on his knees beside him.

"Tyler!" he cried. He turned and yelled up at Dr. Kimberly's window over the Dairy Foods.

"Doc, hey Doc, come quick! Tyler Oglesby's been shot."

Oglesby looked up but did not recognize him. A moment later his eyes lost their focus and glazed over. Dempsey heard his deep sigh and knew he was dead. He looked up at the crowd gathering around and shook his head as Oglesby's young deputy spun around the corner in the city Ford.

"After 'em, Luther," Ben Scoby yelled from the bank door. "It's the Dillinger gang!"

As the getaway car roared down Broadway, Nelson thrust his tommygun out the window and fired a long burst at the hardware store. The bullets shattered the plate window, splintered ax handles and kerosene cans and snapped harnesses like twigs as they hung from hooks in the ceiling. The people inside dove to the floor as the bullets raked the store above their heads, showering them with debris.

"What the hell'd you do that for?" Dillinger yelled.

"Give 'em something else to talk about," Nelson yelled back. "Hey, looks like a patrol car swingin' in behind us."

"That must be the other copper. Step on it, Russell."

"I'm goin' almost seventy now!"

"I'll just slow that son-bitch down," said Nelson.

"No more killing, Lester!" Dillinger yelled.

"Right," Nelson said. He smashed out the back window of the Packard with his tommygun and waited as the patrol car drew closer. When it was in range he fired one burst, then another.

In the patrol car, Luther Conklin saw the window smash out but could not see clearly because of the rain. Then he saw the flash of the machine gun and heard the bullets ripping into the radiator, heard the steam hissing from it. The radiator cap exploded off and steam poured out. Conklin swerved in the road as another burst tore into both front tires. They burst under him and the car veered, skidded wildly on the wet pavement. He frantically fought the steering wheel, trying to gain control, felt the car skid into the shoulder and saw the tree rush toward him, felt it tear into the far side of the car. He smashed against the steering wheel, his breath rushing from his lungs.

Nelson settled back in the seat with a grin. "Cooked that little bastard's goose for him," he said.

"Christ, we killed another cop, maybe two," Dillinger said, shaking his head.

Conklin staggered out of the car, clutching his sprained ribs and fell back against the ruined police car. Rain poured down his face. He stared with frustration and disappointment as the most famous bank gang in history disappeared down the rain-swept highway. Dillinger, Pierpont, Clark, Nelson and Van Meter. He had no way of knowing that within six months all of them would be dead, tracked down by the man they feared most, the G-man Melvin Purvis. Dillinger would be the first to die, exactly two months later. On the twenty-second day of July.

What rotten luck, what bloody, stupid rotten luck.

What was it Vierhaus had said to him once, *it's usually the unexpected that gets you.* He was on the spot because it had never occurred to him that he might be trapped in this town, certainly not by the FBI. But that was exactly what was happening.

Dempsey sat on the edge of the bed, staring at the raindrops making thin tracks down the window. He had been sitting without moving for ten minutes. He looked at the clock: three twenty.

When Ben Scoby contacted the Chicago FBI office, Purvis himself got on the line. He was coming down personally with a team of FBI agents and had ordered Scoby to lock up the bank and send everyone home until they arrived. Scoby had called a meeting at seven P.M. in front of the bank.

Dempsey had to leave before the FBI got to Drew City. He could not risk an interview with the G-men. Nor could he risk taking the bus or hitchhiking; everybody in town knew him. There was only one way out: he had to hop a freight. And even that was risky. If his failure to show up at the bank started a search, they might check the train when it arrived in Lafayette. But it was a risk he had to take.

He made his decision. First, he thought, shave off the mustache and wash the dark dye out of his hair. Dress warmly, it was still quite cold at night. Wool socks and the heavy-soled walking shoes Louise had given him for his birthday. Money was not a problem. *I'm not unprepared,* he thought, *just caught short.*

He got a pair of heavy corduroy trousers and a thick plaid jacket from the closet, dug out socks and shoes. He was on his way to the attic when the doorbell rang. Dempsey fell back against the wall. It couldn't be the government men. It had to

be Louise. He stood motionless for a full minute while the bell
rang a second, then a third time. As he stood there, a plan began
to form in his mind. He thought about it as he slowly descended
the stairs.

It was perfect, he thought. Even if they saw through it later
it would give him time. Once he was in Chicago, he didn't care
what they thought, he would no longer be Fred Dempsey.

He opened the door and Louise rushed into his arms.

"Oh God, my heart stopped when I heard," she said, hugging him to her. "Thank God you're all right. I was afraid they
shot you."

"It was Tyler Oglesby."

"I know, I just left Dad. Are you sure you're all right?"

"Of course. All I did was sit on the floor for five minutes and
listen to John Dillinger brag about what a good guy he is."

"I can't believe it! All the times we've joked about the bank
being held up. And Roger and his cards . . ."

"Easy," he said. "It's over. It's even over for poor old Tyler.
C'mon, let's go upstairs."

"Upstairs?"

"We've got three hours before the FBI gets here."

"Fred!"

He leaned over and kissed her throat.

"But . . ."

"All the excitement, it . . . it excited me." He kissed the back
of her neck and she twisted her head and shivered.

"Gives me goose pimples."

"You *always* give me goose pimples."

He drew her slowly up the stairs, kissing her and caressing
her cheek as they mounted the stairs. He led her into the bedroom, eased her onto the bed. She lay down beside the pants
and flannel jacket.

"What's that?" She asked.

He was leaning over her on stiff arms, staring down at her.

"It's going to be chilly and wet tonight. I thought I'd change
before I went back to the bank. You can take my clothes off for
me, Louise. You can undress me."

"Oh, Demps," she whispered. "I love you so."

It was the first time either of them had mentioned the word.
He lowered himself slowly down on top of her.

"And I love you," he said softly in her ear.

She rolled him over and unbuttoned his vest, took off his tie, unbuttoned his shirt as he removed her blouse. She toyed with the hair on his chest then kissed his nipples, her tongue circling first one, then moving to the other. He unbuttoned her skirt at the back and when it was loose, slid his hand down the front of it, feeling her cotton panties, then her hair.

"Oh God, yes," she said. He moved his hand lower, felt her grow hard under his touch, began stroking her, lubricating her with her own juices. Finally he put his other hand under the band of the skirt and slipped it off. She unbuttoned his fly and her movements were frantic, her breathing quickening as she tugged at his trousers, then reached up and pulled off his shirt. When they were naked they lay on their sides facing each, each stroking the other and finally she rolled on top of him, rose up on her arms, squirming until he slipped inside her. She sighed, rising up and down on him, slowly at first, then faster.

"Oh yes," she said, "it comes so quickly now. So easy. Oh . . . faster, faster . . . God, faster . . ."

Her own passion stimulated his climax. He could feel her tightening on him and he reached up and began stroking her shoulders. Her moves grew faster and faster and her words began to blur together and then suddenly she cried out and as she did, he came too. Thrusting deep into her, he moved one hand quickly under her chin and the other to the back of her head and with one hard snap of his wrists, he broke her neck.

Her cry of joy turned to a gasp. The sound of her spine snapping drowned out her cries. Her mouth fell open and she stared down at him in horror and disbelief for just an instant before her bulging eyes went dead. She fell forward on top of him.

He rolled her off on her back and lay for two or three minutes taking deep breaths. His heart was pounding so hard it felt like it would break his ribs. Finally he turned on his side, his back to her, and rising up on one elbow, reached for his cigarette makings.

The phone interrupted his smoke. The phone was on the wall in the kitchen. He wrapped a towel around his waist and took the stairs two at a time.

"Fred, Ben here. Did Weezie come by?"

"She's here now. She's pretty upset, Ben."

"Everybody in town is. Poor Liz Oglesby is in shock. Doc's with her now. Reason I'm calling, the FBI called back. Weather's given them fits. Better make the meeting for seven-thirty. I'll call everybody else."

"Fine. Listen, I might drive Louise over to Shorty's Steak House in Delphi, get her mind off things. We've got plenty of time."

"Good idea," he said. "You always seem to know just the right thing to do, Fred. Don't know what we'd do without you."

"Well, it's a terrible time, Ben, terrible."

"Sure is. I'll have Mrs. Ramsey come over and keep an eye on the boy till after the meeting."

"Good. See you at seven-thirty then."

He went back upstairs, finished rolling the cigarette and lay on his back beside the body of Louise Scoby, smoking. Then almost as an afterthought, he reached over and with a thumb and forefinger closed her eyes.

When he finished his cigarette he went into the bathroom, shaved his mustache and took a shower, using heavy tar soap to wash the dye out of his hair. He toweled off, went back in the bedroom, opened the bottom drawer of the dresser and reaching back, pulled loose the dagger which was taped to the rear of the cabinet. He went back in the bathroom and fixed the Nazi weapon to his calf with adhesive tape. He went to the attic and retrieved the lockbox, emptied it of its contents: the cash, a new passport and birth certificate, bank books from the New York account. He parted his hair in the middle, sweeping it forward over the areas he had kept shaved to add to his age. He put the cash in an envelope and taped it to his stomach. Then he methodically checked every inch of the house. There was nothing else he needed, nothing to reveal his real identity.

He dressed in long johns, cord pants, a heavy sweatshirt and the flannel shirt over it and got his rain slicker. He went back to the bedroom, dressed Louise Scoby's corpse, carried it down to the car and put it in the trunk with the empty lockbox.

Heavy clouds and rain brought darkness early that Friday. Dempsey parked under a bay of trees near the park. The body of Louise Scoby was propped behind the steering wheel, the stiffened fingers of one hand wrapped around the steering wheel, the other arm rested on the seat. He had pried open that hand and wrapped the fingers around the suit coat he was wearing during the robbery. He had torn the sleeve at the shoulder so it would appear that his body had literally been torn from her grasp. When he was sure nobody was watching, he threw the heavy lockbox and glasses into the river. He checked his watch: five forty-five.

It was time. He started the car and sitting close to the body, he shifted into low and pulled out onto Highway 25. There were no cars in sight. He drove toward the bridge over the river. Just before the bridge there was a steep embankment that dropped straightaway into the raging river. He picked up speed until he was fifty feet from the bank. Then he slammed on the brakes and twisted the wheel. The car skidded onto the shoulder, veered back on the road, leaving heavy black skid marks. Then he steered the car toward the embankment, braking it down to ten miles per hour, opened his door, and as the car rumbled onto the shoulder above the river, he jammed his foot on the gas and dove out of the car door.

He rolled as he hit the muddy shoulder of the road, felt the elbow of his jacket tear out and the sharp sting of pebbles burning the skin. As he rolled over on his back, he jammed both heels into the mud and slid to a stop.

The thrust of gas was enough to send the Buick over the bank. It rolled on its side, rocks and small trees tearing at fenders and doors, then hit the bottom of the bank, hung for a moment, and slipped front end first into the turbulent stream. The racing river carried it downstream, bobbing like a fishing cork, and then it twisted a half turn and vanished under the broiling, muddy water.

Dempsey jumped to his feet and swiftly erased his muddy tracks with his hands. He ran back to the train tracks and trotted toward the railroad bridge. The six o'clock freight would slow down as it crossed the span into the west end of town, a perfect place to jump aboard. When he got to the bridge he ducked down beneath the ties and waited. The train was five minutes late. It slowed down as it always did and headed over the bridge. As it rumbled overhead, the engineer blew a single, mournful blast on his whistle. Dempsey clambered up the bank and ran beside the train. He had to gauge his steps so his feet would land on the ties. He was gasping for breath as a boxcar clattered out of the darkness behind him, its door half open. As it passed, he reached inside, feeling desperately for something to grab hold of. As he did, his foot slipped on the wet ties. He gave one desperate shove with his other foot as he began to founder, grabbed the edge of the open door and twisted himself into the car.

BOOK THREE

"The belief in a supernatural
source of evil is not
necessary; men alone are quite
capable of every wickedness."

Joseph Conrad

23

Bert Rudman liked to write in a small reading room off the lobby of the Bristol Hotel, preferring it to his apartment, which was much too quiet and secluded, and his office, which was frenetic and intrusive. The room was subdued and quiet, its floor-to-ceiling brass lamps flared at the top and mounted against the walls, casting soft indirect light off the ceiling on scarlet-and-black-striped silk wallpaper. There were fringed lamps and brass ink wells on the half-dozen mahogany writing desks in the room. The sofas and chairs were leather and the people who sat in them usually whispered as they would in a library.

If he felt the urge for a drink, across the narrow lobby was the hotel bar, a subdued, intimate watering hole with a twenty-foot-long slate bar running the length of one wall, charcoal carpeting, glass-topped pedestal tables and deep-piled chairs. The bartender, Romey, played his favorite records on a Gramophone hidden in a storage closet, his eclectic taste ranging from opera and classics to the latest jazz recordings. Romey was perhaps the rudest bartender in Paris, greeting occasional musical requests from customers with a dour grunt, followed by *"non."* He refused to indulge in casual conversation and muttered obscenities to himself when asked to make a drink he personally did not like. But if Romey was less than radiant he made up for it with phenomenal recall, remembering the drink preference of guests he sometimes had not seen for six months or longer.

For two years, Rudman had been keeping a daily journal of his activities, his viewpoints and impressions of the escalating crisis in Europe, a chronicle of his innermost thoughts and fears, an evaluation of the gathering storm.

On this night he was writing an essay about the élan of the French who seemed, on the surface, to ignore the threat to the north and east of them. After all, they had the Maginot Line, a string of vertical, concrete buttresses backed up by bunkers that stretched the entire length of the border. That, with the French Army, was supposed to hold back Hitler's *Wehrmacht*. Rudman thought it was a joke and had so stated in several of his columns, an observation which had hardly endeared him to the French government or the military.

Each night he sat in the writing room with a glass of absinthe and let his thoughts ramble, stretching his subjective viewpoint, adding unproven rumors and predictions on the future of the continent he could not use in his newspaper articles. He had been using the free time before going to work for the *Times* to update the journal, which he called *Overture to Disaster,* and trying to ignore a persistent inner voice that told him he was actually writing a book. Rudman was not ready yet to accept that responsibility as a reality.

The Bristol Hotel was a small but exclusive hotel catering to steady customers and celebrities who sought the kind of anonymity they would not find at the larger and more famous Ritz. Keegan always stayed at the Bristol. It was a comfortable hotel and because he was known there, he was treated especially well by the managers. The lobby was a long, narrow corridor leading to a small registration desk and an elevator, an open brass and ebony cage. The lobby was bracketed by the reading room on the left and the bar on the right. Keegan and Jenny always came by the reading room when they returned from their nightly forays in search of entertainment. That was Rudman's sign to quit for the night. They always had a nightcap together.

But tonight they were running late. As Rudman, tired of his own nitpicking rewriting, decided to have another drink, he looked up to see von Meister, the German Embassy attaché, standing across the lobby in the doorway of the bar. Silhouetted by the back-lit glass shelves of liquor behind the bar, he was an intimidating figure, tall and erect, an almost satanic personification of the Third Reich. Von Meister was wearing a dark blue double-breasted suit instead of his uniform, yet Rudman still felt a sudden chill, as if he had walked past an open refrigerator.

"*Bon soir,* Monsieur Rudman," he said. Then, nodding at the journal, "Letting your imagination run rampant as usual?"

Rudman smiled. "I prefer to call it truth."

"Well, one man's truth is another man's lie, correct? I do not know who said that, certainly some astute poet."

"I'm sure," Rudman answered.

"I understand your American friend—what was his name again?" Rudman didn't answer and von Meister waved his hand, as if forgiving the silence. "Ah, yes. Keegan. I understand he is going to marry that German girl."

"That's the story going around."

"I hope they will be very happy," the German said without conviction.

"I'll tell them you care."

Again von Meister indicated Rudman's journal, this time with a faint smile.

"You hardly have an objective viewpoint," he said. "I thought that was the mark of a good journalist, objectivity."

"That what they taught you at Cambridge?"

"What they taught me at Cambridge is of little use to me. What I *learned* at Cambridge is that the British Empire is doomed. The strain is weak. Too much inbreeding."

"That's what you thought the last time you took them on and look what happened. You got your ass whipped."

The German's smile faded. The muscles in his jaw tightened.

"You know, it is a privilege for you to work in Germany. *We* grant you a visa and *we* can always rescind it. I would not forget that if I were you."

"I don't forget anything," Rudman said.

"How interesting," von Meister answered. "Neither do I."

"Christ, you're an educated man, von Meister. Can't you see what's happening to your country? Don't you have any conscience?"

Von Meister stared at him. "Hitler is my conscience," he said.

He turned to return to the bar. *"Bon soir,"* he said without turning back. "Give my regards to Herr Keegan and his *deutsche* lady friend." He lifted his glass in a mock toast.

Rudman was deeply disturbed by the conversation. His mind was in a perpetual whirl, trying to sort out all the dichotomies of the German situation. He had spent fifteen years off and on in Germany and he thought he knew the people. But the reaction of Germans to the startling rise of Hitler from jailbird to absolute dictator of the country astounded him.

He turned back to his ledger and wrote:

"How could the Germans let this happen? How could they simply give up freedom of speech, freedom of expression, freedom from search and seizure?

"The German people are virtually prisoners in their own country. They are choked by censorship and rampant police excesses. Their literacy and taste are controlled by creative illiterates. Goebbels and his henchmen, supported by religious opportunists, have stripped the libraries of the great books—Kipling, Mark Twain, Dante, Steinbeck, Hemingway, Freud, Proust, Thomas Mann, the list is endless—which they have deemed degenerate, and the museums of the depraved paintings of Van Gogh, Picasso, Modigliani, Gauguin, Degas and dozens more.

"How can they abide the destruction of the Constitution by judges who are political henchmen, who make their decisions, not on the basis of morality or justice, but simply to appease Hitler and his mob. Legalize sterilization? Legalize lobotomy? These men are *judges*! They legalize everything he does. My God, what crimes are justified in the name of Justice!

"How can a whole nation of basically decent people turn its collective face away from the wholesale robbery, assault and murder of Jews and political dissidents? Good God, these things are not subtle! It takes an *effort* to look the other way!

"How, indeed?

"Perhaps if we learn the answer to *that* question, we can prevent such a human tragedy from ever happening again.

"But I doubt that we will.

"We never seem to learn."

A few minutes later Keegan and Jenny came in with their arms wrapped around each other, laughing as usual. He closed the ledger.

"What was it tonight?" Rudman asked, gathering up his papers and putting them in a leather portfolio.

"Le Casino de Paris," she said, her words rushing together

with excitement. "We saw the Dolly Sisters and the Duke of Windsor and Maurice Chevalier and, who was the fighter, Francis?"

"Jack Sharkey," he answered and rolled his eyes. "He's only the ex-heavyweight champion of the world."

"Another memorable night, eh?" Rudman asked.

"Oh yes," she said, wrapping her arms in Keegan's. "Every night is memorable."

The memory of Wilhelm Vierhaus's first day in school sometimes intruded on his thoughts without warning, subconsciously triggered by some real or imagined look or word. When that happened, Vierhaus was overwhelmed with awesome fury, made more terrifying by his cold control of his emotions. The object of that fury was always David Kravitz.

He had led a rather sheltered life until that day, his deformity accepted and ignored by family and friends. Although he was aware that the ugly lump of muscle on his shoulder made him different from others, he was not yet aware of how cruel children can be.

The initial offender was David Kravitz, whose family was rich and influential, and who was a kind of self-appointed class leader. It became quickly apparent to Kravitz, an excellent student, that Vierhaus represented a threat. The deformed boy was brilliant, quick to raise his hand in class, always prepared. So David Kravitz set out to demean and discredit Vierhaus, whom he called the "new boy with the mountain on his back." He implied that the deformity was really the result of some dark and horrible genetic secret, carefully guarded by the family. He had once spread the story that Vierhaus, actually an only child, had a sister who was so deformed she was kept in a closet. The other children quickly joined in the conspiracy.

Kravitz was the first person Vierhaus had truly hated and that hatred quickly spread to include all Jews. He reveled in the lies and rumors which the racists spread about them and when Vierhaus read *Mein Kampf*, its racial distortions had fired that hatred. It became his Talmud, his Bible, the Psalms that motivated him. Hitler was God, Jews were the Devil and blood was the holy water of life, to be purified, cleansed, Aryanized for the glory of the Third Reich. He was the perfect Nazi, an intelligent, dedicated man whose blind hatred had replaced moral conviction and whose racism was so vile it was akin to a perverted religious fanaticism in which humiliation, treachery, torture and murder were the rituals.

Vierhaus understood the irony of the fact that he depended so completely on Jews to carry out one of his most important assignments. And so he smiled as he watched through a slit in the door to his sitting room, as Herman Adler was ushered into his office. He checked his watch. He would let him wait for ten minutes. Ten minutes alone in that foreboding room with only paranoia for a companion, what a delicious thought.

Herman Adler sat on the edge of his chair with his satchel clutched against his chest as if he were afraid it would fly away. The room was dark except for two overhead lights, one beaming down on the desk, the other on Adler. The top of the oak desk was empty except for a writing blotter, a telephone and an ashtray. The rest of the office was dark but before Adler's eyes became accustomed to the deep shadows, the door opened and Vierhaus entered the room, walking with a kind of shuffling gait, trying to minimize the hump on his back. He did not look at Adler. He sat down at his desk, slipped on a pair of glasses, opened a drawer and removed a file folder. He took out a pocket watch and put it on the desk, opened the folder and leafed through the contents, stopping occasionally to read something, nodding and murmuring approval to himself as he scanned the contents.

Finally he lit a cigarette and settled back in his chair. His flinty eyes fixed on Adler, who remained seated on the edge of his chair clutching the satchel.

"So . . . may I call you Herman?" He said pleasantly.

"Oh, yes sir, please do."

"You may call me Professor," he said, looking back at the file.

"Thank you, *Herr Professor*."

"You have been remarkably successful working in our Genealogy Program, Herman. I have been wanting to meet you personally but . . . these are busy times."

"Of course, *Herr Professor*."

Vierhaus had learned that the more one did, the more Hitler demanded. First it had been the intelligence unit, then the Black Lily and now this Genealogy Program. He was determined to make the experiment work. While Himmler and Heydrich were busy with the major problem of dealing with the Jews, Vierhaus was quietly performing his own service with mixed-blood subjects, half, quarter, and one-eighth Jews. It was difficult to ferret them out. Adler had turned out to be an invaluable ally in this project.

"I see we share a mutual interest in opera," he said without looking up. He was not in the slightest interested in Adler's love of opera; he simply wanted the Jew to know that the SS knew *every*thing about him.

"Yes, it is my first love. When my wife was alive we would take all our holidays in Italy. We went to La Scala every night."

"How nice. Well, as I was saying, yours is a most impressive record."

"Thank you," Adler answered, his head bobbing nervously.

"What is it now, twelve, thirteen families?"

"Fifteen, sir," Adler said modestly.

"Hmm. Are any of the Jews in your community aware that you are doing this work?"

"No, no, Professor," Adler said with a look of alarm, "nobody would speak to me."

"Of course."

"That is why I come at night to make my reports."

Vierhaus peered intently at Adler again. He was fifty-four years old, a short man, chunky although not fat, with dimpled hands and soft eyes. His graying black hair was receding and his face was lined and chalky. He was wearing a blue serge suit worn shiny at the elbows and his shirt collar was frayed. A thin line of sweat glistened on his upper lip. Neat but tawdry, thought Vierhaus. Grateful—no, indebted—for the smallest favors.

"I am curious about something, Herman. Does it bother you? Turning up other Jews this way?"

Adler did not have to think, he shook his head immediately.

"It's the law," he said. "I think I am lucky to have the opportunity."

For an instant, Vierhaus's eyes glittered and his eyebrows rose with surprise. "I must say, that is a most practical point of view," he said slowly. He looked back at the papers. "You are a jeweler by trade, yes?"

"Yes. I had my own shop."

"Was it nationalized?"

"Yes."

"And your home?"

"Yes."

"You live at 65 Königsplatz now. Is that a flat?"

"Yes, *Herr Professor*. One room and a small kitchen."

"No family, I see."

"My son was killed on the Western Front in 1916. My wife died three years ago."

"Yes, a heart attack, I see."

"*Ja.* She never really got over our son Ira's death."

"And you also have a heart problem?"

"Minor. I had a small attack a year or so ago. I have my pills just in case. I am quite fit."

"Good. We wouldn't want to lose you. You understand, Herman, there are people in the party who disagree with this department's mixed-blood policy. They feel only full-blooded Jews should be involved in repatriation and emigration. Bureaucrats, mostly. They are slow to come around, bureaucrats thrive on the status quo. That will change with time, of course. In the meantime, the Führer has given me the responsibility of starting this experiment. But you do understand the confidential nature of this work, don't you, Adler? You don't even discuss it with other SS personnel."

"I understand, *Herr Professor*."

"Personally I think four generations is far enough to go back. Eventually the numbers will be overwhelming. So, Adler, there will always be plenty of work for you."

"Thank you, sir."

"Perhaps I might even have you elevated to Aryan status. It is done, you know, in cases of special merit. You cannot vote or marry an Aryan woman, but those are minor things. If your success keeps up we can make arrangements for you to move to something a little bigger, more comfortable, maybe get you another shop, eh, even throw a little party business your way?"

Adler closed his eyes. He had heard that the Germans

sometimes destigmatized Jews but this was the first official confirmation that it was possible. *My God*, he thought, *to have my own shop again, a decent house, to have the 'J' removed from my ID. To have a sense of freedom again.* It was too much to hope for.

"That would be most generous, *Herr Professor*," Adler said, his voice trembling. His heart began beating faster.

"I offer you another challenge, Herman," Vierhaus said, standing and walking around the desk. "Herr Himmler would like to bring back some rather influential Jews who have . . . left Germany. These are people who, for many reasons, we would like to have back here. Traitors. Troublemakers in other countries. They are scattered everywhere."

He waved his hand flamboyantly.

"Italy, France, Egypt, Greece, America. Any leads you might get for us would be an even bigger feather in your cap. You would not only earn my gratitude, but *Reichsführer* Himmler's as well. I can provide you with a list of names. You keep your ears open, hmm?"

"I will get on it right away, *Herr Professor*."

Vierhaus patted the Jew on the shoulder.

"Would you like a cigarette?" He took out the package and shook a cigarette loose. "They are French. Gauloises."

"Oh, thank you, sir," Adler said, taking it with a shaky hand. When it was lit, Adler opened the briefcase and took out a sheaf of documents.

"I have something here, I think you will be very excited by this . . ."

He laid them very precisely on the desk in front of him. Almost as an afterthought, he then put the case on the floor beside the chair.

"These are family records," Adler said. "Birth certificates, some interviews with family members, friends. This man Oskar Braun has a bank near Coburg. Very successful." He shuffled through the papers and stopped at a chart. "I tracked back four generations, four, *Herr Professor*," Adler said proudly, holding up four fingers. "His maternal grandfather was a Jew. Joshua Feldstein. He was a cantor in the synagogue and he actually started the bank. I have a list of all the descendants, including nephews and cousins. Forty-six in all."

"Yes, yes, that's quite ingenious. The *Schutzstaffel* will take care of Herr Braun. But," Vierhaus said, picking a note from the folder, "it says you have information for my ears alone. What is that about?"

"Yes, *Herr Professor*. It is regarding the memorandum you sent around about a month ago."

"Adler, I write a dozen memoranda a day."

"This one concerned the Black Lily."

Vierhaus looked up sharply.

"You have information about the Black Lily?" he said, making no attempt to conceal his sudden interest.

Adler nodded.

"Well . . . ?" Vierhaus wiggled his fingers toward Adler as if to coax the information out of him.

Adler shuffled through more papers. "Ah," he said. "Here we are. Uh, you know about the connection with Reinhardt and . . ."

"Yes, yes, we know all that," Vierhaus said slowly, taking off his glasses and placing them on the desk. His eyes narrowed to luminous slits, but his voice never changed. If anything, it became more controlled. He ground his cigarette out in the ashtray. "We arrested Reinhardt, that is past history. I need names, jeweler, *names*!"

"I *have* names for you, sir," Adler stammered fearfully. "And charts."

He fumbled nervously through his papers and as he did, Vierhaus suddenly and radically changed his mood. This was what he called a "neutral interrogation." Nonadversarial. But he used the same methods he would have used in less friendly encounters, employing subtle changes in temperament combined with equal doses of cruelty and generosity, designed to keep his prey off balance and intimidated. Methods he had learned from the master of the technique, Adolf Hitler. The difference was that Vierhaus, unlike his volatile and psychotic boss, was a study in serpentine control.

"Would you like a cup of coffee?" he asked abruptly, with a smile. "It is imported from South America, an excellent brew."

"Oh, that would be very kind," Adler said, taking out a handkerchief and wiping his face. He had been reduced to ersatz coffee months ago. He couldn't specifically remember the last time he had a cup of real coffee.

Vierhaus got up and went to a corner of the room and turned on a floor lamp. A pot of coffee simmered on a hot plate.

"Cream?" he asked.

"Yes sir." *Cream. Real cream.*

Adler sipped the coffee with his eyes closed, savoring every drop.

"Now, tell me what you know about the Black Lily."

"Herr Reinhardt was a frequent visitor at the home of a Jewish teacher named Isaac Sternfeld. Sternfeld taught political science at the university here until he was sent to Dachau."

"Is he a Communist?"

"Nein, a Social Democrat radically opposed to the Führer and the Nazi party. Before the Führer became chancellor, a group of students who were also frequent guests at Sternfeld's started a pamphlet called *Die Fackel.* It was aimed mainly at students, a kind of college humor . . . uh, satire thing with a bit of a sting to it. Then after Herr Hitler . . ."

"The Führer," Vierhaus corrected.

"Yes, the Führer, after the Führer became chancellor it became more pointed. That is when Reinhardt became involved, writing occasionally for it and editing it. Sternfeld was the advisor and it was printed by Oscar Probst."

"The Berlin Conscience," Vierhaus said.

"Ja. When the . . . uh . . ."

"Repatriation?"

"Ja . . . repatriation . . . of the Jews began the students formed the Black Lily to help get Jews out of Germany."

"Where did they get that name?" Vierhaus asked out of curiosity.

"There is no such thing as a black lily, *Herr Professor.* They meant it to be a phantom organization, just like the flower."

"Schoolboy antics," Vierhaus said, waving him off. "What else?"

"They moved money into Swiss banks, arranged forged passports, transportation, everything."

"Students?" Vierhaus said with astonishment.

Adler nodded.

"Students are doing this?!" Vierhaus said, shaking his head. He could imagine Hitler's reaction to *that* bit of news.

"But very dedicated students," said Adler.

"Politicized by Reinhardt and this Sternfeld person, hmm?"
Adler continued to nod.

"The editor of *Die Fackel* was a Jewish boy named Avrum
Wolffson. He is now twenty-five years old. His best friends are
Werner Gebhart and Joachim Weber. It is my understanding
that Wolffson is the head of the Black Lily. Gebhart handles the
movement of Jews out of the country, and Weber handles
money, the paperwork, passports, false ID's, such things."

Vierhaus stroked his chin as he listened to Adler. Other
things were becoming clear to him.

"So, now I think I know what happened to Otto Schiff and
Tol Nathan. These students probably ran them out of the country. And they probably forced Simon Kefar to hang himself."

"Simon Kefar worked for you, too?"

"You didn't know that? Schiff, Nathan, Kefar, all very effective *Judenhascher* like yourself. You knew them?"

"I knew Kefar casually. The others only by name."

Vierhaus stroked his chin for a moment or two longer.

"How do they finance all this?" he asked finally.

"With contributions from rich Jews and sympathizers here
and abroad."

"This Wolffson and a couple of students created all this
intrigue?" Vierhaus said, still unable to accept Adler's theory.

"Actually I think it was Sternfeld who organized it anticipat-
ing the . . . repatriation. But Wolffson was a brilliant student,
very pragmatic the way I understand it."

"How do you know all this?"

Adler stared at him for several seconds. "Joachim Weber is
my nephew," he said. "The boy and I have never been close but
I talk to my sister—his mother—frequently."

"How many people are involved with this bunch?"

Adler shook his head. "Dozens, I assume. In Berlin, Munich, Linz, Paris, Zurich."

"All Jews?"

"No. They are both Jews and Gentiles."

"How did this get so far out of hand!" Vierhaus said almost
to himself. The Führer would be outraged. "And where do we
find this Wolffson?"

"That is the problem, *Herr Professor*, nobody knows. There
are no lists of the members, it is not a military-type organization.

It is like the flower, it seems not to exist. It is like a train that runs whenever necessary. Nobody has seen Wolffson in months. But I believe he must be in Berlin. And I have this."

He handed Vierhaus a sheet of typing paper. There were two columns of names and addresses on it.

"These are forty-eight people who are related to Wolffson. That includes three generations up to fourth cousins and nephews. I have similar lists on Weber and Gebhart in the folder."

Vierhaus was impressed. "That is a remarkable report, Adler." He turned back to the list of names and ran his forefinger down each one. "You did this in a month?"

"Three weeks actually."

"Remarkable indeed. The Gestapo has been investigating this for months with no success."

"They are not Jews," Adler said, almost in a whisper.

"Very true, Herman. It takes one to catch one, eh?" He smiled at Adler, who began to relax. The jeweler wiped sweat off the back of his neck. "If you can find him, sir, I think I can produce enough proof to . . ."

"I do not care about proof," Vierhaus said, waving his hand as he scanned the list. "Give me names and addresses and I will get confessions from these schoolboys. I don't need proof."

Vierhaus started to say something else and then stopped. His finger was poised over one of the names.

"This is his sister? Jennifer Gould?"

"Half-sister, *Herr Professor*. Her mother married the Jew, Wolffson. She is a Catholic, I believe."

"You have no address on her?"

"*Nein.* She moved about three months ago and dropped out of sight."

"Hmm," said Vierhaus. "We seem to have an epidemic of vanishing . . ."

Vierhaus looked up suddenly, his eyes squinting into a dark corner of the room, and then he slapped his hands together. Adler was startled by the sharp sound in the quiet room.

"I *know* where she is!" Vierhaus said. He pulled open a desk drawer and clawed through file folders. He pulled one out. Inside were copies of the weekly reports of military spies in half a dozen major European cities, including von Meister in Paris.

Vierhaus licked his thumb and flipped through the pages, then stopped. "Yes, of course. Keegan!"

Vierhaus leaned back and smiled, proud of himself not only for reading these dull reports every week but for remembering the brief reference to Keegan and the Gould woman.

"She's a singer," he sneered. "She sings American nigger jazz. And she is a friend of that American liar, Rudman." He looked at Adler and smiled. "Perhaps she knows where Wolffson is. Perhaps she is the *Kettenglied* to the Black Lily. And she is in Paris."

Adler scurried down the street toward a small delicatessen with his satchel still clutched to his chest. It had started to rain, a persistent mist that slowly collected on hair, skin and clothing. He hunched his shoulders up. He needed to take a pill. His heart was racing with excitement. A shop, he thought. And a decent place to live, possibly even an Aryan ID card. It was all very dizzying.

As he passed a sedan parked at the curb, a hoarse voice said from behind him: "Herman Adler." He started to turn but as he did two muscular arms encircled his, clamping them to his sides. The satchel fell to the ground.

Adler opened his mouth to speak but before he could get the words out a wad of cotton was jammed against his nose. He smelled the stinging-sweet odor of chloroform a moment before he passed out. As two men shoved him into the car, a small bottle of pills fell out of Adler's vest pocket and rolled into the gutter.

Vierhaus had a few minutes before he had to leave for his dinner appointment. He leaned back in his chair. He had to move cautiously for the time being, particularly in working with Himmler. A great many Germans were sympathetic to the Jews, particularly the officials and bureaucrats in the provinces. Hitler did not want to jeopardize his power over them. At this point the Führer needed everyone's support. Vierhaus's work with mixed bloods and renegades could not become general knowledge, not for a while at least. But there were many who knew and believed in the purification work. Theodor Eicke was one of them.

He snatched up the phone and placed a call to the brutish ex-brownshirt, now a member of the SS and manager of the camp at Dachau. Eicke was known for his inflexible harshness. As a member of the SA he had once beaten a Jew to death with his bare hands. At Dachau he had killed a prisoner with a shovel. Eicke was a man Vierhaus could deal with.

"Teddy, it is Willie Vierhaus," he said when Eicke's harsh voice answered.

"Willie! How are things in Berlin?"

"Excellent. Everything goes very well. And with you?"

"Oh, fine. This is a lovely town."

"And the camp?"

"Running well."

"No troubles?"

"*Nein.* The Jews give us very little trouble, it's the political prisoners who are a problem. But we have it under control. Our only problem is crowding."

"The new camp at Sachsenhausen will be ready in the spring, that should give you some relief. And they are planning others at Bergen-Belsen and Buchenwald."

"*Ja,* very good."

"And Anna? How is she?"

"She complains occasionally. We have had an escape attempt or two and always at night. The wire always gets them but it is quite annoying. The static from the wires wakes her up."

"Get heavier shutters," Vierhaus suggested.

"*Ja, ja,*" Eicke said and laughed.

"Listen Teddy, I have a favor to ask. You have a prisoner there called Sternfeld."

"The teacher?"

"*Ja.* He may have information about a group which calls itself the Black Lily. The Führer is most anxious to get all the information he can about this organization. I thought perhaps you might employ some of your more persuasive methods on this Sternfeld."

"I am sorry, Willie. You are a little late."

"Late?"

"Sternfeld is dead. About a month ago."

"What happened to him?"

"He was allergic to hard work," Eicke said with a chuckle. "But pneumonia actually did him in."

"Damn!"

"Sorry," Eicke said. "Do we have anyone else here who might have information?"

"I don't know," Vierhaus said. His disappointment was obvious in his tone. "I will look into it."

"Well, Willie, if you find we do just give me a ring," Eicke's gruff voice answered. "We could make the Brandenburg Gate sing the 'Horst Wessel' if we had to—but we have no luck at all with corpses." And he laughed.

Vierhaus leaned back in his chair and finished his coffee. He had to break the Black Lily and unless Adler came up with new information, Vierhaus had only one lead left. Jennifer Gould.

Adler awoke with a splitting headache. He was lying on a cot in a dark room. He sat up slowly, his feet groping under him for the floor. Then he saw his satchel, sitting beside the bed. The top was flared open and the satchel was empty. A light suddenly burst on. It was about thirty feet away, a spotlight aimed straight at him. A man sat silhouetted on a chair in front of it.

"Who are you?" Adler demanded, squinting into the light. "Why are you doing this to me? I have nothing . . ."

The silhouetted man's arm moved. There was a flare of light as he threw something toward Adler. The file folders from his satchel smacked the floor and slid to his feet, the contents splayed out around them.

"You are wrong, Herr Adler," the silhouetted man said in a flat monotone that sounded as if he were purposely disguising it. "You do have something. What is this, work in progress?"

"That is none of your business."

"We know everything you have done. Fifteen families, sixty-four people, all sent to the work camp at Dachau. You have become an executioner, killing your own people."

"They are not *my* people."

"They are the same blood."

"Leave me alone!" Adler said miserably.

"We have an offer for you, Herman Adler. We will take you out of Berlin tonight. By this time tomorrow you will be in a neutral country with a passport and tickets to either England or America. But first, you must tell us what you reported to Vierhaus."

"I cannot leave Germany . . ."

"Of course you can. You live in a hovel like a cockroach and you betray your friends. You cannot keep it up, Herr Adler.

Accept our offer and you will be a free man with a job awaiting you."

"As what, an apprentice gem cutter to some English snob? I am a German! This is my country."

"No. It is no longer your country or my country. We can't vote, own property, go to decent restaurants, have a job. For God's sake, man, they took your property, your bank account, your home, everything you own. How can you spy for them?"

"I am trying to stay alive!" Adler cried out passionately.

"We *all* are. That is why you cannot keep this up."

Adler squinted across the room at him. "And what are you going to do if I refuse? Kill me?"

The silhouetted man paused for several seconds. He stood and walked out of the halo of light. Adler squinted and turned his face, blinded temporarily by the spotlight. The man stood in the darkness, the tip of his cigarette glowing intermittently.

"No," he said, finally. "What we will do is this. We will print your face on the front page of *The Berlin Conscience* with a story listing every Jew you have given to them. We will see that every Jew in Germany knows who you are and what you do. Since you will no longer be of any use to the *Judenopferer* Vierhaus or anybody else, they will either kill you or send you to Dachau with the people you have betrayed. Think about that." He used the harsh term *Judenopferer,* which meant "Jew sacrificer" rather than the slightly less offensive *Judenhascher.*

Adler shook his head violently. "No, no! I can't do it. They will kill me." Adler felt a familiar tremor in his chest.

"You have no choice. Freedom and forgiveness now, or you are most certainly a dead man. Who did you give up tonight, Adler? We may still have time to save them."

"Nobody," Adler lied. "Vierhaus sent for me."

"Why?"

"I told you, to meet me." A sudden pain fired deep in his chest. He began to rub his chest with the flat of his hand.

"Why did he want to meet you? Did he want you to make some earrings for him? Or fix his cuckoo clock? Why did he send for you, Adler?"

"He lectured me to do better in the future."

"You are lying."

"No, no, I . . ."

"Shh, shh, shh, Herman." Another voice spoke up, this one from the shadows behind the lamp. "You are lying and we know it."

"You know how we know you are lying?" Still another voice said. "Because you are the best of the *Judenhascher* who work for him. The best, Adler, how does that make you feel, eh?"

"Did he bring you in to give you a medal, Herman? To kiss you on both cheeks and congratulate you for being such a good Jewish Nazi? Is that why you were there, Herman?"

"And what do you get for this?" The first voice said from the darkness. "Your room? It is not much bigger than a prison cell. You do not have enough food to feed an ant. They give you ration food and a few marks, isn't that true? Good God, man, how do you live with yourself?"

"Do you ever consider the consequences of your actions?"

"It is the law!" Adler shrieked. "You are the traitors, not I."

"It is *not* law," the gravelly voice snapped back angrily, and there was a moment when it sounded vaguely familiar to Adler. "It is immoral. It is degrading. It is a violation of everything that is human and decent."

"Why don't you just kill me? That is what it is all about, isn't it?" Adler said with a sudden burst of bravura and anger, straightening his shoulders and glaring into the shadows. The pain had subsided momentarily.

"We don't kill, that is their game. We are trying to reason with you as we did with Schiff and Nathan."

"And did you provide the rope Kefar used to hang himself?"

"*Nein.* His conscience tied that knot," the gravelly voice answered. Adler sat for a moment, staring away from the spotlight, trying to pick out forms in the shadows. The gravelly voice sounded more familiar.

"Listen to me, Herman," the first man said in a sympathetic voice. "Stop now and I promise no one will ever know what you have done. We understand the pressures. But if you continue, there is no way you will ever wash the blood off your hands. Your people will shun you and the Nazis will break you like a twig."

"Stop it!" the little man cried. The excitement of the meeting with Vierhaus coupled with his fear at the hands of his kidnappers began to take its toll on Adler. He was breathing hard. Sweat stained his shirt collar and bathed his face, which had turned the color of wet clay. He squeezed his chest with one hand and his lips pulled back from his teeth in a grimace.

"I need my pills," he said, frantically searching his pockets. "Please, where are my pills?"

"There were no pills in your pockets, Herr Adler. I searched you thoroughly."

"Of course there are pills," he gasped. "I go nowhere without my pills."

He stood up, lost his footing and one of his captors jumped from the darkness and grabbed him.

Adler clutched at the man's shirt. "My pills," he croaked. "Help me please." And then his eyes bulged as he looked up at the man. He was short and broad-shouldered, a young man in his twenties with a heavy black beard and long hair. It took a moment for Adler to recognize his nephew.

"My God, Joachim, what are you doing?" he cried. "I am your Uncle Herman!"

The young man steered him back to the bed.

"Where are the pills, Uncle?" he asked in a calm voice.

"V-v-vest pocket . . ." His voice had diminished into a terrified whine. His hands trembled uncontrollably as he fumbled through the pockets. "Here, they were here." But there were no pills and the realization added to the stress and anxiety Herman Adler was already experiencing. His heart was racing out of control, sending lightning streaks of pain into his chest and stomach. He started gasping for breath.

"Oh my God," he croaked. He clutched his chest with both hands and bent over so his head was almost touching his knees. "Help me. Help me."

The other two captors had joined Weber. They loosened Adler's tie and unbuttoned his collar.

"Take it easy," the taller one, the silhouetted man, Avrum Wolffson, said gently, and began rubbing his wrists. "Try to relax. Your pills must have fallen out of your pocket. Take slow, deep breaths, don't make it worse. We will try to get you a doctor. Get him some water, Werner."

Adler looked up, his breath coming in short rushes. "Why?" he asked pitifully and collapsed on the bed. By the time Werner Gebhart came back with the water, Herman Adler was dead.

John Hammond was one of Keegan's oldest friends. He was the scion of the Hammond Organ family, a jazz aficionado who wrote a column for the jazz music magazine *Metronome* and prided himself on discovering new talent. Hammond would go anywhere, to the smallest town and the dingiest club, to hear any jazz musician with promise. Among others, the young entrepreneur had discovered Billie Holiday and Benny Goodman, the clarinetist engaged to Hammond's sister, who was gaining fame in the States with his swing orchestra. He had set up Holiday's first recording date with Goodman, lured Count Basie from Chicago to New York, discovered the frenetic drummer Gene Krupa, had been the first to write about drummer Chick Webb and his big band, and he had discovered the great piano player Teddy Wilson, putting him together with Goodman. Hammond had produced a couple of records for Columbia Records and his reputation as an impresario of new talent had become indisputable. If Hammond was impressed by Jenny's unique long-distance phone audition, he could open many doors for her—nightclubs, bands, recordings, radio shots.

Keegan had hired Charlie Kraus, an American jazz arranger and pianist living in Paris, to work with Jenny and accompany her during the audition. That had impressed Hammond who knew Kraus to be a tough and discriminating musician, a man who would not waste his time with second-rate talent. A dapper little man who dressed in the fashion of the day with his beret cocked jauntily over one eye, Kraus, whose mother was Negro, had been an arranger for Fletcher Henderson, Duke Ellington, Cab Calloway and other rising stars before he had abandoned the States two years earlier, disillusioned by racism in the music business.

Kraus made a good living as a teacher and arranger and had a small combo which played in one of the Paris clubs on weekends. It was there one night that Keegan had convinced him to let Jenny try a song or two. Kraus had been amazed, talking her into singing with the band for an entire set, then offering her a permanent job. But Keegan had more ambitious plans. He had tracked down Hammond in Kansas City and put Kraus on the phone.

"She's special, Johnny," Kraus told Hammond. "Great breath control. Phrasing's a miracle. Tone's unique, not quite alto but almost. And the lady has great respect for lyrics, doesn't throw away a single syllable. I mean, this lady knows exactly what she wants a song to sound like. Man, she reaches for notes some of us don't even hear in our *head.* Tell yuh, John, she could give me a lesson or two."

Based on that endorsement, Hammond had agreed to the unprecedented phone audition. Keegan's dream was that Hammond would be impressed enough to lure Jenny to New York.

They had gone to Kraus's studio in Montmartre and spent an afternoon there, exchanging ideas, trying new things, working with songs she didn't know. Then Keegan had moved the piano into their suite; she and Kraus had been working together for two weeks to prepare for the event.

Keegan placed the call three times before the overseas connection satisfied him. Finally they were ready. He uncradled the phone in the bedroom and placed it in front of the loudspeaker, then went back in the living room and picked up the extension.

"Ready?" he asked.

"Fire away," said Hammond.

Jenny's first choice was a strange one. The song had become a kind of anthem to the Depression and had been made famous by Rudy Vallee, the nasally Ivy Leaguer turned crooner, who had recorded it almost as a dirge.

Keegan and Rudman sat nervously on the edge of one of the stuffed sofas, sipping champagne. At first Keegan was shocked by her choice. But as she sang, he realized it didn't matter. She closed her eyes and held a finger against one ear, leaned her head back slightly and started singing. She sang with such ardor, reaching for and hitting each note so perfectly, that her choice of material quickly became moot. Keegan sat back and marveled at her incredible control, at her passion when she sang.

> *"Once I built a railroad, made it run*
> *Made it race against time.*
> *Once I built a railroad, now it's done.*
> *Brother, can you spare a dime?"*

She turned the bitter tune into a torch song, almost a love song with an upbeat lilt, as she finished:

> *"Hey, don't you remember, they called me Al,*
> *It was Al all the time,*
> *Hey, don't you remember, I'm your pal,*
> *Buddy, can you spare a dime?"*

Then segueing easily into the next selection, looking across the room at Keegan, she sang:

> *"I got a crush on you,*
> *Sweetie Pie,*
> *All the day and night time,*
> *Hear my cry,*
> *The world will pardon my mush,*
> *But I have got a crush,*
> *My baby on you."*

And from the Gershwin love song she easily turned to a Billie Holiday heartbreaker, shifting the words slightly to suit her, stretching a syllable out for two or three notes, rolling from one note to another, shaving the songs down to the bare essentials, then as she segued into her last number, she looked over at Keegan and wiggled her hips and winked, then in a very upbeat tempo, fingers snapping and staring bright-eyed at her lover across the room, she sang:

> *"Everything*
> *Is fine and dandy*
> *Sugar candy*
> *When I'm with you . . ."*

She ended the set on a high note with Kraus and bass player Chuck Graves jamming behind her. When she finished, Kraus, Graves, Keegan and Rudman all were speechless for seconds before they simultaneously burst into applause.

"Immaculate, lady, im-maculate," Kraus said, flashing a million-dollar smile.

Dead silence for a moment when she finished, then Keegan snatched up the extension phone. "Well?" he asked.

"How soon can you get her to New York?"

"Are you kidding!"

"Not this time."

He cupped the receiver. "He wants to know how soon we can come to New York," he said to Jenny.

Jenny bit her lower lip. Her heart was pounding. This was a chance she had dreamed about since she was a child. But . . . she had other responsibilities. Her eyes began to well up with tears. Keegan was so happy, so happy *for* her. Perhaps they could go to New York for a few weeks and test the waters. Perhaps if she was a success she could do something significant for her friends and family in Germany. Perhaps . . .

"Go . . . go . . . pick up the phone," Keegan said.

"Oh no, no . . ." she said shaking her head with embarrassment. He grabbed her hand and put the extension phone in it.

"Here, say hello to John Hammond," he said, and went to the other phone.

"Hello . . ." she said hesitantly.

"Miss Gould, you have a voice that would put the heavenly chorus to shame. Quite simply, you have a great voice and you know exactly how to use it."

"Oh, thank you," she whispered.

Keegan picked up the other phone. "So . . . Where do we go from here?" he asked Hammond.

"You get her this far and I'll take it from there. We'll introduce her around, maybe get her a guest shot at Kelley's or the Onyx, one of the downtown clubs. I'll get Benny and Bill Basie, maybe even Lady Day herself down there to hear her. With a voice like that she can sing her way through any door in town."

"All right, all *right*!" Keegan cried.

"Do me a favor," Hammond said. "I'll call Louis Valdon at the Gramophone Recording Studio there in Paris and set up a session. Cut all four songs and send them ahead to me. I want to hear what she sounds like on wax. Put Charlie on a minute.''

"Go in the other bedroom and get on the phone," Keegan yelled to Kraus. A moment later the dapper arranger picked up.

"Charlie, we'll do a session with her. All four songs. Maybe you can add drums behind her, what do you think?''

"Sounds right.''

"Can you produce it for me? Francis will pick up the tab, won't you, Francis?''

"You skinflint.''

"Hey, I told you, get her to New York and I'll take over. Listen, if she sounds as good on wax as she does over the phone, I'll have the city hopping up and down by the time she gets here.''

"You're on.''

"I'll call Louis right now and tell him to expect your call. Let me know when you'll be in New York.''

"Thanks, John.''

"Hey," Hammond laughed, "after ten years I finally got something out of you.''

That night they ate alone in a small unknown restaurant on the Left Bank. She would go to Berlin in the morning to say her goodbyes. He would stay on in Paris and make arrangements for the trip, then fly over to Berlin in five days to pick her up. He booked her on the ten A.M. plane to Berlin the next morning.

"We'll fly to London and take the *Queen Mary* over," he told her.

After dinner they walked down the banks of the river. The *bateau-mouche* slipped by and they sat down for a moment, watched and listened to the laughter of the people on the pleasure boat. They walked on, started across the wooden foot bridge that crossed one of the small tributaries at the Quai de Bethune. From the middle they could see the gargoyles on Notre Dame, squatting ominously in spotlights, and beyond it, the Eiffel Tower, a brilliant, luminous triangle.

"It's like a diamond glittering in the dark," Keegan said.

"Why did you decide to live in Berlin when you came from the States?" Jenny asked. "You seem to adore Paris so much.''

"I was doing business in Germany. And I truly liked the

people. That's why I really don't understand what's happened
to them."

"The devil spoke and they listened," she said.

"You really believe that, don't you? That Hitler's the devil
incarnate?"

"Yes," she answered with a bitterness he had not heard in
her voice before. "And Himmler, Göring, Goebbels. All of
them."

He took her in his arms and kissed her lightly on the lips,
but she pressed harder as he started to draw away, clinging to
him almost in desperation.

"Hey, what is it?" he asked softly.

"I love you, Francis. I love everything about you. You're
funny and tough and a little mysterious and you make me feel
safe. And I know in my heart nobody has ever felt toward me the
way you do. And I do love you so for that, too."

"And I love you," he answered. "For all time and beyond.
I promise you, I'll make your life the most dazzling adventure
you can imagine. I'll devote my whole life to making you happy."

She brushed his lips with the fingertips of one hand.

"You already have," she said.

The hawk shrieked as it swept past the domed tower of the Gothic fortress, startled by the rumbling, blazing torches flickering through the window slots. Inside the stone walls, Himmler stood apart from the others, watching the ritual unfold. Even he was stunned by the power of the play and its setting. Vierhaus watched from the side of the tower, jealous of Himmler's moment of glory and yet awed by the power of the ritual. It was the first holy ceremony at the new secret SS headquarters at Wewelsberg. Beside him, etched in lurid flickering light, were Hess, Heydrich, Goebbels and Göring—the powers behind the throne.

This was Himmler's night and he was indeed a genius. No place could be more perfect than this moss-covered, dank castle, its cold halls stalked by Teutonic ghosts who had died jousting for the pleasure of ancient kings or clashing broadswords on some forgotten battlefield.

Himmler's cold, mouselike features wavered in the yellow torchlight and his jaws twitched as he tried to control his emotions. He loved the night. It matched the darkness of his soul and the mad fantasy he had brought to life in this eerie fortress. His ghoulish imagination had created a nightmare Camelot, a flagitious Round Table whose homicidal knights now had a secret headquarters in which to swear allegiance to their new king, Adolf Hitler. Not to the Fatherland—to Hitler.

Thirty-six newly graduated SS officers stood in their black uniforms, eyes ablaze with hypnotic fervor, their passionate oath to defend Hitler to the death echoing in the silolike stone tower while the wind soughed and whipped the torch flames into a frenzy. They stepped forth, four at a time, to touch the consecrated battle standard, the swastika, a perversion of the Sanskrit

svastika, a religious symbol to the Hindus, its four points repre-
senting the animal and spirit worlds, hell and earth. The left-
hand swastika adopted by the Nazis stood for darkness, for Kali,
goddess of murder, for black magic and witchcraft. To simply
touch the cloth of this flag was sexually stimulating to some of
the initiates.

The new black knights of the Third Reich returned to their
places on the winding stone staircase, raised their arms and
cried out:

"Heil Hitler! . . . Heil Hitler! . . . Heil Hitler!"

They had touched the consecrated flag and taken the oath
of fealty to Hitler. Now Himmler walked up the steps followed
by Heydrich, giving each of the initiates a sword and scabbard
to be worn only at official ceremonies. And each was given the
long knife, their dagger of authority.

What a moment for Himmler! Hitler had given him full
responsibility for creating the *Schutzstaffel* and he had gone
about it with a vengeance, combining the mission of the SS with
his own fantasy, spending three million reichsmarks to renovate
the ancient castle known as Wewelsberg outside Paderborn in
the heart of Westphalia. Just as the Nazis had perverted the
swastika, Himmler had perverted Christian holidays into SS
holidays—pagan rituals to celebrate Hitler's birthday, the anni-
versary of the Beer Hall Putsch, harvest and spring festivals; had
created a funeral service straight out of the Dark Ages, a midnight, torchlit ritual climaxed by cremation; had combined
witchcraft and mythology into a pseudoreligious order. And he
conscripted and nurtured men who disavowed Christianity in
favor of darker spirits; who worshipped Ares and other gods of
war; who were matched in marriage to Aryan maidens selected
by their commanding officers; who dreamed chaos, murder and
unspeakable atrocity, their psychoses nourished by the Third
Reich and encouraged to flourish by the Führer.

Thus the SS was born; a madhouse government within the
government, bound by no laws, with awesome powers and its
own secret police, the SD. Hitler's private army created in the
mind of Himmler. But if Himmler had created the machine,
Hitler had given it its perverted soul. Racism, Hitler had written
in *Mein Kampf,* would give the Germans "blood" and "soul." It
would identify a common "enemy." It would restore the self-

confidence and enhance the ego of the German people. So, he had ordered Himmler to create the SS. It would enforce this Nazi tenet and Goebbels would publicize it. Hate, terror, lies, these were the spine of the Nazi Third Reich.

Vierhaus stared down at Himmler, standing at the base of the staircase, looking up at the new troopers spiraling up and around him. Himmler smiled smugly. Treachery begets treachery, Vierhaus thought to himself. The SS would become Hitler's avenging army against his onetime friend Röhm, now turned traitor, and his maverick SA brownshirts.

"You are now members of the greatest order in history, *Die Schutzstaffel,*" Himmler said. "Tomorrow you will take part in a great adventure, one which will tell the world that our great leader, Adolf Hitler, *is* Germany. And *we* are the true knights of the Third Reich. We are his army. *Sieg Heil!*"

"*Sieg heil!*" They answered.

"*Sieg heil!*"

"*Sieg heil!*" They answered.

"*Sieg heil!*"

"*Sieg heil!*" They answered.

Himmler raised his dagger over his head.

"Go with God," he cried.

Everything seemed right but the weather.

Saturday, June 30, 1934, had been the day picked by Himmler for *Operation Kolibri,* "Hummingbird." Hitler had accepted the date without question, for if Göring was the obese Falstaff to Hitler's king, Himmler was the Führer's Merlin. Himmler had relied on his mystic powers, his understanding of the occult, witchcraft, astrology, and numerology, to arrive at the date. He conjured the spirits and advised his leader that the weekend was the perfect time for *Operation Kolibri.* Himmler was the ultimate magician of the Third Reich. He could even manufacture evidence out of thin air if the Führer needed it.

It was Himmler who had invented Hummingbird, as they all had come to call it, and drawn up the basic blueprints, although everyone ultimately contributed something to the dark plot. Theodor Eicke, the sadistic manager of Dachau, had drawn up the initial list, even going back through old news accounts seek-

ing names that might have otherwise been forgotten or overlooked. Himmler and Göring added their own victims to the
growing roll. Then Heydrich dropped a few names in the hat.
Hitler had even invited Vierhaus to add his names to the list but
the deformed little box of a man declined.

"Danke, mein Führer," he said. "My enemies are all dead
already."

So the list grew. Not only leaders of the brownshirt *Sturmabteilung,* but political opponents and old enemies appeared. By
the end of June there were over three thousand names on the
deadly roster.

The schizoid path of deception and betrayal eventually led
to the town of Bad Godesberg, near Bonn, and a quaint hotel
called the Dresen which overlooked the Rhine River. In his
suite on the second floor, Hitler brooded. His round, astonished eyes glared up into the southern skies, prematurely dark
from the storm clouds that were broiling up between Bonn
and Munich. Occasionally a jagged arrow of lightning would
etch the contours of the river, followed by rumbling drums of
thunder.

He stood in the open french doors that led to the balcony,
his hands stiff behind his back, his shoulders hunched. The
weather had to clear, he said to himself, smacking his fist into
his open palm several times. It was crucial that the weather clear.
His dinner of vegetables and fruit sat untouched. The room
seemed to crackle with tension. Vierhaus, who was smugly honored by being invited to sit with the Führer on this important
night, had never seen him look so gaunt and edgy. Hitler's eyes
were ringed with deep, dark circles and they seemed even more
feverish than usual. His cheek twitched uncontrollably.

He had made his old friend, Ernst Röhm, probably the best
recruiter and trainer of militia in the world, head of the *Sturmabteilung* and Röhm had built it from 600,000 men to 3 million in
one year, an amazing feat. And then Ernst had developed ideas
of his own. Dark delusions. Now it was obvious he planned to
use the SA to overthrow Hitler.

A born soldier, Hitler's inner voice screamed, *a street soldier,
only happy when dealing in death. Why did he turn on me? How could
he be so disloyal?*

Hitler saw in these elements a truly Wagnerian tragedy. Two magnificent schemers pitted against each other. One of his oldest friends. Now his greatest enemy. Such irony.

And yet, Hitler could still not bring himself to initiate Hummingbird. He had to be sure. He still had to have *evidence* that his old friend had turned traitor.

He went back in the sitting room. Vierhaus was sitting on the sofa reading a newspaper. He put it aside when Hitler came back.

"I need a cigarette," Hitler said. "You have a cigarette, Willie?"

"Gauloises?"

"Anything. Just a cigarette," he said with a wave of his hand. He took it and leaned over for the light, then strode the room, smoking like an amateur, holding the butt between thumb and forefinger, taking short puffs, blowing the smoke out in bursts.

"I did everything I could for him," he said finally. "Didn't I write him a letter of thanks at New Year's?"

"Yes, *mein Führer.*"

" 'I thank you for the imperishable service you have rendered,' " Hitler said with mock grandeur, wafting his arms as he spoke. " 'It is an honor—an *honor,* yet—to number such men as you among my friends and comrades-in-arms.' "

He stamped his right foot angrily and slapped both fists against his legs.

"What do I get in return," his voice began to rise. "Betrayal. Lies. *Treason!*"

"Yes, *mein Führer.*"

"*This man was my friend!*" He roared, shaking his fists at the ceiling. He dropped his arms to his sides and bobbed up and down on his toes. He picked up the newspaper.

"Did you see this article in *Der Sturm?* He is openly bragging about his . . . his perversion. Compares himself to other *ho . . . mo . . . sex . . . uals.* Alexander the Great, Julius Caesar, Frederick the Great . . ." He stopped for a moment and tried to control his gathering fury. "My God, how many *years* have I overlooked this. Ignored it. But . . ." He waved the paper over his head and slammed it to the floor.

"He has no concept of how important women are to the

Third Reich, to the propagation of the Aryan race. Listen to this, listen . . ."

He reached down, scrambled through the crushed newspaper and pulled out a page, punched a forefinger at the story.

" 'I renounce the political ideology of the new Germany because it gives women an equal place in contemporary society.' " He threw the paper down again. "People think these are *my* thoughts too, Willie!"

And then, as if to justify what was about to happen, still stalking the room, he said:

"On June fourth, not a month ago, I sent for him. 'Ernst,' I said, 'Stop this madness. You must conform to the rules of the Third Reich.' Yes, *mein Führer,* he said. I reminded him of the Beer Hall Putsch when sixteen of our comrades died in the streets and he was himself shot. 'All our ideals we fought for then are within our grasp. Believe in me,' I told him. 'Don't cause trouble.' Yes, *mein Führer,* he said. 'Take a month's leave, all of you. No uniforms for a month,' I said. Yes . . . *mein . . . Führer,* he said." Hitler started to scream. "Now he has called all his top men to Lake Tegern for a meeting . . . and they are all in uniform! He lied to me. *Lies! Lies! Lies!*"

Hitler stopped and shook his head violently. Vierhaus decided to divert his attention, get his mind off Röhm for the moment.

"I, uh, have some encouraging news, *mein Führer.* I had decided to wait, I understand the stress of the evening . . ."

Hitler dropped heavily into a leather chair near the windows. He sat hunched down, his eyes bulging like those of a madman, the whites around his pupils glaring eerily in the shadows. The eyes looked up at Vierhaus.

"No. No you don't, Willie. Nobody understands it but me."

Vierhaus saw in the moment, a chance perhaps to curry favor, to take the edge off the night.

"Perhaps while we're waiting for Goebbels . . ."

"Yes, yes, what is it?"

"I know who the head of the Black Lily is and how to catch him."

Hitler's face did not change but his eyes brightened.

"Who?" His voice was a low rasp.

"The head of the Black Lily is a young Jew, until recently a student. His name is Avrum Wolffson. I also know the names of his chief lieutenants. And best of all, I know how to get to him."

"Do it *immediately,*" Hitler snarled. "The moment this is all over, do it."

"Yes, *mein Führer,* the process has already started. I hope to arrest him as soon as Hummingbird is complete."

"What a moment, Willie! If we can destroy Röhm *and* the Black Lily in one, swift, *Blitzkrieg.*"

"Consider it done, *mein Führer.*"

"Kill him, you hear me, Vierhaus?" Hitler said, his voice beginning to rise. "No trial, no publicity until it's over." He slammed his fist on the coffee table. "Just *kill* him!"

"Yes, *mein Führer.*"

Hitler thought for a moment, then said, "Take him to the cellar at Landsberg and behead him."

"Yes, *mein Führer.*"

Hitler stood up and began pacing again. "And then cremate him and throw his ashes to the winds."

"As you wish."

"I want him *obliterated.*"

"Yes, *mein Führer.*"

"Power is in the muzzle of a gun, Willie. Röhm is about to find that out. And this Wolf . . . what?

"Wolffson."

"*Ja,* Wolffson. They have made their coffins, now they will lie in them."

"*Ja, mein Führer,*" Vierhaus said and to himself added, *It is about time.*

Then the messages started. Couriers, telephone calls, telegrams, all reporting on the preparations for the night's devilish activities. Finally Himmler called Hitler personally.

"*Mein Führer,* we have irrefutable evidence that the SA is planning a *coup d'état* for tomorrow."

"What! Where did you get this evidence?"

"Karl Ernst has alerted the SA troops for a general uprising."

Karl Ernst was the SA chief of Berlin, a longtime friend of Röhm's and a dedicated storm trooper.

"Is Göring there? I wish to speak to him," Hitler snapped.

"Nein, mein Führer. He is on the street. The entire area between Tiergartenstrasse and the Augustastrasse is cordoned off. The SA are trapped in the middle. Nothing gets in or out."

"Excellent. Do not move until I give the word."

"Of course, *mein Führer,"* Himmler answered.

Hitler cradled the phone.

He went back to the window. The storm clouds raced across the night sky. To the north, the lightning still brightened the heavens. But it was clear that the storm was moving on. Hitler took it as a final sign.

He whirled on Vierhaus. "People must be convinced that this plot to overthrow the government was real," he said. "Röhm is not unpopular, you know."

"You can make people believe anything if you tell them in the proper way," Vierhaus said softly.

Hitler shook his head violently.

"Ja, ja! But it must come from me. It must be in my words. The people know my words."

He strolled around the room, stopped and stared at the wall for several minutes.

"Let me tell you something, Willie," he said. "The world is ruled by fear and the most effective political instrument of fear is terror. Terror conditions people to anticipate the worst. It breaks the will. The people must understand that this . . . insurrection . . . cannot—*will* not—be tolerated *ever* again. Hmm?" He nodded approval of his own words.

"So . . . Röhm plans to overthrow the *Führer,* does he?" Hitler said with a sneer of satisfaction. "Well then, call the airport. I want to know when we can leave for Munich. We will initiate Hummingbird immediately."

He looked at his diminutive sycophant.

"Let the killing begin," he hissed.

As they approached Brown House, Hitler could see Reinhard Heydrich standing at attention on the front steps with half a dozen men behind him. There was no mistaking Heydrich. Even in the darkest moments before dawn, his tall, gaunt, ramrod figure was unmistakable. As they drew closer, Heydrich's cadaverous features and dead eyes were highlighted by street lamps.

Hitler felt a sudden chill. There was something about Heydrich. He was almost *too* efficient, like a bloodless robot. But he was integral to Hitler's plans, a man who took orders without hesitation and who performed admirably. When Vierhaus had discovered that Heydrich's grandmother, Sarah, was Jewish, Hitler had officially purged him of his "tainted blood," making Heydrich an Aryan by decree.

One of his men sprang to the armored car and opened the door. Heydrich cracked his heels together as Hitler got out and snapped his arm out in the Nazi salute.

"Heil Hitler."

Acknowledging the salute, the dictator asked, "Well, Heydrich, how does it go?"

"We arrested Schneidhuber and his assistant, Schmid, without incident. They are under guard along with a dozen other SA who were here already, all under house arrest. All protesting bitterly."

"Of course," Hitler snapped. Schneidhuber, a former army colonel, was the Munich chief of police and the highest ranking SA official in the city. It was rumored he would be Röhm's chief of staff if the *Wehrmacht* and SA merged.

"Schneidhuber," he growled under his breath as he followed Heydrich into the lobby of the Nazi headquarters building. Schneidhuber was a heavyset man in his late forties who affected the turned-up wax mustache and monocle of the Prussians. His thick lips seemed permanently curved into an arrogant sneer. He was in SA uniform as was his aid, Edmund Schmid, in stature a smaller version of his boss. Small and rotund, he had the dull look of a typical sycophant.

Upon seeing them, Hitler went into a violent rage. His face seemed to swell up. Veins stood out in his forehead and his color turned from white to red almost to purple.

"You traitor!" he screamed at Schneidhuber. "You miserable pig of a man!"

"Mein Führer," Schneidhuber pleaded. "I don't underst—"

"Shut up! Shut . . . *up!"* Hitler bellowed. He began to shake. Suddenly he reached out and grabbed the SA insignia on the police chief's epaulets and tugged at them, jerking the stout officer back and forth, until part of one of the sleeves tore away.

"You are beneath the contempt of everyone, everyone, Schneidhuber, you hear me! You . . . are . . . a . . . yellow, incompetent, lying . . ."

He stopped and backed away, still clutching the handful of cloth, then dropped it and clawed for his pistol.

Heydrich stepped around him, drew his Luger and held it at arm's length, six inches from Schneidhuber's face.

"Mein Gott!" Schneidhuber screamed, a moment before the pistol roared in his face and he felt the burning gasses scorch his face and the sudden explosion in his brain. His head jerked back and he sprawled on the floor, his forehead scorched by the hot powder. The small, singed, nine-millimeter hole was squarely between his eyes.

Schmid fell against the wall. His knees buckled. He held his hand at arm's length in front of his face.

"Please," he whined.

Heydrich fired the first shot into the palm of Schmid's hand. It ripped through both hands and creased Schmid's forehead. The little man fell screaming to the floor and Heydrich leaned over and shot him behind the ear.

Heydrich turned to Hitler.

"They were beneath your effort, *mein Führer,"* he said.

"Quite right, quite right," a shaken Hitler said. "Where are the others. How many are at the hotel?"

"Half a dozen," Heydrich answered. "The rest will start coming in by train about six."

"Good. Assign a man to the station with a detail. Arrest them as they arrive. Execute them all." He looked down at the spreading red stain on the marble floor. "And clean this mess up. Get rid of the ones that are here now."

"Yes, *mein Führer. Heil Hitler."*

Hitler raised his hand in a hurried salute as he walked out the door. Heydrich took three men and went to the conference room where the six SA officers were under house arrest. He opened the doors leading to the courtyard and grabbed a young lieutenant by the arm and shoved him out the door.

"Heydrich, what on earth is happening?"

"You have been condemned to death by the Führer."

"Why, for God's sakes? We are not guilty of anything!"

"The charge is treason. *Heil Hitler!"* And Heydrich shot him in the chest. The lieutenant grunted as the bullet smacked into his body, knocking his wind out. He fell in a sitting position, and looked up just as Heydrich fired a second shot. It hit him in the eye. The other five were shoved through the doors and as they screamed innocence and pleaded for life, they were gunned down and shot repeatedly after they had fallen.

Later in the day, Hitler sat behind his desk in Brown House, arms stretched out and resting on his desk. In front of him was Eicke's death list. Vierhaus had been checking off the names throughout the day.

Himmler had ordered one hundred and fifty SA cadets and another hundred brownshirt leaders taken to the old military jail outside Berlin and the death squads went to work. Every fifteen minutes, five storm troopers or cadets were led from their cells and marched or dragged screaming to the red-brick prison wall outside. Their shirts were torn off, a circle was marked on their chests, and they were executed by ten SS sharpshooters. That grisly work done, the bodies were tossed into metal-lined meat trucks and hauled to a small village down the road from the barracks. There the bodies were cremated and the ashes scattered in the wind.

Check . . .

A Bavarian who had helped foil the Beer Hall Putsch eleven years before but was opposed to the annexation of Bavaria to the rest of Germany, was taken out into a swamp and beaten to death with a pickax.

Check.

A music critic who was an outspoken socialist was hanged in his basement and shot four times. His death was listed as a suicide.

Check.

An ex-storm trooper named Grünstadt, who had once been Hitler's personal bodyguard before becoming *Gauleiter* of a small German town, was dragged from his farmhouse and had both legs and both arms broken with an ax. Then he was dragged screaming by his collar to a small lake on the farm.

"This is a mistake," he screamed. "Call the Führer. I was his bodyguard!"

"Verräter," one of the SS troopers snapped.

"I am *not* a traitor," Grünstadt begged.

They threw him in a small lake and smoked cigarettes as they watched him drown.

Check.

General Kurt von Bredow, who had been an aide to General Schleicher during the Beer Hall Putsch, left his house at seven thirty to take his dachshund, Gretchen, for her morning walk. He carried the puppy outside and as he stooped down to attach the leash to her collar, a black Mercedes pulled up in front of the building.

"General von Bredow?" one of them asked.

"Yes?"

The three men raised their pistols and fired in unison. A dozen bullets ripped through von Bredow's body.

Check.

Gustav von Kahr, seventy-three, who had also suppressed the 1923 putsch, was found in a swamp near Munich, hacked to death with a pickax.

Check . . .

Check . . .

Check . . .

By dusk, the SS death squads led by Göring and Himmler in Berlin had crossed over 1,500 names from Eicke's list. The Munich operation had slaughtered over 300 more. Before nightfall, almost every name on Eicke's list was crossed out.

Hitler leaned back in his chair and nodded slowly to Vierhaus.

"Done and done," he said with relief.

Only Röhm was left.

In the basement of Stadelheim prison, Röhm sat on an iron cot. He was sweating heavily and had taken off his shirt. His barrel-chest was black with wet, matted hair. He looked up as the cell door swung open and Vierhaus entered. He handed Röhm copies of newspapers with sketchy accounts of Hummingbird. He laid a loaded pistol on top of the paper.

"The Führer gives you one more chance to make your peace," Vierhaus said.

Röhm looked up at Vierhaus and laughed.

"If I am to be shot, tell Adolf to do it himself," Röhm said arrogantly.

"Suit yourself," Vierhaus said and whirling around, he stalked crablike out of the cell. When he got upstairs, Theodor Eicke was waiting for him. Vierhaus shrugged.

"Obstinate to the end," he said. "Do it."

They waited fifteen minutes. Then Eicke checked the clip in his Luger and charged a round into the chamber.

"*Heil Hitler*," he said.

"*Heil Hitler*," Vierhaus answered.

Eicke went down into the musky, dark, basement cell. The guards watched him as he came down the steps, silhouetted against the sunlight on the first floor, a burly angel of death, gun in hand. He said nothing. He walked to Röhm's cell and nodded. The guard opened the door.

Röhm looked up as he entered.

"Well, my friend the exterminator," he said. "So old Adolf does not have the guts to do it himself."

"Chief of Staff, get ready," Eicke said.

Röhm threw back his head.

"*Mein Führer, mein Führer! Heil Hitler!*" Röhm yelled.

The pistol roared in Eicke's fist. The first shot hit Röhm in the chest.

"Oh!" he cried out. He looked down with surprise at the wound. Eicke shot him again. A second hole burst open beside the first, knocking him on his side. He started to get up again, his head dangling, blood trickling from his nose.

Eicke stepped closer and shot Röhm in the temple. Röhm's head snapped sideways and he stiffened. Every muscle seemed to tense up. Eicke stood over him. He was about to fire a fourth shot when he heard Röhm's breath rush out and saw his body go limp.

A few minutes later, Vierhaus entered Hitler's office.

"Röhm is finished," he said.

Hitler glowered from beneath bunched eyebrows. There was a moment when he might have felt fleeting remorse but it quickly passed. He nodded.

"So . . . the opera is over," he said. And then slowly he clapped his hands together.

"Bravo . . ."

And now he is in control of the German Army, Vierhaus thought to himself. *Now the police are under the control of Himmler. In one night, Hitler has eradicated the heart and soul of the SA and almost all of his outspoken political opponents. He is absolute master of Germany. Now all of Europe is within his grasp.*

Hitler looked up at Vierhaus, his eyes glittering, his blood lust still not sated.

"Now bring me the Black Lily," he said.

Jenny left the hotel before eight A.M. and took three different taxis on the way to her destination. It was a trick she learned from Avrum, paying ahead of time, jumping out suddenly, dodging through buildings, taking another taxi, then repeating the same procedure again. She did not check to see if someone was following her; she just assumed someone was, just as she had when she was passing out leaflets and circulating *The Berlin Conscience.* Finally she took the Boulevard Ney south around the perimeter of the city, past the Arc de Triomphe to Montparnasse and walked two blocks to a small café on Rue Longchamps. She bought the morning paper and took a table in the back, from which she could watch the door. She ordered coffee.

She was shocked when she opened the paper. The story was bannered on the front page.

HUNDREDS DIE IN NAZI MASSACRE

What surprised her even more than the lead story was a guest column on the front page by Bert Rudman. Why didn't he call them with this news? she wondered. Then she smiled ruefully to herself, remembering that she and Kee had made love until early morning and that he had left word at the desk to hold all calls.

Bert Rudman's commentary on *Operation Kolibri* was on the front page just under the main story, bordered in black and labeled *Commentaire.*

BERLIN, GERMANY, JULY 1. Last night, in this land of Brahms and Beethoven, of Viennese waltzes and

Dresden china, the word fratricide was redefined in a bloodbath the scope of which has not been seen in modern times.

In 1920, then university student Rudolf Hess, now Hitler's second in command, wrote in an essay: "Great questions of the day will always be settled by blood and iron. Hitler does not shrink from bloodshed. To reach his goal, he is prepared to demolish even his closest friends."

How prophetic.

In one ghastly night of homicide, Adolf Hitler turned the dagger of deceit on his friend, Ernst Röhm, and the brownshirt legions that helped propel him to power. Germany's leader ordered his personal guards, the SS, to execute hundreds of brownshirt leaders, one of whom was Röhm, the pedophile warrior he once called friend and comrade.

It has been reported that Röhm's last words were: *"Sieg heil!* (Hail victory.) *Heil Hitler."*

It is hard to spare sympathy for Röhm or his decimated legions. These storm troopers were the bullies who smashed shops, beat up and murdered innocent people and became the billboard for Hitler's anti-Semitism, one of the tenets of the Nazi party and Hitler's Third Reich.

But the cowardly manner in which it was done during a night and day in which friend murdered friend and brother turned on brother chills the blood.

Like rainwater after a storm, blood collected in deep pools in the courtyard of Stadelheim Prison and the SS barracks as the execution of innocent SA military cadets from the training school continued throughout the day. There are reports that many members of the SS firing squads who executed hundreds of cadets became physically ill from the terrifying spectacle and had to be replaced.

Nor was the butchery confined merely to Röhm and his henchmen. Dozens of Hitler's political opponents were murdered, some as they slept. The SS was given *carte blanche* in its murderous forays. Mistakes were made during this Night of the Long Knives. Several people were killed because of mistaken identity.

We have managed to compile only a partial list of

those murdered during the night of terror. Estimates range from two hundred or three hundred to as many as three thousand. The actual number of people murdered in Germany in the last twenty-four hours may never be known.

One thing is obvious. With the destruction of the *Sturmabteilung,* the brown-shirted storm troopers who helped elevate him to dictator, Hitler's power is unchallenged. His personal elite guards, the *Schutzstaffel,* known as the SS, which number fifty thousand to sixty thousand, are now the undisputed rulers of the streets. The *Gestapo,* the secret police, has replaced the civilian police.

In *Mein Kampf,* Hitler wrote: "Racism gives the Germans blood and soul. It identifies the enemy and gives the People a sense of self-identity and self-confidence." Racism has now become the law in Germany.

But this was different. This was not Nazi against Jew, this was German against German, soldier against soldier, comrades killing comrades. This was power through mass murder. This was an outrageous violation of contemporary morality.

Those of us who have watched the frightening malignancy of Nazism grow within this nation recognize this purge as the prelude to the nightmare. Germany has bowed to the law of terror and Hitler has once again proven himself the master of treachery.

She folded the paper and stuffed it in her bag. As always, she was proud of Bert for being so outspoken. But she was also humiliated by the horrible news—another humiliation she as a German had to endure. The leader of their country had sanctioned *mass* murder, like some psychotic despot from medieval times.

She hurried to the corner and turned into Rue Fresnel, a short, bright street lined with gay shops. A flower stand dominated the center of the block. She went to the stand and looked over the freshly watered bundles of flowers, glistening in the morning sunlight.

"*M'amselle?*" the stand keeper said pleasantly.

"I am looking for something special," she said in French. "Perhaps I can help."

"I am looking for a black lily," she said.

His expression changed only slightly, a shift in the eyes, a tightening of the jaw.

"I am sorry," he said. "Try *deux cent cinq.*"

"*Merci.*"

He tipped his hat and turned to another customer.

She went on down the street, checking the numbers; 205 was near the middle of the block. It was a tiny tailor and cleaning shop, cramped and hot and smelling of steam and cleaning fluid. It was empty except for a young man in his shirtsleeves pressing pants on a steam machine. He smiled as she entered.

"Picking up or leaving off?" he asked pleasantly.

"I came to see Uncle," she said quietly.

"Uncle?"

He was tall and slender with long, shaggy hair and soft brown eyes. He looked out the window, quickly perused the street.

"Uncle Eli," she said. "I brought a flower for him, a rare flower."

His smile grew more cautious.

"Oh? An orchid perhaps?"

"A lily."

"Lilies are not so rare."

"The black lily is."

He nodded, still staring intently at her.

"So it is. And who should I say is calling?"

"Jenny Gould. I am Avrum's sister."

His eyes brightened.

"Ah, yes," he said warmly. "This way."

He led her past the steam machine into a back room. They edged their way through racks of fresh-smelling clothes to a stairway at the back of the shop.

"My name is Jules Loehman," he said, leading her up a narrow staircase to the second floor. "Uncle Eli is my father."

"Thank you for helping me, Jules."

"A pleasure and an honor. I met Avrum a few months ago when he was here. A very courageous fellow."

"He would be pleased to hear you say that."

"Good. Then tell him I said so."

They reached a small hallway at the top of the stairs and Jules knocked softly on a door and then opened it and ushered her into a small, incredibly cluttered sitting room. An elderly man was seated at a rolltop desk, writing in a ledger book. Every cubbyhole in the desk was jammed with papers and envelopes. A small dining room table was also stacked with books, papers, file folders. There were even files stacked on the chesterfield and easy chair that occupied one side of the room. In sharp contrast to the litter, the room itself was a bright and cheerful space, lit from above by a large skylight.

The old man was thin to the point of being frail, his white hair wisping from under a black yarmulke. His skin had the soft, almost translucent look that comes with old age and he had a shawl thrown over his shoulders even though the room was quite warm. He looked up as they entered, squinting over his half-glasses.

"Uncle, you have a guest. This is Jenny Gould. She is Avrum Wolffson's sister."

"Half-sister," she said.

He stood with some effort and took her hand.

"Well, well," he said with a wan smile. "What a pleasant way to start the day." He kissed her hand then waved at the sofa. "Jules, make a space, please."

He led her to the sofa as Jules stacked several piles of litter on the floor.

"I had to leave Germany rather abruptly," Old Eli said, gesturing around the room. "This is the sum total of my possessions. I have been going over these things for almost a year and I am still on the first pile."

"I must get back to the shop," Jules said, excusing himself.

"You are German then?" Jenny asked.

"*Ja,*" Old Eli said sadly. "I taught at the university with Reinhardt and Sternfeld. I got out." He stopped for a moment and then added: "Unfortunately they were not so lucky."

"Yes, I know. I am so sorry."

He studied her through gentle eyes, wise with age and faded with time.

"You have this look of . . . surprise," Old Eli said.

She laughed. "I am sorry. For some reason I expected you to be younger."

"Oh? Subterfuge is a young person's game, is that it?"

"I suppose that's exactly what I was thinking. A ridiculous prejudice."

"Most prejudice is ridiculous," he said with a shrug. "Anyway, my dear, it takes an old head to keep young hands steady. Besides, who would have thought that at the age of seventy-nine I would become the traffic director for a subversive organization. I find it all quite invigorating. So, what can we do for you?"

"I must talk to Avrum."

His face clouded up. He made a pyramid of his fingers and stared across the tip at her. "Very difficult, my dear. In fact, quite impossible at this moment. Have you heard what's happening? Things are insane in Berlin right now. They are saying as many as three thousand of the *Sturmabteilung* and many others may have been killed since two nights ago."

"I just read the paper. My God, what is happening?"

"On a very basic level, it means that Hitler's power now is absolute."

"How can we keep putting up with this? How can the people put up with it?"

"The people?" Old Eli said with great sadness. "Why they ignore it, my dear. They look the other way. Their attitude is simple: they cannot do anything about it so they make believe it is not happening. That is why Avrum's work is so important. He has literally become the voice of Germany's conscience. He keeps reminding them that what is happening is morally repugnant. Not just legally wrong, *morally* wrong."

He leaned back and stared up through the sunlight at the bright summer morning.

"He was one of my students, you know," Old Eli said rather wistfully. "I'm quite proud of that. To have been a mentor to a voice of dissent, what a sweet accomplishment."

"It doesn't seem possible that the chancellor of our country has resorted to cold-blooded murder," she said.

"Oh, he did that long before last night," the old man said.

"And now we hear the Black Lily is number one on his list. That is why it is impossible to call Avrum just now. He is on the move. But I am sure he will be calling me in the next day or so. Can I give him a message?"

She shook her head and then explained why she had to go to Berlin.

"Before I left he told me I should always check with you before coming back. He said you would know if there was any danger."

"You have to do this? Go to Berlin right now?"

She nodded. "I must tell him about my decision. He knows about Francis but he has never met him. Also I have to close up my apartment, see some family. I am leaving for America in a few days. I must say my goodbyes."

"That can all be done for you."

"No, I can not leave without explaining it to Avrum."

"So? Write him a letter."

"Do you think I am on the fugitive list? Is that why you are so concerned about my going back?"

He shook his head. "Not at all. I think we would know about it if you were on the list. But, because of your relationship, it may be a dangerous thing to do right now."

"I know you are thinking that if I am caught they will get information out of me," Jenny said. "Believe me, that is not possible, Uncle. Avrum told me nothing. All I did was help distribute folders and newspapers."

"A beheading offense, did you know that? They take news vendors of *The Berlin Conscience* to the basement of Stadelheim prison and behead them. *Behead them!* Can you believe such . . . barbarism? It hurts my heart to see this happening."

"Will you help me go home?" she asked, pressing the question.

He seemed to be delaying a decision.

"You must admit, it is a bit peculiar, helping someone get back *into* Germany," he said, almost as if bemused by the idea.

"Uncle . . . ?"

Old Eli shrugged and rolled his eyes. "Sometimes I think we Jews put too much on family."

"I'm not Jewish, Uncle. Avrum is my half-brother. But we were brought up as brother and sister. I admire what he is doing.

It scares me to death, but I admire him for it. The least I can do is explain why I am going away."

He wagged his hand as a sign of submission and nodded.

"Excuse me a minute," he said. He hefted himself from his chair and left the room. She sat quietly, listening to his muffled voice in another room. Fear started gnawing at her insides, a small thing to start with but a spark that could grow into an inferno. She tried to suppress it, but her mouth started to get dry and she could feel perspiration breaking out on the back of her neck. It was not herself she feared for, it was Avrum.

Old Eli came back in the room carrying a slip of paper.

"You will fly into Leipzig," he said, reading from his notes. "Then you will be taken into Berlin by motorcar. It is only a two-hour drive, one hundred kilometers or so. You have a place to stay?"

"I moved into a new apartment before I left. The phone is not in my name. I think it will be safe there."

Old Eli pulled a chair over in front of her and sat down. He leaned forward as he spoke.

"But not for long," he warned. "If they learn you are in Berlin and they are indeed looking for you, then you must get out as fast as possible. When you are ready to leave you will come back the same way. Remember, from now on trust no one."

"Not even Avrum?"

"Of course Avrum. But avoid anybody not involved directly with the Lily. And do not look for Avrum, he will find you."

"I understand."

"There is only one flight a day from here to Leipzig. It leaves in two hours. You must use your real name because of the passport. We do not have time to get you a counterfeit. Anyway, they will only be checking the Berlin flights for fugitives."

"I don't think they would connect Avrum and me—different last names . . ."

"Dear Jenny, if they learn his identity, they will know you are his half-sister very soon after."

"Hopefully they do not know who he is. He has evaded them for almost a year."

"Good luck does not last forever," Old Eli said.

She smiled and patted his knee. "Do not be so pessimistic," she said.

"Ha! We Jews are all pessimists, my dear," he said with a smile. "It is part of the diet. To be anything less would not be kosher."

A persistent ringing at the door of his suite awoke Keegan. Half asleep, he instinctively reached over to touch Jenny but she was not there. As he reached for his robe he noticed the time: 9:45 A.M. He jumped up. They were going to miss the plane.

"Jen?" he called out.

Then he saw the note propped up on the dresser. He snatched it up and read it as he walked through the living room to the door of the suite.

Darling Kee,

You were sleeping like a child and I hate good-byes. Am taking a taxi to the airport. I will call you tonight.

Five days, my darling, and then we will be together always.

I love you in my heart.

Thank you for changing my life.

Jenny

He opened the door and Bert Rudman, as usual, burst into the room without being invited. He was waving the morning paper over his head and babbling. Keegan had never seen him quite as agitated.

"Where have you been? Why was the phone turned off? I've been trying to call you all night!" Rudman jabbered, running all the sentences together.

Keegan stared at him sleepily, then looked back at the note.

"Where's Jenny?" Rudman asked, looking around the suite.

"She left already," Keegan said, handing the slip of paper to the journalist.

"Left? For where?" Rudman asked as he read the note.

"Back to Berlin."

"And you let her go?!"

"Let her go? I don't own her. Besides, I'm picking her up Thursday and then we're off for London. What's the big deal?"

"You don't know what's going on?"

"Where?"

"In Germany! Where do you think, on Mars? Goddamn, Kee, the Nazis have gone berserk!"

He handed Keegan a copy of the morning edition of the *Paris Gazette*, reprinted from his *Times* story.

"Christ!" Keegan said when he'd finished reading Rudman's story. He looked up at his friend and his eyes revealed admiration. Admiration mixed with fear.

"I'm going back to Berlin on the afternoon plane for a follow-up."

"You're going to Berlin after writing this? They'll kill you, you silly bastard."

"I keep telling you . . ."

"I know, I know, they won't mess with the American press. Let me tell you something, if they'll knock off three thousand people in one night, your press pass ain't gonna mean *bopkes*. You're worried about Jenny and you're probably number one on their hit parade."

"That's very flattering."

"No, what it is is very true. Look, Dick Daring, I don't like funerals, okay? Particularly when my best friend is the guest of honor."

"I can take care of me. But you've got to get Jenny the hell out of there."

Room service arrived. Keegan signed the check and doctored his coffee. Rudman sat down heavily on the sofa, took a long pull at his drink and sighed.

"You taking the four o'clock plane?" Keegan asked.

"Yeah, four-ten."

Keegan sipped his coffee thoughtfully. A sudden jolt of fear stabbed his chest. *Was she really in danger?* he wondered. *She wasn't political. But the whole country seemed to be going crazy. Maybe Bert was right. Maybe he better get Jenny out of there.* Abruptly he snatched up the phone.

"I'll try to locate my plane," he said to Rudman. "We can fly over together."

A few minutes before noon the phone rang.

"Francis?" the familiar voice said. "It is Conrad."

"Conrad! Are you here in Paris?"

"No, I am in Berlin."

"Is it crazy over there?"

"Only if you read the papers. Francis, I am calling you because Jennifer is in serious jeopardy."

"What do you mean?"

"I have heard through sources that the Gestapo plans to arrest her if she returns to Berlin."

"Where'd you hear that?"

"I can't tell you but believe me, it is most reliable. I am taking a great risk to even call you but I feel I contributed a little to your romance. You must be very careful."

"But why Jenny? She isn't . . ."

He stopped, remembering her explicit instructions. *Don't give my address or phone number to anyone.* And she had moved just before coming to Paris. Maybe she *was* mixed up in something.

"She's over there now, Conrad," Keegan said and checked the time. "She should be arriving home about now."

"Where does she live? I'll warn her."

Could he tell Conrad? He had taken a great risk just calling Keegan. Certainly he was safe. And yet she had said not to give the information to *anyone.*

"It's all right, Conrad, I'll call her. I'm sure she can find sanctuary somewhere until I can get over there and bring her out."

"Please, forget I made this call, understand?"

"What call? Listen, Conrad, thanks. I owe you a big one."

"You owe me nothing. It's the least I can do."

In Berlin, Conrad Weil cradled his phone and dropped heavily into a chair. His tall, elegant body seemed to collapse, like a punctured balloon. Across the room from him, Vierhaus sat with his chin resting on the handle of his cane. He smiled.

"There, see how easy that was, Conrad?" said Vierhaus. "What did you do? Nothing. Warned a friend. Did him a favor. And because of that generous gesture, the Führer will permit your club to continue performing its . . . degenerate show every night—without harrassment."

In the years to come, Keegan would sometimes reflect on the little things that alter our lives forever. Snap decisions. Hasty moves. Something as simple as a phone call. On this day, Keegan immediately flashed the operator and gave her Jenny's Berlin number. It rang a dozen times while Keegan silently urged her to pick up. But there was no answer.

The fear began to mount.

Perhaps he should call Conrad back and ask his help, he thought as he hung up. He looked at his watch again. In two hours the plane would be there. By four o'clock he would be at her door. By five they could be on the way back to Paris. He would wait.

In the switchboard office, the operator who had placed the call for Keegan took off her headset. She handed the phone number to the tall businessman with the German accent.

Von Meister smiled his thanks and handed her two hundred-franc notes. Two hundred francs. Less than fifty dollars. Even in Paris life was cheap.

At Tempelhof Airport, Keegan was waved through customs. He had no luggage and several of the customs agents recognized him from his frequent trips in and out of Berlin. Rudman was not so lucky. They searched through his two suitcases item by item while a Gestapo agent stood nearby watching every move. Then Rudman was ushered into an office for further conversation.

It was five P.M. and Keegan was anxious to get to Jenny's apartment. He waited nervously in the large waiting room, watching through the glass-partitioned office as Rudman argued with the customs agents while the Gestapo agent leaned against the door, his hands buried in his pants pockets and his felt hat pulled low on his forehead. They were obvious, but that was the game. The mere presence of the secret police was a subtle threat. It was clear they knew who Rudman was and were purposely harassing him.

Keegan tried to call Jenny's apartment from a phone booth but there was still no answer.

Where was she?

Tremors rumbled through Keegan's stomach. He sent a note to Rudman telling him he would either call or meet him at Rudman's hotel before he returned to Paris.

The taxi was hardly out of the airport parking lot before Keegan realized he was being followed. A light blue Opel pulled away from the curb two cars behind the cab. He watched the car as they drove down the highway into the city. As they reached the center of the city Keegan ordered his driver to take several sudden turns, weaving aimlessly through the city. The Opel got caught by a light and fell three blocks behind.

"Turn here," Keegan ordered, and as the taxi made the

turn, he handed the driver a handful of marks and jumped out. He hid in a doorway and watched the Opel wheel around the corner and swerve through the traffic after the cab.

He rode in two more taxis before he took to foot, walking down alleys and through stores until he was positive he had shaken his followers. Then he walked three blocks to the three-story apartment building where Jenny lived. He stood across the street for ten minutes more until he was positive he had shaken his tail.

It was an old stone Gothic apartment house but it did have an Old World charm. Gargoyles lurked ominously at the roof corners and there were stained glass windows on each floor over the entrance. Inside, the building was damp and gloomy. A wide staircase wound up through the core of the building. Tall ceilings added to the gloomy interior. The steps groaned with age as he climbed to the third floor. Door locks clicked and hinges creaked in his wake as he went up the steps to the third floor. He sensed eyes peering at him through the gloom as he reached each landing. As he reached the top floor, he turned quickly and looked back down the steps. He heard two or three doors click gently shut in the penumbral halls but he saw nothing.

Apartment 32A was the first door at the top of the stairs. He heard a creak down the hall and he turned sharply to see a woman peering through a door that was open a mere sliver. She closed it immediately.

Fear tapped Keegan on the shoulder.

The first thing he noticed was that the hall light was burned out. The long hallway was cloaked in dark shadows except for a narrow shaft of rainbow-colored sunlight that filtered through swirling dust from the single stained glass window at the far end.

The lock to Jenny's apartment was shattered, the jamb splintered, the door ajar an inch. His mouth went dry, a sudden jolt charged through his chest.

He swung the door open with the back of his hand.

"Jenny?" he said softly.

No answer.

He entered the apartment cautiously.

"Jenny?"

Nothing.

He went down a short entrance hallway and then stopped.

The living room was a shambles. Cushions from sofas and chairs had been ripped open. Little balls of stuffing drifted and swirled idly in the wind from an open window. Drawers hung open with the contents spilled out on the floor.

"Jenny!"

He raced through the one-bedroom apartment, checking the kitchen, the small dining room and the bedroom. The destruction was thorough. In the bedroom, the mattress was thrown half off the bed and split open. Clothes dangled from half-open drawers and littered the floor of the closet.

The apartment was empty.

"Jenny!" he yelled, knowing there would be no answer.

Who had ransacked the apartment? And where was Jenny? If she was in hiding, how would she contact him? She didn't even know he was in Berlin.

He went back into the living room. He heard a sound behind him in the darkness of the apartment. Keegan walked slowly across the room, knelt down next to the desk and started to pick up some mail that was scattered on the floor. The floor creaked. He could feel the presence of someone else in the room. He turned slightly and as he did strong arms suddenly grabbed him around the throat in a choke hold.

Keegan slashed back and up with his elbow, buried its sharp point in the groin of his assailant. The man grunted with pain as Keegan stood and spun at the same time, throwing a hard, straight jab into the face of the man. As he did a second man jumped him, wrapping his arms around Keegan's waist, pinning his arms to his sides. A third man moved swiftly toward Keegan, who raised both legs and kicked him in the stomach, then slammed his head back into the face of the man who was holding him. The man screamed as his nose shattered. Keegan twisted out of his grip and threw a hard uppercut to his jaw. The assailant spun away and fell over a coffee table.

Again Keegan was attacked from the back, powerful arms holding Keegan's arms in check. A thick cloth was thrust over his face. He choked as chloroform stung his eyes and nose. He tried to hold his breath but he was hit in the stomach and his wind rushed out. The cloth was jammed tighter as he gasped for breath. The room began to spin around. His arms lost their strength and his legs went numb. He was aware he was still struggling but the room seemed to shrink around him and grow darker. He fell backward into a void.

He awoke slowly, as if coming out of a long coma. The smell of chloroform was still on his skin. He was blindfolded and tied to a hard chair. He felt nauseous and he swallowed hard, took several deep breaths. The feeling of malaise slowly dissipated.

"Herr Keegan, I am going to untie your hands and remove the blindfold," a voice said. "There is a man across the room from me with a gun. If you try to leave the chair, he will kill you."

The blindfold was pulled off and his hands were untied. He squinted into a blazing spotlight.

"Jesus," Keegan groaned as he rubbed the feeling back into his wrists and hands and then shielded his eyes with one hand. A large man stood silhouetted in front of him, smoking a cigarette. Behind him, another outline, this one smaller and aiming a Luger at him.

"What do you want?" Keegan asked.

"What were you doing in *Fräulein* Gould's apartment?"

"Are you the police?"

There was a pause, then: "We are the state police. You are guilty of breaking into the apartment."

He studied the two shapes more closely. Both wore beards and had long, shaggy hair. They were dressed in work shirts and corduroy pants.

"Well, somebody obviously beat me to it," Keegan answered and an edge began to creep into his voice. "And while we're at it, where is Miss Gould?"

"I will ask the questions."

"Maybe you should check with her before you push this any farther."

"Perhaps you can tell us where she is?"

A tremor of dread rippled through Keegan. *Was this some kind of ruse? If they were the Gestapo, where was Jenny and what were they doing in her apartment? And where was he and why were they grilling him?*

Something didn't play right.

"You came into Tempelhof tonight on your private plane, Mr. Keegan. You walked right through customs."

"So?"

"No customs inspection?"

"I didn't have any luggage. Besides, I go in and out of Berlin all the time. They all know me."

"So they let you through and followed you to her flat."

"No way. *Some*body started to follow me but I dumped them." He stopped and looked at his two abductors for a moment and smiled. "Of course. It was you guys. You're the ones I dumped. And since I dodged you and you showed up at her place anyway, you *knew* where she lived. Hell, you were after *me*. Why?"

"I will ask the questions, you just talk."

"Okay. Want me to tell you what I *don't* think?" Keegan said.

"So? What don't you think, Herr Keegan?"

Keegan again held a hand up so it blocked the harsh light and looked back and forth between his captors.

"I don't think you're Gestapo. You don't look like Gestapo, you don't act like Gestapo, you sure as hell don't dress like them. Your hair's too long and you wear beards. And if you were Gestapo, you wouldn't be asking me about customs. Besides, if you were Gestapo we'd be down in one of those dingy state buildings and I'd probably have electrodes attached to my testicles. Isn't that the way they do it?"

"You are very perceptive, Herr Keegan. But we knew that. What else *don't* you think?"

"Well, if you aren't Gestapo then my guess is you're probably just the opposite. What are you, some kind of vigilantes? Guerrillas? And what am I doing here? And what were you doing ransacking Jenny Gould's apartment?"

"We were not responsible for that."

"Then who was? The Gestapo?"

"You're very clever, Mr. Keegan, the question now is, where do you stand?"

"About what?"

"About Vierhaus. How close is your relationship with Vierhaus?"

"Vierhaus! I don't have a relationship with Vierhaus. I've seen him at a couple of parties and I got stuck in a steam bath with him once. And what the hell business is that of yours anyway? Who the hell are you?"

"Vierhaus is the head of an organization called *Die Sechs Füchse,*" the bearded man said. "You didn't know that?"

"The Six Foxes?" he said.

"It is a special intelligence group, completely separate from the SS. He is head of this group and he reports only to Hitler."

"You telling me that Vierhaus is some kind of superspy?"

The big, bearded man nodded slowly. "He is perhaps more dangerous than Himmler or even Heydrich. Everyone knows what they are up to but *Herr Doktor* is a question mark. We know he advises Hitler so we know he has influence. We also know he has a soul as black as my beard."

"How do you know that?"

"Because it is my business to know it, Herr Keegan."

"Well, just what the hell *is* your business, anyhow? And what's all this got to do with me? I'm not a German."

"You claim to be in love with a German."

Keegan's temper exploded. *Where was Jenny and who were these jokers and what was all this wind about Vierhaus and superspies and the Gestapo?* He jumped up suddenly, sending the chair spinning off behind him. It clattered against the wall. The man with the gun got edgy and held it at arm's length pointed straight at Keegan's head.

"That's none of your goddamn business!" Keegan snarled, walking up to him until the muzzle was an inch from his forehead. "And I'm tired of you waving that thing in my face. Either put it away or use it," he said flatly.

"Don't be foolish, American."

"I think you're all bluff. You didn't bring me here to waltz, you brought me here because you want something. Now why don't you just get to it and stop waving that piece around."

"Don't make light of the . . ."

"Hey, why the hell am I here?" Keegan demanded. He moved forward until the muzzle of the pistol was touching his forehead. "There, you can't miss. Now, either you pull that trigger or tell me what the hell you want. I told you I don't know anything about Vierhaus. And how do you know about my relationship with Jenny . . . and what the hell business is it of yours anyway?"

The bearded man stared at him for several seconds. He reached out and lowered the arm of the man with the gun.

"My name is Avrum Wolffson," he said finally. "Jenny is my half-sister."

"Your *sister!*" Keegan said with shock. He stared at Wolffson for several seconds, then said, "Well, she ought to get after you for playing with guns."

"Do you make a joke of everything?"

"Why not? Life's a joke. And the older you get the funnier it gets. Look, I came over here to get my fiancée and take her back to Paris. I get here, her apartment is a mess. She's gone. I get a face full of chloroform, I wake up in a warehouse someplace with hot lights and guns in my face and you guys giving me the third degree, now you tell me you're her *brother*? What the *hell* is going on?"

"I had to make sure you were not connected with Vierhaus."

"Why? Because of Jenny? Is this some kind of bizarre family tradition, to try and scare the hell out of her suitors? I'm in love with your sister. I've asked her to marry me. I mean, why would I do such a thing?"

"I don't know, but you and I were the only ones who knew where she lived. Somebody got to her place and she's gone. And I didn't tell *any*body, so that leaves you."

Keegan was getting angrier but he controlled himself.

"I didn't tell a soul," he said.

The big question now was, why was *any*body after Jenny? *Why?*

"Why do they want her?" Keegan asked.

"You really do not know, eh?"

"If I knew would I ask you?"

"Perhaps. If you were trying to convince us you are not involved."

"You're very paranoid."

"Yes, it keeps us alive."

Wolffson lit another cigarette. He held the tip of it up and blew a stream of smoke across the end of the cigarette, watching it glow, giving himself more time to make his decision.

"Come on, Wolffson, why would the Gestapo be dogging me?"

"The light is on her. She is the target."

"What do you mean, the target?"

"I mean the Gestapo is onto her. She has been betrayed and we think your friend Vierhaus is the one who is after her."

"Betrayed? By who? And for what?"

"Some miserable *Judenopferer* turned her up."

"A what?"

"A *Judenopferer* is a Jew who hunts other Jews. The word literally means 'Jew sacrificer.' They spend hours going over court records, looking for the most remote Jewish connection, they listen to rumors, infiltrate families . . ."

"You still haven't told me why."

"To get to me."

Keegan sighed. "Okay, I'll play. Why do they want you?"

"Have you ever heard of an organization called the Black Lily?"

"No . . . Wait a minute. I did hear that expression once. At the American embassy."

"The night you refused to help Reinhardt?"

Keegan did not answer for a long time. He felt his pockets for his cigarettes and matches and lit a cigarette and then slowly started to nod.

"That's right," he said. "The night I turned my back on Reinhardt." He rubbed his eyes. "Look, Wolffson, I know a lot of things now I didn't know then. But I don't know what the Black Lily is. And can we do without the hot lights? I'm getting a headache."

Wolffson turned around and made a motion with his hand. The heavy light went out and a small table lamp was turned on in its place. A third man was sitting at a table nearby. The room appeared to be a one-room flat. It was small and contained a bed and dresser, a table and two chairs, a stuffed easy chair and a floor lamp. Black cloth was taped over the windows. In a corner there was a small table that held a hot plate with a coffee pot simmering on it.

The man at the table was unarmed and his nose was flattened and bruised. He was clean shaven, had a conventional haircut and wore wire-rimmed glasses. The shorter man with the gun had a bandage taped to his jaw, which was badly bruised and swollen. He was burly, his muscular arms straining rolled-up sleeves, and had fierce, angry eyes, the demeanor of a man holding himself in check but about to explode. A thick black beard added to his ominous presence. The tall man's left eye had begun to swell. He, too, was in excellent physical condition but his look was intense rather than mad and his beard was more scholarly than menacing. He was calm and totally in command.

None of them could have been more than twenty-five or twenty-six years old.

Well, thought Keegan, looking at the bandages and bruises, *I got in a few licks anyway.*

"One gun?" he said. "You have one lousy gun?"

"We are on the run, have been for months. But it is now more intense. You know what it means in German, *Freiheit*?"

Keegan thought for a moment. He wasn't familiar with it. He shook his head.

"It would be in English something like . . . freedom. We don't blow things up. We don't kill people. We distribute pamphlets and try to help people who are in trouble with the government. Jews, Germans, gypsies, no matter. If they become targets and we know about it, we try to get them out of the country."

"In America, back in the slave days, we called it the Underground Railroad."

"*Ja,* to help Negroes escape to Philadelphia."

Keegan chuckled. "Right," he said. "So what got them so hot on you all of a sudden?"

"We also keep the German people informed of what is really going on here, so they can never say they did not know what was happening. They can never lie about it, they will have to say, 'Yes, we knew and we turned away our eyes.' That is what *The Berlin Conscience* is for. Anyway, a man died a few days ago. A Jew named Herman Adler. He was a *Judenopferer.* He was also Joachim Weber's uncle." He nodded toward the young man at the table.

"Your uncle turned other Jews in to the SS?"

Joachim nodded and looked down at the table. "He betrayed me and Avrum," he said, and nodded toward the young man with the gun, the silent one. "And Werner Gebhart there."

"My God."

"Adler was one of the best they had," said Wolffson. "He was responsible for the arrest of dozens of people. Jews, Gentiles, Gypsies. We tried to reason with Herman, offered to get him out of the country. But he was arrogant about it. There was some yelling, some anger, and then he had a heart attack. Just like that he was dead. We felt sorry for Herman. He was scared. He was doing the only thing he could do to stay alive."

"He betrayed too many of us," Joachim, the nephew, said bitterly. "Our grief over him was brief."

"Then the thought occurred to me that perhaps we could make an example of him, a lesson to other hunters," said Wolffson. "So we wrote a story about what he—and the other *Judenopferers*—are doing. I realize now it was a stupid thing to do. It merely goaded the wolf. The Gestapo has become obsessed with destroying the Black Lily ever since."

"And Jenny?"

"Also Adler. He made the *Kettenglied*—the connection. But we did not know it at the time."

"God, why didn't she tell me? Maybe I could have . . ."

His voice trailed off as the horror of the situation began to sink in.

"She was protecting us," Weber said. "The less people know, the better."

"I should have guessed. She was so secretive about her new apartment. Didn't want anyone to know her address or phone number."

The fierce-eyed one with the gun, Weber, said nothing. He simply glared at Keegan.

"The last time she moved it was because she got one of our pamphlets in the mail," said Wolffson. "She knew it was a trick, we would not mail anything to her."

"I don't understand," Keegan said.

"It's one of the things the Gestapo does," said Wolffson. "Germans are required to report anything of a subversive nature. So they send one of our pamphlets to everyone on a particular street and if these people don't report getting it, they are accused of a subversive act."

"So she moved?"

Wolffson nodded. "And the only way the Gestapo could have gotten her address is by following you or me—or getting her phone number, which was not in her name."

Keegan stared in silence, thinking about what Wolffson had just said. *I didn't even give the phone number to Bert or to Weil,* thought Keegan. *It couldn't have been me.*

"You and I were the only ones who knew where she was, Keegan."

Keegan was getting angrier but he controlled himself. "I told you before, I didn't tell a soul."

"Did you telephone her from your hotel?" Wolffson asked.

"What the hell . . ." He stopped. *Was it possible that they had tapped his phone in Paris, got her number and tracked her down? My God, was* he *responsible?*

"Did you?" Wolffson asked.

"I tried to call her. There was no answer."

"The Nazis are all over Paris. And I don't think there is a hotel operator in the entire city that cannot be bribed. All they needed was her phone number to get her address."

"Jesus." Keegan paced back and forth for a few moments. He lit one cigarette off another.

"She contacted the Lily in Paris. They flew her to Leipzig and drove her into Berlin," Wolffson said. "So Vierhaus had lost her. He was desperate."

It all began to come together for Keegan.

"And had Conrad Weil call me, knowing I would call her. He was in on it. My old friend, Conrad. I should have suspected something was up when he called me. Conrad bends with the wind, he told me so himself. And von Meister was there waiting for me to take the bait." He shook his head. "I'm sorry, truly sorry. But what does Jenny have to do with all this?"

"Nothing, really. I am sure Vierhaus thinks she can give me up but she cannot. She doesn't even know about this place. She delivered *The Berlin Conscience,* distributed some leaflets, that's all. But they think she knows where I am and I am the one they want. Me, Gebhart here and Joachim. We are the leaders of the Black Lily."

"How did you get involved in this?"

"The newspaper was started by our professors at the university. Sternfeld, Reinhardt and Eli Loehman. Now Reinhardt and Sternfeld are dead. Only Old Eli is safe. He is in Paris with his son. He is the one who arranged to get Jenny back here."

"And you boys picked up the banner, eh?"

"*Ja,* I suppose you could put it that way. But now the Black Lily is very important. So important that Hitler has put a price on our heads and the Black Lily is the main target of the SS."

Somewhere in another room a phone rang. Joachim got up from the table and went to answer it.

"Three college boys and one gun and you've set the entire Gestapo on its ear?" Keegan said to Wolffson.

"Not just three college boys anymore," Wolffson said. "There are over two hundred of us in the network. We have connections in Switzerland, France, England, even Egypt and America. So far we have been very lucky. But some of our people . . . have not been so lucky. You know what happens if they catch us?"

"I can imagine."

"I do not think so," said Wolffson. "We are taken to Stadelheim Prison and tortured. And then we are beheaded."

"What!"

"*Ja*, Herr Keegan. Beheaded. And most of them are students."

Weber returned and called Wolffson to the door. There was a whispered exchange, then they walked back into the room. Wolffson looked stricken. The veins around his jaw had hardened into blue ridges.

"The Gestapo arrested Jenny," Wolffson said in a harsh voice that quivered with emotion. "She has been at Stadelheim prison for five hours. I don't know that she is still alive."

Keegan fell back in his chair, ashen.

"You may as well face it, Keegan, they will be very hard on her," Weber said. "They will assume she knows much more than she does."

"And we just sit around and let it happen?" Keegan said. "We don't do anything?"

"There is nothing we can do at this point," Wolffson said.

Keegan panicked.

"We've got to get her out. Get bail, get lawyers! I'll call the embassy, maybe they can help."

But hell, what could the embassy do? And why would they help him? He understood now how Wally must have felt the night he was trying to get Reinhardt out. There was one big difference. The Gestapo already *had* Jenny.

"It will do no good," said Wolffson.

"If we can just get her out on bail," Keegan pleaded. "I'll take her to New York, she couldn't be safer anywhere else."

Gebhart suddenly spoke up for the first time, his voice trembling with suppressed rage. "Damn it, man," he said, "get it into your head. *It's too late!*"

"There is no such thing as bail," said Weber. "There will be no trial."

The shock began to wear off and Keegan slowly realized how desperate her predicament was. *What they're saying*, he thought, *is that she's* gone*!*

"No," he said, shaking his head. "Don't even say that."

Dear Jenny, he thought, *is this what you get for loving me?* Why did this happen? Was it some kind of cruel joke? Crazy things raced through his mind. God, I may never *see* her again! I can't even say *good-bye*. Jesus Christ! What's happening here?

"What's happening here!" he cried aloud, his fists clenched in front of him. Tears flooded his eyes and he tried to fight them back. "It's unacceptable, *unacceptable*. There's got to be somebody we can bribe, somebody we can blackmail, threaten . . ."

They stared at him with sadness but little pity.

"Now you know vot it iss like for us every day of *der* year," Gebhart said bitterly. "Every day they take somebody avay. Friends, lovers, children. Sometimes whole families simply disappear off the street."

"Understand, Keegan, we know your frustration," Wolffson said quietly. "My hatred and anger consume me. I wanted to be a zoologist—work with animals. Look at me. Running all the time. Helping one out of perhaps every fifty or one hundred who get on the list. Throwing pamphlets around the city to people who don't care."

"Then why do you do it?"

"We cannot just surrender our lives without doing something," Weber said.

"I want to kill Vierhaus," Keegan blurted. "I want to kill that son of a bitch slowly. I want him to plead . . . no beg . . . *beg*, for mercy. I want to hang him up by his heels and pour honey all over that miserable hump on his back and then let the rats eat their way through it right into his miserable black heart."

He slammed his fist into the wall and then, exhausted, sat down on the edge of the bed.

"I am sorry, Keegan," Wolffson said. "But we also love her.

She's my sister, not just my half-sister, my *sister* in my heart, you understand? Werner has loved her since they were born, they grew up together, same street. Joachim went to school with them, all the way through college. We share your agony. We understand what is happening inside you. But there is *nothing . . . we . . . can . . . do.*"

Keegan did understand the awesome frustration of the tragedy. Jenny was just one of hundreds, thousands, who had been lost in these camps. And these people were becoming immune to the pain because of the enormity and futility of the problem.

"I can't relate to all that," said Keegan fiercely, pacing the room. "I can't relate to thousands of people, I can only relate to her, that's all the tragedy I can handle right now. Right now I hate the world. I hate you for telling me it's hopeless."

"I think the time has come to get rid of all *Judenopferers,* teach them they must stop betraying their own," Weber said.

Wolffson flicked an ash off his cigarette and shrugged. "And become just like them?"

"Why not?" said Keegan. "For the first time I understand the meaning . . . the true meaning . . . of an eye for an eye."

"Listen to me," Wolffson said. "Please, it is important. What we are doing, it is very delicate, a very fragile thing. A very dangerous thing. But it is important. Even to save one life is important, more important than killing."

"But not hers, right?"

Gebhart stood very close to him, his eyes also misty, his fists also clenched. "Don't you get it, *Ire,* vunce the Gestapo has dem it iss over. No matter who it iss, even your own mother or father, it iss over. Ve are not an army, ve are students and teachers and old men *mit* no training. Ve cannot take on the SS and the Gestapo. Ve must help those who haff not been caught."

"We understand how you feel," said Wolffson. "Please understand our frustration is just as agonizing."

And suddenly Keegan realized how sorry he was feeling for himself. These three men were family, lifelong friends, silent lovers. His anguish was no deeper than theirs.

"I'm sorry," he said. "I was being bloody selfish."

"It is all right," Wolffson said. "We know all the feelings." He stopped for a moment, then said, "Keegan, you must leave Berlin and the sooner the better."

"I won't leave, not without her," Keegan answered.

"Don't you understand, man, if you go on the list, they will torture you too. You know too much about us."

"I don't know anything they don't know already."

"You know about our Paris connection," Weber snapped, moving very close to him. "How we got Jenny over here, how big the network is. As long as you are in Germany, you are a danger to us."

"Or . . ." Wolffson said thoughtfully.

"Or what?" Keegan asked.

"Or you could go to Vierhaus. Pretend you know nothing. Tell him Jenny is missing and ask for his help."

"Ask for his help! I want to kill the little freak."

"Exactly what he would expect, so if you can keep calm you will convince him you know nothing," Wolffson said. "He may give up some information we can use."

"You want me to spy for you?"

"For me, for Jenny, for you."

Keegan settled down again. Maybe the kid was right, maybe he could beat Vierhaus at his own game. It was certainly worth a try.

"All right," he said, "what can I do?"

"Go back to your hotel . . ."

"I don't have a hotel, I was planning to take Jenny out of here tonight."

"You usually stay at the Ritz, correct? Go there and check in. Call Vierhaus. Tell him you came back to get Jenny and she is missing. Her apartment is torn up. That's all you know. It will throw him off, convince him you know nothing."

"That's a long shot. That's about a two hundred-to-one job."

"I'm afraid I don't understand."

"It doesn't matter," Keegan said. "What else?"

"If we should learn they are after you for any reason, we will call," Wolffson said. "The message will be, 'This is the tailor, your suit is ready.' If you get that message leave immediately. Avoid being followed, of course. Go to the city zoo, the *Tiergarten.* There is a phone booth near the carousel. Wait there and we will call you. So you will know it is us, when you answer we will ask if you picked up your suit yet. Your answer will be, 'No, they did not fix the torn pocket.' Then we will give you instructions."

"Come on, all this is conjecture and . . ."

"Keegan, we've been at this for a long time. Believe me, it is not conjecture. If it happens, do not even think, move. Get out of the hotel and to the zoo."

A silence fell over the room. Cigarettes were lit. Wolffson got a cup of coffee. Gebhart sat in a chair and cracked his knuckles, slowly, one at a time.

"Okay," Keegan said finally. "I'll give it a shot. What do you really think they're doing to her?"

"They will torture her. Even if they know she knows nothing, Hitler wants revenge against the Black Lily. They know she is a *Kettenglied.* They'll do anything to find out what she knows. Thankfully it is not much."

"What's the *best* we can hope for?"

"That she can convince the Gestapo she knows nothing," Wolffson answered. "And that they let her die quickly."

"If she survives?" Keegan kept his voice steady.

"If she stays alive? Dachau," said Wolffson.

"What's Dachau?"

"A little town about thirty kilometers from Munich," said Wolffson. "They have built a camp there, an enormous prison stockade for political enemies. It is like a Russian slave camp."

"How long will she be in for? How much time will she get?"

"It doesn't work that way," Weber said.

"There is no sentence," Gebhart said in a low voice. "She will be there forever. Dachau is a forever place."

He lay in bed all night watching the phone, waiting for Vierhaus to answer his calls. He had called three times, talking to the same icy male SS operator on the other end of the line. On the last call the operator became abusive.

"Don't you understant," the *Schutzstaffel* man snapped in his thick German accent. "He iss not here! He vill call you ven he iss ready to call you. *Auf wiedersehen.*"

Sleepless, Keegan lay clothed on the bed thinking about Jenny. Wondering where she was at that moment. Wondering what horrors the Gestapo was wreaking on her. Imagining himself attacking the prison, killing all the guards, and whisking her to freedom in some mad, outrageous rescue scheme that could only happen in the movies. And, too, he wanted to get even. Vierhaus, Conrad Weil, von Meister, each had contributed in a different way to the tragedy, each for a different reason, and each was equally responsible.

The minutes crawled by. Dawn sneaked through the drapes, spreading a crimson stain across the carpet. He watched the spear of light lengthen and widen and slowly illuminate the room.

The phone was a silent threat. He stared at it, reached out, then drew his hand back. He wouldn't call the miserable bastard again. Pain laced his stomach and he reached out again, asked for room service and ordered coffee and rolls. When he heard the knock on the door he opened it, expecting the bellman. Bert Rudman was standing there.

"Can I come in?" he said softly.

Fear cut into Keegan again, a pain now so common he recognized its roots immediately. Bert Rudman had never asked to come in before. Barging in with arms waving, that was his style.

"I didn't know the Gestapo had picked up Jenny."

"Yes. I've known since late last night. I called the bureau and left a message for you."

"God, I am sorry, Kee."

"I don't know what to do. I've never felt this . . . this helpless before."

"You look like hell. Have you been to bed?"

Keegan shook his head. "I couldn't sleep," he said. "What do you know? For sure, I mean?"

"She was arrested at two o'clock yesterday afternoon . . ."

Keegan slammed a fist into the palm of his hand. "Damn it, why did I make that call," he anguished.

"What call?"

Keegan paced the room, burning off nervous energy, rambling in a low voice as if he were talking to himself, as if Rudman wasn't there and he was addressing an imaginary friend, recounting the steps that had led to Jenny's imprisonment.

Rudman walked over to Keegan and stared at him quizzically.

"How do you know all that?" he asked when Keegan finally was quiet.

"Some of it's conjecture, most of it's fact. I know it, take my word for it."

"What else do you know?"

"That they probably tortured her. She may be dead by now. I understand that's the custom."

Rudman took Keegan firmly by the arm. "She's not dead, Francis."

"Are you sure? How do you know?" Keegan said in a rush.

"I got a tip. She was moved about five this morning."

"Moved where? Where did they take her?"

"They're taking her to Dachau, Kee."

Keegan was too stunned to speak for a moment. He was not surprised. The news itself was not unexpected. It was the reality of the news, knowing his worst fears had materialized, that got to him.

Dachau!

"No!" his voice croaked.

"They got four of them. They were arrested for . . ."

"*No!*" Keegan suddenly screamed, his fists clenched.

"Listen . . . listen to me, Francis, there's nothing—*nothing*—you can do right now. At least we know she's alive. She's a political prisoner. If she were tried, she'd be tried for high treason. But there isn't going to be a trial. She's gone for now, Kee. Maybe when . . ."

"Damn, is that the only tune anybody knows? That's all I hear. *Nothing.* I'm tired of hearing that word."

"Kee . . ."

"I'll go to the embassy. Damn it, I'll call the president . . ."

"Kee . . ."

"Goddamn it, we're going to be married! She'll be an American citizen. Hell, she hasn't *done* anything. Her brother's . . ."

"*Kee!*"

Keegan stopped. He was soaked with sweat and his hands were shaking.

"Aw, listen to me, man," Bert said. "If I could storm the place by myself and bring her back to you, I'd do it. And if you weren't my best friend I couldn't say this to you . . ."

"Then don't," Keegan cut him off. "You listen to me. I don't buy nothing. *I . . . can't . . . give . . . this . . . up!*"

"You have to!" Bert answered, his voice rising too. "You don't have any choice!"

"You're telling me that and you claim to be my best friend . . ."

"Christ, I'm trying to be honest with you . . ."

"Bullshit. Bull *shit!*"

Rudman felt his own anger building but he held it in.

"Listen, you're the one used to say it wasn't any of your business, remember?" he snapped back. "This isn't your country. It will all blow over. Used to tell me I was hysterical. Hysterical? Look at you."

"What the hell do you expect me to do? Jitterbug around the room?"

The room service bellman arrived and they both cooled down while Keegan signed the check. Rudman poured two cups of coffee. He sat down on the sofa.

"Every day hundreds—maybe thousands—of people are

dragged off the streets like this," Rudman said shaking his head. "Out of their homes, offices, shops, out of *schools*, for God's sake, and their families never see them again . . ."

"I'm not one of them. I'm an American citizen . . ."

"Immaterial, pal," Rudman interrupted this time. "You've got to get that fixed in your head. All your money, your influence, it doesn't mean anything here. You *are* one of them, Kee. The same pain, same anger, same . . . everything. This thing, you're just one of the crowd. All those other voices drown you out."

"Then we'll tell them. Write a story about Dachau, about what's happening . . ."

"Damn it, don't you understand, nobody *wants* to hear it. I did a story on Dachau for the *Tribune* three months ago. It was buried on page thirty in the New York edition."

"So I roll over and play dead, that it?"

"Kee, you can't get her out," Rudman said slowly. "The whole world feels the way you did, that it's a German problem."

"You won't do anything because it'll jeopardize your precious bloody bureau, is that it?"

"Aw, for Christ sake, Kee . . ."

Keegan whirled suddenly and threw his coffee cup at the wall. It shattered, spraying bits of china around the room, the coffee etching a brown stain down the wallpaper. His shoulders sagged.

"Go on, get out of here." Keegan waved his hand dejectedly. "Leave me alone."

"To do what?" Rudman said. "Wallow in self-pity?"

Keegan dropped into a chair and did not answer. He seemed to shrink from the weight of the tragedy. Rudman sighed and walked to the door. "You're just another member of a very sad club, Kee, and the membership's growing larger by the day."

He left. As the door clicked shut, Keegan jumped up.

"Ah shit," he said, striding across the room after him. The phone rang.

Vierhaus? he thought. *Finally.*

He rushed across the room and snatched it up.

"Yes?" he said, far too eagerly.

"Mr. Keegan?"

"Yes."

"This is your tailor. Your suit is ready."

Keegan, disoriented, angry, completely overwrought, wasn't thinking clearly.

"What? What suit?" he snapped.

"Your suit is ready and we're closing early today, Mr. Keegan."

Click.

Keegan suddenly snapped back to reality. Was that Wolff-son? he wondered. He didn't recognize the voice, not enough time. My God, he thought abruptly, that was the warning. Was the Gestapo after *him* now?

He stopped in the middle of the room, took deep breaths to calm himself down. What was it Wolffson had told him? If they called about the suit go immediately to the city zoo and find the phone booth near the carousel.

Immediately!

He checked the front window of the suite, then the back. Nothing out of the ordinary. He went to the closet and got his briefcase, the only luggage he had. He snapped it open, took out an envelope, checked the contents, and stuck it in his inside pocket. There was nothing else of real value in the case. He left it on the table and checked the windows again. As he was watching, a black Mercedes sedan pulled up and parked on the opposite side of the street. Four men wearing leather raincoats and black hats got out. Two of them entered the front of the hotel, the other two walked around to the rear.

Keegan left the suite, took the elevator to the second floor. He walked quickly to the fire stairs and started down. As he reached the first floor, the door opened. Two black hats barged into the stairwell. They stood two feet away from Keegan.

Leather coats, black fedoras, expressionless faces, blank eyes, lean as jackals. The only difference between the two was their height. One was two inches taller than the other.

The taller one stared at Keegan with surprise for a second, then blurted, "Herr Keegan?"

Keegan reacted immediately. He kicked the tall one in the kneecap as hard as he could. The man howled with pain and fell to the floor. As he did, Keegan slashed his knee into the shorter one's groin, grabbed his collar and slammed his head into the wall. His forehead split open. Keegan slammed him into the wall one more time and as he fell, reached inside the man's coat and grabbed the grip of his gun.

Whirling on the taller one, Keegan stuck the Luger under his nose.

"You make a sound and I'll blow your brains all over that wall. You understand me? *Verstehen?*"

"*Ja.*" The German nodded, his face still distorted with pain.

"Auto keys, *Schlüssel?* Where are they? *Beeilen sie sich mal, beeilen!*"

"I don't . . ."

Keegan jabbed the muzzle of the gun under the agent's chin, shoved his head back.

"You drove the car, you lying son of a bitch. Give me the keys or I'll kill you just for the hell of it."

The agent fumbled in a vest pocket and handed him the ring of keys.

"Take off the coat and hat. *Beeilung!*"

The agent struggled to one knee and took off the coat. Keegan snatched his hat off and put it on. He took the coat, leaned forward and slashed the pistol down on the back of the agent's head. The man sighed and fell unconscious.

Keegan put on the coat and stuck the gun in his pocket. He pulled the hat down low over his forehead, entered the lobby and, without looking to the right or left, walked straight to the entrance and out the door. He crossed the street, got in the Mercedes, cranked it up and drove off. He turned right at the first street, stepped on the gas and wove his way through traffic. In two blocks he turned right, drove another block, turned left and parked. He got out and threw the keys down a sewer trap. He walked to the corner and found a taxi.

"Tiergarten," he said as he got in.

The rain had settled into a fine mist. When Keegan got out of the taxi, he went into a store across the street from the zoo entrance. He waited until the taxi pulled away and rounded the corner, then he walked briskly across the street and entered the zoo. The carousel was in the middle of the park near the lake.

The phone booth was beside the monkey cage across the walk from the merry-go-round.

Keegan stood with his hands in his pocket and waited for the phone to ring.

"Do not turn around, *Ire,*" a voice said behind him. "Listen quick. Ve haf learn Vierhaus is going to arrest you as a *Spion.*"

"I know. They came to the hotel after me."

"You are in serious trouble. Go to the rear of the carousel now. Iss a toolshed there. Go inside."

"Have you heard any more about Jen . . ."

"Beeilen!"

A young couple came by and stopped beside Keegan. They stood with their arms around each other, ignoring the rain, and threw peanuts to the monkeys. *Not a care in the world,* Keegan thought. *Two days ago that could have been us.* He waited until they moved on. When he turned around, there was nobody there.

He walked around the carousel, found the toolshed and went inside. It was a small utility room. A large worktable and chair took up most of the space. A bare bulb hung from a cord over the table. Cobwebs, like gossamer nets, dominated the corners.

Werner Gebhart was waiting. His cold eyes appraised Keegan as he entered the shack. Gebhart took a pair of cord knickers, a tweed cap, a sports shirt, a sleeveless sweater and heavy boots from a rucksack and put them on the worktable. He also produced a blond wig and a pair of glasses.

"Put on *die Verkleidung,*" Gebhart said in a rough mixture of English and German. "*Beeilung.*"

"You're really prepared for emergencies aren't you?" Keegan said, quickly peeling off the coat and hat.

"Ve expected dis," Gebhart said coldly. "Whatever dey found out from Jenny, dey tink you can . . . how do you say . . . ?"

"Corroborate?"

"*Ja.* You should haf left last night."

"They're taking Jenny to Dachau," Keegan said.

"*Heute Morgen* ve heard. *Das Unglück.*"

"Bad luck? That's all you have to say?"

"*You* change, Keegan," Gebhart said firmly. "Ve talk about dis later. *Und ja,* it is all I say."

"You don't like me, do you, Werner?" Keegan said, continuing to change as quickly as he could.

"*Nein.*"

"Why not?" Keegan pressed him.

"Because you are playing the hero. You are reckless and arrogant, *Ire.*"

"Okay," said Keegan. "If I get caught, you go down, too, so why don't you just tell me where to go and I'll get there on my own."

"*Hören sie mal!*" he said in a low, angry voice. "I am not doing this to help you, I am doing it to help us because you are poison to us all. Do not fool yourself, you vould not last ten minutes mittout us. You are . . . uh, *gefährlich* . . . dangerous . . . you play *der* hero *und* vill die and many of us vill die *mit* you."

"Nobody's gonna die."

"You see? Arrogant. People die every day."

"I tried to call Vierhaus all night," Keegan said, changing the subject. "He never returned the calls, sent the Gestapo instead."

"He is very, what you call *schnell.*"

"Fast? Quick?"

"*Ja. Und* he has been at *das Spiel* three, four years," Gebhart said. "You are no match for him, *Ire,* no matter vat you tink. Dat vass a bad idea." He gathered up the clothes as Keegan took them off. "Vere did you get *Mantel und Hut?*"

Keegan took the Luger out of the coat pocket and handed it to Gebhart.

"Gestapo. Here, you might be able to use this."

"Vot happened?"

"I had to get by a couple of agents," Keegan said, pulling on the pants. "I didn't kill them, just gave them bad headaches. I also stole their car and left it on a side street."

"So . . . now the whole city iss out for you," Gebhart said. He pulled the wig down on Keegan's head, shoving his dark hair under the edges and smoothing it down around Keegan's ears and the nape of his neck. He gave Keegan an ID card listing his occupation as a postal worker. Smart. The Nazis avoided offending bureaucrats.

"If ve are stop, I vill talk. Ve are going on holiday to the Alps for mountain climbing."

"Okay."

"Now *der Hut und,* how you call them, *die Brille?*"

"Spectacles."

"*Ja.* The glass iss clear."

Keegan looked across the dimly lit room at Gebhart. "Well, how do I look?"

"Just remember, ve know vat ve are doing. Do as I tell you *und* do not argue. Do it quickly. *Verstehen Sie?*"

"Yes," Keegan nodded, "it's quite clear."

They walked out of the shed and around the lake to a parking lot, got in the blue Opel and drove through the middle of the city and across the main bridge into a *Häuserblock,* a residential section. The shops and commercial buildings surrendered to duplexes, six or seven to the block; heavy Gothic buildings with large arched windows, thick, oak-framed doorways and gray stucco walls, six or seven houses all attached in a single long, gray block. Gebhart pulled behind one of the rows. An alley behind the granite square was lined with brightly painted garage doors. He pulled down to one of them and blew the horn. A minute went by, then the door rolled open. Gebhart pulled into the garage. The door closed behind. He waited for a minute or so in the dark, then turned on the car lights.

The garage was small and empty except for the car. Gebhart nodded toward a door that led into the house.

"Go through there," he said. *"Viel Glück.* I will not see you again."

He held out his hand and they shook.

"Thanks, Werner. *Viel Glück* to you too."

He entered the house and went up a short flight of stairs and through the sparsely furnished kitchen to the living room. Wolffson was alone there sitting on a large packing crate. There was no furniture except for a single floor lamp with a fringed shade. An ashtray filled with butts sat beside him.

"Welcome, Herr Keegan. Pick a box and sit down."

"Moving in or out?"

"In, actually. We travel light, *Ire.* Sometimes we have to leave everything behind. So, we have to kill some time. We will be here awhile."

"Mind telling me what's going on?"

"We have an excellent contact at SS headquarters. Early

this morning, Vierhaus ordered your arrest. Specifically you are charged with espionage."

"Ludicrous."

"But true. And if they catch you, you are a dead man either way."

"The whole thing is insane. It doesn't even make good sense."

"That is right, it is insane. But it makes sense to them."

"So what's the plan?"

"We will leave at dark, drive to Munich. We know back roads where there is little traffic. It takes longer but we will be there before dawn. There will be three of us. You, me, and Joachim."

"Do I have any say in the matter?"

"What is your choice, *Ire*? Go to the American embassy? No way to get out once you are in, you could spend eternity there. If you remain in Berlin they will most certainly catch you and after your skirmish with the Gestapo they will most certainly kill you. Or go with us. We will have you out of Germany in forty-eight hours."

"Why Munich?"

"We have a strong organization in Munich and we need to spend the day there. Much safer to travel at night and it will take us two nights to get to the Swiss border."

"Ah, so we're going into Switzerland, then?"

"Yes. We have good friends there and we know the safe places to cross. If everything goes well, you will be a free man by day after tomorrow."

Keegan lit a cigarette and thought about the alternatives. Of course, Wolffson was right. Nothing could be gained by staying in Berlin.

"I keep thinking once I'm out of Germany I lose any hope of helping Jenny," he said finally.

"If she can be helped, I promise you we will do everything in our power to get her out," Wolffson said.

"How about escape?"

"Virtually impossible. We have tried three breakouts. All failed. Twelve people died."

Wolffson ground out a cigarette and went to the window, peering through the drapes and checking the street.

What a way to live, thought Keegan. Constantly on the run, never trusting anyone, knowing if you are caught some blond moron will cut off your head in the basement of Landsberg prison.

Finally Wolffson turned back to Keegan.

"What will you do when you get back to America?" he asked.

"I don't know," Keegan answered. "This has all happened so fast. I suppose try to wake people up to what's really happening. Maybe try to raise money for you. Try to do something to help."

"And what will you tell them they do not know already? People hear what they want to hear, *Ire*. And right now they do not want their conscience challenged. Much easier to ignore it."

"I have influential friends, Avrum. I may be able to do something."

"Politicians?" Wolffson shook his head. "They will not help you. They lean with the people and the people do not want to hear about our troubles. They have their own problems. Believe me, I know."

Wolffson stretched out on the floor with his hands behind his head and stared at the ceiling. Several minutes passed in silence.

"There is only one way to impress anyone with the horror that already exists here," Wolffson said finally.

"What's that?" Keegan asked.

"See it yourself," Wolffson said. "Nobody can deny what you have seen with your own eyes."

Then he closed his eyes.

"We talk later. I need some sleep, it is a long drive."

Keegan sat against the wall with his knees pulled up and his chin resting on his arms. Here and there, streaks of light sneaked through the heavy drapes. In a minute or two Wolffson's breathing grew deeper, more rhythmic, and he was asleep. Keegan watched as the shadows in the room grew longer. Finally he too dozed off.

31

They were a hundred yards away, hidden in the thick trees and heavy brush of the woods that hid the treacherous stockade from the main road. An area one hundred yards wide had been cleared of all foliage around the entire perimeter of the camp. Signs warned that this barren stretch was mined. A single-lane road led through the trees to the gate and beyond it, railroad tracks glistened in the morning sunlight, the tracks worn shiny from use.

The lenses of the binoculars swept slowly across the terrain, picking up first the gate, then the wire and finally the camp itself. It was a forlorn and desolate place, bleak, disheartening, oppressive; a place of long, drab wooden barracks painted gray, a place barren of foliage except for a failed attempt at a garden between two of the barracks, a sorrowful row of twisted, dead plants that hung from stakes or lay on the hard, brown earth. The earth itself was baked rock hard by the sun, earth so poor layers of it were churned to dust and swirled away by the slightest wisp of wind. The buildings were coated with the dead earth.

Then there was the wire.

Four rows of barbed wire three feet apart, humming with deadly electricity, followed by a ditch and a twelve-foot link fence, which was also electrified. Dogs snarled at the end of short leashes. Powerful searchlights were mounted on tall poles scattered about the sprawling enclosure. Gun towers loomed ominously at the corners of the compound.

As Keegan scanned the enclosure with the binoculars, he stopped suddenly. An old man in striped prison clothes dangled on his back across the inner wire; his arms, stiff in death, were outstretched. One foot barely touched the ground. His flesh was gray and had begun to rot. His white hair fluttered in the breeze.

Flies swarmed hungrily around the corpse. Fifty feet away, an elderly woman with a handkerchief pressed over her nose and mouth numbly watched the flies at work.

"Good God," Keegan breathed.

"His name was Rosenberg. A banker from Linz. He was fifty-eight years old. That is his wife looking at him. His only crime was that he was a Jew. They took his money, his property, destroyed his family and then put them in the camp. They broke that gentle old man and he finally jumped on the wire and ended it all. So they leave him there until he literally rots away. A warning to others."

Keegan lowered the glasses and took several deep breaths.

"You wanted to see Dachau and I wanted you to see it, Keegan," Wolffson whispered. "Now you can believe, now you can convince others that this is not just a foul rumor."

"Oh, it's foul all right," Keegan groaned. "Foul beyond comprehension."

A third man, whose name was Milton Golen, lay beside them with a camera wrapped in cloth to muffle the shutter click. The camera thunked quietly as he shot photo after photo of the ghoulish stockade. He stopped occasionally to jot down notes.

"We try to monitor the condition of the prisoners," Golen whispered, raising the camera again. "Keep track of who has died, who is ill. It is not very effective but we do our best. Coming here is very risky as you can tell."

"We can't stay but a minute," Wolffson added. "They patrol these woods constantly with dogs."

They had driven through the outskirts of Dachau just before dawn. It was forty minutes from Munich, on the main road between it and Berlin. Wolffson had turned off the main road, driven through the village to Golen's farm and parked the car in his barn. His wife had served them breakfast and strong coffee.

"Are you going to the woods today?" Wolffson had asked their host and Golen had nodded.

"Is it safe for the three of us to go?" Wolffson asked.

"As safe as for one. It is never safe. If we get caught, we will be inside, if they don't shoot us."

Wolffson had turned to Keegan.

"So, *Ire,* you want to do something to help? *Gut.* We will give you a memory to take back."

He had outlined the ground rules. Follow orders. Speak only in whispers. Leave when ordered. They left just before dawn in a horse-drawn firewood cart with a hollow core, entering from underneath through a trap in the floor of the wagon. They had left the wagon a mile from the edge of the clearing in the forest and gone the rest of the way by first walking in a stream so they would not leave a scent for the dogs, then crossing beneath an open field through a sewer culvert. They had crawled the last fifty yards on the floor of the forest, dragging themselves through snarls of sticker bushes and bug-infested grass, then suddenly they were at the edge of the security clearing and the dreadful compound loomed before them.

Keegan's mouth had gone dry at the first sight of it. He lay flat on his stomach, one hand holding back the grass, the other scanning the place with binoculars. He continued to scan the yard, hoping, praying for a glimpse of her, to know she was still alive.

The ultimate shock was the inmates themselves. Gaunt, bowed before their time, physically broken, they seemed almost hypnotized. Their eyes told the whole tale. Hope was burned out, replaced by terror and resignation. Like robots, they moved around the dirt yard surrounding the barracks, hardly speaking.

Near one of the corners, an old man in a striped jacket and pants, his white beard brushing his chest, stood in one spot and stared without moving, across the wire and through the link fence. His eyes moved neither left nor right. He said nothing. He simply stared across the twenty or so feet of tangled wire, past the tall fence and the barren perimeter, toward freedom.

There was about the place such an utterly despairing sense of futility and lost hope that Keegan seemed to collapse inside. His shoulders caved in and a pitiful moan escaped from his pressed lips.

"Shh," Wolffson warned.

"My God," Keegan said softly, "it looks so . . . so totally hopeless."

"And so it is for the people inside," whispered Golen. "This place is not just for Jews. Most of these prisoners are Germans.

Political prisoners. Hitler's enemies. God knows what they do to them."

"Come, we cannot stay here, Keegan," said Wolffson. "The dogs will catch our scent."

"Just one more minute."

He swept the glasses across the crowded yard one more time. And then he saw her.

"There!" he breathed. "Over by the barracks. She just came out."

Jenny seemed smaller, withered almost. Her steps were short and faltering. She hugged herself as if she were cold. Her hair was tangled and snarled and she wore a formless dress that hung down to her shins.

"She looks so . . . so frail," he breathed. "Jesus, what've they done to her."

"At least she's still alive," Wolffson said, locating her in his glasses.

"That's not living. That's torture," Keegan answered.

He bit his fist to keep from crying her name, to let her know he was nearby, that there was hope, although in his heart he knew her situation was futile.

Is that really why Wolffson had brought him here, he wondered. So Keegan would know how utterly hopeless it was?

"Keegan, we must leave now!" Wolffson insisted.

A moment later they heard the dogs.

Wolffson grabbed Keegan by the arm and dragged him back into the trees.

"Stay low and run," Golen said. "We must get through the culvert before they catch our scent."

They ran stooped over, dodging through thickets that tore at their clothes like thorny hands snatching at them. Behind them they heard the deep snarling bark of the shepherd dogs drawing closer.

"Faster!" Golen demanded.

Keegan's breath was waning, his lungs were on fire, the muscles in his legs began to knot up. But he kept running, trying to breathe with some semblance of rhythm. Ahead of them the forest grew brighter, then suddenly they were at the edge of the field. They ducked into the culvert, their footfalls echoing in the narrow tube, dashed through it and burst out of the other end. They jumped three feet down into the stream and headed away from the camp, running through knee-deep water. Behind them they could hear the dogs barking, snarling, yipping. Their cries echoed in the culvert.

"*Gut,*" Golen cried out, "the dogs are confused. They are in the tube and have lost our smell. We're almost there."

Golen turned sharply and Keegan and Wolffson followed as he jumped out of the creek and climbed a small embankment. The firewood cart was where they left it, the horse nibbling on the grass. Wolffson dove under the cart, rolled over on his back and opened the trap door. He and Keegan crawled inside the dark compartment. Golen quickly changed from his wet pants and shoes to dry clothes and boots. He rubbed limburger cheese on the shoes and on his wrists and, leaning under the cart, rubbed the foul-smelling cheese around the edge of the trap-door. He threw his wet clothes inside and slammed the door shut. Keegan and Wolffson lay in the dark on the rough floor gasping for breath. A moment later they heard Golen chopping wood.

"What's he doing?" Keegan whispered.

"He is sweating. So he will cut some wood and if they follow us this far, they will not suspect him."

Fifteen minutes passed without incident. Inside the compartment, Keegan felt the cart lean as Golen climbed into the driver's seat. A moment later they began to move, the wagon creaking down the road toward the village.

"You will be in Switzerland before morning," Wolffson sighed. "The rest of the trip is easy."

"I owe you one," said Keegan.

"Which means?"

"It means I owe you a big favor."

In the dark, Keegan fought back tears.

"I wasn't a hundred yards away from her," he moaned. "A hundred stinking yards!"

His defeat, frustration, humiliation were complete. Now he fully comprehended the futility of the situation.

"Use your influence, *Ire,*" Wolffson said. "Go back and tell them what you saw here. Take this."

"What is it?" Keegan asked, then felt the cool, small spool of film in his palm.

"It is the film Golen shot back there. Take the pictures back. Show them what is happening. Tell them if they do not stop this madness, the sin is theirs just as it is the sin of all Germans who turn their faces away from the truth."

Colebreak, Kansas, lay in the southwest corner of the state. The three-story courthouse was the tallest building in town. It provided a core to the tiny hamlet around which clustered half a dozen stores. The only tree to speak of was in the front of the courthouse building and the bench under it provided a meeting place for whittlers to cut and chew and trade lies on Saturdays while their wives did the shopping. The population of the town itself was 250.

Three men sat on the bench. Jack Grogan and Dewey Winthrop were playing checkers, the board laid out between them. The third man, Hiram Johnson, was carving a whistle out of a tree branch for his grandson. It was a Thursday. Armistice Day. Uncommonly hot for November, the temperature pushing 85 degrees. The town was almost deserted.

"Must be the holiday," Grogan said. "Everybody's at home or gone to a parade som'ere's."

"You hear?" Hiram answered. "They canceled the parade over to Lippencott."

"What's the matter?"

"Sand blizzard. They say it's worse'n that winter fog three years ago. Can't see a foot in front of yuh."

"Who says that? Harvey Logan, bet."

"Right, was ol' Harve."

"Shit, you can't believe a word he says," said Grogan. "He'll stand in the rain n'tell you the sun's shinin'."

"All I know, they canceled the parade. All them vets over there in their overseas caps with their medals pinned on and the high school band and all went in the auditorium over to the school t'wait it out."

"If it's like over in Tulsa last summer, it ain't gonna blow over," said Dewey. He pursed his lips and a black streak of tobacco juice squirted into the grass.

"I heard they had a black blizzard so bad it turned day to night in Chicago," Hiram said.

"Yeah," Dewey chimed in. "Read in the papers they could see it in Albany, New York. New *York!* Why hell, that's half the country away."

"Aw hell, Hiram, you don't believe that, do you?"

"Papers don't lie."

"Sez who?"

"Not about somethin' like that they don't."

"Shit."

They saw the LaSalle a mile away as it came down the flat highway toward them, churning up dust behind it. It looked yellow from a distance but as it drew closer they could see the car was pale blue, its paint covered by a thick cake of dust. The car pulled into town and stopped at the square. The driver, his tie pulled down from an open collar and his shirtsleeves rolled up, got out and brushed dust off his pants. Sweat stains spread down under his arms almost to his waist.

Drummer, thought Hiram.

The driver pulled his shirt away from his sweaty chest and strolled over to the Pepsi machine in the vestibule of the courthouse and dropped a nickel in.

"Sure hot for November," he offered.

Hiram nodded.

The drummer took a deep swig from the bottle and swished the fizzing cola around in his mouth before swallowing it.

"Whatcha sellin'?" Grogan asked.

"Ladies' wear," the tall man said with a smile. "Not doin' too well, either."

"Seen any dust?"

"Everywhere. Not like what they had south of here yesterday but I'll tell you, I had to close up m'windows and I damn near fainted from the heat. Dust just seeped right through around the windows. Hell of a note."

He shook his head and took another swig.

"Where you from?" Hiram asked.

"St. Louis."

"Long way from home."

"Well, it takes a big territory and a lot of travelin' to make a livin' these days."

"I heard you say that, all rightee," Grogan agreed. "Nice car."

"Was before I hit that wind yesterday. Look here, like sandpaper. Took the finish off m'hood."

He wiped his hand across the front of the car, sweeping a small dune of dust into the air. It was just as he said, the blue paint was nearly sanded off.

"Damn, would yuh look at that," Grogan said.

"Where you headed?"

"Thought I'd make Lippencott and spend the night. I forgot it was a holiday t'day."

"F'get it," said Grogan shaking his head.

"What's the matter?"

"Black blizzard. Had to cancel the Armistice Day parade. Tell me you can't see your feet, it's so bad."

"Could be blowin' this way," Hiram said.

"You know that for a fact?"

"Just talk," said Grogan. "He's been on the phone with old Harvey Logan."

Hiram shook his head. "Could be blowin' this way," he repeated.

"I'd sure find out," the drummer said. "It can kill you, y'know. Dust is so thick it'll just choke your life out. If it does come, you need to be inside. Maybe wrap a hanky around your nose and mouth."

"I heard of a man who got caught outside and actually vomited dirt, it was that bad," said Hiram.

"There you go again," said Grogan.

"Well, if it's blowing in Lippencott I'm not going near there," said the drummer, walking to the edge of the sidewalk and looked west, down the ribbon of black top toward Lippencott. "Got a hotel?"

"Back down the road about ten miles. Bradyton."

He squinted his eyes, focusing on the horizon, looking for the ominous wave of sand and wind that had plagued these prairie towns for months. The previous summer, the heat in Kansas had stayed at 108 for sixty days in a row and there had only been twenty inches of rainfall in the year. That had started it. The earth, weary from years of poor farming practices, dried up, cracked, turned to shale, then to dust. Then heavy winds came and like a giant hand scooped the earth up and threw it into the air. The clouds of dirt tumbled over each other like waves, built into towering black oceans of dirt, engulfing everything. Roads disappeared before the clouds. Homes were buried in mountainous dunes. Whole towns vanished in a night, buried under the sea of sand. Animals suffocated in their tracks and people died of pneumonia, their lungs ruined by the sod. In nine months, one hundred million acres of topsoil had blown away. The deadly bowl spread from Texas north to the Colorado border. The prairie land looked so much like a beach that a reporter for the *Tulsa Tribune* had written: "I was driving and suddenly the road disappeared. Then I saw the roof of a house, just the very peak of it, sticking up through what looked like dunes at the beach. I almost expected to smell salt air."

The drummer had driven through a small wind storm the day before and that was bad enough. Now as he watched, the black cloud obscured the horizon and grew like a great broiling, black thunderhead. There was no sound yet, just the ominous towering black cloak swirling before gale winds, towering up into the sky even as he watched it. It was headed straight for them.

"My God," the drummer breathed.

The three townsmen joined him at the curb, followed his eyes and saw the deadly cloud. As they watched it kept swirling higher into the sky, darker than a storm cloud, darker than dusk.

"God a'mighty," Hiram breathed.

"Is it comin' this w-w-way?" Grogan stammered, his eyes bulging at the sight of the growing cloud.

"It ain't goin' on vacation," said Dewey.

"I got t'get home," Hiram said. "God, don't tell me we's gonna get what Tulsa got!"

"It's comin', it's comin'," Grogan cried as the three men scurried for their vehicles. The drummer stood hypnotized, watching the storm of sand build. Then faintly he heard the wind, a low rumble, almost like thunder. It was probably fifteen miles away, he thought, and it's already twenty thousand feet high. He bought another Pepsi, got in the car and roared away, back the way he had come.

He drove back toward Bradyton ignoring the thirty-five-mile-an-hour speed limit. Behind him, the giant wave of dirt seemed to chase him down the highway. The drummer wrapped a handkerchief around his face and kept the windows open because of the heat. Farm after farm on both sides of the road was deserted. Signs flapping on the front doors told the world the bank now owned the property. Once he passed a farmer, his wife and their two children, rushing in and out of their small frame home, valiantly struggling to pile possessions on a battered old Model T. The wind was already whipping sand into twirling dervishes around them.

He was three miles outside Bradyton when he noticed the gas gauge. The needle registered empty. He tapped the gauge with his fingers but the needle was frozen on "E." Panic coiled in the pit of his stomach. The black blizzard was already on his tail. Ahead of him, he could see maelstroms of sand whirling onto the highway and he could feel the wind buffeting the car. Then, through the whorls of sand and wind, he saw a small filling station beside the road. He whipped the LaSalle off the road and parked beside the pumps. It was a Sinclair station, a small building of corrugated tin and wood, already shuddering before nature's onslaught. He ran to the door and beat on the glass, then cupped his eyes and looked inside. The place was deserted. He found a rusty old tire iron and smashed the window. It was obvious the owner had left in a hurry. The cash register drawer was open and the power had been turned off. The drummer ran back outside and smashed the Yale lock off the single gas pump and started filling the tank, trying to shield the tank opening against the whirling sands.

The great black wave descended on him, howling like a wounded animal, suddenly turning day to night. Sand ripped at his face and hands like tiny razor blades. He drove the car to the front of the building and pried the lock off the garage door, pushing and shoving it open against the banshee gale. Finally he got the car inside. The wind slammed the door closed behind him. Darkness descended over him like a dark cloth. He turned on the car lights and went back into the office, grabbed a handful of crackers and candy bars and stuffed them in his pockets. He used his crowbar to force open the soda machine and took a half dozen bottles back into the garage. He got in the car, wrapped his jacket around his face, closed the car windows and huddled there.

Outside, a great sea of earth thirty thousand feet high, forty miles wide and nine miles deep, swept down on the small building, engulfed it, assaulted it, battered it mercilessly with sixty-mile-an-hour winds. Around him he could hear metal screaming, things clattering against the small building, timbers groaning. An edge of the roof fluttered loose of its nails and the gale roared under it, peeled it back like the skin of an orange, and whipped it away. Sand poured through the gaping hole in the roof like water. The car began to rock before nature's wrath. The drummer held on to the steering wheel, his eyes closed and his teeth clenched, while the car rocked harder and harder. Fine silt started to ooze in around the windows.

Finally in abject fear and frustration, the drummer cried out:

"*Stop!* . . . *Stop!* . . . *Stop!* . . ."

It was midnight-dark and the nightmare continued.

The drummer cursed himself for taking the job. He had spent three months, driving first through the South, then north beside the big Mississippi to St. Louis. He had spotted the ad in the Sunday newspaper and had taken the traveling job because it seemed perfect. He would be on the road all the time, traveling from one hamlet to the next in the prairie states.

"All you need," said Albert Kronen, the man who answered the phone, "is an auto and a silver tongue." His territory included Kansas, northern Oklahoma and southern Nebraska. He could stay on the road for months at a time, displaying his wares—girdles, cotton stockings and panties, simple frocks—in village after village. Perfect. No time clock to punch, no schedules to meet. He would be on his own.

Kronen did not mention the black blizzards, the towering waves of death that were turning the plains states into deserts and villages into abandoned ghost towns and blowing the farmlands to the winds.

The car rocked harder. The rest of the corrugated roof tore off with a mighty screaming sound and the drummer huddled deeper in his seat, his shoulders hunched up around his ears, his eyes squeezed shut to keep out the fine sand that filtered through every slit and opening in the car. How long would it last? he wondered. How long *could* it last?

The wind howled for half an hour before passing as quickly as it had arrived. It became deathly still. The drummer sat at the wheel of the car with the taste of dirt in his mouth. He looked in the rearview mirror and saw an apparition, a dusty clown face with two black potholes for eyes. He brushed the dirt off his face with his hands and got out of the car. A shower of dust poured down from the top of the car when he opened the door.

Gray sunlight poured through the gaping holes in the roof of the garage. The door was jammed shut. He put his shoulder against it and battered it open a foot or so and squeezed through. Dunes of sand greeted him. Drifts of it slanted down from the sides of the battered building. The road was an indented sliver stretching toward Bradyton. He sank to his ankles as he walked to the front of the filling station. He found a large metal sign half-buried near the pump and pulled it free. A rugged-looking cowboy with a cigarette dangling from the corner of his mouth smiled up at him from the sheet.

The drummer laughed aloud when he read the slogan.

"I'd walk a mile for a Camel."

The drummer looked around. *I could use a camel myself right now,* he thought to himself. *But not the kind you smoke.*

He used the sheet to shovel the sand away from the garage door and make tracks to the main road, ate a candy bar, washing it down with a bottle of soda pop, and backed out onto the highway.

A man who could have been forty or eighty stood near the entrance to the Bradyton House, a three-story yellow brick building in the center of town. He wore bib jeans and his fists were pressed against his chest. The man stared past the drummer, his face caked in dust, his eyes and mouth black scars in the powdery facade. He was shaking uncontrollably.

"You all right?" the drummer asked.

"N-n-never seen anything l-l-like it," the old man stammered, his terrified eyes gazing straight ahead in a fixed stare. "D-d-dirt falling from the sky. Hell on earth. Hell on earth."

A woman, her skin leather-tanned in color and texture, was

sweeping up sand that lay in ripples across the linoleum floor. Oiled rags were stuffed in the sills and sashes of the windows. It was a pleasant lobby with several sofas and easy chairs and a scattering of magazines and newspapers. A door beside the tiny desk led to a restaurant.

The woman looked up as the drummer entered.

"Come to stay the night?" she asked.

"Yes," he answered.

"You're in luck. Kin have any room in the place." She set aside the broom and walked behind the desk, spinning the registration book around so it faced him and handing him a pen.

"Four dollars the night. Includes clean sheets, sink and commode in the room, bath at the end of the hall. Breakfast is on the house."

"Very reasonable," he said wearily and scribbled his name on the ledger. She whirled it back and read the name aloud.

"John Trexler, St. Louis. Tell you what, Mr. Trexler, I can tell you've had a bad afternoon, as we all have. Why don't you just go on up to the top of the stairs and take the suite. Has its own bath and shower. I should be able to feed you in an hour or so. We should have the kitchen back open by then."

"That's very kind of you," the drummer said. "Thanks."

He carried a couple of newspapers up with him and sat in a steamy tub, leisurely reading a four-day-old *Kansas City Star*. In the Help Wanted section, an item immediately caught his eye.

GOLDEN OPPORTUNITY

For qualified men only, a chance to get in on the ground floor of a new winter resort. Must be expert skier and mountain climber and have training in survival tactics. Weekly salary, room and board. Inquiries: Snow Slope, Aspen, Colorado.

He got out of the tub, toweled off and dug his atlas out of the suitcase. Aspen was a mere dot in the middle of the Rocky Mountains about 150 miles west of Denver. Trexler sat on the edge of the bed and lit a cigarette. Twenty-seven had found the perfect place to once again settle down.

BOOK FOUR

"The tree of liberty must be
refreshed from time to time
with the blood of patriots and tyrants.
It is its natural manure."

Thomas Jefferson

Rudman walked down through the ruins of Alicante. The city was virtually leveled. There was hardly a wall more than five feet tall still standing. The civilians were gone. The dogs had been eaten. There was nothing left but the rats and a tattered battalion of Loyalists who were holding the town because it was a port and controlled the main coast road.

It was sweltering hot and there were flies everywhere. Some of the more recent dead had yet to be collected for burial.

Rudman had been in the same clothes for six days, since the hotel had been bombed out. He had bathed naked in the ocean every night but his clothes were stiff with dirt. His beard was beginning to show some gray and he had a slight limp from a piece of shrapnel which had buried itself in his calf months before.

Only one or two restaurants were still open, along with the telegraph office from which Rudman and other journalists covering the civil war filed their daily dispatches. Rudman carried his story into the disheveled telegraph office and the telegraph operator, an old man with thick white hair and a drooping mustache, gave him a weary smile.

"Señor Rudman," he said, "what have you got for me today?"

"Same old stuff," Rudman said wearily. "I've been here off and on since 1935. After three years of writing about this butcher shop it's all beginning to sound the same."

He stood at the counter and read over the hand-written piece once more, marking out or changing a word here and there.

ALICANTE, SPAIN, June 22, 1938. The last remaining Loyalist troops are facing annihilation in this southern coast town today as the Fascist forces of Generalissimo Franco move closer to the city.

There is little left of this town that was once a holiday haven for the rich of Europe. But it is no different from most other villages that have been destroyed in this three-year war, the worst civil strife since the American Civil War.

This morning, vultures have replaced Nazi bombers in the skies above, circling the devastated town in search of a feast.

Looking in horror at this fratricidal holocaust, I am reminded of a time in Africa when I saw a gut-shot hyena, nature's most efficient scavenger, eating its own insides.

In this war, which has pitted brother against brother, neighbor against neighbor, church against state, Spain, too, is devouring itself while its German and Italian "friends" sit on the sidelines crying "Olé!"

They have provided the most modern and efficient machines of death to Franco. What a cynical gesture—turning Spain into their private testing ground and using Spanish blood for their grisly experiments. The weapons perfected here will be the weapons used in the next world war. . . .

He put down the pencil and pinched his eyes.

"Oh, the hell with it," he said, "just send it on, Pablo."

"*Si Señor,*" the operator said.

Rudman went back outside. A Loyalist soldier was sitting on a pile of bricks, digging beans out of a can with his bayonet which he used as a fork. He was thin as a palm leaf, his pale eyes buried deep in black sockets. He wore a rag of a white shirt and torn cord pants and had a bandolier around his shoulder. His toes were sticking through the end of his boots. His rifle, an old Mannlicher, was leaning on the bricks near his leg.

"*Americano?*" Rudman asked.

"Yeah. You too?" the soldier answered.

"Yep. Join you?"

"Sure, pull up a brick and sit down."

Rudman sat down and took a swig of water from his canteen.

"What's your name?"

"What's the dif? I'm just a soldier." His voice was hoarse from the dust that drifted up from the ruins.

"Are you a Communist?" Rudman asked.

"Hell, no. I just hate these Fascist bastards. You don't stop them here, they'll be in Coney Island next. Least that's what I thought when I came over here."

"You don't think so anymore?"

"Hell, I don't know what I think. Y'know, I never seen a dead body before I came over here? Some education."

"Sorry you came now?"

Soldier laughed. "Shit, is anybody ever glad they came? It's something you think you ought t'do. You can't complain when it doesn't go right, can you?"

"Where you from?"

"Boston. Boston, Mass. Land of liberty. You ain't in the Brigade, are you?"

"No, I'm a correspondent."

"No kiddin'? For who?"

"New York Times."

"Hey. You're a big shot, huh?"

"There aren't any big shots here."

"Well, that's a fact," he said. "That's a fact for damn sure."

"How long you been over here?"

"I was in on it almost from the beginning," the soldier said in his hoarse voice. "November 1935, I think it was. Long Goddamn time. I guess I seen it all. I was at Tortosa the day the bastards wiped out the Lincoln Brigade. Only a dozen of us got out. Six of us drowned trying to swim the Ebro rather than surrender. Christ, what a day that was. The tanks just chewed us to bits. That's when I knew it was all over. This ragtag army can't hold out much longer. Thing is, we don't know how to stop. I guess we'll just keep fightin' until we're all dead."

"Why don't you just quit? Walk away from it?"

"Where'm I gonna go?" the soldier answered, staring at Rudman with haunted eyes. "Can't go home. The U.S. says we broke the law coming over here to fight. Some kind of neutrality act or something." He stared out at the harbor. A British ship languished in the cluttered port. "Don't want to rot in some Spanish dungeon. May as well keep killing the bastards until they get me." He looked back at Rudman. "Where you from?"

"Ohio."

"That a fact. Never knew anybody before from Ohio. Been home recently?"

Rudman stared out at the British ship for a long time before he answered. "I haven't been to the States since 1933."

"Jesus! Why?"

"Work. Pretty sorry excuse, actually."

"How long you been in Spain?"

"Off and on since the beginning. Occasionally I go back up to Germany and do something."

"You're here for the finish, ain't that it?"

"I hope the hell not."

"But you know it's true. Italian tanks, German dive bombers . . . you look back on it, we never had a chance." He stopped and changed the subject.

"Don't you miss it? The States, I mean?"

"Sure."

"Don't you miss your friends?"

"I only have one friend in America," Rudman said. "Hell, I don't even know where he is. Been . . . almost four years since we talked."

"Don't ever write, huh?"

"Nah. He's not much for writing."

"So when are you going back?"

"When the wars are over."

"Wars?"

"You don't think it's going to stop here, do you? Hell, this is just the warmup. This is the prelims, soldier."

"You got a pretty dismal outlook."

"Yeah, I suppose so." Rudman laughed. "My job's dismal."

"Ain't that the truth . . ." The soldier stopped suddenly and looked up, his eyes narrowing, head cocked to one side.

"Hear something?" Rudman asked, shielding his eyes with his hand and scanning the sky.

"Thought I did. Sure has been quiet all . . ."

He stopped. Then Rudman heard it. The distinctive rumble of the bombers, their engines roaring in unison.

"Christ, what's left to bomb?" the soldier asked bitterly.

"Maybe they'll pass over. Maybe they're headed someplace else."

"Not a chance. Better get to the shelter, what's left of it."

They stood up and started to walk through the broken bricks and rubble of buildings, picking their way around boards with rusty nails sticking out of them, toward the shelter two blocks away. The roar of the planes became deafening. They looked up and saw half a dozen German Junkers peeling out of formation, engines screaming as they dove toward the ground.

"Jesus, it's the fuckin' Junkers! Let's go!" the soldier yelled and they started to run. The engines screeched as the dive bombers dove toward the earth, then howled almost painfully as they pulled out. Then came the most chilling sound of all, a sound both of them knew well, a piercing scream that got higher as the missiles got closer to the ground. The earth shook as the bombs began to hit, stitching a great trench through the city's debris. The screams got louder. They ran harder. Rudman could see the entrance to the shelter but they were pulling the door shut.

"Wait a minute!" he yelled, "Wait for . . ."

But his plea was lost by the screaming bombs. The screams got higher and higher and louder and louder. . . .

"La-d-e-e-e-s and gent-ul-men, your attention pu-lease. This is the main event of the evening. Fifteen rounds of boxing for the heavyweight cham-peen-ship of the world. In this corner, wearing black trunks and weighing two hundred twenty-one pounds, the U-lan of the Rhine, from Berlin, Germany, the challenger, M-a-a-x Schmeling!"

There was a chorus of boos and catcalls from all over Yankee Stadium as the brutish, glowering, unshaven fighter stood up. He sneered at the insults from the audience.

"He looks like a Nazi," Beerbohm said.

"He's got a head like a rock," Keegan answered. "But Joe's got the hammer to crack it."

He looked around. There were almost a hundred thousand people in the special stands built especially for this grudge fight between the pride of the Aryan race and the Negro from Detroit. It was the largest crowd ever to see a prizefight.

The mob had long since peeled off jackets and ties. Everyone was sweating in their shirtsleeves but nobody cared. This
was a fight to sweat for.

"And in this corner, at two hundred twelve pounds, wearing
white trunks, the Brown Bomber from Dee-troit, Michigan,
heavyweight champeen of the world . . . Joe Louis!"

The crowd went berserk and Beerbohm and Keegan were
with them. Everyone was on their feet as the lean American
strode loosely to the center of the ring, one arm raised. They
were still screaming as the tuxedoed referee called the fighters
to the middle and gave them their instructions.

There was electricity in the air. Two years earlier at the
Olympics in Germany, Hitler had insulted America's running
pride, Jesse Owens, by refusing to attend Owens's gold medal
ceremony because he was an "American *Nee-*gro." That same
summer, Schmeling and Louis had met for the first time. In the
twelfth round, Schmeling had connected with a crushing right
and Louis had taken the count, the only time he'd ever been
knocked out.

Now, two years later, it was get-even time and the crowd
knew it. Grudge fight? Hell, thought Keegan, this is the grudge
fight of all times. This is bigger than David and Goliath.

Louis looked great. Louis looked ready. Louis had death in
his eyes.

"It won't go five rounds," Keegan said.

"I don't know, kid. Schmeling's no pork chop."

"You want to talk or bet?" Keegan said from their second-
row seats, squinting up at the two fighters.

"Name your poison."

"I got twenty says Schmeling'll answer the bell at the sixth."

"Let's see it," Keegan said, peeling off a twenty. Beerbohm
took out two tens. Keegan snatched them out of his hand,
wrapped them in his twenty and tucked them in his shirt pocket.

"How come you hold the money?" Beerbohm asked with
mock suspicion.

"Because I'm rich, Ned. I'm not going to abscond with a
measly forty bucks. On the other hand you are, how can I put
it . . . ?"

"Poor," Beerbohm said.

"Yeah," said Keegan with a nod. "Poor's good. That covers

it." They both laughed. Keegan was feeling good tonight for a change. . . .

A year after Keegan returned, his Uncle Harry had died suddenly of a heart attack, willing him the Killarney Rose. Dispirited, Keegan spent almost a year focusing his energies on renovating the top floor of the building, turning it into his private luxury apartment. Jenny Gould remained paramount in his mind. It was an open wound that would not heal. It was with him when he awoke in the morning and it stayed with him until sleep temporarily eased the ache. Although he knew his anguish was partly caused by uncertainty—was she alive or dead?—he could not push it from the forefront of his mind. Nor did time ease the hurt. He gradually retreated into himself, avoiding old friends, ignoring phone calls. He went to Hong Kong on business, spent months at a time alone on his horse farm in Kentucky and spent the rest of the time in the back booth of the pub, which he used as a kind of ex-officio office.

Beerbohm came into the Killarney Rose every day, Tuesday through Saturday, at almost the same time—4:10. He sat on the same stool near the back of the bar and drank two boilermakers—Seagram's Seven and Schlitz on tap—always left at 5:40 to catch the 5:50 E train to Jamaica, where he lived alone in a two-bedroom duplex. There was no reason for him to rush home except that Beerbohm was, first of all, a man of habit— catching the 5:50 was part of his daily ritual; and second, he was a potential alcoholic. Two boilermakers was his limit. It put him right on the edge. After downing his two drinks a mere whiff of blended whiskey would have made him a slobbering, falling-down drunk.

Keegan had known Ned Beerbohm for twenty years, since Keegan was fifteen and had first worked the bar at the Killarney and Beerbohm was a young reporter. Beerbohm had gone the usual route—reporter, columnist, drunk. He had taken the cure and started over on the copy desk, working his way back up the ladder to news editor. But he still had the haunted eyes and spare frame of the alcoholic. Beerbohm was one of the few people Keegan did not share his tragic story with. Why bother— Beerbohm was a walking encyclopedia of current events. He had heard it all.

He was usually in a rumpled blue or gray suit, red tie hanging down from an open collar, twisted and destroyed, the late edition curled up and jammed in his suit coat pocket, gray homburg perched on the back of his head. Beerbohm was always the first one in, followed shortly by reporters and editors from the *Mirror, News, Trib* and *Journal-American.* The Killarney Rose through the years had maintained its position as one of the favorite watering holes of the city's news community.

The dialogue rarely varied:

"Phew," Beerbohm would say, dropping like a sack of rocks on the bar stool. "This has been one hell of a day," to which Keegan would reply, "You say that every day."

Then Tiny the bartender would bring Beerbohm his glass of draft and shot of Seagram's Seven and Ned would throw the paper to Keegan in the back booth and wait to be invited over.

"Depressing," Beerbohm would say. "Every story is apocalyptic."

"The world is apocalyptic, Ned," Keegan would answer without looking up.

Beerbohm would shake his head, hold the shot glass over the mug of beer and carefully drop it in, watching it sink straight to the bottom of the glass and settle there where the thick, oily liquor would seep up into the brew like an amber trail of smoke. He would tilt the glass toward the ceiling, suck in the whiskey and let the beer chase the bitter taste. Then he would pull his lips back, sigh and hold the empty glass up toward Tiny, the 250-pound ex-wrestler who tended the rear section of the Killarney bar.

Ritual. Five days a week. As certain as the sunrise.

It was that kind of relationship, spiced occasionally by a trip to the ball game or to a special event like the fight. . . .

The gladiators returned to their corners. Nobody sat down. The roar increased. The air crackled with tension.

Louis was hunched over, his eyes cool, staring across the ring at Schmeling, taking his size. The German avoided the stare, talked to his handler, glanced around at the gigantic saucer of people.

The bell.

They came toward each other, Schmeling with his shuffling

gait, moving one foot, then bringing the other up beside it; Louis lighter on his feet, more fluid, his body as hard as a boulder. Louis's eyes were cobra's eyes, watching his victim, waiting for the proper moment. There was a bit of sparring, then suddenly Schmeling loosed his right, the same right that had put Louis away two years before.

It hit hard, a thud against the side of the Bomber's jaw. Louis shook his head and forgot it. It was as if Schmeling had blown him a kiss. He moved past the punch like it never happened and for an instant fear widened Schmeling's eyes. Then the onslaught began.

Louis lashed out with blurred rights and lefts. They sizzled through the hot air under the heavy lights and battered the German into the ropes. Then Louis unleashed a left hook. Schmeling never saw it. It drove him up in the air and against the ropes where he dangled like a drunk, one arm dangling over the top strand, dazed, confused, surprised.

Fear was etched into every muscle of his face. Louis was all over him, smashing lefts and rights into the stricken German. Finally the referee pushed him back. Schmeling was shaking on his feet. He took a one-count and plodded forth for more.

"He's going to take him out in the first," Keegan said. "Say goodbye twenty."

With each wracking thud of Louis's fists, Keegan felt a moment of delirious pleasure, as though he himself were landing the punch. Every splash of blood from Schmeling's battered face gave him another moment of joy. He stood in the screaming, sweating crowd, fists clenched, eyes afire, yelling: "Kill him! Kill him! Kill the Nazi bastard," with such unbridled fervor that even Beerbohm was surprised.

Schmeling looked pleadingly toward his corner, turned and caught a vicious right cross to the jaw. Above the din of the crowd, Keegan heard the bone-crunching sound as it connected. It literally hammered Schmeling to the canvas.

He was hurt. His eyes were roving crazily, trying to focus. He was back up on three, struggling up through air as heavy as oil, almost in slow motion. Arms half up, wide open, wounded and defenseless, he stared terrified as the next right smashed his already swollen jaw. He went down again, his gloves brushing the canvas, legs bent, head lolling. And again he rose, staggering, his senses battered to oblivion, his knees rubber. The Bomber stepped in tight and whacked him again.

"Jesus!" Beerbohm cried.

"Go ahead," Keegan yelled. "Hit him again! Knock the bastard back to Germany where he belongs!"

Briefly, watching this Aryan apostle being demolished and humiliated, Keegan felt a moment of relief from four years of pain and anger, a moment when his hate seemed sated, a moment when he almost forgot Jenny Gould and Dachau. He had used his political connections. He'd sent hundreds of thousands to Germany in bribes. But he had learned nothing, accomplished nothing. He had failed at the only thing he'd ever truly needed to succeed at. So this, watching the fury of the Negro fighter, was an instant of retribution.

Louis struck again, a coiled spring of destruction that battered Schmeling's sagging jaw and demolished his hope. The Aryan apostle fell face-down on the gritty canvas.

Keegan could see the delight in Louis's eyes as he danced to a neutral corner. From the corner of his eye, Keegan saw the white towel float from Schmeling's corner and fall at the referee's feet. He snatched it up and threw it over his shoulder. It dangled from the ropes as he began his count:

"One . . . two . . . three . . . four . . . five . . ."

The crowd was manic. Schmeling's handlers were awestruck.

The referee looked down at the stricken Nazi and stopped counting. He spread his hands sharply apart, palms down.

"Yer out!"

The first round. Pandemonium.

And so on this June night in 1938, Joe Louis had finally gotten even.

As for Keegan, his heart soared as they dragged Schmeling's battered body back to his corner. It was a bittersweet moment, a small taste of revenge. But it was not enough.

Not enough to make up for four years. Four years without a letter or a word from Dachau. Was she alive or dead? Keegan did not know.

How could it be enough?

It could never be enough.

The crowd in the Killarney Rose was rowdy with victory, yelling, cheering, jitterbugging in the aisles to a Count Basie record in the jukebox they could hardly hear. It was like New Year's Eve. Somebody stood up on the bar and started counting:

"One . . . two . . . three . . . four . . . five . . ."

"Yer out!" the gang yelled. Then somebody else struck up a chorus of "Yankee Doodle" and everybody joined in.

Beerbohm and Keegan sat sideways in the back booth, singing, laughing, reveling in this instant of national retaliation.

"What a sweet moment," said Keegan. "You know, for a little while there I felt . . . I felt . . ."

He paused, trying to find the right word.

"Like you got even?" Beerbohm offered.

"Is that all it's about, Ned? Getting even?"

"Look at it this way," Beerbohm said. "Hate is very fashionable these days. The Germans hate the Jews, the Italians hate the Africans, the Japs hate the Chinese, the Fascists hate the Commies and the Spanish hate each other. What I mean is, I'm not knocking it. Getting even helps. When you get rid of all the superfluous stuff, then you can zero in on what's really hurting you. Someday you'll be able to deal with that, too."

"I guess I never thought about it in those terms before."

"Look at it this way. Father Coughlin is finished. Huey Long's dead. The Bund is about to be outlawed. Louis has just destroyed Schmeling. Take heart, pal, that's a lot of little 'get evens.' "

"Not enough."

"You want the big kill, right. Fantasy time—Hitler in your sights."

"How come you got so wise?"

"I got old," Beerbohm said and smiled.

Keegan smiled too and said, "Well, it's been one helluva night, let's not spoil it."

A young man in knickers and a cap sheepishly entered the bar, stared wide-eyed at the party, edged his way to the corner of the bar. He cupped his hands and yelled to Tiny who nodded and pointed to the booth. Completely intimidated, the lad scurried down through the crowd staring straight ahead.

"M-m-mister Beerbohm," he stammered.

Ned looked up and smiled.

"Hi, Shorty, what're you doing in here?"

"Mr. MacGregor on the night desk asked me to run this over to you." He handed Beerbohm an envelope.

"Thanks, kid. Shorty, this is Mr. Keegan. He owns the joint. Shorty here's one of our primo copy boys." He tore open the envelope, took out a sheet of paper.

"How long have you been with the paper?" Keegan asked.

"Almost a year, sir."

"Tell you what, go over there and tell Tiny, the big bartender, to give you a hamburger and a soda, on the house."

"Gee, thanks!"

"Sure."

The boy rushed off and Keegan turned back to Beerbohm. The editor's face was suddenly drawn and bloodless.

"What the hell happened to you, Ned?" Keegan said. "You look like World War Two just started."

"Almost as bad," Beerbohm said and slid a cablegram across the table. Keegan knew before he read it. He knew what it was going to say. He had feared this telegram for four years.

"I'm sorry as hell to be the one to show you that," Beerbohm said.

The cable was simple and to the point:

BERT RUDMAN KILLED NOON TODAY DURING BOMBING RAID ON ALICANTE. RUDMAN WITH THE FIFTH VICTORY DIVISION. AT-TACKED BY GERMAN DIVE BOMBERS. KILLED INSTANTLY. MORE FOLLOWS. PLEASE ADVISE RE REMAINS. MANNERLY, MADRID BUREAU CHIEF.

Keegan stared at it for several minutes, reading and rereading it, hoping perhaps he was missing something in the sparse message. His throat began to ache and the old anger welled up in him again.

"Goddamn them," he said in a cracked voice. "God*damn* those miserable bastards." He slammed his fist on the table.

"I'm awful damn sorry, kid," said Beerbohm. "I know how close you two were."

Keegan was silent for a minute or two and then he shook his head. "No you don't," he said, and there was misery in every syllable. "We haven't been close at all since I left Europe."

"I just thought . . ." Beerbohm said with surprise.

"That he was my best friend? He was. He was one of those people who make life a little sweeter for you, who care about you."

He stopped and took a deep breath, trying to control the hurt. He began to babble, about Rudman and Jenny and that summer in Paris. About von Meister and Conrad Weil and the dirty little hunchback, Vierhaus. About friendship and betrayal and the dumb things we sometimes do and never undo.

"I'm not sure I ever told him how really good I thought he was. Used to kid him all the time . . . fact is, he had more guts than anybody I ever knew. Just kept . . . going back for more. It had to happen sooner or later. Ironic, isn't it? He probably wrote more about what's really going on in Germany than anyone alive and a goddamn German plane kills him in Spain."

He paused for a moment and took several deep breaths.

"Can I keep this?" Keegan asked, holding up the cable.

Beerbohm nodded.

"I don't feel very sociable right now," Keegan said.

Keegan sat for a long time staring off toward the front of the bar. His chest hurt and his throat hurt. Faced with the sudden death of his friend, he wished desperately for just five minutes to tell Bert how much his friendship had really meant to him. How much he had missed him these last few years. How much he admired his talent and courage and insight. How much he had learned about love and devotion from him and from Jenny.

Too late. Too late for anything. He folded the cable several times and stuck it in his pocket. "I'm sorry, pal," he said to nobody. "I'm so sorry."

Finally he got up, walked across to Fifth Avenue and up past St. Patrick's. Then he crossed over to Third Avenue and wandered back down, thinking about his two best friends. Beerbohm was right, he wanted to hurt somebody, to get even. But who was there to hurt? He picked up the *News* at a corner stand. Bob Considine's story was on the front page.

"Listen to this, buddy," it began, "for it comes from a guy whose palms are still wet, whose throat is dry and whose jaw is still agape from the utter shock of watching Joe Louis knock out Max Schmeling . . ."

Christ, he thought, *what am I doing reading about a prizefight?* He threw the paper in a trash can and went back to the Rose, seeking the security of his back booth. But the joy of the crowd was more than he could handle and he went up to his apartment. He got a bottle of champagne from the walk-in refrigerator, took three tulip glasses from the cabinet, went into the living room and took a scrapbook from the bookcase. He sat down on the sofa, popped the cork and poured three glasses. Keegan clinked his glass against theirs.

"Salud," he said.

He had started the scrapbook when Rudman went to Ethiopia, carefully pasting each dispatch in its pages. He had planned to give it to Bert as a peace offering when he finally returned from the wars. He started turning the pages, stopping occasionally to reread a particularly poignant or significant story.

Mussolini Invades Ethiopia; Bombers Attack Civilians

by
Bert Rudman

ADOWA, ETHIOPIA, Oct. 3, 1935. The barefoot tribes of Haile Selassie, Lion of Judah, Emperor of Ethiopia, direct descendant of the kings of the Ras Tafari, and Prince of the ancient tribes of the Nile, were attacked today by the tanks, bombers and booted legions of Benito Mussolini, the barber turned Dictator of Italy.

In what may very well be an Apocalyptic vision of modern warfare, bombs and incendiaries shrieked down from the night sky on helpless civilians. In the chaos that followed, great fires swept the city and the confused and wounded raced through the blazing city like mice in a maze . . .

And less than six months later . . .

Ethiopia Falls in Italy's
Slaughter of the Innocents

by
Bert Rudman

ADDIS ABABA, ETHIOPIA, Feb. 28, 1936. The Lion of Judah has been caged and tamed by the Roman Legions of Dictator Mussolini. But in winning this victory, Italy has fouled its own house . . .

By the summer of 1936, the civil war in Spain had become a reality and Rudman was in the thick of it, where he would stay almost continuously until he died.

Death Rains on Spain's Capital
As Fascists Declare War

by
Bert Rudman

MADRID, SPAIN, July 22, 1936. Spain finally erupted into Civil War last night as the Fascist Rebels of General Francisco Franco attacked this stronghold of the Loyalist . . .

Innocents Die by Thousands in Brutal Fascist Reprisal Raid

by
Bert Rudman

GUERNICA, SPAIN, Apr. 27, 1937. German dive bombers and fighter planes without warning swept out of the skies over this Basque city today, strafing and bombing schools, hospitals, farmhouses and the marketplace and killing thousands of innocent people . . .

His work was a devastating mosaic of a world gone mad. It was as if a great cloak of darkness had been draped over Europe and down into Africa. And as the darkness spread, Dachau was lost in its core, a mere spot in the center of the growing fascist empire.

Triumphant Hitler Marches into Austria as Crowds Cheer

by
Bert Rudman

VIENNA, AUSTRIA, Mar. 14, 1938. Adolf Hitler, who left this Austrian city as a penniless youth, returned in triumph today and claimed this nation as his own.

To cries of *"Heil, Hitler"* and *"Sieg Heil,"* the dictator drove through the streets of this city as crowds cheered and threw flowers in his path . . .

And even more ominously . . .

Germany Readies Several
New Concentration Camps

by
Bert Rudman

BERLIN, AUG. 7, 1938. The Nazis have opened three new concentration camps in Germany and have several others under construction, according to confidential sources . . .

Keegan was struck by the fact that his estranged friend was the harbinger of his own personal despair. With each story, Jenny's plight seemed more desperate. Was she still alive? Had she been tortured, brutalized, in that infamous Nazi cesspool?

There was one story, late in the book, that particularly touched Keegan. Laced with sadness, it had a foreboding sense of doom between every line. It was written as if Rudman had seen the future and knew his string was running out.

A Quiet New Year's Dinner
in Barcelona

by
Bert Rudman

BARCELONA, SPAIN, Jan. 1, 1938. A few of us American correspondents got together tonight for a traditional New Year's Eve party at our favorite bistro.

It is now only a bombed-out hole on the ground littered with the rubble of war. Around us in this beleaguered city, the smell of death hangs heavy in the air.

But we brought a lantern, some cheese and a bottle of wine and sat on broken chairs and at midnight we sang "Auld Lang Syne." We wept for fallen friends on both sides of this bitter struggle and talked about home and family and friends we have not seen for a very long time.

As we sat there, escaping for the moment from this dreadful war I could not escape the realization that if Franco and his hordes succeed in winning this civil war, France will be trapped between Germany and a new Fascist stronghold. Thus Spain may have the nefarious distinction of being the final dress rehearsal for World War II. . . .

Francis Keegan stared at the book, no longer reading, his mind tumbling through time, when the doorbell rang. He tried to ignore it, hoping whoever it was would go away. But the bell was persistent and finally he got up and answered it.

Vanessa Bromley was standing in the doorway.

"Hi, Frankie Kee," she said softly, accompanied by a devastating smile.

He was so surprised at the sight of her, he faltered before he spoke. His mind suddenly leaped back to the Berlin train station, almost five years ago.

Vannie throwing him her beret. Walking back to the hotel alone in the rain, thinking not about her but about Jenny. Sending the flowers without any card.

She looked great, a black Chanel hat cocked over one eye, long legs sheathed in black silk, her magnificent figure flattering a gray silk suit, a black velvet choker with a single diamond in the center. She was dressed to kill and he knew he was the quarry.

Bad timing, he thought, until she said just the right thing.

"I'm truly sorry, Kee," she said. "I just heard about Bert."

"How'd you know I was here?"

"Oh . . . I knew," she said, almost wistfully. "May I come in?"

"Of course, what's the matter with me?" he said and stepped back, swinging the door wide for her.

The living room was the size of a loft with a massive picture window overlooking a balcony and beyond it, the East River. The French doors on either side of it were open and a cool breeze billowed through the drapes. The furniture, lamps, tables, were all rounded at the corners and had a soft, inviting quality, the latest in art deco. The room was painted in light shades of pastel—grays, yellows, blues. There were three Impressionist paintings in the room, one by the recent Spanish discovery, Picasso. An open brick fireplace dominated one side of the room and facing it were floor-to-ceiling bookshelves, both of which offset the pale colors and gave the room a strong masculine quality. On a table in the corner was a picture of Jenny, Bert and Keegan at Longchamp. It was the only photograph in the room.

Vanessa saw the three glasses on the coffee table next to the open scrapbook.

"Oh," she stammered, suddenly embarrassed. "I didn't know you had company. What a brazen thing for me . . ."

"I don't have company," he said flatly.

She looked down at the glasses again and he wondered how it must look, a man sitting alone in an apartment with three glasses of champagne. How the hell does one explain that? he wondered.

"I was . . . I was drinking a good-bye toast to Bert. Why don't you join me?"

"I'm sorry, this was presumptuous . . ."

"I'm glad you came," he interrupted. "C'mon, I'll get you a glass of champagne."

"Why don't you just drop a lemon peel in one of those," she said with a smile.

"Still remember that, huh?"

"I remember every second of those two days," she said very directly. "I also know about your friend and what happened to her. You've had more than your share of grief. But you can't stay alone forever, Kee."

He smiled as he poured her glass. "That carved in stone?"

"No," she said, her shoulders sagging a bit. She took the glass and followed him out on the balcony. The soft summer breeze stirred her collar. She leaned on the balcony, staring at a tugboat put-put-putting up the river. "It's probably carved in desperation."

"Desperation?"

She took off the hat and shook out her hair. She had let it grow down to her shoulders.

"I'm absolutely shameless where you're concerned," she said. "For four years I've gone to every first-night, every gallery opening, every party, your favorite restaurants, hoping to accidentally bump into you. But you don't go to openings or parties. And I guess you eat at home."

"I've turned into a helluva cook, Vannie," he said. "I'm just not ready for the social swim yet."

"After four years! You have friends here who care about you and miss you." She turned to him, leaning her back against the balcony rail. "At least one, anyway."

She was still as splendid as she had been in Berlin but the bright-eyed look of innocence was gone, replaced by the first signs of cynicism, the first cruel lines of maturity.

"I heard you got married."

"So you do still *talk* to the living."

"I was never really a part of your society, Vannie. Your father made that clear to me."

"What do you mean?"

"That I'd only be accepted if I played by their rules."

"Which you didn't choose to do."

"Hell, I'm not an aristocrat. My blood is definitely not blue. The last party I went to was . . . I guess three years ago, after the *Normandie*'s maiden voyage. Marilyn Martin filled me in on you."

"I know. I saw you for just a minute. Remember?"

He nodded slowly. "Sure I remember," he said. "You were the most stunning woman there . . ."

Sleek and proud, the Normandie *steamed loftily into New York Harbor while thousands lined the waterfront, cheering her to her berth. Hundreds of tiny boats clustered around her like puppies around a Great Dane. She had just broken the world speed record on her maiden voyage, easily stealing the honor from Germany's* Bremen, *so the crowd was particularly gleeful. Horns honked. Whistles shrieked. A storm of confetti fell on Wall Street as she passed lower Manhattan on her way up the Hudson. There had been a clatter of fireworks as she negotiated the wide turn into her berth at the foot of West 49th Street.*

Keegan arrived just as the party, which had started on the broad, gaily lit first-class deck, spilled into the main salon. Benny Goodman's Trio kicked off and charged into "I Got Rhythm." The uptown crowd, at least five hundred of them enjoying the hospitality of the French line, jammed against the stage, applauding Goodman's joyous playing, the thunderous beat of Gene Krupa's drums and Teddy Wilson's subtle counterpoint as his fingers barely brushed the keys. At the back of the dance floor, behind the crowd, the more adventurous guests jitterbugged frantically, spinning away from their partners and back, high-kicking, their feet a lively blur. Keegan got a drink and was sampling the hors d'oeuvres when a voice behind him said:

"Francis?"

He turned and stared down at a diminutive redhead. Her hair was auburn, cut short and close to the nape and covered with a sequined cloche. Her green eyes were saucer-round and ebullient. Energy radiated from her. Her white, sequined dress barely contained a spectacular figure, the small stones glittering in the light, twinkling as she walked and turning every step into a shimmy. A true sprite, Keegan thought. A dazzling imp.

"Marilyn," he said. "It's good to see you."

"You remembered!" she cried, obviously pleased. He was surprised himself. He had not seen her for years. Her brother was one of his gang at college and the last time he saw her was just before graduation—before the caterpillar had turned into a butterfly.

"Have you seen Vannie since you got back?" she asked abruptly. The question caught him totally off balance. Before he could answer, she said, "Oh, that was catty of me. I know you haven't seen her, she's my best friend."

"Vanessa Bromley?"

She nodded.

"How about that," he said for lack of anything better.

They started strolling toward the front of the big room to get a better look at the Goodman Trio.

"Is she here?" he asked.

"She will be. She's at the th-e-ah-tah." She closed her eyes and elongated the word with mock sophistication, then she stared up at him and quickly added, "But she'd walk out in a second if she knew you were here."

"Stop that," he said irritably.

The tall, bespectacled bandleader was like the calm in the center of a hurricane. Only his fingers seemed excited, fleeing across his clarinet as though the keys were on fire while the baby-faced Krupa was his antithesis, an entranced whirlwind, turning every drumbeat into a pistol shot.

"Please don't leave until she gets here," Marilyn blurted out. "She's very unhappy."

"Marilyn . . ."

"Anyway, this is fun. I haven't seen you for . . . ten years? Ten years! My dad loved you. Said you were the only crazy one in the whole gang."

"He never met Freddie Armistead?"

"Freddie wasn't crazy, he was hopelessly insane."

Keegan smiled at the memory, despite himself. "Remember when he dug that hole in the Quad and put the horse in it? Took them all day to dig it out. They never did figure out who did it."

"Wonder what ever happened to old Armistead?" she said. "He vanished into thin air after graduation. And remember Lyle Thornton?"

"Old Turkey Thornton?"

"Oh God, how he hated that nickname. Were you responsible for that?"

"Nah," Keegan said unconvincingly. "But he did look like a turkey."

She hunched up her shoulders and giggled. "Looked exactly like a turkey," she said. She squinched up her nose. "That little scrawny neck."

"How about that beak of his?"

"That's cruel, Francis."

"C'mon, he had a nose the size of a baseball bat."

"Did you hear about his father? Got cleaned out in the crash, went out to Chicago and jumped out a window of the Edgewater Beach Hotel. Old Turkey floundered around for a couple of years, then he married rich and his father-in-law bought him a seat on the stock exchange for a wedding present, probably so he wouldn't have to support him."

"Lyle Llewellyn Thornton, the Third," Keegan reflected. "You have to be rich with a name like that. Who'd he get to marry him?"

"Vannie," Marilyn answered bluntly.

"Vannie!" he said. "Vannie married Turkey Thornton!?"

"Doesn't make a bit of sense, does it?" Marilyn said. "One of the true mysteries of the twentieth century."

"Maybe he has some hidden talent we don't know about," Keegan suggested.

"I really don't think so," Marilyn answered. "He got involved in the theater. Turkey got a couple of uptowners involved with a Broadway show. Lo and behold it turned out to be The Gay Divorce. *Now everybody thinks he can smell a hit a mile off. He's been dabbling in it ever since. They have a townhouse on East 83rd, half a block off the Park, and a summer house on Cape Cod." She stopped for a moment and flicked a speck of confetti off her shoulder. "She's absolutely miserable."*

"Miserable?"

"Thornton turned into an absolute ogre. He knocks her around, stays out for days at a time. Once the little SOB got his hands on the

money . . ." She let the sentence die, then added, "She talks about you all the time, has ever since that summer in Germany."

"It was two days, Marilyn . . ."

"And she never forgot it," she said, finishing the sentence.

"What are you, the Upper East Side matchmaker?"

"No. I just hate to see my friends unhappy. I have no complaints, I'm very lucky. Happily married, have two girls who'll knock your eyes out, a big house in Westport, and a husband who dotes on me." She stared up at him with the big green saucers. "Whyn't you just stay long enough to say hello to her," she pleaded.

"We'll see," he said and quickly changed the subject. "Where's your husband? Do I know him?"

"I don't think so. He's from Pittsburgh. A surgeon. He's got an emergency operation at Governor's Hospital. I'm hoping he'll get here before the party's over."

"From the look of things, this brawl will still be going on next Tuesday."

"Look, we're all going to the French Casino on 50th and catch the midnight show of the **Folies-Bergère**,*" she said. "Why don't you come with us? It's supposed to be very risqué."*

"Not when you've seen the real thing."

"That's very snobbish."

"I didn't mean it to be," he said casually. "I just meant the French version is a lot bawdier."

"Well, come with us anyhow."

"Marilyn . . ."

"Or how about Sunday brunch? We're all going out to the Merry Go Round. It's on the Island, Atlantic Beach. Has a revolving bar, hobby horses, these fluffy, crazy-looking jungle animals. It's right on the ocean with an outside dance floor . . ." She did a little shimmy.

"Marilyn . . ."

"Or how about coming up to the Westport theater to see Ruth Gordon in **The Country Wife**? *She's supposed to be quite the screwball in it, you know. We're planning . . ."*

"Marilyn!"

She stopped suddenly. "Yes?" she said innocently.

"The lady's married."

"She's dying inside, Francis," she answered seriously.

"I can't do . . ." he started to say and caught himself. **I can't do**

anything about it. It's not my problem. *Familiar phrases from the past. Embarrassing phrases he had sworn never to use again.*

"It's obviously a bad time for both of us," is all he said.

"Will you think about it?"

The ultimate out—think about it. One could take forever thinking about it.

"Sure. I'll think about it."

"Good. C'mon, dance with me."

"I don't know how to do that newfangled stuff."

"It's called jitterbugging and it's easy." She led him out on the enormous dance floor, shimmering in her spangled dress.

Later he had stood near the bridge of the big ship, looking down at the party. He saw Vanessa come aboard, watched her move majestically through the crowd. She was in a short, black cocktail dress, startling in its simplicity, with a clutch of diamonds at her throat. He realized as he watched her how much time had changed her—from a lively sprite to royalty. She moved with sublime grace, an exquisite creature who exuded stately nonchalance as if she were in some superior caste created for her alone. Confident, imperious, sublime, there was also about her a hint of wanton naïveté. Easily the most interesting and imposing person at the party, Keegan thought. And probably the most dangerous. What a pair she and Marilyn must make. He didn't even notice old Turkey Thornton.

Then suddenly she turned as if by some primal instinct and looked straight up at him. They stared at each other for a full minute while the crowd seemed to part and move around her. Her expression changed very subtly, became more intense, then someone rushed up to her and there were giddy greetings and hugs and squeals of delight. He left the party.

I'll think about it, he had said. That was three years ago.

". . . anyway, Marilyn talks too much," Vanessa was saying.

"She talked like a best friend talks. She was concerned about you."

"I know, I didn't mean that. Fact is, she talked me into coming over here. I didn't have the courage to do it on my own."

"Courage?" he asked quizzically.

She turned her face away from him. Her voice was almost a whisper. "Oh, God, Kee, don't you know why I really came?"

She still did not face him.

"I came because I threw my husband out a year ago. I came because I'm twenty-four years old and I'm lonely and because I've been thinking about you for five years and I've wanted to sleep with you for all five of them. I've never stopped wanting to sleep with you. And if that makes me a hussy or . . ."

"Hey, hold on," Keegan said softly. Then he chuckled. "What the hell, you always did get right to the point."

"Just hold me, will you, Frankie Kee?" she said. "Or let me hold you."

"Hell, I'm no good to you," he said, and it had the tone of a warning.

She shook her head and turned her back to him, looking out toward the river.

"I don't know why I said that anyway," she said. "What I really want is someone to hold me while I fall asleep, share my tears with me, hurt when I hurt, laugh when I laugh. I want someone to believe in me, not laugh at my fantasies." She looked back over her shoulder at him. "Is that so very much to ask of somebody, Kee?"

"No, it's a modest request."

"Don't you want that?"

"I did."

"And you lost all that?"

"I stopped caring."

"Why?"

"When I lost her . . . hell, I don't know . . . maybe it was never quite as good as I remember it."

He stopped and sorted through his darkest thoughts, questioning his memory, as he had done many times in the past, always with the same conclusion.

"No," he went on, "that's not true. It was, it was a very fine time in my life. It just didn't last very long. Maybe we all have just so much happiness doled out to us and we used ours up and now we're paying for it, except the price she's paying is . . . much . . . too high."

"I don't believe that. I don't believe God's that cruel. I haven't given up yet."

"You mean with old Turkey?"

"The hell with old Turkey," she snapped. "I got over him a long time ago."

"Where's he now?"

"He has a place in the Dakota, that big gloomy building on the West Side."

"I know the place."

"I guess that's where he entertains his show girls," she said bitterly. "I hear he likes two or three at a time."

"Are you divorced yet?"

"Twenty-four more days. I mark each one off on my calendar." She stopped to catch her breath. Tears crept into the corners of her eyes and she tried to blink them away. "I tried so hard, Kee. I tried to be a good wife and make him happy. It was never enough. Lyle never gets enough of anything. His appetite for *every*thing is insatiable. Thank God we don't have children."

"That little freak," Keegan said harshly. "He never had anything going for him. He was a cheat in school—and a liar. He used to lie all the time."

"Oh, he's very good at that."

Keegan tried to soften the dark tone of the conversation. "Hell, he wasn't any good at it at all, he just lied so much people got tired of calling him down."

And she laughed and nodded. "Yes! You're right! That's exactly what people do."

"What was it about old Turkey . . . ?"

"Oh God, I don't even know anymore. Sometimes I wake up in the middle of the night and wonder the same thing. And then I think . . . maybe it's me, maybe I didn't *deserve* any better . . ."

"Stop that."

"No, I do . . ."

"*Stop* it! Don't lay off all the misery on yourself. There are lots of Thorntons in the world . . . they use up everything they can get their hands on and never give anything back."

She stared at him with moist eyes. "There's another thing about it. Sometimes I think . . . we had three years together and I think, there ought to be *some* happy memories. I ought to feel *some*thing for him. But I don't."

"I have a partner named Nayles out on the West Coast. When we were in the war together, he used to say, 'Pal, we come in buckass naked and we go out buckass naked and everything in between is gravy.' Maybe that's the right attitude. Maybe we ought to make the best of whatever comes to us."

"You're not doing that."

She looked up at him and her stare seemed to come from a very private place deep within her; a warm, longing, loving look that pierced Keegan's armor like a lance.

"Oh, Kee, what's happening to the world? What's happening to all of us?"

His anger was like a coiled snake he had kept trapped inside him and suddenly it burst free. It was not a shrill outburst but his fists were clenched and he spoke in a voice that was low and full of rage.

"What's happening is that we're living in a world full of people who want us to think the way they do and act the way they do and believe the way they do and if we don't, if we don't conform, they destroy us. And you know the irony? They're always in the minority. We ignore them until we wake up one morning and there isn't any *Times* on the newsstand and our favorite books are gone from the library and they beat up our best friends and drag them off to prison because their hair's the wrong color or their noses don't measure down to their standards. Then it's too late."

"You really think that could happen here?"

He nodded emphatically. "There was a moment, Vannie, when I literally had to run for my life. I mean I literally had to *run* for it. I don't know which was worse, the fear or the humiliation, but I think I have a better idea of what freedom is all about now."

"Is that what happened to her in Germany?"

"That's what happened to *Germany*. She got caught in the sweeper. So you don't need to shed any tears for me, save them for her. She's locked away for life in a cesspool run by psychopaths."

"Oh my God . . ."

She reached up and ran her fingertips lightly down his cheek. Then she wrapped her arms around his waist and held him very tightly and after several moments he reached out, too, and put his arms around her and they stood on the balcony for a long time clutching each other, like two drowning people, each trying desperately to save the other.

They fell into a warm friendship that was shakily platonic. But she did not impose on that part of him. She was happy to be around him, coming to his place, fixing dinner, occasionally dropping by and listening to him and Ned discussing the news of the day. When they went out for dinner they went to offbeat places, usually late at night to avoid old friends. Only Marilyn shared their secret, sometimes spending the evening with them when her husband was tied up at the hospital. Keegan juggled his emotions between past and present. Until suddenly a voice from the past changed everything.

New Year's Eve, 1939, three A.M.

Keegan was returning from Vanessa's apartment. He was fumbling for his keys when a voice, thickly European, whispered from the shadows beside the entrance.

"Mr. Keegan?"

Keegan stopped, squinted suspiciously into the darkness. The man moved partly into the light. In silhouette he was an inch or so shorter than Keegan but ten pounds heavier, all of it in his muscled shoulders, chest and arms, which strained the sleeves of his black cloth coat. The bottom of his face was obscured by a thick black beard and he was wearing a black seaman's cap, pulled low on his forehead.

"Depends on who's asking," Keegan said cautiously.

The man moved into the light.

It was Werner Gebhart. Avrum Wolffson's chief lieutenant in the Black Lily.

"Perhaps you remember me?" he whispered from the shadows. "We met in Berlin."

Keegan was astounded to see the young German. "My God, Gebhart, of course I remember you," he said, motioning him into the open. "Come in, come in."

Gebhart moved quickly. They shook hands as Keegan led him through the private entrance and down the hallway to his private elevator. Gebhart looked frightened, his eyes frantically checking the street as they entered the hallway.

"Is something wrong?" Keegan asked.

"Yes," Gebhart answered. "I am an illegal."

"Not here you're not," Keegan said with a reassuring smile.

"*Mazel tov,*" Gebhart said, and there was relief in his voice.

When the elevator doors closed, Gebhart relaxed. Keegan remembered him as being an innocent, slender man-boy, youthfully arrogant and suspicious. He had put on twenty hard pounds and his face was ridged by hard times. He had tortured eyes, half pleading, half angry, the kind that had seen too much suffering, had lost too many friends and had seen the kinds of things that rob the young of their innocence. His black beard was already streaked with gray. How old was he, Keegan wondered? Mid-twenties at best. Looking at the toll the Nazis and Black Lily had taken on Gebhart in four years, Keegan wondered what the years had done to Avrum Wolffson.

"Avrum?" Keegan asked.

"Alive."

"And well?"

Gebhart nodded. "He has become too hard. It shows."

"And what of your other friend . . . ?"

"Joachim Weber?" Gebhart answered. "Joachim was murdered by the Nazis.

Keegan's shoulders sagged. *My God,* he thought, *the madness never ends.* "I'm sorry, Werner," he said.

Gebhart simply nodded.

"When did you get here?" Keegan asked.

"About ten o'clock."

"You've been waiting here for five hours?"

"Yes."

"How long have you been in the country?"

"Since ten o'clock. I came on a steamer from Portugal."

"Good! You must stay here. It's perfectly safe and all my people have closed lips."

Gebhart held up his hand. "Please, *Ire,* that part of it is taken care of. I have a place. Someone who has worked with us for years. On Fifth Avenue. I understand there is a park across the street."

Keegan smiled. "Central Park. Pretty fancy digs up there, Werner."

"So I have heard."

"You haven't been there yet?"

Gebhart shook his head. "I came here first. It was Avrum's wish that I see you first."

"God, it's good to see you again," Keegan said finally. "I haven't heard from Avrum for all these years. I thought . . . hell, I thought everything."

"It is dangerous even to send out letters. But I have a present from him. And a message for you. He said to tell you it is the one you owe him."

Keegan laughed. "He has a helluva memory. The last thing I said to him, *That's one I owe you.* It was a joke."

"Avrum doesn't joke."

Keegan thought for a moment before he nodded. "I had forgotten."

He was avoiding the big question, almost afraid to ask. The elevator reached the penthouse and he led Gebhart into the kitchen. "I have a cook," he said, "but she won't be here until seven. I'm sure we can scrounge up something. How about a steak and some eggs?"

"Such a lot of trouble."

"Peel off the coat and grab a chair. It's no trouble at all. I can scramble a mean egg and burn a steak."

Keegan opened two bottles of German pilsner and put one in front of Gebhart. Gebhart reached into his duffel bag and took out a package. He laid it on the table and slid it in front of Keegan.

"From Avrum."

Keegan picked it up. It was flat, about the thickness, size and shape of a sheet of typewriter paper and bound with twine. He held it in both hands for a moment as if it were emitting some kind of psychic energy.

"All right, how about Jenny?" Keegan finally asked as he reached into a drawer, took out a pair of scissors and cut the string.

"It's . . . probably . . . in the letter," Gebhart answered haltingly.

Keegan stared at him but Gebhart averted his look, stared down at the beer bottle, took a long swig of beer.

"Werner?"

His visitor stared slowly back up into his eyes.

"Is she dead, Werner?"

The moment seemed to poise in the air before Gebhart finally said

"Yes"

and stared away again.

Keegan said nothing. In his heart, he had known she was gone. He felt no tears, no numbing pain of reality. He felt only outrage and the galvanic anger which had consumed him for almost five years. He looked down at the table, nodded very slowly. There was very little expression on his face. He remembered what Beerbohm had said once about getting even. But how? There was no way to *really* get even. Get even with whom? That was part of the frustration, there was no one to fight, no one to take on.

"I am sorry," Gebhart whispered.

Keegan sat down and held the unopened package tightly between his two hands, then he put it back down on the table.

"Excuse me a minute," he said in a voice that was just above a whisper. He walked over to the sink and, holding cupped hands under the tap, splashed his face with cold water. He sat back down at the table, his hands splayed out on either side of the package, staring at it.

"I'm sorry for you, too, Gebhart."

"Why, *Ire?*"

"Because you were in love with her too. It was obvious—the way you talked about her, the way you looked when you spoke her name, your concern. Your obvious dislike of me. You did love her, didn't you, Werner?"

The German did not answer for a full minute. The lines in his face seemed to grow harder. Then he shrugged and smiled for the first time.

"*Ire,* I fell in love with Jenny the first time I saw her," Gebhart said softly. "I was fourteen and she was seventeen. Her family moved to the house next door. Avrum and I became best friends but she always loved me as sister to brother, so that is what she was, my good friend. My good, good friend. But I do understand how you must feel, *Ire.* To hope for so long . . ."

"I gave up hope a long time ago," Keegan said. "But I kept hanging on to a fantasy."

He went to the stove, cracked two eggs on the griddle and threw the steak on beside them. He put bread in the oven to make toast. When it was all ready, he put the food on a plate and set it in front of his visitor.

"Coffee? Milk? Anything else?"

"This is quite grand," Gebhart said. "The food on the ship was . . . less than desirable."

"So," Keegan said, sitting across from him. "Can you tell me what happened?"

"Are you sure you want to hear, *Ire?*"

"Yes. I want to know everything you can tell me."

Gebhart ate like a starved man, talking between mouthfuls in a monotone, bereft of emotion.

"There was an attempted escape from the camp. Half a dozen of the younger men attempted to breach the fences. They used steel rods they made in the foundry to short-circuit the electricity. Three of them actually got out. The others were shot down on the wires. But the cleared area between the fence and the trees was mined. One of them stepped on a mine and . . . and it . . . blew off his legs."

Gebhart put down his fork and looked away, out through the living room toward the big window. Keegan could tell it was difficult for him to talk about the incident.

"The other two were knocked down by the explosion," he went on. "The Germans machine-gunned those two and left the man with no legs in the field to bleed to death. They left all of them, the man with no legs, the two they machine-gunned, the three on the fence, left them there until . . . until their bodies rotted. Then they lined up all the inmates. Eicke, the man in charge of the camp, walked down the rows with his swagger stick, tapping every third or fourth prisoner on the shoulder, and the guards dragged them from the line. There were fifty of them and they were forced to dig a long trench and fill it with lye. They threw what was left of the six who tried to escape in the pit. And then . . . then the bastards ordered the fifty hostages into the hole and . . . and . . ."

"And what, Werner?"

"And buried them alive with a bulldozer. Then they planted flowers over the entire field so we cannot find the mass grave. Jenny . . . was one of them."

They both sat in silence for a very long time. Keegan's face hardly changed. Except for the muscles in his jaw which jerked in endless spasms, his face was a mask.

"I'm sorry," Keegan said finally in a hoarse whisper. "I . . . I . . ."

"It is all right," Gebhart said quickly. "There is nothing to say. How does one speak about the unspeakable? And to bring such horrible news on this night. I am truly sorry."

"When did it happen?" Keegan asked.

"In September. We would have tried to tell you sooner but it was quite impossible to get a message out and your friend Rudman was not in Berlin."

"Rudman was killed in Spain."

"My God," he said sadly. "When?"

"In June."

"I am really sorry, *Ire*. To lose two people so close together . . ."

"*Danke.*"

"We knew I was going to come to America so Avrum decided to wait until I got out to bring you the news."

"Why are you here? Can I help you in some way?"

Gebhart shook his head.

"I think the package will explain many things. You should know that Avrum has changed a lot. It is like a demon has him by the arm. All he thinks about is killing."

"He's declared his own war, Werner."

"I do not believe in this kind of vindictive violence, *Ire.* I am Hasidic. This eye for an eye is against my beliefs. Even when we threatened you that time, it was an effort to hold a gun—and it was unloaded! But Avrum has the fire of vengeance in him. Finally I told him I could not take part in it anymore. He was very understanding. He sent me here to raise money and arrange for our defectors to get into the States."

"Which I tried and failed to do . . ."

"You didn't know the right organizations," Gebhart said. "And they didn't trust you. I know the people to contact and how to achieve my mission. Avrum has something more important for you to do."

"What's that?"

"Open the package, please."

Keegan tore off the wrapping. Inside was a primitive sketch of an old man in the humiliating striped uniform of Dachau prison, staring with burned-out eyes through the barbed wire. Keegan remembered that man. The vision of his hopelessness was burned into his memory forever.

"I remember this man," he said.

"He is dead now. The painting was smuggled out. You will notice the signing."

In the lower righthand corner was written: "Jennifer Gould, Dachau Prison, 1937."

Keegan drew in a sharp breath. His hand trembled as he turned the painting over. There, on the back, was a letter.

My dearest Kee:

I hope this letter will eventually find its way to you. Just imagining that you might hold this slip of paper in your hand one day makes my heart sing.

How sad that we never said good-bye. How many times I have said it over and over to myself and hoped that perhaps my love for you would be strong enough to carry the message across the miles and through the air and into your heart.

I wish we had lived in a different time when there was love in the world instead of hate, when there was caring instead of cruelty. Such wishful thinking!

My days with you were the happiest time of my life. You shared the world with me and what a splendid world it was! In this misery, that memory makes me smile, makes my heart beat faster, brightens these awful hours.

And I think of Bert, too, and how serious he is and how hard he tries to tell the rest of the world what is really happening. Give him a kiss for me. But save the rest for your lips.

I love you, my darling. Please remember me as someone who gave her heart freely and gratefully and who was rewarded with joy and love and happiness.

My heart's love, sweet Kee. Stay well.

Jenny

September 23, 1938

There was a note attached to the painting:

Keegan:

Werner has a story to tell you. When last we saw each other, you said "I owe you one." Werner will tell you how you can pay it. I am sorry about Jenny. If her blood had been the same as mine, I could not have loved her more. Avrum.

There was one other item in the package. It was the list of the hostages murdered by Eicke. *Jenny Gould* was the first name on the list.

Keegan felt only cold wrath.

"You have a story to tell me," he said.

Gebhart found it difficult to tell the story. Raised within the strict religious confines of the Hasidim, that most disciplined of Jewish sects, he so detested violence that to consciously relive the night he was about to describe was a painful experience. But he had promised Avrum he would take the message to Keegan and he was a man of his word.

"Before I start, I must tell you that I cannot see you again after tonight. I think you understand why. I must trust that you will not give up my identity."

"I might be able to help you."

Gebhart shook his head. "You will understand when I finish."

Keegan nodded. "Whatever you wish. I'm just sorry we can't be friends, but I agree."

Gebhart took a swig of beer, wiped his lips with the back of his hand and then began:

"A *Spion* infiltrated our group in Berlin. He was friendly and very clever, very quick. A young man named Isaac Fish. He was planted by Vierhaus and he came to us very roundabout. Munich, Düsseldorf, Essen, finally Berlin. He worked his way slowly to get next to Avrum. His mission was to kill Avrum. Supposedly he had escaped from Dachau. They have begun now to tattoo numbers on the arms of the prisoners and this man had such a number."

"Tattoo numbers on their arms?" Keegan said incredulously.

"Ja. It has become so bad now, *everyone* is paranoid. So Avrum decided to doublecheck Fish. We got the list of Dachau prisoners and sure enough, there was Isaac Fish and the correct number. The only thing wrong was that the real Isaac Fish was one of the hostages killed with Jenny."

He pointed to the name on the list in Keegan's hand.

"Avrum went crazy! I have never seen him like that before. He howled like an animal when he realized we were being betrayed. We took Fish to a farmhouse outside Berlin. It was supposed to be an important meeting of the Lily. Avrum had gone out beforehand and set up a torture cell in the smoke cellar.

"When Avrum accused Fish, the *Spion* went crazy. He pleaded for his life. Avrum laughed at him and the more Fish pleaded for his life, the harder Avrum laughed. Avrum . . . attached electrodes from a twelve-volt battery to . . . to . . . his testicles. The screaming . . . it was the worst sound I ever heard in my life. We had a woman with us, one of our members, who is a trained secretary, and she took down every word Fish said. He identified three other agents. One of them in Zurich had set up the trap for our friend Joachim. They had ambushed him in the street and cut his throat. He lay there . . . he could not scream from the pain. He could not . . . cry . . . for help . . ."

He paused for a moment. His lips were trembling as he continued.

"Another one had infiltrated our group in Vienna. When it was obvious the man who called himself Fish had nothing else to tell us, Avrum shot him in the head. And then he swore to kill the other three. He killed the man in Zurich and the one in Vienna but the third one was out of his reach.

"After we interrogated Fish, Avrum told me to memorize all the shorthand notes so I could give the information to you. Only three people know about this, *Ire*. The woman who took the notes, Avrum and me. You will make four."

"I'm listening."

"Fish said that when he was in training in the Bavarian Alps there was another agent there. A very special man who was kept separate from the others and known only as *Siebenundzwanzig* . . ."

"Twenty-seven?"

"*Ja*. This agent was being trained for something very special, a mission in America."

Keegan perked up. His eyes came to life.

"He's here? In America?"

"Please, let me continue."

"Sorry."

"Fish did not know the nature of the mission—according to Fish only Hitler and Vierhaus know what he was being trained to do. But he said this assignment could neutralize America if England and France go to war against Germany."

"Neutralize America?"

"It would force the United States to stay out of the war."

"What could that possibly be?"

Gebhart shook his head. "I do not know. We speculated on it for months, imagining every possibility, but nothing made any sense."

"One man is going to pull this off?"

Gebhart nodded. "According to Fish, he will have some help but basically it is to be a one-man job. The other members of Vierhaus's group call him the *Gespenstspion*."

"The ghost spy?"

"*Ja. Siebenundzwanzig* is a lone agent and his true identity is

known only to Hitler and Vierhaus. We have no description and
no name. Only that he is very, how do you say it, *gefährlich*?"

"Dangerous?"

Gebhart nodded. "And he is an expert at *Verkleidung* . . ."

"Disguise . . ."

Werner nodded vigorously. "Also an expert skier. He first
came here in late summer of 1933. But the following spring
something happened—he was caught up in some kind of FBI
inquiry and he had to run."

"But he's here now? Has been for . . . Jesus, almost five
years!"

"If the information is correct."

"And this Twenty-seven, he got in trouble with the government here in 1934? You're sure it was the FBI?"

"*Ja.* But it was not exactly that way. It was more like . . . he
was involved in something as a bystander, a . . ."

"Witness?"

"*Ja,* a witness. But because the government police were also
involved he could not risk an investigation."

"What the hell . . ." Keegan stood up and started pacing the
kitchen. His energy had suddenly skyrocketed. A superspy, here
in America, to perform a job so insidious it could force America
to remain neutral in the event of war with Germany? Well, he
thought, whatever it is, his time is running out. Events in Europe
were escalating. The whole continent could be at war before the
next New Year. But what could it be? And how could he find this
man? He had no description, no name other than *Siebenundzwanzig*, no location. And why did Avrum want Keegan to pursue
him?

"Avrum wants *me* to try and catch this Twenty-seven?"

"*Ja.*"

"Why me?"

"So you get him first, before the police. So there is no
chance he would be tried and perhaps sent to prison instead of
. . . of . . ."

"I'm not an investigator, Werner," Keegan cut him off,
ignoring for a moment Gebhart's last remark. "I have no experience at such things."

"He says you can do it because you are as tormented by
what they did to Jenny as he is."

"There are many, many others far more qualified to do this than me, Werner. The FBI for one. They are trained for this."

"They do not have the obsession . . ."

"Avrum learned a lot about me in a few days."

"Also they would probably not believe you. Also, *Ire,* you cannot tell them that I brought you the message or they will come after me."

"Yeah, the FBI and I have hardly been bosom buddies anyway. Our problems go back aways."

"When you were a gangster?" Gebhart asked innocently.

Keegan laughed. "Yeah, Werner, when I was a gangster." Then he stopped. "Wait a minute, you said he doesn't want him to be tried in a court?"

Gebhart shook his head.

"Then . . . ?"

Gebhart said one word under his breath, a whisper, barely breathed: *"Töten . . ."*

"He wants me to *kill* the spy?"

Gebhart looked down and nodded.

"Avrum reasons that the only chance Germany has is if America, England and France go to war with Hitler. If England and France declare war on Germany do you think America will follow?"

"I don't know," Keegan said. "I seriously doubt it."

"Why? They are your allies."

"I don't know whether you can understand this, Werner, but I have a hard time getting emotional over the plight of one hundred thousand people. Or even fifty people, for that matter. It shocks me but it doesn't touch me personally. But when it became one-to-one, when it was somebody I knew, somebody I loved, when it was Jenny, then finally I understood. I think most Americans are like that. Until it hits home, until people they know start dying, they will stay away from war."

"Do you believe this story Fish told?" Gebhart asked.

"Do you?"

"I told you, *Ire,* I was there," he said nodding. "And I will tell you, this man did not lie or make it up, I assure you of that. What he said he said out of pure terror and pain."

"If you and Avrum are convinced, then I believe it."

"And will you pursue him?"

"Yes," Keegan said without hesitation. He stared at the German sitting across the table from him and saw great sadness in his young face.

"And kill him?" Gebhart asked.

It was not an easy question to answer. For all these years Keegan had been frustrated, filled with anger because he was powerless to help Jenny. He could do nothing. He owed one to Wolffson, now Wolffson had called in the marker and he *could* do something about that. The thought of it excited him. If the security of the country was at stake, that alone was reason to track down the agent known as 27. If he were doing it purely out of need for revenge that was all right, too. And if tracking this dangerous superspy gave his own existence a new purpose, all the better.

"Yes, if it's possible I'll kill him."

"Vengeance is mine," Gebhart replied. "The Lord said that."

"You have to get even before you get well," Keegan snapped back. "Ned Beerbohm said that."

Gebhart looked confused by the remark.

"I cannot give up the things I have been taught. It even troubles me to give you a message which *might* cause violence."

"Let me tell you something, Werner, I used to have this recurring dream. In the dream I would find Vierhaus tied up in different places here in New York. I would be carrying a cage full of hungry rats and I would spread cheese all over him and then I'd let the hungry rats loose on him and watch them literally gnaw him to death. I had that dream a lot for a while and whenever I had it, I'd wake up all sweaty and out of breath. Then as time went on, I had it less and less and finally it went away and I started dreaming about Jenny. Nice dreams at first but then they went sour, too. The Nazis had her and there was this great pane of glass between us and I couldn't break that glass. And what they were doing to her was even worse than what I did to Vierhaus. Pretty soon I started having the rat dream again. It was like waves in the ocean. For five years it's been either one or the other. When I start to get complacent, the rat dream comes back. I guess what I'm trying to say is, I have mixed feelings about all this. I've never killed anyone, except in the war. I have no compulsion to kill anyone, not even this *Siebenund-*

zwanzig, so other factors enter into it. I respect your religious beliefs, Werner, but you have to respect the way I feel."

Keegan stood up and motioned Gebhart to follow him.

"Come here, I want to show you something."

He led Gebhart through the apartment and pulled open one of the French doors. They went out on the balcony. The cold air stirred them both. Keegan turned up the collar of his jacket. His steamy breath was whisked away by the wind. He felt a sudden rush of relief. Now finally, he was shed of the fear of not knowing. Now that part of it was over. But with the relief came a great burden of guilt and there was nothing he could do about that. He would have to learn to live with it.

He pointed to the street below.

"I grew up down there," Keegan said with obvious pride. "That was my front yard, that street right below you. I went to what you call upper school, we call it high school, right up the street about four blocks. A very hard place, Werner. Down there, if some guy does something to you, you do back to him only twice as bad. The reason is simple: he won't bother you anymore, he'll go pick on somebody else. You might call that an eye for an eye or two eyes for an eye or whatever you want to call it, Werner. I call it survival. And if you want to survive down there, you learn three things real fast. You never squeal on a pal. You never go back on your word. And you always pay your markers—your debts. I suppose that's the closest thing to a religion I've got. So I'll tell you right now, I'm going to find this Twenty-seven. I don't know how, I don't even know where to begin, but I'll find him and when I do . . . then I'll decide."

But in his heart, Keegan knew that if he found 27 he would most certainly kill him. Not because he was a threat to the U.S. or because he was a Nazi superspy. Keegan would kill him because he owed Avrum. And Jenny. And, in the end, because he owed it to himself.

Keegan was surprised at how fast he got from the cashier to the manicurist to the owner of the shop, who was also the barber, and finally to the man himself. He recognized the high-pitched, hoarse, voice immediately.

"Who you say this is again?"

"It's Frankie Kee, Mr. Costello. You remember me?"

"Yeah, I remember you. You still drivin' that Rolls?"

"I switched to a twelve-cylinder Packard."

"So you're that Frankie Kee."

"One and the same."

"I heard you was outa the country."

"I'm back."

"You was where, Germany?"

Costello obviously kept in touch. He was a man who never forgot information, no matter how unimportant it might seem. It went into the old memory bank and stayed there.

"That's right."

"What were you doin' over there?"

"Hating Hitler."

Costello broke out laughing, then yelped. "Jesus, Tony, you almost cut my throat . . . well I can't help it, the guy made me laugh . . . you, Frankie Kee, you almost got my throat cut for me."

"Sorry, I didn't know you were getting a shave."

"Okay, you're back. What's your problem?"

"Mr. C., my problem is I'm lookin' for a guy and I've got almost nothing to go on."

"This guy one of ours?"

"No. He's a European. Nothing to do with the business."

"So why you come to me?" There was a touch of irritation in his husky voice.

"Because I need a name. Somebody who can keep his mouth shut and can give me some pointers, like how to find somebody who doesn't want to be found."

"This is personal, am I right?"

"Very personal."

"I heard you never packed a heater."

"That's true."

"This ain't any of my business, but this guy you're lookin' to hire, does he have to do anything else? I mean, if he turns this noogle up, do you want him to do anything else for you?"

"*I* want to turn him up, Mr. C. All I want to know is how to go about it."

"Must be *real* personal," Costello said with a chuckle.

"You hit it on the button."

There was a pause, a long pause. Vaguely in the background he could hear the sound of a razor being drawn across a whiskered face, the sound of an emery board on fingernails and, way in the background, H. V. Kaltenborn was delivering his daily news broadcast on the radio. Finally Costello spoke again.

"It could cost you a bundle, the guy I got in mind."

"The cost doesn't figure in."

"Jesus, you really *do* want this guy bad. You got a pencil handy?"

"Right."

"Eddie Tangier. GRamercy 5–6608. It's a candy store on the East Side. They'll take a message. You can use my name."

"Thanks. That's one I owe you."

"You're okay, Frankie Kee, I'll remember that. Maybe someday you hear from me."

"*Grazie. Addio.*"

"*Addio.*"

At four o'clock a man entered the saloon. He stood in the doorway for a moment, a hazy shape, haloed by sharp sunlight from outside. He was short and square, a boxy little man who kept his hands in his overcoat pockets as he strolled slowly around the room, checking the booths. He went to the back, opened the men's room door with one hand, leaned over and looked under the booth doors. He did the same with the ladies' room, then went back to the front. A moment later a second man, a slender man nearly six feet tall dressed in black, entered followed by two others who stood on either side of the entrance like palace guards.

Keegan sat in his rear booth reading the afternoon paper. He watched the little drama at the door with casual interest, then turned back to the tabloid.

The tall man in black walked cautiously toward the booth. He did everything cautiously. He walked cautiously, he looked around cautiously, he talked cautiously and he sat down as if he expected the seat to be cushioned with nails. He was a dapper man with a pencil mustache and he wore a vested suit under a black chesterfield coat. He walked down the length of the bar, stopped at its corner and stared across the room at Keegan before he finally approached the booth.

"Frankie Kee?"

"Yeah."

"Okay."

He sat across from Keegan, shook out his shoulders and stared at him for ten or fifteen seconds. Then he smiled.

"Eddie Tangier." His voice was low and soft, almost a monotone.

"Thanks for coming."

"This your joint?"

"It's one of my enterprises."

"One of my enterprises, I like that. That uptown talk tickles me to death. So . . . ?"

He held his hands out and wagged his fingers toward Keegan.

"I need some advice," Keegan began.

"From me?"

"Yeah."

"What kind of advice?"

"I'm looking for a guy."

"Whoa, whoa, what do you think, you see any feathers on me? I am not a vocalist."

"It's not like that. This guy isn't connected in any way."

"So why would I know him?"

"You don't. Hear me out a minute, okay. I talked to Mr. C.,

he told me you were the man. He told me you could find God if the price was right."

"Costello said that?" Tangier smiled, obviously flattered. He stretched his neck and sat up a little straighter in the booth. "Well . . . yeah, that's true. Mr. C. says the truth."

"Let me set up a hypothetical case for you."

"Hypo*what?*"

"A make-believe situation. I'm looking for a guy and I've got very little to go on. I want to pick your brains, maybe I can figure where to start."

"This ain't a job then, you looking for something for nothin', huh?"

"I'll pay whatever you think it's worth."

Tangier sat sideways in the booth and looked past his shoulder at Keegan. He drummed his fingers on the table.

"You really do got big ones, call me in off the range like that, I think it's something important, you blow smoke up my ass."

"I'll pay you five grand now and five G's bonus if I find the guy."

"Jesus, that's okay. I'll have a glass of wine. Red. My throat's dry."

"Sure. Tiny, a bottle of the best red in the house for Mr. Tangier. Two glasses."

"Yes sir, comin' right up."

"Okay, so you wanna ride with Eddie Tangier. Shoot, what's the game?"

"You might look at it as if . . . as if it's a patriotic thing."

"Uh huh. Right. We gonna salute the flag here in a minute?"

"I'm looking for a guy. I don't know his name, I don't know what he looks like and I don't know where he is except he's in America someplace. Where do I start?"

"What is this, some kinda gag or somethin'? You're lookin' for a guy, you don't know his name, don't even know what he looks like. What'd this phantom do?"

"Nothing yet. I want to stop him before he does."

"What's he *gonna* do?"

"I have no idea."

"Shit, you're wacky. You got bees in your bonnet there, Frankie Kee. I shoulda known."

"I'm dead serious, Eddie."

"I didn't say you weren't. What I said, you're nutty as a fuckin' peanut farm is what I said."

Tiny came with two glasses of red wine and put them on the table with the bottle.

"Yeah, thanks," Tangier said. He poured an inch or so in the bottom of the glass, held it up, peered at it through the light, took a sip and nodded approvingly.

"Good dago red," he said and filled both glasses.

"Just let me set it up for you, okay? Hear me out. You still think I'm around the bend, you and your boys have a steak on me, we forget all about it."

"You're one strange dude there, you know that? Anybody ever tell you that?"

"Almost everybody."

Tangier chuckled.

"Okay, so you know it. So talk to me." He waved his two men away from the door and pointed to a booth. They sat down. "Feed 'em while we talk, they been on their feet most of the day."

Keegan nodded to Tiny, then toward the two bodyguards.

"Okay," Keegan said, "here it is. Let's say you want to get lost. Disappear, start over someplace else. You need an identity, license, whatever. How would you go about that? What's the procedure?"

"Somebody could still recognize you."

"No. The Phantom's from across the pond. A foreigner."

"Hey, this ain't some kinda spy stuff? Look, I'm not about to screw around with the feds."

"Thing is, Eddie, he doesn't have to worry about his face. What he needs is an identity. I mean, can you buy that kind of thing?"

Tangier leaned back and caressed his lower lip with the rim of the wineglass. He took a sip and put the glass back on the table.

"Look, whyn't you take this to the G-boys? They got the moxie, got the people."

"I tried that."

"And?"

"It's too vague. They don't have the time or the people. They think I'm a crackpot. They're just not interested, blah, blah, blah. Take your pick."

"So forget it."

"I don't want to forget it."

"This a personal thing?"

"Very."

"You gonna whack this guy when you find him?"

"Probably."

"I heard you don't even carry a piece."

"I know how to use one."

Tangier looked around the saloon for a moment, then, "Okay, tell me everything you *do* know about this turkey."

"Then *you* forget it, okay?"

"Hey, I got the worst memory you ever met."

Keegan sighed. He lit a cigarette and blew smoke toward the ceiling.

"The mark is highly trained. A very smart guy. He came here in '33, spent a year someplace. Then sometime in the spring or early summer of '34 he got in a mix-up with the feds. It wasn't something he did personally, it was like he was maybe an innocent bystander, something like that. Anyway, he had to cool off, disappear, start all over. So now he's got a new identity and I don't know where the hell he is. That's all I know."

"No description at all?"

Keegan shook his head.

"That's a bitch."

"Tell me about it."

Tangier finished his wine and poured himself another. He thought for several seconds.

"Once there's this guy called Speed Cicorella, who's a numbers boss up in the Bronx only he's shaving off the top and the boys get wind of it and they put his feet to the fire and it's like, y'know, cough up thirty big ones, Speedy, or it's curtains, so Speed turns rabbit and Mr. C calls me in.

"Now this Speed is a very bright guy except when it comes to tearing a piece off don't belong to him. I got to figure, scheduled for a box like that, he's gonna get real lost. The easiest way to do this, you go to a town, not a big town, not a small town, an in-between town, like, uh, Trenton or Rochester, and you go to the cemetery and you look over the stones and you find where a baby cashed in right after it was hatched, a week or so old, and this mark died about the same time you was born. You know, Baby Smith, born on Tuesday, died on Thursday, we miss you, that kinda thing. The reason you don't wanna pick a small town, probably everybody in the courthouse knows about Baby Smith. You pick a big town like New York, you get lost in paperwork. So anyways you pick a medium town and you find your mark and you go to the courthouse and you get a birth certificate. And you become Baby Smith only now you're like thirty years old."

"How about death certificates?"

"They don't match 'em up. You get born, your stuff is in one place, you die, it's someplace else. They don't match 'em up 'cause it's too much trouble plus who cares, okay? What I'm sayin', it ain't a problem, matchin' up birth papers and death papers. It don't happen."

"Okay."

"So now you got a new ID. You get a driver's license. You get a passport. You get a job. You're Baby Smith, now age thirty. You can do it and do it and do it, man. You can set up three, four IDs, switch back and forth. What it is, you're gone, okay?

"So now I got to find Speed who is thirty-seven and could be anyplace and be anybody so what do I do? I check out his pedigree and he's from this little town in Jersey called Collingswood across the river from Philly. I figure, what the hell, we got to start someplace. The biggest little town near there is Camden. I do the cemeteries. I write down every dead kid I come across who would be thirty-five to forty if he's still kickin'. I end up with thirty-two names outa maybe half a dozen cemeteries. So I pull some strings with some people I know in Trenton and I make a run on driver's licenses. I'm lookin' for a match-up to one of the names from the cemetery, somebody in his late thirties who just applied for a driver's license. I draw *bopkes*.

"Then I start dealin' with Speed himself. He likes big city action. He likes ladies. He likes to play the numbers and the ponies. And . . . a big hit, he's got diabetes. He needs a fix every now and again."

"Insulin."

"That's the ticket. I figure, maybe he went across the river, maybe he's hangin' out in Philly. So I do the same thing with driver's licenses in Pennsylvania and whadda ya know, I get lucky. I come up with three guys, three addresses, and one of the addresses is a phony. Now I figure Speed is a guy name of George Bernhart with diabetes livin' someplace in Philly. I do the hospitals. My story is, this guy Bernhart, I never met him before, he comes by my place with a friend and he leaves his fixins. I'm afraid he needs the stuff. There's twelve hospitals in the Philly area. I get to number nine, bingo again. Now I got a George Bernhart, age thirty-eight, a diabetes freak livin' at such-and-such in Philly. I stake the place, sure enough, here comes old Speedy down the street packin' groceries. I make a phone call. Ten days, the job's old news, I'm back in Manhattan spendin' the felt. See what I mean?"

"I get your point. Sometimes it's the little things that count."

"Yeah, right. Some oddball piece of information you pick up is what dumps them. If you ever get on to this bird, find out everything you can about him. *Everything.* Plus I got lucky."

"You make your own luck."

"I suppose there's somethin' to that."

"What happened to old Speedy?"

"I didn't ask. See, it's not my thing. I'm a tracker, I don't do hits. I don't even pack heat, that's what muscle's all about. Now I'm in industry. I done Lucky Lootch a favor once. Wasn't for him I'd be sittin' in the pen someplace. Or maybe dead."

"What kind of favor?" Keegan asked.

"I'm sittin' in the holding pen down at the Tombs waiting for my bondsman to show up. I'm maybe twenty at the time, a small-time booster, that's all. Anyways I'm sittin' there and a couple of city dicks walk by and I hear one of them mention the name of a gambling house uptown they're about to knock over. It's a place I know is one of Lucky's. So I make a little noise about my bond man not being there and the desk man lets me out to make another call and I ring up a guy I know knows Lucky and I tell him what's about to happen and to get the word upstairs real fast. When the cops got there, the place was dark. Not a soul on the premises. Next thing I know my charges are dismissed and Mr. Lootch offers me a spot. I had this knack for sniffing out people didn't wanna be sniffed out and he kind of cut me loose on my own. I never missed yet."

"Mr. C. was right."

"Bet'cher ass. I think I'll have that steak. Medium well, a potato maybe and a bottle a ketchup."

"My steaks are all prime beef, you don't need to douse them with ketchup."

"I put ketchup on everything. I put ketchup on my Wheaties."

"Tiny, a T-bone medium well and a potato for Mr. Tangier. Bring the ketchup bottle."

"Got it," Tiny answered.

"So where do I start?" asked Keegan.

"Me? I'd start with the screwup. See, you're lookin' for something federal around the middle of '34, right. Something that happened and maybe the feds are lookin' for somebody related to that thing, whatever that thing is."

"Like what?"

"Hell, I don't know. Maybe hot cars, that's federal. Kidnapping. Smuggling. Bank robbery. Maybe somebody movin' ladies around, state to state . . ."

"He wouldn't be involved in anything like that."

"Good thinkin', Frankie. Not if he's a sleeper like you say, waitin' for somethin' to happen, his angle would be to become a needle in the haystack. So, what I'm sayin', somethin' happened that maybe he wasn't directly involved in. Somethin' would make this John Doe turn rabbit. What could that be, a guy who's missin' but the feds wanna talk to him? An eyeball to something maybe? He knew somebody somethin' happened to maybe?"

"And he couldn't afford the scrutiny. What I mean, they'd maybe turn up his cover."

"Now you're cookin'. Look, how many cases that happened during those three, four months were the feds involved in? Already you narrowed things down a lot."

"Where would you go if you were this guy?"

"Get lost out in the sticks someplace. Out in the farmland, someplace out past Chicago. Just melt in."

"How about the South?"

"People're too nosy down there."

"Would he know all this?"

"You'd know that better than me. Anyways, that's the way you do it, pal, hit and miss. Play the logic. Put yourself in his place. What would he do next? See what I mean? I can't take a hand in this, y'unnerstand, with the feds in on it and all."

"Sure."

"You got my nose up, though. I hope you make this bird."

"I'm *going* to make him."

"Uh huh. I think I believe you there, Frankie Kee. Just outa curiosity, how bad you really want this guy?"

"I want to make a spot on the street out of the son of a bitch."

Tangier chuckled in his icy undertone. "Well, look, you run up a blind alley, you got my number, gimme a ring."

"Thanks, Eddie."

"Sure. Where the hell's my steak, they have to kill the cow?"

At three A.M. the phone jarred him out of a deep sleep. He groped for the instrument in the dark, finally got his hand on it and answered sleepily.

"Yeah?"

"It's Eddie again."

"What time is it?"

"Who cares. Listen, I been thinking about this problem of yours. A couple more things occur to me. First, if he come from across the pond, he had to have a passport from wherever he come from. Could be somethin' there. Two, he woulda gone for his new ID quick, he wouldn't wander around with a passport lookin' in cemeteries."

"I get your point," Keegan said sleepily.

"I figure he probably hit the East Coast because he would do this fast when he got here," Tangier continued. "If I was guessing, I'd say he got the name somewhere in north Jersey or eastern Pennsylvania, outa the Manhattan area but close enough by. Then he'd want to put some distance between him and wherever he picked up his ID so my guess, you look out in the middle of the country someplace, leastways for starters. So now you're lookin' for a case happened during those three, four months somewheres out West. See what I mean, I know it ain't much but it's better'n goose eggs."

"I appreciate your help, Eddie," Keegan said.

"You wanna give this thing up, I'd say you got good reason. But I just got the impression there, talkin' to ya, this was a big thing with you."

"It is a big thing with me."

"Then don't crap it up. You can find this guy. But I think you're gonna need some help from the G-boys, looking for what screwed this bucko up back in '34. If the guy disappeared it's gotta be on the books somewheres."

"Easier said than done."

"Think about this. What would be the perfect way to disappear? So they'd stop lookin' for ya?"

Keegan lay in bed staring at the shadowy ceiling for a few seconds then it struck him.

"Dead. Hell, he'd die."

"The perfect cop-out, pal. If he faked his death it would stop right there. He's out clean, comes back later and starts over. Pull all your strings, Frankie Kee. Nothin' comes easy."

"I hear you. Thanks, Eddie."

"Keep in touch."

Keegan lay in the dark for several minutes. *Pull all your strings,* Tangier said.

He only had one string left to pull.

But it was a good one.

Keegan turned off the main highway just before he got to the city limits of Princeton and drove about four miles to the tiny village of Allamuchy. It was dark and the misting rain that had plagued him all the way from New York had turned to fog. He might have missed the railroad station completely had he not been stopped a hundred yards from it by four cars blocking the road.

A tall, gaunt-faced man with his hat pulled over his eyes emerged from the fog and shined his flashlight in the car.

"Excuse me, sir, can I help you?" he said in a flat, no-nonsense voice.

"My name's Keegan. To visit Car C."

"May I see some identification?"

Keegan handed him his wallet and his passport. The agent checked the license signature against the name in the passport. He flashed the light in Keegan's face again, then back down to the passport photo.

"Very good, sir. Mr. Laster will drive down with you if you don't mind."

"Not at all."

Laster was a handsome, pleasant man impeccably dressed, although soaking wet. He shook the rainwater off his hat before he got in.

"Sorry," he said. "I'm afraid I'm going to get your seat wet."

"That's the least of my troubles," said Keegan.

"Drive down to your right, past the station. You can cross the tracks there."

As they crossed over the railroad, Laster told him to take a sharp left. A hulking steam engine loomed through the fog. They drove past the black leviathan. Steam curled from around

its enormous wheels and undercarriage as it hissed idly, waiting
to be stoked up. The private train was seven cars long and was
dark except for slender shafts of light streaming from under
drawn shades. As they drove the length of the train, Keegan
could see the vague forms of bodyguards moving about in the
darkness. Then Laster suddenly ordered, "Stop here," as they
neared the last car.

Keegan slammed on the brakes. A slender woman with a
wide-brimmed hat came out of the last car, her collar turned up
around her ears. A plainclothesman helped her down the steep
metal steps, then they scurried through the mist around the back
of the car. A moment later Keegan saw automobile headlights
flash on the opposite side of the Pullman car. Then he heard an
auto drive off.

"Okay, pull down to the end of the train," Laster said and
after hesitating a moment, added: "You might forget what you
just saw."

"I didn't see a thing," Keegan said.

Laster smiled without looking at him. "This'll be fine," he
said.

Keegan stopped the car and they got out.

"Just a minute, please," Laster said as he mounted the steps
on the back of the Pullman. He disappeared inside. Keegan lit
a cigarette and turned up the collar of his suit coat. The mist was
so heavy it collected on the brim of his fedora and dripped off.

Keegan now understood why the president's private train
from Hyde Park to Washington was sidetracked in this virtually
nonexistent village. Through the years, Keegan had heard news-
men joke among themselves about FDR's "lady friend." It was
a reporter's inside joke; no one ever hinted at it in print. But
Beerbohm had confided to Keegan once that her name was Lucy
Rutherfurd and she lived someplace in New Jersey and that
Roosevelt had been in love with her since before the war; a
twenty-five-year love affair which the press chose to ignore.

A minute or two passed and Laster appeared at the door to
the Pullman car and motioned Keegan in. He climbed the steps
and entered the private car.

It was laid out as an office, its walls lined with dark wood
paneling, the floors covered with thick piled carpeting. A large
oak desk dominated the middle section of the car. Behind it was

a bar and to its left a large leather sofa with Tiffany floor lamps on either end. An antique chair sat in front of the desk. The lighting was subdued and the tasseled silk shades were fully drawn.

President Roosevelt sat behind the desk in his electrified wheelchair, dressed in a scarlet smoking jacket and a dark blue silk ascot, his pince-nez glasses perched on the bridge of his nose, a cigarette holder clamped between his teeth, a glass of scotch at his elbow. His face broke into the familiar warm, broad grin as Keegan entered the car.

"Well, Francis, what a grand surprise after all these years," the president said, offering his hand.

"Mr. President," Keegan said as they shook.

"Pour yourself a drink and sit down there in front of me," Roosevelt said, nodding toward the chair. "Sorry about the rain. I trust the trip from the big city wasn't too uncomfortable."

"Not a bit," Keegan said. He poured himself a sour mash highball and sat down. "I appreciate your taking time to see me."

"I can hardly pass up a chance to say hello to an old friend," Roosevelt said, enunciating every syllable in his refined accent. "I can't thank you enough for your contributions to the party over the years, Francis. You've been a generous and loyal supporter."

"My pleasure, Mr. President," Keegan said. "Are you going to break precedent and go for a third term?"

"Still up in the air, old man," Roosevelt answered. "My advisers have mixed feelings about it."

"For what it's worth, I hope you do," Keegan said.

"Thanks. You look hardy, Francis. I trust things have gone well for you."

"No complaints, sir."

"Excellent, excellent. Before we chat I would like to request that you keep our meeting confidential," the president said. His eyes had an almost mischievous glow. "A policy of mine, permits me to let what little hair I have down."

"Absolutely, sir," Keegan answered.

"One other thing. You mentioned national security. Would you consider letting an adviser of mine, Bill Donovan, sit in?"

Keegan recognized the name immediately. He had heard

that Wild Bill Donovan, of the old Fighting 69th, was organizing an information-gathering agency. It would collect intelligence information and analyze it as part of Roosevelt's attempt to overhaul the entire intelligence system, such as it was—which wasn't much.

"That'll be fine, Mr. President," Keegan replied. But Roosevelt could see a tinge of disappointment in Keegan's face. He leaned forward in his chair with his hands on the edge of his desk and fiddled with a cigarette, finally putting it in a long, ivory holder and lighting it.

"Francis, do you know how many spies we had when the world war started?" he asked, and held up two fingers before Keegan could answer. "Two."

"Two!" Keegan said with a chuckle of disbelief.

"That's right, my friend, ridiculous as it may sound, we had two spies and two clerks supporting them. That was our entire intelligence service. And to make matters worse, what intelligence sources we *did* build up during the war have mostly been abandoned since the armistice. You've been to Germany, Francis, you've seen firsthand what's happening over there. We *desperately* need a first-class intelligence agency. Bill Donovan will take on the task."

"Sir, you don't have to . . ."

Roosevelt waved a hand at Keegan and cut him off.

"What I'm telling you is public knowledge. But if national security *is* involved in this matter, I would appreciate your sharing the information with him. If this is a purely personal thing, he's waiting in the club car so I'm sure he won't get too bored if we leave him there."

"I think intelligence might very well enter into it," Keegan said.

"Good." The president reached under his desk and pressed a button.

A minute or two later a tall, well-built man in his late forties entered the car from the front. Keegan recognized him from photographs. He stood very erect and was dressed in a blue double-breasted suit, starched white shirt and a flaming red tie. He was carrying a drink.

The president made the introductions. "William, this is my friend Francis Keegan. Bill Donovan, Francis."

Donovan's handshake was sturdy and his blue eyes stared straight into Keegan's eyes. "Good to meet you, Keegan," he said brusquely.

"Colonel," said Keegan. "It's an honor."

Donovan's poker face did not change. If he was flattered by Keegan's remark, he did not show it. He sat against the wall on the leather sofa, crossed his legs and sipped his drink. He did not take his eyes off Keegan. Donovan had been a U.S. district attorney in western New York state for several years and Keegan wondered what was going through his mind, sitting in on a meeting with the president and an ex-rumrunner—a man he might have prosecuted a few years earlier—discussing national security. Keegan sensed an incipient skepticism from Donovan. If Keegan had any credibility, obviously it would have to come from the president.

"Congratulations on your new job," Keegan said. "From what I hear, we need you."

"Actually it's pretty dull stuff," Donovan said.

"Dull?" Keegan said.

"Sure," Donovan said. "College graduates sitting in offices monitoring foreign broadcasts, reading foreign publications, sifting through diplomatic reports. They dig up information and then the experts decide if it's pertinent. The fun stuff, the movie stuff, that's a small part of it."

"How about the embassies?" Keegan pressed.

"Embassies?" Donovan asked innocently.

"Come on, Colonel," Keegan said. "Everybody knows the diplomatic services are fronts for espionage. The German embassy in Paris is nothing more than an intelligence unit for a major named von Meister."

Now how the *hell* would he know that? Donovan wondered.

"But," Keegan said, "since Mr. Hull thinks spying is ungentlemanly all our embassies do is give parties and kiss ass."

Roosevelt leaned back in his chair and howled with glee. "Well, what do you think of that analysis, William?"

Donovan's cold countenance softened slightly. He chuckled and said, "Not bad. Want a job, Keegan?"

"No thanks," said Keegan with a smile. "I tried that in 1917. I don't take orders too well."

"You took them well enough to win a Silver Star at Belleau Wood," Donovan said casually.

Touché, thought Keegan.

"Well, what do you have for us, eh?" Roosevelt asked pleasantly.

"Look, Mr. President, I think you know I'm not some nut from the boondocks. I say that because what I'm about to tell you is going to sound pretty crazy. The thing is, I wouldn't be here if I wasn't sure it's true."

"Uh huh," the president said eagerly. He was clearly intrigued. Donovan continued to stare from a poker face.

"A man I consider above reproach has passed information on to me that there is a German sleeper agent living in this country," Keegan began. "He's been here for several years. This man is a master agent and his mission, if he's successful, could neutralize the United States in the event England and France go to war with Hitler."

"Neutralize us?" Donovan said, showing only mild interest. "What the hell is he planning to do?"

"Whatever their plan is, this man—his code name is *Siebenundzwanzig,* Twenty-seven—is working directly for Hitler. According to my information, whatever their plan is, it could prevent us from declaring war on Germany."

"And you have no idea what this assignment is?"

Keegan shook his head.

"That's ridiculous," Donovan sneered, showing his first hint of emotion. "What could one man possibly do that would compromise us to such an extent?"

"I don't know, Colonel, but I can tell you this. The information came from a Nazi agent in Germany who had infiltrated an underground organization. He was caught and tortured. He gave up the name of three agents. The information on the other two was accurate and they were both killed."

"What underground organization?" Donovan asked, his face once again a mask of control. Not a man to play poker with, thought Keegan.

"My source is impeccable," Keegan insisted.

"Where did you get this tip?" asked Donovan.

"I can't tell you that."

"I think I can promise you the information will never leave this room," Roosevelt said softly, his smile still staunch. "Don't you trust us, Francis?"

"Of course I do, Mr. President. But I made a promise."

"I appreciate that," said Roosevelt. "On the other hand, Bill has a point. It would help if we can judge the validity of your information."

"Have you ever heard of an organization called Black Lily?"

A flicker of recognition in Donovan's eyes. Roosevelt looked at him with eyebrows raised.

"Yes," Donovan said.

"It came from the head of Black Lily."

"You *know* the head of Black Lily?" Donovan said, disbelief in every syllable.

Keegan nodded. Donovan was skeptical. He looked at the president and rolled his eyes. Keegan decided it was time to take a round or two in this mental boxing match.

"His name is Avrum Wolffson," Keegan said, and Donovan's amazed reaction told Roosevelt that Keegan had won the first knockdown in the delicate match.

"Does that jibe with your information, Bill?" the president asked.

"I've heard the name mentioned," Donovan said cautiously, still not willing to give up the round.

"Wolffson is unquestionably the head of Black Lily," Keegan said with finality. "He's been head of it since it was formed at the University of Berlin in 1933. One of his chief lieutenants was a young man named Joachim Weber. Weber was murdered by Nazi agents in Zurich two years ago. Wolffson's reaction was radical. He struck back, killed one agent in Zurich and another in Vienna. But the one known as *Siebenundzwanzig* is still alive because he's here in America."

Roosevelt settled back in his wheelchair, getting rather perverse enjoyment out of watching the two men spar with each other. Donovan, a bit flabbergasted by the flood of information, was subdued.

"And how did this Wolffson find out there was a spy in his outfit?" Donovan asked, still skeptical.

"The infiltrator used the name Isaac Fish. The real Fish was a prisoner at Dachau. He was executed along with fifty other inmates as an example after an aborted escape attempt. Wolff- son got a list of the hostages who were murdered . . ."

"Oh, now really . . ." Donovan started but Keegan cut him off. He handed him the tattered list of dead hostages.

"This is the list," said Keegan.

Donovan took the sheet reluctantly and scanned it. He looked up at Keegan suspiciously.

"Where the hell did you get this?" he asked.

"I'm sorry, Colonel, I can't tell you that."

"You expect us to believe you're privy to this kind of infor- mation?"

"I think it speaks for itself," Keegan answered. "Wolffson was . . . coaxing . . . information out of Fish when he spilled the beans about the three agents."

"Wait a minute," said Donovan, shaking his head. "I know for a fact that Black Lily isn't involved in that kind of thing."

"It is now, Colonel. It isn't a *Freiheit* movement anymore. It has become a full-fledged active underground operation. The three agents were members of a unit called *Die Sechs Füchse,* the Six Foxes, a small, elite intelligence unit headed by a psycholo- gist named Wilhelm Vierhaus and accountable only to Hitler."

"Jesus!" Donovan exploded. "Where the hell did you learn all this?!"

"The first name on that list is Jennifer Gould," Keegan said. "She was my fiancée and Avrum Wolffson's half-sister."

There was stunned silence in the railroad car.

"Do you know about this unit, Bill?" Roosevelt interrupted. Donovan nodded slowly.

"And she was *executed*?" Roosevelt asked Keegan, gently.

"She was buried alive," Keegan said. "Along with fifty other prisoners."

"Good God!" Roosevelt exclaimed. A silence followed, a respectful silence that was finally broken by a now soft-spoken Donovan.

"How fresh is this information?"

"I learned it eight days ago."

Roosevelt leaned back in his chair again and stared at a corner of the car. According to Hoover, there were several Nazi agents in America. The FBI had been investigating their ties to the German-American Bund for over a year. But Hoover had never come up with such specific information.

"Do you have anything else on this man?" Donovan asked.

Keegan decided to hedge a little. He knew he had them both going. He shook his head slowly.

"So we've got a sleeper agent with the code name Twenty-seven, living somewhere in the U.S. with a plan to keep us out of the war? *That's it?*"

"Yes sir, except I assure you again, this is *not* hot air. I am convinced that Twenty-seven exists and knowing Vierhaus, I think whatever their plan is, it has *some* validity. Why take a chance?"

"There's no place to start!" Donovan said. "We have no source of information in Germany to back-check. We have no description, no name . . ." The sentence died out.

"On the other hand," said Roosevelt, "can we afford to dismiss it? It seems to me that the closer we come to war, the more frequent these threats are going to become."

"I don't suggest we dismiss it," said Donovan, sighing. "Let's get back to the problem at hand. From a jurisdictional point, this is an FBI matter."

"No way," Keegan said immediately and emphatically.

"I beg your pardon?" Donovan said with raised eyebrows.

"Colonel, I'm not one of Mr. Hoover's favorite people," said Keegan. "He has a long memory, sir. He'd probably laugh at the information, then bury it. I can't give him specifics and I can't jeopardize my contact. I won't do that. That's why I came to you, Mr. President. I don't know who else to turn to."

Roosevelt and Donovan exchanged quick glances. Keegan had a definite point. In the matter of intelligence, Roosevelt had a problem with Hoover, a powerful and popular figure in America. Hoover had invented a weekly roll called the "Ten Most Wanted," plastered the faces of America's most dangerous criminals in post offices and literally declared war on bank robbers. In one year, his college-graduate machinegun squads, led by the hard case Melvin Purvis, whose credo was "shoot first, then ask questions," had killed Pretty Boy Floyd, Ma Barker and her "Boys," Machine Gun Kelly, John Dillinger and Homer Van Meter.

But by 1935, Hoover's G-men were running out of quarry. And since there was still no effective intelligence service, Hoover had turned his attention to the Communist threat, placing known members of the party under surveillance, gathering information on them, and taking over the responsibility for intelligence gathering in the Western Hemisphere.

Hoover had been annoyed by the proposal that Donovan establish an intelligence agency. He had acquiesced only so long as Donovan stayed out of his territory. It was a touchy issue and one which Roosevelt had to juggle carefully, since Hoover and his agents had very little experience in gathering or analyzing intelligence data. The compromise he made was that Donovan's group would operate outside North, Central and South America, leaving the entire Western Hemisphere in Hoover's jurisdiction.

Roosevelt knew the danger in the compromise: Hoover could follow the same path which Himmler had followed in Germany. After the Reichstag fire, Himmler's list of Communists had been used to frame the Communists for the fire, then track them down and murder over one thousand members of the party in the weeks following the fire. The lists being gathered by Hoover might also be used for political rather than national security purposes. The power-hungry FBI director was not above such abuse of his office.

Keegan's request could precipitate a political crisis which Roosevelt could not afford at the moment. And yet the president believed Keegan's information was probably accurate. The ex-rumrunner had presented him with an unusual dilemma.

"Do you have a suggestion?" the president asked Keegan.

"Let me go after him," Keegan said flatly.

"What!" Donovan said.

"Just a minute, William, hear him out," said Roosevelt.

"I need credentials that will get me into the bureau's files and also give me credibility when I ask questions."

"Without Hoover knowing about it?" Donovan said. "That'll be the day."

"I promise you, I'll confine everything specifically to this investigation."

"What do you know about investigating anything?" Donovan asked.

"Logic. It's all logic. That's all we have to go on. Logic and intuition. Maybe we get lucky. Maybe we get on his trail. Maybe we get a fingerprint, something like that. I run it through the system, see what we turn up. This is nothing but a trackdown, Colonel Donovan. It's not a murder investigation."

"I think Edgar might disagree with you there, Keegan," said the stoic Donovan. "Even if he doesn't believe the information, he'd get extremely ugly if he found out someone outside the bureau was stepping on his toes."

"I only need access to the files for about four months—say March through June of 1934."

Donovan suddenly was very interested. He leaned forward on the sofa and put his drink on the floor, his eyes narrowing. "You're holding out on us," he snapped.

"Anything else I could tell you would be pure conjecture."

"Let me judge that," Donovan said.

"What have we got to lose?" Keegan asked naïvely, unaware of the political implications of his request. "We know Hoover will fluff off the information anyway. Why not let me take a crack at it? Does he have to know?"

"Subterfuge, Francis?" Roosevelt asked wryly.

Keegan smiled. "I guess you could call it that, Mr. President."

"What else *can* you call it?" Donovan asked.

Keegan could tell Roosevelt found the idea appealing.

"You're talking about a lot of time and work, Francis," the president said.

"I've got nothing else to do. And if I abuse the privilege you can always revoke my library card."

"Library card, I like that," Roosevelt said with a chuckle.

"I'll pay my own expenses," Keegan added.

"A dollar-a-year man, eh?" Roosevelt said. The idea was beginning to appeal to him. Since he had become president, Roosevelt had surrounded himself with unpaid advisers from many different fields who were paid a token fee of one dollar a year.

Donovan picked up his glass and took a drink without taking his eyes off Keegan.

"We're in a curious situation," Roosevelt said. "I think the three of us would agree that war between Germany and England

and France is inevitable. But the American people don't want to hear about it. I made a speech in Chicago the other night warning the country about the threat of fascism. I thought it would rally the people and I was certainly mistaken about *that,* my friend. *Nobody* supported my position. What an outcry! What criticism. It's a hell of a note, boys, when you're trying to lead the country and you look over your shoulder and there's nobody there."

"America just isn't ready to face up to it yet," Donovan offered. "The last war is still fresh in their minds. We're still getting over the Depression."

"You're right, Bill," Roosevelt said. "Americans won't accept the reality of totalitarianism right now." He paused for a moment and took a sip of scotch. "On the other hand, the capture of a dangerous Nazi spy in this country might have a strong effect on public opinion."

"*If* such a spy exists," Donovan said.

"He exists all right," Keegan said. "I'm just asking you to make the job a little easier because I intend to go after him whether I have your help or not."

"Now just a damn minute . . ." Donovan said angrily.

"Hold on, hold on, boys," Roosevelt said, his face breaking into the wide grin again. "We're all on the same side here."

"There are experts in this field, Keegan," Donovan said slowly. "Why not let them handle it?"

"Why not let them help me?"

"Listen . . ."

Roosevelt stepped in again.

"Just a minute, Bill. Francis, I'm sure your decision to come to me with this information was not an easy one. What do you say we sleep on the matter? Do you have a card, Bill?"

Donovan handed him an embossed business card. His name was printed across the middle and in the right corner, "The White House" and a phone number. Roosevelt turned it over and scrawled "Franklin" across it, then tore it in half. He handed one half to Keegan.

"If we have a deal, you'll be contacted by whoever has the other half of this card. Whatever happens, you must be discreet. Bill and I will know about it, possibly one or two other people. I must ask you to keep what you are doing to yourself, Francis.

It is important that we keep this information quiet. If Hoover gets wind of this there'll be hell to pay and your investigation would be over."

"I understand, Mr. President."

"If you don't hear from me by tomorrow, then you must assume I can't help you."

"However it bounces," said Donovan, "this meeting never happened."

"I understand," Keegan said.

Roosevelt held out his hand. He was smiling broadly, his cigarette holder cocked toward the ceiling—a familiar pose in photographs. They shook hands.

"You've always been a good friend, Francis," Roosevelt said. "And a discreet one. I assure you, I deeply appreciate this information. And I am deeply sorry about your fiancée."

"Thank you, Mr. President. I'm flattered you even remembered me."

Roosevelt's eyes twinkled. "Now how could I forget you . . . Frankie Kee," he said with a chuckle.

Keegan had hardly closed the door behind him when Donovan turned to the president.

"He's awfully arrogant, Mr. President . . ."

"Certainly, Bill, you don't want a bunch of namby-pambies working for you."

Donovan looked at the floor and smiled. *Roosevelt did have a way of cutting through the bullshit,* he thought to himself. He took another tack.

"It sounds preposterous to me," he said. "I can't imagine what the Huns would have up their sleeve that could, what did he say, *neutralize* us?"

Roosevelt didn't answer. He fiddled with his cigarette holder for a few moments. *What indeed,* he wondered. The myriad possibilities fascinated him.

"I classify information by letter and number," Donovan went on. "A-one would be top of the line, A being an unimpeachable source, one being verified information. I would classify Keegan's data as about . . . D-five."

"I won't disagree with your judgment on that, Bill," the president said.

"Hoover is insanely protective of his territory," Donovan said. "He's made it clear that anything happening in the States is his jurisdiction. Why not give him the information?"

Roosevelt's eyebrows rose. "Because I made Keegan a promise," the president said. "Besides, I do agree with Keegan in one respect. If we give this information to the Bureau, nothing will be done. You know Edgar, if his people don't initiate a project, it goes to the bottom of the pile."

"Then he can take the rap if it turns out to be true," Donovan said.

Roosevelt's face clouded up for just a moment, then the lines softened again.

"We're not talking about blame here, Bill," he said. "What if Keegan's information turns out to be A-one and he turns this sleeper agent up? It would be a feather in your war bonnet if Keegan were working for you."

"And if it's a flop?"

Roosevelt smiled. "Then, my friend, nobody will ever know the difference. The project will be classified *secret*. We won't even keep a file on it."

Donovan was still unconvinced. He stood and pressed his fists in the small of his back.

"What the hell could this mission possibly be?" he asked. "Assassination? If, God forbid, they should kill you, it wouldn't neutralize us, the chain would continue unbroken. Sabotage? What could *one man* possibly destroy that would neutralize our position?"

"I have no idea. And obviously Keegan has no idea."

"Mr. President, I don't have the manpower or the budget to send a team out to find some phantom running an unknown and highly suspect mission. I'm still putting my operation together."

"And I don't like surprises, William," said Roosevelt. "Look here, I appreciate your skepticism. I just have a feeling about this one. Hitler's such a devious bastard, it sounds like something he might do. After all, what has he got to lose?"

Donovan lit a cigar and blew the smoke across its tip, watching the end glow. He was deep in thought, considering the pros and cons of having an unattached ex-bootlegger running around the country with White House credentials.

"Bill, before this is over you and I are going to be doing a lot of unorthodox things," Roosevelt said. "I don't want to step on your toes but . . . humor me on this one, will you?"

"Of course, Mr. President . . ."

"I'll get him White House security credentials," Roosevelt cut in. "You assign a contact man to keep tabs on him, kind of give him a hand. All it will cost you is a little of your man's time."

"And we just cut Keegan loose by himself?"

"Why not? He has a certain . . . obsession about this. If there is a shadow agent out there, he might just get lucky."

"We'd have no control over him . . ."

"True . . ."

Donovan stared across the car at the president. "You like this Keegan, don't you?"

"I know he can be trusted. I know he can keep his mouth shut. And he does have interesting connections."

"Because he was a gangster?" Donovan said skeptically.

Roosevelt pursed his lips and sipped his drink.

"Tell me, Bill, where do you plan to find recruits for this outfit of yours? Yale? Harvard?"

"Is something wrong with your old alma mater?" Donovan asked with a grin.

Roosevelt laughed heartily. "Not at all," he said. "But you're also going to need people who have . . . *special* qualifications. People who've picked up a few scars along the way. You're going to need a few ruffians in this outfit of yours. Francis Keegan fits that profile perfectly." Roosevelt leaned back in his chair and looked at the ceiling, savoring the intrigue. "Keegan understands subterfuge. He can handle himself in difficult situations. He's very resourceful, independently wealthy, an honor graduate from Boston College. The fact that he escaped from the Gestapo and he actually knows this man Wolffson and the Nazi . . . ?"

"Vierhaus."

"Yes . . . men you know only by name, that says something for him."

"But he's not interested in joining my operation, he made that patently clear."

"We-l-l-l, if he's any good, perhaps he'll change his mind. He's old-fashioned. Do him a favor and he'll repay it."

"The code of the underworld?" Donovan said with a smirk.

"Possibly. Or perhaps he's that rarest of things, an honorable man."

"He's an ex-bootlegger, for God's sake."

"He's *my* ex-bootlegger," Roosevelt said.

Donovan's eyes widened with surprise. "Is that why you agreed to meet with him?"

Roosevelt took a sip of his scotch. "He also contributed a quarter-million to my first campaign and a hundred thousand in '36," Roosevelt added casually.

Donovan chuckled and held his hands out at his sides. "Well, hell, in that case it's your call . . ."

"No, this is your outfit. We have a deal—you run the outfit, I'll run the country. But if it's manpower and funding you need, I can arrange that. If you're uncomfortable with Keegan or the situation . . ."

"No sir," said Donovan with a shrug. "It's his play, let him run it out. I just hope you won't be too disappointed when he comes up with . . ." He made a circle with thumb and forefinger.

"Oh, I hope he does, Bill," the president said. "I sincerely hope he does."

The president twisted a Chesterfield into his ivory cigarette holder. Donovan leaned over and held a lighter to it.

Then he walked to the bar and poured himself another whiskey. "Actually when you think about it, we're in the same boat as Hitler," he said. "We have nothing at all to lose, either."

Roosevelt leaned back with a satisfied grin.

"Excellent," he said. "Delighted you agree."

The line for the Staten Island Ferry was shorter than usual. It was below freezing and a harsh wind was blowing up from Hell Gate bringing with it the first hints of a snowstorm. Chunks of ice that had broken off the jetty bobbed in the choppy water. Snow flurries danced in the wind.

Why had he picked this cold dismal day to take a ride on the Staten Island Ferry? Keegan wondered. The man had called him earlier that day.

"Mr. Keegan?"

"Yes."

"I'm calling on behalf of the colonel."

"The colonel?"

"I believe you have his business card."

"Oh," he said. *"That* colonel."

"Can you meet me on the upper deck of the Staten Island Ferry this afternoon? There's one that leaves Manhattan at two thirty."

"I suppose so. Who is this?"

"Back end of the enclosed area."

"Who *is* this?"

"Be reading *Life* magazine. Good-bye."

And he had hung up.

Why all the cloak-and-dagger stuff? Keegan wondered. All he wanted to do was look at a few files, for God's sake.

The guard raised the gates and the stream of cars moved slowly into the tunnellike parking deck. Keegan set his brakes and went to the second deck of the ferry, a narrow glass-enclosed room with rows of dark-stained wooden benches. The windows were opaque with frost from the cold outside air. Even though heated, the large room was cold and drafty and smelled of oil, saltwater and creosote. Keegan took a seat at the end of the room on the corner of one of the seats and opened his magazine.

The foghorn bleated as the ferry shuddered and backed into the bay. A minute or two later Keegan heard the sliding door behind him open. A cold blast of air whooshed past him as the door rolled shut. Keegan turned back to his magazine and then a voice said, "Mr. Keegan?"

He looked up at the man.

"That's right."

The stranger was carrying a small brown paper sack which he held out.

"Peanut?"

"No thanks," Keegan said.

He was a tall man dressed in a tweed jacket with its collar turned up, a wool turtleneck sweater and a tweed cap. He carried himself erect like a career military man and had an intense look about him, his narrow face dominated by deep-set, piercing eyes and topped by a shock of thick, black hair. He was wearing aviator sunglasses which he whipped off and stuck in his jacket pocket.

"The name's Smith," he said, holding out his hand. His voice was pleasant with a hint of southern drawl. As they shook hands, Keegan felt something press into his palm. It was the other half of Donovan's card.

"Just to make it official," Smith said.

Keegan took his half out of his pocket and slipped the two sections together. A perfect fit. Keegan smiled up at him.

"Good to see you," he said.

Smith sat down beside him, leaning back, crossing his legs and stretching his arms out on the back of the bench. Keegan shook his shoulders against the chill and looked around the room.

"What's the matter, won't they give you an office?" he asked.

"I've had a tail on me all day," he said. "I dumped them just before I jumped on the ferry. Actually it's quite an effective maneuver. If they do get aboard they're easy to spot, in which case of course, I simply would have ignored you."

"You think the Germans have people following you? Isn't that a bit paranoid?" Keegan asked.

"Not the Germans, Mr. Keegan," Smith said in a patroniz-
ing tone. "Hoover's boys. They have two teams on me. They
know I work for Donovan and Hoover wants to know every move
he makes. That's the reason for all the inconvenience. If they tie
us together they'll be all over you, too. You'll never get anything
done."

"Why is FDR so nervous about Hoover? He's the President
of the United States, for God's sake."

"Because Hoover was appointed for life. Nobody can fire
him without a damn good reason and that makes Mr. Hoover a
very powerful man. The president does not want him as an
adversary."

"Hoover's really that way, huh?"

"Little Napoleon? I'm surprised he doesn't walk around
with his hand in his vest speaking French."

"You mean we're going to have to sneak around and meet
like this from now on?" Keegan said.

"I'm afraid so."

"I feel like a married man cheating on his wife, Mr. Smith."

"Bizarre notion," Smith said.

"I assume we have a deal," Keegan said.

"Yes," Smith drawled. "Here's the situation. I'll be your
contact man. You need anything, anytime, you contact me. You
get in trouble, you contact me. You get arrested, sick, need to
go to the hospital, you contact me. Nobody else. *Me.* Okay?"

"Sure. Kind of like rubbing a bottle and a genie pops out.
Only you're the genie."

His genie ignored his analogy. "I just put a briefcase in your
trunk. It contains everything you'll need to get started. I'd like
the case back. It's my personal property. Abercrombie and
Fitch."

"How the hell did you get in my trunk?"

"I picked the lock."

Keegan laughed. "You and I are going to get along," he
said.

"I hope you don't make my life miserable, Mr. Keegan. I
have this feeling you could make it a living hell."

Keegan laughed. "I wouldn't do that, Mr. Smith."

"I'd like you to run things by me. I'd like to know what

you're up to. Since I'm your only contact with Washington, it's important that you keep me up-to-date."

Smith broke open another peanut, letting the shells drop into the bag. "Sure you won't have a peanut? Straight from Georgia."

"No thanks. Just don't cramp my style, okay?"

Smith glared at him for a moment, then went on. "Now listen, this is important. I don't know what you're looking for, Mr. Keegan, but be as subtle as possible. Anybody asks what you're doing for White House Security, tell them security checks and background."

"Security checks and background."

"Right. You don't mention me or Donovan to anybody and you never even *met* the Boss."

"You call him the Boss, huh? You must be right on up there."

"I couldn't get a private meeting with him on twenty-four hours' notice. *That's* being right on up there."

Keegan chuckled. What it really was was $350,000 in campaign donations and four years selling the old boy his booze.

"You certainly have a lot of muscle to have pulled *this* off," Smith added.

"Just logic," Keegan said.

"It's logical to send a rich businessman on the trail of a Nazi spy?"

"Why not? Look, I'm sure you have the whole résumé on me, Mr. Smith, but let me tell you something. When it comes to advice I have unlimited resources in just about any field you can imagine. Experts, Mr. Smith. If I don't know how to do something, I can find out in short order. If I need information, I can get it. A virgin heater? Nothing to it. And as far as the FBI goes, I'm sure you know I dodged the feds for six years. They never even had a good description of me. I've thought a lot about Twenty-seven. If we catch him it's going to take a lot of logic— and a lot more luck. I'm a logical man and I have my share of Irish luck. True, I'll be flying by the seat of my pants but what's the alternative—give the information to Hoover and have him file it under 'Forget it'?"

"It seemed like a bad call to me, Mr. Keegan, but I'm not calling the shots."

"Just what do you do exactly?" Keegan asked. "Do you have a title? Everybody in Washington seems to have a title."

"No title."

"What's your job?"

"I get things done, Mr. Keegan."

"You're Mr. Smith and you get things done?"

"Precisely. And my name *is* Smith. You might call me an expediter. Are you familiar with the expression *dog robber*?"

"No."

"It's a Navy expression. I was in the Navy for several years. For a time I was Admiral Harry Grogan's dog robber. When the admiral wanted something, I got it for him. When he wanted something done, I did it. Anything, anytime. No matter what it was, I would say, 'Yes sir,' and take care of it. That's a dog robber, Mr. Keegan. Every admiral has one. Now I'm Donovan's dog robber. Just so we're straight, I know vaguely what you're up to and my job is to help you in any *sane and legitimate* way I can. I emphasize *sane and legitimate* because I don't like trouble. The mark of a good dog robber is to get results with an apparent minimum of effort and *no* trouble."

"And I assume you're a very good dog robber?"

Smith ignored the comment. "I know what you're trying to do and you know what I do, that takes care of all the biographical niceties. Now shall we talk about this operation of yours?"

"Ah, so now it's an operation."

"Probably stretching the point a bit. There's you and there's me—part-time. Not much of an operation."

"What's in the briefcase?"

"Credentials, some phone numbers, a contact or two, my card with a day and night number on it. Naturally I prefer day."

"Are you married?"

"I was. I was attached to the embassy in Shanghai when the Japs started their war. My wife was in the street market. She was killed by the first wave of bombers."

"I'm sorry."

"Thanks. The Chief—Donovan likes to be called Chief, by the way—is concerned because he feels this witch hunt of yours . . ."

"It's not a witch hunt, Mr. Smith. I assure you, *Siebenund-zwanzig* exists."

"Uh huh. As I was saying, he's afraid your motive is too personal. People who are too personally involved in these things sometimes act recklessly."

"I'll keep that in mind."

"If by some miracle you do turn this man up, you will give him to us, won't you." He was not asking a question, it was more like a statement of fact. He paused long enough to shell another peanut. "You realize how valuable this man could be to us, don't you, Mr. Keegan?"

"Sure."

"Sure what? Sure you'll turn him over or sure you know how valuable he is?"

"Both."

"You won't do something rash like dropping him in the East River with cement boots on?"

"It's not boots, Mr. Smith, the expression is a cement over-coat and I never did that kind of thing."

"The Chief seems to think you know about eighty-seven exotic ways to dispose of people."

"I said I didn't *do* that kind of thing, I didn't say I don't know *how* to do them."

"I feel reassured."

"Wonderful. Does Donovan believe me?"

"Whether he believes you or not is immaterial. He does think *you* believe the story and that's what counts. He's taking a shot on you. And don't forget, if this information gets to Hoover there will be a lot of hell to pay. And Donovan'll be the first one to catch it."

Keegan smiled his crooked smile and nodded. "I got the message, Mr. Smith."

"If you have any questions after you go over the material in your trunk give me a call. I'll have the briefcase picked up. I think that about covers everything. Anything else you need?"

Keegan liked Smith. There was a surly irreverence about him, a nasty edge coated with humor. He decided to test him.

"So you're the best dog robber there is, huh?"

"I don't like to brag, Mr. Keegan. Why do you ask?"

"There's something I could use."

"Oh?" Smith answered skeptically.

"I think transportation is going to be a big problem for me.
I hate to wait around for trains and buses, that sort of thing. So
I was wondering—do you think you might shake me up an air-
plane?"

Smith's expression never changed. "An airplane," he said
in a flat voice.

"Yeah, with a pilot that knows what he's doing."

"You want an airplane *and* a pilot."

"It would really be a big help."

"I'm sure it would."

Smith peeled another peanut and popped it in his mouth.
He stared straight ahead thinking for a minute or so.

"That's it? An airplane and pilot?" he said sarcastically.

"For now," Keegan answered pleasantly. He sensed that
Smith secretly enjoyed the challenge although he would never
admit it.

Smith ate another peanut and sighed. "I'll be in touch," he
said. And without another word he got up and left the ferry boat
cabin.

"Nice to meet you, too," Keegan mumbled to himself.

Back in his apartment, Keegan fixed himself a drink, put on a
Count Basie album and sorted through the material in the black
briefcase. He was impressed. There was a leather folder about
the size of a wallet containing credentials identifying him as a
member of the "White House Security Staff, Investigation Division" with a space for a photograph; a stapled, typewritten list
of all government agencies with the unlisted phone numbers of
the directors; a temporary pass to the "File Section" of the
Federal Bureau of Investigation; a pass permitting him on U.S.
military bases; and a White House business card ambiguously
identifying Don Smith simply as "staff" with his day and night
numbers on the back; and a note:

Mr. Keegan:
    Please affix a current photograph in the proper places
on both the White House and military credentials. No
glamour poses please, a simple passport photo will do.
    Memorize the phone numbers and dispose of the card.

Your contact at the FBI is Glen Kirbo, 4th floor of the bureau building in Washington. He doesn't know what you are up to and doesn't want to know.

Your military clearance will give you access to all unclassified material.

Discretion is the soul of valor.

Smith

The next day Dryman showed up.

He did not walk into the Killarney Rose, he swaggered. There was arrogance in every step as if he were defying everyone in the bar *not* to know who he was. His dress was almost sloppy. A pair of baggy tweed pants atop scuffed-up cowboy boots, a bright red flannel shirt with a white silk scarf draped from under its turned-up collar, a scruffy leather flying jacket with a pair of Air Corps wings over the heart and an army officer's cap, its crown crushed down around his ears.

In his early thirties, Keegan guessed, tallish and well built with auburn-red hair and a pleasant, cherub face, a cocky grin and twinkling blue eyes; a man who looked like he had the world where it hurts. He swaggered straight to the back end of the bar and took a bar stool across from Tiny.

"Canadian on ice in a highball glass, General, Coke on the side," he said, then spun the stool around and sat with his back to the bar, checking the place out. His eyes fixed on Keegan. He smiled and pointed a finger at him.

"I'll bet you're Francis Keegan," he said. His accent was soft Boston, not quite the long A's and E's, but enough of a twang to root him somewhere in New England.

"What makes you think so?" Keegan asked, returning the smile.

"Well sir, you look like you own the place and since Keegan owns this place, I figure you must be him," he said.

"That's pretty good, pal. And who might you be?"

He walked over to Keegan's table, put his two glasses down and stuck out his hand.

"Captain John Dryman, United States Army Air Corps."

"It's a pleasure, Cap'n," Keegan said, looking over the flier's clothes. "Are you on furlough?"

"T.D.," he answered and took a long pull at the whiskey.

"Oh yeah? Where?"

"Here."

"In New York?"

Dryman looked surprised. "Right here. In this bar. With you. I am on temporary duty here as of," he looked at his watch, "one hour from now."

Keegan's brow furrowed. "To do what?"

"I was hoping you'd tell *me* that. Look, I'm not complaining, Mr. Keegan, I got six months left on this tour and then I'm off to China."

"Maybe you haven't heard, there's a war going on in China."

Dryman winked. "Yes sir, sure is. Ever hear of Major Claire Chennault? The Flying Tigers? He's started his own little air force over there. As of January 1, I will be in Kunming, teaching the Japs a few tricks. Meantime I have been assigned to something called White House Security and I'm to take my orders from you. And Boss," he looked around and giggled joyfully to himself, "I can't think of a better place to finish out my tour. The plane's out at Mitchell Field."

"Plane?"

"Old Delilah, a two-seat AT-6. I wouldn't go anywhere without her." He stopped and checked out the bar again. "I have a hard time believing this," he said. "Let me tell you, this is a pilot's dream. I mean, to get assigned to a *bar* taking orders from the owner. The guys will never believe this."

"The guys aren't going to know anything about it, Cap'n," Keegan said seriously. "From now until you're off buzzing the Himalayas you're going to forget everything you see, hear and do. Okay? That's the first and probably last order you'll get from me."

Dryman looked over both shoulders, then leaned over and whispered, "Is this some kind of spy stuff? I mean, the bar, these plain clothes, uh . . . *you.* What's it all about?"

"You'll find out in due time. What do they call you?"

"H.P."

"H.P.? I thought your name was John."

"It is," he said, still grinning his cherub grin. "H.P.—for Hot Pilot, a nickname, incidentally, I have earned the hard way.

Ten years in the Air Corps, the last two instructing snotty college kids, hoping they'll stay alive through the course. I was a test pilot for two years, had my own squadron for a while. Hell, I am so hot, Mr. Keegan, I could set this place on fire with the seat of my pants."

Keegan was astounded. Smith actually had an Air Corps pilot and plane assigned to him. His respect for dog robbers was growing by the day.

"So tell me, H.P.," Keegan said. "If you're so hot, why are you flying courier duty for the White House?"

Dryman shoved his cap to the back of his head and leaned back in the booth.

"Actually . . . I was grounded when the White House called."

"Grounded!" Keegan said with a note of alarm. "For what?"

"I think the specific charge was 'Unauthorized Flying Procedures,' " Dryman said, taking another swig of whiskey.

"And what specifically were these unusual flying procedures?"

"Unauthorized," he corrected. "Everything I do in an airplane is *unusual*, Mr. Keegan. There're only two things I do well. Flying's one of them—and I do it a helluva lot better than anything else. Let me tell you, I can fly anything that has a motor and two wings and I can fly it anywhere, anytime and in any kind of weather. I was *made* to fly, Mr. Keegan, I'm happiest when my feet are about ten thousand feet off the ground."

"That's very interesting but it doesn't answer my question."

"Flight instructing is shitty business, Mr. Keegan—and boring. The same thing day after day. You got to set a good example for the cadets, do everything by the book. Hell, I came off a year flying airmail in weather so bad I'd put a cup of coffee in my lap to make sure I wasn't flying upside down! Then all of a sudden I'm down in Florida wet-nursing a bunch of college boys. So to blow off a little steam, four of us instructors decided to have a race. Thirty miles. The finish line was a bridge out on the coast highway. Well, hell, I could have flown the last five upside down, there wasn't anybody even close to me."

He paused to finish his whiskey and chase it with a sip of Coke.

"Unfortunately," he went on, "my C.O. was driving *over* the bridge at exactly the same time I decided to fly *under* it. Colonel Frederick Metz. No sense of humor. He never saw the other boys, he was too busy ripping out his mustache when he saw me go under him. I said, 'Colonel, what can I say, I got a wild hair up my ass.' He says to me, 'You got more than a wild hair up your ass, Dryman, you also got grounded for ninety days.' Ninety days! Christ, a lifetime! And then . . ." He leaned back with his flashy grin, ". . . God smiled on me."

He waved an arm grandly around the room.

"And what exactly were you told?" Keegan asked, wondering what Smith's instructions to this crazy man were—and how Smith even found him.

"I was told I was a White House courier—how about that, *courier*—and that I was to come here and report to you and do whatever you said . . . within reason." He chuckled. "Whatever that means."

"It means don't get us killed, H.P."

"Never happen," Dryman said, brushing off the remark as if the idea were ludicrous. "Now, what's the first thing I have to know?"

"For the time being, here's all you have to know. I'm looking for a guy. I don't know what he looks like, what his name is, what he does, or where we might find him. And the way things are looking in the world these days, I probably don't have a lot of time to track him down."

Dryman stared at Keegan across the table for several seconds and then he snickered.

"O-kay." He leaned across the table. "What are we *really* going to do?"

"That's it, H.P. I have no idea where we're going to end up, but we're going to start by flying to Washington tomorrow morning. You'll stay in my guest room in the penthouse upstairs and you'll be on call twenty-four hours a day. When we're not working, I don't care what you do. I have three cars, you can use the Rolls. I don't drive it much anymore."

A look of awe crossed Dryman's face.

"Rolls?" he asked reverently. "As in Rolls-Royce?"

"Yeah."

Dryman's grin broadened to a laugh and then a bellow. He

looked around The Rose again and said, "So this is what it looks like."

"What?" Keegan asked.

"Why, heaven, Boss," Dryman cried out through tears of joy. *"Hea-VEN!"*

The file room of the FBI was as spotless as a hospital operating room. There was not a speck of dust on a lamp or table and the floor was polished to a dangerous sheen. The rows of file cabinets stretched the entire length of the wing; row after row after row of gray metal drawers.

Kirbo was a tall, soft-spoken man with thinning blond hair and gentle eyes. He wore a white lab coat over a white shirt and striped tie and was as impeccable as the room itself. He got up from his desk and limped across the room to greet Keegan and Dryman.

"I've been expecting you," he said pleasantly after the introductions. "You certainly didn't waste any time getting here."

"We don't have any to waste, Mr. Kirbo," Keegan answered. "I appreciate your help."

He led them back to a wooden desk, well scarred from years of use but as neat as the rest of the place. He motioned them to chairs.

"What are you looking for?" Kirbo asked. "Perhaps I can help. I've been the custodian of these files for five years now." He tapped his leg. "Car thief ran me down. Can you believe it? Eighteen-year-old kid. Panicked and stomped on the gas. I didn't jump fast enough."

"That's a tough one," said Keegan. "I'm sorry."

"I think my wife secretly figures it was a good trade. I'm home every night and all I had to give up was tennis. So . . . what are we looking for?"

"I'm looking for a man who was either a witness—or maybe was just going to be interrogated—in connection with a federal crime. I don't think he was directly involved in the case although I'm not positive of that."

"What was the offense?"

"I don't know."

"What's his name?"

"I don't know that either."

"Description?"

"No idea."

"What *do* you have?" Kirbo asked.

"I don't have anything, Mr. Kirbo. I don't really know a damn thing about this guy except that he's a good skier, a master of disguise and he's German by birth, although I'm sure he has American credentials. I know he came here sometime in 1933 and disappeared in the spring of '34 because he was involved in some way with an FBI investigation and couldn't stand the heat. He resurfaced a year later, probably with a new identity, and he's been here ever since."

Kirbo waited for a minute or so before he said, "That's it?"

"That and a strong inclination to find him."

"How are you planning to go about that?"

"We're only talking about three months here. March, April and May of 1934. I thought H.P. and I would go through the files for those three months and hope to hell something rings a bell."

The FBI agent laughed. He got up and limped down a row of file cabinets, pulling out drawers and leaving them open as he spoke:

"We have files on stolen government property, extortion, stolen motor vehicles, kidnapping, bank robbery, unlawful flight to avoid prosecution. We have felony crimes committed on government property—except for Indian reservations, national parks and ships at sea—white slavery, interstate transport of stolen property, forgery . . ."

He turned at the end of the row. "Off the top of my head I would say you're looking at, oh . . . two hundred fifty, three hundred cases—a month."

"A *month!*" Dryman gasped.

"That's my guess. Probably seven hundred cases give or take a few. But look on the bright side, you can forget counterfeiting and moonshining, that's the Treasury Department."

"Ah," Dryman said. "A real break."

"In '34 we would have had about thirty field offices, twenty, twenty-five agents to each office and we stayed busy."

Keegan whistled softly to himself. *Seven hundred cases!*

"Mr. Kirbo," he said. "Given the skimpy information I've given you, where would your instincts lead you?"

Kirbo closed the drawers and sat back down.

"First of all, the subject was obviously involved in some other criminal activity or he wouldn't have run."

"Perhaps, but I don't think the FBI knew that. I think his concern was that they would discover that he was using a false identity."

"Maybe there's a warrant out on him. Of course, that's . . . five years ago. I don't know. Depends on how bad the bureau wanted to talk to him. It's worth a try. We'll see what's outstanding from that period." He jotted a note to himself. Then he put down the pencil and shook his head.

"This could be anything," he said. "He could have worked in a government office that was robbed or something like that . . . I mean . . ." He shrugged hopelessly. "We conceivably would interview seventy-five, one hundred people in a situation like that."

"I figure this way," Keegan said. "Whatever it was, he had a little time to make his run before the G-men got there. I mean, this guy disappeared from *some*place where he was probably known by the locals. He had to move fast before the feds got there and still not look suspicious. So I'm guessing it was probably a small town, possibly in the Midwest somewhere, a place it would have taken your people an hour or two to get to."

"Maybe he was just real cautious," Dryman offered.

"That still doesn't narrow down the categories," Kirbo answered. "I'll tell you what. Why don't we start from the beginning. All these files have a cover sheet—the agent in charge always makes a report, kind of a summary of the case, and they are pretty complete. The director doesn't react well to sloppy work. That cover sheet is backed up by all the testimony gathered in the investigation. If Mr. X was so nervous he took a powder, my guess is that he was either witness to something or knew somebody involved in some kind of criminal activity. I doubt that he would just run like that unless he was sure the bureau would turn up his identity problem. So, first round, let's narrow it down. We're looking for a missing witness or person involved in a federal crime in a small Midwest town."

"I say we start the first week in March and check the cover sheets first." Kirbo looked back and forth between Keegan and Dryman. "A real fishing expedition, gentlemen."

They worked long hours, rarely leaving the file room before ten or eleven P.M. In the first week they waded through more than three hundred folders and dozens of old warrants and had set aside two dozen cases involving missing witnesses, suspects or fugitives. Most of those case folders involved known criminals who had "turned rabbit," as Kirbo put it, because they were either involved in the crimes themselves or were wanted for something else. But they had to be checked out. Keegan pulled every file which, for any reason, involved missing people. The pile to be rechecked grew higher and higher.

The cases were as simple as a stolen car and as complex as a scam to embezzle hundreds of thousands of dollars from a regional office of the Department of the Interior. There were missing husbands, wives, sons and daughters sprinkled among the cases. Most were runaways peripherally involved in another crime and all quickly discarded because of age, sex or because they could easily be traced back ten or fifteen years by friends or family members.

They flew to Akron, Ohio, and Buffalo, both wild goose chases.

As one pile got smaller, the other grew. They started making phone calls, checking out the stories of what they called "maybes." People couldn't remember things. The amateur investigators heard a lot of rumors and gossip. Nothing struck a chord.

They flew to Pittsburgh and chased another wild goose. Dryman loved the trips. He occasionally swooped down to five hundred feet to "check out the sunbathers" or did a sudden slow roll or loop to break the monotony of a long trip. Sometimes he sang cowboy songs at the top of his lungs in his Boston accent. Flying anywhere with H.P. was never dull.

"Hey, Boss, are you ever gonna tell me what the hell this

is all about?" Dryman asked as they returned from another abortive trip to Illinois.

"I doubt it."

"Why?"

"It's classified 'secret.' "

"Are you kidding? I got a top secret clearance. Hell, I'm checked out on the Norden bombsight. You can't get any more secret than that."

"You can if it's *my* secret."

Keegan laughed. H.P. did a sudden snap roll that almost broke his neck.

Vanessa sighed with satisfaction and slid off Keegan, lying beside him and rubbing his chest with the palm of her hand, her left leg still stretched across his waist. He turned to her, drawing her in tight, his hands caressing her back. The only escape Keegan and Dryman had from the monotony of their daily drudgery were weekends in New York where Dryman could blow off steam and Keegan could spend time with Vanessa.

"Christ, you feel good," he whispered.

"Thank you."

"No," he said. "Thank *you*."

"I don't mean just the lovemaking."

"For what, then?"

"Letting me come back into your life. That night, six months ago, I was terrified. I just knew you were going to run me off."

"I could never have run you off, Vannie. Hell, we were friends long before we were lovers."

Keegan was a man reborn, fired by two passions: Vanessa and the quest for the Nazi specter nobody else really believed existed. Before Jenny's death, he had been a man obsessed by a consuming love, a love that had become an open wound. His feelings of culpability and remorse were confused by anger and malice. But her death had released him from his self-imposed bondage of guilt and his wrath was now directed at 27. For the first time in years he had a sense of purpose.

"You saved my life, Vannie. My God, I had stopped laughing before you came back in my life."

She tucked her head down beside his and whispered, "Oh, how I adore you, Kee."

Five months had passed since Keegan had learned of Jenny's death in Dachau. Vanessa had sensed the subtle changes in him almost immediately: the sense of relief that came with the end of the waiting; the gradual end to the guilt that had affected his feelings toward her. Freed by divorce, she, too, had been an emotional bomb waiting to explode. Together, they slowly healed each other and as the months passed, they became as impassioned as they had been years before during their brief flirtation in Berlin.

They had celebrated her thirtieth birthday earlier that night with dinner at an Italian restaurant in the Bronx, then had spent the rest of the evening dancing at the Café Rouge where Glenn Miller was playing. It had been a perfect night.

Keegan got up suddenly and padded naked into the kitchen, taking a bottle of champagne from the wine closet.

"Kee," she called to him.

"Yeah?"

"Daddy wants to know if you want to spend Thanksgiving with us this year?"

"Hell, I don't know where I'll even be on Thanksgiving," he answered, searching for a corkscrew. "Do you really want to go to Boston for the day?"

"They're not going to be in Boston, they're going to the island."

"What island?" He called back, digging the corkscrew out of a kitchen drawer.

"Down in Georgia."

"You mean that rich boys' hangout?" he answered, taking two champagne glasses from a cabinet. "Do you want to spend Thanksgiving playing croquet with a bunch of snobby, crotchety old millionaires?"

"I'll tell him you said that," she joked.

"He knows how I feel about that bunch," he said, returning to the bedroom.

"We've been going there for years but it isn't the same as it used to be. Most of the old gang has drifted away. I don't want to go either, but I promised I'd ask."

"How does he feel about us?" Keegan asked, sitting on the edge of the bed and working the cork out of the bottle.

"He never says. Actually, he likes you a lot, otherwise he wouldn't have asked us to go to Jekyll with them."

"Go ahead and tell him what I said," Keegan said and laughed. "We'll eat here. I'll cook dinner."

"Okay," she said. "I'll set the table."

He handed her a glass of champagne, then reached in the drawer of the night table and took out a small box wrapped in silver and bound in black ribbon.

"Happy birthday," he said.

"Oh, Kee, thank you!" she cried with delight.

The card read:

To Vanessa, who restored my faith in the luck of the Irish. Sharing it—with all my love . . .
      Kee
      Aug. 10, 1939

She unwrapped it slowly. It was a small but elegant brooch in the shape of a shamrock, the four leaves made of emeralds outlined in diamonds with a cluster of diamonds at the stem.

"Oh, God, Kee, it's absolutely gorgeous."

"Too bad you can't try it on," he said with a grin and putting his arms around her, he fell backward on the bed with her on top. The phone rang.

"Ignore it," he whispered.

But it persisted. Finally Vanessa reached over, lifted the receiver and held it against his ear.

"Hello?" he said, trying to sound sleepy.

"Mr. Keegan?"

"Yeah?"

"This is Mr. Smith."

"I recognize the voice," Keegan said.

"Have you been listening to the radio?"

"It's the middle of the night, Mr. Smith. No, I'm not listening to the radio."

"Maybe you better," Smith said. "The Germans are mobilizing along the Polish border. If they invade Poland, England

and France will declare war immediately. If you expect to find this Twenty-seven, you better hurry. I don't think we can keep the FBI out of the case much longer . . ."

"We're almost through all the case records," Keegan said forlornly. "Give me another couple of days. If that doesn't work, I'm out of ideas anyway."

He hung up.

"Who is Mr. Smith?" she asked.

"The world's greatest dog robber," he said.

"The what!"

"Just joking," he said, but there was little humor in his tone. "I'm going to have to go back to Washington tomorrow," he went on. "But I don't think I'll be gone much longer."

"You don't sound very happy about it," she said.

"I made a promise to somebody," said Keegan. "Now it looks like I can't keep it."

"Did you try?"

"I did the best I could," he said.

"Then God will forgive you," she said softly.

"I didn't know there were this many crooks in the world," Dryman groaned as the hours got later and the days dragged on. Kirbo helped when he could, a methodical man who worked slowly and overlooked nothing. Their attention span and energy level began to fall rapidly. Keegan began to wonder whether checking the records was ever a good idea. But they did not have an alternative. They made jokes to kill the deadly boredom, sometimes got hooked on a case that was unusual and spent hours poring over the ancillary reports.

"How about a dead witness?" Dryman said one night as he was leafing idly through one of the reports.

"We got enough live ones, H.P." Keegan answered.

"Geez, this guy really had bad luck, didn't he? First his bank gets robbed by Dillinger and if that isn't bad enough, he gets killed in a car wreck the same day."

"I assure you, the guy we're looking for didn't get his neck broken in a car accident. If you're looking for drama, there's a great report over there on a bank job Pretty Boy Floyd pulled in Wisconsin."

"He drowned."

"Beg pardon?"

"He didn't get his neck broken, he drowned."

"Get on with it, Captain. I want live witnesses."

Dryman threw the folder in the discard pile and moved on to the next folder. Hours later when they were getting ready to leave for the night, he picked it up again and started reading through it, rooting through the reports attached to the cover sheet. He didn't know why, it was an impulse.

"Just seems weird," he said to himself.

"What're you mumbling about?" Keegan asked.

"It seems a little weird, this guy is the loan officer in a bank that gets robbed, then drives into the river on his way to dinner with his girlfriend."

"Bad luck, he had real bad luck," Keegan answered and started putting away the folders they had completed. Dryman kept leafing through the reports.

"They killed the chief of police," he said.

"Who?"

"The Dillinger gang. They killed the chief of police in this little town, uh . . . Drew City, Indiana."

"Uh huh," Keegan said, slipping the folders back in their proper places in the drawers.

Then as he was about to put the folder away, Dryman stopped. He pulled a sheet from the thick file.

"Hey Boss?" Dryman said.

"Yeah?"

"This guy from the Dillinger job that drowned?"

"Yeah."

"They never found his body."

42

Dryman roared across Indiana at three hundred feet with a Sinclair Oil Company road map in his lap, trying to figure out exactly where he was.

"Are we lost, H.P.?" Keegan asked. He had the folder on the Dillinger job in his lap, reading through every sheet of paper.

"Of course not," Dryman said, insulted. "I'm looking for landmarks."

"You're going to knock some farmer's hat off if you don't put some altitude under us."

"I can't navigate from ten thousand feet," Dryman complained and changed the subject. "You're really hot on this one, aren't you, Boss?"

"It's desperation. We're running out of subject matter," Keegan answered sourly. "Just keep flying."

Keegan remembered something Eddie Tangier had told him. *If he faked his death it would stop right there. He's out clean. . . .*

Fred Dempsey had supposedly drowned in an auto wreck but they had never found his body. He was the loan officer in the bank and had actually spoken with Dillinger during the robbery. Certainly he had been a prime witness and one of the first the FBI would have interviewed.

"Hey, there it is!" Dryman said, pointing down as if surprised that he had found the town. "Drew City, Indiana. Boy, there's not much to it. I hope we're not going to be here long."

"As long as it takes, H.P."

Dryman buzzed the town once, "to find a place to set down." Then he did a slow chandelle to the right, circled the main intersection and put the low-winged monoplane down on a road just beyond a cluster of houses.

"Beautiful," he congratulated himself.

"How come we never land at airports?" Keegan said as they climbed out of the AT-6 but Dryman ignored the remark. "Got a reception committee," he answered instead.

A string of kids stretched out from the middle of town, running toward them followed by several adults who approached with more reserve. A police car wheeled around them and screeched to a stop a few feet away.

"Everybody okay?" the young policeman asked as he jumped out of the car. Keegan leaned closer to him. He was wearing a chief's badge.

"Just fine, uh . . . Chief . . . ?"

"Yes sir, Chief Luther Conklin, at your service, sir. Not often a plane lands on Main Street Extension."

Keegan flashed his ID. "I'm Francis Keegan, White House Security," he said. The response was always the same: a flurry of excitement, then curiosity ("Why is he here?"), and eventually, "The White House *what*?"

"We're here to run a check on a man who was killed a few years back. You'll probably remember, it was the day Dillinger robbed your bank."

"I certainly do, sir. My boss, Tyler Oglesby, was killed that day. Shot him down in cold blood. But you're talking about Fred Dempsey."

"Right. Fred Dempsey. You knew him, did you?"

"Real well. Once made me a loan just on my name."

"Nice guy, huh?"

"Yes sir. On the quiet side. It was a real tragedy. Both him and Louise Scoby was killed. Car skidded off the road back at the bridge and went into the river. Her father was Fred's boss, Ben Scoby, president of the bank. Damn near killed him."

"I'll bet it did, Luther. I hear they never found the bodies."

"Oh, they found Louise the next day. But it was during the spring thaw and we had a hellacious rain that day. The river could've taken him . . . fifty miles downstream. Probably stuck up under some log somewheres."

"Probably. Tell me about old Fred. How tall was he? What'd he look like?"

"Tall? Oh, six feet, I guess. Had a good build on him for a bookworm type. Dark hair, a little gray around the edges. Gray

eyes, I remember those piercing gray eyes of his. I think he and
Louise were pretty hot and heavy, everybody expected them to
get married. Roger, her brother, took it real hard. He loved
Fred. Fred was good to him. More like a father than old Ben."

"How old is he, the kid?"

"Let's see, he'd be about thirteen now. Works afternoons
down at the filling station."

"And her father's president of the bank?"

"Yes sir. Fine man. How come you're interested in Fred?"

"We're putting the Dillinger files in the archives," Keegan
said casually. "Just filling in some blanks."

"Oh."

"Would Ben Scoby be at the bank now?"

Luther took out a pocket watch and checked it.

"Probably home eatin' lunch about now."

"Mind running' me by there, Chief? Then maybe Captain
Dryman can check around town, talk to some of the folks who
knew Dempsey."

Ben Scoby was a man aged early by time and tragedy, his
straw-thin hair streaked with gray, his eyes faded and lusterless,
his voice shallow and distant. He ushered Keegan into a parlor
that was neat but dusty, a room choked with furniture, doilies
and doodads, the small treasures of life in a room that looked
frozen in time. He had taken off his suit jacket and his suspend-
ers dangled around his hips. A forgotten napkin was tucked
under his chin and as he sat down he noticed it and took it away
with an embarrassed grin.

"Well," his faint voice said, "never have met anybody from
the White House before. Can I get you something? Lemonade,
coffee maybe?"

"No thanks," Keegan said. "Actually we're closing out
some old files, Mr. Scoby. There still is a question about Fred
Dempsey. You know, his body never turned up and, uh . . ."

He let the sentence hang in the air, hoping Scoby would
respond. But Scoby only nodded and said, "Uh huh."

"I understand that your family was close to him?"

"Yes, sir. M'boy Roger loved him. And I guess I hoped that
maybe he and Weezie—my daughter Louise—might marry. It
was . . . it was a . . . devastating experience. Senseless waste . . ."

He shook his head and looked down at his veined hands.

"Mr. Scoby, can I trust your discretion? What I mean is, if I confided something to you, could you keep it quiet?"

"Suppose so, Mr. Keegan. Never have been much for gossipin'."

"This is just speculation, of course. Supposing I told you that there's a chance that . . . *maybe* . . . Fred Dempsey wasn't killed in that accident. That perhaps he got out of that car and managed to get out of the river . . . or maybe never went in the river in the first . . ."

"That's a lie!" a voice cried from the doorway. They looked up at a skinny kid in scuffed-up corduroy pants and an open shirt, glaring defiantly from the doorway.

"Fred didn't do that," the boy insisted angrily. "Fred would've tried to save Weezie and that's why the river took him under. That's what Mr. Taggert said and that's what happened."

"Roger, you're not supposed to be eavesdroppin' on your elders," Scoby scolded. "This is my son, Roger Scoby. Roger, this gentleman is from the White House in Washington, D.C."

"I don't care where he's from, he's a liar!" the boy said, pointing at Keegan.

"Roger!"

"I said *supposing,*" Keegan said. "I was just speculating . . . playing a little game . . ."

"It's a rotten game. Fred was my friend and you shouldn't play games like that about dead people. You lie and you get out of our house!"

"Roger!" the boy's father snapped.

"It's all right," Keegan said. "Loyalty is a rare enough thing, Mr. Scoby. I admire his spunk."

"Go upstairs and do your homework, son," Scoby ordered.

"Finished it already."

"Then just plain go upstairs," Scoby snapped.

"Yes sir." Roger started to leave, then turned back to Keegan. "Isn't right to talk about dead people like that," he admonished Keegan again before leaving.

"Never has gotten over the accident," Scoby said, closing the parlor door. "They were real, real close. You were saying . . .?"

"Who's Taggert?" Keegan asked.

"County coroner over at Lafayette. Why would Fred do

something like that anyway? I mean, if he got out, why didn't he tell us? Why would he've left without saying anything? Don't make a lot of sense, Mr. . . . uh . . ."

"Keegan. And I agree, it really doesn't make a lot of sense but you know how these bureaucrats are. They can't stand loose ends."

"Why would Fred do that?"

A Nazi spy, hiding in Drew City, Indiana, working in his bank, making love to his daughter? The man would think I'm totally nuts, thought Keegan.

"That's why it's far-fetched, Mr. Scoby. You're right, it doesn't make a lot of sense. It's just that never finding the body and all, we're trying to cover all the bases. Want to close the case up once and for all. Sorry I upset the boy."

"Like I said, he'll never get over it," Scoby said sadly. "But then, neither will I. I'll say one thing for Fred, he made the last few months of my daughter's life very happy ones. She didn't have a very pleasant life before he came along. Lost her mother when Roger was born, had to tend to him and me and the house. Fred put some sparkle back in her eyes. I'll always be indebted to him for that."

"Yes sir. Can you remember anything else about him specifically. You wouldn't have a photograph, would you?"

"No sir. Fred wasn't one for snapshots. Was a private man, Fred was, stuck close to his friends, didn't go in much for show."

"Did he have any quirks? Any funny habits?"

Scoby pursed his lips and scratched his temple with a forefinger.

"I just, uh . . . been a long time, Mr. Keegan. Five years this past May. M'mind strays a bit these days."

"Sure."

"Actually Fred was just an average man who treated me and my children with a lot of love and thoughtfulness. Liked the movies. Liked a glass of beer with his dinner but he wasn't a big drinker. He rolled his own cigarettes. Didn't like the store-bought kind. Prince Albert pipe tobacco, as I recall. Had this gold cigarette lighter he was real proud of. Family heirloom, so he said."

"What kind of lighter?"

"It was rectangular, 'bout three inches long." He measured a distance between his thumb and forefinger. " 'Bout like that. Had smooth sides and a wolf's head carved on the top of it. It was solid gold, not plate. Very handsome thing. Looked expensive. He was right proud of that lighter."

"Could you draw a picture of it for me?"

Keegan handed him a notebook and a pencil and Scoby drew a fair likeness of the lighter with a hand that had begun to shake with time.

"Mother lived in Chicago," Scoby went on as he drew. "She was ailing. He used to go up there occasionally to visit with her."

"Was her name Dempsey?"

"Well, I suppose so."

"What I mean is, she could have been a widow or divorced and remarried."

"Uh huh. Never did ask. He didn't talk a lot about himself, sir."

"Do you remember where he was born, Mr. Scoby?"

Scoby looked up with surprise and then grinned. "Born?" he said.

"Yes sir. Where he was from."

"Sorry to laugh, it just seemed like a strange question. Matter of fact I do remember that. He was born in Erie, Pennsylvania. I remember it from his job application. Looked it up on a map once, just out of curiosity."

"Anything else. College? Previous jobs . . ."

Scoby stared at him for several seconds, then shook his head no.

"Right," Keegan said and rose to leave. "Mr. Scoby, you've been a lot of help. As I told you, we're just trying to clean up some loose ends, put this to bed once and for all. Thanks again for your time."

As they reached the front door, Scoby said, "There was one thing about Fred. I've never told anybody this, not even the board down at the bank. Fred had a letter of recommendation from the First Manhattan Bank in New York. I hired him because I liked him and because he had a good, strong letter. He seemed real smart and honest, told me he'd been looking for work for a long time. This was the heart of the Depression, remember.

I forgot about the letter until about a month later I came across
it in my desk drawer and just kind of force of habit, I called the
bank. They never heard of Fred Dempsey."

"And you kept him on?"

"Well, times bein' what they were, lots of people were desperate. By that time I had found him to be an honest man and
a hard worker, easily living up to the recommendation. Besides,
Roger and Weezie were in the picture by then. I decided to
judge for myself rather than broach the subject with him. Never
said anything more about it to anybody till now."

"I appreciate your confidence. Thanks again. Good luck,
Mr. Scoby."

"Same to you, Mr. Keegan."

On the way back to the plane, Conklin turned off the main
road and drove across a bridge, parking on the opposite side of
the river.

"Thought you might like to see this. Here's where the car
went off, right here," Chief Conklin said. "Must've skidded. The
car was . . ." he pointed fifty yards downstream, ". . . about there
when we found it. Weezie was still in it. She had ahold of Fred's
jacket. He must've been swept away. The river was going crazy
that night."

Keegan looked around. It was a barren stretch. There were
no houses nearby, only the railroad tracks that paralleled the
river. Isolated. If Fred Dempsey had wanted to fake his death,
this was the perfect place.

"I didn't get much," Dryman said as they crawled back in the
plane. "Too long ago. People really don't remember him all that
well. Want to hear something funny? That same night, the night
of the bank robbery? There was a big fight in a hobo camp down
the road. Two people were killed."

"A hobo camp? Where?"

"Lafayette."

"No kidding. Do you think you can find Lafayette, H.P.?
And a real airport? I'm getting tired of landing in people's
backyards."

"What're we going to Lafayette for?"

"I want to talk to the coroner."

* * *

Elmo Taggert. who was both funeral director and coroner in
Lafayette, picked them up at the airport in his hearse.

"After you called, I took the trouble of digging out a copy
of the report I filed on Louise Scoby," he said. He handed
Keegan a brown envelope. Keegan took out the report and
scanned it.

"She was dead when she hit the water?" Keegan asked.

"Yes sir. Probably snapped her neck when the car hit the
water or maybe when it went off the road. Broke her neck clean
as a dry branch. Death was instant, that's why her lungs were
dry."

"Was there a bruise?"

"Had several bruises, what you'd expect. The car fell eighteen feet before it struck water. I figure she was looking back or
maybe out the window when it hit. Kind of made a twisting
break."

"A twisting break, you say?"

"Yep." He cracked his hand from the wrist and snapped his
fingers at the same time. "Crack! Just like that," he said. Dryman
grimaced.

They drove in silence for a few minutes more. The report
did not reveal too much more.

"There's one thing I guess I should tell you, although I
don't really see that it makes any difference," Taggert went on.
"I've known Ben Scoby since high school, Mr. Keegan. Didn't
want to see him get hurt any more than he was already, so I
didn't put it in, but . . . Louise Scoby had semen in her vagina
when she died. Obviously she and Fred Dempsey had sexual
intercourse just before they were killed."

Christ, was he that cold? Keegan wondered. Did he lure her
to his house and make love to her before he killed her and
dumped her in the river? A man on the run from the FBI who
takes time out to get laid before he fakes his own death? He
could not have planned it. He didn't know John Dillinger was
going to rob the bank. Everything he had done that fateful day
had to have been spur of the moment. Was 27 really *that* cool?

"How about Dempsey?" Keegan asked.

"Nothing. She had his jacket in her hand, like she was hanging on to him when she died. My guess is, the door flew open
and Dempsey was swept out of the car."

"Isn't it likely he would have surfaced sooner or later?"

"Not really. River's a hundred and fifty miles long, Mr. Keegan. Long stretches of it are uninhabited. Lots of debris from the spring floods. Hell, he could've been jammed under junk somewhere . . ."

Keegan put the report back in the folder. "Tell me about the fight in the hobo camp that night," he said.

"Know about that, do you?"

"Somebody mentioned it to Captain Dryman."

"Well, sir, nobody here's real proud of what happened that night," Taggert said. "There'd been a lot of grumblin' in town about the Hooverville and how big it was gettin'. And the railroad people were gettin' real put out about it. The railroad bulls decided to clean it out. Some of the tents caught on fire. Pregnant woman had a miscarriage. Twelve people in the hospital. And two dead, one of the railroad cops and a 'bo."

"How were they killed?"

"The cop was beat to death with a baseball bat. The 'bo was stabbed. Deep wound. Under the ribs right here and up into the heart. Nasty wound. Must've been a hell of a knife."

He pulled off the road and parked on the shoulder.

"That's where it happened, right over there in Barrow Park," Taggert said, pointing out of the car. There was a broad expanse of green grass and trees beside the railroad. "The 'bo camp spread along the railroad tracks from the edge of the river there all the way down the road t'the edge a town. Real eyesore, it was."

"Where's the railroad come from?" Keegan asked.

"It's a spur. Runs down from Logansport."

"Through Drew City?"

"Yep."

"Were there any witnesses to the killings?"

Taggert nodded. "One man saw the whole thing, even saw the stabbings. Joe Cobb. Worked for the railroad. Lives over on Elm Street."

"Here in town?"

"Yes sir."

"And he was there that night?"

"Right in the middle of it."

"Can we talk to him?"

"Sure. Old Joe'll tell anybody about it who'll listen to him. Problem is, nobody takes him too seriously."

"Why's that?" Dryman asked.

"'Cause he's blind as a mole."

Joe Cobb sat in a rocker on his porch, eyes hidden behind dark glasses, his hands gripping the arms of the chair as if he were afraid he would fall out of it. Years of inactivity had turned muscle to fat. Cobb had a big stomach which folded over his belt, hulking shoulders and a neck the size of a tree trunk. The chair squeaked as he rocked back and forth.

"Remember that night? Of course I remember that night. Last time I ever saw God's sweet earth," he said. "Look, I never took offense at those folks. They was just unfortunates, got wiped out in the bust, tryin' to make a go of it, y'know. The Hooverville was down to Barrow's Point. There was this spate of robberies around town. Nothin' big, mind yuh, but folks was gettin' nervous. Railroad didn't want em. Town didn't want 'em. Hell, *nobody* wanted 'em. About seven-thirty, the local rattler came in . . ."

"That the train that came through Drew City?" Keegan asked.

"Yeah. Bunch of 'bos jumped off and was runnin' down to the camp. They was maybe ten of us from the railroad chasin' them."

He remembered that night all right, like a nightmare montage burned into his mind. Men silhouetted against campfire sparks twirling into a black, windless sky. Dirt-caked fingers protruding from the holes in a pair of red wool gloves. Cardboard lean-tos, worn-out canvas tents, shacks of tar paper. The tired, burned-out faces of defeat and the frightening sounds of the attack. A woman screaming. The sickening sound of wood striking flesh and bone. Flashlight beams crisscrossing through the camp. People running from shanties, bumping into each other in the dark, scrambling to get out of the camp. The sound of a shot. A crazy-eyed hobo, blood spurting down his face from a jagged crack in his forehead, waving a Bible at arm's length as he cried out. "They's upon us, the heathen screws is upon us. Save yourselves, sinners . . . the wicked draw their bows and aim their arrows, to shoot at good men in the darkness.' Psalm eleven, verse two." And a brutal response: "C'mere, you miserable stinkweed."

Chaos.

Oh yes, he remembered it.

"We come up on two of 'em sitting on the edge of the gulch gasping for wind," Cobb went on. "They jumped up when me and Harry Barker seen 'em. 'Here's two more of 'em,' Harry yells, and we went after 'em with our Louisville Sluggers. He hit one of 'em in the back and that fella turned on him like a tiger, grabbed him and spun him around and wrapped an arm around his neck and snapped it with one powerful wrench of his arm. Harry went down and then the 'bo grabbed Harry's bat and he whales him and then he hits me a good one in the stomach. The other 'bo, he says, 'C'mon, we got to get outta here,' and then the first one, he leans over and he pulls a knife out of his shoe— his *shoe!*—and sticks his buddy, just like that. 'Sorry, 'bo,' he says, 'you seen too much.' It was a helluva knife, I'll tell you, not a hunting knife. Had a long narrow blade sharp on both edges."

"Like a dagger?" Keegan asked.

"Yeah, a dagger. Anyway, I started to get m'feet under me and I looked up just as he swung that damn bat as hard as he could and it got me right in the face, right in the eyes."

"Do you remember what he looked like?"

"Remember? Are you kiddin'? It's the last thing I ever saw. He was tall, maybe six feet, husky, black hair, and . . . the way he was dressed. He weren't dressed like no hobo. Had on a flannel shirt, nice pants and what looked like brand new boots. Hadn't been a hobo for very long, else he stole the clothes he was wearing. And there was one other thing. He had different colored eyes."

"Different colored eyes?" Dryman echoed, looking at Keegan skeptically.

"Yep. One gray and one green."

Indian summer had settled over eastern Pennsylvania. The golden colors of fall were replacing the green of summer and a soft breeze stirred the trees in the cemetery. They walked down the rows of markers, looking for the grave of Fred Dempsey. Keegan was more convinced than ever that Dempsey was their man. Dryman, even though he had made the connection, was still skeptical.

On the flight from Indiana to Pennsylvania, Keegan had finally explained their mission to Dryman.

"C'mon, Kee, you really believe this bank clerk was a Nazi spy?"

"I'm convinced of it," Keegan replied.

"Well, if it was him he's probably been dead for five years. Probably floated up somewhere along the river and the dogs ate him," Dryman answered.

"H.P., the railroad runs right past where the car went into the river in Drew City and ends at Lafayette," said Keegan. "Now, supposing you had just faked your own death and you had to get out of town. How would you do it? You can't drive, can't take a bus or hitchhike. You can't afford to be seen. But . . . you could hop a freight. And if Fred Dempsey jumped a rattler, he would've walked into the middle of that brawl at the Hooverville."

"If, if, if," Dryman grumbled. Then Keegan grabbed him by the elbow and pointed to a plot. It was well cared for, the grass neatly trimmed and small plot of flowers at the foot of the section. A large headstone was bracketed on either side by two smaller stones, one of which read:

Frederick Dempsey
Born: Feb. 3, 1900 Died: Feb. 7, 1900

Taken from this earth after four days
Beloved for a lifetime

"Convinced?" an elated Keegan cried.

Keegan was not satisfied with just one subject. Recalling what Tangier had told him, that people on the run sometimes set themselves up with more than one identity, he and Dryman checked the rest of that cemetery and five others in the city. They strolled through the rows of tombstones, jotting down the names of all male children born between 1890 and 1910 who had died within two weeks of their birth. By the end of the day they had the names of twelve male children to check. It was a long shot, Keegan agreed, but so was the search that had turned up Fred Dempsey.

They had little trouble getting birth certificates of all twelve. Death certificates were recorded on a separate floor in the courthouse. Eddie Tangier was right, the state made no correlation between life and death. The certificates were not cross-referenced. As far as the clerk in the vital statistics department knew, Fred Dempsey was alive and well. Little did she realize how alive and well he was.

Keegan met Mr. Smith in a small Chinese restaurant in Georgetown. By arrangement, Keegan arrived first and was ushered into a small private room in the back. Smith arrived ten minutes later, entering through a back door after taking his usual circuitous route. The tall, enigmatic dog robber listened patiently as Keegan described the trip to Drew City and Erie, Pennsylvania.

"So . . . we know our Mr. X assumed the identity of Fred Dempsey," Keegan concluded. "He lived in Drew City for nine months, never caused any trouble and might have even married Louise Scoby if fate disguised as John Dillinger hadn't walked into his life."

"Seems to me you may be stretching a point, tying him to the killer in the hobo camp," Smith answered.

"Why? It makes perfect sense."

"But there's no proof . . ."

"We're not trying the son of a bitch in court, Mr. Smith. I assure you, if Fred Dempsey and Twenty-seven are one and the same, then he did not die. He's alive and well. He is six feet tall, about one-eighty, green eyes. Obviously he was wearing those new-type colored contact lenses and he lost one in the fight at the Hooverville."

"How do you know that?" Smith asked skeptically.

"We know this guy is a master of disguise. He had gray eyes when he lived in Drew City. Joe Cobb saw a man with one gray eye and one green eye. It's obvious that Twenty-seven lost one of the gray lenses in the fight and his eyes are green. And since he went to all that trouble to change the color of his eyes and he's German, my guess is he's blond. He uses a gold cigarette lighter with a wolf's head on the top, rolls his own cigarettes using Prince Albert tobacco, loves movies and the ladies, and hasn't a trace of an accent. I'll tell you something else, this guy doesn't shake. He's one cool operator. He shacked up with Louise Scoby *knowing the G-men were on their way to Drew City.* And he likes to kill people, Mr. Smith. He shacked up with Louise Scoby for months, then broke her neck and dumped her in the river like that . . ." he snapped his fingers sharply ". . . to set up an alibi. He killed two men and blinded another one because they saw him and might tie him back to Fred Dempsey in Drew City. I'm beginning to understand this guy, Mr. Smith. I'm beginning to know how he thinks and how he operates."

"If what you say is true, he's more dangerous than we anticipated."

"I never doubted that for a moment."

Keegan took a list of names from his pocket.

"I've got twelve names for you. I believe one of them is our German sleeper agent. All of them were born in Erie, Pennsylvania, between 1890 and 1910. If I'm right, he applied for *two* passports in May 1933, one under the name Fred Dempsey, the other under one of those names on that list. He'd want to be able to get to Europe, to be able to escape in case something else happened."

He leaned across the table, his eyes alive with excitement.

"If I can get a look at his passport application, I'll know what he looks like and possibly where he lives now."

"Doesn't it seem likely he's changed identities again since then?"

"Why? He has no idea we're on to him. If he's settled in some place, like he was in Drew City, why would he change? The more accepted he is, the safer he is."

"That's assuming Dempsey was your man."

"He's got to be."

"But supposing you're wrong, Mr. Keegan?"

"Then I'm beat," Keegan said. "But I don't believe I am. I'm right about Dempsey, Mr. Smith, and if any of those twelve names matches up to a passport application, we got our man."

"That kind of information is highly confidential. This is not an easy task."

"C'mon," Keegan said. "Nothing's too tough for the world's greatest dog robber."

Smith sighed. He recognized cajolery and flattery—but he was not immune to it. He toyed with the list for a few moments and shrugged.

"I'll see what I can do."

Keegan and Dryman checked into the Mayflower to await the result of Mr. Smith's investigation. Two days later, Smith met Keegan in the back room of the Regal restaurant a few blocks from the Capitol.

"Sorry I'm late," he said. "I had to drive all over the city to dump the twins."

"What's the latest news?"

"The whole city's in an uproar. Everybody expects it's just a matter of days before Hitler attacks Poland. Neville Chamberlain's 'peace in our time' treaty wasn't worth a lead nickel."

He put a small brown envelope on the table in front of Keegan.

"You better face facts, Mr. Keegan," Smith said as Keegan eagerly checked the contents of the envelope. "If this lead doesn't pan out and Germany attacks Poland, you're off the case. Hoover's gone bananas on the subject of security." He stopped for a moment and nodded toward the contents of the envelope. "And I broke at least three laws to get you that information."

"Isn't that what dog robbing is all about?" Keegan answered with his crooked grin.

He read the passport application and his heart picked up a few beats. There was no photograph, but there was an artist's sketch showing a handsome man with a dark beard, longish hair and spectacles.

"I couldn't lift the photograph so I had a sketch made for you," said Smith. "Of course he could have shaved off his beard, changed his hair color . . . Well, what do you think?"

"Could be him," Keegan said flatly.

He read the passport information:

John Trexler, born Erie, Pa., November 2, 1898.
Passport application: August 12, 1933. Renewed: February 9, 1938.
Occupation: Ski instructor.
Address: Mountain Way, Aspen, Colorado.

He was hiding his excitement. Now he was sure that John Trexler was Fred Dempsey and both were *Siebenundzwanzig,* the Nazi agent 27. Keegan knew the real John Trexler was born in Erie on that date and had died a week later. This had to be their man.

"Listen, Keegan, don't go grandstanding on this, okay?" said Smith, and for the first time he showed concern. "If you're sure he's your man, take plenty of help."

"Oh, absolutely, Mr. Smith. Absolutely."

In the weather room at National Airport, Dryman pored over maps and weather charts, shaking his head as he studied them.

"This could be hairy, Boss, very hairy," he said, holding a thermal chart next to the sectional map. "We got a front moving in from Canada. They already had their first snowstorm of the season earlier this week. There's four inches of snow on the ground and a blizzard coming in."

He looked up at Keegan.

"Mountains all over the place. Big mountains—like fifteen-thousand-footers—and this place is in a pocket. Look here."

He pointed to a large sectional of the area. The town was surrounded by mountains, two of which, to the north and south, were indeed almost fifteen thousand feet high. Dryman traced his finger down a heavy line that coursed south a few miles west of the town.

"That's the Continental Divide. We're gonna have to fly

over it and nose-dive into that airfield, which I'll guess is nothing but a cow pasture with a wind sock. I say we forget it until after the front moves by."

"Why should that bother you, you're the one who prefers to land on highways and in cornfields?" Keegan answered. "How much time do we have before the storm hits?"

Dryman read the weather strip.

"They're expecting bad weather to move in by late afternoon. It's a seven-, eight-hour flight when you figure in at least three stops for gas." He looked at his watch. Five A.M. "If we're real lucky we may be able to sneak in ahead of the storm. Otherwise we'll end up in Lost Overshoe, Nebraska, or some dipshit town in Kansas. That's if we don't wind up in the side of a mountain."

"Hey, Mister Hot Pilot, you crapping out on me? You're the one was bragging about flying through dishwater when you were hauling the mail."

"That's hittin' below the belt, Kee. That's a real shot in the groin. We're looking at mountains and snow here."

"I say we give it a shot, H.P. If Aspen does get snowed in and we have to sit down someplace along the way, remember, he can't get *out* either. At least we'll be close. The minute the storm blows over we can move on him."

"It's gonna be colder'n hell out there."

"Then we'll have to get some warm clothes." Keegan said. "And we need to get ourselves a couple of pistols. . . ."

They had picked up a strong tail wind somewhere over Missouri and were approaching the Colorado Rockies by three P.M. Ahead of them was a wall of ragged, threatening mountains. Black storm clouds broiled over angry, towering peaks draped in snow and ice and surrounded by ragged tors. As they flew toward the mass of rock and snow, howling winds began buffeting the small plane. For fifteen minutes Dryman tried to raise the radio at the Aspen airport without success. The storm rushing down from the north turned afternoon into twilight. The fuel gauge was twitching on empty.

Dryman pressed the button on his mike.

"Aspen local this is Army 457, do you read me? Over."

Nothing.

"Either I can't break through all this interference," he yelled back to Keegan, "or they've shut down because of the storm."

"Let's just find the damn strip and get on the ground," Keegan answered.

"Easier said than done," Dryman answered. "There's a fifteen-thousand-foot mountain between us and the town and so much snow on the ground we probably won't be able to see it anyway. And these clouds aren't helping. It's getting darker by the minute."

"Then put it down on the highway or in a field or any-damn-where!"

"Aspen local, Aspen local," Dryman kept repeating. "This is a distress call. This is Army 457 calling Aspen local . . ."

The radio crackled with static and then a faint voice faded in and out: ". . . is Aspen . . . the air . . . losed . . . you can hea . . . on the phone and . . ."

"Aspen local, this is Army 457. I'm having trouble reading you. We are about twenty miles south of you on the opposite side of Castle Peak. Do you read?"

They were flying below the tops of the mountains and the winds became stronger, more erratic. The plane, buffeted by the turbulence, suddenly dropped off on one wing and spun out. Dryman slammed the stick forward as the plane spiraled out, pulled back on the throttle and stopped the spin. He pulled out of the drive and swept across a snow-swept valley. The mountains towered above them. Keegan could almost reach out and touch the straggly pine trees as the plane slowly started to climb back up. Sheer cliffs surrounded them.

Dryman frantically checked the map. There had to be a way out of the pocket they had dropped into. He began to circle and climb, circle and climb, going for altitude to clear the fifteen-thousand-foot Sawatch Range. But as they hit fourteen thousand feet the engine began to falter again. The plane shuddered as Dryman pushed it to the limit, but wind, storm and thin air were choking out the engine. He circled again as he scanned the sectional map in his lap. Then he saw a notation between two of the mountain peaks, "Independence Pass, 12,095 feet."

"I can't seem to bust fifteen thousand feet," Dryman called back to Keegan. "There's a pass over there to our west. It's our only chance to get on the other side of this range."

He tightened his circles, the plane skimming the treetops as he searched for the cleft in the mountain range.

"There!" Keegan cried. "Off to the left."

It was a narrow gorge that sliced deep into the foreboding wall of mountains. Dryman peeled off and dove straight into the cut. Keegan's knuckles were white. The plane was roaring through a claustrophobic canyon less than a hundred yards wide with sheer cliffs on both sides and harsh winds still wracking them.

As they zoomed out the end of the pass, the radio crackled to life:

"This is Aspen local, Army 457. Our field is closed . . . I can direct you south to . . ."

"Negative, negative," Dryman said, cutting him off. "I'm dodging mountains out here, I'm ten feet in front of a blizzard and I'm flying on fumes. I need some landing instructions fast."

"Repeat, the field is *closed*, Army 457. It's already beginning to snow here and . . ."

"Listen here, Aspen, I'm running out of fuel and it's getting darker by the second. I'm coming down. Give me wind and runway instructions."

"You can't even *see* the runway," came the answer. "We haven't cleared it off since the storm last week. We've still got two or three inches of snow out there!"

"Then turn on your lights and say a prayer," Dryman answered.

"We haven't got any lights! Wait a minute . . . I can hear you. You're north of the field."

"You got a truck or car there?"

"Yes, sir."

"Well pull out on the front end of the runway, aim it down the strip and turn on the lights. I'll have to feel this one in."

"Mister, you're crazy!"

"You're probably right, but I don't have any choice. I'm going to have to dump this into that pocket you're in. Get movin', pal . . ."

There were mountains all around them and the snow was slashing at the cabin windows. Dryman peeled up on one wing and dove down the side of one of the mountains, then pulled out and skimmed across the village at about five hundred feet.

"I think the airport's over there someplace," he said, pointing vaguely to the left.

"You don't know?"

"Hey, Boss, I can't see anything in front of us. I'm really flying by the seat of my pants."

Suddenly in front of and below them, through the slashing snow pellets, they saw headlights flash on.

"Glorioski, Sandy, there it is," Dryman yelled enthusiastically. "All we gotta do now is land."

The plane roared across the east-west strip heading south. Dryman peeled up, stood the plane on her wing and swung around in a tight arc one hundred feet off the ground, did a perfect 270-degree bank, leveled off, dropped down and hopscotched over the top of the car, clearing it by five feet.

"Hang on!" Dryman yelled as he cut power and pulled the nose up. The plane whooshed down and thudded hard on the frozen ground. Snow showered up over the wings and pummeled the cabin. Dryman pumped the brakes, trying to keep the plane from skidding out from under him. The fence at the end of the field rushed toward them. Then he slammed hard on the right brake and the plane spun around twice and stopped.

They sat for a full minute staring out at the snow flurries that fluttered around them.

"Beautiful," the pilot finally said half aloud. He turned and looked back at the rear cockpit. A pale Keegan smiled wanly back at him and gave him a thumbs-up sign.

"Always remember," Dryman said with a laugh. "Any one you can walk away from is a good one."

The airport manager drove up through the snow, the chains on his tires clinking against the fenders of his car. He jumped out, a young redheaded man in his mid-twenties, his eyes still bugged from the spectacle of watching Dryman make it safely to the ground.

"You guys okay?" he said as they climbed out of the plane.

"I'm ten years older than I was an hour ago," Keegan replied with a sigh.

"Amazing! Amazing!" the young man yelled. "I've never seen anybody fly like that!"

"And probably never will again," Dryman said, climbing out of the plane. "You did real good, fella. What's your name?"

"Jesse Manners," he said sticking out his hand. Keegan jumped down from the wing and slogged through ankle-deep snow to shake hands with the young man.

"Keegan, White House Security," he said. "This is my pilot, Captain Dryman."

"Jesse Manners," he repeated, shaking their hands. "I manage the airport here, such as it is. Why don't you taxi over to the hangar? Least it'll keep your plane from freezing up."

"Good idea," Dryman agreed.

"Mind if I drive with you?" Keegan asked. "I need to call the sheriff."

"Sure, but he ain't here. He's over at Glenwood Springs to talk to the sheriff there. I seen him at lunch just as he was leavin'. You might try Duane Harris, he's the forest ranger in charge, usually watches out for things when the sheriff's off somewhere."

"He'll do."

The ranger sounded friendly and a little awed by the fact that they had flown into Aspen in such bad weather. Manners provided hot coffee while they waited for Harris to drive fifteen miles from town to the airport. Keegan avoided Manners's questions while they waited and finally the youthful manager went into the hangar to help Dryman check out the AT-6. Half an hour later a husky forest ranger in a heavy sheepskin jacket entered the airport office. He was in his late twenties, a pleasant, shaggy-haired man with the beginnings of a beard and a quick smile.

"Mr. Keegan? Duane Harris, U.S. Forestry Station," he introduced himself.

"Good to see you," Keegan said. "I really appreciate your help in this. Meet my pilot, Captain Dryman, H.P. for short." He showed Harris his credentials and drew the ranger aside, speaking in a low voice. Manners, one of Aspen's most notorious gossips, appeared to ignore them but his curious ears were keened to the conversation.

"I'm looking for a man named Trexler, John Trexler? You know him?"

"Why, hell, everybody knows Johnny. He works ski patrol for Highlands Resort. Is there a problem?"

"Just need to talk to him," Keegan said. "I hate to impose on you, but the sheriff's out of town and I thought maybe you could help us out."

"Sure enough. Let's get trottin', though, this weather's not gonna get any better. How the hell did you get in here anyway?"

"A great pilot and the luck of the Irish," Keegan said with a smile as they went out into the storm.

Jesse Manners could hardly wait until Harris was on his way before he grabbed for the phone.

In his cabin, John Trexler was mentally tossing a coin. He had planned to drive the fifty miles into Leadville for the weekend but with the storm coming in he was having second thoughts. The phone rang. It was Jesse Manners at the airport.

"Hey, Johnny, you been holding out on everybody?" Manners asked.

"What do you mean?"

"About the White House?"

"What White House?"

"*The* White House. You some kind of big shot?"

"What the hell're you talking about, Jesse?"

"An army plane just put on one hell of an air show out here. Came in right under the storm. Two guys from the White House. They're comin' out to talk to you. What's going' on, old buddy?"

"They're from the White House?" Trexler repeated.

"That's what they said. White House Security."

White House Security? Trexler's mind started racing. *What could that be?*

"It's a secret, kid," he said calmly. "Tell you about it later. And listen, Jesse, keep it under your hat for now, okay? It's a surprise."

"Sure, Johnny."

Trexler cradled the phone and stood motionless in the room, his mind bombarded by questions. What in hell would two men from White House Security want with him? What the hell *was* White House Security? Did it have something to do with immigration? Had someone accidentally stumbled onto his false identity?

Was there a breach in security?

Impossible! Vierhaus, Hitler and Ludwig were the only ones who even knew of his existence. And yet, of all the possibilities that ran through his mind, that one seemed the most logical. While a breach was remote, it was the only thing that made sense.

The question was moot anyway. He could not take a chance, he had to run for it. He needed time and a lot of luck for what was ahead. He had to create another illusion.

He had his knapsack ready. After the incident in Drew City, Trexler was always ready to make an immediate escape. He went into the bedroom and lowered a ladder leading to a storage space in the ceiling of the cabin. He went up with a flashlight, unlocked a footlocker stored there and took out a rucksack. He had everything he needed in it: identification, cash, his long knife, a .45 Colt automatic and clothes. He tied the SS dagger to his right calf and strapped on a money belt containing his cash.

As he outfitted himself, he was working out a plan, one of several options he had formulated through the years. He went back down and threw enough clothes in his suitcase to appear as though he would be away for a couple of days.

He returned to the living room and called the ski patrol office at the lodge. Wes Childress, the patrol captain, answered.

"Wes, it's Johnny," he said, sounding as casual as possible. "I'm heading out for Leadville. Just thought I'd check out. I should be back Monday if the roads are clear."

"You're not going to make it, kiddo," Childress answered. "This blizzard's on us already."

"If I hurry I can run down Route 82 and beat it to the main highway. Is Soapie still planning to make the run to Copperhead Ridge?"

"Yeah, I just talked to him."

"Does he need help?"

"Nah, you know Old Soap. He's used to this shit."

"Okay. See you Monday."

"You're nuts, pal. Good luck."

"Thanks."

Trexler looked at his watch. He had thirty minutes at best. He left the cabin, locked it, threw his suitcase in the trunk of his car and drove down the two-hundred-yard driveway to the mountain road leading back into town. But he didn't turn toward town, he headed up the mountain toward Soapie's cabin.

On the way into town, Harris checked the ski patrol office at Highlands Resort, which employed Trexler.

"Hey Wes, it's Duane. Do you know John Trexler's location?"

"Yeah. He was in his cabin about ten minutes ago. But he's planning on trying to beat the storm into Leadville. I think he's got a lady friend there."

"How's he planning to go?"

"Route 82. It's still open. Why?"

"Got a couple of visitors want to see him."

"You may just miss him."

"Thanks," Harris said. He laid the radio mike on the seat beside him.

They drove through a small quaint village and a mile or so beyond it, Harris slowed down.

"This is the road up to his place," Harris said. "It's a mile or so up the trail. His cabin sits about two hundred yards off the road." He looked out the side window as he turned into a narrow lane that led up through the trees. Mounds of virgin snow outlined the narrow roadway.

"We're in luck," Harris said. "No tracks. He must still be up there."

"Any other road out of here?" Keegan asked.

"Nope, it dead-ends up at Soapie Kramer's ranger station."

"How far's that?"

"Four, five miles."

Harris dropped into low gear and turned up the road.

"How long've you known Trexler?" Keegan asked.

"Oh, Johnny's been around these parts for a few years now.

He's worked for all the resorts through the years. Half a dozen companies have tried to make a go of it and failed. He's with the Highlands people now and it looks like they're here to stay."

"What's he like?"

"Just one of the guys. Everybody likes him. Helluva skier. He and Soapie saved a couple of climbers trapped up on Mount Elbert last year. They were almost to the top, fourteen thousand feet, in weather worse than this. When you said you were from the White House I thought maybe the president was gonna give 'em a medal or something."

"I hadn't heard that," Keegan said sardonically. He reached under his arm, took out an army .45 and checked the clip. Dryman did the same. Harris looked over at Keegan with surprise.

"Hey," he said. "What's going on?"

"Duane, I'm going to level with you," Keegan answered. "If this guy's who we think he is, he's very, very dangerous."

"John *Trexler*!"

"That's right. This is the way we're going to play it. The minute he opens the door, we'll rush him and get the drop on him."

"What did he do?" Harris asked. There was alarm in every syllable.

"For starters, he's killed three people that we know about," Keegan answered.

"Sweet Jesus!" Harris said.

"What if he gets crazy?" Dryman asked. "What if he's got a gun?"

Keegan's heart was pumping overtime but he was outwardly calm. "Then I'll blow his brains out," he answered without hesitation.

"Maybe I better call my boss," Harris said nervously. "Maybe we ought to go back into town and get some help."

"Don't worry about it," said Keegan. "He's not expecting us. We'll just stay calm. Be pleasant as we approach the place. If he's outside, introduce us as a couple of rangers from the district office in Denver. Then we'll take him."

"I've never done anything like this before," Harris said.

"That's okay, neither have we," Keegan answered.

Harris expertly negotiated the snow-piled drive, the back end of the vehicle groaning as its four-wheel drive urged it up the lane. When they reached the driveway leading to Trexler's cabin, Harris stopped.

"Don't see his car," he said. He rolled down the window and checked the road.

The snow was falling harder and the wind was picking up. Harris knelt down and checked the tracks leading up the mountain.

"Funny, no tracks going down, they're all going up the slope," Harris said.

"What the hell's up there, anyway?" Keegan asked.

"Ranger station. Soapie Kramer lives up there. But he was planning to try to beat the storm and head up to Copperhead Ridge to the high station on avalanche patrol—just in case anybody gets lost on the mountain."

He's running, thought Keegan. *Somebody tipped the son of a bitch off and he's running.*

"How good's this Kramer?" he asked Harris.

"Twelve years in these mountains. Don't figure they get any better."

"How good are you, Duane?"

"Not that good. I'm good but I'm not old Soapie."

"How about Trexler?" Dryman asked.

"He's damn good, too," said Harris. "Could have been a real competitor but he wasn't interested. Likes the quiet life."

"Does he smoke?" Keegan asked.

"Smoke? Yeah. Rolls his own."

"Does he have a cigarette lighter?" Dryman said.

"Why, yes . . ."

"Gold lighter with a wolf's head on the top?" Keegan said.

"Yeah," said Harris with surprise. "You must know him pretty well."

"I know him real well," said Keegan flatly. "What d'you say? Let's give it a shot."

Harris shook his head as he climbed back in the car.

"I'll try anything once," he said. "But we got about a twenty-five-degree slope here. I can't promise anything."

"I'm sure you'll do your best," Keegan said.

* * *

Trexler drove as fast as his Hudson Terraplane would safely maneuver the road to Dutchman Flat and Soapie Kramer's cabin. He was reviewing his plan, checking it for holes.

The road finally began to level off. He picked up speed, coursing down through the ridge forest until suddenly he burst out onto the flatland, a plateau near the top of the mountain. Snow flurries were just beginning and thick woolly clouds were tumbling over the mountaintops, bringing the big wind with them.

What has nature got against me? he thought to himself. First it was the dust storms. Now this. But he wasn't complaining. Actually the storm would provide his cover. He needed a couple of days and the brewing storm just might provide them. He parked near the cabin, aiming the car out toward the lake that adjoined Kramer's place. Snow flurries danced across the ice surface. He walked directly to the corner of the building. The phone line was stretched down the side of the cabin, entering it through an outlet near the base of the house. Trexler opened his penknife and cut the wire.

He went around to the front, peered through the glass panel.

Thank God! Kramer was still there.

Snow lashed the windshield and Harris leaned forward squinting as he guided the black '35 Ford, twisting and skidding, up the steep dirt road.

"We're not gonna make this, gentlemen," Harris said. "Need chains. All I got's snow tires."

Keegan was also straining his eyes ahead on the road.

"Keep trying," he said.

The car fishtailed as the road turned to slush beneath them. The tires started spinning faster and the Ford began to slow. Then suddenly the rear end jerked to the right. Harris spun the wheel to compensate but he was not quick enough. The rear wheel went off the road.

There was a ten-foot drop beside them.

Harris slammed down the pedal, trying to get traction. The wheel spun feverishly, spewing mud and snow behind it, hit a fallen tree and caught. Smoke billowed from tire and log as Harris continued to spin the wheels. The Ford tilted slightly, felt for a moment like it was going to roll over, then righted itself.

Harris blew out a breath and lowered his head on the steering wheel.

"Phew, that's a ten-footer there," he said. "Long fall in a car."

Keegan opened the door and jumped out. He was closer to the edge than he realized. His feet foundered in the muddy snow and he had to grab the door to keep from falling into the gully. He pulled himself back up slowly and tried to shield his eyes against the frigid snow which, whipped by a deep, mournful wind, swirled through the pine forest and started to drift against the side of the vehicle. He slowly worked his way to the front of the car, then stared down at the half-frozen creek below. It looked more like a hundred feet than ten. His gaze moved to the rear of the vehicle. The left rear wheel of the Ford was half off the road, wedged against a fallen tree.

Harris got out and appraised the situation.

"Maybe I can bully it outa there," he said, cupping his hands and yelling in Keegan's ear. "If I can jockey it back on the trail . . ."

"How long will it take to drive up there from here?" Keegan yelled back, interrupting him.

"We can't get up this road, sir. Not without chains. Even then it'd be hit or miss."

"How much farther is it?" Keegan asked.

"At least a mile."

"We'll walk."

"In this storm?" Harris said with astonishment. He shook his head. "Not a chance. I know this country better'n I know my own bedroom but in this stuff we could miss the cabin. Easy as fallin' off a roof to get lost. Hell, man, you'd freeze to death up here. A mile is forever in a blizzard."

Keegan slammed his fist on the hood.

"Goddamn it, we've got our fingertips on him!" he yelled. "He's only a bloody mile ahead of us!"

"Okay if we get back in the car and think this out?" Harris yelled. They scrambled back inside the car. Keegan pulled off his gloves and breathed on his frozen fingers.

"He's not going anywhere in this weather," Harris said, breathing hard. "He and Soapie will have to hole up there."

"This guy isn't holing up anywhere," Keegan said. "I know him. He's a survivor. He's dedicated. He's on a mission. And he's on the run. Let me tell you something, Duane. When he's on the run he's harder to stop than the Twentieth Century Limited."

"Hey, Trexler's good but nobody could ski through the storm that's brewing."

"He can and will. And we can't stop him because we're *stuck in the* . . . !"

Keegan suddenly sat bolt upright.

"My God," he said. "I know what he's going to do. Harris, get on the radio. Tell them to get in touch with Soapie Kramer immediately. If Trexler shows up at his station, Kramer is to hold him at gunpoint. He's a very dangerous man."

"They won't believe me!"

"Then I'll tell them. Do it! Your man Soapie's life depends on it."

"Kee . . ." Dryman started.

"Can it, Dry."

"But . . ."

Keegan whirled in the front seat and glared at Dryman. "What?"

He knew what concerned Dryman. Supposing they were wrong about Trexler? Hold him at gunpoint? Dryman was having trouble with that.

"The man's life could be at stake, Dry," Keegan said quietly.

Harris raised base station but the reception was poor. Static crackled from the speaker.

"Base, this is Harris. Mr. Keegan of the White House staff says you should radio Soapie Kramer pronto and tell him John Trexler is dangerous and to arrest him."

The radio popped and snapped and then: ". . . reception. Please repeat . . ."

"Christ, they can't read us," Keegan said.

The ranger repeated the message. Static and a fluctuating signal obscured part of the response but they picked up enough of it.

". . . ler left for Leadville an hour . . . Soapie . . . to Copperhead Ridge . . . camp . . . radio shut down."

Keegan's shoulders sagged.

"He's doing it again," Keegan said half aloud.

"Doing what?" Harris asked.

Just like Drew City, he thought. It worked once, he's going to do it again.

I know you, you bastard. I know how you think. Always ready to run. Always got a back door.

"Doing what?" Harris repeated.

"Getting away," Keegan answered.

Soapie Kramer was leaning over the large Mercator projection, pinned by its corners to a drawing table. He traced a trail with his finger, east, then south.

"I got the mountain between me and the wind most of the way," he said. "It's only six miles up there. The last . . . two hundred yards'll be the worst. I ought to be able to make it before dark."

"Well, far be it from me to argue but base says this one's gonna be a pistol," said Trexler.

"All the more reason for me to be up there," said Kramer, then he snapped his fingers. "Hey, what's the matter with us? I can radio down there, tell 'em not to worry."

Trexler hesitated for only a moment. He had forgotten about the radio. A mistake, but not a serious one. It was time to make his move. Kramer walked into the adjoining room. Large glass windows on three sides of the room overlooked the valley, now obscured by windswept snow. The radio was on a table in front of the center window.

"I already shut 'er down," he said, flipping on the power.

Trexler walked up behind him, leaned over, and reaching under his pants leg, pulled the SS dagger from the sheath strapped to his ankle.

"I don't think I'd do that, Soapie," he said.

The ranger turned to him.

"Why n . . . ?"

Trexler's arm was already making a powerful underhand swing. It arched upward almost from the floor and buried in Kramer's stomach just under the rib cage. The long blade sliced deep and up and pierced Kramer's heart.

"Oh," he cried out, his eyes bulging with surprise.

Trexler grabbed Kramer by the collar, spun him around and dropped him on his back on the rug. Kramer sighed once as Trexler slammed his foot against his chest and pulled the knife out. He stuck the point of the long knife into Kramer's throat just under one ear and slashed it. Blood gushed like a fountain from under Kramer's chin. Trexler quickly rolled him up in the rug before the blood could spread.

A mile away, Ranger Harris was getting fidgety. They had to do something.

"What the hell," Harris said finally, "I'll try to back down to Trexler's place. Least we won't freeze to death."

Shifting quickly between first and reverse, he rocked the car back and forth. The tire dug into the fallen tree, started to jog back onto the road, but as it did the tree gave way and dropped into the gully. The front end of the Ford lifted straight up and twisted sideways.

"Jesus, we're goin' over!" Harris screamed as the Ford's rear end dropped over the precipice and the car rolled over and plunged upside down into the gulch.

At Kramer's cabin, Trexler dragged the ranger's rug-wrapped body down the front steps of the cabin and dropped it beside the trunk of his car. He opened the trunk, stuffed Kramer's body in it, then hurried back inside the cabin. He went through Kramer's rucksack, found an army Colt .45 and a box of cartridges and stuffed them in his own knapsack. He went back outside and threw Kramer's rucksack in beside him. He slammed the lid down, got in and drove to the edge of the lake. He parked, walked out on the ice with a stick and tried to punch a hole in the ice. Too thick. Leaning over, he carefully worked his way around the lake until he spotted a large clear space below the ice, an air bubble about five feet across. He jabbed the stick into the ice until it punched through. An inch thick, he figured.

He hurried back to the car and put it in gear. Driving with the door open, he steered it out onto the lake and aimed at the air hole. Then he slammed down the gas pedal and rolled out of the car, skidding and rolling across the frozen surface until he slid to a stop. He rose to his knees and scurried on all fours toward shore. The car slowed, rolled out to the middle of the lake. Through the wind, 27 heard the ice groan. He reached hard ground and looked back. The car had almost stopped and had skidded sideways. The ice groaned again, then there was a sharp crack like lightning, and another, even louder than the first, and suddenly the front wheels of the car crashed through the ice. The surface shattered and the front end of the automobile plunged through the frozen surface and the car slid nose down into the lake. A large air bubble burst through the hole.

Then there was only the sound of the wind.

Trexler snapped a pine branch off a tree and walking backwards, dusted the car tracks and his own footprints, smoothing them out. Then he hurried back to the cabin.

Keegan was lying on his back against the door on his side of the Ford. It had flipped three quarters of the way over and jolted to a stop, lodged five feet above the ground against a thick pine tree. Harris was hanging upside down, his head in Keegan's lap. He was unconscious. Keegan cautiously looked over his shoulder and out the window. He was staring straight into the deep gully.

Keegan struggled to get his feet under him. He had cracked his ribs but otherwise was uninjured. Harris's right leg was twisted grotesquely above him, caught between the clutch and brake pedals. In the backseat, Dryman lay on his back with his knees against his chest. A large bruise was beginning to discolor his forehead.

"You okay?" Keegan asked.

"Yeah," said Dryman, gingerly touching his forehead and flinching. "Though I'm gonna have the worst headache in history."

"Harris's out. How's your first aid?"

"I took the army course about ten years ago."

"Well, you're one up on me," said Keegan. Hefting Harris with his shoulder, he carefully dislodged the foot.

"His ankle's broken," Keegan said. "The bone's sticking out. We'll have to tie it up and get him back to Trexler's cabin."

Keegan carefully forced open the door on Harris's side and worked his way out of the sedan. He was sitting on its side, staring up at the road. The car seemed safely wedged in the tree.

He stretched out along the length of the Ford and forced open the luggage kit on the back. Inside were a first aid kit, blankets, a coil of rope and a large tool chest. He pulled out the blankets, first aid kit and rope and inched back to the door.

"We're in luck. He's got enough stuff back there to start a hospital," he said. "Tie up that ankle and wrap him in a blanket so he doesn't go into shock. I'm going to wrap this rope around the tree so we can lower him down by rope."

"We ought to be dead, you know that, don't you?" Dryman said, "We ought to be down there in that creek."

"But we're not," Keegan said. He was lying on his stomach, handing the first aid kit and blankets down to Dryman. "That tree's gonna give out if we don't get the hell out of here."

"Then hurry it up, pal."

Dryman stretched out sideways. Reaching between the seats of the wreck, he pulled Harris's leg taut, pushing the shattered bone back with his thumb, and wrapped a bandage around the ruined ankle as tightly as he could to hold the bones in place. Snow fluttered through the open door as he worked.

"Ain't we the lucky ones," Dryman griped as he worked. "Maybe we'll get lucky. Maybe an avalanche'll get us. Or maybe Harris was right. Maybe Trexler's snowed in up there and we can . . ."

"Yeah. Maybe we'll all sprout wings and fly out of here. And maybe we can get the hell off this damn car if you stop talking and fix that ankle."

"I'm fixing it, I'm fixing it!"

At Kramer's cabin, Trexler worked feverishly to get ready for the trek across the mountain to Copperhead Ridge. He carefully checked the cabin, then pulled on an extra sweater and his fleecelined jacket, then a ski mask and goggles and put Kramer's hat on over his own. Important to keep the head warm. If his head got cold, his body temperature would go down accordingly. He strapped on his backpack, pulled on his gloves and headed out into the storm.

The ridge sloped away from him and vanished in the blizzard. He could see twenty, thirty feet around him at best. He knew the trail but not the hot spots, not the drop-offs and the slicks. Half a mile down the mountain there was a sudden fall-off. A three-hundred-footer. He could not afford to drift down the slope, get too close to the cliff.

He slipped his feet through the leather thongs on his wooden skis and tightened the straps around ankle and heel.

The trail ahead was gradual for three or four hundred yards, then it sloped sharply up to the right. The last two hundred yards was a bitch—a forty-degree slope up to the cabin in the open wind. In this wind, a slip there could mean an unrestricted slide—four thousand feet to the bottom of the mountain. Nothing to break it. There wasn't so much as a daisy on that slope.

Trexler smiled to himself. At the top of his lungs, he yelled: *"Heil Hitler!"* And hunching up his shoulders, he pushed off into the face of the storm.

Dawn. And it was still snowing. Trexler had made it to Copperhead Ridge just before dark, crawling up the last two hundred
yards from rock to rock on his belly to keep from being blown
over by howling winds. Once inside, he had built a fire, eaten
and then slept for eight solid hours. Nobody was going to follow
him up there, he was sure of that.

He was up well before dawn and ready to go down the other
side of the Copperhead as soon as the sun permitted. The wind
had died down in the predawn hours. At 6:30 he was on his way
again, skiing cautiously until the sun broke over the Sawatch
range to the east. As his vision improved he went faster, staying
on the high ridges. Skiing cross country to keep on the high side.
By noon he was almost adjacent to Mt. Harvard, which was his
halfway mark. But the wind had picked up and swung to the
west, slowing him. His hands and feet were beginning to get
numb and his visibility was down to thirty or forty feet. He
entered a pine thicket and walked instead of skiing.

Then an instant of panic. Ahead of him, immediately to his
right, the snow was curling upward. A moment later he felt the
updraft. He was almost on the edge of the cliff. He stopped and
traversed up the slope, his breath coming harder. Through the
icy swirls off to his left he saw something. At first he thought it
was the root bowl of a fallen tree. But as he drew closer to it he
realized it was a cave, a gaping hole five feet wide in the side of
the mountain. He worked his way up to it, shoved his knapsack
through the opening and took off the skis, shoving them inside
the cavern. He gathered up some sticks and branches and
crawled into the hole. He took out his torch and flashed it
around the opening. It was a funnel-shaped cleft narrowing to
a smaller opening thirty or forty feet from the main opening.

Leaves and broken limbs, nature's refuse blown from the outside, littered the floor of the fissure.

He made a fire near the opening, letting the updraft suck the smoke out. He took off his boots and socks and warmed his feet and hands over the fire. Then he put on fresh socks. He ate some canned meat and an orange and drank almost a full canteen of water.

An hour passed. The snow shower tapered off and the wind shifted. It got brighter out. But the wind shift blew the smoke into the cavern. He repacked his bag and prepared to get back on the trail.

Then he heard something. At first it was a low growl. A snort almost, like a dog sneezing. Trexler sat up and peered into the dark cave. He flipped one of the tree limbs out of the fire, made a torch out of it and held it at arm's length deeper into the mountain lair. He saw nothing. He reached into the knapsack for the flashlight.

Then he heard it again. This time it was louder, deeper, more threatening. Trexler instinctively backed up a foot or two, the torch still burning in his hand. He reached into his knapsack with the other, rooting around, feeling for the flashlight and his pistol.

Then he heard movement and realized suddenly that whatever was in there was big. And he was between it and freedom. He rustled the fire with his torch so it burned brighter, still groping for the .45, still searching the darkness of the cave.

The beast roared an angry no-nonsense challenge and then it took shape in the darkness. A grizzly bear, awakened from his winter's sleep by the smoke, stalked toward him, half asleep, its black lips folded back over bared teeth, its eyes flashing with anger.

"*Jesus!*" Trexler screamed aloud as the enormous creature came toward him. He threw the torch in its face and started pulling things from the bag, felt the cold steel grip of the Colt and pulled it out of the sack. But as he did, the bear charged, slashed out at him with one paw. The nails tore into Trexler's cheek, ripped three deep gashes from cheekbone to jawline, knocked him backward into the opening of the cave.

Trexler screamed with pain, falling backward and kicking the fire at the enormous animal. It backed off for a moment and he held the gun at arm's length, aimed at the bear's face and fired. The bullet tore into its forehead just above the eyes, grooved the top of its head. The bear charged again, looming up over him as he squeezed off shot after shot. The bullets thunked into its thick body without effect. With each hit it roared louder, became angrier, as Trexler scrambled backward to get out of its path.

He backed into one of his skis and it tipped and slid out of the cave. He reached frantically for it but missed. The ski bounded down the steep cliff and plunged out of sight.

Trexler whirled back as the great beast charged again, rising up over him, its roar booming through the cavern. Trexler swung the gun up and got off the last shot. It hit the bear in the eye. The eye burst like a grape, the bear's head snapped back. It shook its head violently and fell as he tried to roll out of the way. The animal fell across his legs and lay there groaning.

Trexler wriggled one leg free and kicked and pushed at the dying creature until he freed his other leg. He snapped the clip out of the gun, found a box of bullets and nervously slipped six more shells into the clip. He slammed it back in the gun, held it six inches from the bear's head and shot it three more times. Then he dropped the gun and, groaning with pain from the deep gouges in his face, he crawled outside and bathed the three wounds with snow.

Trexler was not cold anymore. Adrenaline was roaring through his veins. He took out his torch and flicked the beam through the cave. It appeared empty. He lay on his stomach and looked down over the side. The ski was gone. A thousand feet down in the valley someplace.

He had another ten miles to go.

He dug out the first aid kit and a mirror. Using a pad of bandage, he dabbed iodine on the wounds. The antiseptic sent arrows of pain into the side of his face. He fell back against the cavern wall, gasping for breath while tears streaked his bloody cheeks. He threw back his head and howled like a wounded animal. The scream echoed down through the gorge and back.

Lamar Trammel was turning off the downstairs lights when the dogs started barking. It was almost ten o'clock and the snow had already reached a foot and a half. The barking was persistent.

"Lamar?" his wife Melinda called down from the bedroom. "What's got into the dogs?"

"Dunno. Maybe there's a bear or a cat out there."

"In this storm?"

His son Byron, a junior in high school, came out of his room.

"Something's raising the dogs, Dad," he yelled down.

"I hear 'em, son. I'm not deaf."

His sister Grace stuck her head out of her bedroom door.

"What's eating the dogs?" the pretty eighth grader asked.

Byron went downstairs and joined his father.

"Shall I get the thirty-thirty?" he asked.

Lamar, a tall, lean, weather-beaten man with wispy brown hair that needed cutting, smiled down at the youth.

"Now what d'ya think you're gonna shoot in this? Probably kill one of our cows."

The dogs, locked in the barn to protect them from the storm, were howling and yapping like hounds on a hunt. Lamar got his heavy flashlight, went to the back door and unlocked it. When he opened it, he reared back in alarm. Behind him, Byron screamed with surprise.

An apparition was framed in the doorway. A man, snow- and ice-caked, his feet tied to pine boughs that had been fashioned into homemade snowshoes, his gloved fingers crooked and frozen. Crazed eyes peered at them from behind a ski mask. The man reached out and tried to say something, then collapsed in the doorway.

Trexler awoke with a soothing wash of warm water on the side of his face. He opened his eyes. A handsome woman, her face leathery from hard living, her long brown hair tied at the back, was cleaning his wound.

"Are you an angel?" he mumbled. "Did I die?"

She smiled warmly. "Thank God you're awake," she said softly, and turning, called out, "Lamar."

A tall string bean of a man sauntered into the room followed by two teenagers.

"How ya doin'?" the older man asked.

"I don't know? Where am I?"

"Pitkin. We're a couple miles up from town."

"Pitkin!" he said with surprise. "How did I get way down here?"

"We're the Trammels," Lamar said. "Melinda, Byron, Gracie. I'm Lamar. You appeared at our door an hour ago. Scared hell out of all of us."

"He means you were a sight," Melinda hurriedly added.

"Afraid we can't get you a doctor," the father said. "Phone's out and besides, the roads are all under two foot of snow."

"I've cleaned the wounds out and dressed them," said Melinda. "Just need to keep them clean."

"I'll be okay," said Trexler. "My name's Clark, Sam Clark."

They shook hands.

"Feel like talkin' about it?" Lamar asked.

"Sure. I was skiing up around Harvard Peak and the snow caught me. Found a cave, was just getting settled in, and turns out I was sharing it with a grizzly bear."

"Holy smokes!" Byron yelped. "How big was he?"

"Byron!" his mother admonished for interrupting.

"Sorry," he mumbled.

"It's okay," Trexler said. "I yelled a lot louder than that when I saw it. He looked bigger than King Kong. Smoke from my fire must've choked him. He came out of hibernation fighting."

"How'd you get away?" the girl asked.

"I shot him with my old army pistol."

"Be damned," said Lamar. "You killed a grizzly with a pistol?"

"Lucky shot. He was right on top of me. Hit him in the eye."

"Wow!" said Byron, obviously impressed.

"Are you hungry?" Melinda asked. "I could warm up some stew or make you a bowl of soup."

"I'm sure you all want to get back to bed."

"Why," said Gracie. "We won't be able to leave the house tomorrow anyway. We can stay up all night and take care of you."

"Mr. Clark is probably tired, Gracie."

Trexler was thinking about energy. He would have to be on his way by dawn. Just a few hours. He needed food and more sleep.

"A bowl of that stew sounds awfully inviting," he said.

"Oh! Great," Melinda beamed. "I'll stoke up the stove. Won't be but a few minutes."

"Great. I can't thank you enough. I probably would've died if I hadn't stumbled on your place."

"That's likely," Lamar said. "I'll help with the stove."

They all left the room but Byron. He lagged behind, stood in the doorway.

"I almost got me a grizzly once," he said. "Up near Crested Butte. But he moved faster than I thought he could."

"What kind of gun were you using?" Trexler asked.

"Winchester thirty-ought-six with a Johnson scope. Dad was carrying his twelve-gauge. You ought to see it. He won it over at the Gunnison Thanksgiving Turkey Shoot two years ago. Got gold curlicues on the stock. Want to see it?"

"Sure," Trexler said with a smile. "Sounds like a real treasure."

There had been two storms in forty-eight hours with a six-hour break between them. Phone lines were still down and they were just beginning to clear the roads. Keegan and Dryman, huddled against the harsh wind, which was beginning to slack off, scurried down the street and entered the ranger station. It was eight o'clock in the morning and the sun was just beginning to rise over the mountains. They had been holed up in their hotel room for two days.

Jack Lancey, a grizzled, white-haired ranger, was sitting behind his desk with his feet propped up, drinking hot chocolate.

"Howdy gents," he said. "Got coffee and hot chocolate on the stove in the other room. It ain't the White House but it'll do."

"How's Duane's ankle?" Keegan asked.

"A little better today but what the hell, a compound fracture. That's gonna smart for a while. You sure did a good job with that splint there, Dryman. He could've been crippled for life."

"I'm sorry I got him into this," Keegan said.

"It's his job, Mr. Keegan. He's faced up to a lot worse."

"Any news from Kramer's cabin?"

Lancey shook his head. "This is a real pisser," he said. "We can't get jack shit on the radio and our phones are down. Don't know whether Soapie went on up to the ridge or stayed at the high cabin. Hell, for all we know Trexler went into the gulch, too. He could be an ice cube by now."

"No such luck," Keegan growled. "Got a big map of this area, Jack?"

"Right in the radio room there, gents. Almost life-size."

They went into the radio room and stared at the map, which covered almost one entire wall of the room. Lancey pointed to a spot with his pencil."

"That's us, right there," he said.

"Let's say he skied out of Kramer's place, just for discussion's sake, okay? Where would he most likely go?"

Lancey stared at the map for a few minutes.

"Well, he probably went to the Copperhead Ridge cabin first. From there it's just about downhill to anyplace you'd want to go. Hell, there's a buncha little villages he might've made it into. But he would've gone southeast, to avoid the river. Over in here someplace. Almont, Gunnison, Sapinero."

"What's this?" Keegan asked, tracing a broken line down the center of the map with his finger.

"That's the Continental Divide."

"Definitely would've gone south, right?"

"Had to. Too rough going north. I don't care how good he is."

"Down in here someplace," Keegan said, kneeling down and looking at the bottom of the map.

"You're talking about thirty miles before you see a smokestack," said Lancey. "Trexler didn't ski thirty miles through that storm. If he tried, he's dead."

"What would he do if he did get to some little burg?" Dryman said. "Nobody's going anywhere. Two, three feet of snow all over the area, roads closed."

"They just got the plows and sand trucks out late last night," Lancey said.

"I'm telling you, he's down there somewhere. Maybe he's holed up, but he's down there."

"How do you know?"

"Because he doesn't think anybody would believe he could make it. And besides, everybody thinks he went into Leadville. He probably figures he's safe."

Lancey sighed.

"Well, hell," he said. "We got a four-wheel-drive with slug chains on it. C'mon, we'll pick up the sheriff and see if we can make it up to Kramer's cabin and take a look."

The sheriff was an enormous man, over six feet tall and weighing about 225, with skin tanned the color of cinnamon. A soft-spoken man with a ready smile and alert eyes, he wore a plaid shirt and cord pants and a bulky sheepskin jacket that made him look even larger. A battered felt hat covered his bald pate. He climbed in the front seat next to Lancey and twisting around with some effort, offered a hand the size of a melon to Keegan and Dryman.

"Sidney Dowd," he said softly. "I'm the sheriff hereabouts."

Keegan shook the big hand.

"Francis Keegan, White House Security. This is John Dryman, my partner."

"White House Security, huh?" Dowd said. "You boys go in and check things out ahead of the president?"

"No," Keegan said. "We're in Special Investigations." He let it drop there, hoping the sheriff would not pursue the point, but it was wishful thinking.

"What'd Johnny Trexler do?"

"We need to talk to him," Dryman said. "Part of an ongoing investigation."

"Took the liberty of callin' the White House," Dowd said. "Talked to a fella name of Smith who seemed a little surprised you were way out here, but he did say you were official and the investigation was highly confidential." He paused for a moment and added, "Whatever the hell that means."

"We just didn't want him to get on to us and turn rabbit," Keegan said. "But somebody tipped him off and that's exactly what happened."

"Don't think there was anything suspicious about the call," Dowd said. "Jesse out at the airport heard you mention John's name when you landed and got all excited. He called to find out if Trexler was going to the White House for some reason."

"Well, that's a relief," Keegan said. "I don't mind telling you I was a little paranoid about that."

"It's a small town, gentlemen. Gossip is not uncommon."

"I thought we might swing by Trexler's place on the way up the mountain, just to check it out," Keegan suggested.

"You think he went up to base camp and killed Soapie Kramer instead of going into Leadville?"

"Yes, we do," Keegan answered.

"I really doubt that," Dowd said and shut up.

They fell silent as they drove through the town and out the highway toward the base camp trail. Snowplows had piled snow deep on both sides of the road and the chains clinked rhythmically beneath them as they crunched over the road. Lancey could handle the vehicle. He wheeled into the mountain road that led to the Trexler and Kramer cabins, double-clutched down to first gear, and started up the trail at about ten miles an hour. The truck snaked up through the snow, its chains biting through the mud and slush into hard ground. Lancey kept a steady speed, made the turn into Trexler's driveway and swung around in an arc so the pickup was facing back out on the road.

They got out and walked toward the cabin. Keegan took Dryman's arm and held him back a little as they stomped a path through almost two feet of snow.

"Find a screwdriver," he said. "And take the handle off the commode. Use gloves."

"The *commode*?" Dryman said.

"Fingerprints, Dry. Nobody wears gloves when they take a leak."

Dryman thought about that for a moment and nodded. "That's right," he agreed.

The cabin was clean and neat. Keegan checked all the closets. No suitcase. He checked the size of a pair of shoes. 11D. Pocketed a hairbrush with strands clinging to the bristles. Trexler's skis and poles were leaning near the back door.

"Doesn't look like he was planning to ski anywhere," Dowd said.

"He wants this place to look like he went out of town for a couple of days," Keegan said. "I'm sure he was planning to use Kramer's skis. Notice something else? Not a picture in the room. Nothing personal."

Dowd shrugged. "Well, Johnny's a little eccentric, maybe," he said. "But that still don't make him a killer."

"Come to think of it, he was real funny about photos," Lancey said, going into the kitchen. "Never would stand still for a picture, said it was bad luck."

Lancey looked in the refrigerator. Ice cream—strawberry. Several cans of smoked herring. Pork sausage. Pancake batter. Three bottles of maple syrup. Two Milky Way candy bars, frozen, in the ice compartment.

"That's one of those new candies," Dowd said. "Never tried one before."

"Never realized Trexler had such a sweet tooth," said Lancey.

"How about this," Dowd said as he opened the cupboard door. They looked in. There was a case of French champagne on the floor.

"Candy bars and French champagne," Dowd said with a shrug. "Got weird eatin' habits. Still don't make him a mass murderer."

Dryman came into the kitchen from the bathroom and winked to Keegan.

"Let's get on up to Kramer's cabin," Keegan said.

It took almost forty-five minutes to get to the top. Dowd got out of the truck and lit a cigar. They were on a broad flat almost at the crest of the mountain. The cabin stood near the edge of a cliff overlooking the valley. Behind it was a large meadow with a lake in its center ringed with stubby pine trees. Beyond the trees, the land fell away again. Below them on three sides a deep valley carved its way through the mountains, leaving deep gorges in its wake. The snow covered many of its traps—the potholes, ice slicks and fallen trees—but even cloaked in new snow, the terrain itself looked awesome and dangerous. It was a stunning sight, this tabletop poised on the edge of the valley. The sheriff nodded toward the gorge.

"I was a fair skier in my younger days," Dowd said. "Grew up here. Hell, I was born not fifty miles away. In my best day and in bright sunlight I wouldn't think of trying a run like that. And you think your man did in that storm?"

He shook his head and hefted his way through the knee-deep snow toward the cabin. Keegan stared at the brutal vista. *Is it possible he actually made it out of here?* Doubts began to creep into his theory.

The cabin was barren. The radio had been shut down and unplugged, which was standard procedure. Kramer's pack and skis were gone. The refrigerator was empty.

Lancey shook his head. "There's nothing out of the ordinary here, Mr. Keegan. Kramer cleaned the icebox out, shut down the radio. Uh, he took a couple of his big sectionals, but you know, maybe he thought he'd need 'em."

"Sectionals?"

"Large-scale maps like the one down in my office."

"Hmm," Keegan answered.

Lancey went into the radio room and swung the telescope around toward a high peak to the west. He squinted into the eyepiece.

"That's Snowmass, the big fella," he said. "A fourteen-thousand-footer. Copperhead Ridge is on the side of her. Come take a look."

Keegan peered through the scope at a snowbound cabin tucked against the side of the mountain. He watched it for several minutes. It was obviously deserted.

The sheriff entered the glass-enclosed room. "No car around," he offered.

Dryman snooped around outside the cabin. On the corner of the building he found the stub of the phone line. He kicked around in the snow and finally found the other section of the line. He went back into the cabin.

"Kee?"

"Yeah?"

"Phone line's cut. Outside going into the house."

Keegan shook his head. "Okay, the phone line's cut, radio's shut down. Kramer's pack's gone. And his maps . . ."

"Hold on, the wind could have snapped the line," said Dowd. "Naturally Kramer took his pack *and* shut off the radio. And anybody'd take maps with them if they were heading out in that storm."

"Uh huh," said Keegan. "Come with me a minute."

He led them back outside and waded through the heavy snow to the edge of the frozen lake.

"First of all, we *know* he came up here," Keegan said. "He didn't turn down to the main highway, we got his tracks. Second, he didn't come back down. We were down there in the storm horsing with that Jeep until dark. By that time nobody could've gotten through. So, why did he come up here? And the biggest question—where's his car?"

Dowd stared at him, his breath misting around his mouth. He looked around as Keegan walked gingerly out on the ice, bouncing cautiously on the frozen pond. He stared out across

it, knelt down and squinted across the surface. It was covered
with several inches of wind-rippled snow, its banks outlined by
drifts.

"My guess is, Trexler's car's in here. And Soapie Kramer's
probably in the trunk."

"Why the lake?" Dowd asked.

"Where else around here could you hide an automobile?"
Keegan looked out over the wide outline of the lake. "If he ran
it off a cliff it would be too easy to spot. But this lake? Hell, it'll
be frozen over for months." He paused a moment, then added:
"Besides, the son of a bitch is partial to water."

"So your theory is he's out there somewhere?" Dowd said,
nodding toward the ragged snowbound mountains.

"Yep."

"I don't know anybody could ski through that storm," Lancey said, shaking his head. "Hell, friend, we had twenty inches
of snow in thirty-six hours."

"If we'd had twenty *feet* of snow, he would've made it,
friend. This guy's dedicated, Sheriff. He's a driven man. He's
diabolical, clever, tough, resourceful, a planner, and completely
without conscience. And I hate to say it, but damn near invinci-
ble."

The sheriff raised his eyebrows.

"I said damn near," Keegan said.

"Sounds a little like you got a kind of begrudging respect
for him," Dowd said.

"No, don't get me wrong. I *understand* him. There's no way
I could respect him. I hate this man with a passion I don't even
think I could explain. And I'll tell you something else, Sheriff,
I'll follow him straight through the gates of hell if I have to. He'll
never get off the hook. I'm going to bring this guy down."

"You sound a little driven yourself, Mr. Keegan," he said.

"I suppose so," Keegan answered with a wry smile.

"Ever read *Moby Dick*?" Dowd asked, relighting his cigar.

Keegan smiled. "Which one do you think I am, Sheriff?
Ahab or the fish?"

One of the sheriff's deputies called to him from the truck.
"Sheriff, you got a call here. Think you better take it."

"Excuse me," Dowd said, and walked to the brown sedan.

He talked on the radio for two or three minutes and then trudged back through the deep snow. He looked troubled. He shifted the cigar to the corner of his mouth.

"Mr. Keegan," he said. "I will admit I thought you were nuttier than peanut brittle on the way up here but I think I just changed my mind."

"What happened?"

"We got a whole family butchered down to Pitkin. Man, his wife, and two high school kids, boy and a girl. Shotgunned."

"That son of a bitch," Keegan said angrily. "How far's Pitkin?"

Dowd looked south, down through the harsh valley.

"Overland? About thirty-five miles," he said with a touch of awe.

There was a landing strip in Gunnison, about twenty miles from the scene of the murders. Dowd begrudgingly agreed to fly down with them. He sat in the gunner's cockpit behind Keegan, stiff-legged and hard-jawed as the plane swept down through the canyons, ducking in and out of the tall mountain peaks. The trip took a half hour.

"Hang on," Dryman said, guiding the plane down through a mountain pass toward the narrow landing strip bulldozed through the snow. "If we skid, we're up shit creek."

Dowd braced himself, his teeth set in a grimace, as the plane leveled off and whooshed down on the hard-packed snow.

"Lovely, Dry," Keegan said with relief as they pulled up to the hangar and stopped.

A youthful police officer named Joshua Hoganberry was waiting for them. His badge was pinned to the crown of a blue campaign hat. It was the only thing he wore that resembled a uniform; he was dressed for the weather.

"Hi, Josh," Dowd said, introducing the cop to Keegan and Dryman. "Sorry to get you way out here in this weather."

"That's okay, Sheriff. We can use all the help we can get. It's a bad mess we got up there at the Trammel place."

"Friends of yours?" Dryman asked.

"Why, hell, been knowin' Lamar since I was born," the policeman said, obviously still shaken by the Trammel massacre.

"Nice man. Quiet, worked his ass off. Good kids, never any trouble. And his wife Melinda was pretty as spring flowers."

"What happened?" Keegan asked.

"Bastard just gunned down Lamar and Melinda where they sat. Old Trammel was readin' the paper. Blew a hole right through it. Shot Byron and Gracie, the kids, in the back as they was running away."

"Who found them?"

"Was a fluke, really. Doc Newton was comin' back from deliverin' the McCardles' new baby and saw the front door standin' open. He went in and found them."

The ranch house was five miles outside of town, between Gunnison and Pitkin, a plain two-story brick place sitting a hundred feet or so from the local road that had been cleared by a snow plow. There were two state patrol vehicles and an ambulance parked in a wide space bulldozed out of the drifts when Hoganberry pulled up in the Ford sedan. A footpath was worn through the snow to the front door.

Trammel and his wife were in the living room. He was sitting in an overstuffed chair, the remnants of a newspaper splattered against what was once his chest. His wife lay sideways on the sofa. One shot from the twelve-gauge had blown away most of her face. The daughter lay crumpled face-down on the stairs, a three-inch hole in the middle of her back. The boy was just outside the back door, face-down in the red-drenched snow. The back of his head was gone.

"My God," Dowd breathed.

They searched the house methodically, one room after the other. In the downstairs room, Keegan spotted a bloody towel in a trash can in the bathroom. There was a half-filled glass of water and an empty packet of B-C powder on the night table near the bed. Keegan wrapped the glass and empty B-C packet in the towel and stuffed them in the pocket of his coat. When he went back outside, Dowd and Hoganberry were standing on the front porch.

"Kind of blows up your theory about him killing Soapie to set himself an alibi, don't it?" Dowd said, lighting a cigar. "He must've known we'd pin this on him sooner or later."

"Not at all. I told you, he's resourceful. All he has to do is get out of these mountains and he'll vanish. He made it this far. Obviously he was hurt in some way. The Trammels helped him and he repaid the kindness by killing them."

"Why? We all know what he looks like."

"To give himself time, Sheriff. He probably figured it would be four, five days before anybody found the Trammels. By that time he planned to be long gone."

Keegan stared out across the rugged landscape, its hidden dangers buried beneath two feet of snow.

"My guess is he skied down into Pitkin. Probably before that second snowstorm. There're no tracks around."

"Well, if he did he's still there."

"Let's check it out."

"I can tell you right now, they ain't been any strangers down in Pitkin, sir," Hoganberry said, stuffing a pinch of tobacco into his cheek. "I live there. If you fart at dinner everybody knows it before you finish dessert."

"Then he went south, down through that forest."

"He must be one hell of a skier," Hoganberry said.

"He got here from Aspen," said Keegan. "Thirty-some miles—in a blizzard. What's south?"

"Salida. Over the shelf there, maybe twenty miles. He'd have to go southeast to get around Antero Peak. It's fourteen thousand feet. By road, close to forty miles."

"How big's Salida?"

"Well, it's a pretty fair-size town for these parts," Dowd said. "Three, four thousand people maybe. Even got themselves a little airport there, 'bout the size of Jesse Manners's place."

Keegan stared at the sheriff.

"They've got an airport there?" he said. "Any planes down there?"

"Why, that's what an airport's all about, Mr. Keegan," the sheriff said with a smile.

"I mean, could he charter somebody to fly him up to, say, Denver?"

"That's Billy Wisdom's outfit," said Hoganberry. "Hell, for the price he'd fly you to the moon. Used to be a barnstormer."

"Phone lines working between here and there?" Keegan asked.

"Yep."

"Let's talk to Mr. Wisdom."

Hoganberry drove them back out to the strip at Gunnison. Dowd had made arrangements for one of his deputies to drive down from Aspen and get him. He'd had enough flying for one day. Keegan and Dryman were flying on south to Albuquerque.

"Well, I got to admit, John Trexler had us all fooled," Dowd said. "Skis thirty-five, forty miles through a blizzard, murders a whole family, skis another fifteen miles and hires crazy Billy Wisdom to fly him down to New Mexico."

"And disappears like a drop of water on a summer sidewalk," said Keegan.

"Wouldn't you know he'd fly three hundred miles south instead of doing the obvious and going to Denver," said Dryman.

"I should have figured it," said Keegan. "He's never done anything obvious yet."

"If I were a bettin' man I'd put my money on you, Mr. Keegan," said Dowd. "You hang on like a damn pit dog."

They pulled into the small airport. As Keegan and Dryman were about to get out of the car, the sheriff turned to them.

"Mr. Keegan?" he said. "It's been a pleasure, although an exhausting one."

"Thank you, sir. The pleasure was ours. You've been a lot of help."

"One other thing."

"Yeah?"

"I'll make you a deal."

"A deal?" Keegan asked, curiously.

"If you'll send me copies of the blood report from that towel and the fingerprints off the glass, I won't arrest you for stealing my evidence," the portly sheriff said. "We don't have any heat in the jail right now, be awful damn uncomfortable. Besides, I don't know anybody south of Denver would know what to do with a fingerprint if they found one."

"Thanks, Sheriff."

"Good luck to you. Hope you find that son of a bitch."

"Oh, I'll find him. Count on it."

Keegan looked out over the snow-drifted vista, beyond the mountains. Somewhere out there, *Siebenundzwanzig* was on the run. Now he knew someone was after him. By now, he had probably changed identity again. But Keegan was undaunted.

"Run, you bastard, run," he said to himself. "I'll be right behind you all the way. Don't even stop to take a breath. If you do, you're a dead man."

Two days later, on September 1, 1939, Germany invaded Poland. World War II had begun.

Keegan sat in the back booth of The Rose. The table was covered with newspaper and magazine clippings. As he read them he moved them from one pile to another. There was a space for a third pile—possibilities—but that space was empty. He had hired two clipping services to scan periodicals, one east of the Mississippi, the other west, looking for murders, offbeat crimes, anything with the number 27. Each day thick envelopes would arrive and he would go through the clippings, looking for something, *any*thing, that might give him a clue to the whereabouts or exploits of 27.

He recognized the tall, lanky man when he entered the bar, even though he was a mere silhouette, framed by the sunlight streaming through the door.

Smith.

This would be bad news.

Smith walked the length of the room and sat down. He motioned to Tiny. "May I have a glass of your best white wine, please?" he asked pleasantly.

"How did you dodge the twins?" Keegan asked.

"Hoover called them in. He's so busy rounding up subversives he needs everybody he's got." He motioned to the clippings as Tiny brought his wine. "What's this all about?"

Keegan explained the clippings to him.

"He's not going to do anything to screw himself up," Smith said.

"He's not perfect," Keegan answered. "Nobody's perfect. He's going to make a mistake and when he does, I'll know it. If I don't read it or hear, I'll feel it. I can feel his heart beating. I can feel the sweat in his palms." He nodded sharply. "I'll know it."

"Mr. Keegan, you've been after this guy for almost a year and you're still no closer to him than you ever were."

"Wrong, Mr. Smith. I was three miles away from him last week. I'll tell you what I know about him. He's six-one. Blond. Probably has green eyes. In excellent physical shape and a real charmer. And he's got three bad wounds on his left cheek. We learned that from the pilot that flew him to Albuquerque. He carries a gold Dunhill cigarette lighter with a wolf's head on the top. I have his fingerprints. We know he used the identity Fred Dempsey. The guy's a chameleon. He can switch identities faster than you can switch hats. He'll do anything to survive. Steal, kill, makes no difference. So far he's killed at least eight people that we know about. When he runs, he makes it appear that he's dead. He killed a forest ranger named Kramer, buried him in a lake and skied out of there—thirty-five miles, some of it through a blizzard. He killed a family of four, then skied *another fifteen miles* and paid some local stunt pilot a thousand dollars to fly him into Albuquerque, not Denver, which would have been the obvious thing. He doesn't do the obvious. If we hadn't been on his ass, he would have gotten away with it. He did the same thing in Drew City."

"But he did get away, Keegan. By now he could be any-where. In any disguise and with new papers. And . . . now he knows somebody's on to him."

"That's not going to change him," said Keegan. "He's a classic psychopath, Mr. Smith. Hell, he kills when he doesn't have to. He killed that family in Colorado, two kids, mother, father, totally unnecessary. Everybody in Aspen knew what he looked like."

Smith shrugged. "He doesn't like to leave tracks," he said. "In the intelligence field that isn't uncommon."

"You mean it's condoned?"

Smith scowled at the question, which he considered naïve. "Nothing's condoned, nothing's forbidden. Those things go unsaid. Cut a man loose like that, his primary objective is sur-vival. He's got a job to do, an enemy agent loose two thousand miles from home in hostile territory. What would you do? Any-way, that question's moot, Mr. Keegan. What do you do next? You've lost him."

"I don't know, but I promise you I know this guy better than anybody in the bureau. I know this guy better than *anybody* and if anybody can catch him, I can."

"Hoover's going to handle this in his own way and in his own sweet time," Smith said matter-of-factly. "And frankly he regards the espionage angle as a joke. Right now his only interest in Twenty-seven is that he's suspected of mass murder and unlawful flight."

"So? Let Hoover put his face up in the post office and in the newspapers. Release the story. Really turn on the heat."

"Not a chance," Smith said, shaking his head. "If it turns out to be a false alarm, he'll look stupid and Hoover would rather blow off his foot than look stupid."

"Tell you the truth, it probably wouldn't work anyway. I promise you this: Twenty-seven has a plan. He is never caught without a plan. Now that he knows he's hot, I'm sure he's got a plan for that, too."

"Suppose he's been activated?" Smith asked.

"I don't know," Keegan shrugged. "Hell, I need a break. If I don't get one, whatever he's going to do, he'll do. And don't ask me what that might be. I've burned up my brains trying to figure that one out."

Smith sighed. He took another sip of wine.

"Look, let them play it their way, and I'll play it mine," said Keegan. "What have we got to lose?"

"It's just a matter of time before the bureau figures out who you are and when it does, we'll need a skyhook to get Hoover down off the ceiling."

"Obviously Hoover doesn't believe a man can reform."

"Are you kidding? If he had his way he'd abolish trials by jury and make jaywalking a federal offense. I'm sorry, Mr. Keegan. Donovan and I are both impressed with what you've done but it's an FBI case now. You're off it."

"What!" Keegan yelled. Everyone in the bar looked back at the booth. Keegan stood up. "Bull*shit!*"

"I'm sorry," Smith said defensively. "The FBI's on it because it's a fugitive case. Espionage has nothing to do with it."

"Then I'll do it on my own," Keegan said venomously.

Smith chuckled and shook his head. "How? You don't have anyplace to start."

Keegan didn't answer. He knew the clippings were a much

longer shot than going through the FBI records, but they were his last gasp.

"Of course," Smith said, "there is one option."

Keegan stared at him suspiciously. "What kind of option."

"Sign a contract with the Office of Information Coordination," Smith said. "That way we can justify an on-going investigation on the grounds that we suspect him of being an enemy agent. Hoover's only interest in him right now is as a fugitive."

"Mr. Smith, I'm not a spy. I don't belong in Donovan's network."

"Takes all kinds," Smith said. "Besides, the Boss and I agree you did a hell of a job tracking him down in Colorado."

"You're telling me if I join this new intelligence outfit, I can keep going on this?"

"For the time being."

"And then what?"

"Then you'll be on our team."

"And at your beck and call?"

Smith nodded slowly. "We'll have a training course set up by the new year. We have a place set up in Boston. Two months. We would expect you to take the course. Hell, Keegan, look at it this way, we'll probably be in the war soon anyway."

"Not if *Siebenundzwanzig* can help it."

Smith opened his briefcase and took out a contract and handed it to Keegan.

"Think it over," he said.

"How about Dryman?"

"I don't think we can justify using an Air Corps pilot and plane any longer. He's due to be discharged in two months anyway. They'll return him to his previous base and begin processing his discharge."

"Credentials?"

"You have to surrender the White House authorization. After you complete the course in Boston you'll get new credentials from the OIC."

"And in the meantime Twenty-seven is on the loose and France and England are at war with Germany."

"With the FBI on his tail."

Keegan snorted. "For the wrong reason."

"Don't sell them short. They just might turn him up with

the information we've given them. They certainly have the re-sources—which you don't have."

Keegan toyed with the contract. Finally he folded it and put it in the inside pocket of his jacket.

"I'll think about it," he said.

"Excellent," Smith said with a wry grin. "Keep in touch."

In the war room of his headquarters in Munich, Adolf Hitler stood before a towering map of Europe, staring smugly up at the colored lines which represented his *Blitzkrieg* of Poland. In two weeks, his troops had swept like two pairs of ice tongs, east across the Polish corridor then south, and east across southern Poland, then back up to link with the northern divisions. Warsaw was surrounded, battered by two weeks of devastating bombing raids.

Poland was his.

He laughed aloud. Behind him, Vierhaus applauded lightly.

"My congratulations, *mein Führer*. The whole world now knows the meaning of *Blitzkrieg.*"

Hitler nodded emphatically several times, his eyes burning with the fever of victory. "Exactly as planned," he bragged softly. "Sixty thousand dead, two hundred thousand wounded, seventy thousand prisoners. And the war is less than three weeks old."

"Next it's France and then we drive the British back across the channel, eh, *mein Führer*?"

The mere mention of the English Channel gnawed at Hit-ler's stomach. He stared at the narrow strip of water separating Europe from Great Britain. Although he never talked about it, the Channel was his greatest threat. He did not believe he had the resources yet to invade England.

"Never underestimate your enemy, Willie," he said, waving his finger at Vierhaus. He strolled around his desk, his fists tight at his sides. "The British are tough. Proud. Dogged. They are exploiters. They are a psychological force embracing the entire world. And they are protected by a great navy and a very coura-geous air service."

"Supplied by the Americans," Vierhaus added.

"Exactly," Hitler said. "You understand what I am driving at, eh, Willie?"

"Yes, *mein Führer.*"

"How fast can you activate *Siebenundzwanzig?*"

"I am ready to order the U-boat south, *mein Führer.*"

"Who is in command?"

"Captain Fritz Leiger."

"Ah!" Hitler said with raised eyebrows. "The U-17. And *Siebenundzwanzig?*"

"We are in touch with him through the newspaper ads. We can activate him immediately."

Hitler eyed Vierhaus with suspicion.

"You anticipated my decision, Willie?"

"Not exactly, *mein Führer,*" Vierhaus said, not wishing to bruise Hitler's fragile ego. "With the war in Europe, I am afraid Leiger may change his plans. Go someplace else. This may be our last opportunity."

Hitler smiled. He put his hands behind his back, slapping the back of one in the palm of the other. "Of course you realize *Operation Gespenst* will force an open confrontation with the Americans."

"They are supplying the British anyway. All they need is an excuse to get into it. They have just approved eighty-five million dollars for new aircraft, most of which we suspect will go to the Allies. Now is the time, *mein Führer.* The longer we can delay the Americans, the better."

"Of course, of course, I agree. We have nothing to lose anyway. When will the U-boat be in position?"

"It should take three weeks."

"And when do you plan to carry out the mission?"

"The third week in November. On their Thanksgiving holiday. The timing could not be better."

Hitler smiled. He went back behind his desk, patting his hand rapidly on it and then nodded.

"*Gut,* Willie. You have done an excellent job and so has *Siebenundzwanzig.* Activate him immediately. He has waited long enough. And so have we."

The conning tower cut the smooth surface of the sea like a knife and a moment later the U-boat silently surfaced. The captain rapidly climbed the ladder up through the narrow con and, opening the hatch, stepped out into a cool September breeze.

Two other officers followed. Below him, two gunners emerged from the deck hatch to man the 8.8-centimeter gun. Nobody made a sound.

The captain peered through his glasses, scanning the black sea ahead of them, keening his ears. In the silence, he heard the deep rumble of engines, barely audible. He strained his eyes. Dimly in the dark, ships began to take shape. He counted them, aware that a hundred yards to his starboard, a second U-boat, the U-22, had surfaced.

"Small convoy," the captain whispered. "I make six ships. No escort yet."

"Shall I signal?" the mate whispered.

"Not yet . . ."

Like many of Germany's U-boat commanders, Fritz Leiger was not a Nazi. A career navy man, he was a militarist with little interest in politics. But like most German military officers, he resented the Versailles treaty for the damage it had done to Germany's pride and economy, so he favored the war against the British and French. He was a short, heavyset Austrian with a thick mustache and a stoic personality. He knew the dangers of U-boat service as well as the stress his crew would suffer before the war was over, so he cultivated few friends among his men. Although he was a fair and compassionate skipper, he felt he could not afford the luxury of comradeship.

In this first month of World War II, there were fifty-two *Unterseeboote* operating in the North Atlantic, type VIIC U-boats with a crew of forty-four men, a single deck gun, two antiaircraft cannons and five torpedo tubes. Leiger had been one of the first of the U-boat commanders. He had helped to develop the wolf-pack strategy, shadowing convoys and summoning other U-boats which would then launch nighttime surface attacks on British ships carrying aircraft and armaments from America to Great Britain. In twenty-eight days of war, the wolf packs had sunk nineteen British ships. Leiger's sleek, gray shark, the U-17, had accounted for four of these, including the passenger ship *Athenia,* which had gone down with 1,400 crew and passengers, twenty-eight of them Americans.

Leiger suddenly stopped scanning the darkness and leaned forward. Refocusing his binoculars, he saw what a submariner fears most, the bubbling white water spraying off the bow of a

British destroyer as it circled wide in front of the convoy and straightened out. The U-17 was directly in its path.

"Destroyer!" he yelled down into the con. "Prepare to dive."

The warning horn blasted as Leiger and the bosun leaped through the hatchway and dropped down the narrow tube to the command deck of the sub. The bosun pulled the hatch closed behind him and locked it.

"Con clear!" he yelled.

"Take her to thirty meters," the captain ordered. "We can't risk a surface shot. Up periscope."

He had his cap on backward and as the sub leveled off and the periscope rose, he swung it around. The destroyer was in the cross hairs, one thousand meters away and closing fast. He could see her silhouette clearly now as she sliced through the ocean toward them. He swung the scope around and focused on the convoy.

"Mark," he said.

"Six hundred and fifty meters," came the answer.

Leiger hesitated for only a moment before making his decision.

"First?" he said, still peering through the periscope.

"Yes, sir?"

"We'll take the two lead ships. Launch four torpedoes, speed thirty-five, then we'll dive immediately to sixty meters and go under the convoy."

"*Under* the convoy, sir?" was the mate's surprised answer.

"That's right. The destroyer's closing fast. When we fire, she'll be looking for us on this side of the convoy."

The first mate quickly nodded.

"Yes, sir."

The captain, ignoring the destroyer, fixed the cross hairs on the first ship in the line. Just behind it, partially hidden by the shadow of the first ship, was a second vessel. By plan, the second submarine would take the last two ships in the convoy. Evasion was up to the individual sub.

"Reading?" the captain asked.

"Five hundred meters."

"Mark."

"Mark."

"Down periscope."

The slender tube slid soundlessly below the deck. Leiger looked at his watch, counted soundlessly to himself.

"Fire one."

"Fire one . . . one away."

"Fire two . . ."

He and the mate repeated the ritual until they had launched four torpedoes. Then:

"Take her to sixty meters, First. Ten degrees left. All ahead full."

The U-boat tilted sharply. There was a clatter of falling objects along the length of the narrow vessel as she dove and leveled off. They could hear the steel fish whining through the water. A moment later they heard the first explosion, then the second.

"That's one," Leiger said with a smile. They waited, heard the sound of the third torpedo diminish.

"Missed," the captain said with disappointment. Then the fourth one hit.

A series of explosions echoed through the sea as the boilers in the first ship exploded. Then the second blew up. The U-boat crew held their positions, staring at the steel hull over their heads as if it were a mirror reflecting the surface above them, wondering where the Brit destroyer was.

Then they heard four more torpedoes screaming through the ocean, heard two more explosions.

"*Gut!*" Leiger said. "U-22 got one of hers."

The thunder of the convoy engines grew louder as the U-17 slid neatly beneath it. The sub was filled with sounds: rumbling engines; tortured steel as the first ship slid beneath the waves; the groaning of steel plates; the sharp *twang* of them buckling and popping from the pressure of the sea as the shattered ship dropped to the bottom; the dull *phoom* of depth charges reverberating through the water as the destroyer assaulted the U-22.

Safely on the opposite side of the stricken convoy, Leiger brought the U-17 up to twenty meters and raised the scope. The black sky was afire. Two of the torpedoed ships were still afloat but ablaze and listing. The rest of the convoy was scattering,

taking evasive action. Beyond it, in the garish red light, the
destroyer was careening through the sea as it launched depth
charges from its stern.

They could easily take two more, Leiger thought. Only one
destroyer and she's occupied. One of the ships, a tanker, her
gunnels almost awash from the weight of her heavy cargo of oil,
made a sharp turn and suddenly was a perfect target. Five hundred meters away.

"Is the rear tube loaded?"

"Yes, sir."

"All back two-thirds . . . prepare to launch . . . four hundred
meters, mark . . . fire five . . . all ahead full."

He watched the tanker through the periscope, counted the
seconds silently to himself, then the torpedo struck. The whole
ship seemed to explode in a great, broiling inferno. A few seconds later they heard the explosion and felt the U-boat shake
slightly.

"Direct hit amidships!" he cried out and the crew cheered.

"She's an oil tanker, burning to sea level," Leiger continued. "There goes her backbone . . . she's breaking amidships
. . . and she's going down. Down periscope, First. Take her to
two hundred and seventy degrees, Bosun . . . all ahead full."

An hour later they were safely away from the stricken convoy and its guardian angel. The crew was quiet, dispirited. They
had heard nothing from the U-22 and presumed she was sunk.

"Excellent show, gentlemen," the captain told the crew to
bring up their spirits. "We'll ride at twenty meters for half an
hour and then we can all get some fresh air."

He went back to his cabin. Ten minutes later, the radioman
appeared at his door.

"I have a message, Captain."

"Yes?"

"It was from Mother. She kept repeating one word . . .
Halloween."

Leiger's expression changed only slightly. He nodded.

"Thank you."

When the radioman departed, Leiger closed and locked his
cabin door.

"Damn," he said to himself, opening the safe and removing
an official envelope marked *Geheim* and below it, *Gespenst.*

"What the hell is this going to be about?" he wondered angrily. He withdrew the orders for this top-secret mission, which he knew simply as "Ghost."

Leiger's eyes narrowed with curiosity and annoyance. He had suddenly been ordered south, out of the killer lanes where the action was and into the clear waters of the southern Atlantic, where the 220-foot-long steel cigar could easily be spotted from the air.

To make matters worse, for the length of this new mission he was under the command of *Die Sechs Füchse,* an intelligence unit of the *Schutzstaffel.* Leiger hated the SS and the Gestapo with a passion, as did most military men in Germany. He considered Hitler and his cronies thugs, psychopaths. This professor, Wilhelm Vierhaus, was to him one of the worst. Although they had only met once, Leiger had taken an instant dislike to the crippled intelligence chief, an arrogant man so thirsty for victory that he had lost all sense of honor.

Leiger pored over his charts with a pair of dividers, measuring the distance to his destination, the eastern coast of Grand Bahama Island in the Bahamas. His ship had a surface speed of about seventeen knots, seven underwater, and if necessary could dive comfortably to a depth of 120 meters. They could stay underwater for up to twenty-two hours at a "creep" speed of four knots.

Calculating his distance, Leiger figured if he traveled at maximum surface speed during the night, underwater during the day to avoid detection, and the weather held up, the trip from his position southeast of Greenland to Grand Bahama would take about seventeen days. He had three weeks to make the journey.

"Verdammt!" he said, angry that he had been ordered away from the action for some stupid "intelligence" mission.

In Bromley, New Hampshire, which had less than 2,500 residents, an old man struggled through the lobby of the only hotel in town. His hair was a white wisp, his face prune-wrinkled. His clothes, though neat and clean, were a size too big and sagged on a body obviously shrunken with age. His back was bowed and he wore wire-rimmed glasses. He used a cane to support his right leg, which appeared to have been weakened by a stroke.

"Good morning, Mr. Hempstead," the desk clerk said.

"Hello, Harry," Hempstead answered in a shaky voice. "Any mail today?"

Harry checked the mail slot, knowing it would be empty. Hempstead had been at the hotel for almost a month now. Every day he looked for a letter from his son but in the time he had been at the hotel he had received no mail.

"Sorry," Harry told him.

The old man shuffled out the door, went toward the diner as he always did. On the way, he stopped at a newsstand and picked up *The New York Times*. As he walked on, 27 felt very proud of himself. The disguise was perfect. The wrinkles on his face hid the three gouges in his cheek. It was unlikely that whoever was after him would look for a seventy-year-old man in southern New Hampshire. He settled in a corner booth of the diner, ordered sausage and rolls and coffee, and turned to the Personals section of the paper.

The code was known as *Schlüssel Drei*, the Three Code. The base message was a fake, identified by a series of numbers within that message. The actual message was then derived by adding three to the first number, subtracting three from the second, adding three to the third and subtracting three from the fourth. Reading through the personals, he stopped suddenly. His heart began to race. There, in the third column halfway down the page, was the message he had been waiting six years to read.

Charles: Have 8 seats for the show on the 14th. Will meet you at 9 P.M. at the 86th Street station. Elizabeth.

Twenty-seven decoded it as 5, 17, 1800 (6 P.M.) and 89.

5.17.1889—Hitler's birthday.

"My God," he said, smiling to himself, unable to conceal his excitement. "The mission has been activated."

Eighteen days later, in the last week of October, the U-17 slipped around the eastern shore of Grand Bahama Island and found a suitable hiding place among the brush on its eastern tip, hopefully hidden from the prying eyes of U.S. Navy PBYs, which patrolled the entire area. With lookouts liberally posted, Leiger decided to permit his men the luxury of swimming, fresh fish and fruit and eggs, which they could buy on cautious visits to the villages a few miles away. He had been advised that he would have to remain in these waters for almost a month, so his plan was to move every three or four days, waiting until dark, then seeking out a new and sheltered cove or inlet in which to hide.

Leiger was to wait for a relayed signal from a mother ship farther out at sea before opening his second set of sealed orders. But now that he was safely alee on Grand Bahama, he could wait no longer. He locked the door to his cabin, opened the safe, removed the envelope and tore it open.

He read the instructions slowly, drumming his fingers on the desktop as he scanned the orders. When he was finished, he slid the sheaf of papers back in the envelope and returned it to the safe. Only then did he sit back and mentally digest what he had just read.

"Mein Gott," he said half aloud. A daring plan. Insane really. And yet . . . it might just work.

The drop was a safe deposit box at the Manhattan National Bank to which both 27 and a courier in New York had access. The courier would leave a message in the box which 27 would then pick up and answer the same day, or vice versa.

Twenty-seven had taken a bus to New York and checked into a modest midtown hotel. He decided to stay in character, although he wore a properly fitting suit. He projected the image of a well-to-do seventy-year-old lawyer or banker when he presented himself to the guard at the deposit box safe. His key to the box had been one of his most closely guarded possessions.

"Box 23476," he said.

"Name?"

"Swan." It had been almost six years since he had used that name. This would be the last time.

"Yes, Mr. Swan. Sign the card, please."

He sat in the small cubbyhole provided for box holders and examined the contents of the small steel container. There was a single eleven-by-fourteen brown envelope inside containing a passport, a driver's license, a leather packet of business cards and a birth certificate, all identifying him as John Ward Allenbee III. Born: 1895 in Chicago, Ill.; an import broker with an office in San Francisco.

He opened a hand-printed note that accompanied the documents.

"You are John Ward Allenbee III," it read. "You are a conservative, very proper American import broker, born in Chicago and operating out of San Francisco. You have an office on High Street (cards enclosed) and accounts in two banks with deposits of $20,000 and $30,000, bank books enclosed. You also have an account at the Manhattan National with $50,000 on deposit. You have been traveling all over the world off and on for the past year-and-a-half. Allenbee is quite wealthy, very refined, dresses in the height of fashion. You must sign the enclosed bank signature cards. There is also a new safe deposit box. The key is here and the necessary signature card. Do this upon leaving. This box is no longer active. Get a new passport photo made and leave a copy of it in the new box. If you need a wardrobe you might try Balaban's on Fifty-third near Park. You will be contacted with further details."

Twenty-seven immediately vetoed the idea of leaving a photograph of himself in the box. He would turn it around, order the contact to leave his picture, which he would use to identify the contact. He dropped a note back in the box:

"No photograph. Leave yours. Assignment, please."

He quickly decided that once he learned the nature of the assignment, he would kill the contact. He would not risk being identified by anyone. He signed the new signature card, left it with the guard and went back to the hotel. He took out his makeup box and his blue business suit. He would steam it out in the shower that night.

He removed his makeup and wig and cleaned his face with cold cream, then washed it off and stared at himself in the mirror for several minutes. The bear scars on his face were still quite visible. The scabs were gone; they were now three thin red lines down the right side of his face. Studying that face, he decided what John Allenbee should look like.

Using scissors, he cut his hair back in a sharp widow's peak then, lathering his shaving brush, he began shaving the widow's peak clean. He opened the makeup case and took out black and gray hair dye, spirit gum, material for whiskers and pale blue contact lenses. Then he went to work.

The next day, Ward Allenbee, as he decided he would be called, went back to First Manhattan and checked the new box. There was a single slip of paper in it. On it was printed a sentence:

Das Gespenst ist frei.

Was this how the contact would identify himself? With the phrase: "The ghost is free?"

He folded the sheet, put it in his pocket and put the box back. Then he went upstairs and introduced himself to the vice president of the bank, Raymond Denton, a sallow, nervous man in his mid-thirties and a fawner. Allenbee did not like to be fawned over, but it was necessary as he began assuming and establishing his new identity.

Lady Penelope Traynor had just cashed a check when she looked across the marble lobby of the bank and saw the handsome man in Raymond Denton's office. He was obviously just concluding business with the bank officer. Quite attractive, she thought. And the way Denton was fawning over him, obviously important. As they got up to leave the office she strolled across the bank toward Denton's office.

Denton saw her and beamed. *Such a little sycophant,* she thought as she smiled back.

"Raymond," she said, extending her hand.

"Lady Penelope, how delightful. Lady Penelope Traynor, this is Ward Allenbee. Mr. Allenbee is a new customer of the bank and we're quite pleased to have him aboard."

When they left Denton, they strolled toward the entrance together, making small talk.

She smiled up at him. "Are you living in New York?" she asked.

"Yes, I've taken an apartment at the Pierre."

"How lovely. My father and I have adjoining suites at the Waldorf. What do you do, Mr. Allenbee?"

"I'm in importing," he told her.

"Really?" she said. "Art?"

"Antiques."

"How interesting."

"It can be at times. Are you over for long? I assume you're from England."

"We have a country house just outside London but we travel quite a bit so we keep a base of operations here, too. Actually I work as a researcher for my father. He writes a syndicated column. Sir Colin Willoughby? The 'Willow Report?' "

"Of course. I've read his articles. Quite perceptive. You were in the Orient recently."

"Yes."

"Interesting observation about the political situation in Japan. Does he really think we can avoid war with them?"

"Well, you certainly should try. The situation over there is quite desperate, you know. The emperor doesn't really seem to know what's going on. Actually the country is under the control of Tojo and the right-wing military faction. The army and air force are quite strong and they have a very powerful navy."

Allenbee smiled. It was refreshing to meet a woman as intelligent and perceptive as she was.

"I have my car," she said. "May we drop you somewhere?"

"May I be presumptuous and offer you a drink? The new bar at the Empire State Building is right up the street. I hear it's quite exquisite."

She hedged a bit, looked at her watch, then finally shrugged.

"Sounds charming," she said. "But I only have an hour."

The car was a chauffeur-driven Packard. Obviously, Sir Colin did rather well with his column. The bar was brass and enamel, its style ultradeco. They sat in a corner booth and sipped martinis. She studied him carefully. Ward Allenbee was a handsome man with pale blue eyes behind gold-rimmed glasses. His thin black hair was graying and archly widow-peaked and he wore a meticulously trimmed Prince Albert beard. His clothes were expensive and stylish, his speech perfect, his voice resonant. And he was intelligent and well informed. Quite interesting, she thought.

Twenty-seven saw a woman in her late thirties, handsome, well groomed, yet oddly cold and detached. Her posture was a little too correct, her classic features a little too perfect, from the angular nose and pale green eyes to the petulant mouth, her red hair a little too tightly combed, her eyes a little too cold and suspicious. A snob who covered priggishness with a veneer of sophistication. She was awesomely well informed and outrageously opinionated and she was a casual name dropper. Some men might have found her intimidating. Twenty-seven saw in her a frustrated and repressed woman of high caste, ripe for the picking, a widow whose husband had been dead for years. A wonderful diversion while he awaited the next step in the mission.

One drink became two drinks and then a third. The first hour passed and they were deep into the second when he suggested dinner at Delmonico's. She eyed him momentarily, her eyes softened by vermouth and gin, then she smiled.

"Why not," she said. "But we must stop by my place, first. I really must change clothes."

She had an ample one-bedroom suite adjoining her father's larger quarters in the Waldorf North Tower. It was pleasantly furnished but hotel furniture was hotel furniture no matter what one did with it.

"I won't take long, I promise," she said. "I'll make you a drink before I change." She went to the bar in the corner and stirred him another martini.

He sipped the drink and nodded emphatically.

"Excellent," he said. "You are really something. You're a walking journal of events, you're quite beautiful and you make a great martini. You're full of surprises, Lady Penelope."

He reached out, very lightly stroked her hair, then her throat. Stepping closer, he cupped her face in his hands and kissed her gently on the mouth. She responded hungrily, a woman who had been chaste, untrusting of men, for years.

She wanted him desperately, feeling he was a safe port in her otherwise stormy life. But that could wait. As he wrapped his arms around her, she buried her face in his neck, then raising her lips slightly, she whispered in his ear:

"Das Gespenst ist frei."

Twenty-seven was astonished when he heard her whisper the code phrase. Was she really his contact, this rich, titled Englishwoman whose father, the internationally famous journalist, had taken so many pot shots at Hitler through the years? Taken completely unaware, he stood flabbergasted as Lady Penelope walked across the room and opened the door to her father's suite.

"Daddy," she said.

The tall, trim, impeccable Englishman strode into the room. He wore a red velvet smoking jacket and a blue ascot. He was a handsome man, his mustache trimmed and waxed, his fingers manicured, his silver hair perfectly trimmed, his posture military. There was about him a cool, tailored, untouchable air. So this was the author of the famous "Willow Report." Looking at them together, Allenbee saw the family resemblance in the painfully correct posture, the classic features, the snobbish air.

Willoughby thrust his hand out.

"Well, well," he said. "At last we meet. We've waited a long time for this moment."

"Sir Colin," Allenbee said cautiously. The Britisher leaned toward him and spoke a simple code phrase, *"Willkommen Siebenundzwanzig, der Gespenstschauspieler."*

They shook hands.

"So . . . time to make our contribution to the Third Reich, eh?" Willoughby said with a smile.

"How did you recognize me in the bank?" Allenbee asked Lady Penelope.

"Since you wouldn't leave a picture, I watched who went to the safe deposit room. You picked up your credentials yesterday so I had a rough idea what you would look like as John Allenbee, although I must admit, the beard threw me. Actually, it was just luck. I was looking for a man I might feel comfortable engaged to."

"Engaged?"

"We'll get to that," Willoughby said. "You know, old man, you gave us a start when we saw the personal in the paper and knew you were on the run. What happened?"

"Somebody got on to me."

Willoughby turned ashen for a moment but quickly regained his composure.

"Who?" he asked, his eyebrows arching with the question.

"Someone at a government department called White House Security."

Willoughby shrugged. "Probably something to do with the guards on the gates and halls . . ."

"I don't think so," Allenbee said. "They knew my name, address, occupation. They asked for the sheriff first, then a park ranger to go with them to my place."

"Where was this?"

"Aspen, Colorado."

"What did you do?"

"I helped set up ski lodges there. Mapped out trails, set up base camps, ran avalanche patrols. It was a good job until these two showed up from Washington."

"How did you get away?" Lady Penelope asked.

Allenbee stared at her for a moment, then smiled.

"With great difficulty."

"What did they want, the two from Washington?" Lady Penelope asked.

"I have no idea. I didn't wait to find out."

"Well, never mind," Willoughby said with a grin. "You made it. You are here. The time is now. Ready to go to work, *Herr* Swan?"

"Not Swan, Willoughby," he said sternly. "My name is Allenbee. Erase Swan from your mind. He no longer exists. And can the German expressions. You're English, I'm American."

"Yes, yes, of course," said a flustered Willoughby. "I'll be more careful in the future."

"See to it," Allenbee said. "So . . . what *is* this plan that we've waited six years to implement?"

"Shall we go to my suite? Everything is there. Actually, the whole gambit is quite simple to explain."

Allenbee followed them both into Sir Colin's suite. Unlike Lady Penelope's hotel decor, his living room had obviously been redecorated in oak paneling and leather furniture. One wall was dominated by an enormous Degas painting. Allenbee stared at it for several moments.

"Early Degas," he said.

"You know your art, John," Sir Colin said.

"It's Ward. I prefer to be called Ward. John is too common."

"Very good, Ward."

"I once had a Degas," Allenbee said. "That was years ago. Willie Vierhaus has it now."

"Help me, would you, please?" Willoughby said, walking over to the painting. With Allenbee's help, he took the painting down, turned it around and leaned it against the wall. Brown wrapping paper was stretched across the back. Willoughby took a sharp letter opener, scored the edges of the paper and tore it off. Beneath it, glued to the back of the painting, were two maps and a detailed blueprint. One of the maps was the eastern seacoast of the United States; the other was a blowup of a small section of the larger map, with an arrow pointing to a spot on the Georgia coast near the Florida border.

"This is where we are going," Willoughby said, tracing his finger down the larger of the two maps to the town of Brunswick, Georgia. "About fifty miles north of the Florida line there is an island called Jekyll Island. This smaller map is a close-up of it. It's just across the marsh from the mainland. Actually, a very short boat ride. The island just to the north of it is St. Simons Island. They are separated by a sound—probably a quarter of a mile wide.

"Jekyll has a somewhat checkered history. Among other things, the last slave ship to come to this country unloaded its unfortunate cargo on the island. I won't bore you with history for the moment except to tell you it is now the richest, most exclusive private club in the world. In 1885, a group of America's richest men bought the island and established it as a private playground. J. P. Morgan, Marshall Field, the Vanderbilts, George Pullman, James Hill, Richard Crane, the Goodyears, the

Astors, the Rockefellers, Joseph Pulitzer . . . you understand what I am saying? The *richest, most powerful* men in the United States. The list goes on and on."

He paused for effect. Allenbee leaned closer, studying its location among a string of other islands that dotted the southern coast.

"Through the years, they have built a rather splendid club-house, two apartment buildings and several what we jokingly call 'cottages.' The first ones were relatively modest. But as time went on and their egos began to clash, these so-called cottages got more and more lavish.

"Since the early thirties, a group of regulars consisting of twenty-seven families have been going every year for Thanksgiving and returning just before Easter. Penny and I first started going down as a guest of the Vanderbilts. We've been going on this jaunt off and on since then. The first trip, the very first time, it occurred to me that it would be a relatively simple thing to lift one or two of them. Then I thought more about it. Why not get them *all*? I took the idea to Vierhaus and he took it to the Führer who was fascinated with the idea."

He turned to Allenbee.

"These men are the fatted pigs of American industry and society," he said, his eyes aglow with excitement. "Think of it, Ward . . . the captains of America's ships of state, some of the richest and most influential families in America with billions in foreign banks . . . all together at one time in one place, isolated from the mainland, literally unprotected. As the Yankees say, sitting ducks.

"Oil, steel, coal, transportation, the press, shipping, arms, munitions, automobiles, banking. The stock market! The heads of two of the biggest brokerage firms in America. My God, these are the men, Allenbee, who will create America's arsenal if it goes to war with us. In fact, they are already providing England with the tools to fight us."

Allenbee lit a small cigar with his gold lighter. He stared at the map without speaking, his face an unemotional mask.

"The plan is simple," Willoughby continued. "We have been invited down for the first three weeks of the season. A U-boat is at this moment sequestered on Grand Bahama Island, approximately two hundred miles to the south. She will come up the coast on the night of November 23rd . . ."

"Thanksgiving?" Allenbee asked.

"Precisely. The U-boat will dock at the yacht pier and we will then take twenty-seven of the richest men in this country hostage, remove them from the island and take them back to Grand Bahama. We will negotiate with Roosevelt. If the U.S. remains completely neutral, when the war is over they will be released."

"How do we get them off this island?"

"Another U-boat will meet us in Andros. The hostages will be split into two groups, to reduce crowding on the submarines. They will be transported to a mother ship in the mid-Atlantic and from there a clipper can take them to Spain. We can have them on our soil in . . . seven days."

"And this was *your* idea?" he said finally.

Willoughby nodded, waiting for his reaction. None came. The man who was now Allenbee stood up and walked to the desk, studying the papers and documents and then the map on the wall.

"The U-boat is already in place," said Willoughby. "The coded message you will send to the U-boat is in this envelope. It is in the *Drei* cipher. Not even I know what it is."

He handed the envelope to Allenbee who tapped it against his cheek for a moment or two.

"And when do we do this?"

"The private train leaves in ten days. The trip down takes five. The timing is perfect. Poland is ours. France is in turmoil. The British have four divisions in France along the western lines. If America is neutralized, France and England will have to sue for peace."

"That's an oversimplification."

"Not at all. The *Wehrmacht* will be on the coast, ready to invade. And jolly old England will be sitting out there all alone with her bloody pants down . . ."

"And," Allenbee said, interrupting him again, "we'll have the industrial and financial power of America in our hands."

"Exactly."

"What made such a good Nazi out of a stuffy old British

bastard like you, Willoughby?" Allenbee said in a monotone, his expression still hiding his reaction to the scheme.

Willoughby chuckled. He sat down behind his desk and leaned back in his chair.

"I interviewed the Führer for the first time in 1927," he said. "He was nothing then—but I could *feel* his power. Then I became a disciple of *Mein Kampf.* I've worked for Jews for years, been exploited by them for years. The Empire is finished, Allenbee. That faggot, Edward, running off with the American bitch. Canada gone. India will be gone. Just a matter of time. A great empire dead of dry rot and run by gutless ninnies. Need I go on?"

Allenbee slowly shook his head. "And you, Lady Penelope?"

"What has England ever done for me?" she said coldly.

He lit another cigar. "What's my cover?"

"Why, you and Penelope are betrothed, old boy," Willoughby said with an almost mischievous grin. "We'll announce it here at a cocktail party two nights before we leave, that way there won't be time for anyone to check on your background, if they so desire, which I doubt. We'll be going down in Andrew Gahagan's private car. There will be twelve private cars on the train. I'll write the first story about the coming nuptials—parental pride and all that. If someone in the press begins to look too carefully into your background, it will be too late. We'll be off to Georgia."

"And what's our story?" he asked Lady Penelope.

"I met you on our last trip to the Orient," she said. "We fell in love in Hong Kong and you followed me back. All very romantic."

"They'll welcome you with open arms," said Willoughby. "I've always written lovely stories about the place so they coddle me. You'll find that the very rich are just as vain as anyone else, perhaps more so."

"Tell me more about the plan. I don't need lectures on human nature."

"Quite. The island's contained, only two miles wide at its broadest and about five miles long. The cottages are all in a nice, tight little cluster around the clubhouse less than a hun-

dred yards from the docking facilities for their yachts—plenty
deep enough to bring our sub in and take thirty people
aboard.''

''I thought you said twenty-seven.''

''Well, there's you and me and Penny, we'll have to leave.
I will act as the negotiator.''

''Okay.'' He stared at the smaller map for a while. ''So there
will be twenty-seven millionaires, their wives and guests, is that
it?''

''Actually thirty-two. When we conceived this plot, twenty-
seven regulars and their guests went down to the island every
year. Since then the players have changed a bit.''

''And we take twenty-seven of them?''

''The list is right here,'' Willoughby said. ''We can take our
pick. But it is my understanding that thirty is the limit.''

Twenty-seven picked up the list and perused it.

''How spread out is this compound?''

''Perhaps three city blocks square. But *everyone* will be in the
dining room at precisely eighteen-thirty hours for dinner that
evening. It's the big meal of the year and by club rule everyone
must eat dinner in the clubhouse.''

''How many total at dinner?''

Willoughby rustled through the papers in a file folder and
separated one sheet from the rest.

''Here is the roster of all the members and their guests.
Thirty-two members; their wives, children, nannies and secretaries total one hundred and twelve. In addition, there will be
a total of thirty-three guests. That comes to a hundred and
forty-five people eating dinner.''

''At eighteen tables?''

''No. Nannies, secretaries and the smaller children eat in
the staff dining room. It's adjacent to the main room right here.''
Willoughby pointed to the smaller room on the plans. ''Actually
the dining room has twelve tables seating eight.''

''So now we have two dining rooms to worry about.''

''But connected.''

''How about security?''

''Just walkabout guards at night, to prevent anyone from
coming ashore and stealing from them.''

"How many?"

"Three."

"Staff?"

Willoughby opened a file folder and sorted through a half dozen sheets of paper, lifting one out.

"Kitchen staff, seven; waiters, twenty . . ."

"Twenty!"

"One for every two tables."

"Exorbitant, aren't they."

"Quite. These men are used to getting things their own way."

"That too will change," Allenbee said with a smile.

Willoughby went on. "Kitchen and waiters, twenty-seven; security guards, three; two radio operators, a switchboard operator and the resident engineer. The teaching staff, maids, caddies, clean-up people, all leave on a six o'clock boat to the mainland."

"That's thirty-four, not counting the rich boys."

"That sounds right."

"145 and 34, that's 179 people."

"Yes, but all you have to do is radio the submarine if everything is clear and keep order until it gets there."

Allenbee laughed. "That's naïve thinking."

"Naïve?" Willoughby was insulted.

"There are radios and telephones on this island. They have to be taken out. There are three security men. They have to be taken out. There will be a hundred and fifty people or so in the dining room, not counting anybody who might be sick and staying home that night. We'll have to cover a hundred and fifty people until the U-boat patrol arrives to help us."

"I, uh . . . am not too good at . . ."

"*I'll* tell you what to do," Allenbee snapped. "This is my operation, we will do it my way. You two will do exactly as I tell you. Is that clear?"

"That's why you were picked for the job, Swan. You . . ."

"It's Allenbee, damn it! My name is *Allenbee.* Swan does not exist!"

"Of course, of course," Willoughby stammered. "It was a silly error. I won't make the mistake again."

"See that you don't. I don't want this whole thing to go down the drain because of some stupid blunder like that."

"I said I'm sorry. It will not happen again."

"So," Allenbee said, stepping back from the map and staring at it with his hands across his chest. "We must single-handedly lay siege to an entire island and hold almost one hundred and fifty people hostage until the U-boat arrives."

"We can't take a chance on bringing anyone else into the plan," Penelope said. "Since the beginning our biggest fear has been a possible breach of security. At this moment only six people know about this. The three of us, Vierhaus, Adolf Hitler and by now, the boat commander. If we bring in more people, the chances for failure will increase."

"Failure?" Allenbee said brusquely. "It's not going to fail! I've been waiting six years for this mission. I will kill anyone who jeopardizes it, anyone who gets in my way—and that includes you two. Is that clear?"

"Perfectly," she said.

"I will remind you, sir," Willoughby said, "that this was *my* scheme. If it were not for me, you wouldn't be invited to the island in the first place . . ."

"And I'll remind you, sir, that if I must I will get on the island and carry out this operation without you and your damned invitation."

Allenbee continued to stare at the material on the table and the map on the wall.

"There will be two changes in the plan. In *your* plan. First, we will kill one of our millionaires before we leave . . ."

"What!"

"We'll select one of them, important but not crucial, and kill him. That way they will know we mean business. Second, ultimately we will divide these men into twos and put them on our U-boats. We will then advise Mr. Roosevelt that every time the British sink a German submarine, they could be killing two American millionaires. And every time two die, we will inform them. *That's* the way to play this game, Sir Colin."

He turned to Penelope.

"So, what do we do about a ring, my darling?"

Willoughby reached into his vest pocket, took out a small

black box and snapped it open. A blue diamond, half the size of a marble, gleamed on a bed of velvet.

"This should be appropriate. Two carats, perfect cut. Straight out of Tiffany's tray."

"How much did I spend for this?"

"A mere thirty thousand."

Allenbee finally smiled.

He took Penelope's hand, slid the ring on her finger, then pulled her to him and kissed her roughly on the mouth. As they separated, he said with a grin, "To a glorious future together, my darling."

Allenbee sat on a fallen tree on the north beach of Jekyll Island, peering through his binoculars, scanning the island a half mile to the north. It had been a balmy day but the wind was beginning to shift from the southeast and the air was getting crisper. The weather report was encouraging. A northeaster was moving in and by the next day the storm would hit, providing a moonless, rainy night for the lift.

He and Penelope had ridden the two miles to the north end on horseback; now she sat at his feet in the sand with a map spread out before her. There were several notations on the map, little things Allenbee wanted to remember. Although navigating the sound that separated St. Simons and Jekyll was the U-boat commander's problem, Allenbee wanted to check everything.

Old Captain Horace Mackelwain, master of one of the yachts that had stopped en route to Palm Beach to drop off a couple of passengers, had explained the island's peculiarities to them over dinner the night they arrived; how the channel that coursed through the sound between the islands was ninety feet deep and curved around the inland side of Jekyll into a wide bay, providing easy access for yachts like the Vanderbilts' *Alva* and J. P. Morgan's *Corsair III;* how perfect the island was situated because even in a storm the channel was relatively calm and easy to maneuver; how the St. Simons lighthouse was a perfect landfall when entering the basin.

Allenbee swept the glasses to his right and checked out the lighthouse, then swung them back to the bay.

"How about the Coast Guard station?" Penelope asked, looking at the location on the St. Simons Island map.

"A good two miles up the beach on the ocean side," Allenbee answered. "They have a small rescue boat, I doubt they'll be out in stormy seas unless somebody's in trouble."

He lowered the glasses and continued to casually study the sound. He smiled to himself.

"A piece of cake," he said. "The whole run won't take more than an hour and we can ride the bad weather halfway to the Bahamas."

Allenbee had been nervous ever since making contact with Willoughby and Penelope two weeks earlier. There had been the cocktail party to introduce him to the bluebloods and a full week of packing and waiting around before the train left. But once the long private train had pulled out of Grand Central Station, Allenbee had relaxed. He could not imagine a safer place to be than on a millionaire's private Pullman car traveling south to the most isolated private playground in the world.

The trip had been a revelation, an introduction to a pampered world of self-indulgent wealth beyond his imagination. The private Pullman cars were a marvel of utilization. Every square inch seemed to be used up. Crammed into a sixty-five-foot car were a parlor, kitchen, dining room, two staterooms, a private bedroom and three toilets. Each car was unique. Tiffany glass fans and windows, chandeliers and candelabras, custom-made Pintsch compressed oil lamps, a homage to earlier days, were common, as were electric fans since smoke and cinders from the engine made open windows hazardous and uncomfortable. The twelve private cars on the train had one thing in common—indulgent elegance.

Allenbee had used the train trip to familiarize himself with his wealthy victims. In the afternoons or after dinner in the evening he sat with them as they sipped Jameson's Irish whiskey, Old Crow or John Dewar's Extra Special scotch, smoked their Overland cigars, and subtly matched egos, each one casually trying to top the other.

Isolationism and profits dominated conversations. The talk was about impending war and the need for America to stay out of it. It quickly became obvious to Allenbee that most of these men wanted the U.S. to remain neutral. Allenbee listened, studying these men who mastered the country's industry and finance. Fortunes—or greater fortunes—could be made by supplying the contestants on both sides without actively becoming involved in the wars now raging in both China and Europe.

On the last night, they were the guests of Grant Peabody, a Massachusetts industrialist who manufactured ball bearings and had the most opulent dining car on the train. It was mirrored, draped in scarlet with satinwood trim, had a crystal chandelier, gilded sconces, gold candelabras and Louis XIV furniture. Fresh flowers were provided at every stop. The meal was a connoisseur's delight: a choice of oysters or terrapin soup, venison, pheasant or grilled salmon, several kinds of vegetables, Piper-Heidsieck Brut and G. H. Mumm extra dry champagnes, along with a variety of fresh berries for desert.

Throughout the meal, Allenbee quietly imagined how this pampered and self-indulgent millionaire would deal with the danger, the heat, the discomfort, the odors, the cramped quarters and rancid food of a U-boat on patrol.

Each night during the five-day trip, Allenbee—and he *was* Allenbee now, immediately entrenched in his new identity—Penelope and Sir Colin gathered in Willoughby's stateroom to discuss the individual millionaires and revise the list of the twenty-seven men they would kidnap.

Now, sitting on the beach, he was savoring the mission, the power of knowing that the fate of America's wealthiest men was literally in the palm of his hand.

Penelope suddenly shuddered.

"Are you getting cold?" Allenbee asked.

She shook her head. "I was just thinking about the submarine. It terrifies me."

"Don't worry about it. Leiger's the best skipper in the whole *Unterseeboot* command."

"I tend to be a bit claustrophobic."

"Well, you'd better get over it by tomorrow night," he responded brusquely.

Since they had arrived three days earlier, he and Penelope had been the talk of the island. Like true lovers, they wandered around the small residential compound, arm in arm, smiling, amiable, whispering to each other as lovers do, except their whispers were hardly the stuff of lovers. Allenbee had observed every facet of life on this secluded isle, revising every phase of their operation to conform to layout, temperament and time.

They had located the radio room, the phone exchange, the gun room, where most of the hunting weapons were displayed in locked glass cabinets. They studied the access to the dock, distances from one place to another, and the idiosyncrasies of the individuals. The previous night they had charted the route of the three guards, who were unarmed.

Allenbee leaned over and stared down at the map. They had walked off the various distances from place to place. The yacht dock, which was empty now, was two hundred yards from the clubhouse dining room. The radio room was a hundred yards beyond the clubhouse adjacent to the indoor tennis courts. The guards spent most of their time on the dock, making a sweep around the cottages, the Sans Souci apartments and the clubhouse, once an hour.

He would make his move after 6:30 when everyone was in the dining room. He had to take out the three guards and the radio operator, destroy the radio and the phone switchboard, and be back to seize the dining room by 7:30, when the U-boat was supposed to dock. Then he would hold everyone at bay until the U-boat patrol came ashore to help load the hostages aboard. He could not count on Willoughby or the woman for anything except to get the kitchen help, children and servants into the main dining room at precisely 7:30.

He looked at his watch. At ten, the radio operator would close down his station for the night. He would have to break into the radio shack and radio the U-boat:

"One, seven . . . the ghost has risen."

Decoded: *U-17 . . . all clear for 19:30 tomorrow.*

At one A.M., Keegan and Vanessa were in his kitchen making dressing for the Thanksgiving turkey. He stood over a wooden chopping block, dicing celery. Vanessa was sitting on the counter behind him, massaging his back with her feet. They had decided to cook dinner for Marilyn and her husband and Dryman, who had decided to spend his separation furlough in Keegan's guest room.

"I had to give up my plane, but I don't have to give up the bar and the Rolls-Royce yet" is how he had put it.

"You're sure this can't wait until morning?" Vanessa asked.

"This is an old family recipe," Keegan answered. "It has to

bubble all night." He plunged his hands into the bready mixture and began kneading it. "I promise you, the meal I cook tomorrow will make the chef on Jekyll Island look like a dishwasher. You'll be glad you stayed here."

"I'm already glad I stayed here." She wrapped her arms around his shoulders.

"A fine time to get cozy," he said, holding up his sticky hands. He twisted his head around and kissed her. "You're sure you don't miss the old days?"

"This year there are thirty-eight or thirty-nine plus guests," she said. "It'll be a zoo."

"I would really have fit in well," said Keegan. "Walking around in my knickers swatting golf balls."

She looked at him slyly.

"You could flirt with the ladies."

"Yeah, sure."

"There's one, Lady Penelope Traynor. She'd catch your eye."

"What's her father do, supply gold to the treasury?"

"He's a journalist. She travels with him everywhere. If he weren't so old I'd suspect incest."

"You really are bitchy at times, Vannie."

"I know," she said with a laugh. "Anyway, you wouldn't have a chance with her, she's found a beau." She arched her eyebrows and looked down her nose at Keegan, "John Ward Allenbee, the Third."

"The Third, no less."

"They make a grand couple, a union conceived in boredom. That cocktail party the other night cured me forever. It was so boring it was sinful."

"I thought they were old friends of yours."

"She is . . . well, not an *old* friend. She and her father have been going down to the island for years. Usually as guests of Grant Peabody. Everybody coddles old Willoughby because of that column he writes in the newspaper. She's quite a dish, but a very cold dish."

"What's her old man's name?"

"Willoughby. Sir Colin Willoughby."

He went to the sink and washed off his hands.

"Hell, I know them," he said. "Met them once . . . my God,

it would have been the summer of '34. Longchamp racetrack, I think. Her husband was a soldier . . . no, he was a test pilot. Got killed."

"That's right, she's a widow. Well anyway, it just isn't like the old days."

"The old days? You just turned thirty, my dear, how old can the days be?"

"Oh, you know what I mean. The old gang was fun. You would have liked them. From the time I was six until I was sixteen, it was a wonderful trip. We went for Thanksgiving and came back at Easter. Had our own little schoolhouse, our own teachers. Nobody was ever in a hurry. Everybody was friendly and got along. Oh, they used to have silly little spats. I remember once, Uncle Billy and Vincent got in this awful argument because Vincent parked his yacht in front of the Vanderbilt place and spoiled the view. Silly stuff like that."

"Uh huh."

"You know, Vannie, I keep forgetting how stinking rich you are."

"Look who's talking!"

"No, I'm talking about rich-rich. The Astors, the Vanderbilts, those guys own the part of the world with the grass. And your old man's one of them. How many of these rich guys were in the 'old gang' as you put it?"

"Well, let's see, there was Cornelius Lee, Mr. Morgan . . ."

"J. P. Morgan?"

"Junior," she nodded.

"Jesus! How about King Midas, did he drop by?"

She giggled. "No, but there were the Goodyears, Ed Gould, Jr., Charlie Maurice, the Rockefellers, Mr. Jim Hill . . . "

"Plus these royal social climbers. Lady Penelope and Whatsisname the Third."

"Hardly social climbers, my dear. Willoughby's a Knight, Kee."

"Hell, half the plumbers in England are Knights," Keegan said.

"Well, I will say they were both incorrigible name-droppers. And the new fiancé isn't much better."

"Really? What kind of names does he drop?"

"How about the Prince of Wales."

"You mean Edward, the one that quit?"

"Yes."

"How does one go about dropping the name of the former King of England?"

"We were admiring his cigarette lighter and he casually pointed out that it was a gift from the prince."

"What kind of lighters does Prince Edward give out as gifts?" Keegan asked, sticking his hands back into the stuffing.

"Gold, of course."

"What else? I'd like to know—just in case I do Eddie a favor."

"It was a Dunhill, I think," Vannie said. "Yes. That's right. A Dunhill. With a wolf's head on the top. It was really quite . . ."

Keegan couldn't hear her anymore. His heart was pounding too loud.

"Listen," he said, his voice demanding, his expression intense. "This guy with the lighter, does he have three scars on the side of his face?"

"Three scars?" She stared into space for a long time, trying to picture him. "He has a beard," she said. "I couldn't tell. Kee, what's gotten into you?"

"Jesus! This old gang you were talking about that used to go down to Jekyll, how many were there Vannie? Exactly?"

"Exactly? Let's see, there was Uncle Joe and . . ."

"My God, do you have to count them all?"

She closed her eyes, counting faces in her mind, and shook a hand at him. "Just a minute, just a minute . . . uh, twenty-five . . . twenty-six . . . and old Crane, the toilet man we used to call him. His cottage has all gold fixtures in the bathrooms and . . ."

"There were twenty-seven of them?"

"As close as I can remember . . ."

But Keegan wasn't really interested in the answer. His mind was racing now. *Twenty-seven millionaires,* he thought. *On a remote island off the coast of Georgia.*

"My God, that's it!" Keegan cried out. "That's *got* to be it. What's his name again?"

"Who?"

"The one who's marrying . . ." he stopped again. "Jesus," he said aloud, "they must be in on it, too. They set it up! They're the connection!"

"Kee . . ."

"Christ, it was probably Willoughby's idea!"

"Francis, whatever *are* you talking about?"

Twenty-seven of the richest men in America, he said to himself. *My God, could that be it?*

He wasn't thinking about their names anymore, he was thinking about associations: steel, railroads, shipping, newspapers, the stock market, oil, automobiles, coal, banking, real estate. You name it, they were there.

Twenty-seven of the richest, most powerful people in the United States. People who controlled almost every facet of business and banking in the country. Isolated on an island two miles wide and five miles long.

Twenty-seven!

Twenty-seven millionaires! *Siebenundzwanzig* was going to neutralize America—and how better than to take these twenty-seven men and hold them hostage on that island!

But . . . that wouldn't work. Couldn't. One man could not hold the whole island captive. Stupid notion, he thought.

Unless he planned to take them off the island. . . .

He dug out an atlas and found Brunswick, Ga. The island was a mere spot on the map. For the next thirty minutes, Keegan was on the phone. But at one in the morning on the night before a holiday, he could not raise Smith and finally gave up.

No one else would believe him. He had no credentials.

And that left him only one choice.

Dryman had been asleep about fifteen minutes when Keegan burst in the room with Vanessa close behind. He had a mug of black coffee and two aspirin in hand.

"H.P., it's Keegan. Wake up."

Dryman was dead to the world. He didn't even groan. Keegan shook him roughly.

"Dryman!" he yelled. "Reveille!"

"Huh," the pilot muttered without opening his eyes.

"Coffee in bed," Vanessa said sweetly.

Dryman rolled over and peered through one half-open eye. "Wha'time'sit?"

"It's late," Keegan said. "Here, wash these aspirin down with this coffee. You'll feel much better."

"G'way. S'a holiday."

"Listen to me, H.P. Wake up!"

"Yeah, yeah," he mumbled.

"Are you awake?"

"I'm awake."

"H.P. I know what Twenty-seven means. I know who he is, where he is and what he's going to do."

Dryman's bleary eyes began to clear. He stared at Keegan.

"You been in the champagne."

"You heard me right, pal. He's on Jekyll Island, off the coast of Georgia. He calls himself John Ward Allenbee, the Third.

"Uh huh. And what's he going to do?"

"He's going to take the twenty-seven richest men in America hostage."

"Aw Christ, Kee. That's bullshit. It's one-thirty in the damn morning and you want to pull practical jokes."

"I couldn't be more serious. You remember me telling you Vannie had been invited on a Thanksgiving trip with a bunch of rich boys?"

"Yeah."

"Well, they're not *just* rich boys! They control shipping, railroads, oil . . . My God, if and when we do go to war, these men will run our war machine. And they're all on one island off the coast of Georgia. Think about it, H.P. They're sitting out in the ocean with no protection and our friend Twenty-seven is right in the middle of them."

"How did you come up with . . ."

"Listen, Captain, I can't get Smith. Everybody with any muscle is off for the holidays. The FBI would laugh me off the face of the earth if I told them this. If I call down there, they'll hang up on me. We've got to fly down there."

"Damn it, Kee, it's all over. We're out of it. You don't even have any credentials. All you've got is this cockamamie story. I'm on furlough and I'll be a civilian in another month. And we *ain't got no airplane!* Are you forgetting I had to give Delilah back to the Air Corps?"

"Drink your coffee. It's not over until it's over, pal. We got a plane ride ahead of us."

"That's a thousand miles down there."

"About seven-fifty as the crow flies."

"What're we gonna do, jump off the roof and flap our arms?"

"We need an airplane."

"Where are we gonna find an airplane on Thanksgiving Day? And anyway, who's gonna loan us their plane. I don't know anybody who even *rents* airplanes."

"C'mon, think. You must know *somebody*, H.P. . . ."

The town of Farmingdale was little more than a crossroads on Long Island an hour's drive out Jericho Turnpike. Dryman turned down a dirt road toward a hangar. It was a delapidated arc of wood and corrugated metal patched with rusty signs and it stood in the middle of a sprawling farm. At rest for the winter, its fields boasted only dead cornstalks and dried-up tomato plants which added to the gloomy atmosphere of the place. The wind sock, a tattered cone of parachute silk, flopped lazily in the calm morning air.

A narrow alleyway had been cut through the fields and leveled off.

"That's the strip," Dryman said with scorn.

"How long have you known this guy?" Keegan asked.

"We flew together for a while. He took the roof off the Officers' Club down in Panama City and they grounded him for life. When his tour was up, he retired."

"Don't they have any sane pilots in the Air Corps, H.P.?"

"I heard there was one up at Westover Field but it's only a rumor."

Barney Garrison was waiting inside the hangar office, huddled between an oil stove and the ruin of a desk. He flashed a winning smile when Dryman and Keegan entered the tiny room.

"Son-bitch, H.P., never thought I'd see you again."

"How's it goin', Loop?" Dryman said, giving his lean, freckled, weatherbeaten ex-wingman a bear hug and introducing him to Keegan.

"Can't complain. Do a little farmin', little crop dustin'. I'm doin' okay. Better'n taking a lot of guff from some chicken shit ground officer. I'm surprised you're still playin' soldier boy."

"I'm on separation furlough. Right after Christmas I'm off for China."

"You gonna fly with Chennault?"

Dryman nodded. "You ought to think about it, Loop. Pay's great. They got P-40's. Gonna be a picnic."

Garrison snorted and shook his head. "Hell, I thought maybe you'd gotten over being crazy by now. China, my ass! Bunch of noodle eaters. Well, come here, take a look at the old lady."

He walked to a door leading to the main hangar and wiped a round spot in the greasy window with his sleeve.

"There she is," he said proudly.

"The old lady" was a blue and yellow PT-17, a single-engine biplane with a homemade canopy built over its double cockpit. It looked like a World War I antique. Keegan stared through the streaked window in stunned silence.

"You're in luck. I got my dustin' tanks off for the winter, cleaning 'em up. Just tuned the engine. Got all new sparks in 'er. She's stripped down to move."

"What'll she do?"

"I'd say if you pick up a little tail wind, maybe one-fifty."

Dryman turned to Keegan with a sullen glare.

"That's six hours in a drafty cockpit with no heater and the temperature's in the fifties."

"Close to freezing up there," Garrison threw in.

"Any radio?"

"Nope. Never use one."

"Intercom?"

"There's that little tube you can yell back and forth through. Works fine. Where'd you say you were goin'?"

"Brunswick, Georgia."

"Where the hell's that?" Garrison asked. He opened a desk drawer and the bottom fell out of it, spilling a dozen wrinkled, oil-stained maps and charts all over the floor.

"Down near Florida someplace," Dryman said.

Garrison got down on his hands and knees and started rooting through the maps, finally finding enough of them to piece together the trip.

"Here it is," he said. "Be damned, they got a little landing strip there. And here's a navy base right down the road from it."

"We can't fly into a navy base without any radio," Dryman said. "They'll think they're being attacked."

"In *that*?" Keegan said, pointing to the biplane.

"What's the weather like down there?"

"It's fine until we get down around South Carolina. Then we're gonna start chasin' a rainstorm—or vice versa. It's moving down toward the coast, if you believe the weather bureau."

"Well," Garrison said quite seriously, "sometimes they get it right. What kind of ceiling you got?"

"A thousand feet and two miles visibility."

"That ain't bad."

"Better than we had in Colorado," Keegan offered.

"I don't want to talk about Colorado. If God hadn't put that pass where he did, we'd be part of the scenery now." Dryman stopped for a moment and shook his head. "Jesus, Kee, can't we ever go anywhere in *good* weather?"

"How about winds?"

"If the storm keeps tracking the way it is, twenty to thirty miles an hour."

Garrison chewed on a toothpick and thought for a few moments. He leaned closer to Dryman. "Listen, I ain't got enough insurance on this crate to cover a flat tire. You sure this guy's good for it, I mean if something happens to my plane?"

"I'll buy you a new plane," Keegan said.

"And he can do it," Dryman said, nodding.

"Okay, if you say so, H.P.," Garrison said, although there was still a touch of skepticism in his tone. He stared back at the maps and shrugged.

"Hell, you might make it," he said. Doubtfully.

When they stopped in Hampton, Virginia, to refuel, Dryman
checked the weather. The storm had increased in intensity and
was blustering toward the coast. Cape Fear, in the tidewaters of
North Carolina, was reporting cloudy skies and intermittent
rain. The weather bureau was predicting the storm would hit the
northern coast of Georgia about the time they got there.

"She's blowing in off the sea and heading right down the
coast," Dryman said, checking his map. "We'll come in right
behind it, if we're lucky."

"And if we're not?" Keegan asked as they climbed back in
the rickety old two-winger.

"We'll get the living shit kicked out of us," Dryman grumbled.

Leiger squinted through the eyepiece of the periscope, twisting
it slowly, watching the shoreline slide past. Pine and willow trees
crowded down to the beaches. Nothing else.

"It's beautiful country," he said to nobody in particular.
"Looks warm. Not like home. Lush. It is very lush. Trees grow
down to the sea. You know what I was thinking? I was thinking
it would be nice to take my wife on a picnic right over there. Just
six thousand meters away." He turned to the chief engineer.
"Take a look," he said. The engineer looked.

"Like a forest growing right down to the beach," he said.
"Is it always this green?"

"I don't know," said Leiger.

Leiger turned to the navigator. "Fritz, what is our position
in miles?"

"Twenty-nine miles south of Jekyll Island, sir."

Leiger took the scope and swept the horizon. The wind was

picking up and it was turning cloudy. There were two shrimp boats a mile off the port bow, bobbing in the churning sea. Then farther out, off starboard, he saw a tanker. A fat, black cat sitting heavy in the water. Loaded with oil and heading out to sea. England bound.

"Mark," he said.

"Four thousand meters."

A sitting duck, Leiger thought. But his orders forbade him from engaging or sinking enemy vessels. He cursed to himself. Leiger looked at his watch. Two-twenty. He had five hours to get into position.

"Chief, bring her up to fifteen meters, all ahead full. Keep an eye on the 'scope. If you see any planes, go to seventy meters. In these seas they'll never spot us at that depth."

"Yes sir."

"We should be at the mouth of the channel with time to spare," Leiger said.

Allenbee sat in his room going over the list he had drawn up. He had decided he would kill one man—Grant Peabody—as they were leaving. It would be an effective shock to the American nervous system.

He would start at exactly 6:30, planning to get back to the dining room at 7:25. If the U-boat was on time, he would only have to deal with the impending hysteria in the dining room for five minutes. If they got out of hand, he would kill Peabody immediately. That would straighten them out.

His adrenalin was pumping hard. He rubbed his hands together and smiled to himself. Three hours. Three hours and he would be on his way home with the richest prize anyone had ever offered the Führer.

The storm looked like a black wall stretching before them. Thunderheads roiled up to twenty thousand feet, their tops swirling even higher, like smoke pouring from a chimney. Lightning streaked from the flat bottoms of the ominous storm clouds, snapping at the earth through rain-swept skies. As they flew closer to the front, they could see winds beginning to pummel the trees on the ground.

Keegan looked at the chart in his lap. He was navigating by pilotage, reporting through the speaking tube to Dryman. They had passed over Ossabaw Island and were approaching St. Catherines, thirty miles from their destination. But it would be a hard thirty miles. Wind began to buffet the small plane and rain pelted the homemade canopy over the cockpits.

Dryman pushed the stick forward, dove down to eight hundred feet to get under the clouds. He had to crab into the wind to keep on course. They had refueled in Charleston so gas was not a problem. He shoved the throttle to the limit to keep up his speed.

They struggled on, passed over the edge of St. Catherines Island and suddenly were swept inland by the roaring wind.

"I've flown through some pretty hairy weather in my day, Kee, but this is the first time I ever flew a papier-mâché kite into a gale," Dryman cried into the tube.

"I have every confidence in you," Keegan answered. "They don't call you H.P. for nothing."

"After today they might."

"Just remember I'm behind you all the way."

"Very funny."

The wind buffeted the small plane like a leaf in a wind tunnel. At first Dryman just let the plane bob with the wind currents, then the turbulence got worse. The roaring winds, circulating through the thunderheads, burst from the bottom of the clouds and suddenly slammed the plane toward the ground. Dryman fought the controls, got the plane under control, pulled it out of its sudden dive. He leveled off at five hundred feet as the plane rocked and tossed in the sky, almost out of control.

Then barely discernible over the howling winds, Dryman heard a rending sound. Looking out, he saw the fabric on the wings begin to peel back, ripped by the battering gale. The struts were quivering. A guy wire snapped with a *twang* and whipped back against the fuselage.

"Christ, Kee, we're breaking up!" Dryman yelled in the tube. "Find us a clear spot, we're gonna have to go down."

As he spoke another guy wire *pinged* loose. One of the struts started breaking loose from the wing. More fabric curled from the wing surface, flapping madly in the roaring winds.

Keegan searched through wind and mist, looking for a clear place on the ground. They were over the coast highway, a two-lane blacktop with pine trees crowding its narrow shoulders. The road was barren except for a small truck fighting its way through the tempest, its headlights swallowed up by the driving rain. To the east was barren marshland and the ocean.

"I think we got a problem," Dryman yelled.

The plane suddenly lurched up on one wing and peeled off, its engine growling as it slipped toward the ground. Lightning crackled around them. As Dryman battled to get the plane back under control, the wing strut tore loose and was ripped away in the gale. The wing, held only by one remaining strut and two guy wires, was vibrating wildly. More fabric peeled loose. They were flying almost at treetop level, at the mercy of the howling squall, when the canopy shuddered and gave way. Keegan ducked as it disintegrated into slivers of glass and wood and was whipped away.

"I got to put'er down," Dryman yelled.

"Where?!" Keegan demanded.

"Edge of the marsh!" he yelled back. "Tighten your belt and brace yourself, we're about to lose a wing, too."

Keegan pulled his seatbelt so tight it cut into his legs. He braced his arms against the control panel as Dryman tried to guide the wildly erratic plane over the trees toward the flat swamp.

The wheels ripped into the treetops and tore loose. The plane dipped and as it did, the top wing wrenched loose. Struts and wires popped as it gave way and the two wings separated. With one last mighty effort, Dryman hauled the stick back, hoping to straighten the hapless craft out.

With wheels dangling loose, it skimmed into the tall grass of the marsh. The wheels tore away and the nose plunged into the windswept bog. The right wings tore away and the gas tank, located in the top wing over the cockpit, split. Water, mud and gasoline showered over the plane as it cartwheeled and splintered to a stop upside down.

Keegan, dazed but unhurt, stared over his head at the soggy earth. He grabbed the side of the plane, popped his belt loose and swung out of the cockpit, landing calf-deep in the murky water. Lightning snapped around them. The engine, torn asun-

der by the crash and sticking up out of the water, burst into
flames with a dull *fumpf*!

"H.P.!" Keegan yelled above the raging storm as he sloshed
through the bog toward the front of the plane. Dryman was
hanging upside down, his foot jammed in the control pedals, his
arms hanging straight down. Keegan supported him with his
shoulder, reached up and snapped the safety belt loose. The two
men fell into the marsh as the flames leaped back across the wet
fuselage toward the gas tank.

Keegan grabbed Dryman under the arms and dragged him
through the water, fighting the wind as the flames lapped across
the belly of the shattered plane, hit the gasoline and exploded.
Keegan shoved Dryman into the marsh and fell across his body
as the craft was totally ripped apart by the explosion. Bits and
pieces splashed around them. A ball of fire swirled up into the
gale and just as quickly was snuffed out.

Keegan rolled off Dryman, struggled to his knees and cradled him in his arms. There was a deep gash in Dryman's forehead and his leg was twisted grotesquely.

"H.P.!" he yelled.

Dryman groaned, squinted up through the rain at Keegan.
"Are we alive?" he stammered.

"Just about."

"How about Loop's plane?"

"Forget it."

Dryman smiled, then flinched with pain. "Good landing,"
he groaned. "We walked away from it."

Through the howling wind, Keegan heard an engine groaning, then saw headlights. A truck lurched down a muddy road
and stopped at the edge of the marsh. The driver opened the
door and leaned out into the rain.

"Anybody alive?" he yelled.

"Yeah, but we can use some help," Keegan yelled back. He
stood up and got Dryman up on one leg. Together they struggled through the marsh toward the truck.

"Man, what a mess," the driver said, looking at what was left
of Loop Garrison's PT-17.

The clinic was a one-story brick building with two offices, a lab,
two examining rooms, a waiting room and two recovery rooms

with adjoining bathrooms. Keegan used one of the washrooms to clean up while the doctor, a short, cheerful man named Ben Galloway, worked on Dryman. Keegan stared at himself in the mirror. His clothes were wet and muddy. One knee was torn out of his pants and there was a splash of Dryman's blood on his shoulder. But he was uninjured except for a few bruises.

He used a towel to wipe off his clothes, tried to straighten up before he went back to the waiting room. The truck driver who had picked him up was gone but there was a tall, lanky man in his late twenties sitting in the room, nervously smoking a cigarette. He looked up as Keegan came back in the room.

"You okay?" he said.

"I'm fine."

"Never knew anybody to walk away from an airplane crash."

"I had a good pilot."

"That him in there?" he asked, jerking a thumb toward the examining room.

Keegan nodded.

"How's he doing?"

"I don't know."

"Old Ben's a good doctor. He'll be okay. Name's Tommy Smoot. Wife just had a little baby boy. I was in with her when you came in."

"Congratulations," Keegan said, shaking his hand. "I'm Frank."

"Where you headed?"

"Brunswick. Actually Jekyll Island. You familiar with it?"

"Sure. I work at the shipyard down there."

"You know anybody with a boat? I need to get out to that island."

"What, tonight?"

"As soon as possible."

"How you gonna get to Brunswick?"

"Be damned if I know. I don't suppose there's a taxicab anywhere around here?"

Smoot laughed heartily. "A taxicab? Hell, I don't think most folks around here ever even *heard* of a taxicab. Why you goin' out to Jekyll?"

"I have a very important appointment."

Smoot thought for a moment, then said, "Well, the rain's

slacked off some, but there's another storm comin' in right behind that last one. Look, Doc wants my wife to spend the night
here. If it's real important, I'll run you down to Brunswick.''

"Mr. Smoot, I guarantee you, it is most important.''

"Well, then, it's done. Only take us half an hour to get down
there. But findin' a boat, I'll have to give that some thought.''

Dr. Galloway came out of the office wiping his hands on a
striped beach towel. He was a gentle man, gentle in attitude and
voice.

"Well, you're lucky, suh," he said softly. "The clinic was
closed for the holiday but Lucy Ann's little boy couldn't wait
until tomorrow.''

"I can't tell you how grateful I am.''

"Why, I'm just glad I was here, Mr. Keegan.''

"We were lucky all the way around," Keegan said. "Truck
happened to see us go down. Dryman in there, got us into a
marsh, otherwise we'd have both bought the farm. How is he?''

"Broken ankle. Two broken ribs. Concussion. Ribs didn't
puncture anything. Simple fractures. We got him fixed up just
fine. He'll be a bit sore for a while.''

"Can I talk to him?''

"Yes, suh, but I gave him a sedative. He'll be passing out
soon. Better hurry on in there.''

Keegan entered the small recovery room. Dryman was
stretched out under a sheet, his head bound in bandages.

"H.P., can you hear me?" Keegan said, leaning over him.

Dryman's eyes fluttered. "Huh?" he asked dreamily.

"It's me, Keegan. Can you hear me?''

"Why? R'you in China?''

Keegan laughed. "No," he said. "We're in Darien,
Georgia.''

"Darien, huh . . . how far?''

"About fifteen miles from Brunswick. I've got a ride down
there. You're going to be okay, pal. Just take it easy. I'll be back
when I finish the job.''

Dryman's eyes roved crazily in their sockets as he tried to
focus.

"Feel great, Kee.''

"Yeah, the doctor gave you a little boost.''

"H'bout th' plane? We lose th' plane?''

"You did great. The plane didn't make it."

He grimaced. "Aw, shit . . . poor ol' Loop . . ."

"Don't worry about the plane, okay? We'll get him a new plane. You just take it easy."

Dryman closed one eye and tried to focus with the other. "Wha'sa matter w'me?" he asked, his speech getting more slurred with each sentence.

"Broken leg, couple cracked ribs. You'll be fine, H.P. I'll be back before you wake up."

"Won't groun' me wi'they?"

"Over my dead body."

Dryman smiled and focused groggily on Keegan. "Do'n say that . . ."

They both laughed.

"I gotta go now, pal," Keegan said. "Take a nap. I'll be here when you wake up."

"Kee . . ."

"Yeah?"

". . . careful, 'kay? Watch y'back door . . ."

"You bet."

"Sorry . . ."

And he dozed off.

Rain began to pelt Smoot's two-door Chevy as they reached the outskirts of Brunswick. The only light came from the headlights reflecting off the macadam pavement. Keegan checked the time. It was quarter to seven.

"The only man I know crazy enough to go over to Jekyll on a night like this is Tully Moyes," Smoot said. "He's a shrimper, lives out on the marsh. But the road may be underwater."

"Get me as close as you can to his place and point me," Keegan said. He reached in his pocket and took out a roll of bills, peeled off three hundred-dollar bills and folded them into the palm of his hand. In the blue light of the lightning, Keegan saw a vast marsh spread before them. A two-story house seemed to be brooding at the edge of the bay off to their right. Beyond it, across the sound, Jekyll Island crouched in the dark. The tide was up and the narrow dirt road leading to the house was beginning to flood. The Chevy began to fishtail.

"Let me out here, Tommy. I can walk the rest of the way.

You don't want to be stuck out here in the marsh with a new baby waiting for you. I can't thank you enough."

"Southern hospitality, Frank. God was good to me tonight, I'm just passing it on."

They shook hands and Keegan pressed the bills into Smoot's fist. The young man looked down at them and began to shake his head.

"Tommy, believe me, you've done a lot of people a great service tonight. The baby's on me. Thanks."

He slammed the door and sloughed up the muddy road toward Tully Moyes's house. It was a rambling shed at the edge of the bay with a wooden walkway from the end of the road to a balcony that surrounded the first floor. Crab traps, fishing nets and loops of heavy ropes hung from the banister. Keegan knocked on the door and it was opened almost immediately by a tall, slender, weather-hardened man with a gray beard and thinning hair. He stared out at Keegan, a drowned rat huddled against the rain.

"Mr. Moyes?" Keegan said. "My name's Frank Keegan. I'm with the U.S. Intelligence Service. Can I talk to you?"

Moyes looked him up and down.

"You're one hell of a mess, Mr. Keegan," Moyes said. "Step in. You got some identification?"

"Mr. Moyes, all I've got's the craziest story you ever heard and one hell of a favor to ask."

Laughing heartily, Moyes brought a bottle of brandy into the living room, put two water tumblers on the table and filled them both.

"So you waded all the way out here in this storm to tell me that cock-and-bull story?" he said, still laughing. He held his glass in a toast. "Here's to audacity, sir, which you certainly got your share of."

The living room was a clutter of old photographs, fishing gear, mismatched furniture and bric-a-brac. There were several pictures of a boy in various stages of growing up, the last one showing him in cap and gown at what was obviously a high school graduation. There were also several photos of a hardy-looking woman. But the room gave no indication that either of them occupied the house.

Outside the windows, the bay was churning up as the storm descended on them again. Rain clattered against windows and walls.

"Mr. Moyes . . ."

"Tully."

"Tully, I know my story sounds outrageous but believe me, it's true. I came out here because Tom Smoot said you're just crazy enough to take me over to Jekyll Island."

"In this storm?"

"Right now."

"You can't be serious."

"I've never been more serious about anything in my life. If you won't do it, can you call somebody who can?"

"Nope," the lean man said, scratching his beard.

"Why not?"

"Phones are out. Been out for a couple hours now. Couldn't call anybody if I wanted to. Besides, if I was to call anybody it'd be the Coast Guard. They wouldn't believe you, but at least they wouldn't laugh at me. No sir, we can't call anybody and you can't walk back to town. It's over two miles and by now the water's up to your knees out there."

"Tully, I'm going over to that island if I have to swim over."

"Look, Mr. Keegan, I'm eatin' my Thanksgiving dinner. Me and Chelsea . . ."

He pointed to a black lab curled before the fireplace. It stared soulfully up at both of them, snorted and went back to sleep.

"Tully, you get me on the island over there and I'll take you to New York and buy you the best turkey dinner you ever ate."

"I'm eatin' king mackerel, Mister . . . what'd you say your name was again . . . ?"

"Frank. Frank Keegan."

". . . Frank. I don't eat anything that has feathers on it and flies through the air."

"Well, whatever you want. Christ, I'll buy you a year's supply of king mackerel. Here, look . . ."

He took out his money clip and counted out ten hundred-dollar bills and slapped them on the coffee table.

"Is that serious enough for you?"

Moyes perused the bills, separated them with a forefinger.

"That's a thousand dollars!"

"You're right."

"You offering me a thousand dollars to take you right over there?" He jabbed his thumb toward Jekyll Island.

Keegan nodded.

"Government must pay you boys pretty well." He took another swig of brandy, then got up and threw a log on the fire.

"Y'know, my son died on a night like this. Playing tug-of-war out in the sound. Kids'd get arguing over whose shrimp boat was toughest, tie two of 'em back to back and then see which one would tow the other. Kind of like playin' chicken in cars."

He walked to the window, leaned over and peered through a brass telescope. He aimed it at Jekyll and waited for lightning to light up the bay.

"Be almost four years ago. Night they graduated from high school, him and his buddy Jimmy Wertz, they had a couple of beers, got challenging each other. So they went at it."

He kept staring through the glass. Seas were running two feet, he estimated. Not bad. Wind was probably twenty-five knots.

"Seas were running about two feet just like they are out there now. Jimmy pulled Ray's stern under. She flooded from the stern and tipped over. Ray was trapped in the cabin. He floated up on King's Way Beach two days later. The boat's still down there. Ninety feet down on the bottom of the channel."

He walked back to the table and washed down the rest of his brandy.

"My wife died last year. She never got over that night. Wouldn't eat worth a damn. Just kind of wasted away. I think she really died of a broken heart. We were married twenty-six years."

"I'm sorry," Keegan said. "I know what it is to lose someone you love. My fiancée was put in a concentration camp by the Nazis. She died there."

Moyes did not respond but his face clouded up. He stared across the table at Keegan.

"I found out about this Nazi agent, Twenty-seven, from her brother. He's head of the resistance movement in Germany. At first nobody'd believe me. Thought I was nuts, just like you did. But I knew he wouldn't bullshit me."

He explained how they had turned up Fred Dempsey and later Trexler in Colorado and described the scene in the murdered family's home.

"Look at it this way, Mr. Moyes. If I am telling the truth, what better time to kidnap these people than now? It's a holiday. Everything's closed. It couldn't be any darker. And this guy has been on that island since Saturday or Sunday . . ."

"Monday morning. Saw 'em go over . . ."

"Okay, since Monday morning. Point is, he's not going to wait all winter to take these people. He's going to do it quick . . . and he's already been over there four days."

He finished his drink. Moyes stared at him for a long time without speaking, then poured him another stout brandy.

"Thanks, I've had enough," Keegan said.

"Drink it, you'll need it. It's less than a mile over there but it's gonna be a tough, wet ride."

"You mean we have a deal?"

"You know anything about runnin' a boat?"

"Not that kind."

"You know port from starboard?"

"That I do know."

"Well . . ." He scooped up the ten bills. "It wasn't gonna be much of a Thanksgiving dinner anyway. Besides, this'll be a lot easier than shrimpin' and a helluva lot more lucrative."

In the dining room of the spired clubhouse, the women arrived in their formal dresses, the men in tuxedos and tails. It was going to be a gala feast and the mood was cheerful, despite the raging storm.

"Part of island life," Grant Peabody joked as they scurried through the rain and sought the refuge of the wide piazza that surrounded the clubhouse.

Twenty-seven watched them from a dark cluster of trees. At his feet lay one of the guards, his heart pierced by 27's SS dagger. Another guard was floating face-down in the inlet, his throat cut. The third guard was making his rounds. Huddled against the storm, he trotted from one cottage to the next, cursing the foul weather. He was hungry and looking forward to dinner. The guards would be fed after the others were finished. He finally found a moment's shelter in the radio shack.

In the flickering flashes of lightning, he and the radio operator saw a man staring through the rain-specked window. He entered the radio shack.

"You gave us a start there, sir," the guard said. "Looked like a ghost starin' through the window."

The man who was calling himself Allenbee smiled.

"I *am* a ghost," he said, and they all laughed.

"Expecting a message?" the radioman asked without looking up. "I'll tell you, sir, the reception is mighty poor and . . ."

Twenty-seven leaned over the radio operator from behind, placed the palm of one hand under his chin, the other hand on the top of his head and snapped his neck. The guard, completely taken by surprise, stared open-mouthed at Allenbee as he let the radio operator's head fall on the desk. Allenbee's arm made a short upward stroke as he thrust his dagger up under the guard's rib cage, slicing deep into his chest.

The guard's head fell forward onto Allenbee's shoulder and the Nazi agent shoved him away. He fell dead at Allenbee's feet.

Allenbee dismantled the radio, then rushed across the compound to the telephone room. It was empty, the phones having been out for hours. He cut all the phone lines just to make sure, then stepped inside the small room, checked the clips in his machine pistol and his .38. He looked at his watch.

It was seven-twenty. Perfect timing. He rushed back to the clubhouse, looked in the window just as the kitchen and maid staffs were herded into the room. Lady Penelope entered with a birthday cake ablaze with candles. She walked to the front of the room. Allenbee walked around to the front of the dining room and entered through one of the French doors that lined one side of the room.

The guests looked at him with surprise. He was wet to the skin, his hair streaked down over his forehead. He looked like a wraith.

"Good grief, what happened to you?" Peabody asked.

Allenbee drew the machine pistol and fired a burst into the ceiling. A stream of plaster splashed on the floor at his feet. There was a chorus of screams. The men looked at Allenbee in shock.

"Everybody shut up!" Allenbee ordered but there was chaos in the room. He aimed the gun at the main chandelier and fired a burst into it. Crystal exploded. The bullets tore through the bracket anchoring the enormous light and it fell straight from the ceiling, crashing into a table.

"I said shut up!" Allenbee ordered.

The room got quiet.

"See here! What in hell do you think you're doing?" Peabody demanded.

Allenbee glared at him and pointed the machine pistol straight at his chest.

"Sit down, Peabody, or I'll kill you where you stand," Allenbee said in a voice that meant business.

* * *

Captain Leiger held the sub at ten meters, its conning tower just below the surface, and watched the St. Simons light spin slowly around, casting its long finger of light across the dark, rain-swept channel. He inched the sub around the northeast tip of Jekyll Island and entered the deep channel.

He swung the periscope around, fixed it on the dark, brooding shoreline of the island, marking the distance. He would hold his course due west, five hundred meters off the shoreline until he reached the northwestern tip of the island, then surface and swing into the inlet. The yacht dock was a few hundred meters south of the point.

Because he had to maintain his distance from the island, Leiger could not check the bay and the sound. If he had, he would have seen Tully Moyes's forty-foot shrimp boat, the *Dolly D,* chugging through the choppy waters, heading for the same destination.

Aboard the *Dolly D,* Keegan shoved shells into Moyes's automatic shotgun, then checked his .45. He had two extra clips which he put in his jacket pocket.

"You mean to kill this man, Frank?" Moyes asked.

"I don't think he'll have it any other way. He's not the surrendering kind."

"You got a plan?"

"Nope. I'm going to get on that island and hope to hell I can get the drop on him."

As they passed the northwestern tip of the island a blazing streak of lightning lit up the entire cove. In its garish white-hot light, Moyes saw a streak on the surface of the water fifty yards off the port side. Ripples running against the wind-borne waves. He peered through the darkness. Another crack of lightning and then another rent the sky. In the flashing lights of the storm, the ripples turned to waves, then suddenly the conning tower of the U-17 broke the surface of the water.

"Christ a-mighty!" Moyes yelled, "A damn sub, fifty yards off our port."

Keegan scanned the turbulent waters. As the sky continued to blaze with lightning, he saw the gray tower rising out of the water and slicing through the small breakers. Beyond it was Jekyll Island and the yacht pier.

"He hasn't seen us yet!" Keegan yelled.

Moyes yelled back, "He's heading for the Jekyll Island dock."

The sub's nose burst through the surface. The long eellike monster bounded atop the inlet, heading straight for the dock. The *Dolly D* headed straight for her.

There was no turning back. If they tried to run, the U-boat would shoot them to bits. But, thought Moyes, if the U-boat's rear ballast tanks were still full, he could ram her. A lucky strike on the conning tower could tip her over. If the hatches were still open, the sub would flood and sink. The dock approach was forty feet deep and the heavy shrimp boat would run right over the bastard.

Moyes's decision was instantaneous. He slammed the throttles full forward.

"I'm gonna ram the son of a bitch!" Moyes yelled to Keegan above the howling wind. "Brace yourself."

Moyes snapped on his floodlight as the hatch swung open and two German crewmen clambered on deck. Startled, they turned to see the bright single eye of light bearing down on them, closing fast. The first man ran toward the machine gun in front of the conning tower. Keegan focused the binoculars on the gray shadow, saw a face appear in the tower. The man was wearing a white, billed cap and he turned immediately toward Moyes's boat, his eyes wide with surprise. He appeared to be shouting orders to the gun crew. Keegan swung the glasses down to the deck as the two gunners pulled a tarp off the heavy deck gun and loaded it. Keegan ran out on the slippery deck, steadied the automatic shotgun against the rail and fired two bursts. The first ripped into the deck a foot or so behind the German sailor. But as he grabbed the butt of the heavy gun, the second blast caught him in the chest. His arms flew over his head and he fell backward, sliding over the side. The sailor's companion grabbed the heavy weapon, swung it around and fired a continuous burst into the cabin.

The windows exploded. Glass and bits of framing showered around Moyes. He wrapped his arms through the ship's wheel to keep her steady but a moment later another burst tore through the small cabin, ripping into his shoulder. He screamed but it was an angry scream, a scream of challenge not pain.

Leiger saw only the ghostly light roaring down on him through the driving rain. Lightning split the sky again, the jagged streaks ripping into trees along the shore. In the glow, he saw the outline of the heavy shrimper as it chopped through the waves ten yards away. They were almost to the dock but the captain realized he would never make it.

Before he could duck back inside the tower, the *Dolly D* struck. The submarine lurched as the heavy wooden boat ripped into the conning tower. Leiger grabbed for the hatch cover but couldn't reach it. He was thrown head-first down the narrow shaft. He plunged into the control room below as the shrimper's heavy wooden bow ground up over the spire. The steel hull sliced through the wooden hull of the shrimper and tore it open. But the U-boat was already mortally stricken. The collision had ripped a jagged crack down the length of the tower; the sub was on its side and still twirling. The captain landed flat on his back on the floor of the sub as it tilted crazily over on its side. The crash horn was shrieking. Men were screaming. The sea poured into the stricken boat through two open hatches and the tear in its con. The one remaining gunner on the deck of the sub was thrown end over end into the inlet.

Debris flew through the air like shrapnel. Rivets popped. Maps, flashlights and anything not tied down was thrown into the narrow shaft. Lights flickered. As they did, the stunned captain felt the burst of cold water as it poured through the open hatchway. The sub kept rolling. Sparks showered out of shattered lamps. The fuses blew. The sub was plunged into darkness—a tomb filled with the screams of the men and the sound of water roaring into it from two open hatches.

The shrimp boat groaned as it rode up the side of the tower, slashing it down sideways into the inlet waters and slamming it into the Jekyll dock. Timbers cracked and snapped as the two boats crashed into it. Keegan was thrown against the bulkhead. Lines snapped and twanged past his ear. The shrimp boat rose high out of the water, riding up over the sub then slamming down on the shattered pier. Its weight and the water rushing into the sub slammed the mortally wounded steel fish down to the bottom, into mud and silt.

Inside the submarine there was chaos. The crew floundered in darkness and panic, disoriented as the big fish rolled over and its tower ripped into the muddy bottom. Throughout the slender boat, men tried in vain to find and close watertight doors but they foundered in the dark or were washed away by the torrents of water gushing the length of the U-boat. In the command center, the captain thrashed frantically, hanging on to a table leg. But as the underwater vessel rolled, he lost his grip and he too was washed like a leaf down through the bowels of the sub, bouncing off metal objects, carrying other crew members with him as he was washed toward the stern of the doomed vessel. The cries of the crew were drowned out one after another until there was only the groan of the sea monster as it settled into the muck thirty feet below the surface.

Keegan staggered to his feet and stumbled back to the main cabin of the shrimp boat. Tully Moyes was draped over the wheel, his arms still wrapped in the wheel, his feet turned on their ankles. He groaned and fell backward on the deck of the shattered cabin.

Keegan rushed to him, saw the bullet hole in Moyes's shoulder and a gash over his eye but the shrimper waved him off.

"Go do your business, Keegan," he said. "I ain't dead yet."

He took the Webley from Moyes's belt and stuck it in his own. Carrying shotgun and .45, he ran to the front of the shrimp boat and jumped down onto the wet wreckage of the dock. He scrambled across the battered pier to the muddy ground. He saw movement to his left, fell against a tree, strained his eyes, then the sky lit up and he saw the gunnery mate scrambling ashore through the marsh grass.

The full fury of the storm was upon them. The German crawled onto hard earth and started running.

"Hold it," Keegan screamed but his warning was lost in the wind. He started running parallel to the German, dodging trees. Both were running toward the tall clubhouse spire.

Inside the dining room there was chaos. Willoughby, his eyes bulging with fear and panic, stared through the windows of the dining room. In the gaudy flashes of lightning, he first saw the sub, then the glaring white spotlight, then heard the wrenching collision.

"My God," he cried. "The sub's been rammed!"

"Shut up!" 27 ordered as the dining room guests started to surge forward. He turned on them, leveled the gun at Grant

Peabody and snarled, "Everyone stand where you are or I'll kill Peabody. Now."

The surge stopped for an instant, then Peabody yelled, "You can't kill us all."

Allenbee leveled the machine pistol at Peabody.

"No, but if anyone else moves an inch, you'll be the first to die."

He backed to the window and looked outside. Through the storm he saw someone running toward the dining room. Behind him was the prow of the shrimp boat, tilted crazily against the dock. No sign of the sub.

Keegan chased the German sailor through the storm but the gunner got to the clubhouse first, scrambling onto the porch and rushing through one of the French doors. Keegan was twenty feet behind him as the sailor burst into the dining room.

Twenty-seven whirled as the sailor staggered through the door and shot him twice in the chest. It was only after the body jackknifed to the floor that the one-time actor realized what he'd done. The room erupted with screams of alarm. Twenty-seven twisted and looked through the open door. For a second, in an explosion of lightning, he saw Keegan huddled in the rain, saw him raise his arm, heard the pistol shot. It skimmed 27's cheek, took off his earlobe and as he spun out of the doorway he fired several shots at the sodden figure. But Keegan had already vanished in the darkness.

Willoughby, totally confused, stared down at the dead U-boat crew man.

"My God! You killed one of our own."

"You damn fool, the sub's finished."

"No," the Englishman cried out. "No, it can't be." He started toward the door which was still open and banging in the wind. With an animal growl, Allenbee fired a burst into Willoughby. The bullets ripped into the older man's chest and knocked him backward across a table in a shower of dishes, glasses and food. He sprawled there, arms outstretched, his legs dangling off the floor.

The dining room went crazy. Screaming guests suddenly panicked and rushed toward the rear doors. Twenty-seven realized he had lost control of the situation. His nemesis was out there somewhere and he was a perfect target in the brightly lit room. He grabbed a chair, threw it through a window and leaped out behind it.

A moment later a sodden Keegan rushed into the dining room. The chaotic mob turned instantly toward him.

He held up a hand. "My name's Keegan, I'm with the U.S. Intelligence Service. Please . . . everybody stay in this room. If you go outside you'll confuse things even more. If he comes back instead of me, kill the son of a bitch. There's a wounded man in the shrimp boat down at the pier. He needs help."

He stared down at Lady Penelope Traynor. "And keep your eye on her highness there."

He jumped through the shattered window after 27.

The machine pistol chattered and a string of bullets ripped the mud behind Keegan as he landed and rolled behind a tree. Another burst tore into the tree. Keegan rolled over on the ground, fired several shots into the rainy darkness, then jumped to his feet, ran back to the side of the clubhouse and crouched in the darkness, listening. He heard only the rumble of thunder, the splatter of rain. He worked his way to the corner of the building and waited for lightning to brighten the compound.

Twenty-seven moved backward through the trees like a cornered fox. He too waited for nature to illuminate their battleground.

A jagged streak in the sky. A dark form dodging from one tree to another. He fired another burst of the pistol, was met immediately by several shots in return. He backed into the wall of a building. Startled, he whirled with a cry. Another shot smacked the wall an inch from his head. He crouched and ran along the side of the building, realized it was the indoor tennis court, found the door. It was locked. He smashed the window with his elbow, reached in, unlocked the door and jumped inside.

Fifty feet away, Keegan heard the window break and hurried toward the sound. He saw the door, its window shattered, in the long, low building and raced up to it, flattening himself against the wall. Inching his way to the opening and facing the wall, he stretched his arm around the jamb and fired two shots blindly into the building. They were answered instantly with a burst from 27's machine pistol. Bullets chewed up the doorjamb. He was obviously across the indoor court somewhere.

Keegan ducked low and dashed into the darkened court. Another burst of gunfire followed him. He felt the hot searing pain as a bullet ripped through his shoulder. But he scampered across the floor and lurked in the darkness next to a scorekeeper's table, listening. He touched his shoulder and flinched. The bullet had pierced the fleshy part just under the shoulder blade and exited.

He squinted in the darkness. The big room looked ominous, with its tennis net stretched from one side to the other and dark corners offering refuge to his enemy.

Where was he? Keegan wondered.

In an opposite corner, 27 lurked and waited in darkness, just as determined to get rid of Keegan. He had to quell his anger to keep it from clouding his judgment. He had come too far, waited too many years, to fail completely. His mind formulated a new plan. The operation was not a total loss. First he had to kill the intruder. *Ja,* he would eliminate his nemesis and then return to the clubhouse. There he would kill Yankee millionaires until his ammunition was gone, then swim across to the marsh and make it to the mainland. He still had funds in New York. With luck, he could make it back to Germany.

But first things first. Where *was* the American?

A hundred feet away, Keegan checked his resources. Too much rain and thunder to hear his enemy breathing.

Keegan slowly reached down to the bucket, took a tennis ball, threw it across the room into a dark corner. Twenty-seven spun immediately and fired in its direction. Bullets ripped into the wall. Then suddenly, the gun stopped firing. There was the unmistakable sound of metal on metal as the firing pin snapped on the empty chamber. Enraged, 27 threw the empty pistol across the room and as he did, Keegan grabbed the bucket of tennis balls and threw them at the Nazi. They bounced around him, bounded underfoot, bounced off the walls and disoriented the German agent. Twenty-seven saw Keegan rise from behind the table and lurched toward him but he stepped on a tennis ball and then another. His legs pedaled frantically under him as he fought to keep from falling. Keegan leaped from the darkness, buried a shoulder into 27's stomach and they vaulted through the window, tumbled in a shower of glass and wood into the mud outside.

Rage replaced common sense for 27 was insane with frustration and anger. *Mein Gott!* he thought. *Is all our planning going to end on this ridiculous spit of land?*

Never!

If nothing else he would kill this Yankee bastard.

Twenty-seven grabbed at his calf, pulled the SS dagger from its sheath. He struggled to his knees and as Keegan jumped toward him, 27 slashed out with the knife. Its blade buried in Keegan's cheek and sliced upward through his eye socket, biting into his skull. Pain exploded in Keegan's face and he almost blacked out. But he was too close, he'd come too far. He wouldn't, couldn't fail. The pain was nothing compared to Jenny's pain, to the pain of all of 27's victims. Keegan grabbed 27's wrist, twisted it up and away from him, heard the bone snap and saw the dagger flip away. Still hanging on, he smashed 27 in the face with his fist, then hit him again and again, knocking the German backward until 27 pulled free. The Nazi staggered out of his reach. In the flashing lightning, he saw Keegan glaring at him with his good eye, his face twisted in hatred and rage.

Twenty-seven darted sideways and slashed his foot out, burying it in Keegan's stomach. Keegan's breath burst from his lips and he was slammed back against the wall of the tennis court. He fell to his knees as 27 closed in on him. Bleary-eyed, he saw the gleaming blade of the Nazi dagger lying in the mud, its handle an inch from his hand. He snatched it up and as 27 grabbed Keegan's shoulder, the American swung his arm blindly. The blade glittered in a flash of lightning. Keegan felt it strike, rip through flesh as he completed the swing and fell back to his knees.

Siebenundzwanzig shrieked in pain. He swayed backward, clutching his throat, hit a tree and collapsed at its base. Keegan pulled a handkerchief from his pocket, pressed it against his throbbing eye. He struggled to his feet and looked down at *Siebenundzwanzig.*

Pain racked 27's body; hot fire coursing down from his throat, down to his fingers and toes. Everything was going numb. In the jagged bursts of light, he saw his enemy face-to-face for the first time. He tried to cry out but his vocal cords were ruined. He couldn't breathe. The salt of his blood filled his mouth. He was numb all over.

His mouth bobbed silently as he made one last attempt to verbalize his rage and hate. Nothing.

The Nazi arched his back against the tree, gasping for breath, his anguished wheeze suffocated by his own blood. His windpipe and jugular had been severed by the slashing dagger. His feet thrashed in the mud and then began to shake uncontrollably as he literally choked to death. He stiffened and cried out, a stifled, pitiful animal whimper. Then he fell sideways in the mud.

Keegan stared down at his dead enemy. Twenty-seven's mouth gaped open. Rain spattered on his glazed eyes. Blood seeped into the murky puddles around his face. Keegan staggered to his feet, leaned against the wall of the tennis court. For the first time in too many years, he was able to breathe a sigh of relief.

He made his way back toward the clubhouse, walked unsteadily into the dining room, a blood-soaked handkerchief pressed against his eye, his shoulder a soggy mess, the dagger still clenched in his hand.

"Get the doctor," someone said.

Keegan did not slow down. He brushed through the confused crowd in the dining room and walked to Lady Penelope Traynor's table. She stared at him with fear. He raised the hand with the dagger and slashed it down. The dagger's point bit into the table and it stuck there. A hint of blood glistened on its wet blade. Lady Traynor stared bleakly at the weapon, at the swastika and the SS runes on the handle, the symbols of her vanished power.

"Sorry, Lady Penelope," Keegan rasped, "the wedding's off."

EPILOGUE

Austria:
May 7, 1945

The American jeep drove rapidly up the dirt road toward the burned-out ruin of a castle, spewing dust out behind it. An American wearing a worn leather jacket with the gold leaves of a major pinned to the shoulders and an army officer's hat cocked on the back of his head sat beside the driver. He wore no other uniform. His pants were brown corduroy and his shirt was dark blue wool. A black patch covered his right eye and a thin scar etched from under it down across his cheek.

In the backseat, a dark-haired, bearded man leaned back with his arms stretched out on the rear of the seat. He was wearing dark work pants, a black turtleneck sweater and a tweed cap. His rifle lay casually across his knees.

Beside the road were forlorn remnants of the Third Reich. Burned-out German tanks, staff cars, a motorcycle or two lay abandoned in ditches along the narrow roadway. Weary but smiling GI's, sitting along the shoulders, tossed half-hearted salutes at the major with the patch over his eye as the jeep passed.

The radio was tuned to Armed Forces Radio. A GI disk jockey was babbling with excitement and had been for an hour. His voice was beginning to crack from the strain.

"That's right, all you GI Joes out there, it's all over! The war in Europe is over. At two-forty-one A.M., Germany unconditionally surrendered. Remember this day, guys, it's *Liberation Day*! May seventh, 1945, the day we won the war . . ."

The major leaned forward and snapped off the radio.

"Geez, Major Keegan," the driver said, "the war's over."

"It isn't over till it's over," Keegan answered.

The bearded man in the backseat said nothing. He stared straight ahead.

The sergeant pulled up in front of the ancient German

castle, swung the jeep in a tight arc and parked in front of a long, wide flight of marble steps that led to the entrance. Keegan and his companion jumped out and started up the stairs. An American flag waved from a flagpole attached to the arch over the door.

The Gothic structure had not fared well in the fighting south of Munich. Its windows were blown out and covered with tattered canvas. One wing of the château had been bombed and now lay in ruins. The roof on the main house was burned out and the face of the old place was scorched.

A military police corporal looked suspiciously at Keegan's makeshift uniform and the leaves on his shoulder before finally deciding to salute.

"Corporal, I'm Major Keegan. This is my aide. I think you're expecting me."

The corporal straightened up when he heard the name.

"Oh, yes sir! Right this way, sir."

He led the two men into the gloomy interior of the place. Ceilings towered above a wide marble hallway. The grand staircase ended abruptly just before it reached the first floor. A gaping hole in the wall behind it had been boarded up.

"This place is a mess," Keegan said.

"Some Kraut general was using it for a command post," the corporal said. "A squadron of P-51s really kicked the shi . . . excuse me, sir, kicked the crap out of the place."

"You can say *shit* in front of me, Corporal," Keegan said. "I'm old enough to vote."

"Yes, sir."

"What happened to the general?"

"I hear they scraped him off the wall. We found the old man hiding down in the wine cellar. He was a sight."

They walked almost to the end of the hall. The corporal nodded toward a door.

"In there, sir."

"Thanks. Congratulations, Corporal."

"What for, sir?"

"Winning the war, kid," he said, and entered the room.

It had once been a library, although one wall had been blown away. Remnants of books littered the room. Soaring bookshelves dominated two other walls while the fourth wall was

an enormous stained glass window which somehow had escaped
the bombardment. A rolling ladder provided access to the upper
bookshelves.

An army cot squatted in a corner of the room with an olive
drab army blanket thrown carelessly across it. The only other
thing in the room was a large, hand-carved oak desk. Like the
window behind it, it was unscathed.

The old man sat hunched over behind the desk, a stack of
books to one side, another opened in front of him. He was
taking notes on a pad of army paper. His disheveled hair was as
thin as mist and pure white. His eyes were dark hollows in a
sallow face. He needed a shave. A hand-made shawl was thrown
over his rounded shoulders.

He looked up through faded eyes as Keegan and his aide
crossed the room, kicking book leaves out of the way. They
stood in front of the desk. The bearded man was in the shadows.

"Professor Wilhelm Vierhaus?"

The old man looked up.

"Ja?"

"You are under arrest, Professor."

"I have been under arrest for over a week, Major."

"No, you've been detained. As of today you would probably
have been free to go, since you are officially a civilian and the
war is over. But I have a warrant here for your arrest. The
specific charge is murder in the first degree."

"I beg your pardon?"

"Murder, Professor. You are a civilian and you are charged
with murdering a civilian."

"Who?"

"Specifically, Jenny Gould."

"Jenny . . ." He shook his head, trying to remember.

"Her brother was Avrum Wolffson."

Vierhaus looked up with shock. His eyes narrowed.

"The Black Lily?"

"That's right. You sent his sister to Dachau and she was
murdered there."

"And you are charging me with *that*?" he said, almost sneer-
ing.

"That's right. Not only charging you, Vierhaus, but I intend
to see that you are prosecuted and hanged."

"I did not kill anybody!"

"You sent her to Dachau to die."

"And who are your witnesses, sir?"

"Her brother for one. Perhaps it's time you met. You've been trying to kill him for twelve years. Av?"

The bearded man stepped from the shadows into the light streaming in the window.

"Professor, this is Avrum Wolffson."

Vierhaus reacted with a combination of emotions: surprise, hatred, curiosity. Fear.

"Jenny Gould was his sister. She was arrested and ultimately murdered in an attempt by you to get her to turn him in."

Vierhaus turned his attention back to Keegan.

"Who *are* you?" he said with awe. "Do I know you?"

"We met once, Willie. In a steam bath at the Grand Hotel."

"Steam bath?" He studied Keegan's face.

"I didn't have the patch then."

But Vierhaus did not recognize Keegan. Keegan took out a pack of cigarettes and offered one to Vierhaus.

"Perhaps a smoke will relax you, stir your memory."

He took out the gold lighter with the wolf's head, held it close to Vierhaus, then flipped open the top and struck it. Vierhaus stared at the lighter, then back at Keegan.

"This is my good luck charm, Willie. Carried it all the way through this stinking war. Every time things got rough I'd rub it for good luck."

Keegan now rubbed the side of the lighter with his thumb and smiled. Vierhaus said nothing. He continued to stare at the lighter, which Keegan held up by its base.

"Quite handsome, isn't it? According to Lady Penelope, you gave this to the actor. And this is what tripped him up. That's where I got it, Willie. From *Siebenundzwanzig,* the night I tracked him down and killed him. And you know who tipped me off, Willie? Avrum Wolffson."

Vierhaus's attention flicked from Wolffson to Keegan to the lighter.

"Think about that. You Germans love irony, so think of the irony here. You sent Jenny Gould to Dachau because of the Black Lily and it was the Black Lily that was Twenty-seven's downfall—and is now yours."

"Who . . . are . . . you?" Vierhaus croaked.

"I'm the man whose fiancée you murdered. I'm the man you chased out of Germany with his tail between his legs. And I'm the man who put *Siebenundzwanzig* out of business."

Recognition suddenly changed the expression on the Nazi's face.

"Keegan," he whispered as if to himself. "The *Ire.*"

"Very good, Willie," Keegan said, and there was a hard edge in his voice. "You pass the course. I chased Twenty-seven for almost a year. And I've waited six more years for this day. You håve any doubt that I'll dog you to your grave? If you think hiding behind a coat and tie is going to save your ass, you're crazy. You're just as guilty as Himmler and Göring and the rest of the paperhanger's boys. That's why it's important to nail you."

The confused professor rubbed the back of his hand across one cheek.

"How did you find me?" he asked.

"An old friend of yours named Danzler at Dachau. We went in when they liberated it. Avrum here convinced Danzler to give up your location."

Vierhaus's eyes bulged as Wolffson stepped closer. He looked up at the man that Hitler had hated with psychotic rage. Wolffson looked down at him without expression.

His shoulders sagged as the pieces fell together. There had been so many murders. So many executions. But now it came back to him.

"So, that is what this is all about? Retribution, eh, Keegan?"

"No, it's for me, Vierhaus. So I can put the last twelve years behind me and go home to my wife, Vanessa, and my little girl, Temple, and enjoy the rest of my life. It's about little monsters like you, too. There's so many big shots ahead of you, they would never have gotten around to you. You would have walked free. But I know what you are, Vierhaus. I know how you whispered your obscenities in Hitler's ear. Killing the actor was self-defense. But you, you're the cherry on the strudel, Willie."

"So you even know who he was, eh?"

"I figured it out with the help of some friends in military intelligence and some old newspapers. You see, I got to know this guy like I know myself. One of his tricks was to make every-

one believe he was dead when he wanted to disappear. So
. . . first we went through the records we seized in Berlin and
found out when he was recruited. After that it was a cakewalk.
I was going through the newspapers, reading obituaries, hoping
maybe something would click. And suddenly there it was staring
at me in big, bold headlines. 'Actor Dies in Mountain Auto
Crash.' The man without a face. The premier actor of Germany.
The man who mastered dialects and spoke six languages.''

Keegan held his hands out to his sides, palms up.

"So this is what it's all about." Vierhaus shook his head in
disbelief. "She was one woman among six million. A moment in
time."

Keegan turned to Wolffson. "Excuse us for a minute, will
you, Av?"

The tall resistance fighter left the room.

"This is an official warrant," Keegan said, laying a folded
sheet on the desk. "You're a civilian, Vierhaus. This is not for
genocide or any of those major, major crimes against humanity.
It officially charges you with one count of murder. And I'm
going to see you tried and I'm going to be in the front row when
they stretch your neck. Of course, I don't know if you can understand this. I hope so. You people killed so many you can't even
comprehend the value of a single life anymore. Except maybe
your own."

Vierhaus didn't answer. He stared down at his dirty fingernails.

"On the other hand, I want to go home," Keegan said. He
took a German P-38 out of his pocket. Vierhaus's eyes grew
narrower. Fear slowly materialized in the bloodshot, lifeless
orbs ringed with deep shadows.

"I don't want to have to hang around here waiting for them
to get around to your trial," he said. "I've had enough of this."

"You don't believe in forgiving your enemies, *Ire*?" Vierhaus said nervously.

"I believe in the old Irish proverb, Willie. Forgive your
enemies—but get even first."

He removed the clip from the pistol, put it in his pocket and
ejected the shell in the chamber. It clattered on the desk and
rolled against a book. Keegan put the gun on the desk.

"*Auf wiedersehen, Willie,*" Keegan said, and walked out of the room. Vierhaus stared after him. He looked around the room, at his cot in the corner, and finally at the pistol on his desk.

Outside the room, Keegan and Wolffson walked down the marble hallway.

"You think it will stick, *Ire*?" Wolffson asked.

"The murder charge?"

"*Ja.*"

"I doubt it."

"You think he'll go free?"

"No. I don't think he'll go free, Av."

"Then what?"

The shot rang out as he said it and echoed through the hallway.

"Christ almighty!" the corporal cried out and ran down the hall.

Keegan walked down the long flight of steps with Wolffson trailing behind him. They got in the jeep.

"Okay," Keegan said. "Now it's over." He leaned over and snapped on the radio. "Whip this baby back to Munich," he said to the driver. "The party's on me."

The same disk jockey was still babbling with joy.

"We're going home, guys! We're going *home*! And here's a classic from a man we all wish was with us to celebrate today. The immortal Glenn Miller and a song that has become an anthem for all of us on this side of the pond."

Keegan leaned back as the song began. He joined in when the Modernaires began their vocal.

Don't sit under the apple tree,
With anyone else but me,
Anyone else but me,
Anyone else but me, no, no, no,
Don't sit under the apple tree,
With anyone else but me,
Till I come marching home . . . .